THE BROKEN MAN

Josephine Cox was born in Blackburn, one [illegible] ten children. At the age of sixteen, Josephine [illegible] and married her husband Ken, and had two [illegible] the boys started school, she decided [illegible] eventually gained a place at Cam[illegible] was unable to take this up as it would [illegible] living away from home, but she went into teachi[illegible] and started to write her first full-length novel. She won the 'Superwoman of Great Britain' Award, for which her family had secretly entered her, at the same time as her first novel was accepted for publication.

Her strong, gritty stories are taken from the tapestry of life. Josephine says, 'I could never imagine a single day without writing. It's been that way since as far back as I can remember.'

Visit www.josephinecox.com to find out more information about Josephine.

Also by Josephine Cox

QUEENIE'S STORY
Her Father's Sins
Let Loose the Tigers

THE EMMA GRADY TRILOGY
Outcast
Alley Urchin
Vagabonds

Angels Cry Sometimes
Take This Woman
Whistledown Woman
Don't Cry Alone
Jessica's Girl
Nobody's Darling
Born to Serve
More than Riches
A Little Badness
Living a Lie
The Devil You Know
A Time for Us
Cradle of Thorns
Miss You Forever
Love Me or Leave Me
Tomorrow the World
The Gilded Cage
Somewhere, Someday
Rainbow Days
Looking Back
Let It Shine

The Woman Who Left
Jinnie

Bad Boy Jack
The Beachcomber
Lovers and Liars
Live the Dream

The Journey
Journey's End
The Loner
Songbird
Born Bad
Divorced and Deadly
Blood Brothers
Midnight
Three Letters

Josephine COX

The Broken Man

HARPER

This novel is entirely a work of fiction.
The names, characters and incidents portrayed in it are the work of the author's imagination. Any resemblance to actual persons, living or dead, events or localities is entirely coincidental.

Harper
An imprint of HarperCollins*Publishers*
77–85 Fulham Palace Road,
Hammersmith, London W6 8JB

www.harpercollins.co.uk

This paperback edition 2013
2

First published in Great Britain by
HarperCollins 2013

A catalogue record for this book is
available from the British Library

ISBN: 9780007419913

Set in ITC New Baskerville by Palimpsest Book Production Limited
Falkirk, Stirlingshire

Printed and bound in Great Britain by
Clays Ltd, St Ives plc

To my darling Ken, as always.

To the musical Murphy family in Ireland. Hope all is well with you. Much love, Jo x

PART ONE

~

Bedfordshire, February

1952

CHAPTER ONE

THERE WAS SOMETHING disturbing about young Adam.

Deep inside, he carried a secret that he could never tell anyone.

Phil knew, though, because he recognised that certain look: the slump of the shoulders; the sad eyes that gave little away.

Having fought for king and country, Phil knew what it was like to carry a secret. Over the years he had learned to live with the vivid memory of terrible scenes he had witnessed.

He could banter with old companions, but the loneliness of guarding his secret was often unbearable.

Though his life was not empty, he ached for the company of a very special person, the one lovely woman he had loved with every fibre of his being. The only woman who was able to bring sunshine into his life, even on a rainy day.

He kept himself busy helping his neighbours and occasionally meeting up with locals down at the pub. He earned his living by driving the school bus, and when the working day was over, he would go home to an empty house, make his tea and, afterwards, sit in his chair and light up his faithful old pipe. Before it got dark, he would take a leisurely stroll through the countryside, his little mongrel dog, Rex, tripping along beside him.

Phil appreciated his few simple pleasures, though he would have given everything to turn the clock back to a time when he was younger and fitter, and fortunate enough to have a loving wife.

Now, though, he would make his way home as always, and except for the faithful little dog who was never far from his side, the house would be empty.

Now at night, he went up to his bed; alone. At first light he woke up; alone. He had no one special to laugh or cry with, no one to slide his arm around when he felt loving. And there was no one close with whom to share any titbits of gossip or maybe a smile at the occasional naughty tricks the schoolchildren got up to on the bus.

There was no one to chastise him when he left the tap running, or when he casually threw his worn shirt on the bedroom floor. It was a hard truth that after many happy years married to a wonderful woman, he was now a man on his own, with only memories and his dog for company.

The loneliness weighed heaviest on him in the evenings. He longed for things once familiar, like making a pot of tea for two, and sharing it over a cheery fire, or maybe cutting fresh flowers from his little garden, and seeing his wife's pretty smile as he handed them to her.

Those precious times had been dearly missed these past four years, since his beloved wife lost her fight against a long illness.

~

Phil's thoughts were suddenly interrupted by a flicker of movement reflected in the driver's mirror. Glancing up, he saw his last passenger, young Adam Carter, climbing out of his seat to make his way down the bus. He was far too quiet and serious for his age. There were times when Phil had caught the boy so deep in thought he was oblivious to the other children around him and he had no particular friend with whom he always sat. In Adam, Phil saw a troubled, frightened boy.

'We're nearly there, son!' he called encouragingly.

Phil manoeuvred the vehicle over to the verge, where he parked, applied the handbrake, and prepared to let the boy off.

'Right then, Adam, here you are, home safe and well.'

'Thank you, Mr Wallis, I'll be all right now.'

'The name's Phil . . .' he kindly corrected the child. 'Everyone calls me Phil.'

'But my father says it's rude to address your elders by their first name.'

'Mebbe, but not if they offer you the privilege . . . which I am very glad to be doing right now. Only if you feel comfortable with it, mind.'

Adam grew restless. 'I'd really like to call you Phil,' he admitted, 'but my father would be angry with me.'

Phil gave a cheeky wink. 'Well, that's easily settled. I won't tell him if you don't.'

Adam gave it a little thought, then with a wide smile said, 'OK. I won't tell him either.'

'Good! That's settled then.' Phil climbed out of the driving seat. 'Seeing as I need to stretch my legs and it's such a beautiful afternoon, I'll walk you down the lane to your front door. That's if you think your father wouldn't mind.'

Adam shook his head. 'He won't mind. Thank you, Phil.'

Phil laughed out loud. 'There you are. It wasn't too difficult to say my name, was it?'

He felt as though, at long last, this lonely boy was beginning to trust him. He hoped the day might come when the child would trust him enough to confide in him.

He now took a sideways glance at young Adam.

At seven years of age, Adam Carter was quietly spoken. With serious brown eyes, and thick dark hair that tumbled over his forehead, he cut a handsome young figure. Not naturally outgoing, he hardly ever laughed out loud, and smiled only on rare occasions. Yet when he did smile it was such a warm, genuine smile, it could light up a room.

Phil had noticed how Adam's nervousness increased

the nearer he got to home. Unlike the other children, who could never get off the bus fast enough, Adam hung back, waiting until the very last minute, almost as though he was reluctant to leave the safety of the bus.

'Right then, son, that's another week over. You go on; I need to secure the bus, especially after that young squirrel got inside and wreaked havoc.'

Adam went down the steps. On the last step he gave a short jump to the ground, his satchel catching on the handrail as he did so.

'All right, are you?' Phil released his satchel.

'Yes, thank you, Phil.'

After following Adam down the bus steps, Phil secured the door behind him.

'I expect you're glad to be home, eh?'

Except for a curt nod of the head, Adam gave no reply, but he wanted to tell this gentle, kind man that no, he was *not* all right; that he was *not* glad to be home. He wanted to confess that he was afraid and unhappy, and that he often dreamed of running away. But he would never do that, because it might be dangerous for someone he loved dearly. So he kept his silence and went on pretending. Even now, as they approached the house, his heart was thumping. Was his father home yet? Had his day been good? Because if not . . . oh . . . if not . . . Quickly, he thrust the bad thoughts from his mind.

Man and boy went down the lane side by side.

'By! This is a real treat.' Phil sniffed the air. 'This time o' day, the pine trees give off a wonderful scent.'

Adam agreed. 'Mum says it's even stronger in the summer. She says when the trees begin to sweat, they create a thick vapour over the woods, and you can almost taste it.'

Phil loved the lazy manner in which the worn path wound in and out of the ancient woodlands, skirting magnificent trees that had been there far longer than he had.

'You live in a really pretty part of the countryside,' he told Adam. 'And now you've got the whole weekend before you, so what might you be up to, eh?' He chuckled. 'By! I wish I were a lad again . . . climbing trees and apple-scrumping. The things we used to get up to, you would not believe.' He gave a great sigh. 'It's all a lifetime ago now. Mind you, I'd never be able to climb a tree these days, not with my gammy leg.' His pronounced limp was a painful trophy from the war.

'I'm not allowed to climb trees.' Adam's voice softened with regret. 'My father doesn't approve of it.'

'Well, I never!' Phil was dumbfounded. 'Climbing trees is what boys do. It's a natural part of growing up, like fishing, and football.' He gave a wistful smile. 'And who could ever forget the first time he kissed a girl?' He rolled his eyes and made the boy smile shyly; he still had that pleasure to come.

'I know it's not my place to ask,' Phil went on in a more serious tone, 'but, what's your dad got against you climbing trees?'

Adam shrugged. 'He says it's undignified.'

'I see.' In fact, he didn't see at all.

Deep in conversation, they were startled and delighted when a deer shot across their path. A few steps on, and Phil resumed their conversation.

'Do you know what I'd do, if ever I had loads of money?'

'No.'

'I don't expect I ever will have loads of money, but if I did, I'd build myself the prettiest little cottage right in the middle of these 'ere woods. And I'd be sure to make friends with every animal that lived here.'

Adam laughed. 'You'd be like the old man in the story.'

'Oh, and what story is that?'

'It's a mystery I once read, about a man who lived in an old shed in the woods. He cut his own logs for the fire, and everything he ate came out of the woods. Sometimes he would even sleep in the forest with the animals, and they never once hurt him.'

'Ah, well, there you go, then. He sounds like a man after my own heart. So, how long did he live like that?'

'A long time . . . years! Then one day he just disappeared, and was never seen again.'

'Hmmph!' Stooping to collect a fallen branch, Phil threw it into the verge. 'So nobody knows what happened to him, eh?'

'No. The story tells how one day he was seen collecting mushrooms; then he was never seen again. Some of the villagers were worried he might be ill, so they went to check the shed where he lived, but though the old man was gone, all his belongings were still there.'

'Sounds too spooky for me.' Phil was intrigued. 'But what do *you* think happened to him?'

'Well . . . I think maybe he got really sick and he knew he wouldn't get better, so he crept away where no one would ever find him. Just like the Indians of old used to do.'

Phil thought about that. 'Well, if that's the case, he's a very lucky man. Not many people get to choose how they live their lives, and then decide where to end them.'

There followed a short silence as they each dwelled on the fate of the mystery man.

'Phil?' The boy softly broke the silence.

'Yes, son?'

'I don't think I'll ever be able to choose what I want to do with my life.'

'Why do you say that?'

'Because my father has my future all planned out.'

'Has he now?' Phil prompted him. 'And you think that's a bad thing, do you?'

'He says I'm his only son and that he's decided there will be no more children,' Adam explained. 'So it's my duty to follow in his footsteps.'

'No more children, eh?'

'That's what he said.'

'And are you sure you don't want to follow in his footsteps?'

'Yes, I'm sure, but when I try and tell him, he gets really angry.'

He was careful not to reveal how his father often took a belt to him; that one time he split the skin on his back and forbade his mother to take him to hospital.

'Have you spoken to your mother about not wanting to follow in your dad's footsteps?'

'Yes, but Mum said it's best if I do what Father says.' He paused before confiding in a quieter voice, 'Sometimes if I disobey him, he takes it out on her. That's cowardly, isn't it, Phil?'

'I'm sorry, son, but without knowing all the circumstances, it would not be right for me to comment on that,' Phil apologised, although his mental picture of the boy's father was now deeply unsettling.

Thinking it might be wise to change the subject, he asked, 'So if you're not allowed to climb trees, what do you do when you're out with your mates?'

'I don't have any mates.'

'Oh? And why's that then?'

'Father says I must not waste my time. He says that if I've got any spare time after school, I must use it for doing extra studies, because I'll never make anything of myself if I don't study.'

He cast his gaze to the floor. 'Can I tell you something, Phil?'

'Course you can, son.'

'I don't like him very much. He makes me study all the time, and I'm never allowed to do anything else. I would like to have close mates that I could bring home and play with. But Father keeps me too busy for that.'

'I'm sure your father thinks it's all for your own good.'

'I know, but he asks too much of me, and he has

such a terrible temper, and if I get the questions wrong, he makes me do them all over again. Sometimes it's midnight and he still won't let me go. Mum argues with him and then . . . he . . . he . . .' his voice tailed off to a whisper. 'Sometimes, I really hate him.'

Saddened by what Adam had told him, Phil made him a promise. 'Always remember, son, if ever you feel the need to talk, I'll be here for you.' Not being witness to what happened in that house, Phil believed it was wrong of him to criticise. Instead, he quietly reassured the boy, 'I expect he has your interests at heart, but you obviously believe he's going about it the wrong way, so all you can do is to keep explaining how you feel.'

'I've made up my mind, I don't ever want to be like him!' A dark look crossed his face.

'Well, I'm sure that's your choice, Adam, but your father has made a success of his own life and, from what you tell me, it seems he wants the same for you.'

'I know that.' Looking ahead towards the house, the boy grew agitated. 'But he's not a good man. Sometimes he's really nasty. He doesn't laugh, and when he gets angry he shouts and screams. Mum tells me not to rile him, or he might . . .'

'Might what?' Phil could see the child was getting agitated. 'Apart from the shouting and wanting you to work harder, is there something else that's worrying you, son?'

'NO! No, there's nothing else.' Fearing he might have said too much already, Adam finished lamely, 'Me and Mum, we just do what he tells us, and then everything is fine.'

'Well, just remember what I said, Adam. If you ever need someone to talk to, I'm here.' Phil brought the subject to an end: 'I've an idea that you and your father will work it out, eventually.' Even so, he was genuinely concerned by what the boy had told him.

'Can I ask you something?' Adam said after a few moments' silence.

'Of course you can!' Chuckling, Phil lightened the mood. 'Unless you're after borrowing a shilling or two, because you know what they say: "Never a borrower nor a lender be", and that's the rule I live by.'

When he saw Adam's face fall, he laughed out loud. 'Take no notice of me,' he said, 'I'm just teasing. So, what is it you want to ask?'

Casting a wary glance along the lane, Adam quietly confided, 'Could you please not tell anybody what I've said, about my father?' Again, he nervously glanced down the lane towards his house.

'Don't worry, son. I've never been a gossip, and I can assure you that what's been said here today will not go any further. All right?'

'Thank you, Phil. Maybe you're right. My father doesn't mean to be like he is. It's only because he works such long hours and he has such a responsible job, he just gets on edge sometimes.'

'I understand that, son, but if you don't mind me saying, what suits one man doesn't always suit another. A man should be able to choose his own path. But you're not yet a man, and maybe your father is looking out for your future. D'you understand what I'm saying?'

'Yes, but I don't want to be bad-tempered and angry

like my father. I want to do something that makes me happy.' Growing increasingly nervous, Adam dropped his voice to a whisper. 'Already my father is training me into his kind of work.'

'How d'you mean?'

'Well, nearly every night he brings home a pile of paperwork and makes me go through it with him. It's all calculations of stocks and shares and money transactions. I don't understand any of it, not really, but sometimes he keeps me at his desk for ages, making me do tests and stuff. He says he's proud for me to follow in his footsteps. He wants me to learn all about high finance and dealing and stuff. And I hate it!'

Phil understood the boy's concern. 'Do you ever get any time to yourself?'

Adam's face lit up. 'Only when Father comes home really late, or stays in London overnight on business. That's when Mum and I have the best time of all, doing the things Father disapproves of. We play card games. Mum keeps the cards in a special hiding place. And sometimes we play loud music on the radio and Mum shows me how to tango and rumba and all that.'

His face broke into a proud smile. 'She was a champion ballroom dancer once. She won all sorts of trophies and she's got photographs of her in these beautiful gowns. She said Father asked her to give it all up when they got married, so she gave her dresses away and never danced again. She kept all her photographs and trophies, but Father locked them away. She knows where the key is, though, and when he's not here, she gets them all out.'

Growing afraid in case anyone was listening, he lowered his voice again. 'He doesn't know that Mum searched everywhere for the key. She found it under the carpet in their bedroom. When he's not here, she sets all her trophies out on the sideboard, and then she teaches me to dance. Oh, Phil, she looks so beautiful. It's not fair. Why would Father lock away all her precious things like that?'

Phil was shocked. 'I'm sure I have no idea, son.'

Feeling decidedly uncomfortable, Phil led the conversation in a slightly different direction: 'So, would your mum ever want to dance in public again, do you think?'

Adam nodded. 'Oh, yes! She says she's still young enough to take it up again. She even mentioned it to Father, but he said if she ever spoke of it again he would have to destroy everything, so she couldn't ever be tempted. I don't think she will ever dance again, though.' Glancing up at Phil, he smiled. 'Not in public, anyway.'

Phil was beginning to see a much wider picture of this family, and it was not good. 'Mmm, well, all I can say is, it's a pity your father has to work such long hours. But it's good that you and your mum get to spend that time together, isn't it?'

Adam nodded. 'It's really nice when Father isn't there. Sometimes, me and Mum go across the fields for miles and miles. We stay out for ages. Then on the way back, we get fish and chips, and sit on a park bench to eat them. That way we don't make the house smell, because then Father would know what we've been up to.' Breathless and excited, he went on, 'Oh, and sometimes we go to the pictures.' His face lit up. 'Last Saturday we went to see a cowboy film.'

Allowing the boy to chatter on excitedly, Phil instinctively eased him round a muddy puddle.

'Do you have a pet? A little dog, mebbe?'

'No. One time, Mum bought me a tabby cat, but it got run over. His name was Thomas and I really loved him. I taught him to do little tricks and he followed me everywhere, though Father would chase him out if he went into the house.'

Phil chuckled. 'I had a cat like that once. Up to everything, he was.'

'Thomas was the cleverest cat I ever knew,' Adam confided proudly. 'I cried a lot when he was run over. Father said I was a big baby and I should be ashamed of myself. And now I'm not allowed to have a pet ever again.'

'He got run over, you say?' That surprised Phil because, in his experience, most cats would head for the woods rather than risk going over a main road. 'That's a real shame. How did you find out?'

'Father told us that he found Thomas in the woods, and that he was hurt so bad that he died, so he buried him where he found him. I wanted to go and say goodbye, but Father wouldn't tell me where he was. He said that way I would get over him much quicker.'

'Oh dear, that's really sad. I'm so sorry.' Having learned a good deal about Adam's bullying father, Phil could not help but wonder about the cat's demise.

He had an idea. 'Look, Adam, being as it's such a lovely afternoon, I'll be taking my little dog for a walk through these lanes before it gets dark. You could ask your parents if you can tag along. What d'you say to that, eh?'

Adam shook his head. 'I'm not allowed.'

'Oh, but it doesn't hurt to ask, does it? You never know. My old dad used to say, "If you don't ask, you don't get."'

Adam shook his head. 'Father won't let me, but thank you anyway, Phil.'

'Ah, well, never mind, eh? Mebbe another time.'

'Yes, I would really like that.'

~

A few moments later they arrived at the house: a fine Victorian dwelling with tall chimneys, large windows and a sweeping drive. Set in beautifully landscaped grounds, it made an impressive sight. 'I'll be fine now, Phil, thank you.'

'All right, son. I'll just watch you go inside the gate, then I'll make my way home.' Reassured by the lit forecourt and drive, he waited for the boy to close the gate behind him.

'Oh, look! Father's home.' Adam pointed to the big Austin saloon parked in the garage entrance. His face fell visibly as he prepared to go in.

In that same moment a man who had to be Adam's father burst from the house. Lingering a moment in the shade of the porch, he appeared surprised to see the two of them at the gate.

'Afternoon, Mr Carter.' Phil raised his hand in

greeting, but the other man gave no response as he scurried to his car.

Leaning closer, Adam confided in a whisper, 'I'm glad he's going out, because now I'll be able to spend time with Mum, instead of being made to work in the office with Father.'

Phil understood, but thought it best not to stir up trouble. In his experience family problems usually sorted themselves out. 'Right, well, I reckon I'd best be on my way.'

''Bye, then, and thank you.' Adam went towards the house, while Phil turned and trudged back down the lane, deep in thought.

He had gone only a short distance when he heard angry yelling.

'You'll do as I say, or you'll feel the length of my belt! Get out of my way, damn you!'

A minute later, Phil heard the sound of a car door being slammed, then the revving of an engine.

Phil thought if that was the father shouting, it was no wonder the boy had little love or respect for him.

Deep in thought, he pushed on down the lane. Suddenly a car skidded past him at break-neck speed, the wheels sending a thick spray of mud all over Phil's trouser-leg. 'BLOODY LUNATIC! TRYING TO KILL ME, ARE YOU?' Shaking his fist as the car bounced out of the lane and onto the main road, he recognised the big Austin belonging to Adam's father. 'Bloody madman!' Phil yelled, brushing the mud from his trousers as he grumbled. 'You want locking up. You've not heard the last of this, I can tell you.'

About to continue on his way, he thought he heard a cry from somewhere behind him. Then he heard it again; this time closer. It was Adam. Running towards Phil, the boy was clearly distressed, 'Phil . . . help me!'

When he fell over, he made no attempt to scramble up. Instead, he remained where he fell, calling out, 'Come back! I need you, Phil . . . please.'

Slipping and stumbling on the uneven ground, Phil hurried back to him. By then, Adam was crumpled on the ground, frantically rocking back and forth, his two arms crossed over his head as though defending himself.

Shocked, Phil lifted him from the ground and held him close. 'What is it, son? What's happened?' It was clear that something terrible must have happened.

'We need you . . . please, Phil.' Trembling in the man's arms, the boy glanced about furtively, his eyes big with fear as he looked back towards the house. 'Phil, you have to come and see.' He lowered his voice to a confiding whisper. 'It was him, I know it was. It was him, Phil. I hate him, I hate him!'

'Ssh . . . take a deep breath, son. Tell me what's happened.'

'I don't know! You have to help me, Phil . . . please!'

'All right, son. Take it easy now. You and me, we'll go back together.' He knew it must be something bad to have affected the boy like this, but now was not the time for questions.

As they hurried back to the house, Adam kept asking over and over, 'He won't come back, will he? I don't want him to come back. Please, Phil, don't let him come back.'

Quickening his steps as best he could, Phil drew him close, constantly reassuring him, though he had no idea of what might have happened.

In the deepening hours of a February afternoon, he took quiet stock of the boy. At first he suspected his father had given him a beating, but the boy appeared to carry no visible cuts or bloodstains. He was thankful for that much, at least.

As they neared the house, Phil tightened his hold on Adam, while continuing to reassure him.

Clinging to Phil, young Adam seemed not to be listening. Instead, he shivered uncontrollably, while constantly glancing back to the main road.

At the gate, Adam drew back, his whole body resisting as Phil tried to move him gently forward.

Then in a sudden burst that took Phil by surprise, he broke away to run up the drive.

Phil quickly followed, then at the porch he hesitated. It went against his principles to enter another man's property without invitation, especially when that man was hostile. His concerns about the boy, however, urged him on.

A moment or so later, on entering the inner hallway, Phil was faced with a scene so shocking, he could never in a million years have prepared himself for it.

Adam was at the foot of the stairs screaming, 'She's dead, isn't she?' his school shirt covered in blood. He ran back to Phil. 'Look what he's done, oh, Phil . . . look what he's done.' The boy's cries were heart-wrenching.

Deeply shaken, Phil crossed to the foot of the stairs and kneeled to examine the woman. He recognised her as Peggy Carter, Adam's mother, and like the boy, he believed she was past all earthly help.

Lying in a pool of blood, she was covered in angry red bruises. Her eyes were closed and there seemed no immediate signs of life. Her body was grotesquely twisted, with both legs buckled. Her two arms looked as though they were wrenched out of their sockets. The right arm was loosely stretched out, while the other hung through the gap in the banister as though she had tried to use the banister railings to break her fall. Phil was of the opinion that she lost her footing as she tumbled down the stairs and had made a brave but unsuccessful attempt to save herself from serious injury.

'Adam! Phone for an ambulance.' There was no time to waste. 'Go on, son! Hurry!' He reminded him of the emergency number. 'Tell them there's been a terrible accident, and that your mother is unconscious. Tell them they must come at once!'

As the boy ran to do as he was bid, Phil called after him, 'Don't forget to give them the address. Hurry, Adam! Hurry!'

CHAPTER TWO

WHILE ADAM RAN down the lane to the public phone box on the main road, Phil attended to the injured woman. Taking off his coat, he carefully draped it over her. He then leaned closer to detect signs of breathing, but all he could hear was a deep, rattling sound that sent a shiver of fear through him. He knew he had to keep her warm and talk to her. Feeling more helpless than at any other time in his life, he mumbled, 'Oh, dear God, be merciful, for it's Your help she needs now.'

Not knowing whether she could hear him, he leaned closer, his tone reassuring. 'Mrs Carter, I want you to try and concentrate on my voice. I need you to keep listening to me.' He tenderly laid his hand over hers. 'My name is Phil. I'm the driver of the school bus. Adam's all right, but he's anxious about you. But don't worry, I'll look after him. He'll be safe enough with me. You just keep listening to my voice. Try and concentrate on what I'm saying, if you can.'

When he felt her hand twitch beneath his, he took it as a sign that he was getting through to her. 'Mrs Carter, listen to me . . . the ambulance has been called. They're on their way. It seems you fell down the stairs. You've been hurt bad, but they'll look after you. Don't try to move; it's best if you keep as still as possible.' Though, in her sorry condition, he doubted whether she could move even if she tried.

At that moment, Adam came running back. 'They'll be here quick as they can. They said we're to keep talking to her, and not to move her.'

Falling to his knees, he tenderly stroked his mother's hair. 'How did it happen, Mum? Can you hear me? Mum! Was it him who did this to you? Did he lose his temper again? Please, Mum, tell me what happened?'

Phil eased him away. 'No, son. That's not the way. For now, your mother needs gentle, encouraging words. I'm sure there'll be time for questions later.'

Adam understood. 'I'm sorry. She won't tell, but I will. If they ask me, I'll tell them how cruel he is.'

Crouching on the carpet, he kept his anxious gaze on his mother's distorted face.

'The ambulance should be here soon, Mum,' he reassured her. 'They said we had to keep talking to you. Me and Phil . . . we want you to listen, Mum. We want you to be all right, because if you aren't all right I won't know what to do. Please, Mum, try your very hardest. Just like you tell me to do, when I find my homework too difficult.'

Choking back his tears, he cast a forlorn look at Phil. 'She will be all right, won't she, Phil?'

'We have to hope so, son.' Realising that Peggy Carter's life hung in the balance, Phil softly measured his words. 'You can see for yourself. Your mother is badly hurt and there's no use pretending otherwise, but she's alive, and we need to be thankful for that. So, keep talking to her. If she can hear you, I'm sure she'll do her utmost to stay with you.'

For the next few precious minutes, Adam continued to talk to his mother, about school, and how his day had been, but all the while his heart was heavy with fear for his mother and loathing of his father. He recalled the many times when he himself had been thrashed; for no other reason than he had missed a question in his homework, or his father demanded more of him than he could give, which was more often than not.

Other times, when he was in the study, struggling over the homework his father had set, he would hear his parents loudly arguing in the parlour. Often the arguments were followed by the swish of his father's horse-whip, then his mother crying out in pain.

Minutes later his father, red-faced with anger, would storm out of the house. When Adam ran to his mother, she would quickly dry her eyes and reassure him that everything was all right, but it was not all right, and they both knew it.

In spite of her efforts to hide the bruises, Adam knew the truth. His father was a bully and a coward. This time, though, he had hurt her really badly, although she would not tell on him. She never did.

In that raw moment, Adam made himself a promise:

that when he was old enough, and however long it took him, he would make his father pay.

Seeing her like this was all too much. 'You won't admit it, but I know he did this to you.' His voice trembled. 'One day, when I'm bigger, I'll punish him, I will. You'll see . . . I'll make him pay for everything!' He tried not to cry, but the sobs took hold of him and he couldn't stop. 'I hate him! I hate him!'

Deep inside, Peggy heard Adam's angry words, and she feared for her child. Everything he said was true, but she could not let him be destroyed by the hatred he felt for his father.

With immense effort, and mustering every ounce of strength left in her, she whispered, 'No . . .' Her eyes flickered open to gaze on him lovingly. 'Don't . . . say that.' Having made this huge effort she was now struggling to breathe.

Seeing this, Adam reluctantly gave his promise. 'All right . . . ssh, Mum. Stay still. I won't say it any more. I'm sorry, Mum.' Ever so gently, he wrapped his arms round her neck and when she shivered, he backed away, sorry that he might have hurt her, and sorry he had worried her by the things he'd said.

Suddenly the high-pitched wailing of sirens filled the air.

'They're here!' Phil scrambled to his feet to go to meet the ambulance crew. 'Stay with her, son. Keep talking to her, but no questions. Just tell her the ambulance has arrived. Tell her she'll be in good hands now.'

Adam tried his hardest to be brave. He was grateful that his mother would get help, yet he was terrified she might be crippled or made to stay a long time in hospital. She would be unhappy about that, because her greatest joy was walking the countryside, just the two of them together.

'Move away, son,' Phil urged him, as the ambulance men hurried in.

Adam backed away as they brought the stretcher forward. 'I love you, Mum,' he whispered. The tears made a bright trail down his face. 'I'm sorry,' he said. 'I'm sorry, Mum. I'm truly sorry . . .'

But he was not sorry about the promise he had made, to make his father pay for what he had done. When he was big enough, he would go after him, and when he found him, he would make sure to punish him.

No, he was not sorry for any of that. The only thing he was sorry for just now was having made this vow out loud, and making his mother anxious.

From the back of the stairway, he watched as they treated his mother to ease her pain. He saw them cut into the rungs of the stairway and tenderly lift her clear, before securing her to the stretcher. Then they carried her to the ambulance where they raised the stretcher to slide her gently inside. In that moment, she made a feeble cry for her son.

He wanted to go to her, but he was too afraid. What if she was calling for him so she could tell him she would never see him again? What if she was in terrible pain and he couldn't stop it? What if . . .? What if . . .? Hopelessly mixed up inside, and more frightened than he had ever been in his young life, he took to his heels and ran.

Panic-stricken, he hid behind the shrubbery, where he sobbed as though his heart would break. 'Don't die, Mum,' he whispered brokenly. 'Please, Mum . . . don't leave me.'

Realising the boy's fears, Phil found him and lovingly drew him away. 'I know she called for you, son, but she's delirious. There is nothing you nor I can do for her. She's getting the best care. If you want to go in the ambulance with your mum, you'd best be quick.'

'Will you come too?'

'I'm surprised you feel the need to ask.' Phil was already hurrying him to the ambulance, where the attendants had executed the necessary safety procedures and were about to leave.

Phil and Adam climbed inside, and then they were swiftly away; the ambulance tearing along the lane with the sirens at full scream.

These fine, experienced men had seen it all before. They had learned to deal with desperate situations in a professional manner.

This particular call-out, however, was deeply disturbing. As they were both family men with young children, they found the boy's distress difficult to deal with. The disclosure that it was the child himself who had discovered his mother lying bloodied and broken on the stairway was shocking. Such a discovery could prove to be the stuff of nightmares for years to come.

Another concern was their shared suspicions with regard to the 'accident' itself. In their considered experience, the woman's extensive injuries did not appear to coincide with a tumble down the stairs.

For now though, getting her to hospital was their main priority.

~

Inside the ambulance, Adam sat quietly beside Phil, his attention riveted on his mum, and his eyes red and raw from crying. Every few minutes he would whisper to Phil, 'She will be all right, won't she?' And Phil would pacify him as best he could, though secretly, he had his own doubts as to whether Peggy Carter could survive.

He wondered about Adam's father, and the way he'd fled from the house like a guilty man. His instincts told him there was far more to Mrs Carter's so-called accident than met the eye.

Throughout the journey, the medic remained by Peggy's side, softly reassuring and constantly tending her while she drifted in and out of consciousness. Not once did he glance across to the two anxious figures seated on the small bench at the back of the ambulance. He had a job to do, and if there was the slightest hope that this patient might survive, then time was of the essence.

~

To Phil and Adam, the journey to the hospital seemed to have taken for ever, when in fact they were there in under an hour.

On arrival, the ambulance doors were thrown open and Phil and Adam scampered down onto the tarmac.

The driver ran from his cab and climbed into the back, where the two men set about securing Peggy to the stretcher again. Phil and the boy waited anxiously, but it was only the briefest of moments before the two medics manhandled Peggy out of the ambulance. With one of them at each end of the stretcher and Peggy now deeply unconscious, they went at a run towards the hospital emergency doors where, having been forewarned, the medical staff were there to collect the patient and rush her straight to theatre.

While Peggy was hurried away, Adam and Phil were taken aside; though Adam tearfully insisted that he wanted to go with his mum. 'Where is she?' he wanted to know. 'What have they done with my mum?' Traumatised by the fear that he might never see her again, he called for her over and over.

The nurse gently assured him, 'The doctors are helping your mother now. Don't worry, she's in safe hands, and they'll come and tell you when you're able to see her. Meantime, there is nothing you can do. She truly is being taken care of, so please . . . I know how hard it is, but you must try to be patient.'

She knew the boy might have a very long wait; especially since the message relayed from the ambulance crew to the hospital as they drove there had described the patient as having suffered life-threatening injuries.

'Look, I'll tell you what . . .' She pointed to the little tuck cabin down the corridor. 'If you go and see Mavis, she might let you have a bottle of pop. Tell her Nurse Riley sent you, then she won't charge you a single penny for it.'

Phil understood her kindly motive. 'That's a good idea, Adam,' he encouraged the boy. 'In fact, I wouldn't mind a bottle of pop myself.'

With sorry eyes, Adam glanced at the green baize door through which they had taken his mother. 'All right then.' Reluctantly, he gave a little nod. 'But you have to promise you'll wait here, Phil. You won't leave me, will you?'

Phil choked back a tear. 'Me? Leave you?' He cradled the boy's face in his hands. 'I would never leave you, never in a million years!' Digging into his trouser pocket he withdrew a shiny coin, which he handed to the boy. 'There! You run off and see Mavis . . . there's a good fellow.'

'Your grandfather is right,' Nurse Riley said. 'Mavis will be pleased to see you.'

Phil and the boy exchanged curious glances at her reference to Phil as 'your grandfather', but wisely, neither of them made mention of her remark.

A short time later, when they had drunk their pop and were seated in comfortable chairs in a small room off the main corridor, the silence between them was heavy.

All they could think of was Adam's mother, who lay just a short distance away, fighting for her life.

Every few minutes either Adam or Phil would go into the corridor and look to see if there was anyone they could speak to about how the boy's mother was doing, but there was no one about, except a man in a long white coat, in a great hurry, and a nurse rushing about with a trolley, piled high with newly laundered linen.

'They all have jobs to do,' Phil reassured Adam. 'I know you're worried, but we have to be thankful that the doctors are looking after her. No doubt someone will come out soon and tell us what's happening. Until then we'll have to be patient.'

Adam was desperately concerned for his mother. He was also concerned about what might happen to him. He reasoned that she would have to stay in hospital for at least a short while. His mother told him long ago that she had been adopted, and that when she met his father, her adoptive parents took an instant dislike to him, and forbade her to see him.

There was a huge row. Having just turned eighteen, she defied them and married his father without their blessing. Shortly after that, her parents emigrated to Australia, and she eventually lost all contact with them.

That was all Adam knew of his grandparents on his mother's side.

The only mention of his father's parents was during a heated argument between his own mother and father. He had learned that his father's older sister and both his parents were devoutly religious, while Adam's own father grew increasingly rebellious against their rigid and highly disciplined way of life. There were constant rows until, in his early twenties, he cut himself adrift from his family.

Now he had no idea where they were, nor did he want to know, because as far as he was concened, they did not exist.

During the many rows with his own wife, he claimed that she was much like his own mother; that she was domineering and saw no worth in him. He argued that instead of being grateful for the good life he provided for them both, she and Adam took him for granted. During his wild, unpredictable rants, he said they were like strangers to him; that they darkened his life and gave him nothing, yet they continued to feed off him like parasites.

He also threatened Adam's mother that if she ever mentioned his parents and sister again, she would be made to regret it. So, knowing from experience that he was more than capable of hurting her, Peggy wisely never again spoke of them.

Once, when Adam was caught eavesdropping outside the parlour, he was punished with the bunched knuckles of his father's fist across his head 'for hiding behind the door and listening in on a private conversation', he was told.

Now, with his father gone, hopefully for ever, he felt able to speak out.

'Phil?'

'Yes, son?'

'Can I tell you something?'

'Of course.'

'All right then.' In a whisper, and with a wary eye on the door in case his father should suddenly burst in, Adam told Phil everything.

He described the awful rows and the things he had learned about his father's family; that his father hated his sister and his parents, and had cut them out of his life. 'He said they were wicked, spiteful people, and that they made his life a misery, and now I'm frightened they might come and take me away, to look after me until Mum's better. But what if they never bring me back? I'm frightened, Phil. I don't want them to come and get me.'

Phil took it all in and when Adam fell silent, looking up at him with fear in his eyes, he assured him, 'If they're as bad as all that, they'll not be allowed to come for you.'

Adam then told Phil of his grandparents on his mother's side. 'Mum said her parents wanted her to go to Australia with them, but she didn't want to, and so they fell out and she left home. Then a while ago, some old neighbour told Mum that they'd gone to Australia, but she didn't know where, and Mum never heard from them again.'

'I see.' Phil nodded thoughtfully. 'By! That's a sorry situation and no mistake. So, it seems you've no close family other than your own parents, eh?'

Because Adam was already in pieces, Phil made no mention of his deep concern with regard to the boy's care. In the light of what he had just learned, he feared there could be all manner of trouble ahead.

'Phil?' Adam grew concerned when the older man lapsed into deep thought. 'Phil!'

Brought sharply out of his reverie, Phil put on a smile. 'Sorry, son . . . I was just dwelling on what you said: no aunts nor uncles, nor family of any kind, except for your parents. By! It doesn't bear thinking about.' Fearing that Peggy Carter might not survive, he was deeply anxious for the boy's welfare.

Adam voiced his own concerns. 'If Mum has to stay in hospital for a long time, I don't want to stay in the house all on my own, so will you please stay with me until Mum gets home?'

Taken aback by the request, Phil wisely avoided answering directly. 'Aw, look, son. It's not good to get ahead of yourself like that. Let's just wait and see how things go, and then we'll decide what's best to do.'

Adam had another question: 'If you don't like to live in my house, can I come and stay with you then?' Growing tearful, he finished lamely, 'Please say yes, Phil, 'cause there's nobody to look after me until Mum comes home.'

Phil glanced about nervously. 'Ssh!' He pressed his finger to his lips. 'It's best not to discuss these things just yet. Let's leave it for now, son. Let's wait and see what the doctor says, then you and me . . . we'll sort summat out. Try not to worry, and the less you say just now, the better.'

'All right, Phil, but if you stay with me at the house, I promise I'll be good. I'll do my homework, and if you want, you can fetch your little dog to stay with us.'

Phil's heart went out to the boy. He knew the situation could never work, and besides, it wasn't right – not for him and not for Adam. And yet he was made to ponder what alternative there might be.

'Listen to me, son . . .' Sidling closer to Adam, he spoke in a whisper. 'It seems they think I'm your granddad, but you and I know that is not the case.'

'We don't need to tell them, though, do we, Phil? You can still pretend to be my granddad . . . until Mum comes home.' His voice shook with emotion. 'Please, Phil . . . please!'

Phil felt torn. 'I'm sorry, son,' he said, being sensible, 'I don't know as I can move into your father's house. It would be wrong of me, and what if your father comes back? Like as not he'll have me arrested, and who could blame him?'

'All right! I'll come to your house and stay with you.'

'Aw, son . . . I don't know.' Phil was growing more unsettled by the minute. 'It's a bad situation. I don't want to think on it right now, not until we see how it goes with your mother.'

'This is all Father's fault, isn't it?'

'I don't know, son. I'm not altogether party to the facts.' Wisely, Phil was reluctant to commit himself to such far-reaching accusations.

'It's true, Phil!' Adam spelled it out: 'He's always hitting her, and she never tells anyone. And now he's hurt her so bad, he's got frightened and run away. He should be locked up for ever!'

Phil didn't really know what to believe, except what he had seen for himself today. And, talking about his father's brutal treatment of his mother, Adam seemed genuinely afraid.

Phil now voiced his own concerns. 'There's a possibility that you could be wrong about what happened. Maybe they had an argument and there really was a terrible accident, and if that's the case, your father will be worried sick when he gets home. I know one thing for sure, though, he will not be best pleased to see me and my dog taking up residence in his house. After all, I'm not even a relative. I'm just the driver of the school bus who's got himself caught up in a shocking accident—'

'It wasn't an accident! He did it, I know he did!'

'Sssh!' Phil instructed Adam, slightly unnerved. 'Like I say, just now, it's best not to talk about it too much. Let's just wait and see how things go. We'll have a better picture of the situation once the doctor tells us what's happening. Until then, however difficult it is, we have to be patient.' He looked the boy in the eye. 'Agreed?'

With a reluctant nod of the head, Adam had little choice but to agree. 'When Mum comes home, everything will be all right, though, won't it, Phil?'

'Let's hope so, eh?' Phil was well aware of the seriousness of this situation.

'Adam?' Phil asked.

'Yes, Phil?' Adam looked up.

'I have an idea to pass the time.' The child's small, anxious face made Phil immensely sad. 'Do you know what I was just thinking?'

'No.'

'Well, I was thinking how you and me could say a little prayer for your mum. What d'you think?'

'Oh, yes, please, Phil, I'd like that.' The tears brimmed over. 'Do you think it might help Mum to get better? I so much want her to come home. She will, won't she, Phil?' Throwing his arms round Phil's neck, he hugged him so hard that Phil found it difficult to breathe.

Phil held him at arm's length. 'Listen to me, Adam. Even if we say a prayer it doesn't mean that everything will come right. It doesn't always work like that. All I'm saying is, at certain bad times in my own life, I've always found a deal of comfort in saying a little prayer; hoping that somebody up there in the Heavens might be listening, and that somehow they would try and help. The thing is, sometimes, however much they might want to help, they just can't do it, and we will never know the reason for that. D'you understand what I'm saying?'

'If you said a prayer, why did they not help you?'

Phil took a deep breath. 'Well, it seems they weren't able to give what I really asked for, but they did help me . . . a little.'

'In what way?'

Phil was beginning to wish he had never started this, because the painful memories were flooding back. 'Well, you see, when my dear wife was very ill, I prayed for the Lord to make her better . . .' Composing himself, he went on in subdued tones: 'Sadly, my prayers were not answered, because that was not to be. Thankfully, though, they did stop her pain and I was grateful for that. Maybe she had to leave me, because she had important work to do in Heaven. Maybe someone up there needed her far more than I did.' Though he could not imagine how that might be, because for almost thirty years she was his world. His reason for living.

And now he had to stop tormenting himself, or the boy would see him cry and that would never do.

Adam's angry voice penetrated his thoughts: 'So, you said a prayer and asked for her to get better, then she died and you were sad. I think that was cruel.'

Phil nodded. 'It was cruel for me, yes, because I miss her every waking moment. But in a way, it was not too cruel for her, because you see, she was no longer in pain. Maybe she would never have got better, and that was why the Good Lord stopped her suffering. Yes, you're right in one way, because she was taken away from me, and I miss her. But I have so many wonderful memories to keep me warm.'

'You loved her very much, didn't you, Phil?'

Phil simply nodded.

'Did you love her as much as I love my mum?'

'Oh, yes. I'm sure I did. Y'see, we were together for a very long time.'

'So, did she say a prayer as well?'

'Well, I don't know for sure, because if she did send up a prayer, she never told me. Maybe her pain was so bad, she prayed for it to be gone, and in their wisdom, and because it was her that was in pain and not me, they decided to grant her wish instead of mine. That's fair enough . . . don't you think?'

'I don't know.'

'Me neither, son, but we have to believe it was the only way.'

His life was not the same since losing his one and only love, and as long as he lived, it would never be the same again. Like it or not, he had to accept the situation.

He returned to his question: 'So, knowing that you can't always have your wish granted, do you still want us to say a little prayer for your mum?'

The boy smiled through his tears. 'Yes, but I only

know the one that Mum used to say before I went to sleep.'

'Right, then!' Phil was glad to have diverted the boy's attention. 'Only you'll need to tell me what it is.'

Adam remembered it well. 'When I lay me down to sleep, I pray the Lord my soul to keep . . .'

'Ah, yes, that's a good prayer. I like that. We'll say it together . . . quietly.'

As they shared the prayer, they had no idea that someone else was listening. Someone who had also heard every word of their conversation.

An auxilary nurse had stopped to stack the linen cupboard next to the visitors' room where Phil and Adam were quietly talking. The dividing wall was thin and she had innocently overheard every word of their intimate conversation.

Some of what she had overheard was shocking, especially regarding the father. Then the fact that the boy had no relatives, except a brutal father who had left the mother battered . . . seemingly to within an inch of her life. Unbelievably, after the event, he had callously abandoned his son to whatever fate awaited him; knowing he had no one to turn to.

Having been made aware of this important information, which she suspected may not have been made available to the duty nurse, she was unsure of what to do. Eventually, torn between compassion and her sworn responsibility, she concluded that there was really no choice at all. She softly closed the wide cupboard doors and made her way down the corridor at a smart pace.

In view of Mrs Carter's life-threatening injuries, she realised there was not a moment to lose.

~

As the auxilary nurse arrived at the door of the main office, the matron entered the room where Phil and Adam were impatiently waiting for news.

'How is she?' Phil enquired.

'She's out of surgery,' the matron said. 'Mr Hendon is a very reputable surgeon. I can assure you no one could have done better. He will answer all your questions, I'm sure, but for the moment he's been called away to advise on another emergency. He needs to speak with you, and of course he's aware you will have questions, so I'm sure he won't be too long.'

'Where's my mum? Can I see her? Can she talk to me?' Anxious for information, Adam pushed between the matron and Phil, his questions coming thick and fast. 'Please, Nurse, can I just see her? Is she awake?'

In a reassuring manner, the matron informed him, 'Your mother is out of surgery and in the recovery room. She's tired and a bit groggy, which is understandable. A moment ago she opened her eyes and asked for you, so I do believe it would do her a world of good to see you. But you must not excite her, and you can only stay for a minute or two.'

Looking up at Phil, she explained, 'She desperately needs to rest, but as she's so very anxious to see her son, the surgeon has agreed for you both to visit, with myself in attendance.' She lowered her voice. 'You understand, she is not long out of major surgery. So when the nurse beckons you away, you will be expected to leave immediately.'

Nervously, Phil dared to ask, 'But she did come through the surgery well, didn't she?'

The matron glanced again at the boy, then she gave Phil an aside look that made his heart sink; for it seemed to warn him that things had not gone as well as they had hoped. 'Like I say, the surgeon will speak with you presently.'

As she turned to leave, the door opened and the surgeon walked in.

A man of impressive stature and authority, he greeted Phil and Adam with a warm, sincere smile. 'I'm sorry to have kept you both waiting, but I was called away.'

Phil's questions were direct: 'How is she . . . really? Are you concerned, or did it all go as well as you would have liked?'

Aware that Adam was also awaiting his answer, the surgeon chose his words carefully. 'As you must understand, there were major injuries to deal with, and yes, of course there were some very worrying moments, but she put up a good fight and we must pray that she makes a good recovery.'

He now directed his advice to the boy. 'Your mother is very weak. You must not expect to be with her for longer than a few minutes, and when the nurse indicates that it's time to leave, you must do as she asks. You do understand, don't you?'

Even though he ached to see his mother, Adam

wanted what was best for her. 'Yes, sir, I understand. I just need to see her.'

'And so you will.' He turned to the nurse. 'Matron, please will you take these gentlemen along to see Mrs Carter?'

'Of course.'

'Thank you. Oh, and I'm afraid I need to commandeer two of your nurses.'

Matron pursed her lips in disapproval, but her smile soon reassured him. 'As long as I get them back.'

'Don't worry.' After working together for many years, these two understood each other.

Before excusing himself from their presence, he turned to Adam. 'From the little your mother could tell us, she lost her footing and tumbled all the way down the stairs. Did you see her fall?'

Adam glanced nervously at Phil before answering, 'No, sir. I wasn't there. I came home from school and found her lying near the bottom of the steps.'

'I see.' He took a breath. 'Your mother will be pleased to see you, but she'll be a little groggy from the anaesthetic. She may not be able to say much, but she will hear you when you talk to her . . . Remember, a few minutes only.'

'Will my mum be strong enough to come home soon?' Adam asked.

The surgeon gave the only answer he could. 'We can't say at this time, because she still has a long way to go. Your mother was very badly injured, but I can assure you, we have done everything possible to help her. I'm sure your mum wants to get home to you as soon as possible. Oh, and you mustn't be too frightened when you see her. She's surrounded by machines; all there to assist her recovery. Both her arms are wrapped in plaster casts, and she carries a great number of nasty bruises.' He deliberately made no mention of the numerous internal injuries; some of which would take many months to repair.

He placed his hands on Adam's small shoulders. 'I'm telling you now so that you won't be alarmed when you see her. All right?'

'Yes, sir.' Adam was shaken, but determined. 'When she gets better, she'll be coming home, won't she . . .? When her bones mend and all that?'

The surgeon tried to put it tactfully. 'We can't really say how long it will take her to recover. Your mum has been through a shocking ordeal, and hours of major surgery, and now it's imperative that she gets rest and care.'

'Then she'll be all right, won't she?' Adam was relentless in his need for reassurance. 'We'll be able to take her home soon, won't we?'

The surgeon was equally determined not to raise the boy's hopes. 'In these early stages of recovery, we must not even think of her as being in a hurry to get home. I'm sorry, I know it's hard for you, but you have to try to understand.'

Tearful now, Adam appealed to Phil. 'Tell him, Phil. I want my mum to come home really soon. I'll look after her, you know I will.'

Phil nodded. 'I know you would, son, but like the doctor says, your mum needs time to recover where the doctors and nurses can keep an eye on her. And besides, I'll bring you to see her every day. Meantime, she'll want you to be attending school and trying to get on with your life as normal. You know that, don't you?'

Reassured by Phil's persuasive remarks, the boy looked up at the surgeon. 'Please, can I see my mum now?'

'Of course.' Being a family man, Mr Hendon was full of sympathy for the boy. 'Matron will take you along.'

The surgeon departed ahead of them, while directly behind him, Matron led Phil and Adam along the same corridor, to the recovery room.

Throughout the long, worrying walk, Adam kept his gaze to the floor, while Phil looked ahead, his mind troubled by the look in the surgeon's eyes when asked about Peggy Carter's condition.

He watched as Mr Hendon, still ahead of them, turned into what looked like the main office. His interest was heightened when he drew alongside the office and he saw the surgeon earnestly talking with two official-looking people.

As Phil glanced in, one of the officials caught sight of them passing by the window. He then beckoned his colleague, and she looked out of the window, directly at young Adam.

Phil's concern intensified. Discreetly, he put his hand on Adam's shoulder and hurried him along.

'Who were those people?' Adam asked. 'Why were they looking at me?'

'They probably heard our clattering feet hurrying along, and were curious,' he reassured Adam.

Phil, however, felt decidedly nervous. He was in no doubt that the officials were interested in the boy. Also, they had appeared to be engaged in deep conversation with the surgeon. Maybe it had nothing to do with Adam or his mother, but Phil had a bad feeling, which he could not shake off.

He glanced at the boy. Such an innocent; his young heart filled with loathing for his cowardly father who had left such a trail of devastation in his wake. And now, he was so afraid his mother would never get well again. Yet through all his crippling unhappiness, Adam gave no thought to himself. Nor did he realise the precarious position he had been put in by his father's abandonment of him.

~

At the door of the recovery room, Matron peered in through the glass panel. 'Don't forget, a few minutes, that's all,' she warned.

After Adam gave an appreciative nod, she turned the handle and pushed open the door to usher them inside.

Phil and the boy were shocked to see the small, vulnerable figure lying in the high bed, her face turned away and her two arms wrapped in thick, stiff plaster. There was a kind of pulley over the top of the bed, with support-joints stretching down; two ends attached to the root of the pulley, and the other ends attached to the plaster-encased limbs, which were very slightly elevated above the patient.

Phil's interest was immediately drawn to the heart-tracking machine.

'Carefully now.' Matron accompanied Adam to the bedside, where she sat him down on a chair right beside the bed and close to his mother, whose badly bruised face was turned towards him. She appeared restless, intermittently shifting her head back and forth, and making a low, whining sound, much like an animal in pain.

Unsettled by this sound, Phil fixed his troubled gaze on the heart monitor; he was greatly relieved to see the screen showed a steady beat.

Taking a seat beside the boy, Phil rested his arm on the back of Adam's chair, while his sorry gaze also travelled the visible dark bruises on Peggy Carter's body. Deeply unsettled, she appeared to be unaware of their presence.

'Mum?' With a shaky voice, Adam called out twice. 'Mum, it's Adam. I've come to see you.' Reaching up, the boy tenderly clasped the tip of his mother's fingers where they jutted from the plaster cast. 'Phil's here too, Mum. He's been looking after me.'

When the tears rolled down his face and his voice began to tremble, Phil slid a comforting arm around him. 'Easy, son. You remember what the doctor said: your mum might not be able to speak, but she might possibly be able to hear you. So, just try and tell her the things that are in your heart. Let her know that everything is all right, that she's not to worry about you. And tell her you'll be here to see her often, until she's well enough to come home.'

So that was what Adam did. He told his mother how very much he loved her. 'I'll be so glad if you can get better really quickly, and then you'll be able to come home and we'll be together, and I'll take care of you until you're strong again.'

Both Phil and Adam were astonished when her eyes flickered open and she looked straight at her son. Her lips were moving, but when she attempted to speak, the mumbled words were lost in a choking sound.

'What's wrong with her?' Appealing to Phil, Adam began to panic.

Quickly now, Matron crossed to the bed. Leaning to examine her patient, she told them, 'It's all right. She's trying to say something, but she's not yet fully awake.' She glanced up at Phil. 'Another moment, and you must take Adam back so she can get her rest.'

As Matron moved away to check the machine readings, Peggy attempted to speak again. This time, Adam drew closer, trying to decipher the incoherent whispers.

With great tenderness, he wrapped his hand about her fingers. For a moment he was silent, painfully reliving what had gone before. Presently, with his other hand he reached out to stroke her thick, wayward hair. 'I love you, Mum. I want you to come home, so please get better soon.'

Peggy heard his every word, and she so wanted to rest, but she had to know first. In a snatched breath, she asked him, 'Is he . . . here?'

Relieved to hear her voice, Adam leaned closer, his

voice small. 'If you mean Father, he ran away like a coward, and he never came back.' Anger consumed him. '*He* did this to you, didn't he?'

'Sssh!' Her voice shivered with fear.

Exhausted, she momentarily closed her eyes. She was not afraid for herself, but for her only child. She needed to take care of him, this precious boy, who had seen bad things that no child should ever see.

'Mum!' Adam leaned closer. 'Don't be afraid, because if he comes back, I won't let him in. Phil's taking care of me, and we'll be all right till you come home. We really will . . .'

When she made a slow, deliberate movement to touch his face, he realised she was anxious to say something else.

'Don't talk, Mum. It will be all right,' he assured her. 'I'll take care of everything until you get home. If he comes back . . . I'll tell them what he's like . . .'

Deeply distressed, Peggy's furtive whispers were for her son's ears only. 'No. Don't say . . . that.'

'But he hurt you, Mum. He did!'

'Please . . . promise me.' Exhausted, she fell back into her pillow.

'All right, Mum.' Adam stood up and, gently laying his face on hers, he reluctantly put her mind at rest. 'I won't tell,' he whispered, 'I promise . . .' He found it hard to believe it was what she wanted, but he would keep his promise.

All he needed was for his mum to get better.

'Love you . . . Son.' Relief shadowed her face and now she was silent again.

'Mum?' Cradling her face, he was shocked at how cold she was. 'Mum!'

There was no response.

'Mum! Wake up . . . Mum!'

Matron hurried across the room. One glance at Peggy and she pushed the panic button. 'Take the boy away now!' she said to Phil.

Glancing at Peggy's face, Phil was afraid. 'Come on, son. We'd best do as Matron says.' Deeply shaken, he led Adam away. As they hurried out the door, a number of medical staff were coming up the corridor at the run.

Keeping a strong hold on Adam, Phil quickened their steps. He did not want even to consider what might be going on in the recovery room.

Quickly now, he took Adam down the long corridor and into the waiting area where they had previously been.

Adam fought against him. 'I have to go back . . . my mum needs me.'

'They're taking care of her, son.' Phil kept a tight hold on Adam. 'They'll let us know how she is, soon enough.' After seeing her so pale and empty, Phil secretly feared the worst.

CHAPTER THREE

IN THE VISITOR'S room, Phil anxiously paced the floor. Occasionally, he paused to look through the window into the corridor, but there was no one in sight.

He turned his gaze to Adam, who was curled up on the couch, quietly sobbing.

With every minute that passed, Phil began to lose faith, though he kept his disturbing thoughts to himself.

Presently, he glanced across at the boy, who was quieter now, deep in thought. Phil's heart went out to him. Again, he made his way over to him. 'I know you want news of your mum,' he started, 'but we must try and be patient, however hard it might be.'

After what seemed an age, there was a tap on the door, and the surgeon entered, his face sombre.

'What happened? Is she all right?' Phil asked.

Simultaneously, Adam ran over, asking anxiously, 'Is my mum all right?'

The surgeon quietly suggested to Phil, 'It might be best if I have a quiet word with you first.'

Sensing the tense atmosphere, and made increasingly nervous by the knowing glances that passed between the two men, Adam backed away. 'What's happened? Why won't you let me go to my mum?'

Moved to tears, Phil took hold of him. 'I'm sorry, son, but you can't go to your mother,' he said gently. Though well aware that it was Adam's right to see her, Phil realized it would not be wise. After all, he was just a child and, at the moment, dangerously vulnerable.

'Why can't I see her?' All of Adam's instincts told him the awful truth. In his heart and soul, he knew she had left him. 'Get off me!' His screams reverberated through the room. He fought Phil off and would have run from the room, but Phil caught him and held him.

'Listen to me, son.' His kind voice was calming. 'D'you recall what I told you . . . about my darling wife and how the only thing I wanted in the whole wide world was for her to be all right?'

Tearfully, Adam nodded.

'And do you recall how, for reasons we may never understand, the Good Lord took her all the same?'

Another reluctant nod.

'Well, then, I've been thinking. Maybe your mum, like my dear wife, could never be made better on this earth. But up there, in God's Heaven, she doesn't feel pain any more; she's comfortable and at peace, and though you will always miss her, she'll be watching over you. She will never leave you.'

Deeply moved by Phil's gentle words, the surgeon cautiously approached Adam. 'I'm so very sorry. I know how hard it must be. I can promise you, we did everything humanly possible for your mother, but her injuries were many and her heart was not strong enough to carry her through.'

Adam looked up, his eyes marbled with grief. He began to sob, and soon it was an avalanche of grief. The devastating loss of his mother and the all-consuming hatred for the man who hurt her could no longer be contained.

In a trembling voice, he murmured, 'One day, when I'm bigger, he'll pay for what he did.'

'Who will, Adam?' Mr Hendon probed for the truth. 'Do you want to tell us about this person . . . the one who must "pay for what he did"? Adam, can you tell me who you mean?'

Adam looked away. The surgeon's words were a timely caution to him, for he knew he must never tell. Not because he didn't want to, but because his mother had made him promise not to.

Just then the door opened and a nurse entered. After she had imparted her message to the surgeon, he politely excused himself. 'I'm afraid I'll have to leave you for a while, but please wait here. Someone will be along in a moment to have a word with you.'

They watched him leave.

'Phil?' Adam's voice trembled.

'Yes, son?'

'When the person comes, will they let me see my mum?' He felt as though his world had fallen apart. It was a strange and frightening feeling. 'I have to tell her something.'

Phil knew that feeling, and he saw it in the boy's face now. 'Adam, listen to me.'

'No! I don't want to.' Tearful, Adam turned away.

Phil persevered. 'Think about what you're asking, son. I know how much you want to see her, but it isn't right for you just now. Later, when everything is in order, I'm sure you can see your mother . . . if you are still of the same mind.'

'Please, Phil, I need to see my mum!'

Phil tried gently to dissuade him. 'I do understand, but do you really think your mother would want you to see her now? Or do you think she'd rather you remembered your last conversation with her, when she was still able to tell you how much she loved you? Don't you think she would feel your sadness, if you were to see her now?'

Phil's wise words reached home. After what seemed an age, the boy took a long, deep breath and tried to be the man his mum would want him to be. 'Is my mum really safe now, Phil?' He needed reassurance.

Phil promised him that she was safe.

Adam accepted what Phil had told him, though he found it incredibly difficult to believe that he would never again see his mother, never again hear her voice. Never again hear her laugh, nor run with her across the fields. In his heart he could see her beautiful smile, and that funny way she had of wrinkling her nose when she laughed out loud.

Suddenly the awful truth began to sink in, and the enormity of it all was too much for him to bear.

In a voice that was almost inaudible, he whispered to Phil, 'I'm really sad.' Winding his arms round Phil's wide waist, he confessed brokenly, 'I don't know what to do.'

'Aw, son, we can none of us do anything, because when the Good Lord calls us home, we have to go.' Phil held the boy tight to him. 'But you're not on your own, son, because I'm here for you. If I'm able, I will always be here for you.'

Thankful that he had Phil, the boy confided in a whisper, 'Phil, I don't know if she heard me promise. I need her to know that I made the promise.'

Choking back his emotion, Phil told him, 'Don't you worry about that, because she heard it all right – I heard it too – but y'know, son, sometimes we make promises and then, later, we regret them. You might need to think about that particular promise, the one you made to your mother. Maybe you won't want to think about it just yet. But maybe later, when you're not so very sad.'

Adam was resolute. 'If Mum had not made me promise, I would have told them everything . . . about how he hurt her, time after time, hitting her and making her cry. I hate him for what he did, but she didn't want me to tell. Why did she not want me to tell?'

Phil measured his words carefully. 'Because she loved you so much, she did not want you to do something that might hurt you in the long run. I believe that was why she asked you to make that promise.' He lowered his voice. 'I think she wanted you not to tell, because if you told, then you would have so many awkward questions to answer. It would be a nasty business, with you caught up in it.'

Leaning forward, Phil placed his hands either side of Adam's face. 'All you need to know is that your mother loved you, and that no one will ever be able to hurt her again.'

Looking into Phil's kind, weathered face, Adam saw such honesty.

'Phil?'

'Yes, son?'

'She's died, hasn't she?'

'Yes, son.'

'Has she gone to the same place as your wife?'

'Yes, I'm sure she has.'

'Will they be friends?'

'I would like to think so.'

'But I'd rather my mum could be here with me, because then, when I get older, I could keep her safe always.'

'Ah, but that's not your job, son, because now she's in the safest place of all. Your mum was an angel on earth, but angels belong in Heaven. She'll be well looked after there.'

'I want her back, Phil. I miss her . . . I really miss her.' Suddenly the full truth had hit home. He could no longer be brave; and his grief was overwhelming. Hiding himself in Phil's musty old coat, he sobbed as though his heart would break.

Holding him close, Phil took him to the couch, where he sat beside him, holding him until he sobbed himself to sleep.

A short time later, Matron arrived. On seeing the boy asleep on the couch, she went out and returned with a fleecy blanket, which she handed to Phil.

She watched him wrap it around Adam before quietly informing him, 'I'm afraid we have to discuss official matters.' She beckoned Phil to the other side of the room, lowering her voice as she told him, 'I am led to understand that you are not the grandfather after all. Is that true?'

Knowing he must, Phil told her his name and the whole story: how he had dropped Adam from the school bus and walked home with him down the lane; how he was on his way back to his bus when he heard the boy shouting. 'In a shocking state, he was, finding his mother like that, and his father running off like a spineless coward. I don't know if it was the father who hurt her, but Adam seems convinced of it.'

'So, why did you not inform us of these circumstances right away?'

'I gave as much information as I could, but it was your staff who chose to believe I was his grandfather, and besides, there were more urgent matters to deal with at the time, as you well know.'

'Well, I'm sorry, but since we have become aware of the truth, I'm afraid it was our duty to call in the authorities.'

'What authorities?' Phil recalled the officials in the office, and all his fears returned. 'Look, Matron, I make no apologies for letting you believe that I was his grandfather, because as far as I'm aware, he's got no one else.'

'I see.' As a woman, Matron was deeply sympathetic, but duty was her priority, along with the boy's welfare. She explained, 'In the light of what we now know, this is a very serious situation. The boy's mother has died under suspicious circumstances, and the father has run away. Moreover, we are led to understand there are no close relatives at hand to take care of the boy.'

'I'll take care of him then. At least until the in-laws can be found.'

'I'm sorry, but I don't think that will be an option.'

'So, what will happen to him?'

'That's for the authorities to decide.'

Before he could answer, she left with the parting words, 'You do seem to have his interests at heart, and he obviously trusts you. If you could please continue to keep an eye on him, I'll be back presently.'

When she had gone, Phil paced the floor. *This is a sorry state of affairs and no mistake,* he thought, walking over to where Adam was sleeping. *I can't imagine what might happen to you now, son.* He gazed down on the boy and he shook his head in despair. *No family to speak of, and no one but me to stand by you.*

He understood the gravity of the situation. Unless Adam's father was found there was little hope of getting the child home. Possibly not even then.

Physically and emotionally exhausted, he sat down in a chair, laid himself back and closed his weary eyes.

Some few minutes later the nurse arrived with two other people.

Phil clambered out of the chair, one eye shut and the other on the boy. He still clung to the hope that, one way or another, he might yet be able to take the boy home.

'These people need to speak with you,' the nurse

advised him. Having waved the visitors forward, she went to sit by Adam. When in his sleep he occasionally whimpered in distress, she tenderly lulled him quiet again.

Phil had been greatly unnerved at the sight of the two very officious-looking people standing before him. The woman was middle-aged, dressed in a dark two-piece. The man was older, serious-looking, smart in light grey jacket and black trousers. He also carried a document case. They were the people Phil had seen in the office earlier.

The woman introduced herself and her colleague: 'My name is Miss Benson, and this is Mr Norman. We're here on behalf of Child Welfare and Social Services.' Her gaze shifted to Adam.

Phil had already guessed at their reason for being there, and he expected the worst. 'Child Welfare, eh? And may I ask, what it is you want from us?'

'I understand you are Phil Wallis?'

'That's right.'

'You accompanied Adam and his mother, yes?'

'I did.'

'Well, Mr Wallis, first, I apologise for all the questions.' She paused to glance at the sleeping boy. 'Please be assured, we're not here to cause distress at this unhappy time, but having been made aware of some rather unsettling issues, we're duty-bound to examine the facts.'

Phil was already on the defensive. 'Well then, I'll explain the "facts" to you, shall I?' He pointed to Adam. 'That poor child there has just lost his mother in the cruellest way imaginable. His father's run off and the boy thinks the world has come to an end. I would not describe that as being an "unhappy time". I would call that catastrophic, wouldn't you?'

'Well, yes, of course. As you say . . . but as I've explained, we have a job to do, and in view of the notification we received, we will first need to clarify the details of your relationship with the boy.' Without waiting for Phil to respond, Miss Benson plucked a black notepad from her document case.

After quickly scanning her own notes, she had a number of questions, which she put to Phil in a quiet manner, being acutely aware that Adam could wake at any moment. 'If you could again confirm that you are Phil Wallis, and that you are no relation to Adam Carter.'

'That's right.'

'I'm sorry,' she seemed genuinely so, 'but I need you, please, to go through what happened.'

Phil was irritated. 'Why can't you let me get him home and we can answer your questions there?' He lowered his voice to an angry whisper. 'What good will it do Adam, sitting here just yards from where his mother lies dead? For pity's sake, let me get him home. I can assure you, neither me nor the boy is about to leave the country!'

'I understand your anxiety, Mr Wallis. Believe me, we also have Adam's best interests at heart. So, if you could, please, quickly run through the events that brought you and Adam here . . .? Once we know exactly what the situation is, we can then decide which course of action to take.'

Phil had no doubt about what she meant. These were official people, and he appreciated that their specific task was to protect children from harm. If they decided Adam needed taking into care, temporarily or otherwise, there would be nothing that he or anyone else could do to stop them. Especially considering not only the seriousness of events, but the fact that he himself was neither a relative nor even a long-term friend. He was merely the driver of the school bus; in the wrong place at the wrong time.

Miss Benson now casually informed him, 'Oh, and incidentally, because of the information we received, the police have been notified. I understand, they are on their way as we speak.'

Her serious-faced companion, Mr Norman, now took a step forward. 'Of course, the father will obviously need to answer to the police. Adam, however, will initially come under our jurisdiction.' Gesturing to a nearby chair, he suggested, 'Maybe you would care to sit down, while we take you through the procedure?'

Phil flatly refused to sit down. 'Ask your questions.'

'Firstly, as we've already established that you are not Adam Carter's grandfather, can you please explain how you came to be here, with the boy?'

Phil explained, 'I drive the school bus and have done these many years. I had already dropped all the other children off, and as Adam was the last, I decided to walk him up the lane to his house. When we got to the gate, I saw the man I assumed to be his father; he came rushing out of the house, and stood on the porch. I greeted him cordially, but he made no reply.'

He paused before confiding, 'It didn't bother me that the boy's father chose to ignore me; he's got a reputation of being a miserable sod, to say the least. Anyway, thinking the boy would be safe enough with his father, I took my leave of them.' He relived the scene in his mind.

'Please, go on.'

'Well, I was on my way back down the lane, when I heard Mr Carter yelling at Adam. Then all of a sudden this car sped past me. Seeing as it was the very same car that was parked in the drive, I thought it must be Adam's father. Whoever it was, they must have taken leave of their senses, tearing down that narrow lane like a bat out of hell! Splashed mud all over my trousers, so he did, damned lunatic!'

'What did you do then?'

'Well, what else could I do but go back and find out why the boy was now calling. I found him in the lane – crying and shaking he was – and then I went back to the house with him and saw his mother, all broken and twisted at the bottom of the stairs. By, she was in a terrible way; she needed help, and quick. So, I did what needed doing: I sent Adam to call for an ambulance, while I sat and talked to his mother. I didn't even know if she could hear me, but I was hoping she could. That's what they say, isn't it – talk to them, just in case they can hear you?'

'So then what? Did the father come back?'

'No! We saw neither hide nor hair of him. It wasn't long before the ambulance arrived. They tended the mother and put her in the ambulance. Me and the boy jumped in alongside. And now we're here, and that poor boy has lost his mother. And there you have it.'

'Thank you. So now we'll need to discuss the implications of what you've told us.'

'What will happen to Adam?' Phil asked anxiously.

Miss Benson's reply was curt: 'We'll be back shortly, and inform you of any decisions made with regard to Adam.'

No sooner were they gone than the door opened to admit two police officers – a woman and her male colleague – who were interested to learn what exactly Phil might know about Adam's father. Concerned that they were not of the same quiet disposition as the Child Welfare officials, Phil inched them over to the furthest side of the room. 'I don't want Adam to hear us talking,' he explained, and they fully appreciated his concern.

Over the next ten minutes or so, Phil impatiently answered all their questions; most of which he had already gone through with Miss Benson and Mr Norman.

The officers were sympathetic, but they questioned Phil about various aspects of his account. 'First, the medical staff were led to believe that you were the boy's grandfather. How did that come about?'

As before, Phil answered truthfully. 'First of all, I can assure you that at no time did I give the impression that I was his grandfather. They just assumed that I was, and because of what was going on I didn't bother to put them right. Mind you, I wish to God I *was* his grandfather, because then I might have some say in what happens to him.' He told them that he was the driver of the school bus, and had fallen into a situation that no one with any compassion could have run away from.

The questions were thick and fast: 'How did you come to be here now, with Adam Carter? How much do you know about the manner in which Mrs Carter's injuries were caused?'

'I don't know any more than I've already explained,' Phil told them. 'I was on my way back to my bus, when the boy called for me to help him. I neither heard nor saw anything of what took place up to that point.'

'All right, so could you just go through it again, say what you do know, and explain how you got involved? Don't leave any detail out, however small and insignificant it might seem to you.'

Quickly, Phil went through it all again: about how he had dropped the boy off and walked him down the lane to his house. 'Like I told the others, his father was with him when I left, so I told the boy cheerio and went on my way.'

'And then what?'

'Well, I heard this man's voice. He sounded angry . . . screeching and yelling, he was. I assumed it must be the father as I'd seen no one else about, and the Carters' house was the only one down that lane. Then the same car I'd seen in the drive went skidding past me and onto the main road like a damned lunatic!'

Uneasy that the woman police constable was making entries in her notebook, he reluctantly continued, 'No sooner was the car out of sight than I heard Adam yelling my name, pleading for me to help him . . . in a right state he was, poor little devil. I ran back to him and when we got into the house I was shocked at what I saw there.'

He described finding Peggy Carter, as before. 'I've no idea what went on in that house, but if you ask me, nobody falls down the stairs and ends up as damaged as that poor woman.'

He was not surprised to see the two officers exchange glances, because he suspected they must be thinking the very same as himself.

Having explained the run of events, he glanced over at the boy. 'No child should ever see his mother like that, and now she's gone, and he's like a lost soul. I gave him my word that I would not let him down.'

'When you "gave him your word", what do you mean exactly?' the male police officer asked.

Phil hesitated. What use was his word anyway, now that Child Welfare had got involved? But then, he must have been crazy if he had ever believed it could be any other way.

'I meant that he was not to worry about anything, because I would look after him. So now I'd like to get the boy home as quickly as possible. It's not right for him to be here just now, especially after what's happened. He needs looking after. As far as I can tell, I'm the only one he's got.'

The male officer was sympathetic, but having dealt with deserted children for many years, he was also realistic. 'I'm afraid it isn't as simple as that.'

'What's that supposed to mean?' Phil's concern was heightened by his remark, even though he was sensible enough to know that what he proposed would never be allowed.

The officer spelled it out. 'As you're well aware, the boy's mother has just died, and as far as we can tell, his father has abandoned him. Then there's the question of how Mrs Carter actually received her injuries. There are still far too many questions left unanswered. As for the boy, he is not altogether your concern. You must understand, it's our duty to see that he is kept safe until every effort is made to locate any relatives there might be.'

'Yes, of course I understand that, but he's a very frightened child, without anyone close to turn to. The thing is, he knows and trusts me. I'm offering to keep him safe, at my home, or if it helps matters I'll stay with him at his house. Either way, he'll be taken care of, and, more importantly, by someone who's known him these past many years; since he was old enough to attend school.'

'I'm afraid this is not an option, Mr Wallis. When a child appears to be in danger, for whatever reason, we have a legal responsibility to examine those circumstances and take whatever steps we have to take in the best interests of that child. From information received, we consider Adam's situation to be highly sensitive; therefore needing an immediate response. As you have already explained, you are not a relative. That being the case, Adam's welfare is a matter for the Child Welfare Department.'

He concluded, 'Under the circumstances, there is no question of allowing the boy to return home. As I understand it, the case has now moved into the realms of a possible murder inquiry. So, until the investigation is concluded with regard to Mrs Carter's fatal injuries, the family home will be cordoned off and kept secure. As for relatives, you can be assured that the search is already underway. Meantime, as I've already explained, the boy's safekeeping remains the responsibility of the courts, and the Child Welfare Department.'

'Yes, and that's what I'm worried about.' Phil spoke his mind. 'I'm worried that they'll put him in the children's home, and if his father doesn't come back, what'll happen to him then, eh? Like as not he'll be fostered out, and how many foster parents would choose a deeply troubled seven-year-old in preference to a younger child? Not many, in my opinion!'

'Have you any idea where the father might have gone?' the woman police officer asked.

'I've no idea at all. How could I?'

'So, you wouldn't know if Mr Carter ever intended coming back?'

'I haven't a clue.'

When the official questions were over, Phil had a few questions of his own, such as what would happen with Mrs Carter now, and when might they be able to make plans to move her. 'When can we begin making arrangements for her to be laid to her rest?'

Again, the answers to all of his questions were negative and unsettling. And he was grateful that Adam had remained asleep; unaware of what was being said.

~

Following an agonising wait, Phil was informed by the Child Welfare officers that, after discussing the case, they had reached the only decision available to them in the circumstances.

Peggy Carter's son would be taken into care until it was established whether or not he had relatives who might want to apply for custody.

Heartbroken, Phil asked if he might be the one to relay the news to Adam. Being sympathetic to the boy's plight, and having already realised the bond between these two, the officials agreed. So, while the officers remained by the door, Phil woke Adam up.

Seated beside Adam, Phil choked back his own emotion as he explained how everyone was concerned that they should do the right thing by him, and therefore every effort was being taken to locate his father, and track down any other of his relatives.

'Meantime, son, you must go with the people whose responsibility it is to keep you safe and well.'

Nervously, Adam looked across at the two Child Welfare people. For what seemed an age he did not speak. Then he looked back at Phil and, in a small, quivering voice he asked, 'Are they waiting to take me away now?'

Trying hard not to show his sorrow, Phil took a moment to reply, and even then was able only to nod, for fear of letting his emotions run away with him.

Then they looked at each other a long while, and the boy fell into Phil's chubby arms. Holding onto him as though his own life depended on it, he confided tearfully, 'I don't want to go with them, Phil. I want to go with you.'

'I know, son, and I would take you home in a minute, but it isn't possible. But you're not to worry. You'll be safe enough with these people. They'll look after you, and who knows, they might even find your real granddad, and possibly a cousin or two. You'd like that, wouldn't you?'

Adam gave no answer. Instead, he asked, 'When can I see my mum?'

'Not yet, son, but when the time is right, I'll be sure to let you know.'

'Will you, Phil? Honestly?'

'Oh, yes! You can depend on it!' It was getting harder for him to hold back his emotions, but somehow he continued to remain calm and reassuring, for the boy's sake.

'And you'll come and see me, won't you, Phil?'

'You bet I will!'

'Are you coming with me now?'

'No, I'm afraid not, but you've got Miss Benson and Mr Norman with you.'

'But I want you there! Oh, please, Phil, don't leave me!' He started to cry again. 'Don't go, *please*.'

Phil addressed the Welfare officers. 'It wouldn't hurt if I went along too, would it?' he asked softly. 'It's been such a bad day for the little chap.'

Of course, they could not deny the sobbing child this request.

'Where are we going?' asked Adam.

'To the place where you'll be living, while they look for one of your relatives,' Phil explained. 'Oh, Adam, wouldn't that be wonderful . . . if they found someone who wanted to love and take care of you . . . someone of your very own?'

Adam looked away. 'I want my mum.'

'I know that, son. But like I said before – and I want you always to think of what I'm telling you now – your mother has gone to a better place. She's not suffering any more, and no one can hurt her ever again.'

'Is she still watching over us, Phil?'

'Oh, yes. More than ever, and she always will be.'

A small, sympathetic gesture from one of the watching pair told Phil it was time to go.

Phil gave a nod, then, as he held Adam by the hand, they were led down the corridor, outside and across the car park, and into a waiting vehicle.

At first Adam resisted, but Phil stayed beside him, coaxing him into the back of the car, before climbing in alongside.

Throughout the short journey, Adam was unusually quiet, head down, his thoughts back there in the hospital with his beloved mum. Occasionally he would choke back a sob, and lean into Phil for comfort.

Phil talked calmly to him. He reminded him that he would come and see him as often as he was allowed, and that he would never let him down.

'I mean to keep track of you,' he said. 'Tomorrow I'll bring you pen and paper, and my home address, so if you feel the need to write to me, you'll have the means. Oh, and I'll fetch you a notebook.'

'What for?'

'Well, if ever there's a time when I'm not able to visit and you might be worried, or sad, or maybe you've done something you feel proud of, you can put it all in your little book. Make sure to keep it safe, and we'll talk it through when next I see you. Mind you, it'll take a herd of horses or the end of the world to keep me from visiting. So, Adam, my boy, is that a deal?'

'Yes, please, Phil.'

Seated upfront, the Welfare officers were touched by the very special relationship between the man and the boy.

'The old fella was right,' Miss Benson confided to Mr Norman. 'If there was any justice in the world, he should have been the boy's real grandfather.'

Mr Norman glanced in his driving mirror to see the boy smiling up at Phil, and he had to agree.

~

Within the hour, they arrived at the children's home. An impressive, proud old building with long windows and a great oak door, it gave an impression of great strength.

'Here we are then, Adam.' Mr Norman climbed out of the car, and opened the door on Adam's side. 'We have many other children here, children much as yourself, who, through no fault of their own, have found themselves in unfortunate circumstances. I do hope you'll be content here, while the search is on to find a relative who might offer you a loving home. In the meantime, I'm sure you'll find a friend or two here. Oh, and I'm sure your good friend, Phil, will be calling in from time to time.'

'Come rain or shine, you can count on it!' Phil assured them all.

Walking across to the front door, Phil felt Adam's hand tremble in his, and his heart was like a lead weight inside him. As was his way, he gave up a silent prayer: *Don't desert him, Lord, for this boy will never need You more than he does right now.*

He glanced at Adam's forlorn face, then he looked up at the impressive building with its long, arched windows and grand oak door, and he hoped it would not be too long before Adam could be reunited with his own long-lost relatives. Or, if that was not to be, then maybe he would be offered a special place in the heart of a loving family.

At that moment, the door opened to reveal a portly woman of middle age. Her pink face, with merry blue eyes, was wreathed in a broad smile, and her mass of brown hair was haphazardly piled on top of her head. She introduced herself as Miss Martin, and brightly invited them to, 'Come in . . . please, do come in.' She had a singsong voice that made Phil and Adam share the tiniest of smiles.

As they were ushered inside, Adam clung to Phil; and Phil felt that Adam was resisting every step. 'It'll be all right, son,' he confided. 'She looks like a nice, jolly sort. Oh, and look!' He pointed to one of the long casement windows. 'The children are waving at you. Oh, Adam! I really think you'll make friends here, but I've a feeling it won't be too long before you're settled into a fine, loving family.'

Adam was not listening; nor was he looking at the

children. Instead, he was thinking of his mother, of her smile and her laughter, and the way she always cuddled him, too tight, and too often; almost as though she could not let him go.

Now, she would never cuddle him again, or laugh out loud, or wave him off when he climbed onto the school bus.

When the inevitable tears came, he quietly wiped them away with the cuff of his sleeve.

Phil had seen the tears, though, and wrapping his arm round the boy's shoulders, he drew him close.

Minutes later, as they walked through the door and into the huge, wood-panelled hallway, Phil had a feeling of dread.

He feared for the future, and with the boy still reeling from the loss of his mother, and his heart heavy with hatred for the man who he believed had caused her death, he was at his most vulnerable.

Phil could not help but wonder how this sad and lonely child would ever again find a sense of peace.

He felt as though somehow he had been appointed guardian. And so, come what may, and for as long as it took, he promised himself that he would watch over Adam as though he were his own flesh and blood.

Miss Martin seemed friendly enough, and as she waddled ahead, they were informed of occasional events that took place in the home.

'We keep an orderly house, but that is not to say we don't ever have fun. We also like to reward hard work and good behaviour. We're privileged to have at least one summer trip to the seaside, and we always celebrate Christmas.'

There were many rooms in the house, and it took the best part of an hour to visit each one. The great hall was very much designed in the manner of the hallway itself, with wall panels above the skirting, and tall, arched windows. At one end there was a raised pulpit.

'This is where we gather for morning prayers and address the various matters of the week,' Miss Martin said.

As they toured the downstairs, Adam remained silent, as did Phil, though the officials did ask questions now and then, in order to gain more information for the benefit of Phil and Adam.

At the front of the building there were classrooms and other, brighter, rooms for play. Adam and Phil had the opportunity to watch the younger children playing happily, with the staff being very caring and supportive.

Of the other rooms, some were dedicated to early learning, while another, with rows of seats and a huge screen, was set aside for additional education and the occasional film treat.

From one small room came the sound of music, and when they peeped inside, Phil and Adam were surprised to see a boy of about Adam's age playing the piano.

Miss Martin was very proud. 'I had to fight the authorities tooth and nail in order for piano lessons to be agreed,' she told them, 'but the piano is mine, so there was no cost to be made.'

She gestured to the old man overseeing the playing. White-haired, and with a slightly bent back, he had his eyes closed, and was obviously intent on the boy's playing.

'That's my uncle,' she explained. 'He's a retired music teacher, and lives quite close. He kindly gives his time freely in order to encourage the talented amongst us.' Softly, she closed the door. 'There is more for you to see,' and with a wide and pleasant smile, she urged them onward.

The back of the house was given over to the kitchens, toilet facilities, and accommodation for junior staff.

Upstairs was divided into two. The lesser area was dedicated to the senior staff. 'We have no need to tour this side,' Miss Martin informed them. 'It's merely private offices and accommodation.'

The larger and better secured half of the upper floors was the children's dormitories, with a small office close by for the duty night officer.

All too soon it was time for Phil to say goodbye to Adam. 'Remember what I said,' Phil reminded him. 'Anything that worries you . . . anything at all, we'll discuss it tomorrow, when I come and see you.' He turned to Miss Martin. 'Do you have specific visiting times?'

'Of course. We can't have people popping in and out at will. It's necessary for both staff and children to work with an orderly timetable, although, of course, in cases of emergency, we can be flexible.'

Bypassing Phil, she enquired of the officials, 'So, does Adam have any belongings with him?'

'I'm afraid not.' Miss Benson walked her away from the group. 'I assume you've been informed of the circumstances?'

'Of course, yes, I do understand. But Adam will feel more comfortable if he could possibly have a few of his own things with him . . . his regular clothes and personal things.'

'Yes, I understand. I can't promise anything, but I will try.'

'Oh, please do. It really will make all the difference to him settling in.'

There followed the inevitable tears, with Adam clinging to Phil.

'I don't want to stay here, Phil.'

Phil's heart ached as he confided, 'For the moment there's nothing we can do about it, son. Just remember. I won't be far away, and I'll be back every day. So you're not alone. Always remember that.'

'Phil?'

'Yes, son?'

'What about my mum?'

Phil took him by the shoulders. 'Listen to what I say now. Your mum is in a safer and happier place, and she's watching over you. If you ever need to confide in her, then do so any time, any place, and she will hear you clear as a bell. As for everything else, just you leave it to me. I'll talk to whoever's in charge, and I'll get all the answers you need, I promise . . .' he laid his hand across his chest, '. . . hand on heart, I truly will.'

'You mustn't worry too much about Adam,' Miss Martin informed Phil. 'We'll soon have him settled in, and he'll be fine. You wait and see.' She smiled at Adam. 'I'll do my best to get some of your personal possessions brought in. It would certainly help if you could make me a list of the things you cherish most.' When Adam gave no answer, she added, 'Just have a little think about it.' She then plucked a leaflet from the hallway table, and handed it to Phil. 'You'll need this, Mr . . .?' She recalled that Phil had been introduced already, and she was irritated that her memory was not what it used to be, although she never lost sight of what was most important: the children and their welfare.

'Wallis . . . the name is Phil Wallis, and you can be sure I'll be back here tomorrow, and every day I'm allowed.'

'I see.' She made a smile, but behind the smile she was wondering if this determined man was a pain in the making. She could see, however, that Phil Wallis was sincere in his concern for the boy.

A few minutes later they were outside in the porch. 'I'll be thinking of you, son,' Phil promised. 'Happen when I come back tomorrow, you'll have made a friend or two.'

Adam began to panic. Throwing his arms round Phil's ample belly, he pleaded tearfully, 'I'm frightened. Please, Phil, let me come home with you.'

It took every ounce of strength for Phil to speak calmly and reassure the boy. Holding him at arm's length, he stooped to his level, and, looking into his eyes, he asked, 'Do you think I would ever lie to you?'

Adam shook his head.

'So, you must know that what I've told you is the truth, that your mother is watching over you, and that she won't let any harm come to you. And don't forget, you'll always have me looking out for you.'

Fishing into his pocket, he took out a pen and a tatty old envelope. 'Look, I'm writing my address down for you, and if ever you need to tell me things that you can't tell anybody else, just write me a letter.' He glanced at Miss Martin. 'He is allowed to do that, isn't he?'

'Of course, but there are certain regulations, so we will need to see the letter before it goes out.'

'Huh! Well, I'm sure he won't be planning a bank robbery with me . . .' He gave an aside wink at Adam.

When Adam chuckled, Phil grabbed him in a hug. 'Aw, son, you'll be fine. Just be yourself. Try not to fret too much, and don't let yourself dwell on the bad things that have happened.'

Fishing into his pocket for a second time, he drew out a handful of coins, which he gave to Miss Martin. 'This is Adam's money . . . for stamps, or whatever other small thing he's able to buy.'

'Thank you, though we do have a small budget for certain incidentals.' All the same, she slipped the coins into her pocket. 'But I'll keep them safe for him.'

''Bye for now, son.' Phil kissed the top of Adam's head. 'Remember . . . the sun nearly always shines after the rain. I'll keep my fingers crossed that the authorities will find your relatives.' He made a point of not mentioning Adam's father.

When Phil climbed into the car alongside the Welfare officers, Miss Martin held onto Adam, who waved until his arms ached. Then, as the car went out of sight, his sobbing was pitiful to hear.

Her heart being slightly softer than her authoritative exterior, Miss Martin slid her arm round his shoulders.

'Your friend Phil has promised he'll be back tomorrow, and I'm sure he will.'

'He will! I know he will!'

'Well, there you are then.'

Adam confided brokenly, 'My mum . . . she . . .' he took a deep breath, '. . . she died. Did you know that?'

'Yes, they told me, and I'm so sorry, but we will care for you here, Adam. We will look after you. For as long as it takes.'

'I don't want to be here.'

'I know, and I do understand.'

'NO! You don't, because you didn't know my mum. You didn't know how kind she was, and how funny, and sometimes she would race me across the fields, and now . . . and . . .' he could no longer hold back the heartbreak, 'I want her back . . . I miss her.' Knowing he would never again see his beloved mother, never again hear her voice or feel her small, strong arms around him, he wept bitterly and his cries were terrible to hear.

Miss Martin understood. 'Listen to me, Adam. I do know what it's like to lose your mother, because I lost mine when I was not much older than you.' She had an idea. 'Do y'know what? I would love to know what your mum was like. She sounds wonderful. So, how about you and I go and have a chat? Then we can talk together, and ask each other all the questions that are in our minds. Afterwards, we can meet up with some of the staff and children. Would you like that, Adam?'

'I don't know.'

'Well, shall we just go and have a little chat on our own? Afterwards, you can decide whether you want to meet some of the children, and maybe one or two members of staff? Is that all right with you?'

Again, Adam nodded, but really he just wanted to run after that car, and his only friend, Phil.

'Right then! So that's what we'll do.' Taking hold of his hand, Miss Martin quickened her steps.

Adam was reluctant. Pulling back against her iron grip and dragging his feet, he glanced towards the windows, his forlorn gaze constantly drawn to where the car had taken Phil out of sight.

He could not understand why or how everything had happened so very quickly, and he was so afraid. This morning he had gone to school as usual, and afterwards, Phil had walked him home. And now Phil was gone, his mother was gone, and his father had run away.

'Come along, Adam,' Miss Martin interrupted his thoughts. 'There's no time for wasting. Lots to do . . . lots to talk about.'

She led him smartly along the corridor and through the house to the parlour, which doubled as her office. 'Here we are, Adam. Now then, how about a glass of fresh orange juice?'

Unceremoniously plonking him onto the sofa, she firmly closed the door and cut across the room to the sideboard. 'I think we deserve a little treat, don't you?' Without waiting for an answer, she took out a small tumbler and a fluted glass.

Humming a merry tune under her breath, she first poured the orange juice into the tumbler, and then she poured a sizeable helping of sherry into the glass. 'One for each of us,' she chirped.

While she bustled about, Adam felt more lost and frightened than at any other time in his life.

Everyone he knew had gone away. Everything familiar had changed, and now he was alone among strangers.

PART TWO

~

The Unwanted Visitor

1957

CHAPTER FOUR

ANNE WYMAN LOVED the little house, formerly her aunt's, on the outskirts of Bedford. It was her pride and joy, but most of all, it was her safe hideaway.

When she'd arrived in Bedford some thirteen years ago, she was a frightened young woman on the run.

Fearful that the man from her past would find her, she would wait until the street was empty before venturing out. When a kindly neighbour might attempt to make small talk, she would merely give a brief nod of the head, before hurrying away.

Back then, after she fled, she was at her most vulnerable. When night fell thick and heavy, she would climb up the stairs to her darkened bedroom and cautiously inch open the curtains just enough for her to peer through to the street below. Then she would kneel by the window and peek out until her eyeballs were sore and her bones ached from the kneeling.

Haunted by the memory of Edward Carter, a madman

who had twice beaten her to within an inch of her life, she had learned over the years to remain ever vigilant. Night after night, and even in the daylight hours, she made herself ready for when he might emerge from the shadows.

At first, having finally escaped from him, she would hardly dare close her eyes to sleep. Instead, aching with tiredness, she would listen to every sound, every slight movement, fearing the moment when he might snatch her away.

So she watched and waited, and eventually she would fall asleep, but it was not an easy sleep. Not then.

And not now.

Today was Saturday. Both herself and her friend Sally had completed their weekly quota of hours working at Woolworths, so this was their day off to do with as they liked.

The thought of spending quality time with Sally brought a smile to Anne's face.

The weather had been bright and sunny all week. Having already decided that, if the weather held, they would drive to Yarmouth, it now seemed that a day at the seaside would be a reality.

Anne hummed a little ditty as she went into the hallway to the telephone. Grabbing up the big black receiver, she dialled Sally's number. It was a while before her friend answered.

'Hello?' She sounded sleepy.

'Sally, being as it's a lovely day, I was wondering, are we still on for Yarmouth?' She kept her fingers crossed, because if Sally didn't go, then neither would she, and she was really looking forward to it now.

Sally, however, was of the same mind. 'Yeah, I'm up for it.'

'Great!' Anne did a little dance on the spot. 'So, d'you want *me* to drive?'

'Well, my car's leaking oil again, so if we go in yours we might actually get there. I meant to deliver mine to the garage but I haven't had time.' She groaned. 'To tell the truth, I keep putting it off, because the mechanic will probably tell me to dump it anyway. He reckons it's well and truly worn out but it's all I can afford, so I'll have to make do with it for now.'

'Look, I've got savings,' Anne said. 'I can lend you some, and you can pay me back whenever.'

Sally would not hear of it. 'I know how long you've scrimped and saved to put a few quid aside. That money is your security and peace of mind, and I would never dream of taking it.'

'It's OK, really. I don't mind. It would be a real pain if your car broke down altogether.'

'Oh, don't worry. It's like an old soldier. It's been patched up before and it'll be patched up again. Meantime, I'll have to stop gadding about and save a few shillings every week until I've got enough to get it put right.'

'OK, so I'll pick you up in what . . . an hour?'

'I'll be ready in half an hour.'

'Are you sure?' Anne knew from experience how

long it took Sally to get ready, and by the sounds of it, she had only just got out of bed.

'I'll be ready, don't worry.'

~

'Right!' Growing excited, Anne resumed her humming as she swiftly cleared away the last of the breakfast things. Glancing at the clock, she saw that it was already half-past eight. 'Crikey! I'd best get a move on.' It was a fifteen-minute drive to Kempston where Sally lived, and at this time on a Saturday the roads could be busy.

Having tidied the kitchen, she made sure the back door was locked and bolted before running upstairs and into the bathroom. She quickly cleaned her teeth, ruffled her fine blonde hair and ran back downstairs; grabbing her coat and bag as she went out the front door.

As always, whenever leaving the house, she made doubly sure that the front door was secured. She then glanced up at the bedroom windows to satisfy herself that they were closed. For good reason, she had learned over the years to keep her wits about her as far as her own security was concerned.

These days, though, she was slightly less paranoid than she had been on first arriving in this quiet back-street many years ago. Even so, the bad memories and a dark, nagging fear that Edward Carter might find her still lurked at the back of her mind.

Clambering into her beloved Morris Minor, she slammed shut the door and then checked through her handbag. She opened her purse: three pound and six shillings, more than enough.

Next, she drew out a stick of rouge and a powder compact. She looked at her reflection in the compact mirror while she dabbed a little make-up over her cheekbones. 'Anne Wyman, you're no oil painting, but you're all you've got, so you'll have to do!' she muttered to herself. Retrieving her lipstick from her handbag, she painted her full, plump mouth with the pale pink lipstick.

She then returned the items to her handbag, started the engine, checked for oncoming traffic, and drew away from the kerb.

At the top of Roff Avenue, she slowed and checked in the driver's mirror. Her eyes were instantly drawn to a tall, dark-haired figure heading away towards the far end of Roff Avenue. He was walking slowly, almost strolling. He seemed nervous, his head turning this way and that, as though searching for something or someone.

Anne's heart skipped a beat. She could hardly breathe. 'Stop that!' she chided herself. The past is long behind you.

The man was out of sight now and, with an irate driver honking his car horn behind her, Anne shifted into gear and drew away.

Some short distance down the road, she pulled over and switched the engine off. Wrapping her trembling fingers around the steering wheel, she gripped it so tight her knuckles turned white.

'Pull yourself together, girl!'

She reminded herself that this was not the first time she'd imagined he was actually in her street searching for her. And each time she'd been wrong.

After a few minutes, feeling calmer, she restarted the engine and set off again. By now, there was no sight of the man who had truly unnerved her.

~

Edward Carter was in a foul mood. Having been up and down the back alley, peeking into yards and hanging about, he had still not been able to catch sight of her. He knew the house was in this street. He'd seen the address in the past enough damned times to know he'd got the right place. Roff Avenue, Bedford.

Unkempt and agitated, he had been on the run far too long. He needed a place to hide to keep his head down for a while. He had a plan, and it involved Anne Wyman, the girl he had married all those years ago. The naïve, trusting little girl who eventually ran off and left him. She owed him, and she was still his wife . . . whether she liked it or not.

He chuckled to himself. If she really thought he might never come looking for her, she was in for a real surprise.

He continued to wander up and down the back alley, growing increasingly agitated, his sharp eyes constantly scanning the houses.

When a couple of people turned into the alley and wandered past him, he flattened himself against the wall, pretending to light a cigarette. As they went past, he nodded amiably to them. 'Morning.'

After a fleeting acknowledgement, the couple walked on, though they turned once to take another look at him. When he stared back, they made a hasty exit.

The policeman had not long turned the corner into Roff Avenue when he saw the man head into the alley, and now, as he noticed the couple hurrying out, he grew curious and crossed the street to investigate.

Edward Carter saw the policeman approaching, and, speaking in his finest voice, he cunningly made his way towards him.

'Good morning, officer. I wonder if you might be able to help me?'

Surprised by this untidy man's refined voice and manner, the policeman replied in a friendly but authoritative tone, 'If I can help you, I will, but it's not wise to be loitering about these back alleys. It tends to make people nervous, and that makes me nervous.'

'Of course. I do understand, but I'm looking for an old friend . . . a woman by the name of Anne Carter. When she moved away from her previous address, she gave me the street and town, but forgot to write down the number of her aunt's house . . . that's where she's staying.'

He began to rummage in his pocket. 'I can show you what she wrote . . . Roff Avenue, Bedford. I promised to visit when I was able. The thing is, her old aunt Ada doesn't have a telephone, doesn't like them, so I'm told.' He gave a warm smile.

The policeman nodded. 'I know a lot of people who

seem a bit timid of the idea. I expect they're used to going down to the red box outside. My mother's exactly the same . . . won't even hear of a telephone in the house.'

Still putting on a show, Carter pulled a crumpled piece of paper out of his pocket, feigning a groan when he read it. 'Oh, wrong one. Sorry, officer. It must be in my inside pocket . . .' He made a big fuss of digging about in his pockets.

The policeman accepted his story hook, line and sinker. 'Look, I understand. I'm afraid I can't help you, but I tell you what –' he pointed back down the alley – 'go back the same way you came in, and turn left. You'll see a pub on the corner. The landlord's always up and working, and there's an old fella keeps the place spick and span. Like as not he might know where your friend is living, especially if there's an old aunt, because the old 'uns do have a communal spirit round these parts.'

'Well, thank you very much, officer. I was about to go and knock on a couple of doors, but I'll have a word at the pub instead.'

'I'm sure that's the thing to do, because you won't find her wandering about in the back alleys, will you?'

'No, you're right. I don't suppose I will.'

'The pub isn't open yet but if you knock on the door, the landlord or his wife will be sure to hear you. Ted and Mary have lived round these parts for some time, so they know the locals better than anybody.' The policeman gave a knowing little smile. 'Oh, and you might even find a few old codgers playing darts in the corner, enjoying a crafty pint out of hours. They think we're not on to them yet, but sometimes we find it wiser to look the other way . . . but don't tell anyone I said that.'

Satisfied that there was nothing to worry about here, he continued on his beat, thinking what an odd sort the stranger was. He found it hard to reconcile the fact that the man was dressed little better than a tramp, while possessing the confident, refined voice of a gentleman. It looked like he'd come on hard times. No doubt he was hoping for a few days' lodgings and a cash handout from his old friend. The policeman did not approve of scrounging, and he thought the stranger should be ashamed, especially when it seemed there appeared to be no reason for him not to hold down a job of sorts.

~

Pausing outside the public house, Edward Carter took a moment to run his fingers through his thick dark hair and briefly brush a hand over his clothes. Best make a good impression, he thought, or they might not be so ready to reveal what they know.

The constable was right. The first thing he saw as he gingerly entered the public house was a group of aged men seated round a table in the corner. They were engrossed in a game of dominoes, and each man had a pint of brown ale before him.

As the door closed behind him, everyone looked up to see who it was. Nobody spoke. Instead, once they had taken stock of him, they resumed their game.

Carter slowly walked past their table. 'Morning. Nice day.' He nodded to each and every one, and they nodded back, curious to know who this weary-looking stranger might be.

'If it's beer you're after, you'll not get it here, at least not till opening time.' The bulbous, whiskered landlord cast a wary glance to the table where the men were now paying attention. 'Oh, and before you go making assumptions, these are friends of mine,' he added warily, 'a private party.'

Carter smiled. 'You've no need to worry about me. I haven't seen a thing,' he assured the landlord. 'To tell the truth, I'm not here for a pint, though I wouldn't say no, especially as I've travelled a long journey to get here.'

'I see. And what is it you want from me?'

'I'm looking for someone. I just thought you might be able to help. I expect you know most people round here?'

The landlord seemed reluctant to answer. 'Maybe I do know a few people, yes, but I'm not the sort to get caught up in gossip. From my experience, poking your nose in other folks' business can get you in a heap o' trouble.'

'That's all right by me, because I'm not the sort to gossip either.' Carter was careful to choose his words. 'The thing is, I'm searching for an old relative.'

'Oh?' The landlord remained cautious.

Carter gave a sad little smile. 'The thing is, when I was sixteen, things got really uncomfortable at home between my parents. Then, when they went their separate ways, Ada took me in.'

The landlord made no response.

Carter continued, 'Ada had a nice, roomy house in Hampshire. I lived with her until I was twenty-one, and then I needed to get out and see the big wide world.'

'Wanted to spread your wings, eh?' The landlord was growing curious.

'I suppose that was it, yes. But my relative didn't want me to leave, so we had a bit of an argument before I left. After I'd gone, I wrote often, but she never answered. Then I was told she'd moved here to Bedford. The sad thing is, she was like a mother to me, so when I heard she was ill, I was determined to find her. I've always regretted us falling out.'

He lowered his voice to a sorry murmur. 'She's quite old now, and I just need to put things right between us . . . before it's too late. If you know what I mean?'

Being a family man himself, the landlord approved of his motive. 'So, if you know where she is, what's stopping you from "putting things right" between you?'

'Because after she moved, I never got her full address. All I was told, was that she'd moved to Bedford . . . Roff Avenue, they thought. I just arrived here this morning and a policeman suggested that I should ask you. He said you might know.'

'What did you say her name was again?' the landlord asked.

'Ada . . . Ada Wyman.'

'Mmm.' He gave it some thought. 'And she's of an age, you say?'

'That's right. I never knew her actual age – you know what women are like about telling – but she must be in her late seventies by now.'

The landlord scratched his head and called for his wife, who was busy washing pots. 'Mary!' his voice rang out. 'Have you a minute?'

'No!'

He raised his voice: 'There's a fella here who's looking for his relative, a woman by the name of Ada Wyman, in her seventies!'

'I don't know any Ada!'

Blowing out his cheeks in exasperation, he apologized, 'I'm sorry. We mostly only know the folk who frequent my pub. Does she have a husband?'

'As far as I know, she never married.' Carter cunningly played his most precious card. 'She might have a niece staying with her, though. Her name is Anne Carter . . . she's in her early thirties. She and Aunt Ada were very close. I was told that Ada was really ill, so her niece might well be taking care of her.'

'I see. And what does she look like, this niece?'

Before he could reply, a voice from across the room called out, 'I know that young lady. Quiet little thing, she is; wild, fair hair and really pretty. Keeps herself to herself, she does. But if you happen to pass her in the street, she always lights up your day with her bright smile.'

Carter could not believe his luck. 'That sounds like her all right!'

The old fellow who'd spoken beckoned him to the table, where they sat together while the other men listened in, waiting to add their own small pieces of information.

'I'm sorry to tell you, but your relative Ada passed

away some years back,' one old, slightly deaf fellow butted in. 'Like you say, the girl did look after her aunt. Did everything for her, she did. She even took her out in the wheelchair most days. You're right, they were very close.'

'That's right!' the little man in the corner who'd first spoken said. 'The old dear was so thankful to have the girl with her, she left her the house, lock stock and barrel.'

'Really?' Carter was so flushed with this discovery, he could hardly sit still. 'Would she be at home now, d'you think?' Carter suppressed his excitement, while feigning the sad expression of a bereaved relation.

'Oh, but you may well have the wrong name for the niece, because this one goes by the same name as her aunt – Wyman. Not Carter . . . Anne Wyman. At least that's how she introduced herself to the postmistress,' said the little man.

Though burning with rage at that unfortunate snippet of information, Carter managed to keep his cool. 'Ah, yes, well, as I recall now, she was indeed a Wyman.'

'Oh, and it's no use you going along there just now because she'll not be back from work just yet.' This further disappointing comment came from a new source. 'Best to leave it till later, I reckon.'

Carter grudgingly thanked the men. Though quietly satisfied with the information he had gathered, he was in a murderous mood. The knowledge that Anne had callously discarded his name while still being married to him was hard to take.

'I wonder if the landlord would mind me having a pint of beer alongside you kind folk?' He needed to keep their confidence. 'You seem to know a lot about my family. It might be nice to sit and chat awhile.'

He was eager to know everything about his runaway wife. Where did she work? How long had her aunt been gone? Did she have a relationship? What was the house worth?

It was beginning to look like he'd fallen on his feet. His bad mood lifted and he had to stop himself from laughing out loud. This morning he was beginning to wonder if he might ever find the woman who was still his legal wife. And now not only had he found his wife, but he'd stumbled across a fine property. As her husband he surely had certain legal rights . . .

He was nobody's fool. He knew that if he played his cards right, he could have it all.

CHAPTER FIVE

'HANG ON! I'M on my way!'

Hopping along the passageway with one high heel on and one in her hand, Sally cursed under her breath, 'Stop pipping that damned hooter. You'll have the neighbours out!'

Slinging her shoulder bag round her neck, she flung open the front door and locked it behind her. She then slipped her foot into the shoe, dropped the key into her pocket and ran down the path.

Seeing her friend make her way down the path, Anne leaned over and threw the passenger door open. 'What did you say?'

'Oh, now suddenly you've gone deaf, have you?' Red-faced from hurrying, Sally clambered into the car. 'Well, I can't say I'm surprised, what with all the noise you've been making. Old Mother Benton next door threw a bucket of water over the ice-cream man, just for ringing his bell. So I reckon she must be out just now, because with the racket you created, she'd have been charging at you with the hose-pipe!'

Anne laughed. 'In that case I'm glad she's out. I'm just excited, that's all. It's been ages since we went to the seaside, and now that we're actually on our way, I can't wait to get there.'

In truth, she had felt oddly uneasy these past few days, and the idea of getting away from Bedford, if only for a day, had eased her mind.

As they drove off, Sally took a sneaky look at her. 'Are you all right?' She had noticed how tired Anne looked, and how every now and then she would nervously glance in her driver's mirror. 'Anne?'

Anne was too deep in thought to hear her name being called.

'Anne!'

Anne gave a little gasp. 'Oh, sorry . . . what?'

'You seem to be miles away. Tell the truth . . . have you changed your mind? Would you rather not go to the seaside? It's a long drive, and I know you're not too keen on driving long distances.'

'No, I'm fine, honestly. I'm really looking forward to a day at Yarmouth. I was just thinking, that's all.'

'About what?'

'Nothing in particular.'

'I'll drive, if that's what worries you?'

'No, like I said, I'm absolutely fine. I just didn't sleep too well last night.'

'Why not?'

Anne gave a little shrug. 'Dunno . . . overtired, I suppose.' She had never told anyone the truth of her past, not even the lovely Sally. She still believed that keeping quiet was the right decision, because that way she had a better chance of putting the horror behind her.

So far, that particular plan was not working.

Sally's voice gentled into her thoughts. 'OK. Well, when we get to Yarmouth, you can park the car and we won't go anywhere near it again until it's time to come home. In fact, if you want to, we could lie on the beach all day, and do nothing.'

Anne laughed out loud at that suggestion. 'Huh! I can see *you* lying on the beach doing nothing. You'd be bored out of your mind.'

'I expect I would, but if it's what you want . . .?'

'It isn't.'

'There you are then! And besides, where's the fun in "doing nothing"? And what's the point in going to the seaside and not trying the rides, or eating candy floss? Or having a go at winning some money in the amusement arcade? And what if we meet up with a couple of good-looking fellas who might want us to be with them for the day?'

'And you a happily married woman! No, thanks all the same . . . about the fellas, I mean.'

'Hmm! So are you saying that if some gorgeous bloke made a pass at you, you would actually turn him down?' She gave a knowing little grin. 'I don't believe that for one minute.'

'Well, you'd better believe it,' her tone darkened, 'because I'm off fellas for good!'

Sally was saddened by Anne's remark, and surprised by the angry manner in which she had said it.

She had to ask. 'Anne?'

'Yes?'

'What's wrong?'

'What d'you mean?'

'I'm not really sure, but you seem to be in a strange mood. Going to Yarmouth was your suggestion, and now you don't seem so sure. Just now, you decided to wake the whole street by honking your car horn, and then you go all quiet on me, like something's playing on your mind. And just now, when you said you were off fellas for good, why is that?'

'Forget about it. I suppose I'm just not ready for settling down, that's all.' She hoped that would be the end to Sally's questions.

'But you sounded angry . . . as though you'd had a bad experience.' Unaware that she had touched a raw nerve, Sally went merrily on, 'Most women look forward to a happy marriage, and children.'

Anne regretted having made that controversial statement. 'I'm sorry if you thought I was angry, because I wasn't.' She gave a little shrug. 'It's like my head's all over the place at the minute. I don't really know what I want, that's the trouble.'

'I reckon you're tired. You said yourself that you're not sleeping. I'm worried about you, Anne. So, what's the problem? We're like sisters, you and me, and you should know by now you can talk to me about anything, and you can rest assured it won't go any further.'

'I know, and I'm sorry.' Anne felt vulnerable. 'There's nothing to talk about. I got out of the wrong side of bed this morning, that's all. And now I'm spoiling everything. Look, take no notice of me. I promise, we will enjoy ourselves. I'll make sure of it.'

Still not altogether convinced, Sally had to accept her explanation. 'Just remember, though, if there is ever anything on your mind and it's causing you a problem, I'm a good listener. And I do know how to keep my mouth shut.'

'I appreciate that, but there is nothing to tell. So now, can we please stop the chatter, and let me concentrate on my driving?'

'OK, and if I open my mouth again, feel free to kick me out.'

Sally's light-hearted remark lifted the mood, but she had known Anne long enough to realise that something was worrying her, and one way or another, she was determined to get to the bottom of it. Meantime, she had to play along.

'Right! So now let's turn our thoughts to enjoying ourselves. OK?'

When Anne seemed deep in thought, Sally asked her again, this time louder, 'I said . . . OK?'

'Yes . . . OK!' Anne gave her answer with a willing smile.

All these years she had kept her dark secret, but now she wondered if it was time to share her fears. After all, Sally was her best friend, and if you couldn't tell your best friend, who could you tell?

And yet the idea of confiding in anyone, even Sally, filled her with dread.

~

Through the final leg of the journey, Anne concentrated on the road, while Sally's thoughts were focused on Anne.

She had suspected for some time now that Anne had a past she did not want to reveal. In all the time she had known her, Anne had never spoken about her family, or the circumstances that had brought her to Bedford.

She had spoken often about her aunt Ada. It was clear she had adored the old woman, but not once had she mentioned her parents or other family. When one of their workmates asked her about her family, Anne always excused herself, claiming that she had something urgent to attend to or somewhere she should be.

Sally, though, remained curious. But her affection for Anne meant that she must respect her friend's right to privacy. Even though, as the years went by, Anne's obvious need to bury her past was of some concern to Sally.

She noticed things that worried her. First, Anne's obvious reluctance to talk about her family did seem unnatural. Also, whenever she had been invited to Anne's house, Sally soon realised that apart from one faded photograph of her old aunt as a young girl, Anne had no photographs on show of either herself or anyone else. And whenever the discussion turned to family, or girlish talk about when they were teenagers and experienced their first love, Anne would swiftly change the subject.

It was a strange and curious thing, but it was Anne's right not to discuss her private life. And it was Sally's intention never to pry.

Over the years, Sally had learned to tread carefully, and because of her discretion, her friendship with Anne had flourished.

She had no idea what had brought Anne here to Bedford, and she had no idea of what her life had been before, or what her future plans were. In the end, it didn't really matter.

Since she came to work at Woolworths, Anne had been a great friend to Sally. She had proven herself to be a kind and compassionate young woman, who cared very much for those close to her. Now Sally could not even imagine what it would be like without Anne. To Sally it seemed as though Anne had always been there, and always would be.

Sally herself had no brothers or sisters, so always having Anne around made her feel complete in a way; kind of warm and happy inside.

Lately, though, she had become concerned that whatever secrets Anne was hiding had begun slowly to destroy her peace of mind.

~

For a time, the two of them were lost in thought: Anne training her attention on the road ahead, which was getting busier by the minute, Sally looking ahead to a wonderful day out, and the fun that might await them.

While she was concentrating on driving, Anne was thinking that she was even more determined than ever to distance herself from the dark memories that had robbed her of a normal life. Sometimes, she could go for weeks, even months, without letting the past invade her peace of mind, then out of the blue something would happen to trigger it all off again – like this morning, when she caught a glimpse of that stranger through her driving mirror.

Try as she might, she could not get the dark-haired man out of her memory. She could see him now in her mind's eye, clear as a bell and larger than life.

It was the way he had walked along the street, in that same, confident manner as her tormentor.

It was the shifty manner in which he had glanced about . . . like a cat watching for a mouse.

It was the shock of dark hair, and the straight shoulders . . . like the posture of a military man.

She had tried so hard to put him out of her mind, and now, thanks to Sally and her innocent chatter, she was beginning to feel a little bit easier.

So, as they neared Yarmouth, Anne promised herself again that she would make a concentrated effort to put the past behind her once and for all. She knew it would not be an easy promise to keep, because Edward Carter had made her suffer badly, and that was not something she could shrug off. It went too deep. It had a life of its own.

That man, that monster, had taken a bright, young girl, and robbed her of all trust and innocence.

He taught her how to be subservient in order to survive. He taught her the very depths of hatred.

Until she met Edward Carter, she had never known the true meaning of fear. Now, try as she might to overcome it, that fear continued to haunt her in her nightmares and in her every waking hour.

All the promises in the world could not make her forget the pain and terror he had put her through. The memories were too strong.

The fear that he might one day track her down still haunted her every waking hour.

CHAPTER SIX

TWO HOURS AFTER leaving home, they were on the outskirts of Yarmouth.

'Look, there's the sign to the front.' Sally pointed the way, straight on.

Anne headed the car towards the sea. 'It's just what the doctor ordered.' She was really looking forward to their day out. 'Sun, sea, and time on our hands.'

'We-hey!' Sally could not contain her excitement. 'Yarmouth, here we come!'

'Behave yourself.' Anne laughed out loud. 'You're like a kid on her first outing to the seaside.'

'Oh, but I do love the seaside!' Sally would not be quietened. 'We'll go on every ride there is. And afterwards, if it's warm enough, we'll go for a swim in the sea. Let's hope there are no sharks or anything nasty like that. Then we'll lie in the sun and get a tan . . . and after that we'll get ourselves one of them pedal-things and whizz down the promenade—'

'Woah! For now, let's just concentrate on getting a parking place.' Anne laughed.

'No worries. We're early enough, so there'll be plenty of space on the front. Look!' She drew Anne's attention to a second sign. 'Parking, turn right.'

'Good. But it's Saturday, don't forget, and it's looking a bit busy already.'

Anne turned right, only to find that this particular car park was full. 'Let's drive along the front. You never know, we might just be lucky.'

She drove the entire length of the front, and there was not a parking place in sight.

'Dammit!' Sally groaned. 'I expect we'll have to park miles away.'

Then she had an idea. 'Why don't we park in that hotel car park?' She brought Anne's attention to the newly refurbished Victorian hotel opposite the beach. 'Perfect!'

'We can't park in there.' But Anne smiled at her friend's mischievous idea.

'Why can't we?' Sally was not easily put off.

'Because all the places are allocated for guests, look.' She pointed to the large white-painted numbers in each parking place.

'But half of them are empty.'

'That doesn't matter. They could turn up any time, and anyway, with our luck the manager's bound to turf us off.'

'Worth a chance, though.'

'Hey! Who's driving this car?'

'You are, more's the pity. If it were me, I'd have been in there like a flash!'

'Then it's a good job I'm the driver, isn't it?' Anne's gaze roved along the seafront. 'Hey! Look! There's a fella pulling out of a parking place . . . up there, d'you see?'

'Where?'

'There, right in front of that little café.'

Sally began to panic when she saw the driver backing out. 'Hurry up, Anne, before somebody else nicks it.'

Anne manoeuvred into position, but as they drew close, the driver of a black Austin Morris tried to edge in front of them from the other direction. 'Cheeky devil!' Sally wound down the window. 'Hey, you! That's our place, so back off!'

Seeing the whites of her eyes, the man backed off, and Anne shot in quick. As the irate driver pulled away he made a rude sign at them.

'And you!' Sally did the same back.

Anne started chuckling, then Sally was sniggering, and now the two of them erupted in laughter.

'You'll get us arrested,' Anne told her.

'Huh! If the arresting officer is tall and handsome, and extra kind with his truncheon, you won't see me putting up a fight.'

'You're a liability, and with a doting husband at home!' Anne was beginning to relax. It was so good to get away for a day.

~

The next few hours were filled with non-stop fun.

Their first ride was in the caterpillar.

'I hope they don't roll the roof over,' Sally whimpered as they climbed in. 'I don't like closed-in spaces. They make me nervous.'

'Let's get out then,' Anne suggested. 'There are plenty of other rides we can go on.'

'Not likely!' Sally was adamant. 'We've paid our money and we're staying on.' She yelled out to the fairground attendant, 'They won't roll the roof over, will they? I don't like it.'

'Naw!' Skillfully throwing his chewing gum from one side of his mouth to the other, he assured her, 'We don't roll the roof down unless it's raining.'

'There you are!' Anne said.

Sally settled into her seat and tried to relax. 'I hope they don't go too fast . . . I get giddy when they go too fast.'

Anne climbed into the seat beside her. 'Let's just enjoy the ride. Oh, look! We're off already.' The ride started slowly at first, then it gathered speed, and as the caterpillar flew round and round the tracks, they held onto the bar, laughing and giggling, and occasionally screaming with delight.

Sally noticed it first. 'Can you hear that?' she yelled above the screams and laughter of other joyriders.

'What?'

'Just listen!'

Anne listened but she couldn't hear anything untoward.

Suddenly it began to get dark, and the screams grew louder. Sally was panicking. 'The roof's coming over! Look at the roof. Bloody Nora, get me out of here!'

She screamed so loud, the ride was stopped and they both climbed off.

'You lied to me!' Sally vented her anger on the ride-owner. 'I asked about the roof and your man said it would not go over unless it rained, and it didn't rain, so I want my money back.'

'You'll not get no money out o' me!' The burly ride-owner sent them on their way. 'You knew what the ride was about and you still got on it, so don't come that old game about getting your money back. Go on, bugger off out of it!'

As they made their way back to the main walkway, he continued to swear and curse after them. 'You want locking up, trying to cheat a poor bloke who works hard for a living. Don't show yer faces round 'ere again, not unless you want a kick up the arse!'

Sally was all for going back to sort him out, but Anne took hold of her and marched her to the goldfish stall. 'Can we please have two fishing-lines?' She handed four small coins over to the homely-faced woman.

Just as Anne had planned, the two of them got engrossed in trying to catch a fish. In the end, though, they came away empty-handed.

Half an hour later, they made their way over to the rifle range.

Whether it was anger because she failed at the goldfish pond, or maybe it was her determination to get the better of something after her row with the ride-owner, but Sally proved to be a hotshot with a rifle.

She quickly won two big adorable teddy bears; one for her and one for Anne. 'Am I a hotshot, or what?'

Punching the air with a clenched fist, she did a little dance on the spot. 'I'm ready for anything now.'

Anne was amazed at Sally's brilliant shooting. She herself hadn't even hit a single coconut, while Sally had sent them all flying. 'How did you do that?' Anne asked.

'Easy. I imagined I was aiming at the ride-owner,' Sally quipped. 'It worked a treat, didn't it?'

Anne smiled but wisely gave no comment. 'Come on then. Let's see what else is on offer.'

A few minutes later, they stopped to rest their aching feet. Sally dropped onto the sandy bench like a sack of potatoes. 'I'm worn out!'

'Stay here a minute,' Anne suggested. 'I'll go and put the bears in the boot of the car.' She took hold of the prizes. 'And no swearing at anybody while I'm gone.'

Just then a couple of middle-aged men sauntered by. They glanced at the two young women, then looked away. Then one of them glanced back to have another look as they wandered on. Unfortunately, Sally was still in fighting mood after the caterpillar ride.

'So what are you two staring at?' she snarled.

'Hey!' Anne calmed her down. 'Don't take it out on strangers, just because that ride-owner got the better of you.'

'It's not that! Did you see them, turning round to stare at us? Did he think we were on the lookout for a couple of paunchy, middle-aged men, or what? Bloody cheek of it! And anyway, that boy on the ride told us a lie, so the ride-owner should have given us our money back.'

'Forget about it.'

'Am I being a pain?'

'Yes.

'Sorry,' Sally apologised. 'It's just that I always panic if the roof comes over.'

'Yes, I got that one.'

'I'll shut up about it, shall I?'

'Might be an idea.'

'Not another word, I promise.'

'Good.'

'We can still have a good time, though, can't we?'

'Course we can!'

'D'you want an ice cream?'

'OK, I'll take the bears back to the car, and you get the ice creams?'

'Good idea!' Sally's sour mood quickly disappeared. 'So, what kind of ice cream do you want?'

Anne didn't have to think too hard. 'A double dollop of vanilla ice cream with a chocolate flake on top.'

'Right! It'll be my treat.' Sally's mood brightened. 'You can get the fish and chips after we've been on the other rides, and no more mention of the caterpillar. Deal?'

'Yes, deal! And you can stop apologising. To tell you the truth, when I saw that cover coming over, I didn't like it either.'

'Ah! You didn't kick up a fuss, though, did you? In fact, you never seem to get het up about anything. I remember when you first started at Woollies and the manager piled more work on you than any of us. And you just got on with it, without a word of complaint. If he'd done that to me, I'd have been up in arms!'

Anne had her reasons for keeping quiet, but she kept them to herself. 'In my experience it pays not to make ripples.'

'Even when you're being taken advantage of?'

'Yes, even then.'

Anne's memories carried her back over the bad years, when she'd been unafraid to speak out. But then she'd been made to pay dearly for her boldness. 'Sometimes confrontation can lead to more trouble than you can handle.' Her answer came in a whisper, almost as though she'd forgotten Sally was there.

'Anne?' Sally had a feeling that something was wrong. '"More trouble than you can handle"? What's that supposed to mean?'

Lost in the horror of her past, Anne did not hear.

'ANNE!' Sally raised her voice.

'Oh . . .' Anne took a deep breath, 'I was just . . . oh, sorry.'

In her mind she could see the baby, small and vulnerable. Her baby. Her own flesh and blood. She shut it from her mind. But she could not shut it from her heart.

'You'd best queue up for the ice creams. I'll only be gone a few minutes.' Grabbing the two bears, she hurried away, while secretly wiping away the tears.

Seeing the stranger earlier had really shaken her and now she could not get Edward Carter out of her mind. She could see his face, angry. Hateful.

She could hear his voice, so refined, so wicked.

Shivering, she quickened her steps, silently praying, *Dear Lord, will I ever be free of him?*

~

At the car, Anne retrieved from the boot two brightly striped shoulder bags, each containing a towel, swimsuit and sunhat. She then climbed into the front seat of the car and sat for a time, her thoughts covering the years before she sought refuge with her beloved aunt Ada.

You're free of him, Anne, she felt the need to reassure herself. *He hasn't found you all these years, and he won't find you now. Besides, he's probably found some other poor woman to terrorize. With luck he's forgotten you ever existed.*

Feeling calmer, she hoisted one bag onto her shoulder, and carried the other over her arm. As she walked back, there was the tiniest of smiles on her face. When she caught sight of Sally, she waved and grinned, and for the moment all seemed well with the world.

'Where the devil have you been?' Sally had expected her back ages ago. 'It's a good job there was a long queue at the ice-cream van. What took you so long?'

'It only took a minute to leave the teddies and collect the bags, but I sat inside the car for a minute or two . . . had to think.'

'What about?'

Anne shrugged. 'Just something and nothing.'

'Is everything all right?'

'Yes, everything's fine.' She reached out to collect her ice-cream cornet. 'Thanks, that looks good.' She licked the trickling ice cream from the sides of the cornet. 'What next then?' She sat down next to Sally.

'What d'you mean?'

'Well, we haven't been on any other rides, and we said we'd spend some time in the amusement arcade trying to win a bit of spending money. Then there's the beach. We promised ourselves a swim and a lie on the beach to try and get a bit of a suntan. But I was thinking, it might be best if we leave that till last. What do you think?'

Sally was in agreement. 'But don't forget, we'll need to get something to eat along the way.'

Anne chuckled. 'You're always hungry.'

'I know.' Sally made a face. 'I reckon I've got worms.'

Anne laughed again. 'What do you want to do next?'

Sally had it all worked out. 'I know I said I was hungry, but I'd rather not eat till later. And anyway, it'll be quieter in the café later on. If that's all right with you?'

'I'm easy.'

'OK. So, how does this sound? We'll finish our ice creams, then we could go on a couple of other rides. After that we could spend an hour on the machines in the arcade, and maybe win a fortune. Then we can go for a swim, and spend an hour or so on the beach, to maybe get a tan before we clean up and finally make our way to the café on the promenade. We'll relax and enjoy a leisurely meal, before setting off home. How's that?'

'Perfect!' Anne clapped her hands in agreement. Whenever she was with Sally, she always felt lighter of heart.

They sat awhile on the beach wall, chatting and finishing off their ice-cream cornets.

'Right!' Having nibbled the small remains of her cornet, Sally wiped her face with a tissue and threw the tissue in a bin. 'Time for action.' She set off down the promenade.

Anne quickly finished her cornet and set off at a run to catch up with Sally. 'Wait for me!'

By 4 p.m., they had seen and done everything they had wanted to. They rode in the flying aeroplanes, and went mad in the crazy bumper cars. They went round and round on the waltzer, and had a wonderful time.

Afterwards, they spent a full hour in the amusement arcade, where between them they won the amazing amount of six pounds.

They had a leisurely swim, and after they had dried themselves off, they persuaded the donkey-man to let them ride on his two biggest donkeys.

'There you go.' He smacked the donkeys' rumps and set them off at a good pace. 'Enjoy yourselves.'

Sally and Anne laughed and squealed as they bounced up and down. Then the donkeys got spooked and took off down the beach with Sally and Anne hanging onto their manes for dear life.

'Help! Get me off!' Sally's cry caused other holiday-makers to laugh at their antics.

Eventually, the donkey-man came to their rescue. 'That's never happened before,' he said breathlessly. 'I never knew they had such spirit in 'em.'

Scrambling off the donkeys, the two women were stunned into silence as they made their way up the beach. Then Anne started giggling, and soon they were both helpless with laughter.

Sally's hair was up on end as though she'd been in a hurricane, and Anne's legs were raw on the inside where she'd gripped the donkey's belly.

'Well, that was fun!' Sally remarked wryly. 'It's the first and last time I ever get on a donkey.'

Anne agreed, but added that she had never laughed so much in all her life.

Afterwards, sore and exhausted, they lay on the towels on the sand, and lapped up the sun.

'This is the life! I could lie here all day, every day, and never do another day's work as long as I live.' Sally sighed.

Anne was also loving the feel of the sun on her bare skin, but time was ticking by, and they still hadn't eaten.

'Sally? I thought you were hungry?'

'I am.'

'So, do you still want to go to the café?'

'Course I do!'

'Do you realise what the time is?'

'No, and to be honest I'm so comfortable, I don't care.'

There followed a short span of silence before Sally asked, 'So what time is it then?'

'Half-past four.'

'Oh, crikey! We'd best get packed up and go, don't you think?'

'What, go home, you mean?'

'No, to the café. We've still got time.'

'I'm a bit peckish,' Anne admitted.

'Me too.' Sally groaned. 'I'm surprised you can't hear my stomach rumbling.'

Anne made the first move. She stood up, brushed the sand from her body and, wrapping the towel around her, she skilfully removed her swimsuit without displaying her attributes to all and sundry.

Sally, though, standing some distance away, was not so careful. Her towel kind of slipped, and when the two young men playing football along the beach wolf-whistled at her, she gave them a quick flash of her buttocks.

'Hey, I reckon he fancies me,' she told Anne, with a naughty twinkle in her eye.

'Behave yourself.' Anne knew only too well what her friend was up to. 'I'm beginning to think I daren't take you anywhere.' She had to laugh, though. 'What would Mick say if he saw you flirting like this?'

'Mick knows I adore him,' Sally said dreamily. 'No one could ever replace him in my heart. *And* he appreciates my sense of mischief.'

Some ten minutes later, as they were trudging along the beach, the football came bouncing their way and landed at Anne's feet.

'See, I was right!' Sally was delighted to see one of the men come running towards them. 'They did that on purpose, just to get our attention.'

As it was in her direct path, Anne stooped to collect the ball and had her arm raised to throw it back, when the fairer-haired fellow of the two bounded up and reached out as though to take it.

'Sorry, I hope it didn't hit you.' His smile was friendly.

'No, it didn't.' Anne thought he was about to take the ball and leave. Instead, he took the ball with one hand and suggestively slid his other hand down her bare arm. 'I don't suppose you and your friend would like to couple up with me and my brother. We could have a bit of fun . . . if you know what I mean?' His knowing wink left nothing to the imagination.

Anne shook her head. 'Sorry. We're on our way to get something to eat, and then we're starting home.'

'Ah, well, me and my brother could do with a bite to eat, so why don't we make it a foursome? It'll be our treat.' Gripping her wrist, he gently drew her towards him. 'Please, say yes.'

From a short distance away, Sally witnessed the exchange between Anne and the stranger.

Moving closer, she was surprised to hear Anne say, 'Thank you, but we haven't actually decided whether or not we will go to the café. We've got a two-hour drive before us, and we have to get back.'

Stepping away, she tried to release herself from his hold, but when he gripped her wrist all the tighter she began to feel threatened. 'Please . . . I have to go now.' Making a determined effort, she pulled free from him.

As she made her way to Sally, her heart was pounding. Then she was panicking. Was he behind her?

Turning to see him already heading back to his brother, she gave a sigh of relief and slowed her steps.

Sally was not best pleased. 'What were you thinking of? He was practically throwing himself at you, and then you frightened him off. Why? I mean, think about it. You haven't been out on a date in ages. All this time, and you still haven't found the right man. For all you know, he could have been the one. As for me, I'm already spoken for, as you well know.'

Anne smiled. 'So, stop looking in the shop window if you don't intend buying. Mick and you have been married for, what . . . eight years?'

'It's just a bit of fun, but having a bite to eat with two good-looking strangers doesn't really mean anything, does it? Besides, I was hoping you might strike lucky.'

Sally had witnessed Anne's nervousness with that man, and she had seen her react like that before when any man got too close. It troubled her.

'Seriously, I'm only thinking of you, Anne. If you don't start going out more, and meeting new people, you may never find the right man.' She tried to lighten the situation. 'Honestly, anybody would think you were afraid of making a commitment.'

When Anne fell silent, Sally realised that somehow, she had touched a nerve. 'All right then, forget I said that. Come on, let's get something to eat, before we head off home.'

Sally continued to chat as they walked down the beach towards the café.

Anne only pretended to listen. She could still feel the strength of the man's fingers gripping her wrist. It had awakened so many memories. Her tormentor had kept her trapped so often by those very same means except, unlike just now, his iron grip had left indentations on her bruised skin for days after.

Often, that was how the real violence began . . .

Anne quickened her steps to escape from the beach and the two men, so that Sally had difficulty in keeping up with her. 'Hey! Slow down.' Running up alongside, she linked her arm with Anne's. 'We're not in that much of a rush.'

As they hurried along, Sally noticed how pale and nervous Anne was, and how every so often she would glance over her shoulder as though worried someone might be following.

'Jeez! You're trembling! Anne, what's wrong? Did he say something to frighten you?'

'No, and there's nothing wrong,' Anne assured her. 'I'm just thinking about the drive home and the traffic getting busy.'

'If it's worrying you that much, we can leave right now. I don't mind one way or the other.'

She did not believe Anne's explanation, especially as Anne was an experienced driver, more than capable, even in the thickest of traffic.

Anne would not hear of abandoning their plans. 'No, we said we'd go to the café and head off home after that. So that's what we'll do. And stop worrying about me, I'm just cold, that's all.' She feigned a shiver. 'I'll be right as rain with a hot drink inside me.' Squeezing Sally to her, she forced a smile. 'I've had a really wonderful time today. I'm so glad I've got you as a friend.'

'Me too.' Sally gave her a little hug. 'We're good together, you and me . . . like sisters, eh?'

'Yeah.' As they climbed the steps to the little café, Anne felt guilty. 'Sally?'

'What?'

'I'm sorry for being a pain just now.'

Sally feigned surprise. 'What? You being a pain? Never!'

They were in brighter mood as they entered the café. 'Can you get the order?' Anne asked. 'I need the loo.'

'Course. What do you want?'

'Coffee. And chips, please, with peas and a slice of bread and butter.'

While Anne went off to the toilet, Sally glanced about, relieved to see there were only two other people in the café, because that meant they would be served quicker, and then they could get a start home that much sooner. That would be a good thing as Anne still appeared to be unnerved by that man's advances.

Sally found a table right in the corner.

'Can I take your order, please?' The woman looked to be in her forties, prim and tidy, with a frilly white cap perched jauntily on her dark hair. 'Is it just the one?'

'No, two; my friend's gone to the loo, but she's left her order with me.'

'That's fine.' The waitress had her pen and notepad at the ready. 'Drinks?'

'One coffee, and one lemonade, please, no ice.'

When the entire order was given, Sally settled back in her chair and gave a lazy yawn. 'Whew! It's been a long day.'

Five minutes passed, and the drinks were delivered.

Then another five minutes, and by now Sally was

growing impatient. *What the devil is she doing in there? The meals will be here soon.*

Picking up the menu, she began to browse through it absent-mindedly. After a minute or so, she replaced it on the table.

In the toilets, Anne washed her hands at the basin, and for a long moment she just stood there, deep in thought.

Leaning against the towel rack, she lowered her head and closed her eyes. She had so much on her mind, what with that stranger this morning, and then the man at the beach. She gave a whimsical smile: he must have thought she was a bit crazy, the way she backed away from him as though he were a mass-murderer.

Her smile slipped away. What was it about today? It was meant to be a fun time away from everyday life. But two incidents had deeply unnerved her. Two incidents in the space of one day.

Over the years she had done everything possible to put it all behind her, but now, because of two strangers, she was taken back, mind and heart, to the most unhappy and frightening time of her life.

~

For what seemed an age, Anne remained in front of the mirror, anxiously murmuring to herself. One minute, she would be staring at the floor; the next, she was nervously glancing about.

'You got Sally really worried,' she chided herself. 'You'd

better get your act together, my girl. Or one of these days, they'll be coming to take you away.'

Leaning forward, she placed her hands on the edge of the basin, her eyes closed and her heart palpitating.

'Edward Carter!' She whispered his name over and over. 'Edward Carter . . . Edward Carter, the monster who ruined my life. Never again will I be able to trust any man. I'll never get married, and I will never have children. Oh, I would have loved to have children, but now I can't. Thanks to him!'

Clenching her fist, she punched the wall. 'I hope you rot in Hell! I hope you suffer like you made me suffer. I pray that you will never have any peace in the whole of your miserable life!'

Unaware that Sally was standing in the half-open door, she began crying; softly at first, and then she was sobbing helplessly.

'Who's Edward Carter?' Sally's voice cut softly through Anne's pain.

'Oh . . . Sally!' Swinging round, Anne was shocked to see her friend standing there. 'He's no one . . . just someone I once knew . . .' Hurriedly wiping away the tears, she was devastated that Sally might have heard everything.

Without a word, Sally wrapped her arms around her friend, and for a long moment neither of them spoke.

Then: 'I'm sorry, I didn't mean to listen to what you were saying, and you don't have to tell me about it. But I want you to know, your happiness means a lot to me, and I don't like to see you hurting,' Sally gently assured her.

Anne felt ashamed. 'It was a long time ago . . . best forgotten.'

'Let me help you, Anne . . . please?'

Anne shook her head. 'I can't.'

'All right. If you'd rather not confide in me, then that's your choice. I'm sorry. I promise I won't ever ask again.'

Leaning into Sally's embrace, Anne tried to gather her senses.

Neither of them spoke for a while.

Presently, Anne drew away, washed her face and, putting on a smile, she said brightly, 'Take no notice of me. I just got upset at something and nothing.'

Sally did not believe a word of Anne's explanation. What she had seen and heard was a woman in turmoil. A woman who was deeply affected by something that had happened to her. 'Like I say, I won't ask you again about what happened, but if you feel the need to confide in me, I'm always here for you. Remember that, won't you?'

'I will.' Anne was greatly relieved. 'Thank you, Sally.'

Deliberately changing the subject, Sally asked her, 'So? Do you want cold chips?'

'No.' Anne was surprised at the question. 'Why?'

'Because I expect they're on the table, waiting for us. The waitress is probably thinking we've changed our mind and run off without paying.' All she wanted was for Anne to come back to the table.

Taking a deep breath, Anne composed herself. 'I'm all right now. Just give me a moment, I'll be right behind you.' Over the years, she had become skilled in the art of putting on a brave face, when inside she was falling apart.

Sally understood. 'OK . . . two minutes, though, or I'll be back.'

Anne watched her go, and gave herself a stern warning: *If you go on like this you'll be put away in some awful place, and they'll never let you out again.*

She tidied her hair and checked herself in the mirror, before going across to the door. Whatever did Sally think of her now? When they got back home, she'd probably avoid her like the plague, and who could blame her? She gave a sad little smile; another friend lost.

Because of her self-imposed secrecy and non-committal, over the years she had lost many friends. And now she convinced herself that she was about to lose Sally, the only real friend she had.

Sally was waiting for her at the table. 'I put a napkin over your chips,' she told Anne. 'Nobody likes cold chips.' She deliberately made no mention of what had taken place back there.

The two of them began their meals, although after Anne's upset neither had an appetite.

'Do you fancy another drink before we head off?' Because of Anne's bizarre behaviour, Sally was not ready to leave just yet.

'Thanks, yes. I'll have a ginger beer.' Right now, Anne was in need of something with a bit more zing than coffee.

'Ginger beer coming up.' Sally went off to order at the counter.

When a few minutes later she returned with the two

drinks, she was concerned to find Anne seemingly deep in thought.

Sally placed the drinks on the table. 'You seem to be lost in a daze. Preparing yourself for the journey back, are you?'

'Not really. I was just thinking, it's so peaceful and pretty here. To be honest, I don't think it would matter if I never went back.'

Sally had no answer to that, but she made an observation: 'You look done in. If you'd rather I drive home, I wouldn't mind one bit. After I see you home safe, I can easily get the bus back to my house.'

Anne dismissed the idea. 'No. Thanks all the same, but I enjoy the drive.'

'Really?'

'Yes, really!'

They sipped their drinks, and talked quietly of anything and everything – except the one thing that burned in both their minds.

'Anne?' Sally's voice was almost inaudible.

Thrusting the bad thoughts from her mind, Anne took a few gulps of her drink and replaced her glass on the table. She could feel Sally's attention on her. 'Oh, I'm sorry, Sally.' She quickly started gathering her belongings together. 'Are you waiting to go?'

'No, we're all right for a while yet. But I do need to ask you something. Don't worry. Like I said before, I won't pry. So if you don't want to answer, that's fine.'

Anne had half expected her to ask questions, and she was ready. 'You can ask, but I can't promise to answer.'

'Earlier, at the fairground . . .?'

'Yes?'

'When I reminded you about the man at Woollies?'

Anne was somewhat relieved. Initially, she feared the question might be linked to what Sally had overheard in the loo. 'Oh, him! Yes, what about him?'

'It's just that afterwards . . . you said something.' Sally had not forgotten. 'It just made me wonder, that's all?'

'What did I say?' Anne grew nervous. 'I can't remember. And anyway, it was probably something and nothing.'

'It might not be word for word, but,' Sally leaned closer, 'as I recall, you said . . . "confrontation sometimes brings you more trouble than you can handle", or words to that effect.'

Anne feigned ignorance. 'Did I really say that?'

'Yes, you did.' Sally was gentle. 'It was a really strange thing to say. So, what exactly did you mean by that?'

Anne measured her words carefully. 'There are times when you might really want someone to leave you alone, but they never do. So you tell them straight. You stand up to them. Somehow, you have to find the courage to speak your mind.' She took a moment to calm herself. 'Sometimes you try and protect yourself, but then you might find that you've made the situation worse. That you've let yourself in for more trouble than you could ever have imagined.'

For what seemed an age, there was silence between them.

Then Anne tried to explain further: 'All I meant was

that you should be careful how you say no. Some people don't like to take "No" for an answer.' Grabbing her drink she took a long swig, then put the empty glass down with a heavy thud. 'Think about it, Sally. I'm sure you've been in that same, uncomfortable situation, at one time or another.'

Sensing a chink in Anne's armour, Sally played along. 'You're absolutely right! Do you remember when the randy foreman asked me to climb the ladder at work. He said he had a bad back and wanted me to get the stock down from the top shelf. I was on to him straight away! Bad back be damned! He thought he'd stand at the bottom of the steps, peering up my skirt and getting an eyeful, dirty old sod! Oh, but he didn't like it when I said no. I pretended I was afraid of heights. He lost his rag. Just like you said, he flew into a spiteful mood. Slamming and banging about, he was, and yelling at everyone for no good reason.'

She gave a nervous little chuckle. 'Nobody ever knew the reason for his bad mood, and I thought it wise not to tell. But I had the feeling he would have loved to give me a battering. As it was, he made some feeble excuse to take me off my regular duties. That same day, he shifted me to the cramped back office, where they carry out stock checks and ordering.'

'But I thought you hated that kind of work?'

'I do. It was my first job on starting there, and he knew it had bored me to tears. But it's what you were saying before, he was just punishing me because I stood up to him. So I do know what you mean. And you're absolutely right.'

'It's true. Some men are like that.' Anne knew only too well. 'They're just naturally vicious. They like to hurt women. They like to see them in pain. They torment their minds, and break their spirit, and they think it's all right. But it's not all right, it's wicked!'

Realising she had already said too much, Anne picked up her glass, and pretended to drain the last few drops.

Sally deliberately ignored Anne's short burst of rage. 'D'you want another drink before we go?' she asked casually.

Anne had lapsed into her own little world again.

'Anne?'

'Yes?'

'Do you fancy another drink?'

'No, thanks. I've had enough.'

'Well then, I'm ready to leave whenever you are.' For one minute, Sally had hoped that Anne might be ready to confide her troubles. Now she collected her belongings. 'Let's hit the road, as they say.'

As always, Sally's bright humour put a smile on Anne's face, although she was fully aware that she had come way too close to revealing the shocking truth. For the first time in all these long years, she had very nearly let her feelings get the better of her.

Yet somehow, even though she had let her guard slip for only that one brief moment, she felt better for it. She felt calmer inside.

The dark memories remained, of course, along with the firm belief that she would never be like others. She would never hold her own child in her arms, or be at the centre of a loving family.

Because of the damage he had done, a normal life was denied her. And as long as she lived, she would never forgive him.

Edward Carter was more devil than man.

At least, she had found the courage to flee from him. In the safe haven that was her aunt Ada's house, she had tried so hard to make a life for herself. But in spite of everything, in spite of all her efforts to shut him out of her mind and her life, he had won.

A short time later, having piled their bags into the boot, Sally and Anne set off home.

'We've had such a lovely day, haven't we?' Sally gave an almighty yawn.

'Yes, and wasn't it great that the weather held out for us?'

'How are we for petrol?' Sally had a phobia about running out of fuel in the middle of nowhere.

Anne assured her that the tank was still half full.

Within minutes of starting out, Sally was fast asleep, her rhythmic snoring making Anne smile.

Glancing down at Sally's crumpled figure and pretty face, she thanked her lucky stars to have found such a loyal friend. *I hope she didn't hear too much of what I said in the café toilets,* she thought.

Even though she knew her friend was the soul of discretion, the idea of her having heard everything played on Anne's mind, especially because Sally had actually asked who Edward Carter was. Somewhere deep inside, Anne desperately wanted to confide in her.

All these years she had been carrying the truth, and

it was a heavy burden. Her fear that one day he might somehow find her was terrifying indeed.

~

As the miles flew by, Anne found herself wondering what Sally would say if she knew the truth. But dare she tell? Was it time? And could she really trust Sally that much?

As they neared Bedford, she constantly tried to push the idea of confessing to the back of her mind, but it persisted.

Eventually, she headed the car down a quiet side street on the outskirts.

Having now parked the car, she gently tapped Sally on the shoulder, 'Wake up, Sally.'

Sally leaped up, eyes wide awake and her voice slurred. 'Oh . . . sorry, Anne! I must have dozed off. You should have woken me. Oh, are we home already?'

'No. We've still got a little way to go yet.'

Feeling groggy, Sally glanced out the window, puzzled by the unfamiliar surroundings. 'Where are we?'

'We're just off the Goldington Road.'

Sally gave a tired groan. 'Oh, bugger it! I knew it: we've run out of petrol, haven't we?'

'No, we've still got more than enough petrol to get us home.'

'So what's going on?' Raising both hands, Sally ruffled her flattened hair.

When Anne hesitated, Sally's concern deepened. Now wide awake, she sensed that something was wrong.

'Anne, why are we parked in a quiet side street?' she asked worriedly. 'I don't understand.'

She knew instinctively that this was to do with the incident at the café and wanted to ask why Anne had been so upset, and who was the man she had cursed over and over. But for now, she thought it best to let things lie. It seemed enough damage had already been done. Besides, if Anne had wanted to confide in her, she would have done so by now.

'Sally . . . what you said back there . . .' Anne began.

'What? What did I say?'

'It was the question you asked me.'

'Well, whatever it was, let's just forget it. It's not my business, and I don't need to know the answer.'

But Anne could not let it go now. 'Sally, can I trust you . . . implicitly?'

'Absolutely! Whatever you tell me won't ever go any further, I promise.'

Anne fell silent for a moment. She needed to be sure she was doing the right thing. She had always intended that Sally should never know anything of her turbulent past, but now, having come to a new decision, there was no turning back. 'Sally, while you were sleeping, I was thinking,' Anne told her. 'And I feel I owe you an answer.'

'You don't owe me anything, Anne. Maybe we should just put it out of our minds and forget it ever happened.'

'No!' Anne stopped her. 'Please listen, Sally. I've never been able to make friends; not even when I was a little girl. You see, my mother had me when she was forty-five years old. When I was born, my parents were already set in their ways. I was not allowed to bring friends home from school, nor play out with them, nor walk to school with them. Mother took me to school and she picked me up, and once she got me home, I was very rarely allowed to go outside, though I could play in the back yard on my own. So, y'see, you're the first real friend I ever had.'

Sally reached out to take her hand. 'It doesn't matter to me what's in the past, because I'll always be your friend. And I hope you will always be mine.'

Anne was grateful for Sally's loyalty, but it was now time for the truth to be told. 'I need to be honest with you, Sally. There are things you don't know about me. Bad, terrible things that I need to share with you. I'm a weak person. What happened was partly my fault. After I've told you, if you want to walk away from me, I won't blame you.'

'It doesn't matter what you tell me, good or bad, I would never walk away from you.'

She was intrigued by what Anne had described earlier. 'You said your mother was in her mid-forties when she had you.'

'That's right, forty-five. My father was three years older.'

'Crikey! So, did you have older brothers or sisters?'

'No. I was an only child, more's the pity. Mother never mixed with anyone, and she raised me to be the same. When I was about ten years old, I was invited to a birthday party, but she refused to let me go. It seemed like a punishment to me, so I argued with her. I wanted to know why she would never let me play out with other children.'

'And what did your mother say?'

'She sat me down and told me I should never have been born. She said I was an accident of nature, that I was never planned, especially at their time of life, that I wore them out and that she had nothing in common with the other mothers. She said if I went to the party she'd be expected to have the other girls back when it was my birthday, but she had no intention of doing parties. She said that Father was coming up to sixty now, and if it weren't for me, they'd have been planning his retirement; looking for a smaller house on the coast. She said all they had to look forward to now was bringing me up, and by the time that was done, they would be too old to make any plans for themselves.'

Sally was shocked. 'That explains why you found it so hard to make friends when you started at Woolworths. It's why I had to tease you out of your shell. I noticed at first you found it so hard to mix with other people.'

'You helped me, Sally,' Anne admitted. 'I could never have done it without you . . . and lovely Aunt Ada. She was older than my parents, but she was so kind and unselfish. She took me in when I needed someone to help me. She made me laugh. She brought me out of my shell, and made me believe that I was special.' She gave a fond little smile. 'She said I deserved a chance to shine.'

Sally remembered the old woman. 'I met her only a couple of times, but I really liked her. She seemed a genuine soul.'

Anne's voice broke with emotion as she confessed, 'I owe her so much, and, oh, I do miss her terribly.'

'I'm sure you do.' Sally knew how close these two had been. 'I don't mean to pry,' she ventured, 'but I've always wondered how you came to be living with your aunt.' She was already learning more about Anne in these few minutes than she had learned these past years. 'Did you leave because of the things your mother said to you? Did you think your parents would be happier if you moved out of the family home as soon as you were able?'

Anne smiled wryly. 'I always knew they'd be happier without me in their lives,' she acknowledged sadly. 'In a way I felt sorry for them. I felt as though I'd ruined their lives. But the truth wasn't as simple as me just "moving out".'

Though she was determined that Sally should know the truth, she was finding it difficult to bare her soul. 'When I was seventeen, I did something really bad. There was a terrible row. Mother threw me out. She told me she and Father never wanted to see me again . . . that I was never to come back. She said, as far as they were concerned they did not have a daughter.'

Sally was beginning to realise what had made Anne so very shy and private. 'Whatever did you do that was so bad it made them throw you out?'

Anne fell silent for a while. In her tortured mind it was almost as though she was back there, caught up in a nightmare.

Having taken time to focus her thoughts, she explained, 'It was a couple of weeks before my seventeenth birthday. Mother had found me a job in the local dressmaker's. I was working long hours and earning decent money; half of which I gave to Mother for my board and keep. She even seemed proud that I was doing so well.'

'So what happened to make it all go wrong?' Sally was intrigued.

'I should have known better. It was the day of my birthday. Irene, the dressmaker's daughter, asked what I had planned. When I told her that my mother did not agree with parties or celebrations, she insisted that the two of us should mark my seventeeth birthday by going out somewhere.' Anne gave a knowing smile. 'Irene was a bit of a rebel on the quiet.'

'So, did you go?'

'Yes, and that's when I deceived my mother for the first time in my life. When Mother asked where I was going, I said I was meeting up with Irene, and that we were going to see one of Irene's friends. When I was ready to leave, Mother gave me the once-over, to make sure I was dressed accordingly. She did not approve of make-up and stockings, and girls who flaunted themselves. She also reminded me that the house would be locked and bolted at 10 p.m. as usual, and that if I wasn't back before then, it would be no use banging on the door, because neither she nor Father would get out of bed to let me in.'

'And were you back on time?'

Anne shook her head. 'Irene insisted on the two of us going out on the town. She said it wasn't every day a girl was seventeen, and that it was cause for a special celebration.' Anne laughed out loud at the memory.

'By the time we left Irene's house I was a different girl. Irene had plastered my face with make-up. My hair was curled, and as we were more or less the same size, she sorted me a strappy dress from her wardrobe. Honestly, Sally, when I walked out of there, I felt like a film star!'

'Wow! And I bet you had a good time, didn't you?' Sally couldn't help but smile at the idea of Anne being plastered in make-up, with her hair curled, and wearing a naughty dress. It was hard to imagine.

'This is where I did a bad thing,' Anne recalled. 'We really enjoyed ourselves. We met up with one of Irene's friends. She was a few years older than me and Irene, but she was so lively, and such fun. I had never met anyone like her. We talked about going to the pictures, but then Irene had an idea, and we ended up dancing to the band at the Palais. Irene's friend got us some drinks. I asked for a lemonade, but she told me to try one of their specialities, which I did.'

'Oh, what kind of "speciality"?' Sally had her suspicions.

'I never knew, but I went with the mood, and I drank it. Then I had another. I felt a bit woozy after that, but by that time I didn't care. For the first time ever, I was out on the town with these lively girls, and I was having fun.'

She explained how, after they left the Palais, they walked the streets looking for a taxi home. 'A big black taxi pulled up and we all climbed in.'

In her mind she could see the driver vividly: long-boned, handsome and dark-haired, he had a smile you believed you could trust. 'The driver was really friendly.

He said his name was Edward Carter, and that he meant to make his mark in the world. He told us he owned the taxi firm and that every now and then, especially on a weekend, he enjoyed coming out of the office to drive a taxi himself. Apparently, his uncle had built up the firm. He had promised Edward he could buy it when he was more experienced, and Edward eventually bought him out.'

'Quite the businessman, eh?' Sally thought he sounded very enterprising. 'Did he get you home safely, though?'

'He took the others home first, then he drove to my house. It was gone midnight. I banged on the door, and called up to the bedroom window, but got no answer. Either my parents were fast asleep and couldn't hear me, or Mother meant what she said and had locked me out.'

'So, what did you do?'

'Well, Edward Carter refused to leave me there in the dark on my own. He asked me if there was a relative he could take me to, and when I told him there was no one, he got me back to the car. He said he could not believe they would lock me out like that.'

'So, where did you go?'

'He took me to a really nice hotel. He even offered to pay my room for the night, but I wouldn't let him. Fortunately I had enough money in my purse to cover it.'

'I think I can guess what happened when you got to the hotel.' Sally was worldy-wise. 'I bet he insisted on escorting you safely to your room. Am I right?'

Anne blushed with shame. 'When we got there, he made a play for me, and like a drunken, gullible fool, I fell for his smooth talk.'

She fell silent, deeply regretting that shameful night, and the fact that it had cost her so dearly. 'I can't put all the blame on Edward Carter,' she confessed. 'I should have been strong enough to resist his advances.'

Sally was angry. 'That's all very well, but don't forget you were a young girl of seventeen. You'd been kicked out of house and home in the middle of the night, with little money and nowhere to go. You must have been really scared. That man took advantage of you. He was the one who should have known better, not you!'

Anne made no response to Sally's wise words.

'So, did you ever see him again?' Sally was curious.

'Yes, I did, more's the pity. My parents never knew, but over the next few weeks, we met up a lot. Things got serious. He began talking about getting married, but I didn't want that. I said it was too soon. I felt I was too young to be married. But then it became clear that I didn't have a choice.'

'What do you mean? Of course you had a choice.'

'No, I didn't, because I got pregnant. Edward didn't know and I was too afraid to tell anyone. I was two months gone, and one morning I was too sick to go to work. Mother guessed and forced the truth out of me. She went crazy!'

Anne choked back the tears. 'It was awful! When Father came home she told him, and there was a huge row, shouting and screaming like I've never heard. They called me a slut. They said I'd brought shame on them . . . that they did not want me under their roof. They threw me out that night, with nothing but the clothes on my back and a couple of personal items. I had a small amount of money, but it wasn't enough to carry me through.'

Sally was shocked. 'That was so cruel. You must have felt really frightened.' She could hardly believe anyone's parents would do such a thing.

'I remember it was pouring with rain,' Anne went on. 'I ran to the telephone kiosk and called Edward's number, but there was no reply. So, I called Irene. When she told me to get a taxi and come straight over, I was so thankful.'

'That was good of her, especially at that time of night.'

Curiously, Anne made no comment. 'When I got to Irene's house, she was watching out of the window for me. She said she knew someone who could get rid of the baby for me, but it would cost. I said no, that it wasn't the baby's fault, and I didn't like the idea of doing that. She got angry, saying I was a fool for having got myself into that situation, and that she couldn't help me, and that I'd best go before her parents found me there.'

Sally was disappointed. 'Hmm! So she wasn't such a friend after all?'

'She was, but I don't really blame her for turning me away. She urged me to go and see Edward that very night, and tell him the truth . . . that he was to be a father.'

'And did you?'

'Yes. I went to his house, but it was in darkness, so I took a room in a small boarding house nearby. I caught Edward at the office early the next morning, and I told him about the baby. He seemed delighted that he might have a son, who he could train up to take over from him one day. He started talking wedding plans and all that, and a short time later we were married at the registry office.'

'Well, at least he seemed to have done right by you.' Sally had been taken aback by what she'd learned. Her quiet, unassuming friend, who most times had little to say, had poured out her heart and soul. She had confided her extraordinary and shocking past, and now those awful times, and her suffering, were clearly evident in her face.

For a moment, Anne spoke not a word. Instead, she sat fidgeting, her head turned away to look out through the car window.

When Sally looked up, she was deeply moved to see tears flowing down Anne's face.

Instinctively, she wrapped her arms round Anne's small shoulders. 'What you've told me won't go any further,' she promised. 'But what happened between you and Edward? The fact that you're on your own now must mean it didn't work out. Am I right? Is that the way it was?'

When Anne merely nodded, Sally went on, 'As far as I can see, you've had a hard time of it. Up to Edward marrying you, there was never anyone there to help you . . . except later, when your aunt Ada took you in. But you've got *me* now, and I'll always be here for you, but I'm sorry things didn't work out with the marriage, Anne, I really am.'

Hugging Anne closer, she asked, 'You take it easy now. I'll drive from here, and when we get back, I want you to come and stay with me for a while. OK?' In the back of her mind, she suspected she had not yet heard the whole story.

Anne, however, was reluctant to leave just yet. 'Please, Sally, I need to tell you everything.' Drawing from Sally's embrace, Anne continued, 'Edward Carter was not the man I believed him to be. He was a spiteful bully. He beat me often, sometimes for no other reason than that he'd lost a good client, or a lucrative hotel-booking had been cancelled at the last minute. Sometimes he beat me so I could hardly walk. When I was eight months pregnant, he came home from a night out. He'd lost a great deal of money gambling. He was in a foul mood and so drunk he could hardly stand up. He was looking for a fight, and things turned nasty. It was awful, Sally . . . I really thought he would kill me.'

Realizing that Anne was badly shaken, Sally held onto her. 'Don't think about it, Anne. You shouldn't be on your own tonight. Please, come and stay with me and Mick, for as long as you like.'

Anne graciously declined the offer. 'I'll be fine, honest. At least I know I'm safe now. Edward Carter is long gone. He can't hurt me any more.'

'Is it helping you – to talk about it, I mean?'

'Oh, Sally! You can't know how long I've wanted to tell you, only I'm so ashamed, I thought you wouldn't want to know me any more.'

'Huh! If I couldn't share your troubles, what kind of a friend would that make me?' She gave Anne a friendly little push. 'You might as well go on, now that you know we understand each other.'

'He hurt me so much that night, Sally. I lost the baby.' Anne fell silent, and for a moment she could hardly breathe. Then, in an almost inaudible voice, she went on, 'Edward Carter killed our baby. At the hospital, they induced me into labour, and I had to give birth.'

The trauma of seeing the baby afterwards was too awful a memory. 'I'm sorry.' At first, she tried not to cry, but then the tears flowed and her heart broke. 'I will never forgive him, Sally. For as long as I live . . . I will never forgive him!'

For a seemingly long time, Sally held her while she cried. And, though silently, Sally cried with her.

After a time, Anne drew away. Her voice was breaking as she continued, 'Afterwards, they brought him to me . . . so tiny . . . a perfect little man.' She gave a muffled laugh. 'He had a look of my mother . . . his grumpy face and that tuft of hair on his head.'

Relieved that for the first time, Anne was able to pour out her heart and soul, Sally urged her to go on.

Anne told her, 'After they took him away, the chaplain came to see me. He said they were bringing in Social Services, because I'd been beaten up. They had pictures of my broken fingers and the bruises all over my body. They said the police had also been informed and would want to ask me some questions.' In her mind, she relived the moment. 'I was frightened they might blame me.'

'So, what did the police say?' Sally asked gently.

Anne shrugged. 'I didn't wait to find out. After the nurses had treated my injuries and settled me down, I waited until they were out of sight, then I scrambled my clothes on, and got as far away from the hospital as I could. I planned to make my way down to Aunt Ada. Edward knew of her existence, but he had never met her, or asked about her. As far as I know, he had no idea where she lived, except it was down south somewhere.'

'So, you made your way down here, knowing you should be safe?'

'Yes. It was my only chance. My parents had disowned me; I had no friends who could help, so the only person I could turn to was Aunt Ada. I thought I'd be safe with her . . . if she didn't mind taking me in. The trouble was, I hadn't seen her in such a long time, I had no idea if I'd be welcome.'

She gave a warm smile. 'I should never have doubted her, because she welcomed me with open arms.'

Sally listened quietly; at times shaking her head and other times shedding a tear.

The longer she talked, the more Anne relaxed. 'When I got there, I was exhausted and close to collapse. Aunt Ada took it all in her stride. She put me to bed, then she sat beside me, holding my hand. When I said I had some bad things to tell her, she said it could wait until I was rested. She reassured me that after I'd had a good long sleep, I could tell her, or not tell her, whichever I felt comfortable with. Either way, she would be there for me, and would nurse me back to health. And that's exactly what she did.'

Sally had met the old woman on only a couple of occasions. 'That was a wonderful thing for her to do, but that's what friends are for. Even so, as a young girl in need, you should have been able to turn to your parents.'

Anne nodded sadly. 'I know,' she murmured, 'but my parents were the last people I could turn to, and to tell the truth, I do understand now. They had me too late in life and it was all too much. Aunt Ada, though, was wonderful! I told her everything: how my parents had turned me out of the house; about Edward Carter, and the spiteful beatings.' Her voice broke. 'I told her about the baby, too, and we cried together. I felt so very sad.'

'What did your aunt say you should do?'

'She said I ought to report him to the police and tell them everything; that it wasn't too late. But she didn't know Edward like I did. If I had reported him, the police would have tracked me down, and then he would have got to me somehow. He would have killed me without a second thought. I know it, Sally. I know it!'

Sally reminded her, 'They would have questioned him anyway, what with the bruises on you, and the baby . . . and everything.'

'Aunt Ada said that, but I know Edward. He would have wormed his way out of it, somehow or another. He probably blamed me. I wouldn't put it past him.'

'Anyway, thankfully, he never did find you, did he? And thanks to Aunt Ada, you now have a whole new life.'

'That's true.' Anne smiled at Sally. 'And I have the best friend in you.' Talking to Sally was as though a great weight had fallen from her shoulders.

For a time, the two of them sat holding each other and thinking of the bad times.

After a while, Sally asked, 'Anne, you don't have to answer this, but something has just occurred to me. How did you divorce Edward Carter, without him somehow discovering where you were?'

'I never did divorce him.'

'Oh, my Lord, why not?'

'For the very reason you just mentioned: because I was afraid that if I applied for a divorce, I would have been found. He would know where I was, and I could not risk that.'

'But doesn't that mean you are technically still his wife?'

'I suppose I must be. I've never really thought about it and, thankfully, no one has ever served me with official papers, but I don't care. I don't want anyone – lawyers or police, or anyone else – to find out where I am.'

'Oh, Anne, you must find someone who can help you. Otherwise, you'll never be free of that monster. Neither of you will ever be able to move on with your lives.'

'I don't care about that!'

'But what if you find someone in the future? There might come a day when you want to get married. But you won't be able to.'

'I will never again want to get married.'

'All right then. But if you truly want to be rid of him, you need to find a discreet lawyer and tell him everything. He'll be able to free you from Edward Carter once and for all. I'll help you, Anne. I'll do all I can to help you, I promise.'

'No!'

'But maybe there's a way in which they can protect your address, so he can never find you.'

Growing fearful, Anne drew away. 'No! I won't do it. Please, Sally, don't ask me to. You can't know what he's like. He's unhinged.'

Sally urged her to think about it all the same.

'I won't ever let myself get drawn into another deep relationship. It's too frighening,' Anne said.

'Anne, listen to me for a minute, please—'

'You're wasting your time. Please, Sally, don't make me wish I'd never told you.'

Undaunted, Sally had one more try. 'If you don't go to the police and tell them what he did to you, who's to say he might not do the same to some other poor, unsuspecting woman? What if he was to hurt her, like he hurt you?'

'It would not happen.'

'But, how can you know that?'

'Because I know I was partly to blame. I was just a stupid, naïve young girl who could not handle a deep relationship like that. I didn't know how to deal with his moods. I was too easily bullied . . . too afraid. No other woman would ever be so gullible. No woman would ever let him hurt her like he hurt me. She would stand up to him, protect herself, or tell someone.' Her voice dipped. 'Only I had no one to tell.'

Glancing about nervously, she suddenly drew closer to Sally. 'I thought I saw him,' she whispered huskily.

'Who?' Sally was taken by surprise.

'Him! Edward Carter!'

'When?'

'This very morning, when I was leaving home. I saw this man, and for one awful minute, I could have sworn it was him!'

'It wasn't, though . . . was it?'

'At first I was sure it was him. He was walking close to the house. I'd never seen him before, but at first glance he looked uncannily like Edward . . . same build. Same dark hair. But then I realised that Edward is older now, so the stranger could not have been him. He couldn't, could he?'

Sally calmed her. 'No, of course not. Can't you see, he's haunting you, Anne. This is why you need to punish him for what he did to you and the baby. Trust me, Anne. You really must take legal steps. Divorce him. Close that episode of your life and stop being afraid.'

'No! You don't understand. If I stir things up now, he will never stop until he's found me. I know him. I know what he's capable of.'

Growing nervous even at the possibility that Edward might somehow find her, she started the car. 'We'd best make tracks.' She grabbed Sally's hand. 'I'm really grateful for you listening to me. You can't know how hard it's been, living with the truth, and not being able to tell anyone.'

Thrusting the engine into gear, she moved the car out of the side street and onto the main road.

~

As they headed further into Bedford, neither Sally nor Anne spoke a word.

And then out of the blue, Anne confessed, 'The odd thing is, even though he was cruel and he hurt me badly, I never hated him.' She took a long breath before finishing. 'Until he killed my baby.'

Sally made no comment, but when she noticed a solitary tear rolling down Anne's face, she reached out and squeezed her hand, to reassure her that she was not alone any more.

And the gesture was enough.

CHAPTER SEVEN

Having arrived at Sally's house, Anne drew up to the kerb. 'I'll see you on Monday then?' She waited for Sally to climb out of the car.

'Wait a minute!' Sally had noticed that her husband's car was not in its usual parking space. 'It looks like Mick's not home yet. He said he was popping in to see his mum on the way from work, so how about I come back with you? Afterwards, I'll get the bus to Mick's mum's, and drive home with him.' She gave Anne a way out: 'Or have you had enough of me for today?'

Still reeling from the shocking things Anne had confided in her, Sally was concerned about her being on her own just now.

Anne, though, was receptive to Sally's idea. 'OK, that'll be nice.'

'Good!' Sally slid back into her seat, a little smile of satisfaction curling the corners of her mouth.

~

Edward Carter was quietly congratulating himself. After learning as much as he could from the old geezers in the pub, he impatiently bided his time while hiding in a derelict builder's yard.

The day had seemed a lifetime long. Twice he'd returned to the house on Roff Avenue, but each time there were no signs of life. Then there was that officious-looking bobby, constantly patrolling the streets, and seeming to peek into every little hidey-hole, presumably looking for the man he saw lurking about earlier.

So, remaining wary of the bobby, Carter watched and waited. When she got back, he would be ready for her.

Yet again, he cautiously emerged from his hiding place. Snaking his way through the maze of back alleys and less inhabited places, he made his way back to the house. 'You've been a thorn in my side for too many years,' he muttered insanely. 'You moved far away, but you should have known I'd find you eventually, and now that I have, we need to finish it, once and for all.'

~

A short time later, unaware that he was lurking out the back, Anne slid the key into the front-door lock and stepped back for Sally to enter.

'You put the kettle on,' she said, 'I'll call the cat in. Little devil! She ran off again this morning, before I could feed her. I've no idea where she goes.'

Sally chuckled. 'Leave her alone. I expect she's got a boyfriend.'

While Anne rushed ahead, Sally followed her down the passageway and through to the kitchen, where she placed her handbag on the windowsill.

Making a small bowl of meaty titbits, Anne then threw open the back door. 'Pusscat! Come and get your feed . . . come on, I won't call you again!'

Meantime, Sally busied herself making the tea. 'Milk, and one sugar, isn't it?' she called out.

'Please.' Anne returned with the bowl of food. 'I expect she'll come back when she's ready. I would leave her food out, but stray cats will wolf it down.' She covered the bowl with a plate and put it inside the sink cupboard.

'Come on then, let's you and me have our tea in the front room, eh?' She placed a packet of gingerbreads and two cups of steaming tea onto the tray, and made her way to the front room.

Anne padded happily along behind her. 'Sounds good to me.'

As they left the kitchen, not for one moment did they realise that they were being watched.

~

A short time later, Sally threw her coat on, jingling the change in her pockets. 'I'll ring you when I get to Mick's mum's house.' She gave Anne a parting hug, 'Thanks for a smashing day out.'

'Thanks for listening to my troubles.'

'Ah, but don't you remember what I said: that's what friends are for?'

'I know.'

'Listen, Anne, about doing something to end the marriage . . . you will think about it, won't you? You never know, maybe you're already free, but you just don't know it. I have heard that they can declare a marriage null and void in certain circumstances, but I'm not sure.'

Anne gave a little smile. 'Don't forget to ring me when you get to Mick's mum's.'

~

Having seen them arrive, Edward Carter had kept his distance. Now he was placed in a vantage point at the end of the alley where he was able to see out while no one could see him.

He watched Sally hurry past the opening. He saw her turn and wave.

''Bye, Anne. See you!'

He smiled to himself. *Will you now?* His plan did not include a third party.

At the bus shelter, Sally checked the time of the next bus. Still twenty minutes to wait. *Oh, bugger, I could have stayed with Anne another ten minutes,* she thought impatiently.

Back at the house, while collecting the tray from the front room, Anne glanced through the window to see the tabby cat, strolling lazily across the busy road. Quickly replacing the tray on the table, she ran out of the front door and swept the cat into her arms.

'You silly little devil! You could get run over.'

Carrying the wriggling bundle inside, she placed the dish of food on the floor, and stood the grateful cat in front of it. 'There! Make sure you eat it all up.'

While the cat tucked into its food, she returned to the front room, and collected the tray. As she walked back into the kitchen, she had a sickening feeling that someone else was in the house.

Through the corner of her eye she saw the swish of a dark jacket. Panicking, she turned to run, but he was on her, gripping her so tight by the neck, she struggled to breathe.

The more she fought to escape, the more his grip tightened, and there was no way out.

'Missed me, have you?' His warm, thick breath fanned her face. 'Long time, no see, but you haven't changed much. Still the same, tight little figure . . . same mop of hair. Mmm!' Gripping a lock of her fair curls in his teeth, he buried his face in her hair. 'You smell real nice . . . all woman.' He gave a long, deep groan as he ran his free hand over her private parts.

Frantic, Anne tried to push him away, but he held her fast. He swung her round to face him, his narrow eyes boring into her. 'You ran away from me. No woman ever ran away from Edward Carter!' Pushing his face close to hers, he whispered in her ear, 'That was not a nice thing to do. You really are a prize bitch, aren't you?'

'Leave me alone!' However hard Anne struggled, she could not free herself from his vice-like grip. 'You mean nothing to me. I don't want anything to do with you.'

His laughter rang through the house. 'Is that so?' he growled. 'Little Miss High-and-Mighty doesn't want anything to do with me? Well, you listen to me, bitch! This is your husband you're talking to. The same husband you dumped back there. The same husband who helped you when even your own parents turned you out. You might be surprised to know that I've made a few friends since I got here, and by the way, I've done my homework. Oh, yes! I know you don't have a man-friend, and you should thank your lucky stars for that, because if I thought you had set up with another man, I would need to deal with him . . . and it would not be nice. If you know what I mean?'

He craftily slid one arm over her shoulders and across her breast. When he began roughly fondling her, she fought viciously. 'Get off me! Get out of my house! My friend has just gone to the shop. She'll be back in a minute—'

'Liar!' Screeching with laughter, he licked her neck from the hairline to the collarbone, making her cringe with disgust.

'I've been watching you,' he crowed, 'and your friend. I know she's gone, and I know she's not coming back. I heard her say cheerio. So, to my reckoning, that leaves just you and me. You may not believe it, but it's been a while since I had a woman. Oh, but that can wait for now; until we've discussed the legal stuff.'

Anne knew the depth of his badness, and she was desperate. 'What are you talking about? What legal stuff? There's nothing between us any more, and never will be. Like I told you, I want nothing to do with the man who killed my baby! I hate you. Every minute of every day, I've wished you dead. Do you hear what I'm saying?'

Her words were cruelly cut short when he grabbed her by the face. 'You want me dead, do you? Well, it won't happen. I'll tell you what will happen, though, shall I?' Lowering his voice, he growled in her ear, 'Like I said, I've made friends. They very kindly filled me in on a thing or two. For instance, I know the old biddy left you this house. Only it's not your house now. It's mine! I'm your husband. What's yours is mine. I'm entitled to whatever you have, and that includes this house.'

'NEVER!' Anne screamed at him. 'You'll get my aunt's house over my dead body.'

'Oh, don't you worry, that can always be arranged.' Thrusting his face close to hers, he took delight in boasting, 'After you ran off, it didn't take me long to find myself another woman. I never loved her, though; not like I love you. She meant nothing to me. She was weak. She had no spirit. I despised her for that.' Anne was shocked when he added casually, 'She died, you know.'

'What do you mean, "she died"?'

'She had an accident. She fell down the stairs . . . broke every bone in her body, I shouldn't wonder. I had a son too . . . Adam. I left them both behind, because of you. Y'see, it's you I want.' He smiled. 'It's always been you. So, what d'you say to that, eh?'

'I say, I've always known that you're completely mad.' Now she was more convinced of that than ever.

'Still feisty, eh?' Her spirit pleased him. 'If I'm "mad", it's prison that made me that way. I did time because of that weak, spineless woman. Even when she was dying, she was too afraid to accuse me.'

'Was it your fault she died?' Anne dared to ask.

'Hmm! Don't you think if it had been my fault she would have said so, and I would have been put away for a very long time?'

He abruptly changed the subject. 'The boy was made in her mould. I've no idea where he is now. Nor do I want to know. He meant nothing to me, and neither did his mother, although I'm grateful that she chose not to say it might have been me who caused her early demise.'

His manner darkened. 'There were others who tarnished my name, though. Apparently, the medical team found a number of bruises on her body, and made certain suggestions. One or two other things were said that marked my card and got me put away. My own son turned against me, and some old man gave an account of me supposedly running away on the day it all happened. I got a prison sentence. Oh, but it was rough in there, I can tell you. The place was filled with rogues, murderers and bad people you could never imagine. But the experience has made me stronger. It's taught me that I must do whatever it takes to survive.'

He smiled. 'It even gave me the will to find you . . . and lay my claim to this house. So now, I'm back in your life, and that pleases me.'

He sniggered. 'You should be delighted to see me. Instead, here you are, calling me all sorts of names, and even wanting to fight me.'

Suddenly, taking him by surprise, Anne pulled away and ran down the hallway, but he caught her and pinned her against the wall. 'Don't make me angry.' He dragged her into the front room. 'You'll only come off worse.' With one mighty shove he sent her sprawling onto the sofa. 'Now be quiet or I'll have to gag you!' Keeping a wary eye on her, he swiftly drew the curtains shut. 'We don't want anyone being nosy, do we?'

In the half-light, he watched her every move. 'No point in trying to escape, my dear. It will only rile me, and make matters worse for you.'

Knowing what he was capable of, Anne remained quiet. Hurt and bleeding, she let him rant on, while training her frantic thoughts on a plan of escape.

~

Sally ran all the way back from the bus stop. *What an idiot,* she muttered to herself, *leaving my handbag on the windowsill.*

She hurried up the front path to Anne's house, and was about to knock on the front door when she heard sounds much like soft laughter. Someone else was there . . . a neighbour, probably. She knocked on the door but there was no answer. She knocked again, louder this time, but still no answer. That was really odd.

Growing curious, she sidestepped onto the lawn, and stretched up to peer in the window, but she was too short to see, and the curtains were closed. Why would Anne close the curtains at this time of day? Sally smiled.

Maybe Anne had got a secret admirer, and didn't want to say.

Tapping on the window, she called, 'Anne, are you in there? I left my handbag on the windowsill . . . I'm sorry!'

When there was still no answer, she grew concerned.

She looked about the garden. Spotting a large plant pot, she dragged it to the base of the window where she turned it upside down, and climbed onto it.

Gripping the windowsill to steady herself, she leaned forward, towards the impossibly narrow slit between the two curtains. Peeping through, she found it difficult to make out anything. There were no sounds, but in the half-light from the hallway, she imagined she could just about see the two figures seated on the sofa. She called out, 'Anne, are you in there? I need to quickly collect my handbag . . . please?'

Suddenly, there was movement, but she couldn't make out what was happening. 'Anne, if you could please hand me my bag, I'll be off and catch the bus.'

Inside, Anne was desperately struggling. Hearing Sally, she tried to call out, but Carter punched her hard across the mouth. Dazed and bleeding, she fell back onto the sofa.

Realising that something was not right, Sally remembered Anne's words: *He hurt me . . . he killed my baby.*

Horrified at the possibility that Edward Carter was inside the house, Sally bunched her fist and banged hard on the window. 'Carter! I know who you are. I know what you did. You'd better not hurt her. I've seen you now . . . I can identify you.' She banged on the window again. 'I'm calling the police!' Scrambling off her makeshift platform, she ran down the path, all the while yelling at the top of her voice, 'Help! Call the police! There's a madman . . . He's got my friend . . . He's hurting her . . .'

She ran to the pub, thankful that the landlord was on the pavement putting out his boards advertising the evening darts match. He saw her running as though her life depended on it.

'Good Lord! What's wrong?' He caught her in his arms.

Breathless, Sally shouted, 'Call the police! Quickly. It's Anne! He means to kill her . . . he will. He'll do it . . . please hurry! Get the police!'

The landlord ran inside, with Sally following. As he dialled the number, Sally told him, 'Hurry! He's got her trapped inside the house, and he's hurting her . . . he means to kill her! Please hurry!'

It seemed like no time at all before the squad cars were racing down the street, sirens screaming.

They found Anne lying on the floor, bruised and bloodied.

Edward Carter, though, had already fled.

Some half a mile away, the foot-patrol officer was on his rounds when he heard the sirens. They alerted his memory of the shifty-looking man who had been lurking about in the back alleys earlier.

Being the kind of officer who took his work seriously, he decided to check the back alleys yet again.

As he came round the corner, Edward Carter ran straight into him. There was a vicious set-to as Carter tried to escape, but he was out of breath and weakened, while the officer was a big, capable fellow, and not one to be brought down easily.

This time, Edward Carter had met his match. Being well trained in the art of apprehending a violent suspect, the officer gave better than he got. There was a desperate struggle, but even though the officer was slightly injured, he soon had his prisoner safe against the wall, arms behind his back, and strong handcuffs securing him there.

While keeping Carter trapped, the officer used his walkie-talkie and within minutes help arrived.

A short time later, Carter was unceremoniously bundled into the car and taken away.

As he went, he glanced out the window. *Don't celebrate too soon, little wifey*, he mouthed in a whisper. *I'll be back.*

~

Pale and shaking from her ordeal, Anne told the constable, 'He's beaten me up before, but this time he really wanted to kill me. I saw it in his eyes.'

'Right! Well, he can't hurt you where he's going.' The kindly constable could see how Carter must have terrified this young woman.

After checking her bruises he made an entry in his notebook. 'I'm sorry, but I need you to tell me exactly what happened here.'

As Anne described the frightening series of events, he meticulously recorded them.

After the police had gone, Sally took charge. 'Come

on. Let's get you upstairs . . . A freshen-up and change of clothes might help you feel better.'

After escorting Anne upstairs and helping her choose a comfortable outfit, Sally told her, 'You finish here, and I'll go down and tidy up. When you're ready, we'll get into your car and I'll drive you over to my house. You're staying with me and Mick . . . and I am not taking no for an answer! Don't worry, Pusscat can come too.'

Anne did not need asking twice.

Half an hour later, the two of them set off. Sally was driving, but she kept a careful eye on Anne, who was very quiet, shaken by what Carter had done to her . . . again.

PART THREE

~

Dangerous Times

1957

CHAPTER EIGHT

When the knock came on her office door, Miss Martin was head down, browsing through paperwork.

'Come in!' She was expecting a senior member of her staff to deliver Adam Carter to her door. In anticipation, she took off her spectacles, laid them on the desk and waited.

Nancy Montague flounced in, ushering Adam before her. 'I've brought Adam as instructed,' she advised Miss Martin. Placing the flat of her hand in the centre of Adam's back, she gently urged him forward.

Miss Martin offered him a smile. 'Good morning, Adam! And are you feeling good, this bright and beautiful morning?'

'Good morning, Miss Martin.' He stood before her, his two hands clenched before him. 'I'm all right, thank you.'

She nodded to Nancy. 'Thank you, Nancy. We'll be

fine just now.' With a flutter of her chubby hand she waved the nervous little woman away.

When the door was closed and she was alone with the boy, she instructed him with a warm smile: 'Please, Adam, do sit down.' She gestured to the deep-bottomed chair strategically placed at the side of her large, well-polished desk.

Adam stepped forward and did as he was asked.

Momentarily, Miss Martin took quiet stock of him, especially noting the subservient manner in which he had stood, hands clenched in front, eyes down. Staring at the floor.

With his thick brown hair and serious brown eyes, he was a handsome boy; quiet with a soulful disposition and a heavy heart.

Now aged thirteen, and having been at the children's home for a number of years, Adam had forged no real friendship here. He was a loner, plagued by events of the past, and ever anxious about whatever future awaited him.

'Please, Adam, look up!' When he raised his head and looked directly at her, Miss Martin asked him, 'Did you enjoy your birthday party last week, Adam?'

'Yes, Miss Martin, thank you.'

'Good! And did you enjoy your outing with Miss Nightingale and your friend Phil?'

Adam's face lit up. 'Oh, yes, I enjoyed it very much, thank you.'

'Excellent!' She always made a point of giving praise where it was due. 'You have a fine friend in Phil.'

Her manner and tone grew serious. 'So, Adam, what are we going to do with you, I wonder?'

'I don't understand, Miss Martin.'

'Very well then, I shall explain. Here you are, now thirteen years old, and still not settled with a foster family. Why is that, do you think?'

'I don't really know, Miss Martin.'

'So, Adam. Now that you've had time to think about your month with the last foster family, can you tell me what really happened there?'

'I'm not sure, Miss Martin. I just wasn't very happy.'

'And why was that? Did someone beat you?'

'No, miss.'

'Were they spiteful in any other way?'

'No, miss.'

'So, they were good to you, then?'

Adam hesitated before giving his answer. 'Yes . . . only . . .' Falling silent, he returned his gaze to the floor.

'Adam! Look at me.'

Reluctantly, Adam raised his gaze.

'Dearie me!' Exasperated, Miss Martin clambered out of her chair, to pace anxiously back and forth. 'This is not good, Adam! After three attempts to place you with fine, God-fearing families, you are still here, with us. Why is that?'

'I don't know, miss.'

'Well, I *do* know! Mr and Mrs Shaler have now officially reported to us. They claim that not once did you even try to fit in. They said you were sullen, disobedient, and that one time, you sat outside in the garden for hours, refusing to come in, even though you had no coat on and it was pouring with rain. Is that true, Adam? Did you do these things?'

'Yes, miss.'

The atmosphere grew heavy, while Miss Martin, loudly tutting, padded her way up and down the carpet.

Meanwhile, Adam closed his mind to that particular foster family and his bad behaviour while living there. He even closed his mind to Miss Martin as she paced back and forth.

Inevitably, his thoughts wandered back to the house where he had lived with his darling mother and the devil who took her from him.

Recently, both Phil and Miss Martin's staff had gone to great lengths to keep the newspapers from him, but he heard the gossip, and what he had learned was more than enough. They said his father had been arrested and locked up for a long time. That it was to do with another woman, that he had beaten her up . . . just as he had beaten his own mother.

So, Edward Carter was in prison. Adam was glad about that.

But it was not enough. It would never be enough!

'I so need to see you settled,' Miss Martin went on, 'but it has not gone well so far. Which is why I continue to ask myself, how on earth *are* we going to get you settled with a good family? Adam, do you hear what I say?'

Miss Martin's question jolted him back to the moment, 'Yes, Miss Martin.'

'Well?'

'I'm sorry, miss . . . I don't know.'

'Hmm.'

Flummoxed by his negative attitude, Miss Martin

stole a moment to study this troubled but capable boy, and reflect on the dreadful experiences he had encountered through his short life. Not for the first time, she was deeply saddened.

'Adam, you do realise you could have a great future, if only you would set your mind to it?'

When he chose not to comment, she persevered. 'I'm told by your teachers that you have a natural talent for painting. I understand they've told you as much. Isn't that so?'

'Yes, miss.'

'Do you enjoy painting?'

'Yes, Miss Martin.'

'Why is that, Adam? What do you see in painting that brings you pleasure? They tell me that most of the images are somewhat dark and brooding, and yet somehow they quicken the heart and fire the imagination.' She paused, before asking softly, 'What makes you want to paint these dark pictures, Adam?'

Adam had never been asked that before. In truth, he had never even thought about it, but now, the answer came to him so easily. 'Most of all, I like painting my mother.'

'Really? And why is that, do you think?'

Adam gave a whimsical smile. 'I paint her when she's walking along the hill rise behind our house, because then she was happy, and so very pretty. It's like springtime. But then *he* hurts her, and everything becomes dark and ugly. It's like . . .' he struggled for the right words, '. . . it's like she's running away, but she can't get through the trees . . . it's dark and shadowy. The trees are like giants. They stretch out their branches and trap her inside, and then it becomes a prison. I can hear her calling for me, but I can't get her out. I can't save her.'

His voice hardened to a harsh whisper. 'That's what I draw, because that's what *he* did to her.'

'And does it help you, Adam? When you draw these pictures, how does it make you feel?'

'Sometimes happy, sometimes sad. Especially when I draw a picture where I make *him* be the prisoner. He's the one in the dark, afraid and trapped. In my paintings, I punish him. And then I feel better inside.'

Miss Martin was shocked at the hatred in Adam's face, whenever he referred to his father. She shared Adam's abhorrence of his father's cruelty to his mother, but to hear the boy talk with such loathing she found deeply upsetting.

More than that, she feared for this sad and lonely boy. He had done no wrong, and yet it seemed his punishment was never-ending. His bad experiences appeared to have crippled him, both mentally and emotionally.

'Adam, I know life has not been kind to you, and I truly am sorry for that. But maybe now it's time to try and put the past behind you. Sometimes, through no fault of our own, terrible things happen to us, and we wonder why.'

Adam simply nodded.

'It's foolish, Adam, but often we blame ourselves when we are just the innocent bystander. You, in particular, have had to deal with things that most children of your age would never encounter. But you really must try very hard to face up to the sequence of events that brought you here, because if you don't face up to them, they will always haunt you. Do you understand what I'm trying to say, Adam?'

Choked with emotion and unable to speak, Adam nodded again.

'No, Adam!' Miss Martin raised her voice. 'A nod of the head will not do! You must say it out loud. Say it, Adam: "Bad things have happened to me, and I have to face up to them. It's the only way I can move forward and build a life of my own." Say it for me, Adam. Say it loud and clear!'

A moment passed and still he could not say it. Miss Martin waited hopefully.

When Adam continued to be silent, she took it to be a simple matter of wills between the two of them. In a way she had always known it would come to this. So, she rose to the challenge in her indomitable way.

Taking a sheaf of typed paper from her drawer, she laid it on the desktop, slowly and deliberately put on her spectacles, and, appearing to ignore him, she pretended to be reading, occasionally adding a little tick alongside the writing, merely for effect.

In the corner of the room, the grandfather clock ticked sombrely. The rhythmic sound of the swinging pendulum was the only sound in the room.

Moments passed, and still Miss Martin kept her head down, seeming not to care if Adam was there or not.

After a while, Adam's hesitant voice began: 'Bad things happened to me . . .' He paused, thinking of his mother, before going on. 'I have to . . . face up to them. It's the only way I can build . . . a life . . . of my own.' There was a moment when his voice seemed to resonate with the ticking of the clock before his muffled sobbing filled the room.

'There!' Miss Martin got out of her chair in a flurry. 'Ssh, child. Well done for being strong enough to say that out loud. I know it can't have been easy. Yes! Well done, my dear.' On an impulse, she wrapped him in her chubby warm arms and held him to her ample bosom for a moment, before dipping into her pocket and flourishing a pretty white handkerchief. 'Here . . . wipe your eyes.'

With a tear in her own eye, she sat beside him, and for a while neither of them spoke.

Presently, she addressed him kindly. 'I do realise how very hard it's been for you losing the mother you loved, and then learning how your father is now imprisoned.' With some embarrassment at showing the softness of her character, she admitted, 'Believe me, Adam, when I say that if I could take away your pain, you know I would.'

'I'm glad he's in prison.' Adam wished that man all the harm he'd caused his mother. 'I hate him! I hope they never let him out.'

Having momentarily dropped her guard, Miss Martin chose not to remark on what Adam had said. Instead, she abruptly returned to her formal self.

'Now then, Adam! I have good news for you.' Having got his attention, she informed him, 'We have another foster family who, I hope, might give you the home you deserve . . . and before you get worried, you won't be the only child, as in the previous home. This family already has two children: an eighteen-month-old baby girl and her nine-year-old sister. Oh, and a dog called Buster.'

Having seen his face light up at the mention of a dog, she asked him, 'Have you ever had a dog, Adam?'

'No, Miss Martin. Phil has a dog, though. He takes it for walks every morning before he drives the school bus.'

Adam's whole manner had lightened, and for the moment he was not consciously thinking of his parents. 'What kind of dog is it, Miss Martin?'

'As I recall, Buster is a little brown terrier. That's all I know. And that's only because they asked if having a dog might stop them from fostering. But in actual fact, we sometimes welcome a pet of sorts. It helps the foster child to fit in. Mind you, if the child is nervous of pets, then that's a different story. We would never send a child where he or she might feel threatened.'

Delighted by Adam's response, she went on, 'So now, Adam, do you have any more questions?'

After giving it some thought, Adam was concerned enough to ask, 'Miss, if they've got two children of their own, why do they want to foster someone else's child?'

Miss Martin began, 'Of course you must understand, that this subject is not for discussion outside of this room?'

'Yes, miss.'

'Very well then, and because I have secured their permission, I may partly share their confidence with you. Suffice for you to know that for medical reasons it is not possible for them to have another child. Apparently, they had planned a large family, and they had hoped their next baby might be a boy. Unfortunately, that cannot happen now, and so they decided to apply for fostering . . . with a view to adopt, if you fit in all right with the family.'

Adam was curious. 'Miss Martin, why would they want me? Why not a baby?'

Miss Martin had gone as far as she was allowed. 'I am not privy to that information, although if I were to make a guess, I would say that as they already have a baby they maybe wanted an older child. Also, they might think a sensible brother could befriend and guide their nine-year-old daughter. But, as I say, that is only my opinion, and you must not quote me on that. Do you understand?'

'Yes, miss.'

'Good!'

Whenever Miss Martin put on her spectacles, she meant business; and she meant business now.

'Now then, Adam. I can tell you that I gave them information on several children, including you. And because I believe in you, Adam, I did not hesitate to sing your praises.'

'Thank you, miss.'

'Fortunately, they seemed to warm to the idea of having you. But of course, I needed to arrange a meeting with them, so they can take stock of you, and you can also take stock of them, so you can see how you feel when you meet them in person. You will spend some time together, approximately half an hour initially, right here in this office. Afterwards, you must say whether or not you feel happy to go with them – if they indeed choose you . . . because, of course, it's a two-way thing. So, Adam, is that all right with you?'

'Yes, miss.' In truth, mainly because of the dog, he found himself growing a little excited. 'I would like to meet them. Oh, and will they bring the dog?'

Miss Martin laughed. 'Bless you, child. You have to look at the family first. As for whether they might bring the dog, I have no idea.' She gave a merry little smile. 'Although I will admit I did not forbid the little dog's presence.'

After Miss Martin dismissed him, Adam danced all the way down the corridor, a wide smile on his face.

Maybe, at long last, things were about to change for the better.

~

Since Adam had first been placed in the children's home, Phil had been a regular visitor. As promised, he continued to remain a constant friend and advisor throughout Adam's feelings of insecurity.

In his own wise manner, he guided Adam through his anger and his sadness, and in doing so, he had not only brought a measure of companionship and love to the boy, but he had unexpectedly found a friend in Polly, one of the staff members at the home.

Whenever Phil had been allowed to take Adam into town to watch a football match, or merely walk along the canal towpath, Polly was officially recruited to accompany them, as part of the security measures.

Neither Phil nor Adam had any problem with that. In fact, through the early months when Adam found it difficult to settle, and through the bad, painful period when he was rejected from his first foster family, Polly had worked with Phil in building Adam's badly bruised confidence.

In the process, both Adam, and Phil in particular, had come to respect and admire Polly; so much so, that whenever he arranged an outing with Phil, he also looked forward to seeing the homely little care assistant.

Today, they had planned to sit by the canal and feed the ducks. It was one of Adam's favourite pastimes.

'Make sure Adam is back here by two-thirty.' Being a stickler for the rules, Miss Martin went on to list the regulated dos and don'ts that accompanied any child on a trip from the children's home. 'Remember, Adam . . . do as you're asked, and always follow Polly's instructions. No changing the plans, or wandering off on your own. And you must stay in sight the whole time. Do you understand?'

'Yes, Miss Martin.'

'Good!' She issued similar instructions to Polly, then she waved the three of them on their way. 'Off you go, then.'

As Phil was about to go out of the door, she called him back. 'A moment, please, Phil.'

Phil hurried back to her, while Polly and Adam waited in the porch.

Pre-empting her reason for calling him back, he assured her earnestly, 'Don't you worry, Miss Martin. We'll have Adam back by two-thirty, as requested.'

Bold enough to speak out of turn, he told her what was on his mind. 'If I may say so, Miss Martin, it really doesn't give us much time together.' He valued his time with Adam; and Polly too, if he was truthful.

Unmoved by his remark, Miss Martin glanced at the grandfather clock. 'It's now twelve-thirty. To my reckoning, that allows you two hours.'

Unable and unwilling to reveal delicate official information, and because Phil was not the boy's official guardian, she gave a certain little smile, which offered Phil the smallest clue to her reason for cutting short the outing.

'The reason I need him back here is because I care about his future . . . as I know you do.' She paused while the remark sank in, then went on in a softer tone, 'Adam might have important visitors arriving to see him. He needs to prepare himself, and I need a short time with him before the important event.' She put on her most official tone of voice, 'If you consider it a problem to have him back by two-thirty, then I must withdraw permission for the outing.'

Again, she gave that certain little confiding smile. 'I'm sure you understand what I'm saying.'

Phil believed he understood exactly what she might be saying, and it brought a smile to his face. 'You can trust me, Miss Martin. I will have Adam back here, in good time for the "important visitors".' He had an impulse to give a little wink. 'Thank you.'

'Ah! So we do understand each other?'

'I believe so.'

'Good man!'

Phil went away with a bounce in his step.

A few moments later, Adam surprised him by saying cautiously, 'I think I might know why they want me back.'

'Oh, do you now? And why might that be then?'

'Because there might be a new foster family coming to see me.'

'Really?' Phil gave a sideways wink at Polly. 'Well now, and if they *were* coming to see you, how would you feel about that?'

Adam gave a little shrug of the shoulders. 'I don't know.' Beyond that, he would not be drawn. After enduring the previous fostering experience, he had grown very wary.

Polly had said very little up to that point, but now she said, 'Try and keep an open mind, Adam. One bad experience does not mean you won't be placed with a good, loving family. In my experience, there are more decent, deserving people out there than there are bad ones.'

While Phil readily endorsed her comment, Adam kept his silence, and brooded on his dark memories.

Though, everything else aside, he was greatly excited about seeing the little dog.

The new family would be bound to ask him questions, and he must answer truthfully, even if it put them off choosing him to be part of their family.

Miss Martin had advised him to ask questions of his own, but Adam decided that he would know anyway if they were kind people and truly wanted him. And, because he had yearned to be part of a real family, he desperately hoped that at long last it might really happen.

More importantly, today was a special day because it was the day when Phil took him to the churchyard to see his darling mother.

Just as Adam was thinking about her, Phil drew him back from the kerb. 'Mind out, son. The bus is here.'

When the bus arrived, Phil saw Polly on, then Adam, then himself.

'Now then, Adam,' he said, 'being as we haven't got much time, we'd best make it hot-foot to the florist and get your mum's posy. Then we'll walk up to the churchyard and spend a few minutes there. After that, we should still have time enough to treat ourselves to an ice cream and a sandwich.'

He consulted Adam and Polly. 'How does that sound to you folks?'

Adam agreed that it was a fine plan and, by way of approving, Polly insisted on paying the bus fares.

~

At the florist's shop, Adam chose a small posy of pink flowers.

'Mum always liked pink best of all,' he told Phil and Polly, who had already learned that from previous visits to the florist.

The florist was a round, smiling woman who always wore green. On more than one occasion, Polly had innocently remarked on how much the florist resembled the flowers, 'all pink and green and wearing a smile'.

Her description brought a little chuckle from the other two.

The florist wrapped the posy in a cornet of stripy paper and tied it with a big floppy bow. 'There!' She was well pleased with herself. 'That's a very pretty posy, even if I do say so myself!'

The churchyard was just a short walk up the hill. When they got to the top, Phil was puffing and panting, with Polly, sprightly as ever, springing ahead. 'You need to do a bit of exercise,' she told Phil, 'get some of that fat off your belly.'

Adam burst out laughing, while Phil replied haughtily, 'I'll have you know, I do a lot of walking and lifting, and I drive a bus full of sprightly children. If you ask me, that's more than enough to keep a fella's weight down!'

Smiling secretly to Adam, Polly took the hint to drop the subject, while Phil took her comment on board and vowed not to beg any more of the children's sweets.

As always, whenever Phil had taken him to the churchyard, Adam ran ahead. Before the other two had even reached the top of the hill, Adam was running down the path to the church entrance, and then through the shrubbery to the pretty green area where his mother lay.

Dropping to his knees, he told her in a whisper, 'I'm here to see you, Mum. Look, I've brought you flowers. Phil's with me . . . and Polly from the home.' He placed a kiss on his fingers and pressed it to her name etched in the stone.

A few minutes later, seeing Adam kneeling there, Phil stopped in his tracks. 'Happen we should stay here for a while. Let the boy have some time with his mum.'

For the slightest moment, Polly was torn between compassion for the boy and her duty to Miss Martin.

Compassion won the day. 'Yes, we'll wait here.' She smiled up at Phil. 'Besides, it's so pretty here . . . don't you think, Phil?'

Phil nodded. 'Pretty it might be, but only for visiting.' He gave a little shiver. 'I'm not ready to overstay my welcome, at least not for some long time yet.'

Polly wagged a finger. 'If you feel like that, then it's more reason for you to lose some of that belly.'

Phil patted his stomach. 'You might be right, but it won't be easy. I've had this belly for a while.'

'There you go then! Cakes and sweets and sticky buns won't help, will they?'

'How do you know I've got a soft spot for sticky buns?'

'Because it's what you order every time we take Adam into a café.'

'That's only once a fortnight or so.'

'Hmm!' Polly gave him a knowing look before seating herself on the nearby stone wall.

Having placed the flowers, Adam told his mother in a whisper, 'He can't hurt you any more, Mum. And now he's been put away.' Leaning forward to wrap his two arms around the memorial stone, he whispered, 'I kept my promise, Mum, but it's hard. I peeped in the newspaper and it said he had hurt this other woman. But they caught him, and he was put in jail, and I hope they never let him out.'

The tears were never far away and now he could not hold them back. 'I hate him! He took you away from me and now everything's changed.'

Wiping his eyes, he told her sternly, 'Sometimes when I'm in bed and I think of what he did to you, I want to hurt him . . . to kill him . . . I really do!'

When the memories became too hard to bear, he cried, because he was sorry, and because he was frustrated that he could talk to his mum but he didn't know if she could hear him. He wanted to see her pretty smile. He wanted to feel her hand over his, and he so wanted to hear her laughter . . . and see her as she suddenly raced him to the top of the hill when they had been walking out together.

'Oh, Mum, I miss you so much. I will love you . . . for ever and ever, Mum . . .' His voice broke beneath the weight of his sorrow, and he could say no more.

Just then, he felt Phil's loving arms about him, lifting him up to his feet and holding him close. 'It's all right, son. It's all right to feel angry, but wanting to kill someone is not the answer. And besides, I have no doubt he'll get his just deserts in prison.'

'Do you know what, Phil?'

'What, son?'

'I hate him! I want to hurt him, like he hurt my mum.' Adam clung to this man who had brought such comfort into his lonely life.

'I understand that.' Phil searched for the right words. 'But . . . like I said, it's not good to harbour thoughts of killing . . . Your mum would never want that, and you know it, don't you?'

When Adam was slow in responding, he asked again, 'Adam, you do know it's very wrong to think of killing, don't you?'

'Yes.' There was a span of silence, before Adam angrily announced, 'I hope they treat him badly in prison. I hope he's really unhappy, just like he made my mum unhappy.'

'Ssh, now.'

Phil held him for a time, while Polly could only look on helplessly.

Over her years at the home, she had seen many friends and do-gooders who might occasionally give a much-needed treat to one of the children at the home. But she had never before witnessed such devotion as she had seen between Phil and the boy. He was more than a friend to Adam. He was more like a father figure. And the love that had grown between these two was humbling to see.

Polly understood how Adam had flourished under Phil's protection. She had long realised that Phil was one of those selfless men – warm and giving – who asked for nothing in return.

She realised it was not too hard to love a man like Phil because, in truth, whenever Miss Martin asked her to accompany Adam and Phil on a trip to town, her heart would turn over. And that had not happened these many years.

A short time later, the three of them made their way down the hill, with Polly walking beside Phil, and Phil keeping a protective eye on Adam.

'All right, son?' Phil playfully ruffled Adam's hair. 'Ready for your ice cream, are you?' After years of coping with the children on the school bus, Phil had a natural way of diffusing a bad atmosphere.

'Yes, thank you, Phil.' Having talked with his mum and rid himself of bad thoughts, Adam was calmer.

'How about you?' Phil turned to Polly with a smile. 'Are you ready for your ice cream?'

'Yes, please, Phil. I'll have a double dollop of strawberry with chocolate sprinkles on top.'

Phil and Adam laughed out loud at that.

'Huh!' Phil tutted. 'And who's been lecturing me to watch my belly, eh?'

'I tell it as I see it,' she retorted with a cheeky little grin.

'There! I always knew it.'

'What?'

'You're a bossy boots!'

Even so, Phil thought her to be a handsome, homely woman, and a fine companion into the bargain.

CHAPTER NINE

'No, Anne!' sally pleaded. 'You're not ready to go back there yet. Please, stay here with us for a little longer. Just until you feel sure.'

Anne had thought about it more and more of late, and though she shivered at the idea of walking into that house again, she was determined that Edward Carter would not defeat her. 'But, I *am* sure, Sally. Well, at least as sure as I'll ever be, I suppose. Besides, I've put myself on you and Mick long enough. If I'm ever going back, the time is now.'

'But you're not strong enough in yourself.' Sally was worried. 'You still have the nightmares, and I know if you go back to where it all happened, it might be too much for you to handle. Please, Anne. Stay here, with me and Mick, for a few more weeks at least. If you're still determined after that, you can go home, and I'll come and be with you for a week or so, just to see how it goes.'

Sally knew only too well how deeply Carter's vicious attack had damaged her dear friend. It was only when she was checked over at the hospital afterwards that it was discovered two of her fingers were broken, and because of Carter's cruel handling of her, they found that some cartilage in her back had shifted, causing temporary damage to her spine. That meant an operation, and weeks of recovery back to full health.

Edward Carter, though, had not only damaged her physically, he had left her in such a bad state mentally that she was a mere shadow of her former self. It soon became clear that while the outward scars were healed, the same could not be said for her fragile state of mind.

In those first few months after she came to stay with Sally and Mick, Anne constantly teetered on the edge of a breakdown.

In the early days after the attack, she was afraid to go outside on her own. Instead, she would huddle indoors, unwashed, undressed, and unable to cope with returning to work.

At night, she could be heard pacing up and down in her bedroom, and whenever Sally took her out, she would never want to stay out long.

On the few occasions that Sally was successful in taking her into town, Anne would be nervously glancing about, watching people passing, and hiding in doorways if she saw any man who bore even the slightest resemblance to Carter.

All that had now run its course, although even now, she was nervous to be out on her own, which was why

Sally was anxious that she should stay with her and Mick for a while longer.

Presently, in the kitchen, making tea for the three of them, Mick heard the exchange between his wife and Anne. Like Sally, he was greatly concerned that Anne should give herself more time to recover before she returned to the house on Roff Avenue.

Having taken it all in, he now had the beginnings of an idea that might just satisfy everyone.

With this in mind, he quickly made the tea and set it on a tray with a box of biscuits, which he carried into the other room.

'I don't know who made me the servant around here,' he joked light-heartedly. 'It's Sunday! Which, as you know, is supposed to be a day of rest . . . and here's me, waiting on you two hand and foot. Right then! I reckon I've done my chores for today, so now it's up to you lovely ladies. You can now pour a drink for the man of the house, while filling me in on all the gossip.'

He put the tray on the coffee table in the bright, spacious room, and sat himself alongside Anne on the sofa, while Sally sat forward in the big brown leather armchair and set about pouring the tea.

'Mick, tell Anne she's not ready to go back to the house just yet,' she pleaded.

'Mmm. Well, I heard what you were saying just now, the two of you, and for what it's worth, I think you're *both* right.

'Really? In what way?' Sally asked.

'Well, from what I gather, Anne wants to go back to

the house, and you want her to stay here. That's right, isn't it?'

'Yes, but Anne is determined to go home. I've been trying to dissuade her, but she won't listen.' Sally appealed to Anne. 'Anne, tell Mick what you told me.'

'I've been here for months now,' Anne explained. 'It's not at all fair on either of you. I've crossed hurdles since I've been here and that's thanks to you two, my best friends. I'm back at work now – another hurdle overcome – and I'm much stronger in myself now. But I need to go home and pick up my life. I really think I can do it. Sally and I have been going over once a week to open and shut curtains, turn taps on and off, and dust around . . . that sort of thing. As you both know, I wasn't at all comfortable with being there at first, but I'm getting used to it now. I'm stronger in myself, and it doesn't frighten me like it did before.'

She appealed to them both. 'I'm sure I'll be OK, and if I'm not, I promise I'll call you.'

Understanding her dilemma, Mick offered his idea of a compromise. 'Look, Anne, what do you think of this idea? Sally is anxious for you to stay here with us for a while longer . . . and so am I. You, however, are anxious to go home, and I fully understand that. But I would not feel right if I let you go back there on your own just yet. So why doesn't Sally come and live with you for a week? I'll pop in straight from work and spend the evening with you both.' He laughed. 'I'll even bring us all fish and chips on my way back from work; save you the trouble of cooking.'

'Brilliant!' Sally was relieved. 'In fact, I suggested

something along those lines.' She appealed to Anne. 'Please, Anne. I would feel a lot better about you going back to the house if you could agree on Mick's plan. Just one week, that's all, and if you feel able to take charge again, we'll back off, although we'll always be here if you need us.'

Mick added, 'Just remember, if you're the slightest bit nervous or worried – about anything at all, however small – then you come back home with us and give yourself a bit more time. The alternative is you and Sally could maybe just go over there at weekends – a small dose at a time, if you get my meaning. That way, you might just reach the point where you feel good about being back home permanently. So, would you prefer that?'

Although still slightly nervous, Anne had to agree with his initial plan. 'I think it might be better to make it the full week as you said, because a couple of days won't be enough. So, if you really don't mind Sally coming to stay with me for that length of time, I would love to give it a try.'

Sally was already thinking ahead. 'I've got clean bedding and towels in the airing cupboard. When we leave work on Friday, we'll go shopping. We'll need to do a big shop: enough for the two of us for a week, and enough to fill the cupboards for Mick.'

'I'm quite capable of getting my own groceries.' Mick could be highly independent.

'I know you are, but while we're there we might as well do all the shopping in one go.'

'OK, Sal. Whatever suits you. So, when are you actually planning to stay at the house?'

Anne had already decided. 'I think we should go over there Saturday. It will be much better to start on a weekend. That way there'll be more people about, and we won't be leaving the house to go to work. It will give us that time to adjust.' She felt as though she was being ungrateful. '. . . If that's all right with you, Sally?'

'Yes, good thinking,' Sally agreed. 'So, this is how it goes. Friday evening after work, we'll go and get the groceries. Then we'll bring Mick's shopping back here, so he'll be all set up. We'll leave our groceries in the boot, except for the milk and such. On Saturday morning, we'll put the bedding and linen in the boot and make our way over to the house.' She clapped her hands. 'Job done!'

'Sounds like you've thought of everything. Thank you, both. I don't know how I can ever repay you,' Anne said.

In a strange and selfish way, she somehow envied Sally's seemingly perfect marriage. From the first meeting with Mick, she had recognised a good and thoughtful man; a man who would never harm a hair on his darling wife's head. Unlike the evil man she had foolishly married as a young girl.

The time came to make one last visit to the house before Sally would move in with Anne.

'We'll draw the curtains as always, and turn on the taps for a while. We'll just spend a couple of hours over there this evening, shall we?' Sally suggested.

'I think so, yes. But why don't we take the bedding and linen tonight?' Anne suggested. 'That way we'll save time on Friday after work. And don't forget the grocery store will be busy at that time on a Friday.'

'Yes, that's very true.' And so it was agreed.

'Do you need me for anything?' Mick asked.

'There's not much you can do, Mick,' Sally reminded him. 'You're terrible at changing beds. And as for housework, if I let you loose it would only have to be done again.'

'Well, thanks for that!' Mick laughed. 'In that case, happen I'll go down the pub, and have a pint or two with the boys.'

'Oh!' Sally sounded disappointed.

'What's wrong?'

'Nothing. It's just that I thought maybe you could put that curtain rail back up, the one that fell down in the back bedroom. Oh, but it's not important, especially as nobody sleeps in there anyway.'

'Mmm!' He had the germ of an idea. 'I'll do the rail, don't worry.'

'No, honestly, Mick.' Sally felt bad now. 'It's all right . . . it's really not important. I don't even know why I mentioned it. I mean, you can fix the rail any time. Go down to the pub. Meet up with your mates.'

'Only if you're sure you don't mind?'

'I am absolutely sure! Honestly, Mick, you haven't had a night out in a while and it'll do you good.' Sally felt mean now even mentioning about the curtain rail, especially as he had genuinely welcomed her friend into their home.

Mick was curious. 'How long do you reckon you'll be gone?'

'Two . . . maybe three hours, I suppose.' She turned to Anne. 'What say you, Anne?'

'Yes. I think that's about right. Check the house. Change the beds and close the curtains. I might just have a quick chat with my neighbour; see if anyone's been hanging about, maybe.'

Sally picked up on her worrying remark. 'Anne, trust me, there won't have been anyone "hanging about". Especially not Carter, because thankfully that madman is well and truly locked up.'

When Anne felt the nervousness creeping up on her, she gave a wide smile. 'That's very true! But I'll go and have a chat with her all the same, if only to thank her for keeping an eye on the house while I've been away. In fact, while we're out getting the groceries, I might pick up a bunch of flowers for her.'

Sally agreed. 'Your neighbour is a real darling. I bet she'd have opened and shut the curtains as well, if you'd asked her. But she's getting on a bit and maybe it would have been too much to ask.'

Mick felt bad about going to the pub. 'I'll tell you what, Sal,' he started, 'I've worked it out. Being as you'll probably be gone the best part of three hours, I can do the curtain rail first and still have time to enjoy a pint or two with the lads. OK?'

Getting out of her chair, Sally went to him and kissed him full on the mouth. 'Course it's OK. I'm sorry if I sounded a bit miffed at first, but I didn't mean it. You go and see your mates. Have a good time, and we'll catch up when I get back.'

Half an hour later, Mick saw them off. 'Drive carefully.' He always worried about Sally in the car. Capable though she was, Sally could be a bit too daredevil at times.

As he waved them away, Mick smiled to himself, thinking how much he loved Sally. He had never had one single moment of regret at having married her. The only regret he had, and would always have, was that Sally was unable to give him a child.

That sorry discovery had floored them both. Yet, even with that, he had never regretted marrying her.

There were still the odd times when he truly ached for a family, especially when he and Sally were out walking, and he saw other men playing footie in the park with their sons, or a father teaching his child how to ride a bike. He missed all that, yet because he adored the ground she walked on, he was always careful never to let Sally know his true feelings.

~

At the same moment that Mick was dwelling on that particular sadness in their lives, Sally too felt a touch of regret at her inability to give Mick the children he craved. She had always planned that the back bedroom should be a nursery, and now, after years with no baby in it, it was looking rundown and neglected. She now felt guilty at having seemed unsupportive when he had mentioned he might go for a pint with his mates instead of putting up the curtain rail.

Anne had noticed how quiet Sally had grown since

they left the house. 'Is everything all right, Sal?' she asked.

Sally nodded. 'Sort of . . . yes. Only I should never have let Mick see how I wasn't keen on him going to the pub tonight. It was selfish of me. I should never have made an excuse for him not to go. The back curtains don't really matter anyway. It's been ages since he went out socially, and the first time he suggests it, I put on a sour face.'

'Well, I'm sure Mick didn't even notice.' Anne had seen the tense exchange, but tactfully made light of it.

Now her curiosity got the better of her. 'Tell me if I'm out of line, but can I ask why you don't like him going to the pub?'

'It's not that I don't like him actually going to the pub,' Sally revealed, 'it's just the tarty barmaid . . . she has her eye on him.'

'Oh, I see!' Anne detected the green-eyed monster. 'And you don't like him going there without you, is that it?'

'Sort of. I'm not being paranoid, but even when Mick and I are there together, she's always stealing a glance at him. It's obvious that she fancies him, and when he goes to the bar I hear the two of them laughing together. I think he really enjoys her company. For all I know, he might even fancy her!'

'You don't believe that for a minute, do you? I mean, he might just be being polite and laughing at her jokes, even if they're rubbish. Mick is a lovely man, Sal. You've often said how he makes friends easily.'

'Well, yes, that's right, he does. But what man can resist when a pretty girl keeps making a play for him?'

'A man like Mick, that's who.'

'Maybe.'

'For goodness' sake, Sal, you must know how devoted he is to you. Anyone can see, he's crazy in love with you. You're a fortunate woman, Sal. You have a good man there. I reckon he would rather cut off his arm than cheat on you.'

The atmosphere grew tense and, for a time, neither of them spoke.

Then out of nowhere, Sally made a heartfelt confession. 'I'm frightened, Anne. I'm really frightened that he might leave me.'

Anne was shocked. 'He would never leave you . . . Why would he?'

Sally took a while to answer, and what she confided rocked Anne to her roots. 'I'm always afraid that he will leave me one day . . . if he meets the right woman. And, to be honest, I wouldn't blame him.'

'But why would he leave you? He loves you far too much.'

'I know he loves me, but sometimes things happen that might make a man do what he might otherwise never do.' She searched for the right words to make Anne understand, without giving away too much.

She had always been afraid to say the truth out loud, hoping that if she never actually said it, then it might not be true.

Anne urged her on. 'What kind of "things", Sal?'

Wishing she had not said anything, Sally gave a little

shrug. 'Just "things". Like if someone was told something . . . so cruel, it could break up a relationship. Something that could never be put right.'

'Such as what?' Anne was intrigued, and a little concerned.

Sally went on, almost as though she was talking to herself, 'Sometimes I think I'm just being selfish . . . none of this is his fault. It's been on my mind for a long time that, however much I love Mick, it's very wrong to try to cling onto him.'

Anne was lost. 'What are you saying, Sal? I don't understand. You and Mick have a wonderful marriage. You belong together.'

Sally shook her head. 'All I'm saying is, maybe the best thing would be for Mick to find some other woman who could make his life complete.' She took a moment to think and reflect. 'If that happened, and he would rather be with her than me . . . well . . . I would have to let him go. It would be cruel of me to try and stop him.'

Anne understood that Sally was sorry for trying to deter Mick from going to the pub without her, but she sensed something much deeper in what Sally was saying.

So, because she cared, and because she and Sal now told each other almost everything, she decided to wait for an opportune moment when she might persuade Sally to confide her troubles.

She needed to know why Sally could even entertain the idea that Mick would be better off with another woman. Moreover, why would Sally be prepared to let her beloved man go? The idea of those two breaking up was unthinkable.

With Sally now lapsed into silence, Anne wisely kept her own counsel. She hoped a quiet moment might allow her friend to reflect on the enormity of what she had just said.

That was exactly what Sally did, and she quickly realised that her problem was too hard to bear alone. It would be good just to talk about it, preferably with a dear friend, who would not judge her. But not now, not in the car. So, gathering all her strength, she told Anne, 'I want you to know everything, Anne. I need to tell you. But it's too difficult just now.'

Gently, Anne laid her hand over Sally's. 'It's all right, Sal. Whenever you're ready, you know I'll be here for you.'

'I know.' Sally was deeply grateful to have found such a loyal friend and confidante.

A moment later, Sally drew up at Anne's house.

After climbing out of the car, each took a bundle of linen from the boot, and as they walked up the path, the next-door neighbour gave a cheery wave from her window.

To Anne, it was a warm and comforting gesture, but not enough to quell the nervous flutter in her stomach whenever she returned to this house.

Yet she was determined to rid her mind of her tormentor, and get on with her life. This was her home, and it was where she wanted to be. She must not let him rob her of that.

Yet, even while her determination hardened, she could still hear his threat: *What's yours is mine.*

She dared not even think about it.

Once inside the house, Anne waited in the hallway for Sal to come in from the street.

She felt nervous, as always. She could feel Carter's presence there. In her mind's eye she could see him standing over her . . . wanting to kill her.

Even now, after all this time, there was an atmosphere of evil here. It lingered, making her blood run cold. *Come on, Anne!* she chided herself. *You can deal with it. You have to realise he can't hurt you from where he is.*

Quickly now, before she lost her courage, she made her way to the kitchen where she put her bedding bundle down. While she opened the kitchen curtains, Sally came in to put the kettle on. 'I think we both need a cuppa,' she sighed wearily.

While Sally was preparing the tea, Anne went into the front room and opened the curtains there. It was a well-practised procedure, which they had perfected daily over these many weeks.

But when Anne came back into the kitchen, she found Sally seated at the little kitchen table, her head bent forward on the bundle of bedding, and sobbing her heart out.

On realising that Anne had returned, Sally quickly wiped her eyes and hurried over to the kitchenette.

Rummaging for the cups and saucers, she said, 'The kettle's just boiled. I'm making us a pot of tea,' and she began setting out the cups.

Having set the tray, she carried it across the room and sat herself down.

For the next few minutes, they sipped their tea and

talked about all things unimportant until Anne could bear it no longer.

'Look, Sal, I know I said I would be there for you whenever you're ready, and I will, but I know something is eating away at you. Please, Sal, you can trust in me.'

'Yes, I know that, but there's no use talking about it because nothing can be done. There's no cure. And there's no real future for me and Mick. I'm just a rope around his neck. I know I should end our marriage but I can't. The truth is, I don't know what I'd do without him by my side. But that's just selfish of me. I understand that now.'

Anne had no idea what Sally was talking about, but she did know one thing for sure. 'Talking about it might help . . . more than you realise. I mean, look how you and Mick encouraged me to talk about what happened here. You helped me through it, and before you got me talking I had it all locked up inside and it was tearing me apart. Don't do what I did, Sal. Don't imagine it will all go away on its own, because it never will. So, let me help. Talk to me.'

'But you can't help, Anne. They've tried, but it seems there's nothing they can do.'

'About what? Tell me what's bothering you. Please, Sal, let me help. Remember how in the worst of my troubles, you told me not to shut you out? I'm asking you the same now. Please, don't shut me out.'

For what seemed an age, Sally did not reply. And then, in the softest of whispers, she confided, 'I can't make him complete. I can never give him the one thing he truly wants.' Hanging her head down, she continued,

'I don't know what to do, Anne. All I can think is to let Mick go. To give him a chance to find happiness with someone else. Someone who can give him what I never can.'

Embarrassed and ashamed, she looked away. 'When we first realised something was stopping me from getting pregnant, I underwent so many different treatments. Mick did the same, but it wasn't his fault. It was me. In the end, they said I should reconcile myself to the fact that I can never have children.'

She took a deep breath. 'So now that you know, I'm sure you can imagine how hard it is. Mick is my life, and it really hurts that I will never be able to give him the child he so desperately wants . . . that we *both* want. I know how much he misses out on being a father. I've seen him looking at the parents with children in the park, and it's so cruel.'

As Sally poured her heart out, Anne realised why the business of Mick going to the pub had been such a problem for her.

'It's unnatural for a man not to father a child.' Sally had suddenly shifted the focus of the conversation. 'The barmaid deliberately keeps making a play for him. She makes me afraid, Anne. She's recently divorced and she's got two small children. She even shows Mick photographs of them. It's as though she knows I can't give Mick the children he longs for.'

When, inevitably, the tears began to flow, Anne held Sally close. It was all the comfort she could give.

~

Left alone in the house, Mick closed his eyes and enjoyed the quiet. For a time he had nothing on his mind. Then he had everything on his mind.

He thought about work, and all the things he had to do. He mentally back-tracked on his day at work and the lorries he had loaded up at the warehouse, satisfying himself that he had not missed anything; that the orders had been properly sent out and all the paperwork was done.

He thought about money. Thankfully, he and Sally had good jobs, so financially they were quite comfortable.

He thought about the future stretching far ahead of him, and he hoped it would be with Sally, because without her, there was no future worth having.

Inevitably, his thoughts reluctantly lingered on the cruel fact that Sally could not conceive. Yet even though the idea of never being a father cut him deep, he felt hugely compensated by the fact that he had a wife in a million. And besides, a man can never have everything, or there would be nothing left to yearn for.

He quickly shifted his thoughts to his mates down at the pub. Should he meet up with them? Or should he not?

He thought about all the work waiting to be done. There was a dripping tap in the kitchen, and last night he had heard one of the roof slates rattling in the breeze. That was another thing that needed fixing. Then there was the curtain rail in the back bedroom.

Oh, yes! The curtain rail.

He thought about the way Sally had grimaced when he mentioned going down the pub.

He knew she suspected the barmaid had her eye on him, even though she also knew he would never look at another woman. And why should he, when he already had the best woman in the world by his side?

Sighing, he shook his head, 'Fancy Sal thinking I would ever entertain that barmaid!' Still, even if he wasn't interested, it was still flattering to know a pretty woman had an eye for him.

Getting out of the chair, he thought he'd better fix that curtain rail, before going to the pub.

Going through the hallway to collect the shed key from the kitchen, he paused by the wall mirror to flex his muscles. 'You've still got it, my boy!' He smiled. 'Oh, yes! You've still got it!'

A few minutes later, he went out of the back door and down the garden to his little tool shed. Glancing around at the many shelves, overflowing with bric-a-brac, he groaned. One of these weekends he'd have to spend a few hours staightening all this lot out. Jeez! It was like a junk shop.

He raked the shelves with his eyes. Some of the stuff had been here since they'd moved in.

He searched the bottom shelf for the big black toolbox, but it was nowhere to be found. Then he looked up and spotted it on the top shelf, sitting awkwardly beside an old packing case. He decided he could just reach it without fetching the ladder from the garage.

Finding it more difficult than he'd first thought, he tugged harder at the toolbox. 'Come on, dammit!' Something appeared to be holding it back.

One more huge tug and he had it almost free, but when he finally slid the toolbox out, the packing case tumbled out with it.

Cursing, he collected the case to replace it on the top shelf, but the lid flapped open, revealing a number of items from the time before he was married.

Intrigued, he followed his instinct to have a little rummage in the old case, which in the event, turned out to be greatly nostalgic. There was a multitude of memorabilia from his past, and some precious items he had thought were gone for ever.

There was his old fishing rod; his brown football boots, all cracked and dirty, and stiff as planks after years of being in the damp. There was a pack of cards and a set of darts from the carefree days when he was a young man, with a young man's wayward habits.

It was like his early life was unfolding right before his eyes.

With most of the contents now laid out on top of a wooden box, he dug deeper. He drew out an old football, now sagging and past use.

A moment later, his fingers gripped what felt like a book.

As he drew it out, he did not instantly recognise what it was. At first glance, it looked to be a brown leather ledger. It was only when he blew away the dust that he realised it was an old photograph album.

The photographs were mostly damaged, with bent corners and cracks; also the damp had badly marred the initial one or two.

There was a lovely photograph of his parents, the

original of which was framed and standing proud on the sideboard inside the house.

Alongside that photograph was the last photo of his mother, before she passed on.

When Mick's father was killed in an explosion at work, his mother lost the will to live. After a difficult year, she too was gone. People understood that her grief was too hard for her to bear, especially as the two of them had been inseparable since their schooldays, and were absolutely devoted to each other.

Mick had the smaller print of his mother's photograph in his wallet, but now, when he held the original in his hand, he felt too emotional for words.

Quickly, he began flicking through the album, eager to put it safely away.

As he folded it shut, he saw the corner of what appeared to be a torn photograph, jutting out from between the top of two pages stuck together.

Curious, he eased the photograph out, and was riveted by what he saw.

The photograph was partly damaged at the corners, but he instantly recognised it, and it took him back to the days when he was in his twenties.

The photo was of himself, and a girl. Mick remembered her vividly: small-built, with dainty features and wild, curly hair. She had the softest eyes, and a pretty smile, like sunshine on a cloudy day.

He was shocked. 'Good grief!' He laughed out loud. 'Peggy Farraday . . . the girl I nearly married!'

Mesmerised, he took the photograph over to the door, all the better to see it. Leaning against the doorjamb, he cast his eyes over the girl in the picture. *Southend!* He remembered it like it was yesterday. They'd been going together for only a few days and had decided on a day out in Southend, with a couple of friends.

He relived the day in his mind.

It was raining, but they were having so much fun, they didn't want to go home. So, after the other two had gone, he and his girl found a telephone box and rang their parents to tell them they were staying over with their mates, although they'd already gone back, after promising not to say anything.

All they could afford between them was an overnight room at a tatty old boarding house. And all because Mick had spent the best part of his money on a silver locket she'd seen and loved.

He couldn't help but smile at the memory and the way it had turned out, and now he was laughing out loud. He recalled how the curtains were paper-thin, and the springs in the bed creaked and groaned, but they hadn't cared a jot.

Now, the laughter died away and his mood grew serious. He had dated a number of girls, but Peggy had been his first real love.

With his finger he traced her small, pretty face, now looking up at him from the photograph. Up to that night, she hadn't even let him touch her in that certain way, but once they got into bed, she was amazing . . . In fact, when it got to four in the morning, he hadn't given a damn whether he got any sleep or not.'

For a while he sat remembering how it was.

It was strange, though, how Fate took you one way and then the other. He looked down again on Peggy's smiling face. They might have gone on to be regular sweethearts and ended up getting married, but they kind of drifted apart after that weekend.

He tried to recall the exact date. That weekend in Southend . . . *Must have been, what, going on for fourteen years now.*

He took a moment to gaze at the photograph. It wasn't meant to be . . . but if the rumours were right, she'd got herself a good catch – some bloke with his own business. As for Mick, he'd found the loveliest girl . . . name of Sally. And he considered himself to be a very lucky man.

Thinking of Sally put a smile on his face. If Peggy and her man were as happy as he and Sally, she wouldn't go far wrong, he thought.

Quickly now, he folded his old life back into the packing case.

He had no reason not to keep the photograph, so he packed it away with everything else.

He replaced the case on the top shelf, collected his tools and returned to the house, a smile on his face. *Who'd have thought it, eh? A real jolt from the past . . .*

Then he made a start on the curtain rail, keen to please Sally. Anything to make her happy.

It took him all of twenty minutes to fix the curtain rail. Afterwards, he stood back to view his handiwork, thinking he'd earned a pint and a catch-up with his mates. He gave a cheeky little grin. There was nothing like a chat and a laugh with your old mates to make a man feel worthy.

Even as he climbed the stairs to get himself ready, the romance from the past was already gone from his mind.

CHAPTER TEN

MISS MARTIN LISTENED intently, while the officer explained, 'We've held on to these personal items for too long. They were passed to us by the new tenants of the Carters' former home. We quite overlooked them and have no legal reason to keep them now.'

Miss Martin was curious. 'But I understood the Carter case was not yet closed. I was of the opinion that because there were no witnesses to the event, and also a certain lack of evidence from the parties involved, it was never actually proved that Edward Carter had caused his wife's death. Indeed, according to the newspaper reports, his wife never once claimed that he was responsible for the injuries that killed her. Surely, if he had caused her death, she would have said so, don't you think?'

'It's not for me to say, but your observations are correct. You would be surprised, however, to know that in matters such as these, nothing is ever black and white.

For my part, all I can do is to apologise for the length of time we've retained these personal possessions.'

'Oh, well, at least they're here now, and Adam will be relieved to have some things of his mother's, I'm sure.'

'Of course, and like I say, I only wish they were returned earlier. It's only now, with Peggy Carter laid to her rest, and Edward Carter sentenced, that we thought to return these files and properties. Having said that, and even though he's proven to be a very dangerous and violent man, we're still not fully satisfied.'

'In what way?'

'I'm afraid all I can say is that we discovered certain documents hidden away amongst old papers that we removed from the house. We suspect there has been another breach of the law, which if proven, could lengthen Carter's sentence quite considerably.'

'What kind of documents?'

The officer gave himself a mental warning. He had a weakness for being drawn in too far. 'I'm sorry, but I am not authorised to discuss that.'

'Well, whatever it is, I'm sure I don't need to know. All I'm concerned about is placing young Adam with a good family.'

Miss Martin was slightly miffed that the officer had cut short the conversation, just when it caught her imagination.

Ready to see him away, she stood up. 'I'm sorry, but if there is nothing else, I'm shortly expecting to receive a family, who might be the right one for the boy.'

'Everything personal to Adam is in that box,' he

assured her, producing an official paper, which she duly signed as temporary guardian.

Miss Martin extended her hand. 'Well, thank you for returning these, officer. I do hope that whatever is in here will bring some kind of closure to Adam.'

'Yes, I imagine it will. These items eventually proved to be of small significance to us, but to Adam, they are part of his mother's belongings.'

'So, there's nothing in here that belonged to his father, is there? Only, I'm not sure he—'

The officer sensed her concerns. 'No. In the light of ongoing enquiries, we have duly retained certain items particular to Edward Carter. Which will in the course of time be returned.'

With that, he shook her hand, bade her goodbye, and left.

On leaving the office, he recognised Adam, seated forlornly on the bench by Miss Martin's office. He greeted the boy, who nodded slightly, but seemed to be miles away in his thoughts.

Once outside, the officer stood a moment, thinking of what that young boy had gone through: no home of his own; his mother lying in the churchyard; and his father jailed for a great number of years. Added to which it had transpired that he had only two distant relatives, neither of which had a yearning to take on a troubled young boy. He hoped that by the time Carter was released, the boy would be a full-grown man. If the police successfully managed to uncover his suspected other illegal activities, this seemed highly likely.

~

A moment or so later, Miss Martin came out of her office and ushered Adam inside. 'We've got a while yet before the family arrive,' she informed him excitedly, 'but in the meantime, I have something for you. Sit down, Adam, please. Sit down opposite me.'

When he was sitting, she informed him, 'The gentleman you probably saw leaving just now was from the police.' Concerned when she saw him press nervously back into his chair, she quickly assured him, 'There is nothing wrong, Adam. He just came to return something that belongs to you.'

Adam was surprised. 'Something that belongs . . . to me?'

'Yes, Adam. This box and everything in it belongs to you, Adam. That's why the officer was here. The police have no further use for this, and so he's brought it here for you.'

'Is it my mother's stuff?'

'Possibly, I don't know. It is not for me to pry into your belongings, Adam. But, he did say there are certain items that might belong to you, and maybe some of your mother's things . . . I have no idea. That's for you to discover.'

Choking back tears, he asked brokenly, 'Can I see it, please, Miss Martin?'

'But of course!' She got out of her seat and gently inched the box forwards until it was within reach. 'Would you like me to leave you alone for a while?'

Adam shook his head.

'So, you want me to stay here, with you?'

'Yes, please.'

'Very well.'

She sat down with a bump. 'Remember, these belong to you, Adam. They're yours to keep.' She added wisely, 'You understand, it may not be good for you to keep it all in the dormitory, but I have a big enough safe here, in this office. I can keep anything precious here, locked away, and of course you may ask to see it any time.'

'Thank you, Miss Martin.' His fingers played on the box lid. 'Can I open it now?'

'But of course! That's why I called you in.'

She asked again just to be sure, 'Are you certain you wouldn't prefer to open the box without me here?'

'No, miss. I'd like you to stay with me . . . please?'

'Of course.'

A moment later, she watched as he tore back the sealing tape and opened the lid.

One by one, he removed the items. There was a diary, beautifully written, seemingly in the delicate, sweeping hand of his mother. Thinking it might be too personal, he put that aside for the moment.

There was his father's old bunch of keys, which he recognised but did not want to touch. Gingerly sweeping them into a corner of the box, he continued to dig down.

He found all manner of things he had never seen before: a small rag doll with one eye; a tray of jewellery, which he tenderly put aside while he continued to empty the box. Then there were a number of items from his own bedroom: a pile of *Beano* comics; his school books; and a tied-up roll of posters.

There were other miscellaneous items, some of which he had occasionally seen and others he had never seen before, such as a pile of documents and letters, neatly rolled and labelled.

Alongside these were his mother's handbag and purse containing little of any significance.

When the box was emptied and all items laid across the desk, Adam began to cry . . . softly at first. Then he was shaking, seared with pain.

He realised how the remains of his old life and that of his mother were now reduced to empty, useless things that only served to hurt him all the more.

Then he felt Miss Martin's chubby arms about him, and he nestled into them. For a while neither of them spoke. Until Adam told her, 'Can you please lock it away?'

'Yes, Adam. I can do that for you. But is there nothing at all that you might like to keep in your own locker?'

He shook his head.

'But you haven't even looked at your mother's jewellery. Maybe you could take one very small thing?'

She understood his pain, but sometimes having some small thing that had been close to the one you love and miss, did actually help. Sadly, she reflected, she knew that more than most, as her fingers now went to the little trinket around her neck.

'I'm sure your mother wouldn't mind. What do you think, Adam?'

It seemed an age before he looked at her with

brimming eyes. It was an even longer age before he told her shakily, 'Yes, please.'

Taking a long, easy sigh, she patted him on the back and smiled. 'I'm glad,' she said, hugging him tight. 'Right! So let's take a look at the tray of jewellery, shall we? And see if anything appeals to you.'

She watched while Adam gently trawled through his mother's precious items. She could see how difficult it was for him, but she also knew it would not be right for her to take charge. This was Adam's moment. It was crucial that he and he alone should complete what must be a very traumatic ordeal for him.

She stayed by his side, occasionally encouraging him, as he lifted one item after another, until finally, he was left with the prettiest silver locket on a chain.

'Mum used to wear this all the time,' he said proudly. 'Father didn't like it. He wanted her to always wear the things he had bought her. Most times she did, because he would get angry if she didn't. But whenever she took me out, she always wore this locket.'

Miss Martin understood. 'It obviously meant a lot to her. Maybe her parents bought it for her, did they?'

Adam tried to remember what his mother had told him. 'No. It wasn't her parents. It was a friend. That's right . . . She said a really good friend bought it for her when they were young. She said it was two days before her birthday. She and some other friends had gone to Southend, and that's when she was given it as a present. She said it was a secret, hers and mine, and that I must never tell Father.

'One time I heard him ask her where she had got

such a cheap thing from, and she told him that she had bought it for herself, because she thought it was pretty.' Adam remembered the conversation he had overheard. 'Father told her she was never to wear it when they went out together, because he did not want people to see her wearing such a cheap and nasty thing, and he certainly did not want his friends to think he could not afford to buy his wife decent jewellery.'

Miss Martin was beginning to grow curious. It was an intriguing story.

'I see. And so, after that whenever she went out with your father, she never wore it, is that the way it was?'

'Yes, I think so.'

'And you think this locket meant a great deal to her, don't you?'

'Oh, it did, yes! She told me it was very special, and she would never get rid of it, whatever Father said.'

'Well, there you go then, Adam. It was obviously a very special present . . . from a very special friend.' She wondered about Peggy Carter and, being a woman, she understood why Adam's mother might cherish that pretty silver locket, though her own romantic past was long gone now.

Adam went on, 'Mum never told me who her friend was, but I think it was a lovely present.'

'And now, it's in your safekeeping. And I think you made a very good choice to keep with you, Adam.'

Adam's tears had subsided and now he smiled up at her. 'Thank you. Miss Martin, would you like to hold the locket?'

'Oh, yes, please. I really would like that, Adam. Thank you.'

When he now raised the silver locket, she held out her hand while he carefully folded it across her chubby fingers.

Turning it this way and that, she took a moment to examine it. Noting the small heart etched into the deep, graceful surface and the raised flowers within, she was impressed by the complexity of craftmanship. 'Your father was very wrong to call this "cheap and nasty". It's incredibly pretty. I can certainly see why your mother might have appreciated it.'

She was convinced that it was a lover's gift and she continued to turn it around, greatly impressed by its simple beauty; so strong, yet so delicate.

She was just about to return it to Adam, when something caught her eye. 'I can't be sure,' she said, 'but I think it opens. Did you know that, Adam?'

'No.' Adam was surprised. 'I've never seen my mum open it.'

Miss Martin showed him. 'Look!' She raised it up to him. 'Can you see that? I might be wrong, and it could be just a natural swelling within the etching, but it does look like a sort of little catch, don't you think, Adam?' She now handed it to him. 'Just there . . . see?' She brought his attention to the rim of the locket and the minutely raised area that was skilfully built into the pattern. 'That's the sign of good workmanship, if I'm any judge at all.'

In fact, the pattern and the catch itself were so cleverly integrated that if she had not turned it over at just the right angle, she would probably have missed seeing the catch.

Excited, Adam tried to move the tiny catch one side and then the other, but it was difficult. 'Do you think there's anything in there?' he asked, wide-eyed.

Miss Martin had seen these lockets before. 'In Victorian times, people would hide a lock of hair in this kind of locket, to remember a loved one, but I'm sure that isn't the case here. And if your mother did put something in there, she obviously didn't want anyone to find it. So, maybe you should let sleeping dogs lie, so to speak.'

Adam had not thought of that. 'What, you think she put something in there to hide it from my father? Is that what you mean?'

'Well, I don't know, and neither do you. But of course the locket is yours now, and it's you who must make the decision to open it or to leave it as your mother left it, well and truly closed.'

Adam was at a loss. 'Maybe there's nothing in it anyway.'

'Yes, that could be very true. As for finding out, I must not persuade you one way or the other. Besides, from the way the catch seems to be stuck hard, it could well be that the locket has never been opened.'

Adam, however, was of a different mind. 'If it has not been opened, then there won't be anything inside, so it won't matter if I look, will it?'

'Well, yes, that's very true.'

'But, if Mum did hide something there, it was so my father could never find it, though I don't think she would mind me looking inside.' Nevertheless, he was concerned. 'But if there is something hidden inside, why did she not show me? She knows I never would have told.'

'Well, of course you wouldn't. Nice people would never tell other people's secrets.'

Adam was in a quandary. 'I don't know what to do now.'

He wanted so much to believe that his mum had been clever enough to outwit his father. That would be just wonderful! But was it too prying to open the locket? What if his mum never wanted him to see what was in there?

'Maybe I should think about it some more,' he suggested.

'Yes, I believe that to be a very good idea. Now then, what shall we do with it while you're thinking?' Miss Martin was relieved at his sensible decision. 'Shall we lock it up now, or do you want to keep it with you?'

'Can I really keep it with me?'

'Of course, but it would not be wise to show it around.'

'I won't do that. I'll keep it safe next to me. I'll wear it under my shirt and when we do PE I'll hide it in my mattress.'

Miss Martin smiled. She had just learned a tiny bit of useful information. 'Would you like me to take care of the other items?'

'Yes, please.'

'Then consider it done.'

At that moment a knock came on the door, followed

by the flustered Mrs Baker, Miss Martin's assistant. 'Mrs Dexter just called.' She explained. 'They apologise profusely. The babysitter let them down, but they've managed to solve the problem, and they hope to be here in about half an hour, if that suits us?'

'Oh, my word, yes, of course. As a matter of fact, it would suit me better. I quite got carried away with other matters and didn't realise the time. Yes, of course. Tell Mr and Mrs Dexter that we're looking forward to receiving them.'

With Mrs Baker gone, Miss Martin smiled down on Adam. 'As you know, it's unusual for me to allow private things of any value to be kept with the child concerned, but I believe you are a sensible boy, that you will be discreet, and inform me if there's a problem.'

'I will be careful. I would never do anything to lose my mother's locket.'

'Nevertheless, if you find yourself growing anxious about keeping the locket safe, you must come and see me. Is that understood, Adam?'

'Yes, miss.'

'Now then, you heard what Mrs Baker said. Half an hour. That should give you time enough to prepare yourself. Off you go then.'

When he hesitated, she asked him gently, 'What is it, Adam? Is there something worrying you?'

'No, miss.'

'Then why haven't you gone already?'

'I just wanted to know, if the dog might be with them?'

'Oh! I see.' Her merry smile was infectious. 'Not this

time, I'm afraid. And nor will the children be with them. The first meeting is just you and the parents. Don't get too worried, Adam. If this family proves not to be right for you, then we shall have to look again. You do understand what I'm saying, don't you, Adam?'

'Yes, miss.'

'Good. Now, run along and be quick. You'll be sent for the minute they arrive.'

'Yes, miss.'

She watched him go out the door. *Dear me,* she thought, *if it isn't one thing, it's another.*

A moment later she was hurrying along the corridor to the library.

As always she muttered to herself. 'Half an hour and they'll be here. All I can say is that it's just as well they did lose their babysitter, considering the amount of time I spent with Adam . . . enjoyable, though. Yes indeed. Quite enjoyable.'

The silver locket reminded her of her own lost youth. *These days I feel so old and lonely*, she thought.

She tutted all the way down the corridor, 'I never did find the right man.'

But Adam was never far from her thoughts. 'They say light will always follow the darkness.' She recalled her own father having uttered those words many years ago. '. . . I hope for the boy's sake, that might be true.'

CHAPTER ELEVEN

LIZ DEXTER SAT at the dressing table, her auburn hair swept up in a ponytail, and her slim figure looking fresh and smart in a long-sleeved blue dress.

Her husband, Jim, stood at the far end of the bedroom, gazing across at this woman he loved. 'You look beautiful, sweetheart.'

'Thank you.' She smiled at him through the mirror. 'Flatterer.' Her face lit up at his warm compliment.

She took a moment to sweep her eyes over him. Of medium height, with the slightest paunch, he had a shock of fair hair, twinkly blue eyes and the features of a handsome puppy dog. 'Change your shirt, Jim.'

'What for?' He examined himself in the long wardrobe mirror. 'A white shirt always goes down well with authority.'

'Maybe. But we're hoping the boy takes to us, and, like you say, a white shirt does smack of authority. Change it –' she gave him a mischievous smile – 'or I might be forced to rip it off your back.'

At that, he rushed across the room, and slid his arms round her waist. 'Ooh! That sounds promising. But I'm afraid it will have to wait because we've got only about twenty minutes to get there.'

She groaned. 'Oh, bugger!' Swinging off the stool, she went to the bed and collected her cardigan and handbag. 'I'd better go and make sure Maureen has everything she needs.'

As she ran out the door, she called back, 'Change the shirt, Jim! Wear the blue one.'

As always, Jim did as he was told. 'I'm a poor, henpecked husband!' he yelled down the stairs, but got no response as Liz went skidding into the sitting room.

Softly whistling, he returned to check himself in the mirror. Finally satisfied that he looked smart and approachable in his dark trousers and blue shirt, he patted his hair down. *That's it! Ready for anything,* he thought.

After a week of nail-biting and worrying, the big day had finally arrived, but it had not been without its problems.

Liz had not slept well, having got herself in a tizzy about whether they were doing the right thing. He hoped he had reassured her.

Downstairs, Liz was talking to Maureen, a sixteen-year-old with a bird's-nest of black hair swept up, and a mouth carefully shaped with the brightest of lipsticks. She was the only daughter of their closest neighbour, and she had babysat many times before. 'I'm off to the flicks tonight,' she told Liz. 'Got a new boyfriend.' She made a swooning noise. 'He's not as good-looking as Danny, but he's all right for now. Anyway, Danny will see me out with my new fella, and he'll get jealous; that'll teach him for giving me the old heave-ho.'

'Well, let's hope the same doesn't happen with this new boy.' Today of all days, Liz did not particularly want to hear about Maureen's turbulent love-life.

'Ah, but it won't happen,' Maureen chirped. 'Hopefully, it'll be me giving him the shove. Y'see, I'm not all that fond of him. I'm only going out with him to get Danny all riled up.'

'Ah! You think that might make him come running back, do you?'

'Oh, yeah!' She giggled. 'He's just sulking. Truth is, he fancies me rotten! Oh, and he's just got a full-time job at the garage. They pay really good money. So, when we go out, I won't have to pay for a thing.'

Liz had to smile. 'Honestly, Maureen. You're incorrigible.'

'What does that mean?'

'Never mind. I'll tell you later. For now, I'm counting on you to take good care of the children. As you can see, Harriet's in her cot. She's been fed for now. I've left the feed times on a list, with the other things you might need. You'll find them all in the basket in the kitchen, with a spare dummy, a pile of nappies and such.'

'OK. Thanks.'

'If there's the slightest problem, go and ask your mum. Now, have I forgotten anything? Do you have any questions?'

'Nope! I've done this job before, and anyway, you told me everything I need to know last night. Don't worry, I've watched the children before and I'm good with them, you know that, Mrs Dexter. I'll feed Buster if you're late back, too, and let him out if he whines to go.'

'Yes, I do know, but this time you've got Alice to look after as well, which is why I'm insisting that you will fetch your mum if need be.'

'I promise.'

'Good. Oh, and do keep an eye on Alice. Let her sleep, though. She needs it after her bad night. I kept her at home today because she's got the sniffles. She was fast asleep just now when I went in. I had a word with her earlier, so I won't disturb her now. I've explained everything to her, so she won't be any trouble.'

'Naw, she never is. Alice and me, we get on just fine. If she comes down and wants to play a game, I've brought some with me – snakes and ladders and all that.'

'That's good thinking, Maureen. There are more games in her room if you need them.'

Jim was getting anxious. 'Come on, Liz.' He burst into the room. 'I've just checked on Alice, and she's still fast asleep. Anyway, Maureen knows the ropes by now. We'd better leave now or we'll be even later.'

He gave Buster an absent-minded pat on the head as he left and Buster retreated under the kitchen table.

~

As they climbed into the car, Liz still had a niggling doubt about their errand today. 'Jim?'

'Yes, love?' Jim was taking extra care as he pulled out onto the road. 'What's up?'

'I can't help feeling just a bit guilty.'

'Why's that?'

'Well, you know, there are so many people out there who can never have babies of their own. We've already got two beautiful children, and now we're about to offer a home to this boy Adam. It does seem a bit greedy, when he might be perfect for any one of those childless people.'

Jim had suspected for some time that Liz was not altogether sure about the fostering. 'Are you saying we should go back, ring Miss Martin and tell her we've changed our minds about having Adam?'

Liz was horrified. 'No! I'm not sayng that. Not at all.'

'Then what *are* you saying?'

Liz was silent for a moment, searching for the right words. 'I'm just asking, do you think we're being selfish fostering this boy? Won't we be depriving another family, who can never have children of their own?'

Jim was not surprised by the question. He had anticipated something like this because of Liz's quiet mood over the past few days.

He took a time before answering. 'So instead of having Adam, you would rather we have another child of our own. Is that what you're thinking?'

'Something like that, yes. And don't tell me you haven't thought of it as well?'

'Yes, I might have given it a passing thought, but

that's all. Because I don't want us to take the risk of you being pregnant again. I know what could happen – what has a seventy per cent chance of happening – and I can't take the risk. I thought you agreed.'

'I thought I did as well. But maybe we should have discussed it further, before raising this poor boy's hopes.'

'No! Haven't we already discussed it until we're blue in the face, and it always comes out the same?'

'What's that supposed to mean?'

'Well, tell me this: would you still want to get pregnant, with such a high chance that our two beautiful children could be left without a mother?'

'It would break my heart to think of leaving them.'

'Yes, and it would break mine too.'

Flicking the indicator, Jim drew the car to the kerb and parked. Then he took hold of Liz's hand to tell her gently, 'Listen to me, sweetheart. I know how hard it is, but I thought we had already faced the situation and come to a joint decision. I love our two girls, and I still have room in my heart for a third child. I honestly don't mind whether it's a boy or a girl, but I don't want a third child if it means losing you.'

He leaned over and kissed her. 'Do you think I don't know just how difficult it is for you? You're a wonderful wife . . . a natural mother. But you seem to have forgotten what the doctor said. He sat us both down and he told us that after the dangerous and traumatic time you had through both births, a third one might well be too much of a risk.'

'I know that. But a doctor can be wrong. It has been known.'

'No, Liz! For heaven's sake, listen to yourself! We almost lost both you and Harriet. Your heart actually stopped! You were in hospital for weeks. Even after you were eventually allowed home, it took you as long again to recover. Have you forgotten all of that?'

Liz had not forgotten the awful nightmare, not for a single minute. 'I just thought that maybe, with a third child, they would monitor me more. That's all,' she said quietly.

'Oh, I see.' Jim made a desperate effort to remain calm, although he was deeply angry at what she was saying. 'So, let me get this straight. You would like us to try for another child. And, regardless of what the doctor said, you think you know better. You think that if they monitor you throughout the pregnancy – if they keep you in for possibly a third or half of the pregnancy – everything will be just fine.'

'But it might be.'

'And the chances are it might not. And what about your two daughters? What if you were kept in hospital in order to "monitor" you? Would you really want them to be without their mother . . . possibly for months? I would take your place with the girls . . . possibly even lose my job. And every minute of every day I would wonder if you were ever coming home to us again.'

Tearful, knowing that he was right, Liz felt ashamed. 'I'm sorry. It's just that—'

'I know it's difficult, sweetheart. But, let's look at this another way. There's a young boy out there who's been through a nightmare. They say he's lost everything: his home, and his family. He has nothing and no one. They've told us what happened to him, and now they're trying to find him a family, some people who might build his belief in humanity again. Some people who might show him that the world is not the ugly, cruel place he has seen so far.' He grew emotional. 'Oh, Liz! We could give this boy so much. And who knows, maybe he'll do the same for us. But we won't do this unless you're happy about it. As for me, I'm ready to show him kindness and love as a substitute father. But before we go on, you have to be sure.'

'You're such a good man.' Liz slid over in her seat and kissed him soundly on the face. 'Jim Dexter, you are the kindest, most sensible man I've ever known. And I love you.'

Jim kissed her back. 'Are you nervous?'

'A bit. But I feel more content about the whole thing now.'

'Good. Now hang on. We're late already!'

Reassured, he pulled back out onto the road and roared away.

~

After seeing them off, Maureen set about her duties.

First, she ran up the stairs to peep in on Alice, who was still curled up in bed, sleeping soundly.

Tenderly, she took hold of the corner of her blanket and drew it up to her chin. 'That's a good girl,' she whispered. 'You sleep, while I see to the baby.'

Running downstairs, she crossed to the cot, where Harriet was happily sucking her thumb. 'It's not your feed time yet.' Maureen collected her from the cot. 'Ooh! You're a fat little lump and no mistake.'

Going over to the sideboard, she switched on the radio, and tuned it to her favourite music, which immediately filled the room. Soon she was jigging and jiving and thoroughly enjoying herself. Even the baby was smiling.

'Like it, do you?' Maureen jiggled Harriet up and down as they went round the room, and the baby laughed out loud. 'You and me, we're a right couple of swingers, aren't we, eh?'

Maureen was never happier than when she was listening to music and dancing the night away. There were all manner of new groups emerging, and she loved the new, exciting sounds that filled the clubs and pubs.

When the song ended, she placed the baby in her cot, dismayed to see that she'd been sick on her bib. 'Too much for you, was it?' She cleaned her up and set about checking her nappy. 'Good! Nice and clean . . . One thing I hate is changing nappies . . . ugh!'

'Maureen?' Alice, woken by the music, had made her way downstairs. 'Where's Mum?'

Small-built, Alice was blessed with big brown eyes and thick, straight brown hair. Normally, she was as sweet-natured as she was pretty, but for some reason she now appeared to be unsettled.

'Mum and Dad have gone out. Mum said you didn't sleep very well last night. Maybe you might be better off going back to bed . . . get some more sleep before Mummy and Daddy come home.'

'I don't want to go back to bed. I want to stay here with you.'

'OK. If that's what you want, that's fine by me.' Maureen could not recall Alice being so irritable.

She brought Alice right into the room. 'I bet you're hungry, aren't you? I'll make you something to eat. I'm sure your mummy's cupboards are full as always, so what do you want?'

'I want my mum.'

'I already told you, she and Daddy have gone out. They'll be back soon, though.'

'Mummy told me about the boy.'

'Oh, did she? Well, there you are then. So, you've no need to worry, have you?'

Maureen had recently overheard her own mother and Liz Dexter discussing the idea of the Dexters' fostering a child. When she later quizzed her mother, she was told never to eavesdrop on other people's conversations, and that she was to forget what she'd overheard. She had effectively put it out of her mind until just now, when Alice mentioned 'the boy'.

Heeding her mother's warning, she changed the subject to take Alice's mind off the idea of 'the boy'. 'I bet you're hungry, aren't you? What if I get you some cereal, or a glass of orange squash and a slice of toast?'

'I don't want anything to eat!' Running across the room, Alice threw herself on the chair beside the baby's cot, where she sat, very quiet and seemingly tearful.

'What's wrong, Alice?' Concerned, Maureen came and kneeled on the carpet beside her.

'Nothing.' Alice turned away.

Maureen persisted. 'There must be something wrong. You've come downstairs in a funny old mood. Why is that? Has something upset you? Or is it just that you're still tired?'

Alice shook her head, but gave no other reply.

Maureen was not so easily put off. 'So, do you want to talk about it?'

'No.'

'I'm a good listener.'

Alice shook her head a second time.

'OK. No more questions then.'

Maureen started on her way to the kitchen. 'I'm really thirsty, though. I'll make us both orange squash. If you don't want it, I expect I'll be thirsty enough to drink the both of them.'

Busying herself in the kitchen, she made two orange squashes and carried them back into the other room. 'Here we are.'

There was no sign of Alice.

Worried, Maureen put the drinks down; and searched around, but Alice was nowhere to be seen. There was just Harriet in the cot, happily kicking her legs and gurgling.

Maureen ran to the window and looked out. She called her name, but there was no sight or sound of Alice.

She ran into the hallway. 'Alice, are you upstairs?'

No answer.

She ran up the stairs two at a time, and found Alice in her bed.

'Why didn't you answer me?' Maureen tried not to sound harsh. 'You had me really worried. Did you not hear me calling?'

'You told me to go back to bed,' Alice answered casually.

'No, Alice! I didn't actually say you had to go back to bed. I just suggested it, because I thought you might still be tired.'

'I am.'

'All right. I'll leave you for a while. Is there anything you want?'

'No, thank you.'

After settling Alice between the bedclothes, Maureen returned to keep an eye on Harriet. She also drank the two orange squashes – waste not, want not – then carried the empty glass and beaker into the kitchen, all the time wondering what was wrong with Alice. Buster was now asleep under the table.

Returning to check on Harriet again, she heard movement from upstairs. Going into the hallway she called out, 'Alice, are you all right?'

'Yes, thank you.'

'You will shout me if you need anything, won't you?'

'Yes.'

'Just try and get some more sleep. I'll let you know as soon as your parents get back. OK?'

'Yes, OK.'

Maureen wandered back to talk to Harriet. 'Hmm! So, Alice knows about the boy, eh?' She tickled the child under the chin. 'You don't know yet, though . . . you're too young to know what's going on, anyway.'

She thought about Alice. 'I'm glad her mum told her they might foster a little boy, because it's not fair when your parents keep secrets and you only find out about them after something happens,' she told Harriet.

She wondered how Alice really felt about having a brother. 'I think it would be nice for you and Alice if they fostered a boy, because brothers look after you. And they don't steal your make-up and clothes like my sister Jan does.' She rolled her eyes. 'She is such a nuisance. I have to hide everything from her!'

Glancing into the cot, she noticed that Harriet was now asleep. 'Oh, I see, don't want to talk to me, eh? You've got your belly full and a nice clean nappy on, so now it's snooze-time, is it?'

Smiling, she went and rummaged in the kitchen drawer, looking for magazines. She found just the one. Bursting with fashion items and kinds of make-up, it was just what she needed.

Curling up in the front room with the magazine stretched out on the arm of the chair, she was soon lost in the many, colourful pages.

Upstairs, Alice sat at the window, silently crying. With her nose pressed against the windowpane she looked up and down the street, watching for the car to bring home her parents. 'Why do you need a boy when you've got me and Harriet?' she whispered.

She went back to lie on the bed. She lay there for what seemed an age, her sorry gaze fixed on the precious rag dolly that her daddy won for her at a fair two years ago.

Taking the doll into her embrace, she cuddled and kissed it. 'We don't need a boy, do we? We just need Mummy and Daddy, and me and Harriet.'

For a while, she hugged the doll tight and softly cried, her tears dampening the doll's raggedy face. She then returned to the bed, where she sat thinking. She was angry, and for the first time in her short life, she felt incredibly lonely.

After a time, loneliness became rejection, and her anger turned to rage. Throwing the doll across the room, she got from the bed and ran across to the window again. 'Don't bring him home. We don't want him here,' she muttered angrily.

A moment later, she collected the rag doll from the carpet and hugged it to her chest. 'We're all right, aren't we, Dolly? Just you and me and Harriet.'

Very gently at first, she painstakingly untied the two bows that tied the doll's plaits. That done, she undid the two thick plaits and, one at a time, she calmly and systematically tore out each hair from the scalp, until there was not a hair left on the doll's head.

That done, she bunched the hair up tight, screwed it round and round until her hands were red-sore, then she dropped the ravished hair into the waste basket.

She hid the waste basket behind her desk and went downstairs. She found Maureen in the front room, intently reading Mummy's magazine. 'I'm hungry now, Maureen,' she said. 'Can I please have something to eat?'

A few minutes later, she was enjoying the beans on

toast that Maureen had made for her, then the two of them sat on the sofa, looking through the magazine together, and choosing the things they would buy if they had the money.

Once or twice, Alice looked towards the hallway door and secretly smiled.

'Maureen?'

'Yes?' Maureen looked up from the pages.

'Can we play match the cards?'

'Yeah, course we can, but no cheating like you did last time, you little monster!'

'I won't cheat . . . honestly,' Alice promised.

But she would if she had to.

~

Adam was nervous.

Having been told to wait in the library, he heard Mrs Baker's excited voice calling out, 'They're here, Miss Martin!' She had seen the car drawing up outside and recognised the driver as Mr Dexter.

'Hurry! Go and greet them, quickly!' Miss Martin tried to suppress her excitement.

While Mrs Baker went one way, Miss Martin went the other, her thick-heeled shoes echoing on the wood-block floor as she hurried to get Adam.

'Quickly, Adam. They're here.'

With great speed, she ushered Adam along the corridor and into her office. 'Don't be nervous,' she told him, fiddling with the neck of his clean white shirt. 'They're just ordinary people, like you and me.'

Adam tried his hardest not to be nervous, but he was excited at the same time. He did as he was told and sat in the straight-backed chair by her desk. 'When they come in, remember to stand up, Adam. Remember to greet them politely.'

Preparing herself for the Dexters, she stood smartly behind her desk; she fussed wth her hair and constantly wiped imaginary fluff from the skirt of her dress.

In truth, she was every bit as nervous as Adam. She so wanted him to be with a good family, and from what she had learned about them, she was satisfied that the Dexters were fine, God-fearing people, with room in their hearts to take in a troubled boy like Adam.

As they walked down the long corridor to Miss Martin's office, Liz and Jim Dexter were somewhat apprehensive.

Although they had discussed the boy with the authorities, and they had met and discussed the matter in great depth with Miss Martin, this introduction to Adam himself was all-important. Everything was resting on it. If Adam was nervous, they were even more so.

As they walked in the door, Adam nervously appraised them. He saw two well-dressed, smiling people. Thinking how much younger they were than he'd expected, he was made easier by the friendly manner in which they greeted him.

Adam took an instant liking to them but, for some inexplicable reason, he was especially drawn to the woman. She had the same soft smile as his darling mother, though there the similarity ended, because where his mother was short and small of bone, this woman was taller and more broad-shouldered. Also, her hair was straight and brown, unlike his mother's wild, curly hair.

Even so, Adam thought she had that same air of graciousness, and when she smiled, it made him feel accepted. He began to relax.

Mr Dexter seemed like a friendly man, who made Adam think he might be a good dad, and friend; something his own father had never been.

Miss Martin introduced them to each other. 'This is Adam,' she announced proudly. 'You've already been made aware of his story and background, and our intention to place him with a good family. This meeting is for you to get to know each other, and for me to answer any questions or concerns that might arise on either side. Before we go any further, I wonder if you might want to be left alone with Adam in order for the three of you to get to know each other better, without myself or Mrs Baker here.'

She looked from one to the other, speaking to the Dexters first. 'Would that help you in any way?'

They thought it would, and Jim Dexter said so.

Liz, however, could see how nervous Adam seemed, constantly fidgeting, and dropping his gaze to the carpet. 'But how does Adam feel about being left alone with us just now?'

From the first moment when she and Jim walked into the room, her gaze was drawn to Adam, this solitary and frightened boy, who needed a family to love him. Right there and then he had touched her heart and banished any doubts she had.

'Well, Adam?' Miss Martin asked. 'Would you like to spend a few minutes getting to know Mr and Mrs Dexter. I'm sure you must have questions that only they can answer.'

Adam took a moment to turn the idea over in his mind. He was nervous and afraid they might not like him. And that would be a shame because he so wanted to be part of a family, and they seemed like kind and decent people.

'Well, Adam? There's nothing to worry about. I won't be far away, and it's only for a few minutes, ten at the most.'

It was the encouraging smile and slight nod of the head from Liz Dexter, that prompted Adam. 'Yes, please, Miss Martin. I would like that.'

'Excellent!'

Both Miss Martin and her treasured assistant departed the office and left them alone. 'Ten minutes,' Miss Martin reminded them. 'Then I'll be back to see how you got on together.'

When the door closed behind her, Jim was the first to speak. 'Adam, for what it's worth – and you don't have to do it if you don't want – but I think it might be best if we don't just ask each other questions. Instead, what if Liz and I tell you all about who we are, what we do, and why we thought you might be the one to come home and live with us, as a son? After that – and only if you want to – you can tell us about yourself. Tell us whatever you feel we need to know. After that, we can ask each other questions. So, Adam, is that all right with you?'

Adam nodded. He liked that idea.

Liz was the first to speak. Without going into details, she told him how she and Jim had always wanted a third child but it was not advisable because her health had suffered greatly when giving birth to her two babies.

She described the baby, Harriet, and her other daughter, Alice, and assured Adam that they would love him as a big brother.

When it was his turn, Jim explained how much they both loved their two children, and that he would be cherished in the same way.

'There's enough room in the house, and enough love in our hearts, to make another child feel as though he belonged. Our preference for a boy is simply because we already have two daughters. Today is the culmination of many meetings that we've already had with the relevant authorities, so we do know a little about you and your background, Adam, and it's only made us want you all the more.'

Soon, it was time for Adam to tell them something about himself. There was much he kept back because he was not ready to discuss some of the really shocking things that had happened.

He told them that his father was a bad man, and that his mother was the kindest and loveliest mother ever, and that he missed her terribly.

He said he thought Mr and Mrs Dexter were kind people and that he would like it very much if they decided to make him part of their family, because he had never had a brother or a sister.

There was one, very important thing that Adam

thought could swing his decision either way. 'My only friend is called Phil, and I would be unhappy if I never saw him again.'

Liz was interested. 'Oh, but I'm sure if we take you into the family, and if you want to stay, then your friend Phil can visit . . . if his parents don't mind.'

'Oh, no!' Adam was taken aback at her remark. 'Oh, no! He's not a boy. He's an old man who drives the school bus. He's my very best friend, and Miss Martin lets me go out with him and Polly to the park, and sometimes we go to the churchyard, where I take my mum flowers.'

Jim was a bit taken aback to learn Adam's friend was an elderly man. 'Of course, if you decide that we're the family for you, then we'll need to meet up with your friend.'

Adam's passion about his friendship with Phil, and the taking of flowers to the churchyard had really touched Liz's heart. 'I'm sure we can work something out about your friend,' she said. 'First, though, you need to decide whether or not you would like to be part of our family. And we must do the same.'

Jim tried to reassure him. 'You'll need time to think, Adam. No one is expecting you to decide here and now.'

Almost before Jim had finished speaking, Miss Martin tapped on the door and entered immediately. 'All done, are we?' She had a good feeling about this particular family.

Jim had a question. 'Adam has been telling us about his friendship with Phil. Could you tell us a little about him, please?'

'Of course. Phil has been close to Adam from the first day he was brought here, and even before that. He's a local man. He drives the bus that took Adam to school every day.'

Being careful with her choice of words, she explained, 'Phil was there on the day Adam's father ran off. At the hospital he remained at Adam's side, and he has seen him through all his trials and troubles. He's a stalwart and well-respected member of the local community, and still remains a very important part of Adam's life. In fact, we actually relaxed a certain rule so Phil might accompany Adam whenever he takes flowers to his mother.' She finished with a bright, proud smile to Adam. 'In fact, Phil is more like Adam's granddad than just a friend.'

Both Jim and Liz were impressed.

Liz had no hesitation in telling Adam, 'It's been an absolute pleasure meeting you, Adam. The first thing for us to do is to agree on the next step, I think.' She turned to Miss Martin. 'What happens now?'

'Well, I believe you were informed by the office that the next step is for Adam to have a trial visit to your home, but first, now that you've met Adam, and he's had the opportunity to talk with you both, you and your husband need to discuss it further, between yourselves. This is a very important decision for all three of you. When you're ready for the next step, let me know, and whichever way you decide, I shall act accordingly.'

Liz glanced at her husband and smiled. 'I think Jim and I have already decided.'

Miss Martin was pleased. 'Even so,' she said, 'in something as important as Adam's future and your own peace of mind, you must have space to reflect. I cannot go ahead with arrangements until you've had time to think and discuss it, away from here. Away from Adam.'

She had seen far too many quick decisions, only for them to be overturned later. After what he had already experienced, she had no intention of putting Adam through further trauma.

CHAPTER TWELVE

Bedford centre was relatively quiet for a Friday, as was the Woolworths store. 'Friday at last!' Sally slunk down into the passenger seat of Anne's car.

Sally and Anne were on their way to work. 'Honestly, Anne, if you'd been just five minutes late picking me up from home, I reckon I'd have gone back to bed.' As though to make her point she gave a long, lazy yawn.

'I know what you mean,' Anne smiled as Sally yawned again. 'I'd much rather be run off my feet than waiting for customers to come to the counter. It just makes the day seem twice as long.'

Sally hunched herself up in the seat, 'Anne?'

'Yes?'

'Are you sleeping better at night?'

'Sort of.'

'And what does that mean?'

Anne shrugged. 'Just that . . . I don't wake up quite as often, that's all.'

'You promised me and Mick that you'd tell us if you were not all right.'

'But I am.'

'It doesn't sound like it to me.'

'Well, if I'm honest I do sometimes wake up at the slightest sound, but I'm getting better. Really I am.'

Sally was not totally convinced. 'If you want me to come and stay with you again, I will. You do know that, don't you?'

She had missed Mick terribly last time, even though he'd come over most evenings to keep them company. Despite this, she would stay with Anne if need be.

Anne graciously refused her offer. 'Thanks all the same, Sal. I do appreciate your concern, but I must learn to fend on my own. Like you said, he can't hurt me from where he is.'

'That's what you need to keep in mind, Anne.' It had been a while now, since Sally had stayed at Anne's house. Only when she thought Anne was confident enough to be on her own did she move back with Mick.

'I really don't know what I'd have done without you, Sal.' Though she would not admit it, Anne still had her bad moments. Sometimes, she was afraid to go into the back garden, even in daylight. And even though she had locked the back gate securely, she still wedged all manner of things against it – wooden garden chairs and even the dustbin – anything to make a noise and alert her if anyone tried to get into the garden.

She was afraid to leave the curtains open once the night closed in. Even now, she did not feel safe upstairs, fearing that if Carter somehow got to her, she would have no way of escaping. She had slept downstairs for a week or so after Sally had first gone home.

Fully dressed, she had slept lightly on the sofa, with a torch beside her, the door secured by the weight of an armchair, and the line from the telephone fed under the door from the hallway, with the phone itself sitting on the pillow beside her.

Nighttime or daylight, and even with the knowledge that he was locked away, Edward Carter still had a hold over her.

She was suddenly startled from her thoughts when Sally said, 'All right, but don't forget, if you change your mind the offer is still there. I've discussed it with Mick, and he's OK with me coming to stay the odd week now and then. Just until you feel one hundred per cent safe.'

'Sally, I'm absolutely fine! Having you for a week was really great.' Anne added light-heartedly, 'Apart from your snoring.'

'I do not snore!'

'You do so! When you get going, it's like all hell let loose.'

Sally was silenced for a minute before confiding meekly, 'Mick said when I snore, it's like a runaway train thundering along the tracks.'

Her throwaway remark soon had the two of them roaring with laughter. 'Poor Mick!' Having experienced Sally's snoring at first hand, Anne had sympathy for him.

'Poor Mick nothing!' Sally groaned. 'Without me knowing it, he sometimes wears the same socks for a whole week! When he takes 'em off, they stand up all on their own.'

They were still giggling as they turned into the car park.

In the cloakroom, they hung up their coats and put on their smart white overalls. 'You and Mick are such wonderful friends to me,' Anne admitted. 'I honestly don't know what I'd have done without you both. You've helped me so much. I know you think I don't listen to your good advice, but I do.'

She hadn't been going to say anything about the positive step she had recently taken, but now she thought it only right that Sally should be made aware of it.

'You might be pleased to know that after the good advice you gave me some time ago, I am now seriously trying to get my life in order. I'm feeling stronger now . . . more like my old self. I'm thinking things through and making decisions that I should have dealt with years back. For all the wrong reasons, I've let things slip for too long, but I'm onto it now, and that's all down to you and Mick.'

Sally was thrilled to hear Anne being so positive. 'That's wonderful, but what kind of decisions are we talking about?'

'Oh, you know, things like I might get the house painted inside, change the furniture and such. It might help me to forget he was ever there.'

She realised she was not quite ready to explain just now. 'I've decided to make an effort to live my life and not be afraid to do things. Important things that have been neglected for too long.'

'Such as what?' Sally was intrigued.

'Like I said, all kinds of things.' Anne realised she would have to be careful what she said, or Sally would never leave her be. 'Just to generally . . . well . . . get my life in order.'

'Oh, Anne, I'm so relieved. It seems to me you have a new fighting spirit.' She reached out and patted her on the shoulder. 'Atta girl!'

Changing the subject, Anne hoped to draw Sally away from asking more questions she was not yet ready to answer.

'Are you going to the works dance tomorrow night?'

'Yes, but you're coming as well, aren't you?'

'I might have other plans.'

'Oh, I see!' Sally playfully taunted her. 'Sounds to me like you're hiding something. So, what are you up to?'

'I'm not up to anything. I just don't feel like going to the dance, that's all.'

'Is that because Tony McDonald asked you to go with him?' She gave a little wink. 'I kid you not, Anne, he's the one bloke that every girl here would love to go with.'

'Except for me.'

'But why? I thought you liked him. You seem to get on well enough. I saw you and Tony chatting the other day and you looked really comfortable with him.'

'I'm not saying I don't like him, Sal, because I do. He's polite and caring, and he doesn't force his attention on you, not like that new maintenance bloke. Bad-mannered oaf. He thinks he's God's gift.'

Sally persisted, 'So, if you like Tony, why won't you go to the dance with him?'

'No reason in particular. I just don't plan on going, that's all.'

As Anne closed the subject, Sally caught her by the arm. 'Anne, I very much doubt if he's the sort of man who would force himself on you, if that's what you're worried about.'

'Huh! I wouldn't even be talking to him if I thought he would ever do such a thing, but he has a kind and thoughtful nature, and like I say, I do like him. I'm not going to the dance, because I have other things to do.'

'Well, I think that's a shame, because he really likes you. He did ask you to go with him, didn't he?'

'Yes, but I'm not ready for dating.' The thought of being close to any man made her shiver.

'Oh, Anne, that's such a shame.'

Sally was used to the shutters coming down where Anne was concerned, but for now she decided to leave the subject alone. 'We're still going out to the café for lunch, though, aren't we?'

'Of course. I'm looking forward to it.'

'Good, because I'm tired of canteen food.'

'Me too. Whatever meal you get, they all taste the same.'

Sally laughed. 'You're absolutely right! But don't let Cook hear you say that or she'll have your head on a plate.'

A few minutes later, the two of them walked through the store and took up their respective places: Sally behind the perfume counter, and Anne fronting the bits and bobs counter, where the selection of threads, needles, wool and bric-a-brac made a lively and colourful display.

As always, there was the initial rush of customers, followed by a slight lull, during which the sales women would have a quick gossip amongst themselves. Today they were all excited about the works dance.

Brazen Pauline from hardware had her eye on a partner for the evening. 'I'm hoping to bag a dance or two with our new assistant manager,' she cooed. 'He's single, probably not short of a bob or two, and he's the best-looking bloke I've seen in a long time.' Clicking her tongue, she gave a knowing smile. 'Oh, yeah! He'll do for me!'

Just then, a colleague nudged her in the back. 'Ssh!' He's on his way. We'd best get back to work.'

As he strolled towards them, it was clear that Tony McDonald was indeed a 'good-looking bloke'. With his wayward mop of dark hair, smiling hazel eyes and a slim body, he walked with a lazy ease that showed authority and a certain sensuality.

He strolled over to Sally. 'How's it going this morning, Sally?'

'Not too bad.' Sally described the initial rush of customers. 'Mostly people popping in on their way to work.'

He thanked her and moved on to Anne. 'Good morning, Anne?'

His manner was different from how it was with Sally. His voice was softer. He stood closer, and when he smiled on her, his kind, dark gaze seemed to look into her soul. 'Everything all right, is it?'

'Yes, thank you, we've already had a flurry of customers.' She felt nervous around him, but not like she was with Edward Carter, because this was a different kind of nervousness. Her stomach danced and she felt hot all over. 'It's always the same,' she answered, 'a bit of a rush first thing, then it goes quiet for a while.'

He shifted nearer to her. 'You look pretty this morning, Anne. As always.'

'Oh?' Not knowing what to say, she shyly averted her eyes, bowed her head and pretended to shift the merchandise about.

Lowering his voice he asked, 'Have you thought any more about coming to the dance with me tomorrow night?'

Anne shook her head.

'If you're worried about driving home late, I could pick you up, and drop you home afterwards. It's not a problem.'

Anne graciously declined. 'Thank you, but I don't know if I'm going. I've got so much to do at home.'

'Can't those things wait even for a day?'

'Not really, no! I have things to prepare for an important meeting next week. And it's kind of complex.'

'Can I help at all?'

'Oh, no!' She began to panic. 'It's private stuff.'

'I'm sorry.' He could see how nervous she was. 'I won't pressure you. If you have important things to do, then I suppose you can't be in two places at once.'

'Thank you, anyway, Mr McDonald. I'm really sorry.' And she was.

His gentle smile enveloped her. 'That's OK. Anyway,

the offer still stands. If you change your mind, it would make me very proud if you could be my partner for the evening.'

Anne nodded appreciatively, and watched him walk away.

She felt a strong urge to call him back, but she resisted.

It was peculiar how he made her feel like a shy little girl, wanting to curl up and hide. In some ways it was a nice feeling.

Tony moved on to Barbara, the smart, middle-aged lady at the help desk.

Out the corner of her eye, Anne was not surprised to see Sally giving a crafty thumbs up as though to congratulate her.

Realising that Sally must think she'd accepted Tony's offer of taking her to the dance, Anne shook her head determinedly, and from the look of disappointment on Sally's face, Anne knew she had got the message.

She thought it comforting, though, how Tony made her feel like she was special. Edward Carter had never been able to do that. For the first time in years, she felt a fluttering of excitement that a fine man like Tony had actually asked her twice to go out with him. It made her feel like a real woman. Maybe, at long last, she really was getting over her fear of men.

Or maybe she was just feeling good because last week she had asked for permission to leave work slightly early, on the pretence that she had a dentist appointment.

The real reason for leaving early, however, was because she had to make a very important decision.

At long last, she had gathered courage enough to take that first step to distance herself from the man who had destroyed her peace of mind for far too long. Sufficient time had passed, and now, thankfully, she was feeling strong enough in herself to deal with issues long overdue.

~

The morning had flown by, with eventually hordes of customers coming in and out of the store, and every assistant run off his or her feet.

It was now midday, and time for the first shift to take their hour-long lunch break.

'Come on, Anne, let's get off before Tony asks us to work through our break.' Sally had already managed to collect their coats.

A minute later they were headed off down the High Street.

'Phew! What a morning.' Sally was glad to get out of there.

They went carefully across the busy road, then through the arcade and on to the café, which they found half empty.

'Good!' Sally made a beeline for the table in the far corner. 'I think you've got something to tell me, and if people start coming in, we won't get overheard back here.'

'Who says I've got something to tell you?'

'Well, let's see. Firstly, you've been acting strangely, such as telling me you're getting your life in order.

Added to which, it's been ages since you wanted to come down here for your lunch.'

'Huh! You know me better than I know myself.'

When Sally continued to hover, she informed her, 'Go on then! I'll have a cheese and salad sandwich . . . and a pot of tea, please.'

'OK, but it's your turn to pay.'

Anne plucked a note from her purse and pressed it into Sally's outstretched palm. 'Go on then.'

She watched as Sally went to the counter, and a warm smile crept over her pretty features. Sally had been by her side through all the troubles. And whichever path her life took from now, Anne knew that she would never be able to thank Sally enough.

Within minutes, Sally was back. 'Oh, dammit!' She took off again. 'I forgot the sugar!'

Meantime, Anne was thinking how best to tell Sally what she'd done. She was wary of saying too much in case nothing came of it. She was also very afraid that it could all go wrong, with her caught in the middle, wishing that she'd left everything as it was.

Sally returned with the sugar bowl. 'Now then, lady!' Seating herself, she poured out her tea and plopped two heaped spoonfuls of sugar into her cup, stirring so vigorously the tea slopped over the brim. 'So, come on, Anne. What are you up to?'

'You're a mucky pup.' Anne laughed. 'Worse than a kid.'

'Never you mind about me, and stop trying to change the subject.' Sally was like a dog with a bone. 'We're here, just the two of us. There are no prying eyes and no one to overhear what you have to say. What's ticking over in that brain of yours? And don't tell me it's nothing, because I know you've got something you're itching to tell me, so come on. Spit it out!'

Anne told her, 'I've been thinking a lot lately, about my life, and everything. You and Mick have given me good advice and so far I've done nothing about it. But, do you remember what Edward Carter said to me, when he trapped me in the house? I told you and Mick about it, and you both said it was imperative that I should seek legal guidance, sooner rather than later.'

'You mean when he made reference to your house, and he said what was yours was his?'

Anne nodded. 'You and Mick were right. I should have done something about it then, and I didn't. But I've been thinking more and more about it lately, and it really worries me. That house was Aunt Ada's home. She and Uncle Bart moved there when they got married, so they enjoyed many good years in that little house. Aunt Ada left it to me, because she wanted me to love it the same way they had.' Her voice dropped to a whisper. 'It really hurts me to think that Carter might get his hands on the house. I don't want that to happen, Sally, and I don't want any link with him any more.'

Sally was delighted to hear Anne talking like this. 'So, have you got a plan?'

'You and Mick were right about a lot of things,' she admitted, 'so I've made an appointment with a solicitor. It's time I stood up and faced the truth. Edward Carter wants to ruin me. He wants to keep me frightened and take everything I have. I know what Aunt Ada would say: she'd say the same as you and Mick. "Fight him!" And that's what I've decided to do.'

Sally was thrilled. 'Good girl! So what did the solicior say?'

'Well, we haven't met yet, but I told him the situation on the telephone, and I gave him as many details as I could. He said he would make a start looking into things, and we arranged a meeting.'

'So, what exactly did you tell him on the phone? What kind of details did he ask for?'

'Well, firstly, he wanted me to bring along a marriage certificate, but I couldn't because I never had one. Edward was such a secretive man. He kept everything squirrelled away. I never knew what he was up to from one minute to the next. I do have the deeds to the house, though. I told the solicitor that I'd get them from the bank, and bring them to the meeting together with anything else that might seem relevant.'

'So, what else did he say?'

'When I asked him about getting a divorce from Edward Carter, he said he would have to make enquiries and such. Beyond that, he said there was much to be done, and that we would discuss the details at the meeting.'

Jubilant but highly nervous, she leaned back in her chair. 'So, what do you think, Sal? Do you think I'm doing the right thing? Or have I opened a Pandora's box? Have I let myself in for more trouble than I can handle?'

'Listen to me, Anne. I won't lie, because even a

normal divorce is never easy. But that man has made your life a misery. He's vicious and cruel, and he doesn't give a tinker's cuss about you. Yes, it might get nasty, and when he's served with divorce papers, he won't be best pleased, but who cares? You and I both know he'll move Heaven and earth to rob you of half the value of your home.'

'He will!' Anne was sure of it, 'I know he will.'

'OK. But everything is in your favour. It will all come out: the beatings he gave you when you were married to him . . . causing the loss of your baby. Then there's the way he tracked you down and held you prisoner, in fear for your life. Don't you worry, the Courts will have a field day with it.'

'I know all that, and I've told myself over and over that if it comes down to it, the Courts will be on my side, but I'm frightened, Sal. You don't know what he's like, not really. You have to live with him before you realise what he's capable of. I've always believed he's a bit wrong in the head. A madman!'

'But he can't hurt you while he's locked up – don't you ever forget that, Anne – and now that you're fighting back, he knows his track record will not serve him well.'

'Yes. Now I'm doing what I should have done years ago. But the thing is, Sal, I'm really frightened it will all blow up in my face.'

Leaning forward, Sally placed her hand on Anne's shoulder. 'It won't. Yes, it's true, divorce is never easy. But you really are doing the right thing, Anne. After you've told the solicitor everything, he'll understand.

I know you're worried, but now that you've found the courage to fight back, you must be strong and see it through. You obviously know that, or you would not have called the solicitor in the first place. And always remember, you're not on your own.'

'I do realise I have to do this, Sal. I'm so weary of being afraid. I just want it over.'

'I know. And I'm proud of you, and if you want me to come to the solicitor with you, I will. I'll tell him everything I know. Calling that solicitor can't have been an easy thing to do, but you did it. Now, like I said, you need to see it through. Mick and I will be right behind you.'

She was greatly relieved that Anne had found the courage to fight Edward Carter. But like Anne, she was nervous of how Carter might react when he discovered that Anne was now taking the initiative and refusing to be the victim.

At the end of the working day, the two of them made their way to the car park. 'Are you sure you won't change your mind and come to the dance with me and Mick?'

'No, but thanks all the same.'

'It seems such a pity, especially as you've made the hard decision to shape the direction of your own life.'

'I know, but I need some quiet time. I intend making a list of every little thing that man has ever done to me. I'm determined that people should know what he is.'

'That's good, but it doesn't mean you can't go to the dance.'

'I know that, Sal, but I really don't feel like going anyway.'

'Is that because Tony asked you?'

'No. Oh, I don't know, Sal. The truth is, I don't think I'm ready for dating.'

'It's not really a date, is it? I mean, it's just the annual staff dance. We'll all be there.'

'I know, but Tony particularly asked me to go with him, and from what I can remember, that's a date. And like I say, I'm not ready for it.'

'OK, but where's the harm in coming along with me and Mick? Just see how it goes. If Tony does ask you to dance, you can always say no.'

Anne could see the reasoning behind Sal's suggestion. 'I suppose it would do me good to get out for an evening,' she agreed. 'Sometimes, the house does seem like a prison. All right then, I don't suppose there's any harm in coming along with you and Mick.'

'Now you're thinking sensibly. So, I'll take that as a yes, shall I?'

'Yes, why not? Besides, I'm sure there'll be time enough over the rest of the weekend to prepare for the meeting.'

'Right!' Sally was delighted. 'So now, the all-important question: have you got a pretty, girlie dress for dancing? And what about shoes? We might have to go shopping. Don't forget the summer sales are still on. Oh, and I'll do your hair, if you like, save you a bit of money going to the hairdresser's—'

She would have gone on, but Anne interrupted her, 'I've agreed to go to the dance, but I am not going shopping for dresses and shoes. There are so many things in my wardrobe that I haven't worn for ages. I'm bound to find something suitable.'

'Oh, no, you don't!' Sally was determined. 'You haven't bought anything really pretty in ages, and everyone will be dressed to the nines. So, the two of us are going shopping. We need a new dress, and shoes, and a hairdo, and I won't take no for an answer.'

And when Sally was in that kind of mood, Anne knew there was no stopping her. In a way, she didn't really want to.

Swept along in Sally's excitement, Anne found herself looking forward to the dance.

More than that, she was also looking forward to a successful meeting with the solicitor, but whichever way it went from now on, she was beginning to feel like she'd been given a new lease of life.

~

Saturday, at the shops, swept by and the moment had arrived.

Right on time, Mick and Sally arrived to collect Anne.

When they drew up outside Anne's house, Mick gave a gasp as she opened the door and stepped out.

Wearing a slinky, black dress and red high-heeled shoes and with a little red bag clutched in her hand, Anne looked like a million dollars.

Apart from one lock of loosely waved hair that hung down to her shoulder, her hair was swept up and gripped in a silver comb. All of this was Sally's doing.

'I know you said she'd knock 'em dead, but she doesn't even look like the Anne that we know,' Mick gasped.

Sally watched proudly as Anne neared the car. 'You have no idea how much persuasion it took to convince her the dress was perfect for her. She's just not used to dressing up.'

Getting out of the car, Sally held the door open for her. 'Oh, Anne, you look lovely.'

'So do you, Sal.' Anne admired Sally's tight-fitting blue dress. Low on the neckline and drawn in at the waist, it swirled out at the skirt. Her pretty blue shoes and bag topped it all off.

When they were settled in the car, Mick drove off. 'I must be the luckiest man ever,' he said. 'I've got the two loveliest ladies right here in my car. When we walk into that room, they'll all be asking, "Where did that ugly devil manage to find those two beauties?"'

Sally kissed him on the cheek. 'You're not an ugly devil. And we're proud to be with you.' She turned to Anne. 'Isn't that right, Anne?'

Anne kissed him as well. 'We're the lucky ones.'

'Mmm,' he laughed, 'you're only saying that because it's true.'

Sally turned round to ask if Anne was all right.

Sally had persuaded her out of her shell, and Anne could not be more grateful. 'I'm glad you made me change my mind about not going to the dance,' she said. 'I'm really looking forward to it now.'

'Good!' Sally was excited. 'Just for tonight, put everything else out of your mind, and enjoy yourself.'

'I will, I promise.'

In this moment, here with Mick and Sal, and wearing a dress she would never have imagined herself in, Anne felt very special, and more excited than she had been for a long time.

When she'd been locking the front door, however, for one fleeting second, Edward Carter crept into her mind. There'd been the slightest, unsettling niggle at the back of her mind that when she came home, he would be there, waiting for her.

But then she'd reminded herself that he was in prison, where he belonged, and that very soon, if all went well, she would be free of him for ever. All these years she had been afraid to stir up the muddy waters, but now that she had started proceedings against him, she felt optimistic. She would not completely rest easy, though, until she'd secured the official papers on which it was written in black and white that she was no longer Mrs Edward Carter.

Twenty minutes later, they arrived at the club. Music blared into the night, indicating that the party was already underway.

'Here we are!' Sally was already twirling as she got out of the car. 'Time to enjoy the evening.'

As Anne followed her two friends into the crowded hall, she reminded herself of what Sally had told her: tonight was her night. It was a night for fun and laughter, with no regrets.

Inside the club, Tony McDonald had been watching for her. When he saw her coming in through the door, he could hardly believe his eyes. She looked so lovely. But then, he thought, she always looked lovely.

Anne saw him striding towards her. For one split second, she almost turned away. But something held her there; maybe his smile, or his genuine delight at seeing her.

Whatever it was, she waited for him. They chatted a while, during which his easy manner made her feel comfortable.

Later, when he swept her onto the dance floor, she went willingly into his arms.

While they danced, he held her tight, and whispered soft endearments in her ear.

Afterwards, they walked out into the terraced garden, where they strolled and talked, getting to know each other. 'I'm so glad you changed your mind,' he said. 'Right up to the minute I saw you walk through the door, I wasn't sure whether I would see you tonight.'

When he reached out to take hold of her hand, she drew away, all her old fears coming back to torment her. 'I'm sorry, Tony . . .'

'What's wrong?' He thought they'd been getting on so well. 'Have I said something to upset you?'

'No. It isn't anything you've done,' she assured him. 'It's just that I'm not looking for a relationship. If I gave you that impression, I really didn't mean to.'

'Look, Anne, I think you already know how much I like you, but I'm not looking for a close relationship either. To tell you the truth, I've only recently come out of a bad situation, and I'm still carrying the scars.' His ready smile was reassuring.

'Oh! I'm sorry if I jumped to conclusions, but the truth is, I need to steer well clear of getting involved with anyone. I don't want to give you any wrong signals . . . if you know what I mean?'

'I hear what you're saying, and I understand.'

'Thank you.' When he smiled down on her, her heart did a little skip. She was both excited and afraid; and ready to flee at the slightest opportunity.

'I'd best go and find Mick and Sal.' Her heart urged her to stay but her head warned her off. 'They'll be wondering where I am.'

Without waiting for an acknowledgement, she hurried away.

She located Sally at the bar, sipping a glass of red wine.

Mick was nearby, talking with the store manager.

Sally turned and saw Anne rushing towards her. 'Where've you been? One minute you were here and then you were gone.'

She noticed Tony McDonald coming in from the terrace. 'Oh, I see.' She gave a naughty wink. 'You've been hobnobbing with the good-looking side of management.'

Anne laughed. 'And you've had one drink too many, by the look of you.'

Sally would not be silenced. 'I want to hear all the juicy gossip.' Taking her drink in one hand, she linked arms with Anne, marching her across the floor to the nearest free table. 'Right, my girl! Spill the beans. I know you've been outside with Tony, so what happened? Did he make a play for you? Was he the perfect gentleman?'

Anne was shocked. 'Ssh! He'll hear you. And yes, for your information, he was a perfect gentleman.'

'Well, that's a pity.' She gave a telltale hiccup. 'I expected him to be a bit more daring that that. One little kiss at least.'

'Well, you expected wrong because there were no kisses, and no canoodling. We just talked.'

'Aw, Anne, I'm sorry.'

'Why? I'm not.' Though in a secretive way, she wondered what it might feel like for Tony to kiss her. But as soon as she thought it, she blocked it from her mind.

'I'll get you a cuppa coffee,' she told Sally. 'Sober you up a bit.'

'Are you saying I'm drunk?'

'No.'

'Right! Then, I'll have another glass of wine. This one's half empty.'

'Oh, no, you don't.' Mick arrived to collect her into his arms. 'You owe your neglected husband a dance.' With a knowng wink to Anne, he swept his wife onto the dance floor.

Anne watched them for a while. She saw how happy they were, and she was genuinely glad for them.

At the same time she wondered why she had chosen a man like Edward Carter. And yet, thinking back, she realised it was he who had chosen her.

Remembering how it was, her mood dropped. Feeling angry with herself, she grabbed up Sally's half-empty wineglass and drank it down in one go.

'Wow! Somebody was thirsty!' Tony McDonald smiled down on her. 'Would it be OK if I sat next to you?'

Taken by surprise, Anne gestured to the furthest chair. 'You're very welcome.'

'Aren't you worried I might pounce on you?' His smile was infectious.

Anne felt foolish. 'Just now, out there . . . what I said, it didn't mean that I don't like you –' the wine was taking an effect – 'because I do. It's just that . . .' She took a deep breath. 'When I was too young and foolish, I trusted a man and I got badly hurt.'

'I understand.' Like Anne, he had not been successful where love and happiness were concerned. 'Sometimes we get swept away with the idea that we'll be happy ever after, but it doesn't always turn out that way. I'm sure it happens to everybody at some time or another.'

'You're right! It's not just me, is it? He was good-looking and charming, and he promised me the world. But he turned out to be a liar and a bully.' She gave a sorry little giggle. 'I wasn't to know what he was really like.'

Sensing a deep confession of sorts, and realising she was not used to the wine, Tony felt like an eavesdropper and decided to bring the conversation to a halt. Getting out of his chair, he rounded the table, slid his hand through hers and bent to whisper in her ear, 'Let's you and me take to the dance floor, shall we?'

'Good idea!' Anne saw a man she might be able to trust; a man who had done nothing wrong. 'Why not? Yes, I'd like that.' And she allowed him to whisk her away again.

Waiting for the music to resume, Mick saw the two of them making their way across the room. 'Looks like Anne has a very keen dancing partner,' he told Sally.

Merry from the wine, Sally waved at Anne, who shyly

put up a hand. 'I'm glad for her,' she told Mick. 'Tony seems to be a decent sort.'

She watched as Tony led Anne into the waltz. She saw how intimately close he held her, and how Anne easily melted into his embrace.

Yet somewhere in the back of her mind, she sincerely hoped that, for the moment at least, Anne would not be drawn in too deep.

PART FOUR

~

Thrown to the Wolves

1957

CHAPTER THIRTEEN

PHIL CLIMBED OFF the bus and started to walk down the road, but he stopped on seeing Adam stitting on a wall at the corner of the street. Adam was so deeply preoccupied with his thoughts, he didn't see Phil heading towards him. He continued to swing his legs, his face looking down and his gaze drawn to the pavement.

Phil was concerned that it was not the first time he'd seen the boy looking so dejected, although whenever he asked Adam if things were all right the same answer was always given with a bright smile: 'Yes, Phil. Don't worry, I'm fine.'

Phil knew he had to be careful. The very last thing he wanted was to stir things up with Miss Martin, and he would never do that, unless he was absolutely certain there was something not right with Adam's situation.

On the other hand, Phil had wondered whether the problem could just be something straightforward, and therefore nothing to worry about. It might be that Adam was still struggling to feel comfortable in his new circumstances.

After all, this new family situation was all very strange to him. It could be that it was taking him longer to settle in than anyone had anticipated.

Phil himself was still fretting because the authorities had flatly turned him down when he offered to take the boy. And whatever he said, they always had a well-rehearsed answer, all tied up in red tape.

Phil had told them, 'You should ask Adam what he wants.' And they assured him it did not work that way.

So, he made up his mind to do the next best thing. He promised both himself and Adam that he would never be far away, and that he would see him as often as the Dexters allowed. It was the only alternative he could offer.

Fortunately, the Dexters had been as good as their word. They had allowed Phil and Adam time enough to be together, to go fishing and walking, and making the regular pilgrimage to the churchyard.

Occasionally, in her own free time, the lovely Polly from the children's home would join them. That was an extra treat for Adam, and especially for Phil, who always looked forward to her company.

To all appearances, Adam was well looked after in the Dexter household. He now had a wardrobe of smart clothes, a fast Raleigh bicycle in the garden shed, and a small amount of pocket money each week. He looked well, and he was growing fast.

Having turned thirteen a short time before he left

the children's home, Adam still had that lean, lolloping gait of a young boy, and that recognisable, ever-untidy crop of brown hair.

Adam had spent two separate visits with the Dexters before approval on both sides was achieved. The next step required formalising the necessary paperwork, along with choosing a school and securing his name on the local doctor's list.

That done, Adam was now a more permanent member of the Dexter family, which included Buster the dog, who had welcomed him with open paws.

With all this running through his mind, Phil slowed his pace. Still unseen by Adam, he took time to study the boy before he should look up and see him approaching.

On his last visit, a week ago, Phil had reason to be concerned. Throughout their wanderings, Adam had very few words to say, and he was distant in his thoughts.

When Phil discreetly questioned Adam, he again assured him that everything was all right. And so, for the moment, he had to be content.

Now, though, he was learning a great deal from Adam's body language, and Phil could see a very unhappy boy. He noticed the way Adam was hanging his head and looking down, as though lost in thought. His shoulders were deeply hunched and there was an air of dejection about him.

He felt troubled. Something wasn't right, and somehow or other, without upsetting anyone, he meant to get to the root of it.

Just then, Adam glanced up, and when he saw Phil,

his face lit up. 'Phil!' Leaping off the wall, he ran up the road, whooping and hollering. 'I've been waiting for you, Phil!'

Adam's excitement was a joy to the old man; so much so that he had tears in his eyes. *They should have let me take him home,* he thought angrily. *Me and Adam, we'd have been just fine. It's true that I might never see sixty again, but I'm not ready for the scrapheap just yet!* His own dear father had lived to be a sprightly ninety years old, and still walked the countryside right up to the day he died.

Adam launched himself at Phil, who was almost knocked off balance. 'Steady on, son!' Catching Adam to his chest, he laughed out loud. 'You nearly knocked the stuffing outta me!'

Adam was so excited, he couldn't stop talking. 'I'm glad you're here,' he confided. 'I've been sitting on the wall for ages. I thought you would never come. I was beginning to get worried.'

'Well, you've no right to be getting worried!'

Taking out his old pocket watch, Phil checked it. 'I'm not late. You should know what time I usually get here on a Saturday morning.'

Adam apologised. 'I know, but it seems like I've been waiting ages, and I was beginning to think you'd never get here. I'm really looking forward to us going across the fields, Phil. I've even got my wellies ready and everything.'

Hoisting his trouser leg up to the ankle, Phil pointed out, 'See there? I've got my new walking boots on, so it seems we're both set for a good old trek.'

When Adam asked why he hadn't got his loyal little

dog with him, Phil explained, 'It's a pity, but since he sliced his paw on that broken bottle down at Badgers Den, the vet said it's best if he doesn't run about. He'll be all right, though. Pat from next door is keeping an eye on him while I'm out.'

He rolled his eyes in frustration. 'She treats him like a baby, and he laps it up, like you would not believe.' Laughing out loud, he confessed, 'I reckon she'd do the same to me, given half a chance!'

Adam innocently remarked how Phil would not want to take up with Pat because, 'You like Polly, don't you?'

Phil was shaken by Adam's observation. 'Well, of course I do. We both do, don't we? Polly is good company.' He added firmly, 'She's also a good friend, to the pair of us.'

He was shocked that Adam had latched onto his fondness for Polly. In future, he would need to be careful, although just now, talking about Polly had brought a warm flush to his old heart.

Side by side, they went down the street together, chatting like the old friends they were, and laughing out loud when Phil described his little dog's antics. 'Rex howled at the window when I set off, but Pat called him back for a juicy bone. It didn't take long for him to choose the bone over me, the little traitor!'

As they approached the Dexters' front gate, Phil had a question. 'Adam, will you be honest with me, son?'

Anticipating the same question that he'd answered last week and the week before, Adam replied with a question of his own. 'Phil! Are you're still worrying about me?'

'Is there any reason why I should worry?'

'No reason at all.' Adam felt uncomfortable. Normally, he would confide in Phil, but on this particular issue, he thought it best if he tried to deal with the situation himself.

A minute later, with Phil going at a steady pace and Adam running ahead, they arrived at the house.

'While you're getting yourself organised, I'll have a quick word with the woman of the house.' He still felt unable to refer to Liz Dexter as Adam's mum.

'But I am "organised",' Adam protested. 'I've been ready for a good hour.'

'Ah! But have you got all your stuff together?'

'What "stuff"?'

'Well, let's see. You'll need a coat in case the weather turns. I've got a full flask, and sandwiches enough for two.' He pointed to the canvas bag he was carrying. 'So we're all right for food and drink, and if we're in need of a treat on the way back there's always an ice-cream cart at the foot of Brent Hill.' He added the most important item to the list: 'Oh, and you'll need your fishing gear.'

'I thought you said we weren't going fishing today?'

'Well, we might, and in any case, it never hurts to be prepared for a change of plan.'

Adam heartily agreed.

As always, Liz Dexter was delighted to see him. 'Phil! Oh, come in. You've time for a cuppa, haven't you? It won't take me a minute. You timed it right, because the kettle's just boiled.'

She led him into the sitting room. 'Make yourself comfortable. I'll be back before you know it.'

Adam ran along the passageway towards the back door. 'I'll just go and sort out the fishing tackle.'

Phil was quietly pleased, because he certainly did not want Adam sitting in while he was talking to Liz. 'We're all right for time,' he called back to Adam. 'There's no rush. Liz is making me a nice cuppa tea.'

As good as her word, Liz was soon back with a tray laden with teapot, cups and saucers, and a plate of shortcake biscuits. 'Help yourself, Phil.' Carefully pouring the tea, she left Phil to add his own milk and sugar. 'So, how's the little dog's paw?' Adam had told her about that the week before.

'Thank you, yes, it's healing well.'

'Oh, I'm glad. It's awful when they're hurt. They look at you with their big, sorry eyes and there's nothing you can do but follow the vet's advice. We had that with Buster last year. He got a thorn in his paw and we didn't even notice it; not until he started limping. By that time, it was infected. The vet confined him to the house and yard. Poor Buster. He was so miserable.' She added casually, 'Jim and Alice took him for a walk. Goodness knows where they've gone, because that was over an hour ago.'

Phil took a long invigorating gulp of his tea before opening the all-important conversation. 'Mrs Dexter, can I ask you something before Adam comes in?'

'Of course you can. But I'd be happier if you'd call me Liz.'

Politely passing over this comment, Phil asked, 'I was just wondering, do you know if Adam is worried about anything?'

'No.' She seemed genuinely surprised. 'Not that I know of. Whatever makes you ask that?'

Phil was careful not to alarm her. 'Oh, it's nothing in particular. It's just that when we were out last week, he was quieter than usual. And just now, when he was sitting on the wall waiting for me, he seemed to be deep in thought.'

Liz was concerned. 'He hasn't said anything to me, and I haven't noticed anything untoward with him.'

Phil was relieved. 'Maybe it's just me. I'm well known for being an old fusspot. That's what comes of keeping a fatherly eye on the youngsters from school.'

Realising he was genuinely worried, Liz made a suggestion. 'It could be that Adam is still finding things a bit overwhelming. Just think of what he's been through, what with the sad loss of his mother and all that terrible business about his father. To be honest I'm not even sure it was right to bring Adam into it, but the authorities claimed they were duty-bound to speak with him.'

Phil harboured the very same sentiments. 'I expect they went by the book. Matters of that sort can be a minefield, if they get it wrong.'

'Yes, I suppose so. But then, as if that wasn't enough to be going on with, he had not long started at a new school and, as far as I know, he hasn't yet made any friends. Then there are all the other intrusions into his young life. Goodness! It's enough to unsettle anyone, let alone a young boy.'

'Yes, of course, you're right.' Phil agreed. 'It's a lot to deal with at his age.'

'It certainly is, though Jim and I think he's coped magnificently. But of course you never can tell how it's affected him inside. But we do talk about these things privately. And we try to keep him busy and make sure he gets plenty of recreation. Jim started teaching him the rudiments of golf, but Adam didn't take to it at all.'

Phil was partly reassured. 'So, do you really think I'm worrying about nothing?'

'Yes. I would say so, Phil. Being fostered into a new family is daunting for anyone. Adam needs time to adjust. But, rest assured, he's doing all right.' She confided, 'Adam and I have an agreement that if he's ever worried about anything at all, he would tell me.'

'That's good.'

Feeling easier, though not altogether convinced, Phil took another long sip of his tea. 'By! I must say, you do know how to make a satisfying cup of tea.'

The sound of the back door being opened heralded the return of Adam, complete with two fishing rods, a basket to sit on, and a small, narrow cart for carrying the load.

Phil was impressed. 'That's a fancy little cart, I must say.'

'Jim made it for him,' Liz declared proudly. 'He even measured the fishing rods so that everything would fit in. It's light and sturdy, so it's easily wheeled over uneven ground.'

Phil got up to take a closer look. 'Well, I never! That'll take the weight and no mistake.'

'I'll pull it,' Adam decided.

Phil was all smiles as he told Liz, 'Let's hope me and Adam catch enough fish to give you a feast at dinnertime.'

A short time later, she waved them off. 'Mind how you go.'

She watched as they went down the street, heading for the bottom lane, which led directly to open countryside. From there it was a ten-minute walk to the canal.

'You might cross paths with Jim and Alice on your way,' she called out as they rounded the corner.

Adam responded with a cheery wave of his hand, but his heart sank at her parting words.

'All right, are you, son?' Phil asked, sensing a sharp change in Adam's mood.

'Yes, Phil. I'm really looking forward to our outing.'

What he was *not* looking forward to, however, was crossing paths with Alice.

~

As it happened, they did not see hide nor hair of Jim and Alice.

Phil was happiest when he and Adam were spending time together. They chatted and laughed, and when they sat down to do a bit of fishing, Adam confided that he really liked Liz and Jim.

'They're so kind and thoughtful,' he said. 'They don't treat me like a baby. They talk to me as if my opinion really matters, and they never force me to do anything I don't want to do . . .' his mood darkened at that point, '. . . not like my father did.'

Phil wisely let him talk on, and eventually, in one unguarded moment, Adam revealed something alarming. 'Alice doesn't like me,' he told Phil. 'She hates me being there.'

'Really?' Phil was taken aback. 'What makes you say that?'

Adam shrugged. 'I just know, that's all.'

'Has Alice actually said she doesn't want you there?'

'Not yet, no.'

'So has she done anything to make you feel she resents you?'

'Not really.'

'So, you could be wrong . . . couldn't you?'

Growing impatient, Adam drew his fishing line out of the water and looked Phil in the eye. 'I'm not wrong, Phil. Alice hates me. She wants me out! And even if she doesn't say it, she tells me in other ways . . . like the time she left a frog in my bed. When I tackled her about it, she laughed in my face. She said it was a joke, but I know it wasn't.'

He glanced about nervously. 'Sometimes she follows me about. It's like she thinks I'm looking to steal something. She makes me feel uncomfortable, Phil. She does it on purpose, because she doesn't want me there.'

For a long, awkward moment after Adam's heated revelation, neither spoke. Adam flicked the line back into the water, and continued fishing as though nothing had happened, while Phil pondered upon the anger in Adam's face when he'd spoken of Alice.

He tried to allay Adam's fears. 'Listen to me, son. It might not be what you think. Girls have a habit of playing tricks. It's just their way. They seem to get a laugh out of it, but I'm sure it doesn't mean she wants you out.'

Adam gave another shrug. 'Well, it feels like it to me.'

'But she's never actually said it to your face, has she?'

'No, but she will. I just know it.'

Phil continued to smooth over the situation. 'It might just be that she's a bit jealous of you.'

'Why would she be jealous of me? What is there to be jealous of? She's far better off than I am. She's got her mother and father. And she's got a little sister. Before I came to live there, Alice had them all to herself.'

'Ah! Well, there you go. I think you've hit the nail on the head.'

'What do you mean?'

'That could be why she's playing tricks on you. Maybe she's jealous. Like you said, before you came along, she had her family all to herself, and now she has to share them with you. Like when Jim gave you a lesson in playing golf, she might have felt a bit left out.'

Phil felt for the boy, but he could also see Alice's side. 'The tricks she played on you, they didn't do you any real harm, did they?'

'Don't suppose.'

'So, maybe you should try and forgive her. Just like you, she's trying to adjust to a new and strange situation. She might be worried that the family haven't got enough love and attention for all of you, and that she might be the one to lose out. It doesn't mean she wants you out of the house. It just means she's desperately trying to hold on to what she's got. It's difficult for her . . . as it must be for you. So can you understand what I'm trying to say, Adam?'

Torn in his thoughts, Adam chose not to answer.

Phil persevered. 'Listen, Adam, try not to worry about it. She's just a little girl, playing silly, childish pranks. It's probably all very innocent.' He lightened the atmosphere with a throaty chuckle. 'You'll find out soon enough that women and girls have a very strange sense of humour compared to us men.'

Adam was curious. 'How d'you mean, Phil?'

'Oh, yes. It's a well-known fact. Women and girls are not at all like men and boys. They get all these silly, immature ideas, and sometimes, no matter how hard we try, us men don't know what to make of 'em.'

He was pleased to see a smile on Adam's face. 'Try and ignore it if you can, son. I reckon she'll soon get fed up of playing tricks.'

He thought it wise for the moment to play down the business of Alice. At least now he had a plausible reason for Adam's sorry little moods.

Though he'd advised Adam otherwise, Phil wondered if the boy might be right. Maybe, Alice really did want him out of the house. If that was so, and it wasn't nipped in the bud quick enough, there might be a real danger that the situation could escalate.

He wondered if he might have a word with Jim and Liz Dexter, but then he instantly thought better of it, because there was still a chance that it really was innocent game play on their daughter's part.

Over the next couple of hours, Phil and Adam enjoyed each other's company. Adam caught three fish, and seemed more like his old self. He made no further mention of Alice and her little tricks, and Phil decided to let sleeping dogs lie. For the moment, he turned his thoughts to giving the boy a memorable outing.

Having secured a good catch of fat, juicy fish, the two of them washed their hands in the water, and wiped them on the towel Phil had thoughtfully put in his old canvas bag.

Then they set about enjoying their sandwiches, before heading back.

'Can we go the long way back?' Adam liked that particular route. 'We can get an ice cream and stop at the ruins.'

Phil had no objection whatsoever. In fact, he was about to suggest it himself.

It wasn't long before they arrived at the ice-cream van.

Parked beside the canal, the van and its colourful owner were a welcome sight to any weary traveller.

'Hello, you two!' Dressed in his blue-and-white-striped overall, the ruddy-faced man was a familiar figure hereabouts. 'Been fishing, I see?' His beady little eyes latched onto the two fishing rods protruding from the cart. 'Hello! What's that contraption, then?'

'It's a purpose-made fishing cart.' Phil liked to wind him up. 'Good grief, have you never seen a fishing cart before?'

'No. Can't say I have. Is it any good?'

'Well, o' course it is. That little cart is carrying two

bags, two nets, a haul of fish and two fishing rods. So you tell me if it's any good.'

'Hmm!' Leaning forward, he peered so hard over the counter, the other two were sure he would fall out. 'I wouldn't mind one o' them for myself. In my spare time I like to do a bit of fishing, but I reckon you could use that little cart for anything and everything.'

'That's my thoughts exactly!' Phil said.

'Oh, yes! I could use that little cart to carry the vegetables home from the allotment. I've got a good strong wheelbarrow, and it's served me very well over the years but it's only got the one wheel and it gets stuck in the ruts when it's wet underfoot. That little cart, with its four wheels, is perfect for the job. So tell me, how much did it cost?'

'Jim Dexter made it,' Adam answered. 'He drew up a plan, then he measured the rods, and he built the cart in his garage.'

The ice-cream man was really impressed. 'Does he sell 'em?'

Now it was Phil's turn. 'He might.'

'Well, if you let me know how much he charges, I might buy one. I know one or two friends up the allotments who would love a little cart like that, too. Does it fold up so's you can hang it in the shed?'

'He can make them any way you want,' Phil said. 'We'll have a word with him and we'll let you know.'

The ice-cream man was so thankful he refused to take payment for two large, chocolate-topped cornets.

'That's what you call drumming up business.' Phil felt proud as he and Adam set off, happily enjoying the biggest ice creams ever, which were all the more tasty because they were free. 'By, I reckon Jim could make himself a small fortune with that little cart.'

On the way home, Adam seemed content enough. When they reached the house, Phil was pleased to see how Adam ran on in front, as though he couldn't wait to tell Jim about the interest his cart had created.

It was as though the worrying conversation about Alice and her pranks had never happened.

Being a belt-and-braces man, however, Phil decided to keep Adam's comments firmly in the back of his mind.

Jim was home. When Adam told him about the ice-cream man and the interest he'd shown in the cart, Jim was most impressed. 'Well, isn't that a turn-up for the book?'

He told Phil how he came to build it. 'Whichever way you look at it, those fishing rods can be a bit awkward to carry,' he said. 'I just thought the cart would make life easier for the two of you, when you're off on your treks.'

Phil thanked him. 'Well, it certainly made an impression,' he said. 'We even got two free cornets.'

'Yes!' Adam spoke up. 'Extra large, they were, with chocolate on top an' all.'

Jim was bemused. 'Maybe I should copyright the design for the future, for when I'm old and worn and I need an income on the side.'

Liz playfully thumped him. 'Don't say that! You'll never be old and worn in my eyes.'

She asked Phil if he'd like to stay to dinner, 'being as you and Adam caught the fish?'

Phil respectfully declined. 'I promised I'd be back by a certain time. Pat, my next-door neighbour, very kindly offered to look after the dog till I get back.'

Liz understood. 'Another time then?'

Phil thanked her. 'Yes, another time. I'd like that.'

'Good! Meantime, you must take the biggest of the catch home to Pat as a thank-you for looking after your little dog . . . Rex, isn't it?'

'That's right. I think I told you . . . I named him after my late father because they've got the same straggly beard.'

Liz chuckled. 'Well, I'm sure Rex would love a bit of fresh fish as well, don't you think?' Without waiting for an answer, she hurried into the kitchen to sort out the biggest fish in the catch.

A short time later, with the fish gutted, cleaned and packed up, Adam accompanied Phil to the bus stop.

'Tomorrow's Sunday,' Adam reminded him. 'I've already got Mum's flowers.'

Phil had not forgotten. 'You're a good boy, Adam. You never forget, do you?'

'No.' Adam's voice shook. 'And I don't forget what Edward Carter did to her.'

Phil understood Adam's bitterness, but nonetheless, he was saddened. 'Justice prevailed and he's being made to pay for his wickedness.' He knew that was not much consolation to Adam.

'I know how hard it must be . . . impossible, even, for you to put him behind you,' Phil told Adam. 'At the same time, I would be distressed if the rest of your life was overshadowed by a man who does not deserve one minute of your thoughts.'

Adam hardened his heart. 'I hate him. He hurt my mother so bad. It's his fault she died.'

'I understand how you feel, Adam. All the same, I'm sure your mother would not want you to spend your life filled with hate and revenge. Nothing good will ever come of it. And besides, if there's any justice at all, Edward Carter will spend the rest of his life behind bars.'

Adam was not convinced. 'I want him to suffer, like he made my mum suffer! I want him to hurt, and be afraid, just like she was.' His voice shook. 'Even if he's in prison, he's still alive, but my mum is in the churchyard.'

When Adam fell silent, Phil feared the boy would never feel any different. But then, why should he? After the shocking ordeal that both he and his mother had gone through at the hands of a maniac, the memories would stay with Adam for ever.

Phil wisely changed the subject. 'I must say your mum would have loved the many bunches of pretty pink flowers you've bought her over time.'

Adam glowed with pride. 'Pink is Mum's favourite colour.'

'I know, son.' Many times he'd watched Adam lovingly arrange the pink flowers in the memorial case, and he did it with such tenderness it always brought a tear to Phil's old eyes.

'Now then, Adam, don't forget to keep the flowers in water overnight. I'll be round here to collect you about midday tomorrow. We'll place your mum's flowers first, then we'll use that little hand spade we hid behind the trees, and we'll tidy round where the rabbits keep digging. After that, we'll go down to the canal and feed the ducklings. I've got half a loaf going stale at home. We'll break it down, throw it in, and before you know it, the ducklings will come out of nowhere and there won't be a single crumb left. So, what do you think? After we've been to the churchyard, would you like to go to the canal?'

'Yes, Phil. I really would.'

'Me too.'

For now, at least, Phil thought the change of conversation had rid Adam's mind of Carter. Though like Adam, Phil firmly believed that such a man should be made to pay the ultimate price for the shocking things he had done.

~

As they made their way up the street, Phil and Adam had no idea they were being watched.

Hidden from view at her bedroom window, Alice followed their progress. When the other two were out of sight, she turned away from the window. Grabbing her doll, she hugged it tight to her chest. 'Don't worry. After he's gone it will be just like it was before.' The idea made her smile.

Collecting the tiny hairbrush from the dressing table, she sang softly as she brushed the doll's long, auburn tresses.

Downstairs, with the dinner almost ready, Liz and Jim were enjoying a few minutes playing with Harriet when they heard Alice singing.

'She sounds happy,' Liz commented.

'That's because she knows we're going out for an hour or so after dinner. She seems to enjoy Maureen coming round.' Jim smiled at the baby. 'See that? It comes to something when your own daughter thinks more of the babysitter than she does her parents!'

Liz laughed. 'Don't be silly!'

'Oh, well, whatever makes her happy.'

He made a monkey-face at the baby. 'Listen to me, Harriet! Don't *you* go shifting your affections to the babysitter, will you? Can you hear your sister singing like a canary because Mummy and Daddy are going out? Most kids would be grumbling, but not our Alice.'

Using two fingers to create long donkey ears above his head, he waggled them at the baby, who stared at him with big eyes.

Liz had to smile. 'Stop it, you big kid! You're frightening her.'

Just then, little Harriet laughed out loud and Jim was forgiven, though there was something else playing on Liz's mind.

'Jim?'

'Yes, sweetheart?' He looked up and paid attention.

'Have you noticed anything different with Adam?'

'In what way?'

'I mean . . . do you think he's happy, here with us?'

'Hmm! That's an odd thing to ask. Yes, I think he's happy enough. I reckon he's fitted into this family really well. But what's brought this on? Has something happened? Has Adam said anything?'

'No! In fact, he never does say how he feels. I was just wondering, that's all.'

'Well, I think he's very happy here with us. Maybe the fact that he doesn't say anything about how he feels, actually means that he's content, and that's all we need to know. So, stop fretting. Adam is an important part of this family now, and as far as I'm concerned, he's our son, in all but name. If he was unhappy for whatever reason, I believe he would confide in one of us.'

'That's what I thought.' Liz was greatly relieved.

'There you are then. You've answered your own question.'

From the landing, Alice was disturbed by the conversation she'd overheard. So, Adam was a son in all but name?

Silently tiptoeing back to her bedroom, she closed the door behind her.

Half an hour later, Liz called, 'Alice! Dinner's nearly ready, sweetheart. Maureen will be here soon.'

A few minutes later, Alice came into the room.

'Goodness! You've been up there a long time, Alice.' Jim was curious. 'So, what have you been up to?'

'Nothing much. Just brushing my dolly's hair.'

Liz gave her a hug. 'You did remember Maureen's coming to look after you later, didn't you?'

'Yes.'

'And you're all right with that, are you?' As if she needed to ask.

'Yes, Mum. I like Maureen.'

'Maureen will probably bring a selection of puzzles and such. So the three of you should have a good time.

I'll have Harriet already fed and changed. She'll be that sleepy, I'm certain she'll be no trouble.'

Alice smiled sweetly. 'If she cries I'll rock her pram and she'll go back to sleep. I've done it before.'

'I'm sure you won't need to do that,' Liz said. 'Maureen is well versed in what to do. Harriet's been crawling all over the place today, so she'll probably sleep well. I wouldn't be at all surprised if she started taking her first steps very soon.'

Jim winked at Alice, admiring the pink ribbon in her hair. 'You look very pretty, Alice.'

'Thank you, Daddy.'

'Would you rather we didn't go out tonight?' She seemed unsually quiet, he thought.

'No! You and Mummy go and enjoy yourselves. Me and Maureen will be fine.'

'And Adam . . . don't forget him.'

'I won't.' She gave a slight nod of the head.

'You know we'll only be gone for a couple of hours, don't you?'

'Yes, and it's all right, Daddy,' Alice assured him brightly. 'You and Mummy don't have to worry about us. Maureen always takes care of us very well.'

'Thank you, sweetheart.' Thinking how Alice was sometimes like a little woman in her manner, Liz returned to the kitchen to collect the condiments. Alice had made her smile. Talk about an old head on young shoulders.

On returning to the table, Liz sat herself down. 'Come on, Alice. Tuck in.' Apart from Adam's meal, which was warming in the oven, everything was served.

Alice's meal was already set before her: boiled baby

carrots, buttered mashed potatoes, and a slice of pink, juicy fish, gently cooked in milk, the way Alice liked it.

'We've got Adam and Phil to thank for this lovely fish meal.'

Liz made the casual remark as Adam arrived to seat himself next to Jim. It wasn't long before he was ravenously tucking in.

'Woah! Slow down, son.' Jim was surprised.

'Sorry,' Adam apologised, 'but I'm really hungry.'

'I expect that's all the fresh air,' Liz suggested. 'Still, you don't want to give yourself indigestion, do you?'

Realising he'd been wolfing his food, Adam slowed down. 'Sorry.'

Jim playfully ruffled his hair. 'Aw, that's all right, Adam. I was the same when I was your age. I remember after we'd been out playing footie, me and my brother would run home, cram our food down, and be off out again, before anyone else had finished.'

The meal continued in a civilised if lively manner. There was much laughter at Jim's descriptions of his boyhood pranks, particularly the one about the time when he'd gone home with the bottom of his pants worn clean through, where he and his mates had spent the morning racing each other down the slide.

When the meal was over, Liz noticed that Alice had eaten everything except the fish, which was pushed to the side of her plate.

'What's wrong, sweetheart? You've always liked fish.'

'Well, I don't any more.'

'Really?' Liz glanced at Jim, 'And why's that then?'

Alice shrugged. 'I just don't, that's all.'

Jim sensed an underlying atmosphere. 'That's OK, Alice.' He smiled. 'You're allowed to change your mind.' Though, like Liz, he thought Alice was being unusually picky, for some reason.

By the time Maureen arrived, Jim and Liz were all dressed up and raring to meet up with their friends at the local pub, which was just a ten-minute walk from the house.

Liz wore her new red dress, while Jim looked every inch the sportsman in his dark trousers and black blazer with the darts club badge on the pocket.

'You're dressed a bit severe for a pint and a game of darts, aren't you?' Liz joked.

'No, I am not! I intend for our team to win,' he declared, 'so I thought I'd put on the gear.'

He did a twirl on the spot and was dead pleased when Adam told him proudly, 'You look really good.'

'Thank you, Adam. So, what do you think, Alice? Do you agree with Mummy, or do you agree with Adam?'

'I agree with Mummy.' There was no way she was about to agree with Adam.

'Well, I'm afraid you women are wrong.' Jim placed a kiss on the top of her head. 'To be a winner, you have to look the part, and I think I do. So this time, the men have it!'

After going through the usual check list with Maureen, Jim and Liz started off up the street, with Alice waving them off at the door.

'Have a good time,' she called.

'We will!' Liz called back.

'And don't be late, will you?' Alice reminded them.

'We won't.' Jim replied, and he had an instruction of his own: 'Alice! Go back inside and lock the door.' He waited for Alice to do as she was bid.

He thought it amusing how Alice had seen them off, so concerned and caring. 'When did it swing the other way?' he asked Liz.

'What d'you mean?'

Jim gave a whimsical little smile. 'Alice, just now. She's nine years old, and there she was, standing at the door, telling us to have a good time and not to be late home.'

Liz agreed. 'You're right. It's like we're the kids and Alice is the concerned parent.'

'She's always been like a little woman, though,' Jim said. 'Always so fussy and protective of her family.'

Liz laughed out loud. 'She's always been a little bossy boots!'

'Well, there you are. Now then, will you please stop creating things to worry about. We have a wonderful baby, a bossy young daughter, with an old head on her shoulders, a fine son, who fits into our family like a hand in a glove, and a dog called Buster, who rules the roost.'

Greatly reassured by his wise words, Liz gave him a quick kiss on the mouth. From now on, instead of looking for things to be anxious about, she would remind herself of how fortunate they were.

CHAPTER FOURTEEN

FOR THE BEST part of an hour, Maureen and the children played on the mat with big coloured balls. It was really a game for baby Harriet, who, with screeches of laughter, rolled the balls haphazardly back and forth to the others, while Buster the dog looked on, too lazy to get up and play along.

'Where's Adam?' Maureen asked. 'I haven't seen him since your parents went out.'

Alice simply shrugged her shoulders, as she often did to avoid answering a particular question.

Maureen was concerned. 'Alice, can you keep an eye on Harriet for just a minute,' she asked, 'while I go and see if he's upstairs?'

Scrambling to her feet, she collected Harriet and placed her in the baby pen, but as she went to leave the room Alice called out, 'He's not upstairs.'

'So, where is he then?'

'He's in the shed. He asked Daddy if he could paint

the little cart, and Daddy said yes.' A deep frown betrayed her disapproval.

A few minutes later, Maureen found Adam busy in the garden shed. 'Hi, Adam. I thought I'd come and see if you were OK.'

'Hi, Maureen. Look, what do you think?' He proudly pointed to the cart, all wet and shiny in its brand-new coat of dark stain.

'Great! Looks like you're doing a good job.'

'Did you want me for anything special?' Adam asked.

'No. I just wondered where you were, that's all.'

'Oh, I'm sorry. I should have told you, but I just wanted to come straight in here and get on with it. I'd like to fnish it before they come back. I'm hoping it'll be a nice surprise.'

'I'm sure it will.' Maureen excused herself. 'Now I know you're all right, I'd best go and sort the girls out.'

'Call if you need me for anything.'

'Thanks.' Maureen did not intend taking him up on his offer of help. She had always seen herself as more than capable.

An hour later, with Harriet still happily playing in her pen, Alice was in the kitchen looking out the window at Adam, who she could see through the open shed door was putting the last few strokes to the little cart.

When he stood back to check that he had covered it thoroughly, Alice dodged back, not wanting to be seen.

Suddenly Maureen called out, startling her, 'Alice, are you in the kitchen?'

'Yes.'

'You're not touching the kettle or anything, are you?'

'No!'

'So, what are you doing?'

'Just having a drink of lemonade.'

'Oh, you wouldn't fetch me one, would you, please?'

'OK.'

Carrying the glass of lemonade, Alice found Maureen stretched out on the sofa, her head buried in Adam's *Beano* comic.

Maureen sat up to take the glass of lemonade. 'Thanks, you're a darling.'

Throwing the *Beano* aside, she asked Alice, 'Do you want to play that new Donkey card game?'

'No, it's boring. Mum says I need to tidy my toy box, so I'm going upstairs now.'

'All right then. See you in a while.'

She watched Alice leave. 'Don't go lifting anything heavy,' Maureen advised her. 'If you need any help, just shout down.'

Five minutes after Alice had gone upstairs, Maureen heard the back door open and shut. 'Is that you, Adam?'

'Yeah. I've finished painting the cart. I'm just about to wash my hands.'

'Make sure you don't tread any paint into the house, or I'll get the blame!'

Taking her advice, Adam retraced his steps to the back door on tiptoe and slipped his shoes off on the mat; Maureen was none the wiser.

She did, however, pop into the kitchen to return her empty glass. 'Alice is cleaning out her toy box,' she informed Adam. 'Apparently, her mum's told her it was well overdue, so you'd best do what I'm doing, and leave her to it.'

Adam gave a wry little smile. 'I'm sure she wouldn't thank me if I interfered anyway.'

From upstairs, Alice heard the two of them talking together, and it wasn't long after that when she heard Adam coming up the stairs.

Quickly, she ran to softly close her bedroom door, while not actually clicking the lock.

Adam called out as he walked past her bedroom, 'Hi, Alice.'

'Hi.'

Going softly to peer through the chink in the door, she watched him go into his room, which was directly opposite.

She watched as he went to the wardrobe and chose a pair of clean trousers and a jumper.

When he turned round and seemed to look straight at her, she ran quickly to the back of her room, where she sat on the toy box, wondering if he'd seen her peeking.

She bided her time, and when she again heard Adam clattering about in his room, she edged towards the door. Stooping down to peer through the narrow chink, she followed Adam's every move. She saw him tidy up the clothes he'd taken off, then he was behind the wardrobe door, hauling up his trousers, and now he was slipping on a clean shirt and rolling up the sleeves.

That done, he came nearer to sit on the edge of the bed, head down, and seemingly faraway in his thoughts.

After what seemed an age, he stood up and, going across the room, he seemed to be reaching down into an area near the wardrobe.

Highly curious, and irritated that she could not see clearly what he was doing, Alice cautiously inched open the chink and watched him return to sit on the bed.

She was excited to notice that he was holding a small, decorated box.

Unaware that Alice was spying on him, Adam held his mother's box for a while. Just to hold it in his hands was an emotional experience for him.

He was in no hurry to open it. Instead, he ran his fingers over the ornate brass panel on the lid. He thought of his mother and the wonderful, happy times they had enjoyed together; the laughter they'd shared. The small adventures they had enjoyed were unforgettable.

And now, for the umpteenth time, he lived the memories again. In his mind, he could almost touch her. He could see her lovely smile and hear her laughter.

He now recalled the many times he had seen her holding this very box.

For the longest moment, he simply sat there forlorn, his eyes closed while he brought his mother's face into his mind and heart. And as always, the pain was unbearable.

With aching curiosity and a deal of resentment, Alice watched his every move. Why had she never seen that box, especially when twice before when he was out, she had gone through his things? So, where did he hide it? What was in it, and who did it belong to?

When Adam held the box close to his heart, it took but a moment for her to realise that it must be his mother's. For one fleeting moment she felt pity for him, but that rare moment of weakness was forgotten as she eagerly watched him open the box and take out what looked to be a long neck chain, which he wound into his hand.

Attached to the chain was a locket, not as flat and small as the one her own mother had, but, oh, it was so pretty. Just now as it emerged from the box, the light caught its brilliance, and the locket seemed to come alive.

Alice was mesmerised.

She saw how Adam caressed the locket in his hands, and she felt his joy. She saw how he pressed it to his face and when she heard him softly crying, she looked away.

In that moment, for whatever reason, Adam instinctively walked across the room and quietly closed his door.

Alice was not best pleased, though in her mind's eye she saw the bright, shimmering locket still, and knew she would not rest until she had it in her hands.

In his bedroom, unaware that Alice had been snooping on him, Adam quickly replaced the locket and hid the box underneath the deep, wooden skirt of the wardrobe, where he believed it to be safe from prying eyes.

Suddenly, he could hear the telephone ringing downstairs, and then Maureen's voice calling up: 'Can somebody please get the phone? I'm changing Harriet's stinky bottom!'

Adam was there in no time. Grabbing up the receiver, he asked, 'Hello, who is this?' Then: 'Oh, right. Yes, we're all fine. Maureen's changing Harriet's nappy, and you'll be pleased to know that Alice is upstairs tidying her toy box.' There was a moment when he just listened, and then: 'Yes, I will. Yes . . . see you later.'

Replacing the receiver, he went into Maureen, who had already guessed from the short exchange: 'That was either Liz or Jim, so is everything all right?'

'They'll be about an hour later than expected. Some friends they haven't seen for a while have just turned up.'

'That's OK.' Maureen was ready for every eventuality. 'I hadn't planned on going out anyway.'

With the baby struggling in her arms, she gently pushed the lazy dog aside with the tip of her toe. 'Shove up, Buster! Harriet wants to play ball.'

She placed the baby into the playpen and watched as she quickly crawled away to get the big, blue ball from the far side. 'I reckon Harriet's gonna be a footballer when she grows up.' Maureen reached down and gave the ball a gentle pat; she laughed out loud when Harriet screamed with delight as she scuttled across the playpen after the ball.

Adam, meanwhile, had gone to make sure he'd locked the garden shed.

Up in Adam's bedroom, Alice was on her hands and knees, frantically searching for the box. She had just about given up when she spotted the corner of the eiderdown oddly tucked up at the bottom of the bed. Quickly now, she ran her hand beneath the bed but found nothing. Then, she reached under the skirting of the wardrobe and there it was: a square object with raised features on the lid. Yes! It had to be the box.

Delighted, she withdrew it and, quickly locating the silver locket, she plucked it out, closed the lid and slid the box back again. Hurriedly, she went to the door and peeped out. Satisfied that it was safe, she went straight back to her own bedroom.

As Adam ran up the stairs, she was already sliding the locket underneath her mattress.

She almost leaped out of her skin when there came a tap on her door. 'Alice. You've got a bit more time to tidy your toy box.' As the door was slightly open, Adam poked his head in. 'Do you need any help?'

'No, thanks. Oh! Was that my mum on the phone just now?'

'Yes. She said to tell you and Maureen that they should be back within the hour.'

'That's good, because I haven't really started on my toy box yet.' This was her moment, just before her parents were due home.

Smiling sweetly, she invited him in. 'Come and see. Honestly, Mummy makes such a fuss. I think it's tidy enough already.'

Adam would rather have got on with his own tasks, but thinking to humour her, he came across the room.

When he was almost beside her, Alice calmly opened the lid, deliberately watching Adam for his reaction.

Adam was horrified by what he saw. Lying neatly on top of a mountain of toys, six mutilated dolls lay in a row, each with her hair pulled out by the roots. Their raggedy arms were hanging off, as though they'd been viciously swung round, and their pot faces were busted to a pulp.

Unable to speak for a while, Adam was visibly shaken, then he was gabbling, 'Alice, what's happened to them? Who did that?'

'*You* did that, Adam!' Alice was calm. 'You came into my room when you thought I was asleep and you broke all my dolls. I saw you, but I was frightened in case you hurt me too.'

Adam was shocked, but from her manner and the way she was smiling, he knew the truth. 'You little monster! You did this yourself, didn't you?' He was so shaken he could hardly think straight: 'Alice! Why did you do this? And why are you blaming me? I would never do such a terrible thing!'

She came back at him, calm and smiling. 'But you *did* do it! You thought I was asleep but I wasn't. I saw you do this, Adam. And when Mummy and Daddy get home, I'll tell them what you did, and they'll send you back to that children's home, where you belong! You don't belong here with decent people.'

'Oh, now I see!' Adam grabbed her by the wrist. 'I should have known. All your snide little glances; the way you always butt in whenever I get some attention from your parents; and I know why you wouldn't eat the fish even though it's your favourite. It was because me and Phil caught it. And now this . . . busting up your best dolls, so you can blame it on me, and get me sent away. Well, it won't work! Because you can tell Maureen what a bad thing you've done!' He grabbed hold of her wrist. 'Come on . . . tell her right now!'

When he tugged her forward she started to yell and scream at the top of her voice, 'Help! Maureen, get him off me!'

Alerted by Alice's frantic cries, Maureen ran up the stairs; she was horrified to see that Adam had Alice by both wrists and was trying to force her downstairs. Greatly distressed, Alice was sobbing as she tried to fight him off.

'Stop it!' Grabbing Adam by the arm, Maureen managed to pull him off Alice. 'What the devil do you think you're doing?'

Breaking free, Alice clung to her. 'I know what he did!' she yelled. 'That's why he wants to hurt me . . . because I saw him do it. He broke all my dolls. He did it, Maureen. I saw him.'

'Sssh.' Maureen calmed her, before asking Adam, 'Did you do what she said? I want the truth, Adam.'

Although Adam vehemently denied it, Maureen chose to believe Alice. 'I can only go by what I see now.' She pointed to Adam. 'You were deliberately hurting her, and she's got the bruises to prove it. What's wrong with you, Adam? Why would you do that?'

Adam could see that he had little defence and, not for the first time, he felt alone and vulnerable. 'What's the point?' He glanced at Alice, who was nestling up to Maureen; a look in her eyes that told him she would lie through her teeth until everyone saw her as the victim.

It was then that he realised no one, not even

Maureen, would believe him against Alice, because she was a part of this family, while he would always be an outsider.

'I'm waiting, Adam.' Maureen was insistent. 'I want to know why you hurt her like that?'

'I was not hurting her. I was trying to get her to come and tell you the truth, and she began screaming and fighting me.'

Maureen tenderly stroked Alice's face. 'That's not true. I saw you with my own eyes. You were deliberately hurting her. The poor kid was terrified. So don't you try and lie your way out of it, because I know what I saw.'

'Well, you saw wrong. I didn't mean to hurt her, but she was like a crazy thing, kicking and screaming. I promise you, I never touched her dolls. I just wanted her to tell the truth about what she'd done, and how she deliberately put the blame on me.'

He gave a wry little smile. 'I can see you've already made up your mind that I'm a liar, when the truth is, it's *her* that's lying. But if you can't believe me, then nobody else will.'

He was not surprised to see Alice smile at him from Maureen's protective embrace.

Deep down, he'd always known Alice hated him. He had even confided in Phil, but being the caring man he was, Phil had tried to dismiss Adam's fears.

'You don't know her,' Adam told Maureen. 'She's worked this all out. She's never liked me being here. She told me that I should go back to the children's home, where I belong. She said I don't belong with decent people. And now, that's what you think as well.

So she's won and I'm the bad one, and if you can believe the tale she's told you, they will all believe it.'

Maureen could feel Alice trembling in her arms. She could not believe how Adam was desperately trying to justify what he'd done. 'Adam, I don't know what to say, except that I'm shocked at what you did. I really am sorry that it's turned out like this . . . for Alice's sake mainly. But she could be right. Maybe you did leave the children's home too soon.'

She looked at him, and what she saw was a boy not much younger than she was herself; a boy who had seemed the perfect son for Liz and Jim; a boy who had been much loved by those good people. And, seeing the look on his face now, she saw a goodness there, and for one split second she was actually made to wonder if Alice was lying.

But then she recalled the evidence of her own eyes, and she quickly dismissed that fleeting instinct. The truth was, Adam had hurt Alice. That was what she had witnessed, and Alice had been terrified. She was the one who got hurt. She was the one in distress. She was the one who carried the bruises.

Moreover, from what she had learned through various sources, Maureen reminded herself that Adam had come from a violent background, while Alice's family were decent, God-fearing people, whose only mistake was making a wrong judgement.

'The truth is, Adam, you hurt a terrified nine-year-old child. She was screaming for you to let her go, and you wouldn't. I have to believe what she's told me, and what I saw with my own eyes.'

She looked at him, at his soulful expression, and the way he kept glancing at Alice as though warning her. It only confirmed her belief that he was a bully and a liar.

Maureen held on tight to the girl. 'I'm sorry, Adam, but from the little I know, I believe you must take after your father.'

'*I'm nothing like him!*' Her cutting words ignited a fury in him. 'Don't you ever say that!' He took a step forward, his anger focused on Alice. 'She's the warped one, not me! She never wanted me here. That's why she's done this . . . to make me look bad. To get rid of me!'

When Alice clung harder to her, Maureen slowly backed away from Adam. 'I'm calling the pub to speak to Liz and Jim,' she said coldly. 'You can explain yourself to them!'

'Maureen, I'm not lying,' Adam pleaded with her. 'Please . . . you have to believe me. If one of us is lying, it's her! I never went near the dolls! And I did not deliberately hurt her. She was fighting me because she didn't want me to bring her down to tell you the truth.'

Maureen was already halfway down the stairs, with Alice clutching onto her. 'Stay away, Adam!' she warned him. 'After what I've seen, I don't blame Alice for wanting you away from here!'

When they were out of sight, Adam stood at the top of the stairs for what seemed to him a long time, though in fact it was only a matter of minutes.

Realising that he might be sent away, he was frantic. Liz and Jim were bound to believe Alice over him, and why shouldn't they? Alice was their flesh and blood, after all. Maybe Maureen was right; maybe he did take after his father. Maybe he really was a monster in the making.

He could hear Maureen on the phone. 'No, she's OK now. I've got her down here with me and Harriet. No, he's still upstairs. I don't know . . . but I'll keep an eye on things until you get here.'

On hearing that conversation, Adam could see no alternative.

He went into his room and collected his hessian bag from inside the wardrobe. He filled it with the basics, together with a complete change of clothes and a spare pair of boots.

Next, he took out all his savings, which he had in a jar under the bed. After transferring all the money to one of his clean socks, he stuffed the sock into the deepest crevice of his travel bag.

The money was not a vast amount – well-earned from his paper round, and other odd jobs – but it had filled the jar, and now it would help him get by until he decided what to do.

For now though, he must be quick. He needed to be out of here before Liz and Jim got back.

Quickly, he checked in his mind that he had enough for his immediate needs.

I'll need to get a job, he decided as he hurried about his business. He'd lie about his age. No one would guess he was not yet fourteen. Everyone always said he was tall for his age.

He now collected the most important item of all: his

mother's box, which he withdrew from under the wardrobe and carefully placed in the bottom of the bag. He had an idea for keeping it safe. Taking a pen and paper from the chest of drawers, he pushed them into his pocket.

Shortly after that, he crept softly down the stairs, and out of the house at the back. He had no idea where he might end up, or if the authorities would catch up with him and put him in care again. He desperately hoped not. He had no intention of going back to the children's home. He longed for the day when he would be out of their jurisdiction; when he would be free to do as he pleased. But that was many long months away yet.

~

Following Maureen's frantic phone call, Liz and Jim left the pub to hurry home.

Jim broke the silence. 'I still can't believe it!'

'It's not like Adam,' Liz agreed, quickening her footsteps.

'Liz, think back. Did Maureen actually say that Adam had hurt Alice . . . that she was bruised and upset?'

'Well, yes, as far as I could understand her.'

'But why would he want to hurt her? What's happened? He's never done anything like that before. Jeez! When I get my hands on him, I'll make him answer for this.'

Seeing how he was getting worked up, Liz tried to calm him. 'I can't help but feel Maureen might have got the wrong end of the stick,' she said, breathlessly, hurrying along beside him.

'No. She's a sensible girl. All the same, I'm damned if I can understand it, because Adam's never shown any sign of violence before. What's going on, Liz? Is it maybe something we've done wrong?'

'We've done nothing wrong, Jim. We've given him a good home and we've looked after him like our own. I don't know what's happened exactly, but I do know one thing for certain: if he has lashed out at Alice, he can go back where he came from; and the sooner the better.'

Yet, even though she was concerned, Liz was convincing herself that Adam would not deliberately hurt Alice.

Jim quickened his space until he was almost running. 'I'm sorry, Liz, but it's beginning to look like we've made a big mistake.' He couldn't get home quick enough. 'Come on, Liz. Hurry up!'

Hobbling along in high heels, Liz urged him on. 'You go ahead, Jim. I'll be right behind.'

Just then, as they passed the bottom of the street, Liz caught sight of Adam out the corner of her eye. 'Jim, it's Adam . . . over there, look!'

Jim caught sight of him. 'It looks like he's making a run for it. So there's your answer! Why would he run off like that if he hadn't done anything wrong? You get home and check on Alice. I'm going after the bugger!'

By this time, unaware that they'd seen him, Adam was away like the wind. As he neared the canal, he realised he was being pursued.

On recognising Jim, he was tempted to stop and explain that Alice had set him up, that he had not deliberately hurt her. But then Jim began shouting, 'Come back, you devil! Face up to what you've done!'

Jim was relentless. As fast as Adam ran, Jim was right behind. 'If you're innocent, come back now. Or maybe you're just a coward, like your father!'

The idea that he was being seen in the same light as his father only fired Adam to keep going, to get away from here, and never come back.

Breathless and stumbling, Jim kept after him, over the fields and onwards, towards the canal. Intermittently calling Adam, he had to stop a couple of times to draw breath, but though the terrain slowed him down, he soon renewed his pace, determined to make Adam face up to what he'd done.

When Adam scampered over the stone wall alongside the water, Jim did the same, though being less fit and lithe than the boy, he paid the price.

As he swung himself over the wall, he caught his foot in a deep crevice between the boulders. Propelled forward out of control, he tumbled headlong down the rough, slippery bank until there was nowhere to go but into the murky waters below. He tried desperately to keep himself from going under, but the harder he struggled, the quicker the waters seemed to cover his head and draw him down.

Being some distance ahead, Adam had no idea that Jim was in trouble, though he wondered why he'd given up the chase.

Jim had been yelling for him every few minutes but

now there was only an eerie silence. Adam was puzzled, but somewhat relieved.

Stopping to catch his breath, he smiled to himself. Jim wasn't as fit as he thought. But something felt wrong. It wasn't like Jim to give up.

In the short time he'd been with the family, Adam had grown close to Jim. He knew his ways and, knowing them, he now grew uneasy. Jim's family were everything to him. If Jim thought he'd hurt Alice, he would never give up. So, Adam thought, Jim had either found a different route and he was planning to waylay him at the other end or, for whatever reason, he had decided to let Adam go. But that idea didn't feel right to Adam.

Now convinced that Jim was in trouble, he stuffed his travel bag between the knotted roots of an ancient tree, then he ran as fast as his legs would take him. He carefully retraced every step and kept his eyes peeled at every turn.

When he got to the canal, he saw that the boulders had been disturbed, and the earth was stripped in a jagged line from the boulders to the water. He suspected Jim might have slipped.

'Jim, where are you? It's Adam. Answer me!' he shouted.

On hearing a weakened cry from somewhere beneath the canal bridge, he swiftly ripped off his jacket and shoes, and eased himself into the water. Straightaway, he caught sight of Jim. Visibly shivering, and badly bleeding from the head, he was desperately clinging to an overhanging branch, which was too thin to hold his weight so he might climb out, but it was sturdy enough to help him keep his head above water.

'Hold on . . . don't let go, I'm here.' Adam swam to him. 'I'll get you out, but you'll have to trust me. All right?'

Jim nodded. He was never more relieved than when he saw Adam approaching.

'Don't worry, we'll get you out, Jim,' Adam continued to reassure him, though he soon realised it would not be easy. It was obvious that if he were to go for help, Jim would not have the strength to hold on. 'There's no time to go for help, but you'll be all right . . . I promise. I'll get you out.'

Going under the water, Adam discovered an even more desperate situation than he'd feared. Both of Jim's legs were badly tangled in a mass of thick, binding weeds. Also, judging by the gaping wound and the peculiar angle of a jutting bone, his left knee appeared to have been broken in the fall.

Coming up for air, Adam was concerned to see Jim drifting in and out of consciousness. 'Stay awake, Jim. You have to stay awake!' he yelled. As gently as he could he explained that the weeds were tangled round both his legs, and that his knee appeared to be broken.

He saw the despair in Jim's eyes. 'I will get you out,' he promised again, 'but you have to help me. It's going to hurt, but I need to free your legs. You must try to stay awake!'

Growing weaker, Jim was concerned for Adam. 'Leave me,' he said. 'Go for help!'

Grabbing the collar of his jacket, Adam yelled back, 'There's no time! I won't leave you here to die, like a drowned rat!'

Cold and weary, Jim could hardly keep his eyes open.

'Keep awake, Jim. Hang on. You can do it, I know you can.' Smacking Jim's face, Adam hardened his voice: 'Jim! Don't make me ashamed of you!'

When Jim smiled at his last remark, Adam felt a huge surge of relief. 'You have to trust me, Jim. I need to release you from the bindweed, and then we'll work together and get you out of here. OK?'

Jim gave a curt little nod, then he laid his head on the crook of his shoulder, and watched as Adam slid back under the water.

Adam quickly set about loosening the bindweed that was tightly coiled about Jim's legs. It was a long and laborious task, but eventually the legs were free. With the removal of the bindweed, the broken knee was now hanging open.

From above the water line, he could hear Jim screaming in pain as the dead weight of the lower leg seemed to be tearing the knee apart.

Adam came up for air, before going back down.

Breaking off some lengths of the drifting weeds, he loosely plaited a makeshift bandage. Tying one end above the knee, he wound the bandage down the leg, to secure the other end around Jim's ankle. That done, he drew the two ends together as far as was possible without actually bending the leg until the gap in the knee was made smaller, thereby taking away the drag of the lower leg.

Jim's agonised cries told Adam it was a painful procedure for him to bear, but he urged Adam on.

On surfacing, he could see the pain etched in Jim's

face. 'I'm sorry,' he said, but there was no time for explanation.

Hauling Jim out of the water was the most difficult part of all.

Hoping that someone might be walking the fields, Adam cried out for help, but no one came so the task of heaving Jim onto the bank was left to him alone.

Little by little, Adam managed to get him onto the upper bank, where the two of them lay side by side, totally exhausted, with Jim slipping in and out of consciousness.

Jim's knee was a real concern. When he'd got his breath back Adam knew exactly what he had to do next.

'I'm going for help.' Adam threw his jacket over Jim's wounded knee. 'I'll make you safe so you don't fall down the bank . . . I'll be as quick as I can.' With Jim lying prostrate, eyes closed, and his breathing unsteady, Adam was beginning to fear the worst.

'No . . .' Jim raised his hand. 'Please . . . help me . . . up!'

Adam refused, but Jim was in such a state that Adam feared if he didn't somehow take him from there, Jim would try to follow and end up in the water again. With Jim so determined, and no time to argue, Adam reluctantly decided to help him up.

~

The farmer's wife was at the kitchen window, when she saw two figures struggling up the field.

Alerting her husband, who went outside to check the strangers, she continued watching from the window.

She then followed her husband out, and the two of them watched in amazement as the boy continued towards them, part supporting, part carrying a man. They both looked to be in trouble.

Realizing the emergency of the situation, they began running towards the boy.

Adam saw them coming. 'We're all right,' he said to Jim, who made no reply. By now, he was too far out of it.

Bent double with the weight of Jim, Adam was hardly able to stagger on, but seeing the couple hurrying towards them gave him renewed strength as he pushed himself forward. He'd promised Jim he would get help, and he had kept his promise.

When the farmer took some of the weight onto himself, Adam was close to collapse, but between the two of them, they managed to get Jim to the house, where they laid him on the big oak table in the kitchen.

In the front parlour, the farmer called the ambulance while his wife tended to Jim, who was slightly delirious and making little sense.

Adam bent to tell him, 'You'll be all right now, Jim. The ambulance is on its way.'

Adam had given Jim's name and address to the farmer, urging that he should call Liz, and the farmer went quickly away to make his calls.

A short time later, after Adam was rested and Jim was made more comfortable, Adam whispered in Jim's ear, 'I need you to know, I did not hurt Alice.'

Not yet fully conscious, Jim seemed not to have heard.

Deeply unsettled, Adam sat on the bench outside the farmhouse door for a while. His every bone ached, and his heart was heavy. What to do now?

He thought about going to see his dear friend, Phil. Then he wondered if he should see Liz. But Alice had put a bar between him and the family, and knowing he would not be welcome, he quickly dismissed that idea.

So, while the attention of the farmer and his wife was on Jim, Adam decided it was time to leave.

He did not say goodbye, nor did he linger for them to ask questions. He simply walked away, and kept going until he found a good spot from which he could think.

His plan was to collect his bag and make his own way in the world.

He did not plan on going back to the children's home. Nor did he feel comfortable returning to the family who had taken him in. The family he had come to love.

He thought of Alice, and he was sorry it had turned out the way it had. But thinking back to Phil's earlier explanation, he understood how she felt about his being here.

Now, though, it was time to leave all that behind, and move on.

More importantly, it was time to leave the boy behind, and become the man.

Again, he thought of Phil, and decided to contact him at the first opportunity.

Now, though, for what seemed an age, he sat down on the grassy bank some distance away from the house, just watching and waiting.

When finally the ambulance arrived, he stood up to see the ambulancemen bring Jim out on a stretcher.

Satisfied, he gave the whisper of a smile, and reluctantly turned away.

~

In the ambulance, Jim constantly asked for Adam, but no one knew where he was. No one had seen him leave.

All they knew was that the boy had saved the man's life, and now he was gone.

The ambulanceman questioned the farmer's wife as to the boy's condition. She told how the boy was completely exhausted and in considerable pain when they took him in, but that he was given a hot drink and some clothes that had hung in the wardrobe since her husband was a young man. The boy had changed into them, and seemed much easier in himself. He was not injured as such, but he was very concerned about his companion. 'When we told him the ambulance was on its way, he was greatly relieved,' she said.

When the farmer had called Liz and explained the situation, she was shocked, but as the ambulance was already on its way she decided to head straight to the hospital.

When the ambulance doors were closed, ready for departure, the farmer and his wife could still hear Jim calling, 'Adam . . . where is he? Where's the boy?'

By then, though, Adam was long gone.

~

It took a deal of searching before Adam located the tree under which he'd left his travel bag. He was devastated when he discovered that the bag was gone.

With his bare hands, he dug deeper into the roots of the tree, but it was definitely not there, and he was in pieces.

For a long time, he sat on the ground, rocking back and forth, thinking of Jim, hoping he would be all right. He thought of Alice and the way of things.

When he crossed his arms over his knees and the tears began to fall, it was not because of the small amount of money he'd lost. It was not for Alice, nor the lost bag, and it was not even for Jim, whom he believed was safe now.

His bitter tears were for the loss of his mother's precious locket.

It was the only part of her he had left. And after all he'd been through this was the hardest loss to bear.

Emotionally and physically exhausted, he curled up beneath the tree. It was not long before he drifted into a deep, troubled sleep.

CHAPTER FIFTEEN

It was late when Liz got home from the hospital. Maureen had managed to get the children to sleep at long last, but was so tired herself, that she'd fallen asleep on the sofa.

On hearing the key in the front door lock she leaped up, desperate to know that Jim was all right.

Liz looked haggard. 'His knee was badly damaged,' she revealed, '. . . his leg was in a shocking mess.'

'But will he be all right?' Maureen was very fond of the family; it pained her to see their suffering.

'They operated, and the doctor said it went well, but that there was a long way to go yet,' Liz explained. 'Jim had lost so much blood, they had to give him a transfusion. He's sedated now and they seem pleased with his progress. I wanted to stay, but the doctor said he would be out of it for quite a time, and it wouldn't hurt for me to come home and get some sleep. They promised to call me if I'm needed.'

Maureen thought Liz was right to come home. 'I'm sure they would have let you stay if they were unduly concerned about him,' she said. 'And anyway, if you don't mind me saying, you do look like you need a good night's sleep.'

Liz didn't argue with that, though she was more concerned about the children. 'Have they slept?' She recalled how upset Alice was at the awful business of Adam running away, and her daddy having to go into hospital. 'I've been troubled about Alice,' Liz quietly admitted. 'I hope she didn't get herself in a state again after I left. Did she?'

'Well, Harriet went to sleep straight after her milk, and she hasn't woken since. But it took Alice ages to get to sleep, and even then she kept waking up and coming down . . . getting herself upset all over again. In the end, I lay in bed with her until she went to sleep. She kept saying it was all her fault that her daddy nearly died and Adam ran off.'

Liz was surprised. 'How can it be her fault? Unless it was that business with Adam hurting her.'

'That's exactly what I thought,' Maureen said. 'But I told her that even though he got her daddy to safety, it still did not excuse what Adam did to her. I said it was not her fault, and she should never think that.'

'You're absolutely right,' Liz agreed. 'I will never be able to thank Adam enough for getting Jim to safety, but then again, if it hadn't been for Jim chasing after him because of what he did to Alice, Jim would never have got hurt in the first place.'

When Liz sank into the nearest chair, Maureen went

off to the kitchen to make them each a cup of cocoa. 'It'll help you sleep,' she told Liz.

Upstairs, Alice had got out of bed and was sitting at the top of the stairs. She'd been waiting for her mother to come home. She needed to see her. To know her daddy was all right.

Just now, she'd overheard the conversation between Maureen and her mummy, and she felt afraid. She returned to her bedroom. There was something important that she needed to do.

Liz and Maureen were sipping their drinks when Alice came into the room. 'Is Daddy all right?' she asked her mother tearfully. 'He won't die, will he?'

Liz ran across the room and led Alice back to the chair, where she told her sincerely, 'No, sweetheart, Daddy's not going to die. He's had an operation, and he has to stay in hospital for a while, but the doctor told me that he should be all right. It might take a long time, but he'll be fine.'

When Alice burst into tears, she kissed her on the forehead. 'Listen to me, Alice,' she said, stroking her face. 'None of this is your fault. If anything, I'm sorry to say, it's Adam's fault, because if he hadn't hurt you, Daddy would never have been chasing him.'

'Maureen said Adam saved Daddy and got help for him. Did he do that, Mummy?'

'Yes, sweetheart, he did. Daddy told me that he was in a bad way. He was trapped in the water and badly hurt, but Adam managed to get him to safety, and we should all be very grateful for that. But I will not forgive Adam for what he did to you, because that was a cowardly thing.'

'But it's all my fault, Mummy!'

'No, sweetheart. None of this is your fault. Adam did a bad thing when he hurt you. When he ran away, Daddy went after him to bring him back, to explain what he had done, and why. But Daddy was hurt. It was not your fault, and you must never think that.'

Liz was surprised when, without a word, Alice got off her knee and went away upstairs.

'Shall I go after her?' Maureen asked.

'No. Let her go for now. I'll go up in a couple of minutes and see if she's asleep. I think she just needed reassuring, that's all.'

A few minutes later, just as Liz was about to go upstairs, Alice returned. She didn't say anything. Instead, she stood before her mother, her hand outstretched and tears running down her face.

'Alice? What's wrong?' Looking down at the girl's outstretched hand, she was surprised to see a locket and chain, so pretty, and shimmering in the light from the table lamp. 'Alice, where did you get that?' Liz had never seen it before. 'Whose is it?'

'It belongs to Adam.'

Liz was confused. 'If it belongs to Adam, what are *you* doing with it?'

'I stole it.'

'You did what?' Liz was shocked. 'Why would you do such a thing? Was it because he hurt you? Is that why you stole it – to hurt him back? Because if you did, it was wrong to steal, and you know that! Adam was very wrong to hurt you, but you had no right to take his belongings.'

'Adam didn't hurt me, Mummy . . . not on purpose.'

'How can you say that? You had the bruises. You told Maureen that Adam had done it, that he had deliberately hurt you.' But from the look on her daughter's face, Liz knew she was now telling the truth. 'I think you'd better explain yourself, young lady.'

Growing nervous, Alice went on: 'It was me who broke the dollies. I did it to blame Adam, so you and Daddy would send him back to where he came from. I showed Adam the dollies and I told him that I would tell everyone it was him who did it. He got upset and tried to get me downstairs to tell Maureen the truth.'

Liz was shocked, but she sat silent as Alice finished.

'When I didn't want to go downstairs, he got hold of me and I started fighting him. That's how I got bruised. He didn't do it on purpose. I did it, because I wanted him to go back to the children's home.'

Liz was truly shaken by what Alice told her. 'How did you get Adam's locket?'

'I stole it from his bedroom. I saw him looking at it and he was crying, because, I think, it was his mummy's locket. He hid it, and when he went downstairs, I went into his bedroom, and found it.'

When Alice now broke into tears, Liz made no move to hold her. Instead, she told her firmly, 'Give me the locket.'

When Alice passed it over, Liz folded it into her plam. 'What you did to Adam was very wrong. Do you understand that?'

'Yes . . . and I'm sorry, Mummy. Truly, I am. I want to make it better. I want to see Adam. I want to say thank you for helping my daddy, and I want to tell him I'm sorry.'

Reaching out, Liz drew her close, her voice firm yet quiet as she told her daughter, 'You did a very bad thing, Alice. You destroyed your beautiful dollies and turned us against Adam, when he'd done nothing wrong. And then, to steal something that obviously meant a lot to him was cruel. If you were so unhappy about Adam being here, you should have told me or Daddy. You must never, *ever* do such bad things again.'

'I won't.' By now Alice was in floods of tears.

Liz made no effort to comfort her. Instead, she said, 'We need to find Adam, and you must return his mother's locket to him. Then you apologise . . . for everything. And hope he can forgive you.'

'I'm really sorry, Mummy.'

Liz could never have imagined her daughter doing such wicked things. She had always believed that if Alice was unhappy she would confide in her and Jim. But at least she had found the courage to own up, and though it was not enough, it was something. 'Well, I suppose there is one saving grace. At least you've now told the truth about what you did. And I can see that you really are sorry. So, maybe now, we can put the record straight.'

She held Alice at arm's length. 'We know now that Adam was not the villain you made him out to be. In fact, as far as I'm aware, he's done nothing wrong since we took him in. I truly hope you've learned a very valuable lesson here, Alice. Have you?'

'Yes, Mummy.'

'Well, that's something. But I'm shocked and disappointed that you found it difficult to confide in me or your father. In future, if you find yourself worried, about anything at all, you must talk with me or Daddy.'

She gently pushed her away. 'Now, I want you to go back to bed, and think about what you did. I want you to think about how Adam must be feeling, and what you might say to him when we find him.'

'If he's run away, how will we find him, Mummy?'

Liz had been thinking about that. 'I'm hoping Phil might know where he's gone. Now you get back to bed, and remember what I said.'

'Good night, Mummy. Good night, Maureen.' Feeling very sad, Alice gave them each a kiss.

With Alice back in her room, there was no more talk of what she had done. Instead, feeling shocked at Alice's deception, Maureen went home, and Liz slept, fully clothed, on the sofa.

It had been a worrying day, during which she had learned a great deal about human nature.

~

It was dawn when Liz opened her eyes.

Aching in every bone, she struggled to sit up and for a moment she sat stretching her arms and thinking about Jim. Then she began to panic. She had to phone the hospital and check on his progress.

She hurried across the room and into the hallway, where she dialled the hospital.

It seemed to take an age before anyone answered.

'Oh, hello, I'm Liz Dexter. My husband, Jim, was operated on yesterday. Can you please tell me how he is?'

Tapping her fingers on the top of the small table, she waited, and she waited; and just as she thought no one was coming to put her mind at rest, a warm, caring voice lifted her spirits.

'Hello, can I help you?'

'Oh, yes, please. I'm calling about my husband, Jim.' She paused while the other person confirmed Liz's identity. 'Please, how is he this morning?'

She listened again and her fears were soothed. 'Oh, thank you so much. So, he had a good night?' She gave a sigh of relief. 'That's wonderful, thank you. Could you please tell him I'll be there very shortly? Thank you.'

She decided not to tell Jim what Alice had done. There would be time enough for that when he was stronger.

With an easier mind, she replaced the receiver and made her way upstairs on tiptoe. Satisfied that the children were still fast asleep, she went down to the kitchen and made herself a cup of tea, which she carried into the other room. Placing the cup and saucer on the arm of the sofa, she opened the curtains.

Already the street was coming alive. John Miller, opposite, was off on his bike to carry out his postman duties, and down the street she could hear a car revving up. Liz gave a hint of a smile. Through thick and thin, good or bad, life still went on. Thank goodness.

Returning to the sofa, she collected her cup and saucer, and as she sat down, something glittering on the carpet caught her eye. On closer inspection she saw that it was Adam's locket.

Realising she must have dropped it in the night, she feared it might be broken. She carefully examined it. On first sight it seemed intact, but when she turned it around, she was concerned to notice a slight twist on the side, where it seemed to have a split along the rim.

Curious, she took it to the window and examined it closer. 'That's strange . . .' She moved her finger along the side rim, and, yes, she could feel the slightest bump. A closer look revealed the tiniest catch, woven into the pattern in such a way that it was hard to see at first glance.

Liz was curious. She guessed it was probably hiding a lock of hair, maybe Adam's from when he was a baby.

She knew lockets were often used for that purpose. She examined the filigree patterns and the intricate raised heart on the front. The design was very special and unlike anything she had seen before.

She turned it over in her hand, thinking it had to be a lover's gift. The way the morning light danced off the front, reflecting its glory, was simply breathtaking.

Liz was curious. From what she knew about Edward Carter, she could never imagine him buying such a lovely thing.

When taking Adam for fostering, she and Jim were officially made aware of Adam's background. They knew Edward Carter was now imprisoned.

Curious, she turned the locket over again to see if

there was an inscription anywhere, but she could see none. The only marks on both chain and locket were official hallmarks.

She ran her fingers over the tiny catch. Feeling guilty, she put the locket down. A moment later, intrigued, she picked it up again.

Twice, she tried to shift the catch and each time it held fast.

Frustrated, she laid the locket on the arm of the chair while she finished her tea, before taking the cup and saucer into the kitchen.

On returning to the front room, she stood a moment just gazing at the locket until her curiosity got the better of her. When she now made a determined effort to open it, the catch suddenly popped up, and the locket sprang open. To her surprise, a small square of folded paper fluttered to the carpet.

Liz bent to pick it up and carefully unfolded it. The writing was tiny, but readable:

> My darling Adam,
>
> This locket was a gift from Michael Slater, a man whom I loved as a girl. You are the only one who knows where I keep the locket, so if you now have this note, I am probably no longer alive. You need to know that Michael Slater is your true father. He gave me this locket before I met Edward Carter, who always thought you were his son.

Please forgive me, Adam. Be strong. I love you so very much.
Mum x

Liz was mortified that she'd pried into the locket, for the message was both revealing, and extremely private. It was not meant for a stranger's eyes.

With the locket clutched in one hand and the note in the other, she sat heavily on the sofa and wondered about the ramifications of what it meant for Adam.

Edward and Adam Carter believed they were father and son, when in fact his true father was a man called Michael Slater. She worked it out in her mind: Adam's mother said she loved this Michael Slater *before* she met Edward Carter . . . so she must have been pregnant with Adam, when she married Carter. And he never even knew.

She wondered about Adam's father, Michael Slater. Why had she and Adam's true father gone their separate ways? Maybe Michael Slater was already married. Or maybe she told him she was pregnant, and for whatever reason, he didn't want to know.

It was a mystery, and one that was not altogether uncommon. Sometimes, these things happened, and the girl might have no other choice but to trick a man into marriage, because she needed the child to be legitimate.

Liz paced up and down for a time, wondering how she might deal with this information. *Talk to Phil! Yes, that was it!*

Her first priority for now, though, was her own family,

not least the love of her life, who she may so easily have lost for ever if it had not been for Adam. A boy not quite fourteen years of age, with no home, no family, and nowhere to go, and he was out there, possibly alone, and afraid.

Unless Phil could help to locate him, that innocent boy, through no fault of his own, was headed for a bleak future.

CHAPTER SIXTEEN

THE SUN HAD risen, but Adam was still sleeping.

Having run ahead of its owner, the dog quickly found Adam, fast asleep and bundled up against the chilly night. Excited, it pounced on him, licking his face with its leathery tongue.

'Hey!' Taken unawares, Adam scrambled up, greatly relieved when he saw it was just a friendly, scruffy little dog. 'Hello, you.' He ruffled its coat and waggled its ears, and not for the first time, he wished he had a dog of his own.

'Come 'ere, boy!' The dog's owner was a ruddy-faced man with a walking stick. 'Sorry about that,' he told Adam. 'He were just being friendly.'

Adam assured him it was all right, and the man went on his way with the dog, occasionally glancing back. Wiping the dog's slaver from his face, Adam gave him a little farewell wave.

After the man and dog were out of sight, he leaned

back against the tree and glanced about. The skies above were morning grey, while the sun was trying its utmost to break through. The ground beneath his feet was hard and rocky. There was not a soul about; not even a bird singing. All around was eerily silent, save for the gentlest whipping of the tree branches when the breeze began to play.

In that moment, it seemed to Adam that he was the only person left in the world. It was an exciting, though somewhat disturbing, feeling.

'Come on, Adam. Move yourself!' he said aloud. Drawing his coat about him, he knew he had better get well away from these parts.

He thought of Jim, and he truly regretted what had happened, though he was greatly relieved to know that Jim was now in safe hands.

He took stock of his own situation. *I'd best get word to Phil*, he thought. *But I'm not going back, not ever.*

He was the one who had made the decision to leave, so why did he feel abandoned? *What do I do now? Which way do I go? How do I live?* So many questions passed through his mind, and so many fears, too.

He stood up straight, shoulders taut and head high. He dismissed each question with an answer. *First, you find work. Then you find lodgings. You say nothing about your age, or where you come from.* The sad truth, for now at least, was that he had no idea where he might be headed.

After living with Jim's family, he now felt incredibly lonely, but he also felt stronger, more able to face the obstacles life might put in his way. *Don't lose sight of who you are,* he told himself. *What you do from now on is up to you and no one else. It's time to make your own way in the world.*

Before he set off, he spared a moment for his mother. 'Someone took your locket, Mum,' he whispered sadly. 'They took everything.'

When the inevitable tears fell, he sat on the ground; folding his arms over his head, he sobbed as though he would never stop.

When the tears were spent he felt a rush of anger. 'I hope Edward Carter gets what he deserves,' he said aloud, his voice grating like the hatred within him. 'I hope he suffers for what he did to my mother!'

He shook the bad thoughts clear and stood up. Where to go?

He glanced back in the direction of the farmhouse where he'd left Jim. He wanted to thank the farmer and his wife for what they did, but in the end he could not bring himself to go back. It was enough for him to know that Jim was now being taken care of.

Turning his head, he looked in the direction of the place where he had found a family, and a measure of peace for a time, and he thought of Liz, and Alice.

For a moment, he was sorely tempted to go back, but the moment passed and he decided to take the same route as the man with his dog.

The minute he started walking he felt as though he had the body of an old man; every bone creaked and groaned. This was the price he must pay for having got Jim to safety, and for choosing the cramped and rocky place where he'd laid his head to sleep.

He kept his pace steady, and the further he walked, the easier it seemed to get. When he got to the neck of the canal, which was far from the spot where Jim got caught up in the bindweed, he walked along the towpath until he found a private little curve in the bend. Here was where the water narrowed, and the risk of anyone seeing him was remote.

Stripping naked, he rolled his belongings into a tight ball and with great care he hid them under a pile of leaves and branches. Then he dived lazily into the water, shivering as he floated free for a time.

The experience was heavenly. The weight was gone from his joints and the water was immensely soothing. And now that the sun was coming alive, he could feel the warmth caress his bare, wet skin. He closed his eyes and let the water take him where it would.

After a time, he spun over and swam back to the place where he'd hidden his clothes. He clambered out and, finding his clothes, he quickly put them on, before anyone might come this way.

Feeling cleaner and fresher, and much easier in his bones, he walked on, following the path taken by the man and his dog.

The dog had reminded him of Phil's little dog, Rex. He missed Phil. He wondered how long it might be before he would see him again.

First, though, he had things to do, and places to go. But wherever he went he would let Phil know. He owed him that much at least.

As his journey progressed, he wondered about that boy who had been taken to the children's home. He made himself forget, for that boy was not him. Never again would he be that boy.

Time had moved on, and life had taken his childhood.

He had lost not only his darling mother, but, with her, the only real and true love he had ever known. Nothing on earth would ever replace that.

It was time to face up to the harsh truth. From now on, he must take responsibility for himself. It would not be easy, he realised, but he would learn, because life itself, with all its trials, joys and impossible journeys, was the best teacher of all. Like it or not, he was already on the longest journey.

At this moment, in this place, he had no idea where the journey might take him.

It was a daunting thought.

PART FIVE

The Girl

1959

CHAPTER SEVENTEEN

PHIL HAD MADE this journey many times when Adam was living at the children's home, but this time he was angry, and deeply worried.

Miss Martin had grown to know Phil very well since Adam had gone missing, some months back. 'Hello, Phil. Come inside,' she greeted him. She led him down the hall to her office, talking as she went. 'I'm afraid there is still nothing to report.'

After ordering tea and biscuits from the kitchen, she told Phil, with much regret, 'Although the police have not been able to find him, they do assure me that they're still on the case.'

Phil had heard it all before. 'That's not good enough.'

Dipping into his pocket, he slid the letter across the desk. 'That one arrived this very morning. It's the fifth letter I've had in these past months, and they're all stamped from different parts of the country. And still they haven't been able to trace Adam. Why is that? *Tell me . . . have* they given up on him?'

Miss Martin was adamant. 'Dear me, no, Phil! The boy is not yet fifteen. It's their bounden duty to find him, and they will. They have traced the letters as far as they can, but still no sight of Adam. We just have to be patient.'

'So what do we do?'

'There is very little to be done, except to let the police get on with it,' she answered sadly. 'I know it's frustrating, but sooner or later they will find him. You mark my words.'

'I'm worried about him.' Phil had suffered many sleepless nights since Adam had been gone. 'In the letters he tells me he's well, and that I'm not to worry, but how can I not worry? He says nothing about how he lives, or where he gets his money from. Or what kind of work he might be taking on. And what kind of people would take him on, anyway? He's just a boy. I can't even write back to him because he never gives me a return address.'

Growing emotional, he could hardly keep his voice steady. 'To tell the truth, I'm at my wits' end.' Dropping his sorry gaze to the floor, he gave a long, drawn-out sigh. 'Oh, dear lady, why doesn't he come home?'

Miss Martin gave a sympathetic little smile. 'I'm sorry, Phil, I can't answer that question. But for now, we must be content that he's keeping in touch. At least we know he must be safe. Isn't that so?'

Phil nodded his head, but he was too choked up to speak.

Just then the assistant arrived with tea and biscuits.

Miss Martin thanked her, and the woman quickly departed.

Phil grew unusually quiet, his mind heavy with troubling thoughts.

Liz had only recently entrusted him with the information concerning the stolen locket and the ensuing discovery of its contents, which Phil so wanted to share the amazing news with Miss Martin. But he realised how strongly Liz and Jim felt about not releasing the information to anyone else.

They had rightly argued that it was Adam's private business and no one else's for the time being. They pointed out, quite rightly, that Michael Slater was a complete stranger, and that Adam might not even want to know him. Also, it was painfully clear that this man had not stood by Adam's mother when she needed him, or he would have been with her and Adam from the start. So, the question remained, what kind of man would desert a woman who was carrying his child?

With that in mind, Liz and Jim were adamant that it was for Adam to decide whether he wanted this man in his life, or not.

Phil himself was undecided as to the best way forward; although his every instinct urged him to discuss the issue with Miss Martin. After all, she seemed a wise and kindly woman, who Adam liked and respected. Moreover, she had many contacts, and she had a canny way of getting to the bottom of things.

Phil's deep thoughts were interrupted by Miss Martin's kindly voice. 'Are you all right?' She smiled at him across the desk. 'You seem to be miles away in your thoughts.'

'I'm sorry,' he answered lamely, 'it's just that I'm so worried about Adam.'

'I understand that, but I can't help feeling that you have something else on your mind.'

Phil confessed, 'You're right. I do find myself in a sort of dilemma, and I'm not sure which way to go.'

'Is it something I can help you with?'

'I'm sure you could, but I believe I'm not at liberty to confide in you.'

'Really?' She was both curious and concerned. 'And why might that be?'

Phil was hesitant. 'I wonder . . . if I was to share something with you . . . something very private and a little difficult, d'you think you could be discreet?'

She smiled. 'People do say that I'm the soul of discretion. Yes, you can rely on me, I promise. I can see that you're deeply troubled about something or other, and in my experience a niggling problem is always better out than in. So, if you want to share the burden, I can just listen. Or, if you want, I can maybe give advice.' She gave a little knowing smile. 'Or I can do absolutely nothing . . . if that's what you want.'

Miss Martin was nobody's fool. She had come to know and like Phil, and she could see he was deeply troubled. 'If you're concerned about me gossiping, have no fear. Whatever confidence you share with me, will never go beyond these four walls.'

Phil believed her, but still he agonised with his conscience. He desperately needed to confide in this dear soul; to tell her of the exciting discovery regarding the locket and the note within it.

Suddenly he was confiding the knowledge he had learned from Liz and Jim. And when he was finished, he shook his head despondently. 'I should never have told.' He felt guilty, and yet curiously relieved.

Growing hopeful, he dared to ask, 'So, will you help us then?'

'Yes, but firstly, I think you must speak with Liz and Jim. I will help, of course I will, and they must remain determined in their efforts to find Adam. However, if he does return, you should persuade them not to tell Adam of their new-found knowledge regarding his father; at least, not until we can substantiate it. Conversely, once Michael Slater *is* located, then of course Adam should be made aware that he may have a father whom he knew nothing about.'

Phil was in full agreement as she outlined her terms. 'There are too many unknown issues here that must be dealt with before Adam is brought into the equation,' she went on. 'Firstly, it might take months, even years, to track him down. Secondly, suppose it turns out that this man is not Adam's blood father? Thirdly, even if he is, it does not follow that he would want to take on a boy he doesn't even know, and possibly doesn't even care about.'

'I agree with everything you say.' Phil was delighted by her response. 'It's just that Liz and Jim are eager to give Adam the news that the unsavoury character he believed to be his father was never his real father at all. The thing is, nothing is certain yet.'

'So, do you think you might persuade them to keep this discovery to themselves, at least until I've had a chance to verify some of the possibilities?'

Phil was thrilled. 'I can't thank you enough, because I know if anyone can locate this man, and get to the truth, it's you.'

'You know I can't promise anything, except to do my utmost, for you, and Adam. I do have numerous contacts in far-flung places, and if you promise to speak with Liz and Jim, I can get on to it straightaway. So, do you think you can persuade them not to tell Adam . . . at least for now?'

Phil did not hesitate. 'I know they'll understand when I tell them that you've decided to help us. With you searching for the man we all hope is Adam's real father, that leaves us able to throw all our efforts into finding Adam.'

They shook hands, and while Phil left with a smile on his face, Miss Martin was already sifting through her contacts list.

~

On a fine, dry day, Miss Martin turned her little black car into the street, some time after Phil's visit to see her.

Parking the car halfway down, she shifted it out of gear and turned off the engine. She then gathered her small briefcase into her arms, and got out of the car. After a glance up and down, she mentally registered the number sequence on the doors. 'Ah . . . this way,

I think.' She proceeded to walk along the pavement, checking the door numbers.

The house with the two flowerpots outside was numbered to correspond with the number in her notepad.

She made her way up the path and knocked on the door. By nature, she was a stalwart and confident figure, but this particular errand today felt more like a part of her own life than a matter of professional interest. Realising how important the outcome of this meeting was to Adam, she felt decidedly nervous.

When there was no answer to her modest tapping on the door, she took a deep breath and gave a resounding knock on the door panel.

Inside the house, Sally was running the upright Hoover over the carpet, and had not heard the first knock. 'Oh, who the devil's that?' It had been one of those mornings. She had already changed the bed, done a pile of washing and baked a cake for the woman next door – it was her daughter's tenth birthday tomorrow and she was hopeless at baking.

'All right! I'm coming.' Switching off the Hoover, Sally rushed to the door and flung it open. She was surprised to see a very matronly looking woman standing on her doorstep. 'Can I help you?'

Miss Martin was relieved to see this very ordinary though pretty woman answering the door. 'Thank you, yes. I hope you don't mind this intrusion, but I'm looking for a Michael Slater. He does live here, doesn't he?' After flicking through her notepad, she showed it to Sally. 'This is the right address, isn't it?'

'Well, yes . . . that's our address.' Slightly frazzled by piles of housework and a late Friday night that left her tired, Sally was somewhat impatient. 'Sorry, but . . . might I ask what you want with my husband?' Thinking her visitor both polite and official, she was a little concerned.

'I'm sorry, please forgive me, but it's a rather delicate matter and I do need to speak with Michael Slater . . . if he's at home?' She felt awkward. She had hoped he would be alone, but now that she was faced with his wife, she was uncertain as to whether it might be wise to come back another time. The news she was bringing, would no doubt be a shock to Michael, but possibly even more of a shock to his wife, who in the event must surely be made aware of her purpose for this visit.

Miss Martin, however, felt her responsibility was to speak with Michael. It was then for him to speak with his wife.

Suddenly he was there. 'Yes, I'm at home.' Having come in from the shed, he was still in his work overalls and with oil stains on his smiley face. He opened the door wider. 'So who wants me?' He smiled at Sally, but Sally was not amused.

Miss Martin was staggered to realise how much Adam resembled Michael: the same bright eyes and smiley face. The same thick, wild hair. She was deeply shaken but excited, yet managed to compose herself. After all, a smiley face, and a mop of wild hair was not enough to go on.

'This lady asked for you, Mick,' Sally said lightly. 'She

needs to discuss a delicate matter, but doesn't seem at all keen on talking to me.'

She opened the door wider. 'Please . . . do come in.' After ushering Miss Martin inside, she then ordered her husband, 'You go and get cleaned up, while I put the kettle on.'

Gesturing to the lounge door, she asked Miss Martin, 'Please . . . go and sit down, while I make us a pot of tea . . . or would you prefer a cold drink?' She was curious as to why this woman might want to speak with Michael.

Upstairs, Mick was wondering the very same. 'What the devil does she want with me?' he muttered as he washed and changed. 'I don't believe I've ever clapped eyes on her before.'

Miss Martin thanked Sally for her kind offer of tea, which, after her journey, would go down very nicely. 'Tea would be lovely,' she said, and watched as Sally went away. She hoped her visit here today would not wreck this marriage.

It seemed no time at all before Sally was back with the tray. 'So . . . what's this "delicate matter" you mentioned?' She set the tray down and poured out three teas. 'Sugar . . . er . . . I don't know your name?'

'It's Miss Martin . . . and please, forgive my manners.' She smiled up at Sally. 'Oh . . . yes, two sugars, thank you.'

She felt awkward. 'I'm sorry, but . . . would it be possible for me to see Michael alone?'

'Mick and I have no secrets. I'm sure he would want me here.'

'Yes! Of course I want you here.' At that moment, Michael returned to find the visitor seated in the armchair. Sally was seated a distance away, on the sofa. 'Right! So, what's this all about?' He addressed the visitor, but glanced at Sally. When she looked away, it made him curiously uneasy.

Miss Martin was also uneasy. She felt awkward with Sally in the room. 'It's difficult,' she said, as Mick sat down in the chair opposite. 'I'll be honest with you both. I was hoping I might talk with Michael, first, and then the two of you could discuss the matter after I've gone.'

'Nonsense!' Mick was adamant. 'Sally and I always deal with everything together. So, who are you, and what's the purpose of your visit here?'

Miss Martin first verified that he was the right person. She checked his name, recent addresses, and ran through the information she'd collated. When he asked light-heartedly if she'd come to tell him he'd been left a deal of money by an aged unknown relative, she chuckled. 'No, nothing like that, I'm afraid.'

She informed him of her name and her work, and both Sally and Mick were taken aback. Why would someone in charge of a children's home be coming to see Mick? Sally was unsettled by the information.

Mick, too, was irritated. 'Why in God's name would you be wanting to speak with me?' he asked impatiently. 'Where do I fit into all that?'

Miss Martin drew out a sheaf of details. 'Firstly, let me tell you that there is no certainty in anything I have to say, or show you. Like I say, it's a difficult situation.'

She glanced at Sally, who was now on the edge of her seat and thinking the worst.

Miss Martin went on: 'We're here simply to determine whether or not this has anything to do with you, or means nothing at all to you. In the latter case I beg your forgiveness, and I'll be on my way.'

Sally was growing increasingly nervous. 'What have you to say?'

And so, she told them about Adam, and how her enquiries had brought her here, to their home.

She informed them of what she knew of his mother, while carefully withholding her name.

'His mother was a lovely lady, but she married a monster, and that monster hurt her so badly that she died. The husband was arrested and is now safely locked away. With his father secure in prison and his mother buried, young Adam became an orphan and was subsequently brought to my children's home. He is now with foster parents.'

Sally was intrigued. She felt for the boy, Adam, but wanted to know, 'What has all this to do with us?'

'Please, I'm getting to that.' Miss Martin went on: 'Adam has his mother's gentle nature, and though he appeared to be content with his new foster parents, the daughter resented him being there and there was a disagreement. Adam ran away, and despite everyone's efforts to find him, he has not been seen since. And of course we are all deeply concerned for his safety.'

She took out Adam's birth certificate and held it out to Michael. 'Does this tell you anything at all?'

He took the certificate and as he ran his eyes over the page, he took in a great gasp of breath.

'What is it?' Sally leaned over to see. 'What's wrong, Mick?' She saw the blood drain from his face, and her heart turned over. 'MICK! TELL ME! Please?'

He handed her the certificate and while she perused the details, he paced the floor, saying not a word, but looking as though his world had fallen apart. 'I knew her,' he said quietly. 'The boy's mother . . . I knew her.'

Sally flung the certificate onto the couch. 'What are you trying to tell me, Mick? What has this boy to do with you?'

Suddenly he had her by the shoulders. 'Please! Listen to me, sweetheart . . . it was a long time ago. It was before I met you. It was a fling, that's all. A young man's fling, and it meant nothing to me. It was one night, and I never saw her again.'

'So . . . what are you saying to me?' She had an idea, but dared not say it out loud.

When Mick looked at her, he realised that one way or another, their lives were about to change, and he prayed he would not lose this woman, who he loved with all his heart. With tears in his eyes, he explained, 'The boy's birth-date . . . he could be mine. I can't know for certain, but it all tallies.' The tears flowed shamelessly. 'Oh, sweetheart! I'm saying . . . that boy could be my son!'

When Sally turned away and ran to the bedroom, he sat for a while on the chair, his head in his hands and his mind in pieces.

'You need to see something else.' Miss Martin gave

him the tiny note Adam's mother had written, and as he read it, she told him, 'I don't think there is any doubt, do you?'

When he sank down into the chair, she knew it was time for her to leave. 'I'm leaving my contact numbers here,' she told him. 'Whether you get in touch is now up to you.' Lowering her voice, she told him, 'I can see now . . . you did not abandon her. You just didn't know . . . did you?'

When he looked up, he seemed a man devastated.

'Go to your wife,' she murmured. 'Anyone can see that you and she are devoted to each other. You have a lovely relationship . . . strong enough to come through this, I'm sure. But right now she needs you, more than ever.'

She told him, 'Whichever way you decide, I would be grateful if you let me know . . . for Adam's sake.'

Through his tears he asked, 'The boy . . . you said he was missing. Will he be safe, do you think?'

She nodded. 'He has many friends, people who love him dearly. And we won't rest until we find him.'

He gave a little smile. 'I'd best go and talk with Sally.'

'Yes, I think you should.'

She left copies of all the information she had collated. Then she let herself out.

~

Late the same evening, Jim and Liz sat talking together.

'Jim, are we wrong in not trying to contact this Michael Slater?'

Jim poured out two glasses of wine, and passed one to Liz. 'No. It has to be Adam's decision. That aside, I've been thinking.' He took a sip of wine and placed the glass on the side table. 'The last letter Phil got was from Dorset. Oh, I know it's a long shot, but what if I went down there and drove about for a while? You never know, I might just catch sight of him.'

'Look, I'm just as desperate to have him home as you are, but Dorset covers many miles,' Liz reasoned with him. 'How could you even hope to get a sight of him? He could be anywhere. In fact, by the time you got into Dorset, he could well have moved out of the area.'

'Yes, you're right.' Jim let out a long sigh. 'I just worry about him . . . what he's doing . . . who he's with, and why won't he come home?'

Liz quietly reminded him, 'He went away thinking Alice doesn't want him here. That's maybe why.'

Jim had no answer to that.

'Jim?' Liz knew how concerned he was.

Jim looked up. 'Yes, sweetheart?'

'If you could get time off work, and you really want to go and look for Adam, I'd be right behind you. You do know that, don't you?'

Jim came to sit on the arm of her chair. 'I do know that.' He slid an arm round her shoulders. 'I also know how lucky I am to have a wife like you.'

They talked for a while and when they were weary of talk and weary of worrying, they went off to their bed.

Another day was ended.

Another day when Adam continued to weigh heavy on their minds.

CHAPTER EIGHTEEN

IT WAS SATURDAY, and the work was almost over. In the relatively short time he had been here, Adam had become accustomed to the noise, colour and excitement of a day working on a fairground. His particular training had been on the waltzer. One of the main attractions, the waltzer consisted of a wide ring of large metal chairs, which spun madly round on their own axles as the machine rotated at great speed. The riders would scream and laugh, as they were thrown every which way, out of control. Adam's job was to collect the money and keep an eye out for anyone who might want to exit early.

His working day was long and hard, but he enjoyed the independence and freedom of having a reasonable wage at the end of the week, and a place to stay, however humble it might be.

Now, as the last ride finished, he noticed the boss heading towards him. Jack Langdon was a man of some considerable size, a kindly but firm man who was well liked by the workers. He ruled his large, nomadic family with a mixture of sternness and humour; the one exception being his second wife, who had an acid tongue, and a delight in seeing men fight amongst themselves.

Apart from Adam, and another, older, man, all the fairground workers were of the Langdon family. Following long and often dubious traditions, the family were close knit and fiercely independent. Occasionally flirting on the wrong side of the law, they answered to no one, and on the first sign of interference into their cherished way of life, they would swiftly move on.

When Adam came looking for work, they did not ask his age or situation. Instead, the boss-man gave him the once-over and, satisfied that this boy looked well capable of doing the job, he was given a month's trial period.

In return, Adam worked hard and long. He kept himself to himself, and made no ripples. At the end of the month, he was taken on for another month and then longer, until now he was just a stride away from his fifteenth birthday.

In the evening, after everyone and everything was accounted for, Jack supervised the securing of the stalls and rides for the night.

One of Adam's late duties before settling into his tiny caravan was to feed and groom the two riding horses belonging to the boss-man. Jack Langdon was an accomplished rider, and the horses were his pride and joy. Everywhere Jack went, the horses went with him, being drawn behind the convoy, in a smart, motor-driven horsebox.

Today, while Adam made his way to the stables, Jack embarked on his regular check: making sure nothing had been missed and that every ride and stall was safely locked down for the night.

From the main caravan window, the girl watched as Adam made the trek towards the portable, makeshift stables. Built from large wooden panels and securely bolted to the ground, the stables were sturdy and warm, with two doors that swung to and kept the horses safe. Inside, the earthy ground was dressed with a thick layer of straw for the horses to lie on.

When moving on, the stables would be taken up and packed onto the wagon, ready for the next stop.

While she watched Adam, her grandmother watched Amy. She had always thought the girl was far too pretty. Small of face, with her sleek black hair and sea-green eyes, she was a magnet for any man, even at sixteen years old.

'Amy! What are you doing looking out the window?' The shrill voice of Maggie Langdon startled the girl. 'I hope you're not fawning over that boy . . . because if you are you'd better forget it. I've told your grandfather he should send the bugger on his way, and the sooner the better. So if you're planning to throw yourself at that boy, you'd best think again, 'cause we don't want no little bastards running about here!'

Amy shrank away from the window. 'That's a dreadful thing to say!'

Like many members of the family, Amy had no liking for her grandfather's wife. 'I wasn't looking at Adam,' she lied. 'I wasn't looking at anything in particular.'

Amy had learned long ago that however hard she tried to please this bad-tempered woman, nothing she did would ever be enough.

The older woman would not let it go. A small creature with birdlike features, she poked the girl in the chest. 'Little liar! I've seen the way you fawn over him. You're turning into a slut, just like your mother. You've got the look of her, and the same appetite for men. If you ask me, you're getting to be a handful. No wonder she ran off and left you. I must have been crazy to let your grandfather take you on; especially when we've already raised our own children.'

When Amy tried to defend herself, Maggie shouted over her, 'Don't lie to me! I saw you gawping at that boy the first day your grandfather gave him work. I warned him not to take him on, but what did he do, eh? He went against me, that's what – like he always does. And now it's only a matter of time before that boy proves me right. He's a lazy article and a waste of space.'

Amy was used to her grandmother's spiteful tirades, and normally she would just walk away. This time, though, she was not only hurt by her grandmother's cruel remarks regarding her and her mother, but she felt the need to speak up for Adam. 'You're wrong, Grandma! Adam is not useless. He works hard. He doesn't steal, and he doesn't fight, not like the others. Grandfather says he's doing really well.'

'Huh! He does, does he? Well, more fool him! It wouldn't surprise me if that little devil hasn't already dipped his hand into the money-bag. Your grandfather's too soft. Too trusting. If this was my business, I'd run it the way it should be run. Unfortunately, it was handed down to your grandfather long before I met him, so he thinks he knows best. If he'd listened to me he would never have taken that boy on . . . same as I never would have taken you on, if that silly old fool hadn't kicked up the divil of a fuss.'

'I never asked you to take me on.' Amy was always hurt by that particular comment. 'It wasn't my choice to stay here with you.'

'Maybe it wasn't, but I had no choice either. I certainly didn't want a bawling kid round my backside . . . not again. But your grandfather has no backbone. He insisted you stay with us, and no matter what I said I could not change his mind. Anyway, you're coming up seventeen. It's almost time for you to take off in the big wide world and make your own living. Oh, but why should you, eh? When you've got it so cushy here.'

Tutting and ranting, she stomped to the bedroom, where she could be heard slamming and banging about.

Within minutes, she was back. 'That boy . . . what did you say about him fighting?'

Amy thought back. 'I said he would never fight, not like the others.'

For the longest moment, the old woman remained silent; and then she was chuckling. 'There you are then. So, he's a coward into the bargain.'

'I never said that, and he's not a coward. Anyway, I'm glad he doesn't fight. He's a decent boy, not like the ones Granddad had to get rid of.'

'Oh, decent is he? Well, if I know anything, it's that the

boy will show his true colours soon enough.' With that she went away and shut herself in the bedroom.

Amy took the opportunity to sneak out.

Once she was free of the caravan, she took to her heels and ran to the stables, where she looked through the door to see Adam gently stroking the long neck of one of the horses. She could hear Adam softly talking to him.

'You're a real beauty,' he was saying. 'It's no wonder Mr Langdon wants you everywhere with him.'

He dropped his voice to a whisper. 'Whenever that wicked old woman has a go at him, at least he's got the two of you to come and be with.' Nuzzling up to the horse, he continued to whisper, and as though understanding, the horse rested his head on Adam's shoulder.

This was always Adam's favourite time of day, when his ordinary day's work was done and he came out here. Trusting and friendly, the horses settled his fears and warmed his heart, and he was glad that Langdon had trusted him with such a special task, because settling the horse for the night also settled him.

Their gentle natures reached him deep inside, where no one else could, except for his darling mother, and, like her, these magnificent horses seemed to know when he was sad and lonely and needed reassurance.

Taking the brush, he ran it over the horse's mane. 'You and your pal are lucky to have each other. I have a special friend too. His name's Phil. I haven't seen him in a while, though, but I send him a note whenever I can to let him know I'm all right, and to say that he's not to worry.'

Thinking of Phil made him think of Alice and the family, and as always the sadness crept over him. 'I ran away,' he whispered, 'so now I have to pretend I'm older than I really am. I can't wait until I'm sixteen, when I'll be free to go and see Phil and the others.'

That particular birthday could not come soon enough for him, because he so wanted to see his dear friend. Phil had been with him through all his trials, and Adam sorely missed him.

Listening from outside, Amy was surprised to hear that he'd run away, and that he was not yet sixteen, and now she was unsure whether or not she should make her presence known. Wanting to be with him, she pushed everything she'd heard to the back of her mind, and stepped back a few paces, calling his name as though she had just arrived.

'Adam . . . it's me . . . Amy.' She shuffled her feet as though she was coming along the path, and when she got to the door, she stood outside looking in. 'Grandmother's off on one of her rampages, so I thought it best to get out of her way.'

'Hello, Amy.' Adam was pleased to see her. 'I'm just finishing off here,' he said. 'Come in, if you want.' He hoped she would, because he really liked her.

Amy went inside. 'You really love these horses, don't you, Adam?' Reaching out, she stroked the neck of the stallion. 'They seem to trust you, and you're so natural and easy with them. Did you ever have a horse, Adam?' she asked.

'No.' Visions of his father dampened his spirit. 'My father would never have approved.'

'Oh, that's a shame.' Noting the bitterness when he spoke of his father, she wisely changed the subject. 'So, did you never have a pet?'

'I once had a cat, but my friend Phil has a dog, and we used to take it on long walks through the woods.' He cautioned himself not to talk about anything connected to his background. 'But that was a while ago now.' He made an effort to close that particular subject.

Amy sensed his concern and changed tack. 'Do you like it here, Adam?'

Adam's face lit up. 'Oh, yes, I really do. I'm earning money and I'm kept busy, and, oh, I do love to be with the horses.'

Amy smiled. 'Did you know that, apart from me, you're the only person grandfather allows to be in here, with his precious horses?'

'Really?' Adam felt a surge of pride. 'He never said.'

'Ah, well, I'm telling you now. These horses are his pride and joy. He bred them, raised them, broke and backed them, and they've both won him championships.'

Adam was in awe. 'Wow! No wonder he doesn't want anyone else near them. But why does he trust me to feed and bed them? I mean . . . I know nothing about horses.'

Amy smiled. 'You don't have to know anything about horses,' she explained, 'because the horses will know whether or not you're safe to be with. I was ten years old when Grandfather first took me to see these horses, and I remember when I stroked this stallion I was really nervous. But he stood tall and let me stroke him, and he even nuzzled me. I was not afraid after that. Granddad told me that a horse has a sense about you. On first meeting, he'll either back off and refuse to come to you, or he'll let you touch him. If he responds like that, it means he feels safe with you, and that you would never harm him.'

Adam was amazed. 'But that's exactly what happened to me. On my second day here, your grandfather brought me to see the horses. He told me to approach the mare and raise the back of my hand near her face. I had to wait until the mare came up to sniff my hand, and then I was to very gently stroke her nose and move away, to see if she would come to me. And she did. It was amazing.'

Amy smiled. 'Grandfather told me that the back of the hand does not represent a threat. If you had gone straight up to the mare with your hand flat out, and she didn't like your scent, she might have bitten your fingers off. Granddad was introducing you to her, like he did with me. The horses obviously liked you. That's why he lets you feed and bed them down.'

'Well I'm so glad he did, because I really like being with them.'

From a short distance away, Grandmother Langdon spied on them. She could not hear their conversation, but she heard them laughing together. She inched closer. Enraged by the sight of Amy leaning in to the horse, with her hair touching Adam's face, she made her way back to the caravan, where she sat by the window, impatiently waiting for Amy to come home. *I should go and get her,* she thought, *but then she would only defy me even more.*

It was half an hour before Amy came back; her face warm with pleasure at having spent time with Adam.

'What have you been up to?' Grandmother Langdon assumed the worst.

'What do you mean?' Amy was angry. 'I haven't been up to anything. For your information, I've been in the stables with Adam and the horses. We just talked, and I helped him so he could finish early.'

The older woman gave no reply. But she was determined to finish this relationship. Maybe Amy was telling the truth and nothing happened this time, but there would surely be another time, when things would not be so innocent. She had never wanted that boy on site. She neither liked, nor trusted him.

When it came down to it, that boy would have Amy, take his pleasure and then he would move on, leaving her with child. They were all the same; only ever after one thing, and then they were gone in the night. She knew about these things.

She also knew she had to do something about it, before these events came to pass.

Retiring to her bedroom, she could not get the idea out of her head. She began pacing back and forth, her mind alive with plans. *If he stays here, before you know it, he'll have her in the sack and there'll be a young 'un to care for,* she thought. *And who would end up being expected to look after the little bastard? Me, that's who! Well, they're wrong. I've done my baby-raising, and there'll be no more of it!*

Soon, her plan was hatched in her mind and she could not wait to put it into action.

~

The following afternoon a horse-trader, Bob, called in on Jack Langdon, telling him there was a young thoroughbred up for sale in the village some fifteen miles away. 'I heard you were on the lookout for a high-class filly, being as your one isn't as young as she used to be. As you know, the best filly thoroughbreds are not only hard to come by, but they fetch such prices as might put anyone off. But being as you can swing a bargain, I reckon you might fetch the price down to suit.'

Jack was excited. 'What made you think of me?'

'That's easy, Jack. You helped me out once, so I thought it was time to return the favour. The filly is out of a top thoroughbred, so you don't want to hang about if you're interested.'

Jack could hardly hide his excitement. 'I've already had three foals from the mare I have now, and sold them on at a tidy profit. And you're right, I've been looking for a filly to bring up alongside her; get it ready for breeding, so to speak. So, what d'you reckon, Bob? Should I go tonight?'

'Well, that's up to you, but if it were me, I would not leave it till tomorrow, that's for sure.'

Before he left, Bob gave Jack the name and address of the breeder, and left him to think about it.

As the visitor left, he looked up to see Grandmother

Langdon at the caravan window. They exchanged a knowing smile. These two were long-time buddies.

~

Adam had just finished his day's work, when Jack approached him. 'I've to go out for an hour or two this evening,' he told Adam. 'The other blokes are already off, and Pete's been called away unexpectedly – there's a spot of trouble with family, or something of the sort. It means I'm one security man short, though. So d'you think you're man enough to fill the breach?'

Adam was thrilled. 'Yes, Mr Langdon. I already know Pete's routine. I walked round with him the other night, and I can do it, no bother.'

'Good! So, after you've seen to the horses, go and check with Seamus. He'll put you right. Just make sure everything is as it should be. If there's the slightest sniff of trouble, you must call Seamus. He won't be far away, but you probably won't need him. I'm counting on you, young Adam. Don't let me down.'

'I won't let you down. Thank you, Mr Langdon.' Adam was pleased to be trusted alongside Seamus.

~

A short time later, after Adam had seen to the horses, he went to his caravan and hurriedly cleaned himself up. He then made himself a sandwich, but he was so excited he couldn't eat it. He put the sandwich aside, collected his torch and went off to find Seamus.

Seamus had already been briefed by the boss-man and he showed Adam the ropes. 'Every half-hour, you check all the locks. You look for anything suspicious, like a flap of tarpaulin turned back, or a light on somewhere, or some little thing that doesn't seem right. You check everything, however insignificant it might seem, but if you do find anything untoward, don't take any chances, just call me and I'll be there in a jiffy. Have you got that?'

'Yes, I've got that.' Every word was emblazoned on Adam's mind.

Some hour and a half later, he and Seamus had done the rounds three times, and the only misdemeanour they could find was that one of the workers had left a bucket across the walkway. In the gloom, Seamus accidentally knocked it over, startling both himself and Adam. Other than that, everything appeared to be normal.

'I'd best go and tell the women not to worry.' Seamus thought the clatter of the bucket might have made them nervous. 'I'll not be a minute,' he told Adam. 'You just hang on here.' He left him by the caterpillar ride.

Adam did as he was instructed. Keeping his eyes and ears open, he waited for Seamus to come back. Everything was quiet. There seemed nothing untoward.

He almost jumped out of his skin when Seamus came up behind him. 'It's all right. Young Amy is safely locked in the caravan, listening to her music. Apparently, the grandmother's in her bedroom having a nap.

Seamus was relaxed. 'Look, Adam, I'll go round and check the rides. You have another walk round the stalls. We'll meet up at the candyfloss stall. Oh, and we should swap torches. Yours looks a bit low on battery, I reckon. I'd much rather it died on me than you.'

Adam thanked him. 'It's all right, Seamus.' He gave the torch a shake. 'I'm used to this one. It's never let me down yet.'

Seamus took him at his word, and each went his way.

Halfway round the site, Seamus thought he heard a noise. Standing still and quiet as a mouse, he listened a while. 'Damned cats!'

Taking out his cigarette packet, he plucked one out and pressed it to his lips, then he struck a match and lit the cigarette. Relaxing, he sat on the steps of the carousel and took a few puffs, blowing the smoke out in perfect circles.

Leaning back, he thought of his girlfriend at home and enjoyed the cigarette all the more. *Adam's a good boy,* he thought, his mind now back on his responsibilities. *Not many young boys actually listen to what you say . . . at least not some o' these chaps we often hire through the summer. Think they know it all . . . lazy little sods!*

On the other side of the fairground, Adam was investigating the very same noise that Seamus thought he had heard.

When a cat ran out from under the tarpaulin, Adam breathed a sigh of relief. But the relief was ended when suddenly he was spun round and before he could shout for Seamus, his mouth was taped and a sack was thrown over his head. Propelled forward, he had no idea what was happening, or who the men were that held him in such a lock-hold he thought his arms would break.

Terrified, he felt himself being dragged over rough ground, and then he was lifted and thrown into what he imagined must be a vehicle of sorts. He could hear an engine running, but he couldn't see or even cry out.

Behind him, Seamus heard the vehicle take off at speed. He ran as fast as his legs would carry him, only to see the back end of a vehicle, partly hidden by flying dirt, and thick smoke rising from the exhaust. Just a fleeting glance, then all he could see were the lights as the vehicle sped away along the top lane. 'Adam!' He screamed his name as he ran back to the stalls. 'Adam, answer me, dammit!'

When it became obvious that Adam was nowhere to be found, he ran towards the Langdons' caravan, only to be greeted by a frantic Amy.

Having heard the speeding vehicle and then Adam's name being called out, she was already running down the caravan steps. 'What is it?' she screamed at Seamus. 'What's happened? Where's Adam?'

Seamus wasn't altogether certain exactly what had happened. 'I sent Adam to check the stalls while I checked the rides. I heard a sound and ran round to the stalls, and there was this vehicle racing off – a van, I think, but I can't be sure.'

Amy was fearful. 'Where's Adam?'

Seamus threw out his hands in despair. 'I can't find him. I've searched high and low and I can't locate him. I checked the horses, but he's not there either.'

'So, where is he, Seamus?' Amy was beside herself. 'Where could he have gone? And who did the vehicle belong to?' She had a really bad feeling. 'I'm frightened, Seamus. What if he's lying hurt somewhere? We've got to search. We've got to find him.'

'I've searched every nook and cranny, and he's nowhere on site,' Seamus told her again. He took hold of her by the shoulders. 'Listen, Amy, it's no good us looking again. You'd best call your grandmother.'

'No!' Amy was adamant. 'Leave her be. She doesn't care about Adam.'

Inside her bedroom, Grandmother Langdon listened to the conversation for a while, and then she turned over, a devious little smile on her crinkled old face.

Outside, Amy ran past Seamus. 'I'll find him,' she said. 'He must be here somewhere.'

Going after her, Seamus held her back. Looking down on her tearful face, he told her what he suspected. 'I don't know who was driving that vehicle, but whoever it was, I think they took him.'

'No! Why would you say that?' Then Amy remembered what Adam had told her. 'He said his father was a controlling man. He ran away. He said he couldn't go back. Oh, Seamus, maybe Adam's father took him?'

'But why snatch him like that? Why not come here himself, in daylight? Why did he not speak to your grandfather, like any other man would do? Amy, fetch Grandmother Langdon. Maybe she can get hold of Jack. Maybe he'll know what to do.'

Fearful for Adam's safety, Amy relented, and ran into

the caravan bedroom where she shook the older woman. 'Grandmother! Get up, quick!'

Opening one eye, the older woman cursed. 'What d'you want?'

Impatient, Amy shook her again. 'We need Granddad. Adam's gone missing.'

'What? You mean he's run off? I knew he would. I said all along he was trouble, but nobody would listen.'

'No! He hasn't run off. There was a van. Seamus thinks someone's taken Adam. We need Granddad. Where is he, Grandmother? Can we call him?'

'No, we can't, and even if we could, he wouldn't thank you for it. He's doing an important deal just now. You know he won't like to be interrupted.'

'He'll want to know about Adam and the van. Please, Grandmother, give me the number and I'll call him.'

'I can't! I don't have a number. And if I did, I would not give it to you. I knew all along that boy was trouble. Good riddance to him. I won't be shedding any tears at his going. Now get out and leave me be!'

When the door suddenly opened to admit Jack Langdon, Maggie was shocked. Drawing the covers over her, she demanded, 'What's brought you home so early? You said you'd be gone for most of the evening doing a deal or something . . . buying a filly thoroughbred, so I was led to believe.'

'Really? And who told you . . . about the filly?'

'Well, I don't know. *You* must have done.'

'No, I didn't. There wasn't time.'

'Well then, I suppose Bob must have told me . . . We had a few words before he came to find you.'

Jack was suspicious. 'We'll continue this conversation when I get back.'

'Where are you going?'

His face set with anger as he stared down on her. 'You get back to sleep. You and me . . . we'll talk later.'

Hurrying outside, he shouted for Seamus. 'Fetch the Land Rover. Be quick! And think hard . . . which way did they go?'

When Amy came running down the steps, he told her, 'Go back. Lock all the doors and windows and keep an eye on your grandmother.'

'I'm coming with you two. I'm coming to find Adam.'

'Do as you're told, Amy!'

Amy's answer was to fling the caravan door shut and run across to climb into the back seat of the Land Rover. 'I'm coming with you, Granddad.'

'Well, if I'm right, there'll be no time for arguing. So keep quiet, sit still, and hold onto your hat!'

When he put his foot down hard on the accelerator, the capable Land Rover responded at speed. As they fled along the lanes, Amy clung on with both hands. She had no idea where they were going. She had a feeling that her grandfather knew something, and from the way he spoke to Grandmother Langdon, maybe she knew more than she was saying. It was a bad situation with undercurrents she did not understand, and Adam was right in the middle of it.

She could hear the two men talking in the front. 'They wouldn't have gone along the main route,' Grandfather Langdon was saying. 'Not from the way you described how the lights were bouncing up and down as they sped off. I reckon they went along the top lane?'

'That's right. I could see the lights clearly bobbing up and down, which means they were on a rough surface. Besides, if they'd been along the bottom lane, the spinney would have blacked out the lights, but I could clearly see the lights travelling on.'

'Right! So, that's the way we'll go – along the top lane – and let's hope to God we're right.'

~

After a rough and frightening journey, Adam was yanked out of the van. Blindfolded, and completely unaware of why this was happening, he could feel himself being dragged along rough terrain. He heard the voices of his attackers, but he was not able to recognise them.

Suddenly his abductors came to a halt and he was dropped to the ground. All was quiet and for a moment he thought they'd gone, but then came the vicious kicking, and a harsh warning. 'Somebody doesn't like you! So don't come back. You won't get a second chance.'

Time and again, Adam felt the impact of their boots against his battered body. Then he was rolling away, faster and faster before the darkness swept over his mind, and took away the pain.

~

Jack Langdon senior had grown up in the countryside. What he didn't know about tracking was not worth knowing. Amy's grandfather was his only grandson, and it had given the old man the greatest pleasure to teach him everything he knew.

It was this knowledge that Jack drew on now.

While he walked in front, following every dip and scar in the road, Seamus crawled on behind in the Land Rover. Amy watched her grandfather and she knew if anyone could find Adam, it would be he.

The abductors' van had left behind a trail of clues: the peculiar swerves, and the deep tyre tracks were still fresh and telling a story.

Amy had wanted to walk with him, but Jack told her to stay inside, and so she hung her head out the window and watched her grandfather's every move. When suddenly he stopped to call out, 'Here! They pulled in here!' both she and Seamus jumped out and ran to see.

The evidence of a vehicle having swerved towards the edge of the steep bank was clear. The ground was stirred up by the heavy-booted footprints from at least two people, and between the footprints the track of flattened dirt suggested that something heavy had been dragged along the ground.

Jack drew their attention to where the flattened ground carried on right to the recently broken edge. 'Here!' Jack knew straightaway, and his fears were very real. 'Go back and lock yourself in the Land Rover,' he instructed Amy. 'If anyone comes near you, press the horn, and we'll be right there.'

When she opened her mouth to argue, he told her firmly, 'Amy! Do as I say. We don't know what we might find down there.' He had an idea, and it was not pleasant. If Adam had been thrown down there, Jack knew his chances of survival were very slim indeed.

For a painfully long time, Amy sat in the car, frantic and increasingly impatient. She wanted to go after them, but the lane was dark, and she was nervous. Granddad had looked really worried.

All she could think of was Adam. 'Please, let him be all right,' she whispered, over and over again. There was no comfort, no reassurance, and now Seamus and her grandfather had been gone for so long, she began to worry about them too.

She was curled up, eyes closed, when a gentle tap came on the window. It was Seamus, and he looked fraught.

Quickly, Amy unlocked the door, and Seamus jumped in and started the engine.

'Seamus! Did you find Adam? Is he all right? Where's Grandfather?' The questions came thick and fast.

'Yes, we found him.' Putting the engine into gear, Seamus sent it hurtling forward, keeping a sharp eye on the road ahead. 'He's bad, Amy. I'm sorry, but Adam's real bad. He's alive, though, thank God. Your grandfather's watching over him.'

'Did Adam tell you who took him?' Amy could not hold back the tears.

Reluctant to tell her that Adam was in no fit state to speak, Seamus avoided the question. 'We've to find a telephone quickly. There's one in the next village. Hold on, Amy!' he warned her again, as he sent the Land Rover surging forward. 'Hold on tight!'

Amy remained silent. There were no more questions. Just a desperate prayer, that they had found Adam in time, and that he would recover.

PART SIX

~

Home is Where the Heart is

1960

CHAPTER NINETEEN

'I'M NERVOUS ABOUT meeting up with Jim and Liz.' Sally linked her arm through Mick's. 'And I've got my fingers crossed that Adam will let you explain.'

Mick reassured her: 'Stop worrying, sweetheart. Miss Martin told him everything, and for now, I'm just delighted that at least, he's agreed to see us.'

Sally relaxed. 'You're right. If he didn't want to know us, he would have said no straight off.'

Mick was also nervous, though he was determined not to let his nerves get the better of him. This first meeting with Adam was too important. 'I can never thank Miss Martin enough,' he said now. 'If it hadn't been for her, and the others, I would never have known about Adam.'

He glanced at Sally. 'As for you –' he squeezed her hand – 'you're amazing. That day when Miss Martin came to see me, you could have packed your bags there and then. Instead, you took the time to listen to what

I had to say, and once you understood, you supported me all the way.' Leaning down, he kissed her on the cheek. 'I loved you from the first day I saw you. Truth is, my life would be empty without you.'

Sally smiled up at him. 'I'm sorry I couldn't give you children.' Her smile brightened. 'But you now have a son . . . *we* have a son, and I so hope he'll accept us, because from what we've been told, he's had a bad time of it.'

'Yes, he has, but if we're given the chance to make it up to him, we'll turn all that around, won't we?'

'Yes, God willing.' She gave a private little smile, 'Oh, Mick . . . just imagine . . . a son, to love and care for. We'll help him forget the bad times, and look forward with him to a better future. Oh, Mick! With us, he'll have so much love.'

Mick was filled with emotion by Sally's enthusiasm. 'You do realise that if he accepts us—'

'Yes . . . what?'

He gave a happy smile. 'There might come a day when we'll be granddad and grandma. What do you think to that?'

Her smile said it all. 'Babies . . . oh, how wonderful!' She clung to him. 'First, though, we need to be thankful for Adam. Like you say, if he accepts us, all the lovely things will follow. And I for one won't mind having grey hair, with a bouncing grandchild in my arms.'

Falling silent, they walked on, growing more excited, more nervous. This was a major day in both their lives. Miss Martin would be waiting for them at a café near to the hospital, where Adam was recovering, along with

Adam's foster parents, Liz and Jim. Also, they would finally meet Phil. According to Miss Martin, it was that dear man who had kept Adam under his wing, and never once faltered in his loyalty to the boy.

Deep in thought, Mick remained anxious. Meeting up with all these fine people was a daunting prospect. Suppose they took against him and Sally? Suppose they were able to persuade Adam against accepting them?

When he voiced his concerns to Sally, she told him in no uncertain manner, 'Stop worrying. Adam will see how genuine you are, and I just know he will love you.' Looking up at him with adoring eyes, she squeezed his arm. 'I mean . . . who wouldn't?'

Meeting up with the others in a café near the hospital, Mick saw them all as having Adam's welfare at heart. He confessed his anxieties.

'I'm just a stranger to him. I'm concerned that he might not give me a chance to explain. He could even reject me out of hand.'

Phil assured him, 'In spite of his bad experiences, Adam is a good and balanced young man, without an ounce of spite in him.'

'He might think I abandoned his mother, but I didn't know she was with child. She never told me.'

Phil put his mind at rest: 'Miss Martin and I have already spoken to him, and though he was deeply shocked, I think he's had time enough to mull it over in his mind. I'm sure he'll listen when you put your case. Like us, he'll see you both as good people, and to tell you the truth, although all of us sitting round this table have done our best for Adam, we are not his parents, and that's what the boy needs, more than anything.'

He smiled at Mick. 'Don't be nervous, either of you. I'm sure Adam will like you both straight off. Trust me.'

~

Adam had been in hospital for two long months.

His broken bones were mending, and the deepest scars he carried from that terrifying ordeal were the memories of it. There was a faint scar along his cheekbone, but apart from that his face had escaped unscathed.

Today, the nurse would take him for final X-rays and a check-up. If everything was headed in the right direction, he would go home this afternoon. Phil was due to arrive before too long. And if all went as planned, maybe Liz and Jim would be with him.

'Excited, are you?' the nurse asked.

Adam told her he was grateful for the care he'd had there, but that he would be pleased to leave now. 'I can't wait to see Phil and the others,' he said.

'Well, I'm sure they'll all be excited to get you home again. You're a very lucky boy to have such good friends.'

Adam smiled. 'I know that.'

'And that little Amy is lovely. I know I shouldn't ask, but I'm naturally nosy. Is it serious between you and her?'

Adam blushed. 'I don't know yet.' For him, it was.

The check-ups all showed that Adam was well on the mend. The doctor was delighted with his progress.

'I'd feel comfortable if you use the wheelchair for at

least another two weeks or so, and then you can progress onto crutches. Within a month or so after that, you should be strong and able enough to climb Mount Everest.'

Adam was slightly disappointed that he needed the wheelchair for a while yet, but at least he was mending, and that was the most important thing.

As the nurse wheeled him back, she suggested, 'You should get a couple of hours' sleep before your folks start arriving. It will stand you in good stead for the travelling.'

In the ward, she tucked him up in bed and left him drinking a glass of orange juice. 'Miss Martin brought your clothes in yesterday. They're hanging in the wardrobe to loosen the creases. Oh, and I'll have the medication waiting for you by the time you're ready to leave. Meantime, you get some rest.'

After finishing his orange juice, that's exactly what Adam did.

First, though, he checked the clock: half-past one . . . another hour and they would be there. He was disappointed that Liz had not offered to take him back, but he accepted it because he thought maybe Alice was uncomfortable with the idea of him living there again.

Still, he comforted himself with the knowledge that it would not be too long before his sixteenth birthday, when he could choose where he might live.

He thought of Amy, and his heart melted. Wherever in the world he went from now on, he would not want to be far away from her.

~

Seated in the nearby café with Phil, and Liz and Jim, Sally and Mick grew increasingly nervous. 'I'm worried that Adam might be upset when we tell him the truth,' Mick said. 'Maybe he won't even like us.'

He was highly nervous of speaking with the son he had not even known he had. He spoke to Liz on that point. 'It's thanks to Miss Martin's valiant efforts to track me down that I found out I had a son. But that was months ago. I should have talked to him about it long before now. He won't forgive me, will he?'

'There is nothing to forgive,' Liz promised him. 'You couldn't tell him when he was lying at death's door, and you certainly couldn't tell him while he was recovering. But you came here every day to see him, while he was unconscious and such dedication tells its own story. Adam will see that, and of course he won't be upset. One thing I would say, though: when you do tell him the truth, do it gently. Think of how the truth came as a shock to you. And as you're well aware, he's already been through a lot these past months.'

Phil endorsed that. 'Adam is a surprisingly mature boy for his age. He has a depth of understanding. I know, when you tell him, he'll be shocked at first, yes, but I can assure you, Adam will be greatly relieved to know that the monster who raised him was not his blood father.'

Sally had a different concern. 'What if he doesn't want to come home with us? We can't force him, and neither would we. So, what do we do?'

'I think we should leave it to Adam,' Mick decided. 'One thing we are sure of, he won't have to go back to the children's home, not now he's got me and Sally. And don't forget, I'm his father – named and verified by his own mother – and I think that means I can say whether or not Adam can stay with friends if he wants to.'

Sally agreed. 'But we would love him to be part of our family. To call us Mum and Dad would mean so very much to us.'

She smiled shyly. 'I'll admit, it was a shock when I first found out that Mick had fathered a child. When Miss Martin traced us and showed us the locket and the note Adam's mother had written, I was truly shaken. I didn't know what it might mean to us. But now, after being by Adam's bedside for hours on end when he didn't even know we were there, I've grown to love him as a person in his own right, and as a son. And I really would love him to come home with us.'

Phil ended the conversation, with wise words: 'Trust me to let the boy know the truth, and we'll go from there.'

~

Adam was surprised to see Phil on his own. 'I thought you were bringing Liz and Jim with you?' he asked. 'Or did they not want to see me?' He was disappointed.

'I came alone because I have something to show you.' He took the locket from his pocket, and pressed it into Adam's hand. 'This belongs to you.'

Adam was amazed and confused. 'Oh! It's my mother's locket! But it was in my bag. Someone stole it . . . However did you find it, Phil?' Holding the locket in his hand again brought tears to Adam's eyes. 'Oh, Phil, I don't know how you found it, but I'll never be able to thank you enough. Where was it? Did the thief try to sell it, or what? I don't understand.'

'The locket was not in your bag when you left Liz and Jim's house,' Phil carefully explained. 'Alice took it from the box. She hid it and told Liz about it later. Now then, I have something here that will change you life for ever, Adam. Something very precious. Liz found it when she took the locket from Alice.'

Intrigued and somewhat afraid, Adam held out his hand. 'What is it, Phil?'

Phil laid the folded note into Adam's palm. 'This was inside the locket. It's a beautiful thing,' he said, 'and it's in your mother's hand.'

With great trepidation, Adam unfolded the tiny piece paper and read what his mother had written for him.

When he had read every word, Adam looked up at Phil, his eyes filled with tears. 'I never knew,' he said, 'I never knew.' He put his face in his hands and he closed his eyes. His mother was strong in his mind. He was sad for her, for the way she had lived with Edward Carter all those years, not because she loved him, but to give her child a father.

He looked up at Phil. 'She made a terrible sacrifice, Phil . . . for me. She lived with that man for all those years, and she probably never even loved him.' The tears ran down his face. 'She did that, for me, Phil. For me!'

Phil warned him against feeling guilty. 'Your mother

was a very strong woman, Adam. She had a choice and she took it. It was what she wanted. And as long as she had you, she was a happy, contented woman. You must never, ever forget that.'

Adam nodded. 'And this man . . . my father. Does he know about me now?'

'Yes. He's a good man, Adam. I can see why your mother fell in love with him. But he never knew she was pregnant with you. She never told him. He's married now but, ironically, Mick and his wife, Sally, can never have children. Miss Martin told them about the letter, and they have been at your side from when you were first brought in to when you began to open your eyes. That's when they decided not to come any more, until you knew the truth. And you could make up your mind as to whether or not you want him in your life . . . him and Sally.'

Adam shook his head. 'I don't know, Phil. I'm confused at the minute. I need to think about it. Are they here now?' he asked suddenly.

Phil nodded. 'They're waiting, but they will go away and come back again to see you . . . if that's what you want?'

Adam was about to answer when both he and Phil became aware of someone bearing down on them.

Mick had decided he needed to know what his son thought of him.

Phil stood up. 'Adam . . . this is Mick, your father.'

For the longest moment neither of them spoke. Instead, they looked at each other and the moment was heavy with emotion. Then Adam opened his arms and

Mick went to him. 'I'm sorry, Son,' he whispered. 'If I'd only known, I would never have let your mother go. She was so very special. But I have a wonderful wife now, and in many small ways she's very much like your mother. She's kind and loving, and she so wants you to be with us . . . if it's what you want too.'

Adam thought of the horses at the fairground, and how they could sense whether they would be safe with a particular person. Just now, he felt the same way with Mick.

In that precious moment he could see his mother's smile; he could hear her voice. And now, having read her heartfelt letter, he knew she would be content if he were to accept this man who was his father.

In answer to Mick's request, Adam smiled and nodded, and his future was sealed.

~

Later, Phil made him aware of Carter's downfall.

He told Adam of a recent report, detailing how Carter had tried to install himself as the big man inside prison. Unfortunately for him, he had set himself against hard and dangerous men, who meant to teach him a lesson.

Edward Carter earned his comeuppance.

After a fierce and bloody skirmish between the prisoners, the officers found Carter, crouched in a corner, badly injured and mentally unstable.

After treatment in hospital, he was transferred to a mental institution, where he was destined to spend the rest of his days.

Phil said it was an eye for an eye; despite all the pain, fear and suffering he had heaped on others, his innocent victims had grown stronger, while Edward Carter was now a broken man.

CHAPTER TWENTY

THROUGHOUT HIS RECOVERY, Amy was never far from Adam's side.

Amy's grandfather, also, was a constant visitor and had neglected his work duties to be there for Adam. Throughout Adam's painful recovery, Seamus had yet again proven himself to be a loyal friend.

When Adam was strong and able enough, he was determined to return to the fairground, of which he had wonderful memories, alongside his darling Amy.

Also, it gave him a measure of pride and satisfaction to repay their loyalty and love.

One evening, after a busy day, Adam made his way across the yard to check that the horses were all put away safely.

Having checked around the buildings and grounds, he then went over to the young colt's stable. The colt had only recently been separated from his mother, and like other young horses weaned from their mothers for the first time, he was somewhat fretful and jittery.

Inside the stable, Amy pacified the colt. 'Ssh . . . you're a big boy now, and you can't cling to your mummy for ever. You have to learn to be on your own at night-times, but don't worry, you'll see her tomorrow in the fields.'

She nuzzled its face. 'I think I know how you feel, though,' she confessed. 'I can never imagine being too far from Adam. When I'm not near him, I feel empty inside, and so very sad. And then –' her eyes lit up and a warm passion coloured her voice – 'when I'm with him, my heart sings and jumps for joy, and I feel kind of . . . complete somehow. Sometimes, when he smiles at me, it's like I can't breathe. I love him so very much, but I'm afraid to tell him, in case it might frighten him away. Oh, I think he does like me a lot, but I don't know if he loves me in the same way that I love him.'

'Then you must be blind,' Adam's voice gentled across the stable.

'Oh, Adam!' Flustered to see him there, she was lost for words, and then she was in his arms as his tender words brought tears to her eyes.

'Oh, my darling Amy . . . how could you not know, I've loved you from the first time I saw you?'

Taking a small, red box from his pocket, he told her, 'I've been carrying this about for over a week, not daring to give it to you, in case you might turn away.'

When he handed her the pretty red box, she gingerly opened it. Inside was a tiny ring, with a bright, blue stone set in a heart-shaped centre.

With tears streaming down her face and her heart about to burst, Amy was lost for words.

'Well?' Adam whispered teasingly. 'Will you marry me . . . or have I got it wrong?'

Amy gave her answer by flinging her arms round his neck. She held onto him as though she would never let go.

'I love you,' she whispered softly in his ear. 'I've always loved you.'

After slipping the ring on her finger, Adam held her for what seemed an age. Then they were laughing, and running hand in hand, so excited. And impatient to tell everyone the good news.

Find out more about Josephine COX and her bestselling books

Dear Reader,

The first thing I do when I'm about to start a novel is to profile the main characters, and, from that moment, it is they who write the story. Along the way, I might laugh or feel sadness with all the characters – I share their every emotion. Sometimes my characters catch me by surprise when they commit an act of cruelty that I might never have originally anticipated. But I remain true to my instincts. The characters are alive, the plot is shaped by what they do – just as in life, we as readers are swept along in their world. In our own lives, we have no say in who we are, and just like the characters, we have no idea how our lives will shape us – and often we are at the mercy of life itself, helpless to change our journey.

In this book, the character that shapes the story is Edward Carter, more monster than man. Through devious actions and callous intent he drives the other characters into situations that will either make or destroy them. But along the way, there are some wonderful characters who cross Edward's path, characters who are as good as he is evil. So, as in life, this story touches upon fear and hatred, but there is also laughter and joy, and a sense of fulfillment.

I am thrilled to live in my characters' world for a time, and I hope you are too – enjoy the journey!

Lots of love and take care,

Jo x

JO ANSWERS QUESTIONS FROM HER READERS

If you could live in another time, which era would you choose?

It would have to be Dickensian London – I'm absolutely fascinated by the world of Charles Dickens.

Are you superstitious?

No, I'm not superstitious, but I always carry a sports whistle in my bag when I travel. I like to think that if the plane went down in water, I could attract attention, which gives me a bit of security.

Have you always told stories? Can you tell us a bit about your earliest memories?

Yes, I've told stories for as long as I can remember! I remember one teacher at school in particular who encouraged me, Miss Jackson.

When I was young, my family was very poor – we often went without, and our clothes used to come from the rag and bone shop. I used to collect up newspapers and take them to the paper factory to save up enough money for something 'off the rack', which was the height of luxury to me then!

One of my earliest memories is of my granddad. He always wore a flat cap and a really long overcoat. He had long whiskers, and a terrier that followed him everywhere. I remember that the shoes I had from the rag and bone shop were hurting my feet, and one day we walked past a shop displaying a pair of red shoes with ankle straps – I pressed my nose up to the window and said to Granddad, "Look at those!" They were so beautiful, and I couldn't ever imagine owning a pair of shoes like that. But my granddad went back to the shop and bought them for me. They were the only pair they had, and they fitted me perfectly – it was meant to be! I've always loved shoes from that moment – so much so that my husband, Ken, built me some cupboards all along the bedroom wall to keep them in, but I still manage to have some in boxes on the floor!

What would you do if you won the lottery?

I would share it with my friends and family – by paying off their mortgages and other bills, for instance. I always try to help anyone who is in trouble if they come to me, and helping the people I love most in this way would be a great joy to me. I think I would also treat myself to a really fast sports car! If I won enough money to do it, I would also really enjoy helping to grant the wishes of children who are very ill, or in difficult family circumstances. I would love to do that, and to see the look on their faces when they got their wish!

How do you come up with new ideas for your books?

New characters just present themselves to me; I see them everywhere, quite often when I'm halfway through writing another book. They stay with me and simmer along until I'm ready to give them their story.

I have writing pads all over the house – I covered eight pages of A4 last night writing a story I've called *The Kissing Tree* – it meant that I only slept for about three hours, but it was worth it!

What have been the proudest moments of your life and career?

The proudest moment of my life, without doubt, was giving birth to my sons. I think the greatest achievements in my career are the beautiful letters I receive from my wonderful readers, and receiving the Outstanding Achievement Award from the RNA in 2011.

Which famous person, and which of your own characters, would you most like to meet?

Without doubt, I'd like to meet Kirk Douglas! I've got every edition of *Spartacus* ever made (and quite often with an extra copy for back up), except for the original unedited film. My brother even bought me a huge framed picture of Kirk Douglas in his loincloth in

Woolworth's years ago. I had it enlarged, and it still hangs in my office. Recently, my wonderful agent Luigi surprised me with a copy of *The Broken Man*, signed by Kirk Douglas himself – needless to say, I was absolutely thrilled! Kirk wrote that he's looking forward to reading my next, 50th book…

Of my own characters, I'd most like to meet the bus driver in *The Broken Man* – he's a wonderful friend to Adam. He is a really warm and lovable person, and he certainly lingered with me after I'd finished the book.

Which character from your books is most like you?

I think probably Emma Grady, from *The Emma Grady Trilogy* (*Outcast*, *Alley Urchin* and *Vagabonds*). I really put myself in her shoes – her uncle, who was supposed to be her guardian, frames her for murder, and she is transported to Australia. She is lined up with all the other convicts and picked out to work for some awful men. I could really feel everything she felt, and I just wanted to cuddle her and tell her that it was going to be all right. I won't give the rest of the story away, but I will say that I made sure she came back to England and gave her uncle his comeuppance!

What's your favourite book?

My favourite book of all time is Charles Dickens' *Oliver Twist*. I heard that story at school when I was about seven years old and was mesmerized. The characters are amazing – you never forget them. It definitely inspired me to become a writer.

What is your writing routine?

I don't have a routine as such. I don't have eight hours sleep, eight hours work and eight hours play – it just doesn't work like that for me. If I wasn't sleeping well I would go into the office and work for four or five hours – I love being with my characters. The story and characters just take over so I have pen and paper in every room of my house in case I need to hurriedly jot something down.

What do you do in your spare time?

That's a very difficult question because I don't have a lot of spare time. I like to go dancing, swimming or walking – basic things make me happy. When I've finished a chapter, I often sing and dance around the kitchen with the radio on. I'm a creative soul.

Are any of your stories based on real life events?

My stories are a mixture of real life and make believe. Sometimes I feature a street that I grew up in or a character that struck me as a child. But often a character just pops into my mind without me even realising.

How do you feel when you finish a book?

I live with my characters while I'm writing a story so when you come to the last page, you do feel sad. There is an element of excitement that the story is written but you miss the characters, as they become so real. A lot of readers say they re-read my novels if there are characters that they particularly relate to.

I have to clear my mind and have a break once I've finished a book so that the new characters can materialise. I'm soon living with them and I have a new set of people in my life.

How do you choose the settings for your books?

I pick up the setting on location – how a street looks, the houses...

I also set a lot of my books in and around Blackburn because it's where I grew up. I think it's natural for most writers to go back to their roots. It was my stamping ground when I was a kid – we used to play in the streets, swing round the lamppost and dream of the future. When you're a child your emotions are very raw and you live life full on – it was a fantastic time and so I feature most of my childhood, filled with memorable characters that I transfer into my stories.

Josephine
COX

Have you read all her
No. 1 *Sunday Times* bestsellers yet?

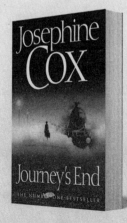

THE LONER

Home is where the heart is – but it's also where the pain lies…

Young Davie Adams is all alone. Devastated, he flees his hometown of Blackburn to escape the memories of the worst night of his life. With little more than the shirt on his back he sets off on a lonely, friendless road, determined to find his father.

Two people are stricken by his departure – Judy, his childhood friend who is desperate to reveal a secret she has kept close to her heart for so long, and Joseph, his grandfather, who is racked with guilt about that fateful night.

Exhausted and afraid, Davie finds friendship and a place to stay but when fate deals him another disastrous blow, he must decide whether to keep running or return to face his demons …

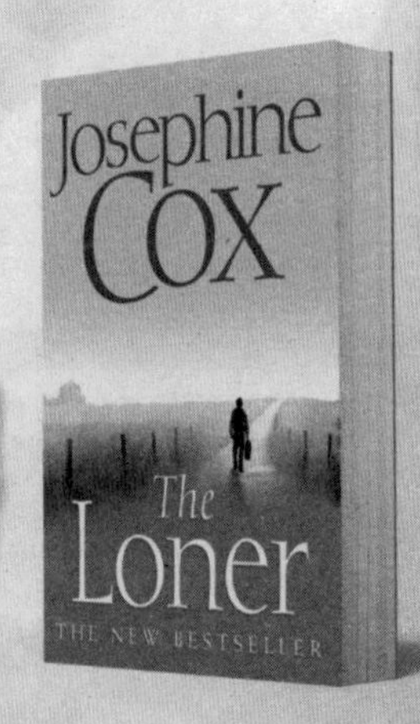

ebook • audio

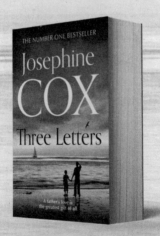

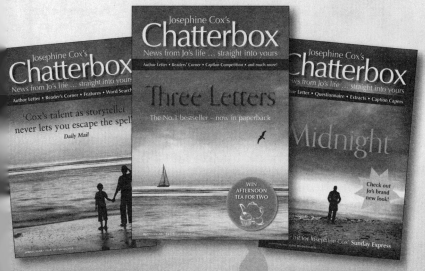

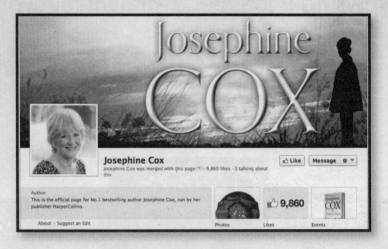

AN ENEMY TRANSF[illegible]ED BY MAGIC'S S[illegible]

is just one of the deadly [illegible] be faced in such [illegible]

"A Wolf in the F[illegible] was chosen to be a Guardian, to fi[illegible] olves with only the strength of he[illegible] nds. And not until a man raised his sword [illegible] nst the fanged and furred foe, did she learn the true nature of the enemy she faced. . . .

"The Cloud of Evil"—Expelled by his masters for dabbling in Dark Magic, he leagued with a sorceress to explore long-forbidden knowledge, a study which might lead to undreamed of powers—or to a doom beyond imagining. . . .

"Heart of the Matter"—Her father's sorceress, she was sworn to do his bidding, and his command was to bring him the heart of one who had betrayed him. But she was also sworn not to kill. Torn between conflicting oaths and her love for the one she was condemned to slay, could she find an answer that would not break either oath?

SWORD AND SORCERESS VII

MARION ZIMMER BRADLEY
in DAW editions:

DARKOVER NOVELS

DARKOVER LANDFALL
STORMQUEEN!
HAWKMISTRESS!
TWO TO CONQUER
THE HEIRS OF HAMMERFELL
THE SHATTERED CHAIN
THENDARA HOUSE
CITY OF SORCERY
THE SPELL SWORD
THE FORBIDDEN TOWER
THE HERITAGE OF HASTUR
SHARRA'S EXILE

DARKOVER ANTHOLOGIES

DOMAINS OF DARKOVER
FOUR MOONS OF DARKOVER
FREE AMAZONS OF DARKOVER
THE KEEPER'S PRICE
THE OTHER SIDE OF THE MIRROR
RED SUN OF DARKOVER
SWORD OF CHAOS

OTHER BRADLEY NOVELS

HUNTERS OF THE RED MOON
WARRIOR WOMAN

NON-DARKOVER ANTHOLOGIES

SWORD AND SORCERESS I
SWORD AND SORCERESS II
SWORD AND SORCERESS III
SWORD AND SORCERESS IV
SWORD AND SORCERESS V
SWORD AND SORCERESS VI
SWORD AND SORCERESS VII

SWORD AND SORCERESS VII

AN ANTHOLOGY OF HEROIC FANTASY

Edited by
Marion Zimmer Bradley

DAW BOOKS, INC.
DONALD A. WOLLHEIM, PUBLISHER
375 Hudson Street, New York, NY 10014

Cover art by David Cherry.

DAW Book Collectors No. 836.

First Printing, December 1990

1 2 3 4 5 6 7 8 9

PRINTED IN THE U. S. A.

TABLE OF CONTENTS

INTRODUCTION

Every now and then, there are times when I wonder why on earth I ever had the idea I wanted to be a writer—or an editor. It was so long ago now that I really don't remember how I originally got that idea.

Like every other job, it has its drawbacks. For instance, if you're on the stage, you have to be careful of developing an allergy to the greasepaint; and one of the many reasons I never sought a stage career—quite apart from the question of whether or not I had talent for it—was my utter inability to sleep in the daytime. No matter how late I was up, I found myself obdurately awake at five in the morning.

In case you are in the enviable position of not knowing what the world looks like at five, I can tell you it's not particularly attractive. Your job isn't open, so you can't work; the rest of your family is asleep, so you can't enjoy their company; you can't work in a shut library; you can't shop, because the stores won't be open for hours.

But you can *write;* and I imagine that's why I became a writer; it was one of the very few things I could do during the wee small hours while all the rest of the world was asleep. Maybe it's because (or the reason that) I married two men who felt ill-done-by if they were expected to rise and be coherent before noon. It was definitely one of the few things I could do and still keep an eye on my kids. It's hard to raise the kids when you're selling shoes in Macy's or being a registered nurse.

And this kind of reason is the reason, I suppose, behind a lot of career choices. I'm *awake* at an hour when even the radio is quiet. (Or it was when I started writing; even the TV went off at about two o'clock. Perhaps from that you can divine my age. When I was a kid, there wasn't any television.)

Writing for a living, you develop a particularly split mind. Almost every man I know finds it hard to work unless he has the equivalent of Marcel Proust's legendary cork-lined room; while every woman writer I know learned to write on the equivalent of a city desk—interruptions all over the place. The women who write for my anthologies are all experts at juggling; instead of waiting until we have "time to write" we just write. We don't have time to write, we *make* time.

There's a very famous essay by Virginia Woolf; it's called "A Room of One's Own," and, if my memory serves me correctly, she comments that this is the reason why women don't make progress in the arts; because they never have that basic necessity: time, space, and quiet in which to create. I often wonder, then, whether Ms. Woolf would ever have written any of her famous novels if she had had to get out and work on a newspaper's city desk?

Most of the woman writers I know don't have time to write; they *make* it. And if that means getting up at four in the morning, or writing on a clipboard, as one prize-winning short story writing English professor I knew used to do on the ten minute interval while her classes were passing, that's what you do.

You can write with kids all over the house, though it's easier to do it when the kids are in school. I don't think it gets any easier as the kids get older; babies only demand a dry diaper and they sleep a lot, toddlers only require a peanut butter sandwich now and then, while teenagers demand almost constant attention to their volatile souls. Of course you have to feed the kids now and then, and do some laundry, (not to mention shoveling out the house often enough that you escape the imminent visits of the Health Department). But if I had a nickel for every woman who has said to me that she wanted to write *when she had time*, I would be a lady of leisure. Here is the bottom line; *nobody ever has time to write.* You make time. You snatch time from sleep if you must, or like Abraham Lincoln, you sit down on the end of the log. You steal time; you don't kaffee-klatch, or have dates, or go dancing. But then I never cared about those things anyhow. My first husband used to refer to my writing as an "anti-social disease" because I used it—ruthlessly—as a good excuse not to go kaffee-klatching when I lived in Texas.

Does this sound grim to you? If you'd rather have a job where you can sleep till eight o'clock, well—nobody told you not to be a plumber. You get, in this life, just about what you want; but be sure you want it before you start.

I once asked my daughter—a gifted dancer—if she was sorry she never had a career in ballet. She replied that she was not: "I could have been lame, illiterate, and washed up at thirty."

And I could have been teaching second grade on Staten Island.

AT THE TOLLING OF MIDNIGHT

by Stephanie Shaver

One of the remaining pleasures, after the novelty of actually editing an anthology wears off and editing becomes slog work like all other chores, is to discover a really fresh original voice, and to discover that the writer is very young.

Stephanie Shaver was just fourteen when she submitted this story, and it's a little different from the average 'first story.' When I was fourteen, I was writing—I think all born writers are—but the stories I was writing then were strictly conventional, and no one, reading them, would have suspected that I had any talent whatever.

Stephanie says of herself that she's a "mediocre artist"—adding that it's too soon to tell about that—and the owner of a cat called "Momma Hitler because of her temper and her unusual mustache." She also describes herself as an avid writer of letters, stories, and bad poems.

After a lifetime of reading the work of young writers, I no longer feel that it indicates anything very much except an active mind which may take any turn when the owner of the mind grows up enough to know which of their many talents they will develop as they grow up. No one nowadays remembers Francoise Sagan, who shocked everyone with an intense and perceptive novel written at the age of sixteen; on the other hand; Robert Silverberg was writing and selling science fiction when he was seventeen and now has become one of the biggest names in the field. At present it's quite enough to know that an active young mind is writing instead of sitting around watching TV or doing something passive.

And then, of course, she might keep writing; kids are no longer being told, as I was in high school, and doubtless many other potential great entertainers are, not to "waste their good minds on such stuff." (I wonder how many potentially good entertaining writers were put off by such pernicious advice when they were fifteen or so?)

Far, far off in the distance, over the din of the Bloody Saber Tavern, I could hear the sound of the great tower bells of the town tolling the midnight hour. I wasn't drunk (yet), but I also wasn't sober. I *was* still capable of seeing without half the room doing a somersault, and—scarcely a minute after the hour—my eyes just "happened" to stray to the door, see it open, and see who entered.

It was Scaz.

She was cloaked head to toe in black with that enormous cowl thrown back so that every outline of her ugly, scarred face was clear before my eyes. She was *not* pretty, but then again, no sailor (or pirate, we were both on the *Albatross*) ever really is. The alternating cold and hot weather that chafed and darkened our skin and the days of rowing for hours at a time made us look more like demons from the Nethers rather than men.

And it should have been worse for a woman.

Yet Scaz took the job on easily; in fact, when she had first come to the *Albatross* we thought her a man, and only later found out she was not. And it wasn't her appearance that had fooled us, for she had come looking like any mercenary-turned-sailor, but her *voice*. It matched her face, which was a demon mask of scars and leather-tough skin, with two ferret eyes sunk deep into her skull; her voice was *ugly*. Harsher than a raven's caw, more unnerving than metal striking rough metal, Scaz rarely spoke, and when she did, glass broke. Thus, when she entered the tavern, the inevitable happened, and I pitied her.

"Sing! Sing! C'mon ye ugly toad, sing!" Someone roared from the back of the room. Drunken laughter followed and Scaz bent her head over her mug of ale, sitting down at an empty table and, obviously wishing to be left alone, turned her back on the laughter.

It didn't stop the men, for the taunts rose, so that all that could be heard was the shouts of, "Sing! Sing!" Even the bar wenches could be heard sneering the word out.

I almost felt sorry for her as she was pushed up to the front of the bar. Someone pushed a lap-harp into her hands as she seated her tough, spare body onto a stool.

"What'll you sing, toad?" someone sneered.

"I will sing 'At the Tolling of Midnight,' " she replied in her rasping voice. Her hand ran down the strings of the harp, emitting a sweet sigh that echoed in the now still room. Then she began. And everyone fell silent.

Even as an old man I *know* I will remember the voice of Scaz, for it was beautiful. More beautiful than anything ever uttered by mortal lips. It wafted through the room and tantalized us with its beauty, encircling everyone in nightingalelike loveliness. Yet even in that voice, I noticed sadness and tears that could never be shed. 'At the Tolling of Midnight' is a lament of sorts, sung when a sailor meets the Dark Reaper. I wondered for whom Scaz was singing. But not for long, for her song obliterated thought as soon as it began. She sang, and anyone within earshot froze.

At the tolling of midnight the stars glow bright,
Burning eternal into the night,
And down they look upon the forest and desert sand,
With them my heart follows to my homeland.

At the tolling of midnight silence enfolds,
Creeping deep into castle and hold,
The ships sit silent as the ocean rolls,
And always behind follows my soul.

She went on and everyone listened. When she came to the final fourteenth verse I almost wished she'd sing another verse, and amazingly, she did.

At the tolling of midnight Death is abroad,
And soon new ghosts are following along,
Most have neither grave nor tomb,
Always in vain searching for home.
Only and always home.

I had never heard *that* verse sung! Nor, I doubt not, anyone else in the room. As Scaz finished, her eyes lifted to meet mine. My soul chilled at the touch of her eyes, and I turned away, shuddering. When I looked again, she was gone. But the touch of her eyes still chilled me, and I shivered. Those eyes were like the Reaper's . . . !

I made an immediate decision to get drunk.

Three days had passed since the night I had heard Scaz singing at the bar, and I still had the residue of a hangover. In fact, the past days had become a mental blur, except for the lingering feeling of those two cold, dead eyes on me. (And the fact that my money pouch was considerably lighter from the many drinks I had bought That Night.)

Something worried me, however. It had been awhile since I had seen Scaz, in fact, not at all since That Night. When at dinner I had still not seen her I asked Joriv, the man sitting next to me, where she was.

His answer was hardly the one I wanted to hear.

Joriv stared at me. "You don't *know?*"

"No, I don't, Joriv, tell me." I answered.

"I can't *believe* you don't *know!*" Joriv repeated, astonished.

I was getting irritated. I snatched the man's tunic

and pressed his face close to mine. "Tell me," I gritted between clenched teeth.

"She—she's dead! Slipped up in the crow's nest and fell to her death." My hands dropped from Joriv's tunic.

"When?" I asked finally.

"What do you mean 'when'?"

My hand balled up in a fist. Joriv noticed and said quickly, "Oh! You mean the *time!*" I nodded and looked him in the eyes. "I'd say about three nights ago," he went on, "at—oh, how many times did that confounded clock toll . . . ?"

I scarcely heard him as my mind reeled. Words came back from what seemed to be an eon ago, words to the fifteenth verse of a song. . . .

. . . .*Most have neither grave nor tomb. . . .*
. . . .*At the tolling of midnight* Death *is abroad. . . .*

And then a new line, one that just seemed to jump into my mind as if it had been placed there. . . .

Always in vain I will search for home,
The Harper of Death. . . .

Joriv's voice broke through, "It was midnight! That's it! Twelve rings for midnight!"

. . . .*when the midnight bells toll. . . .*

THE BUDDY SYSTEM

by Laura Thurston

Sometimes preconceived notions can be an awful drag. When I first looked at this story, I almost didn't read it, because I encountered not one but two of my pet hates, and I have never been known for having a particularly long fuse. When I encountered the character called "great Octogon" I said "Oh-oh," and then when later I came across "Gladriel" I said "Huh; right out of Tolkien's *Galadriel*"; later when I saw the character *Orian* I groaned and then when I found a grammatical error which was one of my pet hates, I actually threw the story on a pile of rejects and almost didn't read it through.

But on another day, fresh at the top of a new stack of manuscripts, and not exhausted by a flood of perfectly awful stories which for some reason all came in at once, I read it through and found it rather fun.

Which goes to show that nobody's perfect, so now I tend to give every story a second chance; if I'm tired out, I read the story again when I'm feeling a little fresher.

But it's still a good idea to think up fresh original names and to proofread your own stories carefully for stupid mistakes; because there are always more stories—and you might not find me in a forgiving mood.

Laura Thurston is 21 years old and works in an electronic parts store. This is her first story, and she dedicates it to her brother, Craig.

"Forgive me, O Great Octogon, for doing the terrible deed of healing—" prayed Friar Orian.

"Would you shut up and let me get some sleep?" Gladriel complained. "It's a wonder you haven't attracted the bandits. Anyone can hear you miles away." Her voice was filled with annoyance. She'd learned to live with his wailing prayers to his dubious Great Octogon in the middle of the night. She'd never heard of any Great Octogon until she met Orian.

Orian ignored her and continued praying loudly in his nasal, singsong voice. When he finished, he glared at Gladriel. "It isn't me who's endangering us. If bandits come, bandits come. What are a few bandits?"

"You never fight them."

"That's not the point. One look at you and the Octogon-cursed farmers attack. Farmers! Farmers who would normally leave us alone."

"It's not my fault. You're the one who told me that the water in that spring was good to drink. You're the one who prayed over it purifying it. All I did was drink it."

"How was I to know it was cursed?" He went into his tent angrily, ending the argument. If it was possible to slam the entrance to a tent, he would have.

Friar Orian was a small man, quite scrawny looking. Although he'd been trained in the use of weapons, he wasn't very good, and let Varsh Nitza and Gladriel, his hired companions, do the bulk of the fighting. They were looking for his brother, Korellis, and the reward would be quite substantial. He hinted at sharing it but had no intention of doing so.

Varsh Nitza was a warrior from the south. She was the tallest woman either of the others had ever seen; her skin was almost pitch black, had it been a shade lighter, they would have noticed the bruises, cuts, and scars she bore. She had little respect for Friar Orian, yet she had no problems with letting him bind her wounds after a fight.

Gladriel didn't know what she wanted out of life,

and when faced with two choices, chose them both. She'd been offered training in fighting and the Arcane Arts. Her teachers told her, "Choose one. You can't have both, you'll divide your energy, and won't be good in either." But she'd proven them wrong.

Gladriel was also the victim of a curse (or the recipient of a blessing depending on how one looked at it). She'd drunk from a cursed spring and immediately had grown a pair of beautiful and fully-functional wings. Right now, her wings were a curse, for in this land any kind of magic was outlawed and very severely punished.

Nitza had ignored what was going on behind her, too intent on keeping watch over their campsite to worry about their argument.

Gladriel tapped her on the shoulder. "Nitz, I'll take over the watch. The Wailer woke me up."

"Doesn't he have any brains? Somebody might hear him and think he's making magic."

The rest of the night, though, passed uneventfully.

After they'd eaten, Gladriel pulled the map out of her backpack. "We crossed the border yesterday. We're here." She drew an X on the map. "There are two options. We can—"

"Follow this road here or take the long way through the mountains. The choice is obvious. We'll take the mountains rather than announce to the world we're here and Gladriel has wings."

"Orian, I wasn't even considering the road. We can either take the mountain route, or if we want to save time, we can go straight north through the blank spot on the map."

Nitza studied the map thoughtfully. "I'd rather go through the mountains. We don't know what's north of here."

"There's probably a reason why the map isn't complete. And it could be something simple: such as, this isn't a current map, or it could be that no one's ever made it back alive."

"I'm not taking any chances," said Friar Orian. "I say we turn back and tell the Council that we found his corpse and by default the inheritance is mine. And what I say goes."

"And suppose they could truth-see? Let's put forth an honest effort. We've been looking for him for a year, and we can't quit. At least we know he's in Stomal." Gladriel started to put the map away.

Orian rolled his eyes. He was the leader on this quest, but every time he tried to assert himself, he'd be overridden.

"Why don't you fly over this mystery ground and see what's there?" Nitza asked.

"I'm not flying anywhere. What if I'm seen? This whole kingdom forbids magic. Including people who are victims of curses."

"In that case, we'll go through the mountains. The quicker route would probably not have been much quicker anyway."

It took them five days to navigate through the mountains, trying to stay in the lower foothill region. On the sixth day, Orian sighted a band of traders.

"Gladriel, hide. If they take one look at you, we're goners."

"Maybe I'd better hide, too," said Nitza. "We'll get them to underestimate our strength, and if they're hostile, we'll surprise them." Nitza and Gladriel hid behind a large rock. Nitza strung her crossbow, while Gladriel prepared to call on the Arcane Power.

Orian approached them with open hands in a gesture of friendship.

The leader of the trader caravan approached him, "Stranger, what brings you to these mountains alone?"

"I am a simple priest on a pilgrimage. But my pilgrimage has ended, and now I'm on my way to Stomal."

"Be very careful. There have been rumors of creatures ruled by magic wandering in the area."

It seemed to Orian that the traders would leave him and his companions alone.

"It's the Abomination!" screamed a mercenary suddenly, as he grabbed his bow and aimed at Gladriel.

The mercenary, and a dozen others, mercenaries

and traders both, immediately fell to the ground and began snoring loudly. The remaining five mercenaries grabbed swords and raced behind the rock. Varsh Nitza let fly a quarrel, dropped the crossbow, and waded right into the midst, a sword in one hand, a dagger in the other.

Gladriel's wings took her aloft and she slashed at the leader from the air. He was terrified but fought to save his own life.

Orian noticed that one of the traders was trying to escape. He pushed through two others to chase after the one that was getting away.

Nitza stood in a pool of blood. Five dead men lay around her. She had a bloody gash on her leg and limped toward the two who were trying to keep Orian from letting their companion escape. Her sword sank deep into one of them.

Gladriel flew higher into the air, and swooped down, her sword leading the way. The leader had no time to scream before she skewered him. The last of the traders saw this and took to his heels.

She hesitated a moment before chasing him.

Nitza killed the last mercenary as Orian tackled the trader. "How far to Stomal? If I like your answer, I'll let you live."

"I don't know."

"You lie."

"Never been there, I don't know."

"Sure you haven't. Traders go everywhere."

"Two days."

"Is it that way?" asked Orian, pointing east.

"No. North."

"Try again."

"East. But first you have to go north."

"That's better. Where do you turn east?"

"You'll come to a creek. Cross it. A mile later, turn east. There's a path. It'll turn into a road."

"Very good, friend. I'm going to give you a present. I'm going to give you your leader's dagger." After he thrust the blade into the frightened man's hand, he dragged him toward the sleeping mercenaries. "Slit their throats."

Aghast, the trader refused.

"All right. Gladriel, do you want to make him do as he's told?"

"Orian, don't make somebody else do your dirty work," said Nitza. "We shouldn't slit their throats. They're harmless. It's cowardly to kill someone who can't fight back."

Gladriel finished cleaning her blade. "Orian, I agree with Nitza. I'll take care of our prisoner."

Gladriel took the man behind the large rock. Soon, they rejoined the group. He was apparently willing to guide them to Stomal.

"Gladriel, what did you say to him?"

"All I did, Orian, was to ask him to help me. He can't refuse, he's been spelled. Let's just hope it lasts," she whispered. Then she introduced Sardok the trader to Friar Orian and Varsh Nitza.

Now that the fight was over, the pain of her leg wound hit Nitza full force. "Orian? Can you take a look at my leg?"

"You know what the Great Octogon thinks about using the Healing Touch on just anybody."

"If we run into any of these people's friends and I can't fight . . . we all know you're hopeless with any kind of a weapon. You're healing me to save your own skin. Tell your Octogon that."

Orian considered. The Great Octogon wasn't generous with healing gifts, or any gift. Orian knew that if either one of his companions died, he'd have to give up, and maybe he wouldn't make it home alive, and it was a very long way home.

He whispered, "Forgive me," and laid his hands on Varsh Nitza's leg.

Meanwhile, Gladriel was asking Sardok who had outlawed magic and why.

"Declaration of the king. His palace is in Stomal. I don't know why he made the declaration, but there are plenty of rumors. Some say the land is cursed, no magic will work here."

"If that was true, I'd be free of my curse."

"Another rumor is that magic killed his brother in a horrible way and he was made to watch. It so disgusted him, that he forbade anyone—good or evil—to make magic."

"Of course these people don't agree on what the horrible manner of his death was."

"Of course. I don't think it would be a good idea for you to make this trip to Stomal. Your wings would be impossible to hide. Some have already seen you and word travels fast."

"I'd guessed."

Three days later (Sardok having misjudged the distance), the group arrived outside the gates of Stomal. Sardok was ahead of the rest. Friar Orian was next. Bringing up the rear, but hanging back a complete horse length, was Varsh Nitza. All were on foot.

The guard at the gate demanded to know what their business was.

"My name is Sardok. I am a trader. My caravan was attacked by bandits in the Makrai Mountains. Only I survived. The good friar allowed me to travel with him. I plan to earn some money so I can hire some mercenaries to avenge my companions."

"I am Friar Orian, priest of the Great Octogon." The blank look of the guard was familiar to Orian by now—his was a very obscure sect. "This is my bodyguard, Varsh Nitza. We are looking for my brother. He has come into a lot of money and a title. Perhaps you know of a resident foreigner here. Tall, bony, and red-haired. His name is Korellis."

"I know of no one by that name or description," the guard answered. Orian's face fell, but he was still full of hope.

Somebody sneezed. Varsh Nitza said in an exaggerated Southern accent, "Excuse me. I am used to a warmer climate."

"It wasn't you who sneezed," said the guard.

"Oh, but I did," she insisted, sniffling. This, too, was faked. And she coughed.

"I know you didn't sneeze. I was looking in your direction the whole time. I've never seen anyone as black as you before."

A whispered curse, wind suddenly rushing by on a windless day, and not one of the three strangers' mouths moved. The guard was suspicious. Someone was making magic. He could denounce them at once or make them pay him to keep quiet. He decided to make them pay. A gate guard just did not make very much money to live on. A supplement to his income would be very welcome. . . .

Fortunately, Gladriel's invisibility held until the group was in the Golden Dagger Inn. Nitza went to the tavern downstairs to play dice games, while Orian went to at least ten different taverns to drink, bribe taverners, and try to get information about his brother.

When daylight came, the three were sprawled out on the floor of their rooms. Nitza was five crowns poorer, Orian had the worst hangover of his life, and Gladriel was bored. She'd done nothing the night before except study the Arcane Arts and sleep.

Orian held his throbbing head in his hands. "What a hangover. But at least I got some information. Nobody knew Korellis, but they all complained about the king, and how he's a tyrant beyond belief. The taverners I talked to told me some graphic stories of violence. Such as how he'd rip out with his bare hands—"

"Spare us the details. How's that going to help?"

"Patience, Gladriel. The king's a tyrant. And he's the one who outlawed magic. He sounds like the kind of lowlife my brother used to hang around with. As a matter of fact, he used to study the Arcane Arts and was pretty good."

"What's he doing in Stomal, if magic's been outlawed?" asked Varsh Nitza. "Could be another wild goose chase."

"I'm sure he's here. But even if he's not, we paid our room and board for a week, so we might as well stay."

"You did better than I for once. All I did was lose. I swear those dice were loaded, but I can't prove it."

"Shouldn't be gambling. The Great Octogon says—"

"You shouldn't be drinking. You spent as much as I did and you can't even heal your own hangover."

"I guess since I'm such a lousy healer who can't do anything right, you'll just have to suffer after fights from now on. If your leg hadn't been healed by me, you might not have it."

Varsh Nitza ignored him. He'd forget what she said, he always did. She told the others she was going to the hiring hall. She could get a temporary job, and possibly someone there would know something.

Orian lay on the floor snoring loudly.

Gladriel smoothed out her wings, stepped over Orian, closed her eyes and whispered, "Seeing, they see me not." She said this over and over until she faded from view.

The door opened and closed.

From the air, it took only a few moments to get to the palace. There were heavily armored guards everywhere. No one noticed a gentle breeze blowing past them on a breezy day. No one noticed that the wind was blowing in the wrong direction.

Gladriel was now inside the palace. *If I'm right, Korellis should be here. From what Orian told me about his brother, he and the king are the same person,* she thought. She glanced down and saw nothing.. Nobody could see her smiling as she walked down the corridor.

Huge double doors were at the end of the long hallway. Gladriel opened the door a crack, trying to do it unnoticed. Though the doors were ornately carved and gold-plated and inlaid with precious stones, the door squeaked like a common servant's room door.

A heavyset, flame-haired man stared right at the door. "Show yourself, or I'll call the guards."

He sat on his throne tapping his foot. His mouth curved up in a sadistic smile. He waited.

Gladriel felt hot. She somehow knew that the king could see her, though she was still invisible. She opened the door and walked into the room.

Gladriel looked at the bright red hair. She hadn't seen hair like that in Stomal on anyone. Orian had described his brother as having hair like fire. Could this be Korellis? From what Orian said, he'd been a nightmare to live with. His parents favored Korellis, who seemed to be everything they'd ever wanted in a son. Strong, highly intelligent, beautiful. Unlike Orian.

But beauty could change. The man that sat in front of her was not beautiful at all. He could have grown fat and lazy from soft living. But his bullying nature wouldn't change.

"You dare to cast a deceitful spell before the king. But a simple spell does not deceive me. I see what no mere rabble can."

Gladriel knew she'd be severely punished no matter what she did. Killed, perhaps tortured. If her guess was right, perhaps rewarded.

"You are King Korellis, brother of Friar Orian of the Great Octogon. I have—"

The King laughed. "I knew he should never have joined such an obscure sect. Great Octogon indeed. And how do you come to know him?"

"I am Gladriel. He hired me to help him find you. He has news for you, but I think it's best that he tell you." Gladriel started to fade in. "Orian's told me so much about you."

"You have wings."

"I had no choice but to make myself invisible. I knew I couldn't get an audience with you otherwise."

"How? Are you something other than human?"

"No, just a person who drank from a stream I shouldn't have drunk from." And Gladriel told how Orian blessed the stream, but didn't realize that blessings alone don't remove curses.

Korellis said, "That sounds like Orian. He's totally inept. He's also a coward. He should have been the first to drink. Bring him to me. I'll straighten him out."

In a short time, Gladriel, Varsh Nitza, and Friar Orian were standing in front of the King.

"Korellis! And I thought I'd never see you again."

"Better for you if you didn't. I suppose you wouldn't have made it here without these two. You haven't introduced me to the tall one."

"I am Varsh Nitza. I'm pleased to meet you. Your brother told Gladriel and me about you. We wanted to see how much is truth, and how much is exaggeration."

"And what did he say?"

"That you are handsome, fearless, strong, and a very accomplished wizard. If this is true, why is magic forbidden?"

"Because it is the law."

"Korellis, our parents died. Their will specified that you are to get everything. All their savings, the land, everything. The Council sent me to find you. You can come home with me and claim your inheritance, or you can stay here as King of Stomal."

"In other words I can renounce my inheritance and stay here ruling Stomal, or I can renounce Stomal and claim the paltry estate that our parents left me. You're hoping I'll stay here and good riddance to me. Right? Wrong. I'll claim my inheritance, Orian. To keep it out of your hands. A good thing, too, because you can't keep up the land and the house. You can't manage any estate to save your life. I am going to accept the inheritance, and put my most trusted Officer of the Guard in charge of it. Stomal will grow, and many lands will pay tribute to me. Emperor Korellis. Brother, it is truly good news you bring. Sorry to disappoint you."

The three left the city with a sealed message from Korellis. They were all complaining about this most recent turn of events.

"A wizard," mused Gladriel. "So that's why he outlawed magic. He can't accept that anyone might be better at something than he is. His head is too big for the rest of his body."

Orian said, "How dare he? All my life he's been taking food right out of my mouth and stuffing his face. He'd cheerfully rob a beggar just to get a few pennies."

"He could at least be properly grateful to you. We should have turned back. You were right all along."

"He's wrong about you, Orian," said Varsh Nitza. "If I've ever called you a coward or derided your healing gifts, it was only in anger, I never meant it."

"Do I take this to be an apology? If so, I accept."

"I wonder what the Great Octogon thinks of this," said Gladriel.

"I'm sure the Great Octogon is very offended by Korellis's greed against one of Octogon's own priests," Nitza said.

"We'll expose him as a coward—that's exactly what he is—who can't accept competition from other wizards. We'll show him to be a wizard." Fire was in Gladriel's eyes. Her guild would surely hear of this, and they did not take kindly to such cowardice.

Orian smiled. He put a skinny arm around each of his two companions. "I may have lost a brother, but I have gained two sisters."

THE CLOUD OF EVIL

by Mark Tompkins

Mark says, "Although I've been writing since I was seven or so, 'The Cloud of Evil' is my first professional sale. Writers whose works have especially influenced my fiction include Clark Ashton Smith, H.P. Lovecraft. Ray Bradbury, Robert E. Howard, Robert Bloch, and Harlan Ellison, but the kind support of Marion Zimmer Bradley has been the greatest influence of all. Without her encouragement I probably would not have bothered to write 'The Cloud of Evil' in the first place.

"My goals for the future include becoming a professional author within the field of fantasy, and playing guitar or keyboards in a professional rock band.

"As of this writing, I'm eighteen years old, a college student, and living in New Jersey. I'm told by my parents that I was born in Manhattan, but vivid and recurring dreams have revealed to me that I was actually born in Dunwich, Massachusetts, on the peak of Sentinel Hill." Weren't we all?

So many of Mark's stories have been so completely in the horror genre—which I define as "perfectly horrible things happen to perfectly nice people for no reason at all," while fantasy may take the luxury of making sense of the world—that I had despaired of getting anything from him which I could use for this anthology. But when this one came in, I decided it had enough structure and fantasy feel to be worth publishing. But it's really horror, so be warned—some people hate horror.

"We live on a placid island of ignorance in the midst of black seas of infinity, and it was not meant that we should voyage far."
—H.P. Lovecraft, from "Call of Cthulhu"

I shall tell you of Niandra the Sorceress, and I shall tell you of the Cloud of Evil; and then I shall make thousands of replicas of this message and disseminate them to every corner of the land, in hopes that at least one of these copies will be discovered and read by some wizard more well-versed in the ways of magic than I, so that he or she can make use of the information presented herein and attempt to thwart the hideous doom which threatens to engulf us all. Time is growing frightfully short—especially for me, it would seem—yet in the interest of magic, in the interest of the well-being of the land, and in the interest of history (should there remain anyone to read history when this nightmare is over), I shall be as complete as possible in my account of the events that preceded the coming of the terrible menace which we now must face.

My name is Slonich, and I was born in the harsh deserts of Khrali where men and women survive or perish according to the power with which they wield their swords. As my parents were both widely respected and feared warriors, they became very disappointed—embarrassed—as it became apparent that I was growing at a much slower rate than my peers, and that I was destined to be smaller and weaker than any of them. In order to compensate for this deficiency, they trained me rigorously throughout my childhood in hopes of making me such a skilled fighter that my lack of height and natural strength would be negated by my prowess in mortal combat. Alas, their plan did not succeed, for I was a rather recalcitrant student, and resisted them whenever I could; living the grueling life of a warrior seemed, and still does seem, a very simple and uninteresting occupation, especially for someone of my unusually capable intellect, and I was very much opposed to having my life controlled by the crude brutalities of the society into which I was thrust. As a result, I spent a great deal of my childhood being the defenseless object of mockery, derision, contempt, and violence at the hands of peers. With each incident of mistreatment that I suffered, my parents lost more and more hope in me—indeed, they became ashamed that I had been born in the first place, and they took the liberty of making this painfully clear to me many times. I had, they said, tarnished their image as great and noble warriors, I had diminished their prestige, and I had made them an object of mockery, for the notion that two warriors as fearless and dreaded as my mother and father could produce from their iron loins such a feeble runt as myself was, to many, hysterically funny and ironic in the extreme. I had disgraced them, and they despised me for it.

When I came of age, my father suggested to me, several hours after I had my head bloodied and my nose broken by a gang of crazed ruffians, that I should depart the desert and journey to the Academy of Magic and Wizardry to study there. "The ways of the world are too overpowering for one as pathetic and worthless as yourself," he said, as blood dripped from the gashes in my head and into my eyes. "By some terrible misfortune, you were not born in the mold of a warrior, and hence the only way you will be able to survive is if you acquire the power of magic."

The suggestion was a very tempting one for me, for several reasons. Firstly, the opportunity of leaving this wretched land, where I was persecuted and treated as an outcast, was a gift from the gods. Secondly, magic intrigued me; for I had heard much of magic and wizardry through legends and lore, and the idea of actually learning magic and being able to apply it filled me with delight. I agreed instantly, and that night, set out on my own for the Academy of Magic, my only guide being the stars and the directions with which my mother had eagerly provided me.

Now, in the grim shadow of unfathomable peril which promises to annihilate all the land, my impertinent reminisces may seem appallingly trivial, but please understand my plight; for soon my life shall be extinguished like a dying flame, and in my last moments, I am compelled to try to relive and remember my life, as now is my last opportunity to do so. No doubt, everyone in every corner of the land is doing the same thing.

After six days of tiring travel over the rugged terrain of the desert, I finally spied the massive, sandy cliff atop which the legendary Academy is situated. My heart fluttered with joy when I saw its massive black structure looming against the azure sky like an abode of the gods. It took me a day to scale the steeply sloping cliff, and when I finally reached the top, I collapsed, but I was wearing a smile. I was now free of the iron bonds which had bound me to the callous, unrewarding land of Khrali, and ready to embark upon a new life.

I was awakened by a grizzled old man wearing a blue robe, and he made me feel instantly refreshed merely by uttering some strange words. Upon bringing me inside, the wizard, whose name was Klote, inquired as to why I had come to the Academy, and I told him the tale I just told you. Klote sympathized with me, for the story of his life was a similar one, filled with all the misfortune and alienation of being born a scholar in a land of warriors. After consulting with several of his colleagues, he informed me that I would be accepted into the Academy, provided that I performed various chores, which all students were required to do in exchange for being taught magic, and provided that I took an oath never to succumb to the allure of Dark Magic. I agreed without hesitation and took the solemn oath, even though I did not know what Dark Magic was, and was then brought to a comfortable chamber, where I slept soundly through the night. The following morning, my lessons began.

In the four years I spent at the Academy, I was taught how to summon djinn and fairies and gnomes, how to use the powers of transformation and telekinesis, how to levitate, how to hurl lightning from my fingertips, how to control flying carpets, how to make myself the size of a giant or the size of an insect, how to pacify hungry beasts, how to read, write, and speak in hundreds of ancient and forgotten tongues, how to make myself invisible, and dozens of other useful spells and abilities. In those four years, I became the pride of my teachers and the envy of my peers, for, as Klote once told me, few possessed natural magical ability to the degree I did, and few were able to apply magic with such skill and facility; Klote also told me that I possessed the potential to become "one of the truly great wizards of all time."

In retrospect, the years I spent at the Academy were probably the happiest years in my life; for at the Academy I had earned the friends, respect, and self-esteem which I never achieved anywhere else.

One day, a week after the four-year anniversary of my advent at the Academy, I became tempted to explore a certain section of the immense library which all students were warned by our mentors never to enter. Since all of the wizards were away for a few days to attend a wizard's convention on the other side of the land, I quickly succumbed to the temptation and explored the forbidden room. It soon became clear why this room was deemed strictly off limits: the mahogany shelves within were crammed with forbidden tomes written about the practice and application of Dark Magic—that branch of magic dealing with forces of darkness, death, evil, demonism, and the unknown. Perusing the dust-covered tomes, I became irresistably intrigued, and began to take volumes off the shelf and read them at random. With each book I read, I became more and more fascinated with the secrets that were revealed to me, and I vowed to read all of the forbidden volumes. One of the advantages of being well-schooled in magic is the capacity to read practically any language, archaic or modern, with phenomenal speed, often at a thousand pages a minute, and thus absorb knowledge at inhuman rates. So, by applying this skill, I read every single one of the volumes of Dark Magic in less than a day, and was galvanized by all the blasphemous marvels I had unearthed.

The next day, while I sat in my chambers contemplating the unfathomable wonders writ of in the tomes of Dark Magic, the wizards returned. Klote stormed suddenly into my chambers, a look of horror and shame on his aged, rumpled face.

"You have read the forbidden tomes!" he said, and before I could speak, he added, "do not attempt to deny this, for the invisible elves who watch over the library have informed me of your ignoble deed. You have not only disobeyed the wizards who have taught you all you know, but you have broken the oath which you took upon your admittance into the academy. I hereby banish you from the academy in shame and disgrace, with the promise that you may never return, and never achieve full wizardry anywhere in the land!"

Before I could conjure up a feeble retort in my defense, Klote uttered a terse incantation, and suddenly I was once again at the bottom of the cliff, atop which the academy loomed, seeming to glare balefully down at me. Surprisingly, I felt hardly any regret at my abrupt excommunication; I almost felt a kind of relief, knowing that I was once again free to do as I wished.

But what should I do? Where should I go? Should I return to my homeland of Khrali to show my parents what became of their son, and possibly to exact revenge upon those who mistreated me? No, I decided, such a venture would accomplish little. As ominous black clouds began to invade the azure sky and rain assailed the land below with a vengeance, drenching my silken robes, (Klote's doing, no doubt) I instantly remembered a line I had read in one of the tomes of Dark Magic: "Those who have been repudiated by the wielders of Light Magic may always seek solace in the castle of Niandra the Sorceress." Instantly, a flood of other passages erupted in my mind, all of which were somehow related to the legendary Niandra, the ultimate master of Dark Magic. Yes, I thought, to her castle is where I am destined to journey; to learn the ways of Dark Magic under her wing is what fortune had determined for me. So, conjuring a flying carpet from the sand, I soared above the stormy clouds and headed toward the legendary sorceress' castle, recalling passages from the books which provided detailed directions from all corners of the land.

For more than seven days, I glided over sprawling deserts and massive cities until I reached her massive, obsidian palace, which is situated on a cliff which overlooks a vast, foaming sea. It was nighttime when I arrived, and as the three gibbous moons shone their emerald, crimson, and amber light upon the rambling spires, gables, cupolas, belfries, and towers which comprised the massive castle, I could actually sense the incredible powers which emanated from it, and I felt an exhilaration the like of which I had never experienced. I entered the castle by flying through one of the open windows into a shadow-shrouded chamber, where, not entirely by coincidence, Niandra the Sorceress was waiting; she was sitting in a jewel-studded, ebony throne in the corner of the room, staring at me curiously, though without the slightest hint of surprise.

She was unquestionably the most beautiful woman I had ever seen. She was slim, lithe, and infinitely attractive, especially in the black, gossamer gown which she wore on that night. Her ebony hair was long and flowing, her eyes were light green and lambent, her skin was the color of buttermilk, and her face was placid and seemingly innocent with its gentle curves and contours. Her beauty entranced me instantly, and for several minutes I could only stare at her, admiring her godly body.

"So you have come, Slonich," she finally said, and her voice was gentle as a whisper.

Astonished, I responded, "You knew I was coming?"

"We of the Dark Magic know many things." She

rose and walked over to me, seeming to glide over the black, tiled floor, and took my hand in hers as I stepped down from the hovering carpet. "Come with me."

Suddenly there was a flash of many colors, and then Niandra and I were flying naked through the crimson clouds of some forgotten land, exchanging fervid kisses and caresses while the warm winds carried us through unimagined dreamlike heavens. We glided on for an indefinite time in this timeless wonderland, until finally my ultimate lustful desires were quelled; and from that heavenly moment onward she had me completely under her control. So irresistible was her allure and her power that I could think of nothing but to serve her forever, to be her eternal slave in the unholy ways of the Dark Magic.

Then, abruptly, I awoke in a massive golden tub filled with warm blood, with Niandra sprawled nude on top of me. As little as a day ago, the idea of bathing in blood would have seemed ineffably repellent, but now, as I lay there, exhausted, the blood seemed to revitalize me, to fill me with power and verve which would last me the rest of my life.

"We are now one," Niandra whispered as she gently massaged my bare, blood-soaked chest. "We are now one unified force of the Dark Magic, and we shall do whatever we wish." And with these gently whispered words, I submitted my soul willingly to the Dark Magic, and knew that wonderful things awaited me in the future.

The next twenty years of my life I spent exclusively with Niandra the Sorceress. During those years we summoned demons from Underworld, condemned countless people to eternal torture, ate the flesh and drank the blood of all manner of beasts which ever existed, traveled through hell and other dark dimensions, inflicted chaos upon hundreds of people, performed thousands of bloody, unholy rituals, worshiped dark and ancient gods from forgotten aeons, created and destroyed beings of all descriptions, uttered millions of blasphemous incantations, brought life to the dead and death to the living, journeyed uninhibited through time and space, experienced every emotion which ever existed, satisfied every one of our most powerful desires, realized every one of our whims, and learned virtually all of the forbidden secrets of the Universe by communicating with every sorcerer and sorceress of Dark Magic from the beginning of time to the end of time. During those twenty years I acquired unspeakable, illimitable knowledge which would overload and obliterate the minds of ordinary men; with Niandra as my mentor in evil, I became a wielder of dark, incredible powers beyond the comprehension of ordinary beings. With ease we could have conquered whole worlds, including our own land, but to do so would have been next to nothing compared to our other mind-blazing, transcendental experiences.

In my twentieth year with Niandra, on a sunny and mellow afternoon, we were strolling lazily upon the expanse of sandy shore which lay beneath our castle, for even though we were virtually godlike in our powers and knowledge, we were still woman and man, and even something as mundane as strolling across the beach was enjoyable now and then, a pleasant break from our usual unearthly endeavors. I think Niandra noticed the vase first; yes, for I remember that she pointed to it when she saw it gleam in the sunlight, and ran to it with excitement. As she picked it up from the wet sand and commented on its deceptive lightness, we saw that the vase, which had apparently washed up on the shore recently, was made of something like brass, except this material was lighter in color, and radiated a faint but definite amber effulgence which was not caused by the white light of the sun. The vase was about the height of a person's forearm, and the width of a person's head, though shaped somewhat like an hourglass; it had no handles but could be grabbed easily around its narrow center with one hand.

As we brushed away the sand which clung to the vase, we saw that innumerable odd-looking heiroglyphs had been etched into it, arranged in a hundred or so circular columns. The characters, which were comprised of circles and ovals of varying sizes arranged in a multitude of different manners, were quite unlike anything we had ever seen. Indeed, this was a most unusual and disconcerting discovery, for we had thought ourselves to be well-versed in all tongues that had ever been or would ever be writ or spoken by any known being, yet these characters were totally new to us.

"We must find out from what land or age it comes," I said resolutely, "for we can allow no shred of knowledge to pass us by without our fully understanding it."

"Then, come; let us learn."

Taking the vase with us, we returned to the castle swiftly and entered one of the vast, dark chambers where we frequently summoned apparitions. Here, we drew several symbols on the floor with a special powder made from pulverized human bones; then we knelt down in opposite corners of the room and began to recite a lengthy and involved incantation in unison. Almost instantly, the center of the dark chamber began to glow with a weird scarlet light, and from the light, the bearded, stooped figure of a long-dead sorcerer appeared.

Holding the vase before the sorcerer, Niandra said, "Utholon, we have summoned you to perform a duty for us. We have discovered this strange artifact of a civilization unknown to us, and we command you to find out from whence it came."

"It shall be done," said the sorcerer, and, gently accepting the vase, he vanished into the red light. Only seconds later he returned, and said, "I fear I cannot determine the origin of this strange vase. The writing etched into it I have never seen, nor have any of the beings with whom I have just conferred."

"You useless and contemptible fool," Niandra spat, and uttered a foul curse. The dead sorcerer let out a terrible cry of agony and then faded away, but not before Niandra could seize the vase from his spectral hands.

We spent the rest of that day, and the next four days, consulting dozens of other sorcerers from other ages, but none of them could be of any more assistance than Utholon. Finally, after she had cursed the last sorcerer to fail us, Niandra rose and announced, "We shall consult our books."

With that I picked up the alien vase and we headed for the vast library which lay beneath the ground, where innumerable tomes concerning Dark Magic were preserved. There we spent the next week, tirelessly looking through hundreds of thousands of books, trying vainly to match the hieroglyphs on the vase with the hieroglyphs in the books. But it was no use; the hieroglyphs were singular, and, apparently, unknown to any author of any book in our library.

But Niandra and I were not easily dissuaded. "We will not rest until we find the origin of this vase!" Niandra said determinedly, after she had fruitlessly consulted the last book which could conceivably have been of help to us. "If no book or spirit can enlighten us, then we shall consult the gods!"

Kandra, the Goddess of the Aeons, was the one we decided would be most helpful to us. To summon her we required the blood of a virgin, and so I located a suitable subject in the nearby land of Cradd. At midnight, we placed her squirming body on the stone altar on the roof of our castle and slit her throat. After drinking her blood, we uttered the necessary incantations; suddenly, the clouds overhead seemed to glow with an eerie white light, and the unearthly, indescribably alien visage of the goddess peered down at us from the heavens.

"What do you want?" the voice thundered.

"We seek to know the origin of this vase," I said, indicated the vase which lay beside me, "and the translation of the hieroglyphs that are writ on it."

"The vase," boomed the deafening voice, "was created by a race of terrible beings who existed when the world upon which you dwell was in its infancy. They were called the Yangerronians, and possessed magic infinitely more terrible and more powerful than the magic you know. Little is known regarding the Yangerronians; the gods have erased practically all knowledge of them from the minds of mortals, for the power which the Yangerronians possessed was not meant for mortals to know."

"Tell us, tell us of their magic, I beg you!" Niandra pleaded.

"I shall not," said the goddess.

"Then tell us what is written on the vase!" I implored.

"I shall tell you what is written on the vase, since it represents only an infinitesimal fraction of the Yangerronians' secrets, and as both of you have served me and worshiped me more loyally than many other mortals, you are entitled to know some things which no one else may know. But you must understand that the information I disclose to you is only for your own edification; you must never apply this information, for it will unlock long-forgotten doors that were not meant for you to open, and the magic that is hidden behind these doors will rush forth like a beast escaping its cage."

"We understand fully!" I exclaimed. "Tell us, tell us!"

The goddess translated the writing on the vase, and as she spoke, both Niandra and I memorized each word Kandra said. She described for us a complicated ritual whose ultimate purpose was not included among the writings, though many allusions were made to strange types of unholy magic with which we were completely unfamiliar. Most of what was written on the vase the goddess translated into tongues we could understand; however, large sections of the writing were comprised of chants and litanies which were meant to be uttered in the original tongue, and these we memorized with extreme care.

Finally, Kandra was through speaking, and she faded abruptly from the clouds, leaving Niandra and me there on the rooftop with the vase and the bloodless corpse of the sacrificial maiden.

"Such an incredible ritual," I commented. "I wonder what it is for."

"Come," Niandra said, rising from her kneeling position with alacrity. "We shall find out."

"But you heard Kandra's warning!" I said, appalled. "We were not meant to know the secrets of the Yangerronians. We were not meant to apply what was just divulged to us!"

"You yourself said that we must never let a shred of knowledge pass us by without our understanding it. Think of it—with this ritual, we will discover knowledge we never knew existed."

"But we cannot disobey the goddess!"

"It is a risk we must take!" She strode over to me, and clasped her soft hand tightly around mine. At her touch, I was instantly placated. "Kandra said that the magic the Yangerronians possessed was even stronger than the magic we know—infinitely stronger, in fact. Think of the power which awaits us! If we unearth the secrets of the Yangerronians, we can practically become gods ourselves. Listen, my love . . . we have an opportunity to obtain power which even we never fathomed. You cannot honestly tell me that you can resist this temptation."

She stared at me with a burning intensity, and the hypnotic luster of her green eyes gradually caused me to yield and assent to her request. "We shall perform the ritual," I said.

"Quickly, then," she said, grabbing the vase, "for the ritual must be performed at sunrise, and sunrise is slowly creeping upon us."

Surging with the excitement generated by the prospect of delving into the forbidden Unknown, we descended to one of the dozens of massive, dark chambers within the castle and began to prepare for the ritual. The ritual was a highly involved one, and, serving from memory, we prepared for it meticulously. With our own blood we drew various complex symbols on the floor, and then we erected fifteen shoulder-height candles at specified locations in relation to the blood-writ symbols and lit them. This done, we procured numerous chemicals, spices, and herbs from our storage room overhead and mixed them into a rancid-tasting broth, with which we drenched ourselves. The next preparation of the ritual required that we drink each other's blood, and this we did by sucking on gashes which we carved into our own flesh with razor-sharp knives. The head of a demon was needed to preside over the ritual, and we obtained this easily by going to another chamber and summoning a demon from hell, whose head I hacked off swiftly with a broadsword the second he materialized. This we impaled on an erect iron stake at the front of the chamber in which the ritual would be performed. One more preparation was required: fifteen dead male bodies were needed, and Niandra procured these by ordering a horde of demons to raid a certain graveyard and bring the rotting cadavers to us. We placed the bodies at various points in the chamber which, like the burning candles, were arranged relative to specific points on the blood-writ symbols on the floor. Once the putrefying corpses were in the proper positions, we set them all alight, and then we were ready to begin the ritual, just as the sun began to creep over the distant horizon.

Kneeling at specified points on the floor, we chanted the strange litany which Kandra had taught us and we had meticulously memorized, speaking in the tongue which the Yangerronians had spoken countless eons ago. It was somewhat difficult to create the sounds as the goddess had created them, for the Yangerronian language clearly had not been spoken by humanlike mouths.

By the time the lengthy litany was complete, the chamber reeked with the stench of frying flesh, and the corpses were burned to cinders. Using our hands, we took the smoldering ashes of the corpses and introduced them into the vase, uttering the same alien phrase each time we added a new handful. It was then that I noticed that the amber phosphorescence which the vase perpetually radiated was more intense than it ever was; indeed, the light was pulsating, like the beat of a heart. When all the ashes were in the vase, we placed the vase at a certain intersection of blood-writ lines on one of the symbols on the floor, and whispered a few more alien expressions.

Next we were to kiss the lips on the grotesque head of the demon, and we did this without qualm. Then, we performed the penultimate stage of the monstrous ritual, which was to lick from the floor the blood-writ symbols until they could no longer be seen. By this time our anticipation was almost unbearable in intensity.

Finally, we performed the last act of the ritual, which was simply to kneel at opposite corners of the room and glare at the vase while repeating the same guttural, inscrutable phrase over and over in a low, controlled tone. As we did these things, the vase began to glow brighter and brighter with each passing second, until soon it illumined the entire room with its blinding light. As we watched, galvanized, a dark crater began to yawn open in the floor like a giant mouth; and into the black abyss the vase fell, taking with it the golden light. Abruptly, the room was plunged into darkness. Niandra and I continued to chant the monotonous phrase, captivated by the spectacle, not having the slightest idea what would happen next. Amid the low drone of our voices, we could hear strange, muffled cries, which were issued from the crater in the floor, cries which were not produced by the mouths of ordinary beings.

Suddenly, a weird green light shone from the hole, and from the incredible depths a singular and unearthly entity rose, causing both Niandra and myself to gasp in astonishment. It was a luminous, amber cloud, about the height of ten men and the width of five men, in whose swirling vapors hundreds of alien visages flickered and faded continuously, being born and being destroyed with the incessant churning of the miasma.

For an indeterminate time the cloud hovered there above the abysmal crater, and Niandra and I, still absently chanting the same inscrutable phrase, stared at it in fascination, watching as countless nightmarish faces contorted before our eyes, only to vanish seconds later into the cloud's amber mist and be replaced by faces more hideous and more inhuman. Although we had witnessed innumerable sights which would seem initially more impressive than this, neither of us had ever experienced the incredible power, nor the unreal evil which the cloud emanated; its power and its evil were oppressive, tangible forces, pressing down hideously upon our bodies like hundreds of warm hands, and causing us to actually sweat in fear. The cloud meant us great harm; this much was instantly clear.

Slowly, the frightful cloud began to drift toward Niandra, pulsating with its weird amber light as tormented faces blossomed and shriveled repeatedly within its miasmic whorls. I did not know what to do, and I sat there dumbly, petrified with fear as Niandra was reduced to gibbering in terror. The cloud was unquestionably an evil, malignant force, and it commanded a magic infinitely greater than any with which we were acquainted; against the cloud, we were utterly helpless. The terrible cries which were issued from the dark pit grew louder and louder, growing almost unbearable in their volume, and as they reached a deafening crescendo, the cloud swooped down upon Niandra and engulfed her as she let out a final, bloodcurdling scream.

The cloud rose once again, revealing empty space where Niandra had kneeled just seconds before, and began to drift menacingly toward me. Horror-stricken, I forced my fright-paralyzed muscles to move, and I dashed out of the room and out of the castle, leaving the terrible cloud in the chamber. Seconds after I reached the sandy shore below, the castle exploded into a shower of enormous fragments, and had I not instantly conjured a magic carpet and soared away on it, I almost certainly would have been crushed by one of the immense, falling chunks.

As I glided over the churning waves of the sea, I shot a glance back at the ruined castle, and at that moment, I realized that Niandra and I, in performing the horrible ritual, had made a fatal error; for dozens upon dozens of swirling amber clouds were rising from the obsidian ruins, being spewed from the hellbound abyss, and they soared in every direction to engulf all beings they encountered.

Summoning what little powers of reason I still retained, I conjured some parchment and a quill and began to compose this hastily-written letter. When I am through, I shall use my magic to make many, many copies of this letter, and onto each I shall attach feathery, magical wings, so that each letter may be whisked to a different area of the land. I will empower each of these letters with the ability to locate other men and women of Light Magic, and hopefully, at least one of these letters will fall into the hands of a capable wizard, and if we are lucky, the wizard will be able to make use of some of the knowledge presented herein in ways I do not know, so that he may attempt to stop the terrible clouds from obliterating all that exists.

I realize now, as my carpet glides swiftly on toward some unattainable solace, that Niandra and I have committed an unspeakable crime; we have knowingly and foolishly meddled with that which was not meant to be meddled with, and the consequences of our imprudence shall fall upon everyone in the land. I cannot describe the horror and guilt which I feel; I have almost certainly brought about destruction of the entire land, and from this sin I can never be absolved.

Oh, dread! . . . a cloud is racing in my direction. It is gaining on me . . . I can feel its repellent power, its illimitable evil . . . I can see the alien faces twisting and writhing within its vapors . . . it is too swift, I cannot outrun it . . . I shall be engulfed . . . what a horrible fate! I can see Niandra's tormented face squirming within the cloud . . . she is screaming and weeping in pain . . . !

I am about to join her. . . .

HEART OF THE MATTER

by Rowena A. Bathgate

Even after a lifetime of reading fantasy, where virtually endless changes are rung on a few major themes, I can still be surprised—pleasantly—by a really surprising and original story.

If I had a nickel, for instance, for every vampire story I've read, I wouldn't need to edit anthologies—I'd have my own publishing house.

Rowena Bathgate was born in Western Australia, where she is now living, but married an American and has lived in Nevada. She has been writing fifteen years but—inspired by her teenagers—has only recently taken up the fantasy genre. This is her first published story, although she has completed a first draft of a fantasy novel. She asks realistically, "Who hasn't?" She says that she likes to walk her dog and ride her horse, adding that "housework is extremely low on the list of priorities." Of course; like me, if you could stand to do housework, you probably wouldn't be a writer. I made a virtue of necessity by doing my first drafts over—or in—the dishpan.

"Father?"

The tall, slim girl in white robes stood before her parent, trembling as she always did in his presence. The duke was sitting in a window alcove, reading, and lifted cold gray eyes to his daughter.

"Vascha. You have found out why Dako left? Why my trusted commander betrayed his liege?"

"Yes, my lord."

"Is it a woman?"

"Yes, my lord."

"She must be beautiful that he would break his oath to me."

"Some have said so, Father." Vascha swallowed and lifted her warm brown eyes to meet the cool ones of her father.

"And does she love him?" the duke sneered his contempt of any person who would lure his most trusted servant from him, knowing the penalty for such treason. The Commander of the Keep in any duchy of this realm was oathbound to celibacy for the period of his service. In all instances the Lord of the Keep chose the punishment, usually death to all parties involved.

"I do not believe she knew that he loved her, Father . . ."

"But does she love him, Vascha?" her father's voice was ice.

"I think, now that she knows his feelings, that she loves him," Vascha's voice trembled.

"Enough to die for him, I wonder?" the duke spoke quietly, his control returned. To his daughter he said, "Bring me her heart."

"Father?" Vascha could not believe his words.

"Dako must suffer for his treachery! His freedom will taste bitter when you bring me the bitch's heart!"

"But Father . . . !"

"Do you betray me, too, daughter? Do you break *your* oath as my bondswoman?" There was quiet, infinite menace in his words.

"I would not wish it so, my lord, but you know I am sworn . . ."

"You are sworn to do my bidding." The duke turned away from her, the audience ended.

Outside her father's chambers Vascha stood, still shaking, hands clenched tightly at her sides. She was honor bound to do as her liege commanded, and Wizard Sworn not to.

"Daughter?" Ursula, her mother, touched her lightly on the shoulder. "Have you found out what your father wanted to know?"

"Yes, Mother. Now he wants me to bring him the heart of the woman Dako loves."

Ursula paled, "Then you must bring it to him," she whispered.

"Mother, you know I am Wizard Sworn not to kill."

"You are a powerful sorceress, Vascha, surely you can find a way to do this thing without killing," her mother's voice trembled, too, and for a moment mother and daughter gazed at each other in despair, then Vascha sobbed and turned away.

In her rooms Vascha gazed out over the green fields, her mind recoiling from the horror of her father's demand. It was impossible to take someone's heart without killing them, unless they . . . suddenly galvanized into action, Vascha almost flew across the room to the shelves of books that lined a wall of the room. A large, little-used volume floated at her command down from the top shelf into her hands. With a gentle puff she blew a stream of dust from it and straight out the window. Into the night she searched, stopping briefly only to light candles as the evening shadows lengthened. The pages of the book turned themselves, sometimes quickly, sometimes slowly, as she read missives and spells on the graying parchment. Sometime before the orange moon shone in through the casement Vascha gave a short, triumphant yelp. Leaving the book open at the page she had found, she lit large tallow candles at the seven points of a star, permanently and deeply etched into the stone floor. Now she turned to the book, read the words carefully, and began to chant softly as she gathered the other components necessary for the spell.

The words of the book began to take on a luminous quality, and a texture of their own, leaping off the page and swirling together as they gathered the forces of magic and the energy required. In the center of the star the sorceress stood, arms at her sides and head thrown back as she added her own energy to the churning above her.

Once again Vascha stood before her father, a large crystal chalice in her hands. "Lord, I have done as you asked. Here is the heart of the woman as you . . . requested."

The duke took the vessel, and gazed at the bloody mess it contained, then looked sharply at his daughter. "The heart here still beats."

"Yes, my lord." Vascha's eyes met her father's gaze, unwavering.

"Then the woman still lives?"

"Yes, Father, but while you have her heart she cannot love anyone."

He smiled viciously, "So, you have found a way to do my bidding, and still not break your oath. You are clever, daughter, each test I set, you have passed." He placed the chalice on the desk. "Go now, you have outwitted me again, but you have done as I asked."

Vascha let the breath escape slowly from her lungs, then backed the customary three paces before turning and walking slowly from the room. She trembled weakly as she closed the doors, then leaned against them, all her strength gone. Within the room she heard her father utter a violent oath, then a crash as the crystal chalice shattered against a wall.

In her rooms she snuffed out the thick candles at the points of the arcane star, and drew back the heavy drapes from the windows. For a brief moment she looked out over the green fields, and thought of Dako, his broken vow, and all the things he had revealed to her two nights before. Sadly she closed the volume of magic she had studied so frantically the night before. She caught her own reflection in the mirror, a soft and comely young woman who had so briefly tasted love

. . . and touched the quickly healing scar over her right breast. A new and fierce resolve steeled her against those she had held dearest. With grim satisfaction she thought of how her vain and foolish mother would react when she realized Vascha was not coming for her heart; of how her arrogant father had not even asked whose heart he held, and how he had forgotten, if he ever knew it, that witches have two hearts.

A WOLF IN THE FOLD

by Deborah Wheeler

One of the many pleasures of doing this anthology year after year is that I have built up a little group of writers of whom I know ahead of time their stories will be worth reading. One of these is Deborah Wheeler, who managed even to overcome one of my long-standing prejudices. Over the years I have printed many stories about wolves, and when I see a story with "wolf" in the title, I tend to groan and reach for a rejection slip. But I read it—because I know from experience that any story by Deborah will be worth the trouble of reading even if I can't print it; and when I finished this one, I couldn't resist the temptation to share it with my readers.

And that's what makes an editor.

As Bijara waited outside the bronzewood meeting hall door, listening to the voices inside fall silent, it seemed the world held its breath with her. The new moon shone palely on the little village of Meata as it huddled around the river, a thread of light in the vast, brooding forest. Down by the pier, boats sighed under their cargo of furs and carved amber, then fell quiet for an instant. The wolves had ceased their howling this past week, as if there were not enough of a moon to be worth singing to. They prowled Bijara's dreams, waiting and hungering, pressing in on her like the trees pressed against the village walls.

What would the Elders do with her? Would they sell her downriver, as the Master threatened when she'd been caught listening at the Guardian's window instead of tending to her proper tasks? Or would they work her so hard she'd never have a moment to think about the Meata wolves or anything else? Why had the Guardian herself taken an interest in a mere bond-girl?

Bijara took a deep breath and squared her shoulders. At sixteen, she was almost as tall as a man, with broad cheekbones and sandy hair so different from the dark, wiry villagers. When she first came to Meata, half-starved and still numb from the loss of her family, the place seemed like any other forest trading town, safe enough on the surface, but in truth living only at the sufferance of the wolves. Then she'd emerged from her grief enough to realize that these wolves might howl as fiercely as they had in the south, but they never breached the flimsy town walls, not even in the full of the moon. Strangers who dared to travel through the nearby forest were always safe. People said it was the Guardian's magic that kept the wolves away, they said—

Suddenly the meeting hall door opened, spilling out firelight and the smell of spiced wine. Bijara caught a glimpse of the Elders inside. Although she'd scrubbed the hall many times since the town bought her bond, she'd never been allowed inside when it was in use.

Akheer, Guardian of Meata, stepped across the wide river-stone threshold and let the door fall closed behind her. Starlight glimmered on her intricate silver braids and narrow, hawkish nose. She sniffed twice, caught Bijara's elbow in an iron grip, and pulled her down the street. Mutely Bijara followed, wondering if the Elders had given the old Guardian the task of punishing her.

As she stumbled along, Bijara remembered all the nights she'd stolen a moment at Akheer's window during the candidates' class, hoping for some clue to the

Guardian's magic. There must be something she could learn, something she could use against the wolves. . . .

Finally, three nights ago, the words came to her—"The first thing to remember about fighting wolves is that there is no defense, only defeat."

Fighting wolves? Bijara's feet had stuck to the spot, the basket of herbs and onions for the Master's table forgotten. The twilit village at her back, full of dinner time bustle, receded to stillness.

Akheer had continued lecturing in her dry, steady voice. "Every wolfish talent—their reflexes, their muscles, the curve of their eyeteeth—is designed to overcome a *retreating* prey. You cannot win free against them."

"So what are we supposed to do?" That was the smith's son, folding his muscular arms across his chest. "Stand there and let them slaughter us? It's all very well to say 'I'm a holy Guardian,' but even here in Meata, nothing will keep us safe when the moon's full."

"No," the old woman replied. "You must attack before they do—end the conflict before it begins, convince the wolf you are already the victor. The Guardian's oath means only that it will be *you,* and not some innocent traveler, who faces the pack."

"With all respect," a stocky, crow-headed girl said in a voice which clearly indicated she thought the old woman daft, "how can we be expected to fight *wolves* with our bare *hands*—and why this silly rule about never using steel, when our knives are as sharp as anyone's—"

Her eyes lit on Bijara, standing at the window. "It's that bond-girl! She's been *eavesdropping!*"

Bijara's next awareness was of the gnarled old woman not two inches from her nose. "Call the Master. I must speak with the Elders about this."

Now, three nights later, Bijara stumbled along at the Guardian's side and vowed that somehow, no matter how she was punished, she'd never give up, not until she'd learned the secret of fighting wolves.

At the low stone wall which bordered the compound, Akheer came to a sudden halt and pulled Bijara around to face her. "Listen, girl. I want to train you as my successor. But I won't have you unwilling. You can either come with me now, or go back to digging turnips."

"You aren't—I'm not—being punished?"

"Not unless you propose to stand out here all night jabbering!"

Speechless, Bijara followed the old woman inside.

The next morning, Bijara wondered if she'd only exchanged one form of bond-service for another. In Akheer's house, pots still needed scrubbing and potatoes needed peeling. In addition, the old Guardian set her to making herbal medicines. After Bijara laid the evening fire, she brought Akheer a cup of joint-pain tea. The old woman held it in both hands, as if its virtue could seep directly into her swollen knuckles.

After she'd finished the tea, Akheer showed Bijara the path-stones, which glowed mysteriously when a traveler had passed their counterparts along the forest trails, and the amulet she always wore, by whose power she could locate the wolves, even in the deepest darkness. Bijara reached out her hands to the smooth-carved stone, hardly daring to believe it was real, that it might be hers to use.

Akheer tucked the amulet back inside her woolen vest. "It will only work for a Guardian, and you've much to learn before you take the Oath. Now tell me, what was so interesting the other night?"

"You were talking about—the wolves." Bijara kept very still, silent except for the thunder of her heart. If the Guardian guessed her true purpose . . .

Akheer nodded, her eyes glittering like dew on berries in her wrinkled face.

"But you said *fighting* them," Bijara blurted out. "I thought—I thought the wolves never attacked here."

"You come from the south, where the wolves are lawless. Do you know why? Because men hunt them with steel, hacking away at anything weaker, with no sense of decency, until all that's left is a pile of dead bodies, wolves *and* men. But here in Meata it's different. Here we abide by the Pact. The wolves will attack, oh yes, but only in their own place and season. In the forest, when the moon's full. We protect those men foolish enough to be abroad then, but we use only our natural weapons. And so we do fight wolves, but we do it to protect them, for if steel is ever turned against them—"

"*Can* you fight a wolf with your bare hands?" Bijara interrupted.

Akheer's eyes went flat black. "And kill them if need be. It's a bloody business, and I wish I could promise you'd never have to do it. I know you will. Hopefully, not often. But you must always be *prepared* to."

Bloody . . . Bijara's senses swam with desire. Wolf blood on her hands . . . Wolf bodies strewn in the drifted snow, even as she'd found her father and brother's, a death for each death . . . She reeled with it, praying that if Akheer saw the fire in her heart, she would think it devotion.

The winter forest brought too many memories, memories that not even months of intensive training could dissolve. Bijara followed Akheer through the snow, stepping exactly in each footprint. They wore bells tonight, jingles that carried through the night.

Since the summer evening when Akheer had dragged her home from the meeting hall, Bijara had studied wolf lore until she recited it in her sleep, drilled for hours at basic fighting techniques—kicks, leverages, chops, punches. She'd trained until she was so tired and sore that only her tattered pride kept her on her feet. She might still lack the old Guardian's timing and balance, but her strength and reaction speed were even better. Now, at last, she was ready to test her new skills.

Akheer paused to catch her breath, and Bijara glanced up at the moon, so round it looked pregnant. Bijara said, "Here, let me lead."

"You ought not to—tire yourself—on your first time,"

Akheer said, but she let Bijara pass her. "It always takes—energy—to face the wolves."

"There must be some easier way of knowing if they'll attack," Bijara said, breaking through the snow crust in big, gobbling steps.

"This *is* easy, child. The path-stones were clear, so there are no travelers to watch for. Only Mikkel the nutgather, who went out this afternoon." Akheer held up the amulet. "We're close."

Bijara kept her eyes on the snow-layered trail. If the nutgather were somewhere out here, he would certainly draw the wolves to him. She saw herself closing with a huge gray wolf, saw him falling at her feet, blood streaming from his gouged-out eyes . . . She wanted to run, to make it happen faster.

They heard the man before they saw him. He'd heard their bells in the snowy silence, and called out. Bijara spotted him, propped against a fallen tree, a dark, amorphous shape in his rabbit-fur parka. She started to plunge ahead, but Akheer grabbed her sleeve and pointed.

Bijara saw them then—silver eyes set in shadow, ringing the little clearing. She thought she heard them growl, low and sullen.

Ours, they seemed to warn. *He's ours.*

Mine, she answered. *You're mine.*

Akheer pulled her into the clearing and knelt at the nutgather's side.

Bijara looked down at him with a shock. She'd thought he was old, driven to nutgathering by feebleness, but he was young, the age of her next-older brother when the wolves came howling at their gates for the last time. The snow-reflected moonlight was so bright, she could see his boyish beard and round, cold-roughened cheeks. He winced as Akheer ran her hands over his outstretched leg.

"My knee . . ."

"Bad sprain," Akheer muttered.

He nodded and hauled himself straighter. Bijara thought, *He could have hobbled back, except for the wolves.*

She looked up. The wolves melted from the shadows—gray, black, one almost white. As they inched forward, they carried their heads low, ears invisible against their necks.

"Which is the leader?" Akheer's voice rang out over the toneless rumble of their warning.

"The white one."

"Good. When do you take him?"

"I break the distance when he forms the point," Bijara recited.

The other wolves halted, as if frozen to the snow. The white male kept coming. Bijara's heartbeat grew so quiet she didn't seem to have one. She saw the wolf's pale eyes, ringed with black and set slantwise in his tapered skull, saw the individual hairs standing up along his spine. She heard his breath lashing through his nostrils, and the pounding of his heart, far louder than her own. She took a deep, lunging step toward him, then another, her eyes seeking the vulnerable target areas.

The wolf paused, a snow-crusted paw upraised. One ear flicked forward. He raised his head and whined. Bijara's chin dipped towards her chest, her breath rumbling through her throat like a barely audible growl.

"Loup's love, girl, back off!" Akheer hissed. "You've already won. Don't force him—"

Bijara heard her, dimly. She could no longer feel her body, half-crouched in battle stance. Her awareness telescoped down to the animal before her.

Mine, pounded through her brain to the beating of his heart. *You're mine.*

The wolf broke first, zigzagging toward her side.

He'll hamstring me! Bijara whirled and caught him on the side of his head with a snap kick. The wolf yelped, rolled, and scrambled back to his feet. His pack-mates surged forward.

Bijara slammed into the unyielding frozen earth as a heavy furred body crashed into her. Curved teeth sank into her jacket sleeve, searching for her flesh. Over the wolf's shoulder she saw Akheer whirling like a dark tornado, so lithe and quick the wolves seemed to slide off her.

Even as she plunged her fingers into the stippled gray fur, Bijara was filled with the sense of disjointed time. A thousand times before, she dreamed she'd been with her father when the wolves struck. Her blood had ran hot and slick down her chest as the beast tore at her throat. The frozen air had burned her lungs—but it had been only in her dreams.

The wolf shifted its grip upward, toward her unprotected neck, and its hind feet scrabbled at her belly. Bijara rolled with it, bringing her knees up and into the wolf's abdomen. The teeth loosened momentarily and she shoved one hand down the animal's throat.

The wolf sputtered frantically, jaws open wide, and threw itself backward. There was a chorus of yips from the others and suddenly Bijara was alone in the snow.

It took her a moment to realize the attack had ended. Slowly she pulled herself to her feet. She knew she was hurt, but she couldn't feel the pain yet.

Mikkel crouched over a dark lump. "No, no . . ."

Bijara forgot her savaged shoulder and the torn skin on her hands and wrists. She threw herself down beside him on the dark-stained snow.

"Akheer, no . . ." she whispered. She put her arms around the fragile, wool-wrapped body.

"She took on three of them . . ." Mikkel murmured.

So I had only the one, and not even that if I'd had the sense to back off when she told me to. Bijara felt the slight, fluttering breath. She laid her head against Akheer's chest and heard the old woman's heartbeat falter and then grow steady. Through the blood-damp wool, she touched the severed tendons behind one knee. There'd be no infection, thanks to Akheer's herbal remedies, but no medicine known could make her whole again.

Bijara jerked upright, unable to breathe with the wolf stench filling her head. Her eyes swam with the reflected moonlight. Mikkel patted her good shoulder. "Not your fault, girl. You did well for your first time. A fine Guardian you'll make us."

* * *

Light woke Bijara, light from the full moon which no curtains could screen completely, light from the path-stones which Akheer insisted she keep at her bedside. The house was silent except for the old woman's snoring. Bijara swore under her breath and sat up. Then eagerness swept all traces of sleep from her brain. This time she'd go to the wolves alone. She smiled as she pulled on her warmest clothing.

She knew from the pattern in the stones where to search along the paths. The night seemed dense and still, her bells jarringly loud. But not loud enough to drown the whinny of a frantic horse.

"I'm here!" Bijara shouted, and broke into a run. Around a sharp bend, hidden by a knot of thick-boled ashleaf, a lone rider wheeled his spotted mare to face her. Costly moon-metal glinted on the horse's bridle and the hilt of the man's long, slightly curved sword.

"Crom's bloody ass, girl! What the hell are you doing out here?"

"I'm the Guardian! Put away that sword!"

Bijara scanned the sides of the trail. She spotted four wolves, one a lanky, gray-muzzled bitch. The leader, black as a moonless night, towered above the others. They hadn't made up their minds to attack yet, and her arrival confused them.

The mare whinnied again, dancing on her hind feet, and Bijara jumped clear. "Now I've got to protect you, too!" the man cried.

"No, you don't," Bijara replied with all the authority she could muster. She'd noted his arrogant bearing and costly fur cloak. He'd see her as nothing more than a little village girl, no one to take orders from.

"Don't you know about the Meata Guardian? You have nothing to fear as long as I'm here. Now put away your sword, as the Pact commands, and let me do what I'm trained for!"

In those few moments, the wolves had tightened their circle, the coal-black leader moving to point. Bijara stepped toward him. She'd run out of time. She searched her heart for the heedless rage which had swept away all fear last time, and was surprised to find herself truly frightened. This wolf was so much bigger than the others, his bared fangs like pearly sabers. She forced herself into another step, lowering her body-center in preparation for quick movement.

The mare screamed again and grazed Bijara with her shoulder as her rider spurred her forward. Bijara stumbled and caught herself on her hands in the snow. She looked up to see the upraised sword as a blur of silver through the night.

The black wolf swerved like an inky shadow, twice as fast as the white one she'd faced before. He landed, recovered, and leapt, all in one motion. *The power in him!* Bijara thought.

The mare made a gurgling sound as she crumbled sideways into the snow, her throat torn out. The swordsman fell with her, cursing Bijara and the wolf with equal fervor. He struggled to jump free, but one leg twisted under the horse's body.

Bijara fumed at the waste of the mare's life. Now they were right back where they started, before the man embarked upon his foolishness. She steeled herself to face the black wolf.

And her heart quailed within her. Where once his eyes had shimmered like bits of moonshine, they glowed now like embers, lit from within by their own unnatural luminescence. An eerie reddish aura rippled over its body.

The wolf seemed to hunch in upon itself and then to swell in size. Bijara could almost hear the rasping of ligament over bone as its body stretched and elongated. The proportions were all wrong—head too narrow, forequarters too massive, an unholy marriage of weasel and bull.

Then it lifted its misshapen head and the moonlight reflected off the red blood trickling down one shoulder. The man's sword had touched the natural wolf, and before her stood something quite different, something out of a nightmare—no, something she had once seen in a priest's book of demons.

What had Akheer said? *"If steel is ever turned against them . . ."*

She tried to warn me, Bijara thought. *To tell me why it was so important that we protect the Meata wolves.*

The thing which had been a wolf lowered its head again, sniffing the man pinned beneath the dead horse, and did not growl. The rest of the pack rolled their eyes and whimpered, tails pinned to their bellies.

Suddenly Bijara knew that the wolf still lived, hidden inside the monster and as helpless as the swordsman behind her. Unless it were stopped now, the malevolent spirit would spread like wildfire through the pack, devouring them from within, turning them to its own purposes.

The wolves would be forever beyond her reach.

"Out, foul demon! The wolf is mine!" Bijara screamed. Slowly the red-eyed thing swung its skull around to her. Faintly glowing slaver dripped from its gaping jaws. Its hindquarters bunched for a leap.

Bijara darted forward a moment before the demon wolf launched itself into the air. Her boot toe collided with the underside of its jaw, ripped through the soft tissue of its throat, and snapped the massive skull up and back. The thing rolled in the air, twisting like a cat, and landed.

Akheer's teachings flowed through Bijara as if she'd always known how to fight wolves. She leaped forward as it silently hurled itself at her again, jammed its heavy body in midair, then whirled, using her smaller turning radius to catch it with a knife-hand chop just below the base of its skull.

The wolf thing yelped and fell, scrabbling in the snow. Trying to rise again. Bijara straddled it just behind its shoulders, and pinned it to the ground with her weight. She reached around and caught its lower jaw, jerked it around and up—*up*—until she felt the joints lock. A hard jerk would break the wolf's neck.

One eye rolled back toward her as she gathered her strength for the final effort. An eye at once beseeching and scornful.

Free me, pleaded the wolf.

Kill it for all I care! laughed the demon.

Carefully, Bijara loosened the grip of her knees and allowed the wolf's body to roll slightly. She kept her leverage tight, turning until both eyes met hers.

"I *will* kill it," she said. "Slowly. Painfully. And *you* will die with it."

Bijara stared at the wolf beneath her as the red light flickered once and then died. Pale, moon-reflecting eyes stared back at her. This time they held no pleading, only quiet acceptance as the wolf waited for its life to end at the hands of its sworn enemy.

I'll kill you . . . when I choose . . .

Quickly she released its head and jumped free. The wolf lay panting on the snow for a few moments, then jerked to its feet. Limping, it followed the others into the shadows without a backward glance.

Bijara ran her fingers over the amulet's seductively smooth surface. She felt it singing in her blood, singing of visions and power. All hers for a word.

She laid the stone in Akheer's lap and stood up, wiping her hands on her thighs. "I cannot take the Oath."

"The trader told me how you fought the wolf. And spared it. I wasn't wrong about you, girl."

"You only say that because you think you won't have to train another. Because you can't—go out next full moon. I can do that for you, for a while. I can teach the drills for you, but I can't—can't—"

"Can't what?" The old woman pulled herself straighter on her padded chair.

"Can't vow to protect them. Don't you see what I've been hiding from you all these months? I only stayed because I wanted to learn how to *kill* the wolves."

"Why didn't you?"

"Give the wolf to that *thing?*"

Slowly Akheer smiled. "I was right about you all along. Do you think mere *duty* can give a Guardian the strength to face the pack, season after season? Do you think any of those feather-brained village louts has one tenth of your passion?"

"But I *hate*— I've *sworn*—"

"And whoever said that hate was not a suitable basis for fighting demons?" Unsmiling, the old woman held the amulet out again.

Bijara felt the pulse of the warmth as it touched her bare skin. It sat in the palm of her hand, glowing with an inner fire. *Her* inner fire. She clenched her fingers around it and walked through the door, to the snow-drifted yard. Oblivious to the cold, she stood at the low stone wall, looking toward the forest.

Behind her half-closed eyes, she saw them, lithe and deadly sparks of silver light. Haunting the forest. Skimming the darkness.

Mine, she thought. *You're mine*.

A THING OF LOVE

by Vera Nazarian

One of the reasons why I always look forward to reading Vera Nazarian's contributions to this anthology—like many of the things she has submitted, they're frequently too long to print—is that I always know ahead of time that they will be very much worth the time I spend reading them; highly colored, really original and with a true sense of wonder.

This is why I wanted to be an editor in the first place, and why I keep at it. I remember reading in MOBY DICK that people who hunted whales "went out to get the brightest and freshest lamp oil" and while the bringing of electric light has made the hunting of whales a dispensable luxury, editors go out to hunt the best and freshest stories and get them all at the source before they're all picked over and with eyetracks all over them.

It was said that Faelittal the Executioner had neither a soul nor a living human heart. A soul had never been given to her, it was rumored, by the will of gods. And a heart—that fragile organ thought to be the seat of emotion—her heart, or any semblance of it, Faelittal had long since cracked in twain, splintered, and then ground the fragments to dust, ever since her sword had first cleaved, with exquisite precision, a human neck.

She would do this, cleave human flesh, without a single twitch of her pale sublime face, without a blink. They who witnessed executions, had the chance to observe this, for unlike any other executioner, the queen's sister looked into her victims' eyes and wore no mask.

Lyksandias, the queen, called for executions frequently. To her they were "things of love," the means by which people were taught the letter of the law, unhealthy displeasure was subjugated, and the vile canker-sores of different thinking were uprooted. The queen's rule was absolute, and those not yet aware of this fact were forced to taste the chilling mercy of her judgment. Lyksandias was stonelike thus, in her "love."

All manner of men and women were executed. Ordinary villains, freemen, those involved in trade were normally hung. The warrior class were shot by marksmen, or strangled with a silk cord. That same cord was offered to the more affluent women and upper class ladies—the latter also had the choice of poison.

The priesthood was allowed by the queen to burn heretics at the stake. There were, of course, numerous other means.

And then, there was the High Execution, either by great sword or ax, to be performed as the highest form of chastisement of traitors to the queen. Faelittal was the greatest practitioner of this very art.

Originally, the somber sister of the queen merely bore arms as a warrior in the service of the God of Defense, one of an elite honor guard, first instituted in deep antiquity. Once it had merely been ceremonial in nature, but at present, things were turbulent, and threats real enough to warrant the presence of a genuinely skilled guard elite.

But Faelittal rose above her already exhalted rank. She was an ascending meteor, and a warrior's status was beneath her potential. Icily composed, placid in demeanor, and brilliant, Faelittal became the original High Executioner.

"My little loyal tigress-cub," the queen would say, with a fond yet secretly awed look, to her not so little younger sister. She, in turn, would look down at Lyksandias, columnlike, from her man's height and stature, and reply: "I am yours to command, my Bright Sister, O Queen." And there would be a certain look in her eyes that was not there at other times.

Lyksandias had many lovers. In fact, this was one of the original reasons that the High Executioner's position came into being. It was some years ago that Faelittal had to slit the throat of a maddened young aristocrat who personally threatened the life of Lyksandias. He had achieved the fleeting rank of consort, but beneath it all was planning treachery and the queen's overthrow. And Lyksandias decided to turn this into an example. The dead but still warm body was carried to a public scaffold where Faelittal, with flashing uncovered eyes, threw down her warrior's emblem, and instead, donned the ebony cloak of night and death. There was one difference to this cloak, however—a fine silver starburst graced its back, a symbol never previously seen.

The High Executioner's symbol it became. And on that day, with a long shining blade, Faelittal executed the body of the traitor.

With time, other such occasions arose, and the queen's sister gained fame for her weird elegance and impassivity while dealing out death. Some went before her pleading and crying, up to the very final stroke that cut their life. Others stood in dignity, and there were yet others that had to be carried up senseless, not able to fathom the horror and hopelessness of their positions. To all of these Faelittal showed only a blank oddly receptive face, not cruel, but never sympathetic—simply *aware.* It was at such times that a superstitious fear of her first occurred to the onlookers, for they could understand most other kinds of effect—pity, guilt, fear, even sadistic glee—but not *this.* And so, they concluded certain things, one of which was that she had no heart, was not really human.

A female demon in human form.

The queen heard of these rumors and laughed. It only helped maintain the particular nature of her reputation. Faelittal, however, did not laugh. Not being the laughing kind, she merely shifted the expression in her already ambiguous eyes.

That had been a long while ago. Now, yet another man stood to be executed by the queen's judgment, a young nobleman of wide popularity both with the court and the masses. He was of a good family, but too liberal, frank, and outspoken. And that became his downfall.

He was Remialt, of the house of Kellen. He had never been the queen's lover. And yet, when he insulted the queen's authority, Faelittal guessed by the particular nature of her sister's reaction, that Lyksandias had wanted him.

The court, meanwhile, was aflame with rumors and turbulence. Such a turn of events was indeed unprecedented; no one expected Remialt to say or do what he did.

For the Kellen had stood up in the presence of all court, and called the queen a "golden whore." And then, still facing her with unflinching eyes, he brought into question her competence and the regal status that had been hers by birth, through a centuries-old chain of succession.

The queen, normally in suave control of herself, allowed a tremor to pass her lips. And then, ignoring the present court and saying nothing to him in her beautiful despotic dignity, she summoned Faelittal. Which meant that here was to be no mercy.

The queen's sister entered, blankly looked at her victim to be, then paused.

Remialt's dark-eyed gaze was so keen, so righteous, that he caught her attention. Therefore she asked him, in her rarely-heard soft voice, something that only a privileged few condemned were entitled to hear: "Is this true, O man, what you say? Do you really believe and stand by your words?"

"Yes," he answered firmly, honestly meeting her eyes with his flashing ones. "I will always stand by my words."

"Then," Faelittal said blankly, "by my hand you must die."

And the guards took him unprotesting.

The eldest son of the house of Kellen was then given the customary week to prepare himself for the High Execution.

The following day half court donned mourning, and there was outrage. The family Kellen went about like the living dead, both due to tragedy, and to dishonor. Rumors, angry rumors, sent mercurial sparks everywhere, and those who understood such things, predicted that at last the queen had done something that would bring consequences beyond her imagining.

"The truth . . ." whispered everyone, "he had simply spoken the truth!"

"But truth is not to be," spoke brokenly the old and blunt lord Kellen. "My son will die. Oh, why couldn't he be like all others, and be satisfied with—with *self-delusion?*"

There was no answer to this. Only, the Kellen younger son decided to do something that might let him retain his sanity, retain a belief in some form of ultimate truth. Chiarn Kellen secretly went to plead for his brother's life, before Faelittal.

He was a darkly thin and tall youth, Chiarn. He would have appeared wraithlike, if not for the proud stiffness of his posture and keen searching eyes. Toward evening, as he was finally allowed into the High Executioner's presence after his long wait, he never lost that pride, only gained an edge to his inner anger.

Faelittal stood before a small window in a dark room, looking out somewhere. She turned to him, a silhouette, clad like a man, and he still could not see her very well. *She must be afraid*, he guessed, *to face what I have to say*.

"Who are you?" said a woman's quiet voice, as she looked at him, he was not sure how intently, in the twilight.

"Chiarn Kellen. The second son. You are to execute my older brother on the third day from tonight."

"Ah, yes." She paused. Inside him, blood pounded; anger and outrage seethed, as he wanted to cry out, strike her. For, like a post she stood, face unreadable, taller than him, and somehow *eternal.*

And he felt then, without even beginning to speak, that no matter what he would say, no matter how he pleaded, he had come all for nothing.

"I am here," he began, hopeless and awkward because of this new awareness, "to speak for my brother's life. To find out, O High Lady, if there is anything I can do, if there's any way to convince you—"

"To spare him?" She cut him off. "You must know that I only do my sister's will. Why speak to me and not her?" Her eyes, like a night animal's were liquid and glittering, while her face was shadow.

Why indeed? He paused, as if this thought had never occurred to him. And then coldly, rationally reasoned out loud: "Maybe because she will not be moved. And you—you have less to do with this, less personal involvement. What is my brother's life to you, but a thing? To be thrown away or spared, think, how really significant! You have no real interest in his death. And therefore, I presume, you might be swayed. Somehow. To spare him. Please! Have mercy on our family! In the name of all and any gods, name your price!"

He waited, and in the dusk he thought he saw her faintly smile. "I have never been swayed before . . ." said Faelittal. "Luckless boy. You've come here to ask me this, knowing very well what my answer would be, beforehand. But your pride insisted. It insisted that I would treat *your* words differently somehow, honor *your* request. Don't you know, boy, who I *am?* Don't you know that I have no sympathy, no senses, and no heart?"

In his overflowing anger he was never to be sure if it was irony that he heard in her voice.

"Then I call all curses upon your head!" he blurted, the knot in his throat that had been building up all along, about to release a flood of tears. "You are a beast indeed, a she-demoness! I am not afraid of your anger, I tell you this straight; I would kill you now myself, and you would see I am no boy, but a man!"

"I see . . ." she said almost tiredly, "I have insulted you. So then, O man who is not a boy. Kill me, if you think you can. . . ."

In response, a thin pale dagger flashed in the folds of his clothing. But before he could even move, she was at him, like a black leopard, across the length of the room. Her lukewarm fingers clamped his wrist and held him there. And, then with a gasp from him, and a flick of her hand, his dagger clanged onto the floor.

She continued to grip his wrist as he first snarled in frustration, and then hot silent tears burst forth, as his body shook, and slowly he sank to the floor. On his knees before her, he silently shook with sobbing. "My brother . . ." he cried, "Remialt . . . my brother!"

And then he felt a light touch on his hair. She had released him and now, oddly, passively, stroked his soft dark hair. "Child . . ." she said.

And in her voice there was no evil, yet no soul.

In surprise, Chiarn stared up at her, then grasped her feet with his two hands, and buried his face and his hair against the coolness of her stark leather boots. "Lady . . ." he mumbled, choking on his words, "Oh, lady, he—he loves life! There's a noble fair woman that is waiting to marry him, this very autumn. And—and there is so much that he would do yet, for all of the family, for—me. . . . Like before, I remember, we would go riding together at harvest time, and he'd give me crunchy apples smelling of autumn sun, and . . . and oh, how he chased me through the house when we were boys. . . . And once, I remember—he mostly smiles, but—I remember I had seen him cry. Only once! Our mother lay in fever. And at dawn, she died. And he would touch my hair, lightly, just as you have done, and—"

Sobs cut him off, as the room went reeling before his eyes and now the pressure of weeping was more than he had ever known.

"Poor youth . . ." said Faelittal. "You do not sway me. You cannot."

Chiarn's anger burst forth anew, incredulous. He

stared with volcanic eyes up at her distant face-shadow. "Don't you—love anything? Care for anything?" he whispered, no longer sobbing, due to shock.

The executioner said softly, impassively, "I love. That which is truth."

"What of the queen? She is your sister, do you love her? What would you do if she were condemned to die?"

For an instant he thought he *saw* something move in her, a flicker of the shadow.

"You do not—ask the proper question . . ." she replied, very oddly, gently. "What I would do as a sister is one thing. As an executioner—another. . . ."

"Then you would execute your own sister! Gods!"

"Yes. Only *I*. You—" she paused, inexplicably gathering herself for something—"you do not *understand*."

"Yes, I don't understand. . . ." Chiarn was feeling slow fear move within him. There was something so peculiar about her, about the whole situation, he now knew—something far more complex than he originally guessed. A gathering of paradox. And yet so far he could not explain it to himself.

"You are not human, O High Lady . . ." he ventured.

"Wrong," she said matter-of-factly. "I am human. If you'd moved fast enough, your dagger would've killed me. Only—praise gods it did not. For I must be the one to kill your brother. Know, that only I can do it the *right* way."

"The right way?! There is a right way to *kill?*" His voice was sarcastic bitterness.

But the next words she said, froze him.

"Yes. There is a right way. As the High Executioner I have been given this knowledge. Now, ask me no more of this, boy!" She was brisk now, harsh. "It is already too much that you have heard. Because of your brother, and the nature of his offense—or better yet, the nature of his person—I have tolerated you. Only because of *him* . . . Now, go!"

"But—" Chiarn began, a knot again in his throat.

"Go!" Her voice boomed. And then, almost as an afterword, her voice followed him away. "Do not think,

Chiarn Kellen, that you have come in vain. For—you have clarified for me *what* exactly is to be your brother's death."

The incomprehensible words rang in his head as he walked. Later he only remembered that the whole time they had spoken, there had been no candlelight, and he had never really seen her face.

At dawn of the execution day, Faelittal came to stand at the high palace walls, a customary ritual before she performed her Act. Already, crowds of sickly-curious onlookers milled beneath, staring, whispering, and pointing at her, from the city streets far below. Chiarn stood, one with the crowd, somewhere down there also. He had never been present at such an event, and now was perversely compelled to witness every minute detail of this day, every single one of her movements. . . .

As usual, the crowd was a many-faced beast. "Kill him, Dark Lady!" they cried. And yet others cried, "Spare him, spare the fine son of Kellen!"

The midnight figure of the High Executioner, oblivious to all, stood motionless. Only when the sun pierced the horizon with its incandescent rose simmer, did she raise her hands skyward, and invoke the god that she served.

And then, she left the palace walls.

Somebody next to Chiarn nudged him, to whisper: "Who knows why she does this every time? Before she kills 'em? I don't—gives me a chill in my back, it does! Feels like—like you're one with *her,* one with the *condemned.* Like it's *your* execution being prepared, not his!"

"I don't—know," Chiarn answered faintly. He wanted to run somewhere, badly, but something gripped him here. He had to see, to *see* the death of his brother.

Meanwhile, Faelittal still let her gaze travel about the audience, looking at each and all. It was only the condemned himself that she appeared to ignore.

"Sister," said the queen somewhat hastily, "Proceed." And her royal voice again almost shook. Lyksandias, too, only now remembered how odd, how terrible these moments in the Executions had always felt. Why did she never think not to attend? Why come and masochistically pain herself?

Faelittal's normally soft voice now boomed. "Remialt, heir lord to Kellen! Are you prepared to die?"

The prisoner did not even blink. "As well as any man!" he retorted in a strong voice, defiantly. Only Chiarn saw the deeper tiredness in his gaze. Somewhere a few feet away, a man's shaky old voice sent up a keening wail. Chiarn recognized the voice of his father. His heart twanged. He had almost forgotten all about *that.*

On the scaffold, Remialt flinched, hearing it also.

"Speak your last words." said Faelittal

"My only words are for the house of Kellen." The condemned man bowed in the general direction of his father, his eyes hungrily searching the crowd. He waited, and then said simply: "I hope that *he* who hears me now, blesses me. . . . I have only spoken the truth."

And then, impassioned, he exclaimed: "And I still say, Lyksandias your queen is a golden whore! *You,* all of you have the means, the power to end this—" He was cut off by a heavy slap on the face by one of the guards. But Faelittal raised a threatening gloved hand at the abuser, and Remialt was released.

She beckoned Remialt to draw near. And then, for the first time, the High Executioner truly looked into the eyes of the condemned man.

A timeless moment. A nothing. All his despair, wildness, righteousness, soul—immortalized in a still glance. And then, all she said was: "Come, O man. Meet your true death."

Holding his breath, Chiarn watched his brother, watched with a sick hunger every movement of his face. And it was then that maybe he alone, of all those present, knowing Remialt the way he did, saw an instant of *difference* in the expression of the condemned man. An expression of peace replaced the stifled anxiety and despair on the face of Remialt. That, for a fraction of an instant. And then, that, too, was gone. Instead, what was left was an oddly familiar blank *receptiveness*—where had Chiarn seen this before?

All around, the multitude, like a single beast, sucked in its breath. And now Chiarn knew that he was not the only one who had sensed all this, stood in nearly full empathy with the condemned. *In fact,* he now thought, "awakening," and also surfacing for breath, *I am not special at all, not different from them. . . . They, too, can feel! Because—because I can feel them in turn! It is like a great mirror with endless facets, all reflecting to each other back at themselves. I feel Remialt's emotion. The crowd feels it. I feel the consequent emotion of every person in the crowd. And every person feels the emotion of every other person, including myself. . . . And what we all feel, is Remialt's approaching death. . . .*

And—

Faelittal the Executioner meanwhile, silent as the sun's shadow, removed the great sword from its sheath, and raised it high overhead.

The condemned man, with blank *receptive* eyes, as though he predicted her every next move, in perfect sync with her, stepped forward silently, then sank on his knees before the neck-rest, and the basket. He slightly inclined his head forward.

The frozen dilated eyes of the glittering doll Lyksandias, and the rest of the crowds were upon his figure.

When the sword fell, it made no sound. Neither did the head, as it fell into the basket ready for it. So clever the blow, that for several instants the headless torso remained upright, as though unaffected by it all.

Another pulse-beat, and the crowd wailed, as the psychological spell—that had lasted since dawn—was broken at last. They were all free of it, free, and so the people—to show themselves that their will was theirs again—made audible cries, exclamations, gasps, or whatever it is that affirmed their beings under such circumstances.

Chiarn could at last avert his eyes (something that subconsciously was his only goal, since dawn). To quickly take his mind off the approaching numbness of despair, he now began making his way toward his old father where the rest of the Kellen gathered.

On her throne, Lyksandias, stricken by something she herself could not explain, recalled again that this was exactly how she felt after each High Execution—as though her being had been rended inside. And yet, this feeling would always "close up," and recede deep inward, and she'd forget. . . . Truly, it was already beginning to do so now.

Faelittal stood alone. Odd, how everyone's attention had all of a sudden shifted now, away from her, from the corpse, from the scaffold. Such was the ending to all High Executions—no cheers went up, no harsh crowds screamed for more blood. Never. In the end, they desired above all to leave the place. Already the square was emptying.

Faelittal stood columnlike. Her keen faraway gaze took in the exquisite form of her sister, royally escorted, and briskly leaving the square. She never looked back, had already forgotten the dead man.

And when Faelittal was sure that there was no one left to observe her—that is, no one who would observe her and *understand*—she, too, took a deep breath, like a sleeper surfacing, and felt all *feeling* and *sensation* rush back into her, on soft delicate sterile wings of truth. And then, because now the sun shone brighter, the air filled her lungs with crispness, and the fresh scarlet blood still dripped from her Sword's blade in a small pool at her feet, she blinked, and there was wetness in her eyes.

One of the guards under her command covered the body, knowing automatically the routine. Faelittal did not need to see the one she killed. And yet, the wetness continued in her eyes, and would not stop.

It was not the *man* she was crying for—it was the wretched *body*. The poor flesh and the nerves, that had to feel the harshness of the parting, the rent neck muscles and the spine. . . .

Faelittal knew that the *man* himself had felt nothing—his silver cord of life she had gently *severed* beforehand, when she looked into his eyes. She had learned enough about him to do it properly, from the necessary conversation with his younger brother. *Too bad,* she thought, *that the youth Kellen would never know how he had in fact facilitated his brother's gentle way of dying.*

Faelittal always allowed a condemned one's relative to meet with her, so that she would know the nature of the fine fabric of their souls. For, souls were exquisite things, unique, yet one could be fathomed through a close other. . . .

And always, she would release each man's soul, gently, with the utmost care, and then execute merely a body—like that very first time. Only, *these* executions were different. *Fear* and *responsibility* for each death had to remain here, to rest heavily on someone, for the sake of balance.

And for that purpose, there was the great crowd, the "audience." They were executed vicariously. And the queen also. . . .

But why, one might think, did she bother with it all, Faelittal? Why tolerate the whim of the queen, the tyranny? So much easier it could be just to end the dark reign, to render Lyksandias powerless, to *execute*—

Faelittal watched the rose-stained sword in her hands, and thought, as always she did afterward.

There were so many others like Lyksandias in the world, too many. Remove one, and another would spring up—straightforward or subtle—to take up the reins of power.

But as long as Faelittal stood as the High Executioner, that dark ultimate power and responsibility was in her skilled hands. She would do occult justice with it.

But even more so, Faelittal stood crying for Lyksandias. Because once again, for what innumerable time, the queen, having her soul opened for her to the truth through such costly means, allowed it again to close up. She had turned away, gilded and radiant, having forgotten.

And Faelittal the Executioner wept, because she knew so intimately the fine nature of her sister's—and hence, her own—soul.

THE SWORD SLAVE

by Diana L Paxson

Fond as I am of the new writers, it's always a pleasure to get in something from an experienced writer which I know, ahead of time, will be worth the time and trouble of reading.

Diana Paxson says that she "married into a family of writers, and thus became aware that writing was not only possible but could be taken for granted."

Her first sale, "People of the Wind," was printed in the anthology GREYHAVEN (DAW 1983). Since then she has never looked back. Like many writers she has held down a variety of strange jobs, and has published a little of everything. She has taught reading to adults in local California colleges, and has two teen-aged sons, one of whom, Ian, is a noted convention-goer and member of a tech crew in theater.

She has written several novels in the "Westria" series which overlap science fiction and fantasy, being at least partly post-holocaust novels dealing with ecology, and partly fantasy; she has also published a group of urban contemporary fantasies laid in Berkeley, including the splendid BRISINGAMEN (Freya's Necklace) and the more recent THE PARADISE TREE. She has also published a major Arthurian novel about Tristam and Iseult, THE WHITE RAVEN.

"So—this should soothe the pain . . ."

Shanna sighed as Tara spread cool salve across the rope burn on her arm, her nostrils flaring as its minty fragrance diffused through the air. The lamp hissed and light flickered across the stretched leather of the tent. From outside came the whicker of a horse, footsteps, the small sounds of the caravan at rest.

The pale blue robe of a novice among the Moonmothers slid back from Tara's cool fingers as she worked. Shanna was reminded of Mother Elosia, who had tended her in Otey. She had been with Bercy's caravan ever since then, and in another day their journey to the imperial city of Bindir would be done. Now that they were almost there, she felt a curious reluctance to actually complete the journey. It had been so long since she had sworn so arrogantly to bring her brother back to Sharteyn, and so many things had changed. If she failed to find Janos, the past five years of strife and wandering meant nothing. If against all odds she succeeded in bringing him back, would a throne still await him? And for her, would Sharteyn still be home?

Tara put the stopper back into the pot of salve and Shanna roused herself.

"It does feel better. You do this as if you've been at it for years."

"I have been—" Tara looked up with a shy smile. "The Mothers pledge no maiden until after her rite of passage, but I was an orphan, left in their care. I've been studying with the healers since I was five. Come back to me tomorrow and—"

Outside, a man screamed.

Shanna's own blade was already in her fist and her other hand sweeping aside the doorflap when she heard the first clangor of metal. She pounded across packed earth, blessing the Goddess that she was still wearing her riveted leather brigandine and mail. A tongue of flame licked up the side of a wagon; shadowshapes danced across the yard and she swerved, sword coming up to guard as light flared on metal. Steel chimed; she let trained reflexes guide her arm in another parry while she tried to see.

Wrapped furs made her opponent look larger—not a soldier, then. He swore in a southland accent as Shanna nicked him, then came swinging in again. A quick slice across his throat silenced the cursing. She heard Bercy giving angry orders, then three more shapes came between her and the light.

Chai! By the burning wagon—to me! Silent wings bore the falcon through the darkness in answer to Shanna's mental call. One man screamed as the bird struck and his blade clattered across the ground.

They must be bandits—escaped slaves and masterless men—they plagued the Empire, but what were they doing so close to Bindir? And more kept coming. She was being driven toward the horse-lines. Someone had cut the picket ropes, and drumming horses drowned out men's cries. Shanna glimpsed her mare, Calur, and whistled. The horse's head came up and she checked, turning. Bercy and her sons were battling back to back. Shanna struggled to reach them, but another group of yelling bandits ran between.

"Bercy, get Calur!" she cried. Then something struck her unprotected head, and she fell down into the dark.

Shanna coughed and struggled upward through a sick swirl of shadow, opened her eyes and gasped as a pulse of fire lanced through her skull.

"You're awake. Now look at me—" Cool hands held her still. Shanna focused and saw Tara bending over her. The other girl was naked and dirty, but she seemed to be unharmed. "Pupils both the same size—good. You've had a nasty knock on the head, but you'll heal."

Shanna drew breath carefully. The surface beneath her jolted and shuddered to the complaining squeak of wagon wheels. A ray of sunlight stabbed through a tear in the canvas above her. As the pain ebbed, awareness of her body returned. Through the blanket beneath her, straw pricked bare skin. She could feel the ache of old bruises, and a cold weight on her ankles. She forced herself up on one elbow and saw that her feet were chained.

"The bandits sold us—" said Tara flatly. "We're in a slavewagon now, on our way to Bindir."

Shanna stared at her. Then the interior of the wagon blurred, and she slid down into darkness once more.

For the next two days she grasped consciousness in short, painful snatches. On the third day, their captors saw that she was awake and chained her hands. And so it was that Shanna, who had once been the Royal Daughter of Sharteyn, first saw the Imperial city of her ancestors as a shackled slave.

In its beginnings, Bindir had been a fortress, built with its back to the limestone cliffs above the brackish waters of the Worldriver that flowed to the western sea. But long ago it had spread down the slopes to the harbor which was its southern gate. The remains of the ancient walls still girded the citadel, warm gold in the afternoon sun. Above them the great houses of the nobles rose in a mosaic of gilding and multicolored stone around the white palace of the emperor with its coronet of towers. The great trade road approached from the north, but on that side lay the Gate of War and the encampments of the army. Skirting them, the wagons turned onto the road that led eastward around the city, so that it was through the Gate of Produce that the slavetrain finally entered Bindir. By then, Shanna was already doing muscle-work to build her strength back and planning escape.

For a week she ate what she was given and made no trouble. The slavers guarded their merchandise carefully, and she understood that she must wait until she was sold before making her move. At the end of that time she was paraded, still bound, in a line with others, and sold.

They told Shanna that her new master was Lord Irenos Aberaisi, a prince of Mesith whose family had long ago traded its own freedom for the gilded servitude of the court. But once he had purchased her she never saw him. Her new world was to be the women's wing in his palace in the citadel, where his first wife, Lady Amniset, ruled.

* * *

"You have your strength back?" The thin woman behind the low table surveyed Shanna dispassionately and she stiffened, then eased back into the balanced fighter's stance she had adopted instinctively when they brought her into the room.

"I can see that you do—" said Lady Amniset, dismissing the male guards who had escorted Shanna with a wave of her hand. "That is well. We have purchased you as a sword slave, to guard." Her fingers were long and white, laden with jewels, but the nails looked sharp and strong. She sat upright on heaped cushions before a filigreed screen, her layered silks arranged in sculptured folds. As the door closed, Shanna heard a rustle of fabric behind the screen and realized that they were not alone. Lady Amniset watched her from glittering dark eyes, apparently undisturbed by the knowledge that they were being observed.

Shanna stared back at her mistress, understanding now why they had restored her red leather brigandine and the undervest of gilded mail when they gave her the tunic and breeches of black cloth. Lying on the table she saw the well-worn scabbard and familiar falcon hilt of her own sword. But where was her warhorse now? Where was the falcon who had been her friend? She swallowed, her throat dry as it had been ever since she arrived in Bindir.

"You are silent—" said Lady Amniset. Shanna frowned. "You are defiant," the Lady went on. "Do you think it will be easier to escape now that you are here?"

"I am not a slave—" Shanna began, and heard muffled laughter from behind the screen.

"Everyone is a slave to something," came the cool answer. "How many understand their chains?" The lady lifted a flagon from the tray on the inlaid table and poured wine into the cup beside it. Shanna licked dry lips, and her captor smiled.

"Are you thirsty? Don't try to deny it—it's a common side effect of the drug the slavers have been giving you." Shanna's face must have shown something then, for Lady Amniset began to laugh. "For two weeks it has been in every meal you ate, and two days would have been long enough to addict you. It is a derivative of lotos, but knowing that will not help—it has been magically altered to affect you alone. When we bought you, we also purchased the spell."

"I don't believe you . . ." Shanna began. Her gaze fixed on the swirl of the wine.

"Try fasting—" the woman said. "Long before lack of food weakens you, your muscles will begin to spasm. Your body will tear itself apart and you will die in unbelievable pain. We have no need of chains to control you. Your own flesh will compel obedience." She held out the cup. "Serve us well, and we will reward you—" The ring on her forefinger glowed crimson, incised with some design like the currents in the wine.

I don't believe that—thought Shanna. *I dare not! But I must seem to obey, for a time. . . .* She took the cup, and even as she drank, wondered if her defiance was already a delusion. Was there an odd aftertaste in the wine? Dimly, she began to recognize one link in the chain that bound her, and its name was Fear.

The rustling began again as the Lady dismissed her, but Shanna paid no attention. Only when she saw the maidservant waiting outside to show her to her quarters did she tense, for it was Tara, smooth limbs draped in gauzy muslin and wheaten hair shorn. She reached out and the girl's blue eyes flickered to hers in swift warning.

"My name is Ti—" she said as they passed down the corridor, and then, more softly, "—and you must not seem to know me. They do not love the Moonmothers here!"

As the days dragged onward, Shanna came to understand the truth of Lady Amniset's words. If there had been more challenge to her work it might have been easier—but a five-year-old child with a broom could have guarded the women's quarters from such dangers as she had seen in the citadel. Here were no bands of masterless men, no dissident soldiers; not even a drunken drover troubled the perfumed peace in the inner courtyards here. She patrolled the gardens and the shaded corridors, lean and graceful as one of Lord Irenos' hunting cats, and as apparently uncaring when murmurs followed her.

But she heard them. Did they think she could not hear the whispers, the cheap wit, or the laughter? In addition to his Lady Wife, Lord Irenos had three contracted concubines born of noble houses, and a dozen slave girls who had been gifts, or won in dice games, or purchased on impulse when he traveled for the Emperor. Some of them had children; all of them had servants; and not one of them had enough to do. Shanna was new, exotic, and possibly—though it was only when they watched her daily workout in the garden that they remembered this—dangerous.

Their reaction did not surprise her, for in many ways the women's quarters in Sharteyn had been the same. But she had not expected it to hurt when the other women wondered if a body so hard-muscled could ever grow a child, or called her by the name that means a eunuch whose male parts are entirely gone. The Dark Mother's curse should have no power to pain her now, when her body conspired with her masters to keep her in captivity. But grief knew no reason, and so she slashed and swirled through her practice as if each stroke decapitated an enemy.

While other captives grew plump and indolent, Shanna ate as little as she dared and drove herself, though it no longer mattered whether she was fat or thin. When her workout was done, there was only the endless patrolling, or the occasional diversion of bodyguarding Lady Amniset to the scented seclusion of some other Great Wife's domain. Shanna could not help hearing some of their chatter: the emperor was ill, some said dying; the bands of masterless men in the provinces grew ever bolder; the power of the Spear-Priests was growing, and there were rumors of suppressed cults stirring, striving, by means magic or mortal, to regain their power.

She heard, but even when they spoke of the Dark Mother who had cursed Shanna so long ago, she could not find it in her to care. "I have tamed her," Lady Amniset would say. "See how she stands like an image by the doorway. None of you understand how to rule slaves. . . ." And then she would smile.

The first month of her captivity passed. In the evening, Shanna danced death in the garden and the fires of sunset kindled from the swift sweep of her sword. The overhead cut that cleft downward . . . the figure eight feint that brought the blade around from the back to slice through neck or waist or knee . . . the slanting upward cut that could sever a man's leg at the groin. Only a soft hiss followed the flashing blade; there was no more than a whisper of dust where her feet fell. The movement was everything, its own excuse for existence. For a moment, mind seduced to stillness by the perfect coordination of sinew and sword, Shanna was at peace.

Some sense more acute than hearing warned her; turning, blade already slicing down, a shift in balance diverted the razored edge. Still whirling, she swept the sword upward through the flowers, and one wisp of hair from the head of the child who had been walking into its path floated to the ground. Shanna finished the movement, let her own momentum spin her around again and stood, shaking, staring into the child's wide eyes.

"Pretty—" said the boy, picking up a severed stem of olanth and holding it out to her. "Cut pretty flowers!" He was plump and golden, too young yet to wear anything but a medallion on a gold chain.

Shanna shivered, visualizing the child's head rolling among the scattered blossoms. Small as he was, she should have noticed him. How could she have been so oblivious to her surroundings? *Because.* came an inner voice, *this is the only escape from those surroundings that you have. . . .* But she had almost killed the boy. She was not yet so crazed as to revenge herself upon the offspring of her enemies. If captivity had already so distorted her skills, then how was she different from the hound bitch she had owned once that had gone mad and had to be destroyed?

The child was still offering her the flower. Forcing a smile, Shanna started to take it from his hand. Then she heard a rustle of silk and running footsteps.

"Tinu, Tinu—" the words died as the woman came around the olanth hedge and saw Shanna standing there. Silver bangles tinkled as she grabbed the child. She was no slave-nurse—one of the mistress' ladies perhaps.

The boy must be important, then. Perhaps the heir. . . . If she had killed him, thought Shanna, her own troubles would have been over, too!

"Naughty Tinu!" the woman dashed the flower from the child's hand, clearly relieved to find a problem she understood. "Mustn't eat that! It would make you a very sick boy!" Her glance flicked toward Shanna's face, then slid quickly away.

"He would have been a dead boy, if he had run upon my sword!" Shanna said coldly. "In the future, keep a closer eye on your charge!"

The woman's grip must have tightened, for Tinu began to cry. Her face went pale, then reddened, and still without a word to the swordswoman, she hurried back into the women's wing.

When they were gone, Shanna picked up the fallen flower. The olanth was poisonous, yes—she remembered her own nurse saying the same. In small amounts, the flowers were used to make a soporific tea, more led to paralysis and death. But first, thought Shanna, they brought a sweet sleep without dreams. Her arm seemed to move of itself, and as she struck, the waxy white flowers cascaded down.

Dreams of darkness . . . dreams in which Shanna's soldiers died around her, or she fled the stench of the Worm of Saibel, she wandered through the wilderness, or struggled against her shackles and heard the curses of the Dark Mother's priestesses again as the temple began to burn. By the time she realized that her old nurse's lore about the olanth's effects had been a lie, it was too late to escape them. She could only accept the fear, could only fall endlessly into it, seeking the final darkness that would set her free.

Hard hands vised her arms. *Saibel! Saibel! The Dark Mother will devour you!* demon voices cried. She struck out at them; a spear pierced her stomach with a point of flame. Crimson swirled around her; the hangings were falling, their embroidered symbols writhing in lines of fire. A moment of prismatic vision showed her a ruby ring carved with the same symbol, bleeding light into a cup of wine. . . . Lady Amniset's ring. . . .

Apalled understanding brought her convulsing against her restraints again. Fire spewed from her belly. Throat burning, she tried to scream, but only a tortured croak would come.

"Swallow, Shanna—please, you've got to try!"

The demons pried at her lips. But when she whimpered, she felt coolness, and for a moment the flames faded and she glimpsed cropped fair hair and anxious blue eyes. Reflexively, she swallowed and the pain flowed back again, but it was dulled this time. Even when more retching conquered consciousness, the flames continued to recede until finally she knew that she was lying in her own bed, and though every muscle in her body throbbed dully, she was alive.

"Shanna . . . drink this now and it will ease you."

Again she swallowed. This drink was sweeter, and it took the edge off her pain. She forced her eyes to focus and saw Tara holding the beaker.

"Why?" With difficulty her lips formed the word.

"Because the Goddess still has work for you." Tara's voice was stern.

Shanna had no strength left to dispute it. Even as her eyes closed, her spirit saw another face, beneath dark hair crowned with stars. Then even that vision faded, and this time the sleep that came to her was as deep and dreamless as the rest she had sought from the olanth flowers.

This time, when she awakened, she thought she was in the slavewagon again. But the bed beneath her was smooth and clean, and did not move. When she opened her eyes, she saw the woman who had been in charge of the child she had almost killed.

"Water—"

"You're alive, then." There was an almost malicious satisfaction in the woman's smile.

Shanna grimaced. There was no pain in her body, but neither was there any strength in her limbs. Alive? She supposed that she must be, but she felt like an empty vessel waiting to be filled.

"Where is . . . the fairhaired girl?" Shanna's lips closed. For a moment she had almost given Tara away. The woman smiled again.

"You mean the witch who poisoned you? Her spells have been bound by steel. She lies in the lock-cellar now, until Lady Amniset decides what death will best banish her wickedness."

They thought that *Tara* had poisoned her? Shanna tried to steady her breathing, realizing that even now the other girl was protecting her. But it was Lady Amniset who was the poisoner. As for sorcery—she remembered now the ring she had seen on the Great Wife's hand. Did Lord Irenos know that his lady served Saibel? And did Lady Amniset know that Shanna was the one who had destroyed the Dark Mother's temple north of Fendor?

The waiting woman bent over her with a beaker. The water was clean. She lay back again, and felt new life begin to stir within. Lady Amniset thought Shanna tamed. She was a valuable piece of property. The Lady would not have given an enemy so high-born a nurse.

And if she finds out, thought Shanna, *what can she do? Torture or kill me? I tried to do worse to myself!* She took a deep breath, realizing that there was less of the drug in her body now than at any time since her capture. But that was not why she felt this sudden freedom. It was neither the drug nor her chains that had kept her captive, but her own despair. She thought now that even the agony of withdrawal could not be greater than what she had already endured.

"The Lady will be happy to hear that you are recovering," said the waiting woman. "She does not wish to destroy the sorceress until you can testify."

Shanna stared at her. She had been wrong, she thought then. By one thing she was still bound. She was obligated to live until she could end Tara's captivity.

Shanna brought her blade to her brow in salute as Lady Amniset swept into the room, feeling the appraisal in those cold eyes as if the woman had touched her. She must still be pale, she knew, but one snapped back quickly when one was in hard training. She could fight if she had to. Her pulse quickened as she realized how much she wanted that.

"Mistress, I await your command." She forced her voice to calm, remembering her plan.

"You have recovered well." Silk rustled as Lady Amniset settled on her cushions.

"I am eager for revenge," Shanna answered her. "Those who serve the Dark Goddess do not forgive injuries." She had reason to know it—the servants of Saibel had pursued her even into the catacombs of Fendor.

Lady Amniset's fan paused in midair. Shanna withstood her gaze without blinking, aware of the risk she was taking. But she had learned already that Tara was too well guarded to be reached unless she could become not only the Lady's servant, but her ally.

"Are you one of us?" The great ruby blazed balefully from the Lady's hand.

"I have stood before the altar and seen the sacrifice," Shanna said carefully. She had, in a fashion, officiated, watching the priestess burn while the child who had been the intended victim sobbed in her arms.

"And they made you a slave! Thus are our people persecuted!" Lady Amniset said furiously. "That girl must have known what you were somehow, or perhaps she was getting you out of the way so that she could attack me! I would have simply had the bitch flogged, but when they stripped her, they found the mark of our Mistress' enemy. When the Great Ones battle on this earth they use human weapons—are you the sword that She has set into my hand?" The crimson flare of the stone fixed Shanna's vision so that she could not look away.

"I have been the Sword of the Goddess before . . ." Shanna's voice rang with echoes of her own words of dedication before the altar of Yraine. "Give me this sorceress to deal with, and let Her will be done!"

"Can I believe you?"

Shanna touched the pommel of her sword. "May this blade betray me if I have lied!"

"I hear truth in your voice," said Lady Amniset softly. "What must we do?"

"It must be at night," said Shanna, thinking furiously. "And outdoors, where I can swing my sword. Let the girl be prepared for sacrifice."

"I cannot manumit you now, or it will cause talk," the woman began. "And to alter the drug so that you can be freed from it will take time."

For a moment Shanna shut her eyes. She had thought she was resigned to her own sacrifice, but suddenly she understood how she could be freed from both captivities. She had only to carry through with this charade. To save her own life, all she must do was to kill her friend. She took a deep breath, and her hand clenched on the hilt of her sword.

"It is not necessary. What matters is the fulfillment of my vow."

Lady Amniset stared at her. "Who *are* you?"

"I cannot tell you that . . ." Shanna brought her hands together as she had seen the priestesses do in the Dark Mother's ritual. If the Lady was a high initiate, this might be a self-betrayal, but she saw the other woman's eyes widen. "Will you obey?"

"In the name of Saibel!" Lady Amniset exclaimed, and bowed.

Shanna forced herself to stand as unmoving as the altar she had told them to build in the lower garden, though her pulse rushed in her ears like the night wind in the trees. It had rained earlier, and clouds still swathed the heavens, curdling and extending now as the wind rose, with only a glimmer to mark the path of the moon. The trees were whispering in the darkness and Shanna strained to hear above the sound. The others who waited with her in the garden were as still and silent as she. There were only two men with the four women, but one of those was Lady Amniset herself, and one of them was the nursemaid, and she had brought the child.

Shanna frowned, not liking that, but at least there were only six, not the whole household. When she had told the Lady to invite believers only to the sacrifice she had not dared to ask how many there would be. The rest of the servants were in their beds or tied to duties in other parts of the House, and Lord Irenos, thank the gods, was on duty at the Palace. Shanna loosened her sword in her sheath, grateful that she would only have to face these few.

Red light gleamed suddenly between wet leaves and spilled like blood across the pools left by the rain. Shanna heard bootheels crunch gravel, and let out her breath in a long sigh as the two torchbearers strode into the garden. Behind them came two others, dragging a limp figure. Had they hurt her? *"Give the prisoner food,"* Shanna had told the lady. *"I want her to know what is happening!"* But there had been no way to warn her. If Tara was conscious, she must think that Shanna had gone mad.

The captive moaned as the men hoisted her onto the framework before the altar and bound her there. Then they eased back to join the half circle facing the altar, watching Shanna expectantly.

"Within the dark seed of life is sown!
Into the dark the spark of life is flown!"

Shanna motioned to the men to douse their torches, trying to remember the rest of the chant she had heard in the Temple of Saibel. Darkness extinguished vision with a sweep of black wings; words came to her.

"And when into the dark the spark has fled,
The spirit walks the pathways of the dead . . ."

Were those the right words? The worshipers were swaying, already half entranced. *"It seeks the path of silence and release—"* said Shanna, remembering how she had sought oblivion. *"In the Great Mother's womb alone lies peace. . . ."*

That was no lie, thought Shanna. But these days, the servants of Saibel forgot that She was Lady of Life as well. The wind was growing stronger; stars gleamed through thinning veils of cloud. Tara had pulled herself upright in her bonds, her white face a ghostly blur in the gloom.

"All that falls and is consumed by Earth,
In its due season will attain rebirth,
And certain as the rising of the sun,
The Justice of the Lady will be done!"

"I am Her Sword!" Shanna cried. "To spare, or to slay!" Memory resonated with the rest of the oath she had taken to Yraine. "And all of you are in Her hand! Call upon your goddess, girl, and see if She will save you now!"

"Moonmother!" whispered Tara. "One last time let me look upon Thy face, and show me Thy will!" For a moment no one moved.

And then the wind spoke suddenly. Shanna felt a strange warmth tingle through her limbs as the clouds parted and the moon flooded the garden with cool radiance. Tara's head tipped back and she called out, but Shanna was looking beyond the moonlight, and the Face she saw in the heavens was that of the Lady of Stars. A breath of wind kissed her cheek and she laughed.

"Lady, receive my offering!" The sword leaped and moonlight wheeled across the dry stones. Down and around and up again flashed the bright blade. Shanna caught Tara as she slumped, and the same movement drew them both forward just as the others began to realize that what the sword had slashed was not the prisoner's breast, but her bonds.

Another sword shivered in the moonlight. Shanna's

blade took the shock of steel and slid onward into flesh. Women were screaming. Lady Amniset's voice came cool and furious from the shadows and two men rushed forward.

"Tara, run!" cried Shanna, laughing. "The Dark Mother doesn't care whose blood feeds Her now—"

"Not without you," Tara threw one of the altar stones, and a woman squealed in pain.

"Traitor. Saibel will destroy you!" hissed Lady Amniset.

"She has already tried—" answered Shanna, breathless. Steel clanged and scraped, and another man fell, black blood splashing across the altar. She could hear shouts from the other wing. She drove toward the woman who had enslaved her.

And there, before her blade, was the contorted face of the child. Stretched muscles screamed as Shanna diverted the blow. It bit the hand with which Lady Amniset was pushing her son in front of her. Leached of color by the moonlight, the great ruby arced like a falling star into the trees.

The women gathered to their mistress as she began screaming, but the guards lay still. Tara turned to Shanna, panting.

"Quickly, or others will come," the swordswoman said. "I've left the kitchen gate unlocked. I'll get you to the Moonmother's hostel before—"

"Before it's my turn to save you once more?" Tara laughed. "Clearly the Goddess has work for both of us, my dear."

Shanna found her own lips curving in answer, and the light of the Lady of Stars blazed from the blade of her unsheathed sword.

FESTIVAL GATHERERS

by Diann Partridge

Diann Partridge says that "I've sold four stories, all of them to Marion," from which you might rightly assume that there's something about her work I like. Perhaps some day other editors will discover what it is that I like about her work. I think it's just a fresh way of looking at the world.

She lives in western Wyoming, is married with three children, of whom two are teenagers, and right now she is currently employed in "making a charted design in petit point of Wyoming wildflowers onto canvas for one of the 24 formal dining room chairs in the Governor's mansion." Well, better you than me; I no longer do needlework—my eyes aren't up to it. She adds that "other than that, not much changes in this little town." This is why I remain horrified at the thought of living in Wyoming. Still, there's no accounting for tastes; some people would be horrified at the thought of living in Berkeley. I guess the answer is—if there is one—to rejoice along with my character Aratak in "the diversity of creation."

"It smells of sorcery, my lord," warned the mage Eldrin, looking up at the open palm on the pennant above the shop door.

"Of course, Eldrin," answered Lord Hazen pleasantly, "I should think it would. After all, this is a place for telling fortunes." His tone implied he didn't believe it, but he smiled graciously at the two young women he was escorting and ushered them inside with a bow.

The four of them crowded the cluttered little room. Hazen yanked at a bell just inside the door. From the rear of the shop, behind a tinkling beaded curtain, came sounds that someone had heard the bell. He rang it again, then an ancient crone pushed her way through the beads. She blinked blearily as she focused on the group.

"Come to have yer fortune told, have ya, dearies?" she cackled hoarsely. "Well, ya've come to the right place. No one else can tell yer fortunes as true as this old auntie."

"Old woman, mind your tongue," replied Hazen in a sharp tone. "This is the bridal Princess Tandra. The Princess is here in Malterick awaiting the arrival of her betrothed, the Throne Prince of Canmal. To pass the time she has desired to visit the Festival grounds and enjoy the celebrations. This is her cousin, the Lady Sarsal." He added this last as an afterthought. "Canmal's Prince will be here in two days. And then we—"

"My lord!" coughed Eldrin sharply. Hazen pulled himself up, flushing angrily when he realized he had been babbling to the old woman.

She made a frightened sound at his look and backed away, but the princess stepped forward and laid a soft hand on Hazen's arm.

"Lord Hazen, please. You are scaring our host. Please, mistress," she turned wide blue eyes on the crone and smiled appealingly, "Won't you tell my fortune now?"

It was a command even though framed as a polite request. Shuffling forward at the kind voice, the old woman gestured toward the low-backed chair in front of a small table. Lord Hazen held the chair and the princess sat down gracefully. The crone plopped down on a stool, arranging her rags in a grotesque imitation of the princess smoothing her silks.

A gnarled claw opened the princess' plump, smooth hand. Tandra controlled a shudder of distaste as a cracked, dirty fingernail traced the lines of her palm.

"This'un's yer life line, princess. Very long, do ya see? And this'un's yer heart line. And ya see this line? Well, this'un shows ya will have at least three children, maybe more. And the first one will be a boy."

Tandra smiled happily and glanced around to make sure everyone was smiling at her good fortune.

The old woman muttered something to herself. Tandra leaned forward with a concerned look. Suddenly the hag looked up, her wrinkled face only inches from Tandra's. She grinned wickedly, revealing a few stained broken teeth. Tandra jerked up in shock and would have pulled her hand away, only to find that it was gripped quite securely.

Hazen instantly shifted forward at the princess' sudden move. The mage clutched the seer stone that hung from a chain around his neck.

"Here now, here now," she crooned softly, "I didn't mean to startle ya, dearie. Just needed a closer look at what yer fortune will be."

Everyone relaxed.

"Well, what is it?" Tandra almost snapped, wishing now they had never come into this shop. She shot a frown at Sarsal that seemed to say this was all her fault.

The old woman's rheumy eyes missed nothing. She chuckled a little, looking down into Tandra's palm again.

"See here, princess," and she traced a short line around her thumb, "This is yer love line. See how deep it runs? That means that no man ya set yer cap at will be able to resist ya."

This restored Tandra's good humor. After a few more favorable divinations Tandra rose and motioned Sarsal to take her place.

It was quite evident that this young woman didn't want her fortune told by the way the crone had to pry her fingers open. Muttering to herself, she noted that this hand had long strong fingers and light calluses across the palm. It was also evident that the two young woman weren't that closely related. Tandra was much shorter, lushly curved and artfully draped in the best southern silks. Her black hair had an auburn cast to it where Sarsal's was raven black. Sarsal's silks were not as rich or as finely embroidered either.

"So what is the lady's fortune to be, old woman? We don't have all day for you to doze in."

She peered closer into Sarsal's hand.

'Hmmm, I see a long life. But it will be clouded by unhappiness unless ya make a change in the near future. And ya have a deep strong heart line." She traced the lines that formed a star in the palm and kept the hand from jerking back. "Who're ya to marry, dearie?"

Sarsal stiffened as Tandra answered for her.

"She's going to marry Lord Nelthrinz, a dear friend of my father's. He is a councillor at King Canmal's court. No one else would offer for Sarsal. She has a reputation, you know. Why, she tried to run off with the horsemaster's son this past spring! So when Lord Nelthrinz offered for her, Father decided we would travel together and have our weddings in Canmal. Of course, Lord Nelthrinz *is* a little older than Sarsal, but what else can she hope for."

Sarsal's green eyes flashed as she bit her lip in rage. The beaded curtain rustled as though a wind had blown through the room. Staring into the angry face as she gripped the hand, the old woman muttered several other dim prophecies before she sat back.

Lord Hazen threw down two silver pieces, then escorted the women outside. The mage Eldrin found himself sweating as he stepped beyond the door into the cobbled street and repressed the urge to shudder. He could have sworn there was sorcery in that room, but there couldn't be any power to that dirty old hag. She couldn't even read palms correctly. He shrugged, putting the incident from his mind.

The princess fluttered gaily down the crowded street, with Sarsal in tow. They stopped at first one shop, then another. She preened happily in a bit of mirror as she tried on a necklace of pearls, twirling around for everyone to admire her.

Sarsal smiled around gritted teeth. Then she glanced back down the street to where the pennant with the open hand hung and frowned.

The old woman pushed herself to her feet. Gathering up the silver pieces, she shambled back through the beaded curtain.

A flash like sunlight reflected off the beads. Behind them, in a room much larger than the front, the hag was no more. In her place stood a tall woman well past middle age. Her hair was shot through with white, but she was still strong and supple. Two younger men sat around a table playing a dicing game. When she entered, one gathered up the cubes.

"Is she the one, Zarka?" he asked quickly.

"Well and true, Relf, I should say she is," answered Zarka. She circled her head a few times to relieve the stress from her neck. "She bears the star in her hand just as we do. And Nelthrinz is still trying to lay hands on one of us. Gods above, that degenerate is older than I am. He wants to marry that child!"

"Is she Sarseth's child, do you think?" Relf came over and began to work the knots out of Zarka's shoulders. It was hard for her to hold such an unnatural form for so long.

"I would bet on it. She has a look of him about the eyes. His temper, too, though she has better control over hers than he ever did. You should have seen her face when the princess blurted out that bit about Sarsal's 'reputation.' I had to bite my tongue to keep from laughing."

"It won't be easy to get her away from here. Hazen has two troops with him, plus the mage. I heard him say that Canmal will be here in two days. That doesn't give us much time."

She shook off Relf's hands and stood up. Gods! It

was irritating not to be able to just take the girl now and go home. Relf grinned at her, understanding her frustration. She shook her fist in his face.

"Why did I get picked for this Gather? Why should this fall to me and not someone else. I would rather be trying to get rid of Nelthrinz."

Relf juggled the dice expertly, then flipped them to Zarka.

"Because, dearie," he answered in a voice like the old woman's, "you were once promised to Nelthrinz. Remember? And when we men come out of the mountains, we just can't remember to keep our britches buttoned. These valley people don't understand true magic. I would imagine that is why Sarsal has a 'reputation.' If Nelthrinz were to capture someone special like Sarsal, how would you feel? We have been watching for her ever since the Festival started and now we only have two days to get her away from Hazen. Did you see anything in that little feather-brained princess' hand?"

Zarka shook her head. The other man, Krogha, spoke up. His voice was full of old bitterness.

"She's the only true one that's been found in the last generation, Zarka. It's bad enough that our own women are barren because of their magic, but on top of that we are forced to breed children on strangers."

"You seem to have been breeding well enough since we got here," shot back Zarka sharply. The men's addiction to coupling with valley women made her angry. She didn't understand what caused it, anymore than she understood why her own race could not produce children together.

"Speaking of breeding, I have to see to that little beauty in the shop down the street. Her husband is three times her age and goes to bed early." Relf grinned as he stood up and stretched.

"I suppose you are going out, too?" she asked Krogha.

His bitterness was replaced with a sheepish look and he nodded.

She threw the dice back to Relf. "Just be back here

before the last bell. I want to try and find Sarsal tonight and I will need both of you reasonably sober and in one piece. Do try and remember that, all right?"

They left quickly to escape any further cutting remarks. But she yelled one last warning at them.

"Someone may have to gather up your offspring in another generation, just remember that!"

It was late. Far after last bell. Zarka paced up and down the room. Damn them! They should have been back by now. Where were they?

Looking out the window she saw that the first moon had risen. In her mind's eye she saw the mountains that surrounded her home, saw the small group of her people that still existed there. The power of the mountains was also their power; magic as these valley people called it. But this power had its price. It gave them long life, but no children. The men would sometimes father a child if they spent enough time away from the mountains, but it was rare for the child to breed true.

When someone like Sarsal was sensed, a group would be sent to find her. It was rare for someone to go undiscovered as long as she had. Even with these two witless men to help her, they had been searching for over a month. The men tended to forget their mission unless she reminded them periodically.

Zarka clenched her fists in her hair, gritting her teeth. She had gone to Lord Nelthrinz as a child, before she was Gathered. His memory still gave her nightmares. But they would have Sarsal before that happened to her.

Unable to wait any longer, she buckled on her sword and took up a short cloak. Slipping out into the night, she assumed the guise of an old soldier. It required only a little altering of her own outward appearance. The shopkeeper's wife that Relf was sporting lived only a few doors away. Deep, gargling snores drifted down from an open upstairs window.

Zarka climbed up the uneven brick work and pulled herself cautiously to the open window. The sword clattered a little as she hooked an elbow over the sill and climbed through. The fat old man snoring in the bed was alone. He roused, but Zarka expended a little energy and sent him back to sleep. The bed slats groaned as he rolled over.

In the dark hall she cast about for Relf and was drawn toward a small staircase at the end of the hall. Wondering how he had gotten up there from the outside, she slipped up the steps and opened the door. Moonlight let her see two figures curled around each other in a bed against the wall. Zarka crossed silently and laid a hand on Relf's shoulder.

He awoke instantly, reaching for his sword at the sight of an armed man next to him. Zarka grimaced and dropped the facade. Relf relaxed, but the girl woke up. He clapped a hand over her mouth and held her still.

"I told you to get back before last bell," whispered Zarka furiously. "This tart isn't worth getting killed for. Now tie her up or knock her out and get dressed. We still have to find Krogha."

Relf shook his head. "I can't knock her out, Zarka. Tear a strip off the sheet and tie her hands for me."

"I'd like to knock you both out," she hissed, but did as he asked. He pulled the girl toward him and Zarka captured her hands. The girl struggled until Zarka slapped her hard, then she lay still. Zarka tied the hands tightly, then knotted a length of sheet and motioned to Relf. He released his hand long enough to kiss the girl one last time, then Zarka pushed him away and gagged her.

She threw his clothes at him and he dressed quickly. He went out the little window first, catching hold of a drain pipe. Zarka followed cautiously. Relf lowered himself from the eaves and dropped to another roof. He crossed the slippery tiles in a graceful slide and jumped. Following him as best she could, Zarka lost her balance, slipped, and fell.

She caught herself on one hand, then stifled a cry as one of the heavy roof tiles hit her ankle. Others clattered down around her. The noise set a dog to barking, then another joined it. Not far away, a sharp metal drumming began. The alarm of the night watch.

"I'm sorry, Zarka," whispered Relf as he helped her up. Pain shot through her ankle as she put her weight on it. "I just forgot. Do you think you can walk?"

She longed to refuse his help, but the pain made her dizzy and sick.

"I can't run on it, that's for sure. Gods help us, if just once you men could think with your heads and not with your balls. Do you have any idea where Krogha is?"

He had the grace to look ashamed. Pulling her arm across his shoulder they set off. Behind them came the drumming. Lights went on in several upstairs windows.

"If we are caught out now, they will lock us up until after the wedding. Krogha had a friend a couple of streets from here. Do you think you can make it that far?"

She nodded, gritting her teeth. More lights went on behind them. Curious voices called to each other from windows. Relf and Zarka ducked down a narrow alley and hid in the shadows. He braced her against his chest so she could take the weight off her injured ankle.

They froze as the night watch swung a lantern down the alley. Zarka extended herself, enough to cover the two of them better with darkness. The watch passed on. Then, leaning against Relf, she closed her eyes and searched the extent of her injuries.

Her hand throbbed, but it wasn't broken. Her knees were scraped. The ankle was the worst. She found two little bones that were cracked. The muscles were bruised, too. Healing wasn't a thing she did well, especially when she didn't have the time or energy to attempt it.

"We will have to strap it tight," she whispered to Relf. "There isn't anything I can do right now."

He nodded and helped her deeper into the alley. She called up a faint light. Relf took his knife and cut a long strip from the edge of her cloak and used it to bind her ankle. Getting her boot back on was sheer torture. She was gasping in a cold sweat when it was done.

She could walk on the ankle now, but Relf still lent his shoulder. Because of the pain it was hard for Zarka to search for Krogha. The street on which they found themselves was full of upper-class hostels. What did he think he was doing in such a fancy area, Zarka wondered? It was hard to concentrate on Krogha.

Finally, faintly, she caught a thread of his presence. They made their way around to the heavily barred rear gate. It was flanked by a tall wooden fence set atop a low brick wall. There was no way she could get over it.

She took several deep breaths to calm herself. This time she remembered to search for a barking dog, found him and put him to sleep. At her nod, Relf scrambled over the fence and unbarred the gate from the inside.

"He must be in with a servant girl," Relf breathed. Zarka listened hard, then motioned to the left.

The kitchens and servants' quarters jutted out at an angle from the main building. Zarka laid a hand on each door in turn. When her senses told her Krogha was there, she nodded to Relf and he opened the door.

A candle stub guttered fitfully enough for them to see two beds shoved together in a space that would have been crowded with one. Two pale figures slept on one bed. Krogha lay stretched out on the other, bare arms crossed behind his head. The bed's other occupant straddled him, bouncing up and down.

Anger flared up in Zarka, drowning out the pain. Her anger increased as Relf, with an amused grin, walked past her toward the other bed. She yanked him back hard. Before Krogha or his friend could react, she drew her sword, crossed the floor and rapped the woman hard on the back of her head. Catching her by the hair, Zarka lowered her to the floor.

"Gods damn you, Krogha!" she snarled in a hiss.

"Get up. Get dressed. We have things to do. Now move!"

In Zarka's presence, his memory came back. He dressed quickly. She wasted another precious bit of her energy to keep the other women asleep. *When we get back from this*, she promised herself silently, *I am going to ask that all the men be sent down here forever. They are worse than useless*.

Once outside she was still fuming, but her temper was appeased when Krogha told her his news.

"The princess and Lord Hazen have taken over this hostel, waiting for Canmal to arrive. She and Sarsal have rooms on the second floor. The soldiers are on the ground floor, with a double guard at each door. But I think we can get in if we go across the roof."

Roofs again. Zarka winced. She wanted to go back to the shop and tend her ankle, but she couldn't send these two alone after two young women. And they only had two days left. She bit her lip and motioned for Krogha to lead the way. Not for the first time she wondered if these valley women didn't have some kind of magic that only worked on mountain men.

Even with help, it was slow and painful. The second moon rose. She could feel the ankle swelling each time she put her weight on it.

Once on the roof, Relf pointed to an open window above and to the right of them. Zarka took a deep breath and probed. For once, luck was with them. Sarsal was asleep there. Relf jumped, caught the sill, and swung himself up and through. Zarka knew she had no choice but to follow him. She jumped awkwardly and grabbed the sill, but her sprained hand slipped. Dangling, she tried to grab the sill again, afraid to dig in with her boots and make a noise. She began to slip, but before she could fall, Relf grabbed her wrists and pulled her in. Krogha crossed with no trouble.

"I shall yell for the guards if you come any closer," spoke a calm voice behind him. "What do you want?"

They turned as one to see Sarsal sitting up in bed.

"We are not here to hurt you, Sarsal," whispered Zarka, "but to help you escape."

"You are the old woman from the shop, aren't you?" she said suddenly. "Believe me, if I could have escaped before now, I would have done so." She raised her arm. It was manacled by a length of chain to the bed.

Zarka felt a flare of admiration for the girl. Coming closer to the bed, she gave Sarsal a brief explaination of why they were there.

"I'll gladly go," answered Sarsal softly. "But how will you get this off?"

Zarka motioned to Relf. He grinned as he turned Sarsal's arm to the moonlight. With a few deft twists and probes of a tiny knife, the iron bracelet fell open. Sarsal removed her arm, then snapped the manacle shut.

Krogha stripped the sheets from the bed. He knotted them together, tied one end to the bed post, and threw the rest out the window. Then he climbed out and down, hand over hand.

They followed him. Just as Zarka hit the ground she heard the sharp snick snick snick of the watchdog's claws on the flagstones. She motioned for them to be still.

The struggle this time to dredge up enough energy to divert the dog involved more than just deep breathing. Sweat glistened in fine beads on her face in the moonlight. The dog came closer, whining a little, head cocked to one side. She pictured a cat on the other side of the courtyard. The dog hesitated, nose twitching. Then he turned and trotted away.

"That won't hold him for long. Let's go."

They slid silently through the shadows toward the back gate. Then once again from behind them came the dog. He spotted them this time and began to bark. A door crashed open, shattering the silence, and someone yelled. A light went on.

Zarka pushed Sarsal toward Krogha. "Take her back to the shop. Don't wait for us."

He grabbed Sarsal's hand and they ran. Relf slipped

Zarka's arm over his shoulder again. She would have fallen otherwise. Her leg was numb to the knee. She threw a desperate last thought at the dog as it ran out the gate, causing it to turn in the wrong direction. The guards followed it.

After that, everything was like a bad dream. Hazen's guards followed the dog for a few streets, then doubled back. Relf was carrying her over his shoulder by that time. He forced a window open in a stinking tanner's shop and they hid there until the dawn moon rose and first bell rang.

The short rest gave her enough strength to assume the guise of the old soldier. With Relf supporting her, they staggered home, mingling with early rising shopkeepers and servants.

Sarsal jumped up, ready to run again when the two soldiers came through the back door. Then Zarka dropped the cover and sagged into a chair.

"I knew there was something funny about this shop yesterday," exclaimed Sarsal. "All my life I thought I was the only one who could change my appearance."

Zarka couldn't even smile. After looking at her foot, Relf shook his head, took out his knife, and gently cut the boot off. To take her mind from the throbbing pain, she began to tell Sarsal who they were and why they had come for her.

The young woman first looked amazed, then relieved. "I knew I could fool people from the time I was about nine. But I made a mistake when I showed Tandra what I could do. She told her father and eventually Lord Nelthrinz heard about me. They would bring me out like a freak in a Festival sideshow, to perform my little tricks in front of company. Eldrin could break my illusions with his seer stone, otherwise I would have run away a long time ago. Then they decided that I would marry Lord Nelthrinz. When we got here, they started chaining me at night. Hazen was afraid I would escape before Nelthrinz arrived."

Her voice was bitter and Zarka reached out a hand to comfort her. Suddenly there was shouting from the street. Krogha slipped through the beaded curtain to see what was going on.

"They are searching each shop," he explained when he returned. Your little friend from down the street is missing, Relf. Her husband is badgering Hazen's guards to look for her."

"I'll have to go out as the old woman again," said Zarka, struggling to get up.

"You can't go out there. You hardly had the strength to get back here. If the mage is with them, he will see through you in a second. She will have to do it." Relf pointed at Sarsal.

Krogha and Zarka started to protest, but Relf waved it aside.

"We have no choice, at least for this one time. She said she could alter her looks. We won't be able to leave the city until after the wedding. If no one answers the door, the guards will break it down and search the whole shop. The room is spelled to fool the mage. It worked yesterday, remember."

Sarsal nodded and started toward the beaded curtain.

"Wait," called Zarka. "Remember, girl, you have to *be* that old woman. Her walk, her talk, inside and out. Don't think of yourself for even a second. That's the trick to it. If you slip and they recognize you, your freedom, as well as ours, is over."

Sarsal swallowed hard and nodded. As she put out a hand to part the beads, there came a pounding at the door. She took a deep breath and walked through.

The guards that peered through the tiny window in the door saw a ragged old woman hobbling toward them. She threw the bolts and was nearly thrown to the floor as they surged in.

"Here now, here now," she croaked loudly. "No need to be in such a hurry, dearie. Come to have yer fortunes told, have ya? Ya've come to the right place, laddies. This old auntie tells the best fortunes in town."

The wedding was sumptuous, extending the Festival for more than two weeks. It was a sad thing about young Lady Sarsal, cousin to the princess. Always sad when someone so young died. But those things did happen. A change in diet or strange water—no one could figure it out. Lord Nelthrinz had been furious, but the body had been burned before he arrived. The Prince of Canmal and his lovely bride went happily back to his estates east of Malterick.

A group of four rode out when all the celebrating was over. They turned west, toward the distant mountains. Two young men, one old soldier, and an even older woman. It seemed a bit odd that such a feeble beldame like that should ride a horse, but then there had been odder things seen at the Festival.

THE TALISMAN

by Mercedes Lackey

Every year since I discovered the writings of Mercedes Lackey she has written a story for me of Tarma and Kethry; this is one of the many rewards of being an editor. I still get a kick out of them, and was delighted to see in print a whole volume of Tarma and Kethry stories, called THE OATHBOUND, published by DAW Books. This only goes to show that one of the best ways to succeed at this very tricky business of writing is to write stories about a character, or characters, about whom people want to read. (But a word of caution; you're likely to get so bloody sick of your own characters that you want to blow them off the face of the earth; Conan Doyle got so sick of Sherlock Holmes that he resolved to bury him "even if he buried his bank account with him." So choose wisely.)

Fortunately, I'm not yet sick of Tarma and Kethry. Nor, I suspect, are my readers.

It was hard for Kethry to remember that winter would be over in two months at the most. The entire world seemed made up of crusted snow; it even lay along the bare branches of trees. From this vantage point, atop a rocky, scrub-covered hill, it looked as if winter had taken hold of the land and would never let go. The entire world had turned into an endless series of winter dormant, forested hills, hills they plodded over with no sign that there was an end to them. Although the road that threaded these hills bore unmistakable signs of frequent use, they hadn't seen a single soul in the past two days. Kethry stamped her numb feet on snow packed rock hard and frozen into an obstacle course of ruts, trying to get a little feeling back into them. She shaded her eyes against snow glare and stared down the hillside while her mule pawed despondently at the ice crust beside the trail, hoping for a scrap of grass and unable to break through.

She heard the creaking of Tarma's saddle as her partner dismounted. "Goddess!" the Shin'a'in croaked. "I'm bloody freezing!"

"You're always freezing," Kethry replied absently, trying to make out if the smudge on the horizon was smoke or just another cloud. "Except when I'm roasting. Where are we? Is that smoke I'm seeing out there, or a figment of my imagination?"

There was a rattling of paper at her right elbow as Tarma took out their map. "I could make a very bad pun, but I won't," she said. "Yes, it's smoke, and I'd guess we're here—"

Kethry took her watering eyes off that far-away promise of habitation, and turned to see where on the map Tarma thought they were. It wasn't exciting. If the Shin'a'in was right, they were about a candlemark's ride away from a flyspeck too small even to be called a village, marked on the map only with the name "Potter," and the symbol for "public well."

"No inn?" the sorceress asked wistfully.

"No inn," her partner sighed, folding the map and tucking it back inside the inner pocket of her coat. "Sorry about that, Greeneyes."

"Figures," Kethry said sourly. "When we've finally got the money to *pay* for inns, we can't find any."

Tarma shrugged. "That's fate, I suppose. We'll have to see if we can induce some householder to part with hearth- or barn-space for a little coin. Could be worse. If it hadn't been for everything that happened in Mournedealth, we wouldn't *have* the coin."

"True—though I can think of easier ways to have gotten it."

"Hmm." Tarma made a noncommittal sound, and swung back up into her saddle. Kethry cast a glance at her out of the corner of her eye, and wondered what she was thinking.

We're still not—quite—a team. And she worries about me a lot more than I think is necessary.

"I don't regret any of it," she said then, trying to sound as if she had intended to continue the sentence. "It's just that I'm *lazy*. That little set-to with my former spouse was a whole lot more work than I would have preferred!"

Tarma's grating laugh floated out over the hillside, and Kethry relaxed a bit.

"I'll try and spare you, next time," the Swordsworn said, nudging her mare with her heels and sending Kessira picking her way through the ruts down the hill. Kethry could have sworn as they passed that the elegant little mare had her lip curled in distaste. "If you promise to give me a little more warning. This could all have been taken care of quite handily by waylaying Wethes and your brother and—ah—'persuading' them that everyone would be happier if we were left alone."

"I thought you Kal'enedral were bound by honor," Kethry mocked, as Rodi lurched and slipped his way down the hill in Kessira's wake.

"*Her* honor, not man's honor," Tarma corrected, not taking her attention from the path in front of her. "And in matters where Her honor has no bearing, we're bound by expediency. I'm rather *fond* of expediency. It saves a world of problems."

"Except when you have to explain your notion of 'expedient' to the City Guard." Rodi took the last of the slope in a rush that made Kethry grit her teeth and cling to the saddle-bow, hoping the mule knew what he was doing.

"You have a point," the Shin'a'in admitted.

It took most of the remaining daylight—*not* the single candlemark the map promised—to get to the cluster of houses alongside the road. That was because of the condition of the road itself; as hummocked and rutted as the hill had been, Tarma didn't want to push the beasts at all, for fear they'd break legs misstepping. So they picked their way to Potter with maddening slowness.

So maddening that at first Kethry did not note the increasing pressure of her geas-blade Need on her mind.

She was tightly bound to the sword; as bound to it as she was to her partner, and *that* binding had the blessing of Tarma's own Goddess on it. The sword repaid that binding by healing her of anything short of a death-wound in an incredibly short period of time, and by granting her a master's ability at wielding it—a fact that had saved *Tarma's* skin now and again, since no one expected blade-expertise from a mage. But Kethry paid for those gifts—for any time there was a woman in need of help within the blade's sensing-range—and Kethry had not yet determined the limits of that range—she *had* to help. Regardless of whether or not helping was a prudent move—or going to be repaid.

Hardly the most ideal circumstances for a would-be mercenary.

Need's "call" was like the insistent pressure of a headache about to happen—except when the situation was truly life-or-death critical, in which case it had been known to cause pressure so close to pain as made no difference. Tarma must have learned to read or sense *that* in the few months they'd been together—she suddenly looked back over her shoulder almost as soon as Kethry herself became aware of the blade's prodding, and frowned.

"Tell me that expression on your face isn't what I think it is," the hawk-faced Shin'a'in said plaintively.

"I would," Kethry sighed, "but I'd be lying."

Tarma shook her head, and turned her ice-blue eyes to the settlement ahead of them. "Joyous. Well, at least there shouldn't be much trouble figuring out *who* and *what*. If there're more than a dozen females down there, I'll eat a horseshoe."

Kethry urged her mule forward until she rode knee-to-knee with her brown-clad partner. "I'll say what you're undoubtedly thinking. If there's a problem in so small a settlement, everybody is likely to know about it. Which means everybody may well have a vested interest in keeping it quiet. *Or* may like things the way they are." The vague splotch beside the road ahead of them resolved itself into a cluster of buildings as their beasts brought them nearer. A few moments more, and they could make out the red-roofed wellhouse, set apart from the rest of the buildings.

"*Or* may simply resent outsiders interfering," Tarma finished glumly. "There are times—heads up, *she'enedra*. We're being met."

They were indeed. Even as Tarma spoke, something separated itself from the side of the wellhouse. Shrouded in layers of clothing, for a moment it looked more bearlike than human. But as they neared, they could see that waiting beside the public well was a stoop-shouldered old man, gnarled and weathered as a mountain tree, with a thick thatch of snow-white hair tucked under a knitted cap the same bright red as the wellhouse roof.

"Evening," he said, peaceably enough, as they came within conversational distance of the half-dozen houses beside the well.

"Evening," Tarma returned the greeting, crossing her wrists on her saddlebow and leaning forward—though *not* dismounting. "What kind of hospitality could a few coins purchase a tired traveler around here, goodman?"

He looked them up and down with bright black eyes peeping from beneath brows like overhanging snowbanks—eyes that missed nothing. "Well-armed travelers," he observed mildly.

Tarma laughed, and a startled crow flapped out of the thatch of one of the houses. "Travelers who aren't fools, goodman. And two women traveling alone who *couldn't* take care of themselves *would* be fools."

The old man chuckled. "Point taken, point taken." He edged a little closer. "Be any good with that bow?"

Tarma considered this for a moment. "A fair shot," she acknowledged.

"Well, then," the oldster replied tugging his knit cap a bit further down over his ears. "Coin we got no use for till spring an' the traders come—but a bit of game, now—that'd be welcome. Say, hearth and meal for hunting?"

Tarma nodded, and seemed satisfied with the tentative bargain, for she dismounted. Kethry was only too glad to follow her example.

"I can't conjure game out of an empty forest, old man," Tarma said warningly as he led them to a roomy shed that already sheltered a donkey and three goats.

"There's game, there's game. I wouldn't set ye to a fool's task. Just we be no hunters, here." He helped them fork hay into the shed; for bedding the mare and the mule would have to make do with the bracken already layering the floor.

"Not hunters?" Kethry said, puzzled, as they took their packs and followed their guide into the nearest house. "Out here in the middle of nowhere? What on earth do you—"

The answer to her question was self-evident as soon as the old man opened the door. The house was a single enormous room, combining sleeping, living, and working space. It was the working space that occupied the lion's share of the dwelling. In one corner stood a huge sink and pump, several wooden boxes of clay, and a potter's wheel. Various ceramic items were ranged on two long wooden tables in the center of the room according to what stage they were in, from first drying to final glazing. The back wall was entirely brick, with several iron doors in it. It radiated heat even at this distance; it had to be a kiln of some sort, Kethry reckoned. Most of the windows were covered with oiled parchment, but there was a single glass window in the wall opposite; directly beneath that was a smaller workbench with pots and brushes, and a half-painted vase. The rest of the living arrangements were scattered haphazardly about, wherever there was room for them.

It was, to Kethry's mind, stiflingly warm, but Tarma immediately threw off her coat with a sigh of pure bliss.

"Put yer bedrolls wherever, ladies," the old man said. "There's porridge as supper."

Kethry rummaged out a packet of some of their dried fruit and tossed it to the oldster, who caught it deftly, grinned his thanks, and added it to the pot just inside one of those iron doors.

"Directly supper's finished, we'll be gettin' visitors," their host told them, as they found places to spread their bedrolls on the clay-stained, rough board floor. "I be Egon Potter; rest of the folks out here be kin or craft-kin."

Kethry's curiosity had turned her attention to the half-finished pottery. It was more than simple pots and bowls, she realized as soon as she had a good look at it. It was really exquisite work, the equal or superior of anything she'd ever seen for sale in Mournedealth.

"Why—" she began.

"—are we way out here, back of the end of the world?" Egon interrupted her. "The clay, lady. No match for it anywhere else. Got three kinds of clay right here; got fuel for the kilns; got all winter t' work on the fancy stuff an' all summer t' trade. What else we need?"

Tarma laughed. "Not a damned thing else, Guildmaster." At his raised eyebrow and quirky, half-toothless grin she laughed again. "I've always wondered where the best of the Wrightguild porcelain and stoneware came from—it certainly wasn't being made in Kata'shin'a'in. You think I can't recognize the work of the Master when I see it?"

"Then there be more about you shows on th' surface, swordlady. But you tol' me that, didn' ye?"

"Oh, aye, that I did." They matched grins in some kind of wordless exchange that baffled Kethry, then the Shin'a'in edged her way past the crowded worktable to the oldster's side. "Here. Let me give you a hand with that porridge."

As darkness fell, Kethry came to appreciate old Egon's craftmanship even more, for he lit oil lamps around the room with shades of porcelain so thin that the light glowed through it easily. And when the first of the lamps was alight, the rest of the inhabitants of the little settlement began to arrive.

They crowded about the newcomers, treating them with friendly reserve, asking questions, but free enough with their own answers. Fairly soon everyone had found space on the hearth, and Kethry was able to examine them at her leisure. They seemed amiable enough. None of the women seemed to be in *any* distress. In fact, it didn't look to Kethry as if there was anything at all wrong here—and this despite Need's unvarying pressure on the back of her mind.

Finally, while Tarma entertained the company with some Shin'a'in tale or other, the sorceress edged over to where old Egon was sitting alone a little off to one side.

He nodded to her but waited for her to speak. She cleared her throat a little, then said, trying not to sound awkward, "Egon, is everyone in your settlement here?"

He seemed surprised by her question. "Oh, aye; all but the little ones. Well—barring one."

This sounded a little more promising. "One?" she prompted.

His eyes went wary. "Well—she bain't a guildsman. Stranger. Settled here, oh, three or four winters ago. She don't have much t' do with us, we don't have much t' do with her. Unchancy sort." Egon blinked, slowly. "Trades with us, betimes. I think she be grubbin' about in the ruins, yonder. Bits of metal she trades, old stuff, gone t' powder mostly, but good for makin' glazes."

Something about this "stranger" evidently made Egon more than a little uneasy. Kethry could read that in his shuttered expression, and the careful choice he made of his words.

"Are the ruins forbidden, or something?" she asked, trying to pinpoint his uneasiness.

"Forbidden?" He flashed her a startled glance, and chuckled. "Great Kernos, no! It's just—she seems witchy, like, but she ain't never *done* nothin' witchy." He gave her a sidelong glance, as if gauging her response to that. "It's like she was looking for something out there and mad as hops 'cause she ain't finding it. 'Cept lately she been acting like she had. Her name's—"

The door opened, and a bundled figure half-stepped, and was half-windblown, into the circle of light. She blinked for a moment, her eyes sunken into pale, pudgy cheeks, her flabby arms hugging her fur cloak tightly about her.

She'd put on so much weight since Kethry had last seen her that at first she didn't recognize her former schoolmate.

Then—"Mara?" she said into the silence the woman's abrupt arrival had imposed on the group.

The woman whirled; peered past the heads of those nearest her at Kethry. Her mouth worked soundlessly for a moment; one plump, pasty hand flew to her throat—then she turned and bolted back the way she had come in a clumsy run.

The door slammed behind her. The rest of those gathered sat in embarrassed silence.

Finally Egon self-consciously cleared his throat. " 'Tis a bit late, and we all have work, come the morning light . . . "

His kin and fellow guildsmen were not slow at taking the hint. Before too very long the house was silent, and empty of all but Egon and the two women.

There seemed no way to break that silence, and after a few halfhearted attempts at conversation, Egon excused himself and went to bed.

Kethry took a long while falling asleep, and not because of the unfamiliar surroundings. Mara Yveda was the *last* person she expected to see out here.

I wondered where she went, after she'd disappeared from White Winds. Poor Mara. She was so certain that we were hiding something from her—that control of magic was just a matter of knowing the right words, having the right talisman. . . .

I'll never forget the night she ran off. Right after she stole Master Loren's staff—then found out the only thing that was unusual about it was that it was cut to exactly the right height to most comfortably help him with his lame leg.

She broke it in two when it wouldn't magic anything up for her. And then—she ran away.

She would never believe that power isn't a matter of "magic," it's a matter of discipline . . . .

She's the one that's in trouble. She's found something, I know she has, and she's gotten into trouble over it. What's more, Egon knows it, too.

So what do I do about it?

She fell asleep finally, without being able to come to any conclusion.

Kethry watched her partner dress the next morning, still in a decidedly unsettled state of mind.

"Swordlady," Egon said hesitantly, as Tarma prepared to set off at dawn to make good her side of the bargain, "there's something I need to tell you. About the game."

Tarma didn't even stop lacing up her boots. "Go ahead," she said. "I'm listening."

"There's a bear about."

Now she left her lacing, to raise her head and stare at him. "A what? Are you sure? That—that's hardly usual."

"Aye," the old man replied, shifting from one foot to the other. "But we've seen it about, not more than a day or two ago."

Tarma took a moment to secure the lacings, and straightened up, her face dead sober. "Do you have any notion what that means, that there's a bear, awake and walking this deep into winter?"

Egon shook his head.

"That is a very *sick* bear, Egon. Either it didn't eat enough to keep it going through winter-sleep, or something woke it far too early, and only illness can do that. In either case, its body is trying to make it go down for sleeping, and it's going completely against those instincts. It's going to die, Egon—but before it does, it'll be half mad with starvation. It could be very dangerous to you and yours."

The old man shook his head. "It's left us alone; we're minded to leave it alone. Don't kill it, swordlady. Leave it bide. Deer, boar, even a mess of rabbit or bird—just—not the bear."

Tarma checked the condition of every arrow in her quiver before attaching it to her belt. Then she looked at Egon and frowned. "You're not doing that beast any favor, old man."

Egon's face set stubbornly. "Not the bear."

She shrugged. "On your head. By the time it's trouble, we'll be gone past calling us back." She half-turned to face her partner. "I should be back by afternoon. One more night here, then we'll be off in the morning, if that's all right with you."

Kethry smiled. "Who am I to complain about another night under shelter? Good hunting."

"Thanks, Greeneyes." The Shin'a'in slipped out the door, leaving Kethry and the Guildmaster alone, sitting across the worktable from one another. The silence between them deepened and grew heavier by the minute. The sorceress stared at her hands, trying to decide what to say—and whether now was the right time to say it.

Finally, when Kethry couldn't stand it any longer, she opened her mouth.

"About that bear—" she began.

Egon spoke at exactly the same moment. "Lady, be you—"

They looked at each other, and laughed shakily. Kethry nodded, gesturing to Egon that he should speak first.

"Lady, I wasn't sure, you wearin' steel and all, but then seemed you know Mara—be you witchy? A sorceress, belike?"

"Yes," Kethry said slowly, wondering if he was

going to be angry at the idea of having sheltered a mage without knowing it. There were some who would be. Mages were not universally welcomed.

"Thank the God," Egon breathed fervently—

Oh, terrific. He isn't going to throw me out, but—

"It's that Mara, lady. I tol' you she been pokin' about in them ruins. Seemed like maybe she found somethin'. Them ruins, there's stories that the people there was witchy, too. Shapechangers." Egon swallowed. "We—we think maybe Mara found something of theirs."

Kethry put fact on top of surmise, and made a guess. "You think Mara's the bear."

He looked relieved, and nodded. "Aye. Exactly that. We figure maybe she found some kind of witchy thing of theirs, what let her shapechange, too. Now she's strange, but she bain't *bad*, or bain't been before. But she's got stranger since we started seein' the bear. There be bear tracks about her house—she *says* 'tis 'cause the bear comes to her feedin', that it's harmless if it's left be—but we don't think so. So—I dunno lady, I dunno what t' ask, like."

"You want to know if she's dangerous?" Kethry asked. She got up from her seat and began pacing, her hands clasped behind her. "Yes, dammit, she's dangerous all right. The more so because I don't think she ever really listened to a single word anyone ever told her at mage-school. Do you know why most mages *don't* shapechange? Why they use illusions instead?"

Egon shook his head dumbly, his wrinkled face twisted into a knot of concern.

"Because when you shapechange, you *become* the thing you've changed to. You're subject to *its* instincts, *its* limitations. *Including the fact that there's not enough room in a beast's head for a human mind.* That usually doesn't matter, much. Not so long as you don't spend more than an hour or two as a beast. You don't lose much of your humanity, and you can *probably* get it back when you revert. But it's not guaranteed that you will, and the stronger the animal's instincts, the more of yourself you'll lose."

"She been spendin' whole days as bear, we think. She don' come t' door, when a body calls, till after sundown," Egon whispered hoarsely.

"And at a time of the year when bear instincts are strongest." Kethry twisted the Shin'a'in oath-ring on her left hand. "No wonder she put on weight. Bears go into a feeding frenzy in the fall—and she *can't* have gained as much as a bear needs to winter-sleep. No wonder she looked like hell." Abruptly she stopped pacing, and went to her bedroll, picking up the sword-belt that held Need and strapping the blade over her breeches and tunic.

"Lady? What be you—"

"Oh, don't worry, Egon." Kethry turned to smile at him wanly. "I'm not going to use this on her."

For one thing, I don't think it would let me.

"I'm going to go talk to her," the sorceress continued. "Maybe, just maybe, I can help her."

She must be being torn nearly in two by now, Kethry thought unhappily, as she, in turn, slipped out into the dawn-gilded, frozen air. *Caught between the bear and the woman—if I can get her to take Need, I think the blade can rebalance her body for her. I hope. I'm no Healer, and that's what she needs most right now. That assumes she'll let me, of course.*

She picked her way across the lumps of frozen snow to the farthest house of the cluster—a cabin, really. It had never been intended to be used for anything more than living quarters, unlike the rest of the dwellings in the settlement. That cabin was Mara's, so Egon had said. It looked deserted.

Kethry pounded on the door for several moments, and got no answer.

With my luck—

She circled around to the back, and found what she'd been dreading. The back entrance was unlatched; the cabin was empty. And among the many tracks leaving and entering the cabin from the rear, there were no *human* footprints among them. Only the half-melted and near-shapeless tracks of a small bear.

Damn!

So many tracks suggested that Mara had fallen into a pattern. And that was bad; it meant she wasn't thinking in her bear-form, she was just acting. Then again, that she was following a pattern meant that if Kethry followed the old tracks, she'd probably be able to find Mara along the trail she'd established.

Whether or not she'd be able to reason with her—

I don't have a choice, Kethry decided. *That's why Need's been after me. Mara's going to get trapped in her bear-shape—and she's going to die.*

The trail took her deeply into the woods; without the trail, Kethry knew she'd have been lost. There were no signs of any habitation, no traces of the hand of man in this direction—except for certain rock outcroppings that didn't quite look natural. Gradually, as the sun rose higher and crept toward the zenith, it dawned on Kethry that these outcroppings were becoming more frequent, as if they marked some kind of long-vanished roadway.

She's going out to these "ruins," she must be going there every day. But why? And why in bear-form?

She was never to have an answer to that question, because as she rounded the torn-up, snow-covered roots of a fallen tree, something stepped out of the shelter of a cluster of pines to block her progress.

"You!" Mara spat. "You've come to steal it, haven't you?"

Her eyes were dull and deeply sunken; her hair was lank and unwashed. As she lumbered clumsily toward Kethry, the sorceress got a whiff of an unpleasant reek—half unwashed clothing and stale sweat, half an animallike musk.

"Mara, I—" Kethry swallowed. *If I say I haven't got the vaguest notion what she's talking about, she'll know I'm lying.* "—my partner and I are here by merest chance. We're on our way down to the Dhorisha Plains. Mara, I'll be blunt; you look awful. That's why Egon asked me to follow you. He's worried about you. Are you ill? Can I help?"

Mara's hands came up to her throat. "Liar! *He* wants it, too! He sent you to take it away from me!"

Kethry raised her chin and looked squarely into those mad, glazed eyes. "Mara, Egon is a Mastercraftsman. He doesn't *need* magic. And *I* don't need some stupid trinket to shapechange; I can do it myself. I don't, because it's dangerous—"

"Oh, yes, I remember you! Dear, bright, *pretty* Kethry! You never needed anything, did you? They *gave* you everything you ever wanted—power, magic, secrets—all those old men just fell over themselves to give you what they kept from me, didn't they? And the young men gave you—other things—didn't they?" Mara's face contorted into a snarling mask of hate. "Well, I've got secrets now, secrets *they* tell me. They made me their lover, just like those old men made you—they come to me when I change and they make love to me, and they whisper their secrets—"

As she babbled on about her "secrets" and her "lovers," Kethry realized with a sense of growing horror what must have happened. She'd changed, possibly for the first time, during mating season. And now she had convinced herself that the male bears that had mated with her were the long-gone shapechanging builders of the ruins.

Never particularly stable, perhaps it had been the shock of mating as an animal—and being unable to cope with it—that had pushed her over the edge.

"Well, you can't have it!" Mara shrieked at the top of her lungs. "It's mine, it's mine, it's—"

The words blurred, the voice deepened, the shapeless bundle of fur took on a shape. The words were lost in the roar of the enraged bear that balanced manlike on hind legs, and advanced—no longer clumsy—on Kethry.

"Mara—*Mara!*"

There was an oddly shaped metal pendant slung about the bear's neck on a blackened thong. Kethry *reached* for it with her own magic, to try and nullify it—and met nothing.

This "talisman" was not magic at all! Mara's shapechanging was not the result of some ancient sorcery; it was only that she *believed* the medallion could work the change.

And in magic, as Kethry had often told her partner, belief is the most important component.

"Mara, I don't *want* your talisman! It's worthless!"

The bear ignored the words, dropping to all fours and continuing to advance, saliva dripping from her snarling jaws.

Kethry flung a sleeping-spell at the shapechanger. It was the most powerful spell she had in her depleted arsenal at the moment. She'd used so much trying to escape Wethes' makeshift prison—

The bear ignored the spell; ignored the mage-barrier she tried to erect to hold it off.

She convinced herself she can change shape—she's probably convinced herself she can defend against spells, too.

So she really can.

Kethry stumbled backward, tripped and fell over the blade strapped to her side.

Need!

She tried to draw the sword—

—and discovered that she couldn't. It *would not* clear the sheath. It wouldn't allow itself to be used against a woman.

The bear reared up on hind legs again, as Kethry backed into the tangle of roots and frozen earth and found herself trapped. She drew her belt-knife; a futile enough gesture, but she was *not* going to go down without a fight.

And an arrow skimmed over her right shoulder to bury itself in the bear's throat.

The bear screamed, and pawed at the shaft, and a second joined the first—then a third, this one thudding into the shaggy chest.

A fourth landed beside the third.

The bear screamed again, and Kethry hid her face in her hands. When she looked again, the bear was down, its eyes glazing in death, a half-dozen arrows neatly targeting every vulnerable spot.

"Next time you take a walk in the woods," Tarma

said harshly, grabbing her by her shoulder and hauling her to her feet, "don't go alone. I take it this isn't what it looks like?"

"It's Mara," Kethry replied, trying to control her shaking limbs. "She learned to shapechange."

The Shin'a'in nodded. "Uh-huh; what I thought. Especially when you didn't give her the business-end of Need. Hanging about with a magicker taught me enough to put two and two together once in a while on my own." She prodded the stiffening carcass with the tip of her bow. "She going to change back? I'd hate to get strung up for murder."

Kethry held back tears and shook her head. "No. She froze herself into that shape—Goddess, *how* did you manage to get here in time?"

"I got Egon's deer almost before I left cleared lands; came back, and found you gone." The Shin'a'in poked at the medallion around the bear's neck. "What's this? Is this—"

"No," Kethry said bitterly. "It's just a bit of trash she found. She was so busy looking for 'secrets' that she never learned the secrets in her own mind. *That's* what killed her, not your arrows."

"That could be said about an awful lot of people." Tarma cocked an eye up at the sun. "What say we make a polite farewell and get the hell out of here?"

"Expediency?" Kethry asked, trying not to sound harsh.

Tarma shrugged.

The sorceress looked down at the corpse. She'd offered Mara her help; it had been refused. Staying to be accused of murder—or worse—wouldn't bring her back.

Expediency.

"Let's go," Kethry said.

WIDOW

by Kathleen A. Varnado

One of the things I repeat ad nauseam in my rejection slips is: "This is a clever idea; but ideas by themselves do not make a story; you need plot and character, especially character."

The one exception to this is the short-short story, which is based on an *idea;* and because of its brevity, all it needs is a clever idea.

Of course it doesn't hurt to have an intriguing character, too, as this one does.

The man trembled with ecstasy, brutally thrusting himself for the final time into the girl-child whose slight form lay pinioned beneath him. Laughing, he lifted himself from her, enjoying the feelings of assuaged lust and thrilled anticipation. He reached for her, his hands easily spanning the fragile neck from which issued a wisp of song . . . and died before he had time to realize he was ended.

Those in the village who had occasion to speak of her referred to her only as "the widow." She lived quietly with her daughter Maura on the outskirts of the village, raising herbs and vegetables to sell. They were both adept at spinning and weaving, so the villagers brought them wool and flax from which to make fine cloth.

The widow and Maura kept to themselves, secretive and private. There was much music there in the simple cottage. They sang, and the little breezes came to listen, bringing with them exotic seeds. The earth listened to their song, and swallowed the seeds, nourishing them gladly. The fruit trees, the rows of herbs and vines, and the flowers listened to their song, and accomplished full growth in a single span of the sun, dawn to dusk. The bees, the birds, and the gentle afternoon rains, all came to hear the widow and Maura sing. The wool and the flax brought by the villagers listened to their song, and danced into cloth, untouched by spindle or loom. Berries and barks flitted lightly to join sweet water, making wondrous dyes for the cloth.

Those who were too curious about the widow and her pale slight daughter heard a fragment of melody, and found themselves calmly going about their own affairs, curious no longer. Thus, none expressed surprise when the widow sent Maura alone to the mountains to find a husband where there were only brigands, thieves and murderers, who preyed on the weak and the innocent. Astonishment was forgotten, as indeed was Maura herself. They remembered only the widow.

How could they know about my mother and me? We are not of their kind, whatever we may seem to be. What could they know of the trade my mother made with the Winds of Fortune? She whispered her heart's desire to the wind while still carried on her own mother's back, and the bargain was struck, fecundity for song. The wind lifted her, changed her, gave her longings voice and power. In return, she and all those of us who will follow her will bear but one child, a female. Our sisters, still crawling and spinning their silken webs, bear many young, but they cannot sing. In a single span of the sun, dawn to dusk, we mate and feed, reach the fullness of our inches, and bear our young. Any who discover us soon forget, or die.

As for the brute who lies dead at my feet, well, only a wicked man would have taken to himself one seemingly so young and helpless. I will be nourished now, and I will thrive, providing for my daughter as did my mother. We will sing to the Winds of Fortune, and prosper.

I step into this new village, seeking a home to my liking. "My name is Maura," I say softly. "I wish to buy a cottage for myself and my daughter." Settling my black robes more closely about me, I tell them, "I am a widow."

JUST DESSERTS

by Elizabeth McCoy

One of my pet hates in stories is the reinvention of the wheel; characters mouthing worn phrases like "we don't send a girl to do a man's work," which should by now be taken for granted. One of the reasons, I think, why this anthology survives, when the conventional wisdom is that short stories don't sell, is that I refuse to re-repeat old cliches. Like all my rules, though, this can be suspended if I think it's appropriate.

This is a wry little story on the "biter bit" theme which demonstrates where and when cliches can be appropriate.

Elizabeth McCoy is another example of a very young writer and a short-short story where a very short story provides a touch of irony, or a character, which lifts it out of the hundreds of short-shorts which are only a set-up for a bad joke.

She is 17 years old, already the author-artist of a children's book, and her class valedictorian. Come fall, she hopes to enter the University of Texas on advanced placement as a sophomore. We probably don't need to express a hope that this young woman will do something important with her life—she seems to have already started. It's nice to see youngsters who can do something more than sit on over-cushioned fannies and watch passive entertainment on the boob tube.

Once upon a time, when women warriors were rare (but not unheard of), there was a town that was plagued by a dragon.

The mayor of the town, therefore, sent messengers to find someone who would kill this fearsome beast.

A few days later, a warrior arrived.

The mayor was happy to see that this fighter was female, for the mayor was a miser and thought himself cunning. He had devised a plan to trick the lady into fighting without pay.

The mayor walked over to where the armored woman stood beside her lizard-horse, and asked why she had come.

"I've come to kill the dragon and collect the reward," she replied.

Good, the mayor thought, *I shall trick her and she will kill the dragon just to prove she can.*

"Really?" the mayor said. "In *this* town we don't send a *girl* to do a *man's* work."

"Is that so?" The woman shrugged and got on her lizard-horse. "In that case, I'll leave for the next town. Good-bye." And she rode out of the town.

The next day the dragon attacked the town, ate the mayor, and died of indigestion.

MENDING WOUNDS

by Gary Jonas

One of the themes we get again—a new stereotype or maybe an archetype in the making—is the woman healer as opposed to a fighting woman or a sorceress.

Here is a story with one of the hundred thousand changes I get yearly on this theme. I do get very fed up with the constant cliche treatments of this theme which assume that good will is enough to cure everything, and Love Conquers All—where the facts of the case may very well be that there are no easy answers to everything.

This, Gary Jonas' first sale, takes a refreshingly hardheaded look at some old cliches. Tough-mindedness can be a refreshing breath of fresh air to remind us that sometimes there are no easy answers, even in fantasy fiction.

Gary Jonas says he has lived in Japan but was "too young to remember anything about it." Perhaps that's what gave him a sense of strangeness or an ability to avoid the easy answers? He lives in the Denver area and is a member of a science fiction critique group headed by Ed Bryant.

I'm not much on the wholesale sharing of embryonic manuscripts, but if you have to choose a mentor, you could hardly have chosen a better one.

She didn't mean to do it. Not really. Couldn't they understand that? Lucinda felt the tears welling up; they threatened to overflow, but she kept them in check. She was thirteen and as of now, on her own; they wouldn't take her back after what she'd done.

She ran through the veldt, hoping the pursuit would give up before she reached Shadow Wood. In places, the shrubs grew high enough to offer cover. She was frightened, confused. The dark twisted forest lay ahead. She slowed her pace, stopped. Shadow Wood was haunted. She almost turned back, preferring to face her death at the hands of the town council. Shadow Wood held the promise of pain and perhaps a death far worse than the people of Cardin could even imagine. Weren't there bolons and wild jereds and other animals in the forest?

Voices, at first distant, grew more distinct. Closer. They were catching up. Lucinda turned back for a moment, but she knew that even a chance at life was better than certain death. She entered Shadow Wood.

The forest was aptly named. Shadows threw themselves across the ground. An occasional beam of light penetrated the ceiling of leaves, but these weren't welcome. Lucinda wished the darkness was absolute—at least then the movements around her wouldn't be noticeable.

Her ears strained. Was that a twig cracking underfoot? Had they followed her into the woods? No, even with her father leading the pursuit, they wouldn't dare enter Shadow Wood.

Another crack. A shuffle as if through a pile of dried leaves. Lucinda turned full circle. She wanted to run back home. But she didn't have a home. Not any more.

Crouching, Lucinda scanned the path ahead. She wished she had a lantern or a torch. Then something stepped out of the trees onto the path.

"A bit past your bedtime, isn't it?" the figure said.

From the voice, Lucinda assumed it was an old

man. She knew she had to respect her elders. No. She was free of all that. Part of her regretted that. It had been comfortable. She'd been happy. Why did she have to be different?

"You didn't let them cut out your tongue, did you?"

"Who are you?" Lucinda asked.

"That's more like it. Step forth, girl."

Lucinda tried to resist, but something about the man demanded her compliance. She rose, but held her ground. "Leave me alone! I'll scream."

"I'd rather you didn't; loud noises are irritating. But if it'll make you feel better, go ahead." He inserted his index fingers into his ears.

He looked ridiculous and Lucinda almost laughed. He didn't seem half so scary now. And yet there was a feeling of power about him. The air crackled with intensity and it seemed as if a voice were whispering assurances in her ear. She felt a bond forming between the old man and herself.

Lucinda shook her head, trying to chase away the voice on the wind, but it was within her mind. "Wizard," she said. "What do you want of me?"

He didn't answer, just stood with his fingers in his ears.

"I know you can hear me."

"Are you going to scream?" he asked, his voice louder than necessary.

"No." She felt more at ease now. Safe. That in itself caused her alarm. She had to remain alert to possible deception.

The old man unplugged his ears and grinned as he stepped into the light where she could see him better. "A wizard would be a wise old man. I grant you the old, but there are many who would disagree with the wise part. I'm here to provide you with a home and an education."

"You don't sound too happy about it."

He shrugged. "We all must bow to greater needs than our own. Shall we go home?"

"I have no home."

"Very well. Shall we go to my home? You can stay

there as long as you wish, provided you're learning your art. And no, you won't pay for my teachings with sex. I may be a dirty old man, but I have a few scruples left and the teacher/student bond is more important than momentary gratification of a physical urge."

Lucinda caught the gist of his message and felt more at ease. "I'm hungry," she said.

"Then let's go eat."

The old man's cabin was typical for a wizard. The outside seemed small and rundown, but the inside was enormous with many rooms. He told her his place was tucked between the dimensional veils, and she'd nodded knowingly, though she hadn't the slightest idea what he was talking about. Large as the place was, it was cluttered. The front room, where they spent much of their time was stuffed with old dusty furniture—chairs, tables, a desk, bookshelves. And everywhere she looked were knickknacks, doilies, pictures, books, vials, beakers of noxious fluids. One shelf was devoted to cans labeled with such things as crushed lizard testicles, roasted bat wings, sliced frog eyes and stick cinnamon.

Piles of dirty clothes dotted the floor and surrounding the mounds were stacks of papyrus and odds and ends. "Your first task," he said, "is to clean this place up."

"Is that what you plan to teach me? How to be a proper *kiena*?"

"I'm going to teach you to use your magic to help instead of harm, Lucinda. But first we need some room to move around in." He sniffed the air. "And I don't suppose it would hurt if I burned some incense."

The first lesson was simple. "Slap yourself on the face," the old man said.

Lucinda looked at him like he was crazy.

"Slap yourself," he said again.

"Why don't you slap *your*self?"

"Because I, like you, passed lesson number one: don't listen to everything everyone says."

Lucinda stayed with the old man for several days before she learned his name. Almegnon. When he'd told her, he seemed to expect a reaction from her—as if he were famous or something, but she'd never heard of him. He shrugged his disappointment aside.

Soon, Almegnon changed his tactics. He pulled out a small knife and ran the blade along his thumb, slicing it open. Blood spilled on the floor. He held his hand out toward her. "Heal me," he said.

"I can't!"

"You were able to do great harm back in Cardin."

"What do you know about that?"

"I know about Shen," he said.

Shame flooded through her and poured out through her eyes and down her cheeks. "I didn't mean to hurt him! I tried to help, but I couldn't. I'm sorry. I can't help people; I can only hurt them."

"Yes, destruction's easy," Almegnon said. "But it's possible to turn it around. Watch."

He held out his hand, blood dripping from the wound. He placed the index finger from his other hand on one end of the cut and ran it along, sealing the flesh. He turned his hand so she could see there was no sign of an injury.

Lucinda stared in awe. "How did you do that?"

"Simple concentration. The body knows how it should be, but it lacks the ability to pull itself together. All I did was provide the guidance and the extra energy to speed up the natural healing process."

"Can you teach me that?"

Her excitement was contagious. Almegnon laughed. "That's what I'm here for."

"Cut yourself again," Lucinda said.

"You will find that if you visualize the way you want the body to look and guide the healing with your mind, you can heal virtually anything. There are some things beyond even your range, though. If a person has lost too much blood, he may be a goner. If a person loses a limb, you can't help him regrow it. There are limits."

"I want to go out and help people," Lucinda said.

"You aren't ready for that. People will fear you if they know the truth. Magic brings out people's greatest fears and their worst emotions."

"It also brings out their best."

Almegnon nodded. "But not as often."

"People like magicians."

"Yes, but that's all sleight of hand. Illusion. There's no real magic. You are a healer, which if you want names, puts you in the class of adept. That's why you must try to keep it a secret."

"So I can't help people?"

"You've come a long way. But you still lack the energy and the technique."

"I'm good. You said so yourself."

"Yes, but there are emotional concerns as well."

"I can handle it."

"I'm against this, but the elders said it would come down to proving it. You want to heal people who need you desperately?"

"Yes."

"Very well." Almegnon waved his hands and they were no longer in the cabin.

They stood atop a foothill gazing down into a valley. Bodies littered the ground. The dead and dying sprawled alone and piled atop one another. The battle had ended and the victors moved on. It was still a battlefield though, as men fought for their lives. This was a war they fought not with weapons, but with willpower. The will to survive the arrows and sword slashes and burns that left them breathing the fumes from their own blood.

A maelstrom of emotion slammed into Lucinda. She staggered at the impact. Almegnon had told her she was empathetic to the needs and feelings of others, and she found she had no shields to filter the effect. Their pain became hers. Their fears tore her world apart.

Almegnon raised his voice and called out to victims of the sea of death. "I bring you Lucinda. She fancies herself a healer!"

"No!" Lucinda cried. "Don't say that! Please. I can't . . . "

Almegnon folded open a doorway and stepped out of the battlefield, leaving her alone.

The pain brought her to her knees.

A man moaned as he dragged himself toward her. "Heal me."

She turned, startled by his proximity. "Go away!" she shouted, the tears flowing. She tried to push herself back but he crawled one arm outstretched, pleading. She rolled aside. "I don't know what to do!"

"Help me."

"I can't!"

"Try," the man said. His face was caked with blood. A long gash ran down his left side. "Please try."

She had no choice. She was a healer. Fighting back the impulse to run, she reached out to him with trembling hands. At first contact she felt his pain so acutely she thought she'd lose herself. Her mind reeled in anguish. Only her shame gave her an anchor.

She tried to concentrate—to teach the flesh to knit itself back together, but the wounds were too deep; there'd been too much blood loss. The strain of being near the man almost made her black out.

"I'm sorry," she said. "I'm sorry. I just can't do it."

She struggled to her feet and ran away, paying no attention to where she fled. She wanted Almegnon to come and take her away from the agony. She stumbled and fell. As she raised her head she saw dying men clawing their way toward her—using their last vestiges of strength for one last chance at life. And she could do nothing to help them—nothing to ease their pain even for a moment. Overconfidence had set her up for the big fall and she had taken the plunge headfirst. No mercy.

"Please leave me alone!"

The men begged her for assistance. One even cried out for her to kill him, reminding her of her brother. Hadn't he begged for death? Why had she done it? The reasons for her anger seemed so trivial now. She couldn't even recall the specific argument. But the suffering she'd caused . . .

Again she pushed herself away from the mob and tried to run away, but a man blocked her path. He held his hands against his stomach, trying to keep his insides where they belonged. From the looks of him, he wasn't succeeding. "You were our salvation," he said, his voice a shade above a whisper. "You came to us in our time of need." He fell to his knees and crawled toward her. She didn't run; there was nowhere to run to. He reached out to her, clutched her tunic. "Why won't you help us?" His grip loosened and his hand slid down, leaving a trail of blood.

It was his final accusation.

Almegnon found her lying amidst a dozen broken corpses. They never spoke of the incident, but more than anything the old man ever said or did, that day changed her. She could have gone one of two ways. She could have let her failure cripple her so she'd close herself off to humanity or she could use it the way it was intended: as a lesson in which she could find strength to grow and learn to do better.

She chose the latter.

She became more attentive. She was quiet and rarely smiled. She feared that she was worthless, but refused to accept it. She was young and there was time. As her mentor had told her, there were always people in need of healing. She had the gift; she simply had to learn the techniques.

One goal lay at the forefront of her desires. She wanted to help her brother. She felt that if she could heal him, her family would take her back and things would return to normal. It always came back to Shen.

"You've taught me all you can," Lucinda said. She'd learned much in the three years she'd studied under him; it was time to put his teachings to good use.

Almegnon stared out the window into the forest. "You still don't understand. You haven't grown up. You have childish hopes to regain what you lost, but what you lost was innocence, and once lost, it's lost forever." He turned to face her and she saw tears in his eyes. "I love you as much as life itself, Lucinda. To see you hurting hurts me."

"You used to think of me as a necessary evil. A child to train because the Elder Wizards demanded it of you."

"No, I used to think of you as a pain in the rear, but somewhere along the line that changed. The Elders didn't think you'd make it after your breakdown. They wanted me to give up. You still hold onto dreams of childhood. Times of no responsibility. You can never go home, Lucinda. You haven't accepted—"

"You don't know me!" she screamed. "You don't know anything about the way I feel. Maybe I can't go home, but I have to *try*."

Almegnon sighed and bowed his head. "Then go."

Cardin hadn't changed since she'd left, but to Lucinda there was a contrast of two vantage points. She saw people she'd grown up with, children she'd played with, boys she'd dreamed of getting joined with and adults she'd feared and respected. People recognized her as she strode into the town; no one dared approach her. She could smell their fear.

Part of her felt contempt for how they'd treated her, but she could see it from their viewpoint and she forgave them. Magic was something they didn't all possess. It was an unknown; therefore it was evil.

Lucinda ignored them and continued toward her parents' home. She didn't know what to expect. When she stood before the cottage her heartbeat doubled. The dwelling which had been a place of happiness for thirteen years now filled her with dread. It was time to try and go home and she steeled herself for whatever might happen. There could be no turning back now. She had to help Shen.

The door was open so she walked inside. Her mother sat at the table, a mug of water in her hands. She looked up at her daughter, then closed her eyes.

I'm no longer your daughter, Lucinda thought. *As far as you're concerned, I died three years ago.*

Her father stepped through the hallway into the living area. "Haven't you caused enough grief?"

He looked tired and Lucinda wished she could do something to rejuvenate him. But she'd come for Shen. If things worked out properly there would be time for the others, but Shen came first and to help him she'd need all her strength. "I need to see him," she said.

"So you can finish what you started? Get out!"

Lucinda stepped toward her father. Perhaps he feared her. Perhaps he thought she'd kill him or worse. Perhaps he still felt something akin to love for his daughter. Whatever the reason, he let her pass.

Shen's room was dark. A blanket hung over the window blocking out the sun. Shen looked like a corpse there in the bed. His eyes opened and locked onto hers overflowing with unspoken accusations and blame. *I deserve that*, she thought.

"I've come to heal you," she said. She was aware of her father's presence in the doorway, but since he wouldn't do anything she focused on Shen. "Words can't tell you how sorry I am, but perhaps you can find it in your heart to forgive me."

Shen just watched her. She pulled the covers off. His legs were twisted even worse than she remembered. A new wave of shame washed over her. Why had she done this? Shen had started an argument with her; he'd always known how to provoke her. But on this occasion he'd pushed her too far. This time her latent abilities surfaced and she struck out, not realizing what would happen. She wished she could go back and prevent her actions, but the best she could do was to try and heal him now.

Placing her hands on his legs and closing her eyes, she allowed images to form. She pictured his gnarled limbs straightening. Her hands glowed white and moved over his thighs, shins, ankles, feet. She softened his legs with the white light—made them pliable and then molded them into the proper shapes. Perspiration beaded on her forehead as she delved deeper, working on atrophied muscles, correcting the tissue damage and restructuring the bones.

As she worked, she thought of happier times. How they used to play together. And how, even though he always seemed to be in the way, she still loved him and allowed him to participate. The good times were still there, she just had to clean away the blackness of her shame and his agony to see them.

At last she'd finished. She took a few minutes to relax and recuperate, then stepped back. "Get up, Shen. Walk."

Shen had observed the entire process with a combination of fear and fascination. He took a long breath and forced himself to a sitting position. Using his hands, he moved his legs over the side of the bed and pushed up to a standing position. Lucinda moved to help hold him up. His legs wobbled, but she couldn't help smiling at his success.

"Bitch!" His fist rushed forward and her face exploded with pain. She fell back and he fell atop her, still trying to hit her.

"Shen! What are you doing? I'm helping you!" She rolled away from him and wiped blood from her face. She saw her father smile.

"You never should have come back," Shen said.

Lucinda shook her head and refused to release her tears. "I thought that you'd be able to forgive me."

"You can't imagine what it's been like. You stole three years of my life, made me helpless, and you expect to be forgiven? What you stole can never be replaced! Get out of my life! I never want to see you again!"

She swallowed her pain, slipped past her father and moved toward the door. She stopped and looked back at her mother but the woman didn't look up.

Lucinda left her family behind. *There's nothing more I can do for them.* She headed back toward Shadow Wood. Why did losing them have to hurt so much?

Almegnon met her at the forest's edge. Silently, he embraced her, crying the tears she couldn't cry.

ST. GEORGE AND THE DRAGON (REVISED)

by Nancy Jane Moore

As I seem to have said, there is one story I have to handle again and again. Still, this theme turns up so often that there must be something in human nature to which it resonates. So, without too much apology, here is another St. George and the Dragon story . . . with a twist.

Nancy Moore lives in Washington D.C. and works at present for a nonprofit law firm. She says she has been writing almost all her life but only recently got serious about it. Well, sooner or later it happens to everybody. Her first sale was to SWORD AND SORCERESS VI.

The dragon swooped low over the village, sending all of the maidens scurrying for cover. Not to mention all the matrons, children, grown men, and anybody else who was about.

He cornered Maura in the churchyard. "Someone go find St. George," she yelled, cowering behind a tombstone.

The dragon leered. "I had St. George for breakfast," he said, indicating the remains scattered nearby. "And I'll have you for lunch," he added, lunging for her.

"Oh, hell," said Maura. "I guess I'll have to rescue myself." She dropped to the ground and kicked the dragon in the groin. Hard.

Now it's a little known fact that male dragons, like the males of most species, are very tender in the testicular area. In fact, most people aren't even aware that dragons have testicles. This is because the Victorians have written most of the dragon stories up to now and they didn't want to discuss such delicate subjects.

Anyway, as soon as Maura kicked him, he doubled over in pain, giving her a nice shot at the unarmored spot on the underside of his neck. She drove a foot into that as well, and then, rolling to her side, found George's sword and stuck it through the dragon's neck for good measure. (It's not a good idea to walk away from live dragons, no matter how injured they are.)

The villagers were very grateful and honored Maura with all the usual parades and statues and things. The death of St. George was hushed up, though, so he still gets all the credit. But in one small village the stories have been handed down over the generations and they know who really killed the dragon.

HER FATHER'S DAUGHTER

by Sue Isle

Sue Isle concluded her letter of biographical data by saying, "I am presently owned by two pet rats." She adds that her tastes include martial arts and history—she is an ex-member of the SCA—hard sf, fantasy, and stories about everything from wolves to were-wolves. I seem to have said some things in these introductions about repeated themes; and one of those I keep getting is "wolves." Personally I can't understand the attraction—but at least it's a change from *cats.* I have never understood the fantasy writer's attraction to cats—but by now I take it for granted, though I don't share it. Some famous poet said that God invented the cat to give humanity the pleasure of petting the tiger; I have revised this to say God invented dogs to give mankind the pleasure of knowing wolves intimately. They seem very much worth knowing; I'd give up all the cats I've ever known for a good German Shepherd. Now—while I duck the inevitable flow of letters to tell me how wrong-headed and perverse I really am—you can read a slightly different story about a werewolf.

There's really no accounting for tastes in pets; my first husband kept a snake in the railroad depot—to the dismay of the little old ladies who came to send telegrams.

Under the Changer's Moon, the woman came alone to Hazor town, late of an evening. On this summer evening, the open-air market was still open, as was usual during the fiery months. She walked among the stalls, staring about her with a strangely innocent wonder. The stallholders marked her, returning her glances with amused looks of their own, for this was no great market. Hazor was a central town, far from any lake or sea. Charn Forest pressed close about the city walls, try though men might to cut it back. What farming lands they had won must be continually defended against the trees . . . and more.

Her tunic was the color of blood, some sign of an old service, perhaps; some great house now vanished. Women mercenaries were not something Kalek encountered very often, but he had met lords who swore they were better than men . . . especially in the interrogation chambers. Because they did not have strength to waste, they were careful fighters, quick and deadly. Because they were life-bearers, they didn't waste lives. At least, he thought to himself with a grin, that was the theory. This one didn't look the sort to soften to a babe. Gray and silver, she was. Gray breeches, boots and cloak, her eyes gray, even her hair a queer off-white, neither white nor cream.

Kalek of Eren was a man who found such behavior intriguing. He was not one who pushed his presence on a woman—indeed, he was a loner himself to such extent that there was at least one well-known song detailing Kalek's supposed preferences for sheep, that had been sung from the rooftops of Vorn's tavern. (By the time Kalek had scaled the roof, blood and blade well and truly raging, the unknown singer had vanished).

On this occasion, he stood on Vorn's terrace and was able to see her coming. She wore her red and gray; the sword peace-strapped, but still present to warn against trouble. In Vorn's tavern, she asked for a red wine and retired to a corner table. Kalek had seen her enter, but stayed where he was for a few moments, then rose and walked to her. He was graceful as the beasts he hunted; not with the outward beauty of some of the young townsmen, but where they must bluster for attention, Kalek would already have it.

"May I sit with you?"

Her gaze lifted to his face calmly; she had not been startled despite his quiet. She looked at the fur jacket Kalek wore.

He took this for inquiry. "My name is Kalek. Kalek of Eren, but they call me Kalek the Bounty Hunter." He grinned. "As though I were the only one."

"You *are* the only one!" Those were the booming tones of Janor Hark, a farmer who had reason to appreciate the skills of the hunter. "Nobody else could rid me of that damn rogue."

"The red wolf?" Kalek couldn't repress a grin. "He was not clever enough against cold steel teeth."

She had not spoken, but the man seated himself, looking inquiringly again at her. "I see you here every few weeks," he explained. "Do you live outside the town?"

"Yes. Quite far."

"I took you for a hired sword." He nodded at the blade. "But such don't stay around the one town for long."

"I have fought for pay," she agreed softly. "But I was called home for a task, and then, perhaps, I will go elsewhere."

Kalek found himself enthralled by her voice. It was low and clear, each word accentuated as though it was a foreign language to her, needing careful thought to speak it. But she was still staring at the jacket, not at his face.

"What hide is that?"

"Wolf." He grinned. "The red bastard that I trapped for Janor. Killed his best ram and not a few of the good ewes."

"Perhaps the wolf couldn't tell what a man thinks is good?"

Kalek shrugged and drained his mug. "I daresay they don't think as men at all . . . but men must live."

She extended a lean hand toward him then, touching the sleeve like a child. Kalek remembered her innocent delight in walking about the market, and wondered whether she was childish. She didn't *seem* to be.

"Have you ever killed a man?"

That question was cold and direct as an arrow of ice. Kalek's muscles tensed under her light touch. "Yes, lady. Twice in my life, bandits have had the misfortune to choose me as their mark." But she didn't answer his smile.

"And some beasts I have killed—are more than beasts."

She nodded somberly. Even a farmgirl from outside the walls—*especially* such a girl—must know of the werekind. Most were very careful where they changed form. Kalek himself had never killed under the Changer's Moon. There was dispute over whether the werekind really were men, possessing souls, or simply beasts. He'd even met a few, mostly serving in mercenary units, and they had been as human as anyone. But those who were rogue were the most dangerous of enemies, and they tainted the name of all their race, so that most werekind kept their nature secret.

"May I buy you a drink?"

She did meet his eyes then and smiled slowly as though liking what she saw. "Yes. You may."

Kalek could hardly believe his fortune. They stayed until Vorn announced closing time—for the second time—and then he walked outside with her and the few remaining customers. The night was brilliant and clear, with a full harvest moon brightly orange above them. Kalek breathed in the clear air.

She paused on the steps and said. "I'm weary this evening. Could your horse carry double for a short distance?"

"I thought you said you lived far from Hazor," Kalek said, puzzled. "It is no matter, of course . . . I . . ."

She smiled, patting the neck of his grey gelding. "Not far as the horse runs, Kalek Bounty Hunter." And her eyes spoke a promise against which he was helpless.

He noted absently that the moon was already on her

way to harbor. Vorn had been generous to let them stay as long as he had. It would be a dark ride home, unless she could be persuaded to let him remain with her. He'd done far better with the woman than he had thought. The man whose skill in the wild was unsurpassed, who could hunt alone and dwell alone, was less expert when it came to the complexities of women. They had left the fields behind and were now in the forest fringe.

"Here," she said. She twisted about to look at him. Kalek shrugged, seeing no dwelling.

"Is your father a woodcutter, then? I will see you to your door."

She jumped lightly down from the saddle of the patient gelding, and turned again. Her pale features were very calm.

"My father is dead, Bounty Hunter."

"Don't call me that. My name is Kalek . . . I would be pleased if you would use it. Would you tell me your name? You . . . you are very beautiful, lady." He leaned down from his horse towards her and said shyly. "You are like a forest elf. May I not know your name?"

She reached a hand up to his shoulder, caressing the red fur of his jacket.

"Give me this . . . as a keepsake, and I will tell you my name." Coquettishly she smiled at him, and Kalek laughed. He pulled the jacket off and handed it to her. "I will get you better, lady. The pelt of a white bear for a cloak . . . soft deerhide for a wrap."

She reached again to touch his wrist. Her grip was cool and firm.

"I want no more than this from you, Bounty Hunter."

Kalek sighed and made to sit up. It was late, perhaps next afternoon he could come riding here . . .

Her grip didn't loosen, as he'd expected. "Let me go, lady," he said gently. "If you will not tell me your name, why, I must ride away in sorrow."

And then he looked at her and saw what he'd been blind to, enthralled with her.

"You're werekind. But the Changer's Moon . . . "

Her eyes glowed yellow in the moonlight . . . the fading moonlight. With that one hand, she pulled him from his horse, which shifted away to avoid trampling him. Kalek tried to rise, but that grip of iron held him.

"I don't have very long, Bounty Hunter," said that clear, low voice. "But whatever shape I hold, I know my father's pelt."

"No!" Kalek cried. "I saw the red wolf dead! He was no changer!"

Her pale hair fell forward around her face, seeming to cling to her slender neck, her pointed face, and the yellow eyes staring down at him. He felt the rough earth of the trail hard at his back.

"You are not as wise as you believe," she whispered. "Ask my name of Silvia, who ran with a wolf of the Pack on a night of the Changer's Moon, a score of years ago. And I—I fight for the wolf nation of Charn, and have this night only to walk among men . . . and find the one who killed my father!"

Her final shouted words lost all coherence, and became a snarl out of the blur of mist and flesh that was a woman . . . and it was the jaws of a white wolf that met in his throat.

Then there was only the red thundering of pain, and nothing.

Kalek Bounty Hunter woke with a raw and bleeding throat, in the muddy trail by the cold light of day, some hours later. His horse lay dead, not far away, savaged by beasts in the night. But he lived to return to Hazor, oddly silent about the terrible accident that had befallen him, returning from escorting a beautiful girl to her forest home. No one could understand why he hunted no more, and he didn't expect them to. Men could not be expected to understand that the wild beasts of the forest were more merciful than they.

WINTERKILL
by Laurell K. Hamilton

Laurell Hamilton has appeared in my anthology SPELLS OF WONDER and she has also appeared in MEMORIES AND VISIONS: WOMEN'S FANTASY AND SCIENCE FICTION.

I seem to have had rather a lot to say in these introductions about strange pets; Laurell Hamilton has "a yellow-naped Amazon parrot with a vocabulary of several hundred words. My familiar is a cockatiel that just loves to have her head scratched. We have a canary named Hobbes." Well, there's—as I seem to have heard somewhere—no accounting for tastes. I once kept a couple of baby parakeets—named Robin and Miranda—who were kept in the same room with two dark gold canaries; and since parakeets will imitate anything, and the canaries listened all the time to classical music, all the birds sang constantly. Alas, one night there was a blizzard; the window of our old house blew open and in the morning all my birds were dead. I have never owned another cagebird; it's cruel in a house where cats are honored residents. (Yes, in spite of all my comments on cats I have owned many—if cats can be owned, which I doubt.)

Laurell says she is "happily married," she grows African violets, and collects dragon figures and a few select teddy bears. At least the glass figurines and the teddy bears are noncontroversial pets. People usually don't get into fights over teddy bears. At least I never met anyone who did; my teddy bears are all pacifists.

Jessamine Swordwitch stood among the ruins of Threllkill village. The forest had moved in to reclaim the small clearing. Twenty houses it had been at its largest, a tiny inconsequential place, but it had been home.

One of her mother's roses had gone wild. It climbed over the broken chimney, pale pink flowers clustered against the sun. The air was thick with its scent, cloying sweet. The black-limbed cherry still stood against the shattered pile that had once been the garden wall.

Jessamine felt her mother's magic pulse through the wild growth. An earth-witch's touch stayed with a plot of land. Mother would not have minded that orange-flowered trumpet vine strangled her garden, or that wild grass grew where she had tended her strawberries.

The thought that her mother's body could still be there, hidden in the green growth, came suddenly. She caught her breath, eyes darting for a glimpse of white bone amidst the wildling strawberries. But there was nothing left of her mother save the roses and the cherry tree. Scavengers had long since picked apart the bones. Twelve years was a long time this close to the forest.

"What happened here, Jessa?"

She jumped, startled, and turned. Gregoor leaned against a soft green mound that had once been part of the kitchen. "I'm sorry; my thoughts were elsewhere."

He snorted. "I could see that." He gestured, arms wide. "What destroyed this place?"

"Old age, an act of the gods."

He frowned and crossed arms tight over his chest. "Are you going to tell me the story behind this place, or not? You drag me out to the wilderness. Tell me nothing. You accept a job without consulting me and then tell me I don't have to come along." He pushed a hand through his short brown hair. "Jessa, we've been swordmates for a year. Don't I deserve some kind of explanation?"

She smiled at that and walked over to stand against the leaf-covered wall, beside him. Her hazel eyes looked at a place somewhere over his head, while her small, strong hands stroked his hair. "In Zairde there are no peasants, only the poor. We were poor, but I didn't know that as a child. We had food, shelter, toys, love. I did not think we were poor, but we were not rich. My mother was the village earth-witch. She never used her magic for personal gain or to harm, unless attacked. Even then she was squeamish of the kill. She wouldn't understand my entombing people in living rock."

"You've only done so twice, and each time it saved our lives."

She smiled down at him. "Yes, there is that. But I stand here with my mother's magic still strong in the earth and I shield myself."

"Why?"

"I'm afraid, Gregoor." The summer wind stirred her dark hair. "I promised my mother I would never use my power for evil. I have broken that promise many times."

"You're afraid her disapproving ghost will haunt you?"

"Yes."

"Jessa." He hugged her to him. "Please, tell me what happened here."

"One day an old sorcerer and his son came to spend the night. I had never seen a truly old sorcerer, for they can live a thousand years. But this one was old. His son was young and strong and handsome; the village girls watched him out of the corners of their eyes. During the night the old sorcerer died." Jessamine's hands stopped moving. She stood absolutely still. "The son accused us of poisoning his father. He destroyed our village with fire and lightning, storm and earthquake. My father and my brothers, were all killed. When it was over, only my mother and I crawled away."

Jessa took a deep, shaky breath. "My mother, as the village earth-witch, took our grievance to the Zaridian courts. They did nothing. Two days after they declared him innocent of wrongdoing, an assassin killed my mother." She looked down at him, meeting his eyes.

His brown eyes were wide, astonished, pain-filled. "Jessa."

She placed finger tips over his lips. "It was a very long time ago, Gregoor, very long ago."

He gripped her hand. "What happened to the sorcerer that destroyed this village?"

"He died." She smiled down at him. It was a smile he had seen before—a slow, tight spreading of lips that filled her eyes with a dark light. He called it her killing smile. "He was the first wizard I ever killed."

"And that is why we specialize in assassinating wizards?"

"That is why I do. I do not know why you do it."

He stood, eye to eye, no taller or shorter than she. "I do it because you do it."

"Ah," she said and gave him what no one else had received from her in twelve years—a smile full of love. "You took this job so you could come home, then?"

"I took this job because the sorcerer I slew had a mother, as I had a mother. It seems she has gone mad. The entire province wants her dead. The sorceress is Cytherea of Cheladon."

"You have sent us to kill Cytherea the Mad. Jessa . . ."

She stopped him with a gesture. "She seeks her son's killer, Gregoor, and has killed hundreds seeking me. I think it is time she found me."

They came to the first town at dusk. A gibbet had been erected in front of the town gates. Three corpses dangled from it, moving gently in the summer wind. They had been hung up by their wrists, and there was no mark of ordinary violence upon them. No hangman's knot, no knife, no ax had killed the three.

Gregoor hissed. "Mother Peace preserve us, I've never seen anything like that."

Jessa could only nod. The corpses, one man and two women, had been drained of life, magic of the blackest sort. The flesh was a leathered brown like dried apples. Their eyes had shriveled in their heads. They were brown skeletons. The women's hair floated around their faces that were cracked with horror, mouths agape in one last silent scream.

Jessa shook her head: that was nonsense. The dead did not retain the last look of horror. The jaws had simply broken and gaped open, nothing more.

"Come, Gregoor, let us get inside."

He was still gazing at the dead. "This is Cytherea's work?"

"Yes."

"And you have set us the task of killing her?"

"It would seem so."

Gregoor pushed his horse against hers and grabbed her arm. "Jessa, I am not a coward, but this . . . Cytherea drained their lives like you and I would squeeze an orange dry."

Jessa stared at him until he loosed her arm. "We have killed sorceresses before."

"None that could do this."

Jessa nodded. "She took their magic when she took their lives, Gregoor."

He caught his breath. "I am only an herb-witch, I can't tell. Did she steal their souls?"

Jessa shivered. Though she shielded her magic, protected herself, she could still feel the answer. She understood now why she had thought the corpses were screaming, silently. "No, their souls are still there, trapped in the bodies."

"Verm take that pale bitch."

Jessa nodded. "That is the plan, Gregoor, that is the plan."

They were challenged at the town gates. A woman called down, "What do you want here, soldiers?"

Jessa answered. "A room for the night, food if you have it to spare, and stabling for the horses."

"Don't you know that you ride into a town that is cursed?"

Jessa kept the surprise from her face. "Cursed? What do you mean?"

The woman gave a rude snort of bitter laughter. "Did you not see the gibbet and its burden?"

"I saw three corpses."

"They are the mark of our curse. You would be better to ride on, soldiers."

Jessa licked her lips and eased back to speak with Gregoor. "I don't feel a curse, except on the corpses, but I am shielding myself."

He looked surprised. "You've been wasting energy shielding yourself, for how long?"

"Since we entered the edge of Cytherea's blight."

"Blight, what are you talking about?"

It was her turn to be surprised. "Look around you. Look at the plants."

The summer trees hung with limp black leaves. The grass was winter dead at the side of the road, crumbling and brown. It was utterly silent.

"Where are the little birds, the brownkins. There are always brownkins."

"Not here, not anymore." Jessa wanted to ask him how he had not noticed, but she knew the answer. He was herb-witch, a maker of potions, his magic was a thing of incantations and ritual. Her magic was tied to the earth and what sprang from it. This desolation wounded her in a very private way. This was blasphemy. And Gregoor had seen nothing in the summer twilight.

"If you will distract the guard, I will spy out the curse and see if it is safe to enter."

He nodded. "They might not be happy to see more spellcasters after Cytherea."

"Yes, and I would rather not be advertised as an earth-witch."

He rode over to the gate. "What has happened to your land?"

Jessa turned inward and did not hear the rest. She listened to the rhythm of her own body, blood flowing, heart pumping, breathing, pulsing. She came to the silence deep in her own body where everything was still. Jessa released her shields and swayed in her saddle. It took all she had not to cry out. The land wailed around her. Death, the land was wounded, dying. It was not just the witches on their scaffold that Cytherea had drained, but the earth itself. She had taken some of the life-force of the summer land. It would not recover. The town was doomed. It could not survive where no crops would grow. There were no brownkins because the tiny birds had fled this place; everything that could had fled this place. Everything but the people. And they would leave soon enough. When autumn came and there were no crops, they would leave.

The destruction was so complete that it masked everything else. Jessa was forced to turn the horse so she could look at the town, concentrate on it, and see if it was indeed cursed. Her eyes passed the gibbet and three sparks of life fluttered in the corpses, bright and clean. The souls wavered and struggled. Jessa turned away and stared at the walled town.

She stretched her magic outward, no longer flinching from the earth-death around her. The town was just a town. There was no curse. A curse would have been redundant after what Cytherea had done to the land.

Jessa rode up beside Gregoor. She whispered, "There is no curse on the town. We can enter safely."

The guardswoman called down. "What was your lady friend doing so long?"

Jessa answered, "I was praying."

The woman was silent a moment. "Prayers are a good thing. Enter, strangers, and be welcome to what is left of Titos."

There was only one small tavern in the town, and they were the only strangers. The windows were shuttered though the summer night was mild. An elderly woman muttered in her sleep, dreaming before an unnecessary fire. Jessa wondered if they thought fire and light would keep out the evil, like a child crying in the night. The place stank of stale beer and the sweat of fear. The tavernkeep himself came to take their orders. He was a large beefy man, but his eyes were red-rimmed as if from tears.

The tavern sign had said simply, Esteban's Tavern. Jessa took a chance. "You are Esteban?"

He looked at her, eyes not quite focused, as if he were only half listening. "Yes, I am he. Do you wish to eat?"

"Yes, but more than food we would like information."

She had his attention now. His dark eyes stared at her, full of anger, and a fine and burning hatred, like the sun magnified through glass. "What kind of information?"

Gregoor brushed her hand, a warning not to press this man. But Jessa felt a magic in the room, untapped but there. It was not coming from the tavernkeep. "A gibbet stands outside your town gates. How did it come to be there?"

Large hands knotted the rag he had stuck in his belt. His voice was a deep whisper. "Get out."

"Excuse me, tavernkeep, I meant no offense, but such a sight is uncommon."

"Get . . . out." He looked up at her as he spoke, and there was death in his eyes, death born of grief.

Jessa knew about such grief and how it ate you from the inside out until there was nothing left, and you died, or you satisfied your vengeance. She spoke low and clear. "Where is your wife, tavernkeep?"

He threw back his head and screamed, then flung their table to the side and advanced on Jessa. She kept out of his reach, a knife in her hand, but she did not want to harm him. The magic she had felt flared and crept along her skin, sorcery.

The old woman by the fire was standing now, leaning on her walking stick. One hand was clawlike in the air before her. "Enough of this!" Power rode her voice, a lash of obedience. The big man stood unsure, arms drooping at his sides, tears sliding down his cheeks.

Jessa sheathed her knife unable to do anything else. Very few people could have forced an obedience spell upon Jessa.

The old woman turned angry eyes on her. "Did you have to hurt him?"

"You would not show yourself."

"Well, I am here now, girl. What do you want? And I warn you if it is not something worthy of the pain you have caused, you will be punished for your rudeness."

Jessa bowed never taking her eyes from the woman. She felt Gregoor close at her side and caught the glint of steel in his hand. So the obedience spell had affected only Jessa and the man. That was something to remember. "I seek the death of Cytherea the Mad."

The woman stared at Jessa for a space of heartbeats. Jessa knew she was being weighed and measured, tested. The old woman laughed then, an unexpectedly young sound, but the body remained old. "An assassin, two assassins."

Jessa and Gregoor shifted uncomfortably for there was nothing that should have given them away. "We are not . . . "

The old woman said, "Do not lie, whoever you are. I have the gift of true-seeing."

Jessa swallowed. It was a rare talent, and one that was proof against all lies, magical or mundane. "We did not enter this town under false pretenses. If you are a truth seer, then you know I mean what I say. I am here to kill Cytherea."

The woman's face was solemn as she studied them. "You believe what you say, that much is true. But saying you will kill her and doing so are not the same thing."

"That is true. We seek information to aid us in our task."

Esteban said, "Can you kill her?"

Jessa looked at him. His eyes were grief filled wounds. "Yes. I am Wizardsbane, and this will not be the first or even the tenth wizard I have slain."

The old woman said, "And you, who follow her like a shadow, who are you?"

Gregoor sheathed his blade. "I am Gregoor Steelsinger, also know as Deathbringer."

"Such auspicious names, young ones. But can you live up to them?"

Jessa said, "We are willing to risk our lives to prove worthy of our names. Are you willing to help us destroy the mad woman that raped your village?"

"I will tell you what I can, Jessamine Wizardsbane, but it is precious little. I am Teodora Truthseer."

Esteban brought food out to them, then sat to listen. Jessa would have protested, but Teodora said. "His wife and daughter hang on the gibbet outside our town. Surely he deserves a seat at this table."

Jessa nodded.

"The first we knew of trouble was a snow storm from a clear summer sky. It was a storm driven by an ice elemental, cold as the netherhells. Cytherea came out of that storm, a demon of ice at her side. She told us her terms for saving our town." Teodora paused and took a drink. "I fought Cytherea when she arrived at our gates. I challenged her to win safety for my town." Teodora smiled and looked at her age-gnarled hands. "I lost. But I did not lose through sorcery. There I could have matched her. She wore a ring on her left hand, an enchanted ring. I walked out the town gates a woman of thirty and was carried back in a woman of sixty."

Jessa and Gregoor exchanged glances. "What sort of ring could age a woman like that?" Gregoor asked.

"Cytherea did not age me, so much as curse me with old age. She wears a ring of curses."

Gregoor gave a low whistle. "That is an expensive item."

Jessa said. "Is that how she bound . . . "

Teodora interrupted her. "Esteban, could you please refill my glass."

The man looked suspicious but got up to do as the sorceress asked.

Teodora spoke low to them. "You were asking if the ring is how Cytherea bound the souls to the bodies?"

"Yes."

"Esteban does not know that his wife and daughter

are still in torment. I think it would be unwise to mention it in front of him."

Gregoor said, "Is it what she used?"

"Yes."

Esteban sat the mug down, and Teodora said, "Thank you, Esteban."

Jessa asked. "How did she take the earth-witches' magic and the land's magic as well?"

Teodora stared at her full mug, brown-spotted hands tight gripped. "She wears a necklace, a square-cut emerald set in gold. It is a unique enchantment. It is attuned to earth magic and steals only that."

"So this necklace contains all the earth-magic she has stolen?"

Teodora nodded.

"You are a truthseer. Is there a way to release the magic, or to destroy the enchantments?"

"The ring of curses is not unlimited in power. It has so many curses in it just like a human curse-maker. If the ring is used up, empty before being reenchanted, then all the curses the ring caused this time will be undone."

"You would be young again?"

"Yes." Teodora studied the food on her plate and talked without looking at anyone. "The necklace is different. It has perhaps an unlimited ability to absorb power. The only way to release the magic is to destroy it."

Gregoor asked, "And how do we do that?"

"You must give it back to the earth from which it came."

"The exact earth," Jessa asked, "or metaphysically speaking, so that any earth would do?"

"Any earth will do."

Jessa smiled.

Gregoor said, "You've thought of a plan, haven't you?"

"I've thought of a possibility."

Teodora asked, "How can we help?"

"Gregoor will need some herbs to make a potion.

And I was wondering if your town can boast a curse-maker."

Esteban and Teodora exchanged glances. "Why, yes, but he is old and not powerful enough to curse Cytherea."

"I don't want him to curse Cytherea, I want him to curse me."

Two days later they rode out of Titos, a new potion at their belts and a curse for each of them.

Gregoor grunted and twisted in his saddle trying to scratch the middle of his back.

"It will only be worse if you claw at it."

He looked at Jessa through red, inflamed eyes, nearly swollen shut. "You said pick a curse, so I did. How was I to know that the Verm cursed rash would grow this bad."

Jessa sighed. "I suggested a curse that would have been serious enough but would not have hampered your fighting skills."

He clawed at his hand. "You wanted me rendered impotent. No, thank you."

She almost laughed. "I am childless until my curse is removed."

"But that's different. You were taking a potion to prevent children any way. I have a use for my manhood."

Jessa smiled, but she felt a heaviness in her stomach; an empty heaviness. She felt the loss. "If this rash grows any worse, you will be all but useless by the time we face Cytherea."

He rode up beside her. "I am sorry, Jessa. I did not understand. If I had known, I might even have let him unman me." He shivered in the sunlight, skin twitching. "I would not have you be killed because I was distracted by this infernal itching." He clawed at his arms, raising welts.

"You're going to bleed if you keep scratching. Don't you have a ointment to help yourself."

"Yes, but I was hoping to save it until we were nearer our destination."

"I think we are close enough. Use the ointment before you flail yourself alive."

Gregoor rummaged in his saddle bags and came up with a sealed pot. "This will take some time."

"We have time. I have a spell to do myself."

He nodded and dismounted. The grass was shoulder-high to him and brushed the horses' bellies. Wild Bellis flowers filled the air with their delicate scent. A swift quarreling flock of brownkins flew overhead. Jessa breathed in the summer bounty. Her magic pulsed and swelled with the ripening grass, the swift flight of birds, the tiny hidden creatures. Everything was magic for the taking for an earth witch.

Gregoor came to stand at her stirrup. His face was coated with an oily lotion. "You sparkle like pale flame."

She grinned at him, stretching arms skyward. "I feel like I should burst into flame, swollen with power."

He frowned.

Jessa laughed. "There's no danger of that, Gregoor. Don't frown so; it'll make you itch." She touched his shoulder.

He jumped as if burned. "Your power poured over my arm. It was . . . unexpected."

"Surely making your herb potions fills you with magic?"

He shook his head. "Nothing like that. I'm an herb-witch, Jessa. Our magic is a quieter thing. You could pass for a sorceress, now."

"It's always like that in spring and summer, but winter," she shivered, "winter is a poor time for earth witches."

"Then what will you do behind Cytherea's spell line?"

"I have absorbed enough power to do a few spells if I'm careful."

"Then what?"

"Then I won't be able to pretend I'm a sorceress anymore. Cytherea will know me for an earth witch, and our plan had better work."

Gregoor looked up at her, the swelling and redness already leaving his eyes.

"You look much better. How do you feel?"

"The best I've felt in three days of travel. I'll be able to watch your back."

"I never thought you wouldn't."

Gregoor remounted, and they pushed through a stand of pine trees. Bushtails chattered and scolded overhead, showering them with pine needles. Jessa felt the first cool tendril of power, someone else's power. She slammed down her shields, cutting herself off from the land, but protecting herself from what lay ahead.

The horses pawed nervously at the top of the ridge. Up through the trees, mist was oozing. Sunlight cut through the mist, sparkling on a line of ice-covered trees. The summer leaves were crumbled, blackened, ice-coated. Frost and snow lay in glittering drifts at the foot of the ridge.

Jessa glanced up at the waving greenery overhead. Yellow snake lilies nodded on the forest floor. "Definitely the work of elementals and demons."

"Do you think we can bargain with the demon?"

"Our plan depends upon it."

"What if it doesn't agree?"

She smiled at him. "Then, Gregoor, we will see if the god Magnus truly does cry tears of blood."

"I did not plan on meeting Him so soon."

"Nor I. Let's get out the winter gear."

Sweat trickled down Jessa's spine. The fur hood was oppressive. Gregoor waited beside her, sweat-carved runnels melting the ointment on his face.

Cool mist swirled round the horses' legs, but the summer sun beat down on them. Winter was a slash of brilliant diamond ice. Snow lay inches deep. The green belt of summer had been sliced cleanly and completely.

Jessa urged her horse forward. The hooves crunched in the snow's edge. The chill breath of winter cooled the sweat on her face instantly. Her breath fogged and began to crystallize on the fur trim of her hood. Something large moved in the trees. Jessa signaled Gregoor to wait.

She could see nothing, and yet she knew something had moved. The winter-ruined trees were utterly still. Snow stretched smooth and untouched. But . . . there was a spot near a large straight elm tree that Jessa could not look at. No matter how hard she tried to stare at it, her vision kept slipping by it. Don't look at me, it seemed to say. I am not here, but of course that meant something was there. The question was, what.

She signaled Gregoor to come up beside her, slowly.

They had ridden only a few strides when the air wavered, and a demon was leaning against the elm. Both sets of arms were crossed over his chest. He was about ten feet tall, only a little less white than the snow. His scales shimmered like mother-of-pearl. Two slender horns grew from his head. His tail twitched in the snow. Jessa was reminded of a cat about to pounce.

The demon's bat-ribbed ears curled and uncurled. "I am the guardian of this spell line. If you cross even one step farther, you will be trapped until the spell is complete."

"When will that be?" Jessa asked.

He blinked large purple eyes. "When Cytherea the Mad wills it, and not before." A forked tongue licked his lips, exposing teeth like ice daggers. "So turn back while you may. You have been warned."

"Thank you for the warning. If we ride farther, what will happen to us?"

He shrugged one pair of shoulders. "Cytherea will decide."

"What will you do if we ride farther in?"

"I," he said, placing a claw on his chest, "nothing, yet. You will have to huddle in the town while Cytherea does her business."

"How long will that take?"

The demon looked up at the ice trees. He smiled flashing fangs. "Not long, I think."

Jessa said, "Then we will cross and wait if we must."

"Come across, then." The demon made a sweeping bow, motioning with his many arms.

They rode forward, skirting out of the demon's reach, though distance alone would not save them, if the demon chose to be nasty.

The demon called, "Herb-witch."

Jessa looked back at Gregoor. He was staring at the ground, very determinedly.

"Look at me, herb-witch, look at me," the demon hissed.

"Stop it," Jessa said. "He does not have the magic to resist you."

"And you do?" He turned his gaze upon her, perfect violet, like the eyes of the blind. Jessa would not meet his gaze. The demon laughed.

"You said you would not harm us if we passed."

"I lied."

She looked at him without meeting his eyes. "Will you stand in our way?"

"Not now, but when Cytherea is done with her little . . . chore, then she will let me choose my reward." The demon was suddenly standing before them. Jessa's horse screamed and reared, hooves lashing the air.

The demon grinned as Jessa fought to control the animal. "Perhaps I will ask for you, sorceress."

Jessa glared at him. "Will you beg for a treat like a well-trained dog?"

The demon's ears curled into tight rolls. His claws flexing the air. "I am no dog, woman. I am ice demon, and I will show you what that means."

"You will harm me before Cytherea has seen me? Is that wise?"

The demon roared, clawing at the trees, raking ice and wood into splinters. The horses went wild. When Jessa and Gregoor slowed the trembling animals, Jessa found a splinter of ice in her cheek. She pulled it out and found it bloody. She would have thrown it on the ground, but the demon was watching her, eyes intent, a strange eagerness in his scaled face. She held the bloody crystal, unsure what to do with it.

Gregoor whispered, "Jessa, try not to make it more angry than you have to."

"Cytherea is your enemy, not us. She has bound you into her service. What if we could free you?"

The demon stared at her. "How?"

"If she is dead, then you are free."

He snorted. "You cannot kill her with sorcery."

"We will not kill her with sorcery."

"Why tell me, when now I can warn her?"

"You want freedom. We want her death."

"What do you want of me, sorceress?"

"An oath that you will not help Cytherea against us."

The demon flashed fangs. "Of course, I promise I will not hurt you, either of you."

"No demon, an oath to Verm and Loth."

His ears furled in surprise. "A vow to the dark ones will sever Cytherea's control over me. Will allow me to stand and watch." He grinned. "One of the few things that will. You are not just a sorceress, are you?"

"No," she said.

"And what do you vow, mortal?"

"We vow to free you."

"I simply watch while you kill Cytherea. Then I am free."

Jessa nodded.

"The exchange is fair, and because of that I cannot take it."

Gregoor started to protest, but Jessa silenced him. "I understand, demon, you must come out the better in the bargain."

He nodded. "You have dealt with demons before."

"Perhaps." She caught Gregoor's shocked look and ignored it.

"What do you offer to sweeten the bargain?" the demon asked.

She held up the bloody splinter. "Blood."

The demon licked his lips. "And from the man."

Gregoor said, "No."

Jessa frowned at him. "Will you bargain with just my blood?"

"If I cannot harm either of you, then I must have blood from both, or we fight here and now."

"Gregoor, just a few drops . . ."

"Look at its face."

The demon's face was lined with hunger, he seemed almost to have grown thinner. He shimmered with a horrible eagerness. "I see him," Jessa said softly.

"Then how can you offer him our blood? I am an herb-witch, and I could kill with a single drop of it. What could a demon do with blood?"

"I will taste your soul," the demon whispered.

Gregoor said, "I will not give that thing my blood."

"Then we fight it here and now. It is your choice, Gregoor. I understand your uneasiness, and I will abide by your decision."

He shifted in his saddle, hand stroking his sword hilt.

"Fight me, wizard. I will have your blood one way or another."

"No," Gregoor suddenly said, "I will give what is asked."

Jessa held out the bloody shard. The demon reached for it, and she covered it with her hand. "Swear, demon, swear by Verm and Loth."

"Let the wizard draw blood first."

Gregoor took off his gloves and drew his dagger. He nicked one finger, letting three drops of blood fall into the snow. "There is your blood." He wiped his dagger clean and applied pressure to the small wound.

Jessa said, "Make oath, demon."

"I swear by the birds of Loth and the hounds of Verm that I will not harm you by direct actions."

The demon grimaced, claws clicking like ice breaking, but he repeated it word perfect. Jessa handed over the ice shard with its cold blood. The demon's claws took it delicately and licked it, dainty as a cat with cream. He licked it clean, but the ice did not melt. He chewed up the ice, crunching it in his teeth.

Then the demon knelt in the snow, all glittering in a stray shaft of light. He rolled his eyes at Gregoor and scooped up the bloody snow. Sucking sounds filled the forest, obscene and joyous. The snow did not melt at his touch, and he swallowed it. He grinned and stood, stretching arms wide. "I will see you in your dreams." He vanished.

Gregoor asked, "What does that mean?"

"We will relive this in our nightmares, with certain changes."

"Jessa, what have we done?"

"We have bargained with a demon. Did you think to come out of it untouched?"

He stared down at his gloved hands. "I don't know what I thought." He drew a deep shuddering breath and looked at her. "Let's go kill this bitch and get out of here."

Jessa smiled, her eyes full of a strange dark-light. "Let us go hunting. May Magnus guide our strokes and strengthen our spells."

The village of Bardou lay in a small hollow, trusting to being hidden rather than protected by a stout wall. Perhaps a dozen houses huddled in the snow. There was activity near one end, people moving. A scream carried through the cold air. Two figures were left isolated in the snow as the rest backed away to the houses. A tall figure in a red, furred cloak stood alone before the two who had been cast out.

Gregoor said, "It would be better to wait until she is in the middle of her spell. We could catch her by surprise."

Jessa shook her head. "Enough have died in my place already. I cannot let these two die while I watch." She met Gregoor's eyes. The killing light had faded from her face, replaced by something he could not decipher. "By saving these people our plan falls apart."

"I know, but this is your choice, Jessa. I will abide by your decision."

Jessa smiled. "Perhaps I have been playing the mercenary too long." She kicked her horse into a gallop and Gregoor followed. The red cloaked figure was chanting, strange twisted words that slid across Jessa's mind and left a stain. Jessa called, "Hold, Cytherea, mother of Solon."

The woman looked up, startled. Jessa glimpsed a pale face. As she rode closer, the woman stared at her with eyes the cold gray of good steel. There was no expression on Cytherea's face, only a blank waiting. Thin yellow hair blew in strands round a fox-lined hood. The reddish-brown fur made the face paler.

"You seek the earth-witch who killed your only son. Is that not true?"

There was no change in the pale eyes, but she nodded.

Gregoor had a potion open in his hand, waiting.

"Let these poor fools go; I am here."

Cytherea shook her head, slowly. Her voice was as flat and unemotional as her face. "You are a sorceress. Do not stand in my way, or I will destroy you."

Jessa rode her horse between the two huddled earth witches and Cytherea. The first flicker of emotion passed those gray eyes: anger. Gregoor dismounted, staying off to one side.

"Do you remember the village of Threllkill?"

Cytherea frowned. "They killed my husband, and my son destroyed them for it."

"Your husband died of old age. Even sorcerers die, Cytherea."

"No," she said.

"Your son destroyed innocent people, but I survived. When I was grown, I hunted him down and I killed him."

Anger flared and turned the eyes a darker color, the color of storm clouds. "Get out of my way, little sorceress, or I will kill you as I kill the earth creatures that slew my son."

Jessa dismounted and pushed back her hood. Gregoor poured the potion upon the ground.

Suddenly, the world was cold, the cold that numbs bone and steals the air from lungs. A glittering figure of ice appeared beside Cytherea, a vague mouth and eyes appeared but nothing more. The ice elemental whispered to the sorceress. "The man spilled a potion on the ground."

Cytherea blinked as if trying to focus upon what was happening. "Demon, where are you, Jecktor?"

The demon appeared and bowed before her. "Kill them, Jecktor. Get them from my sight."

The demon said, "I fear I cannot."

She turned on him, anger flashing sorcery like embers on the wind. "What?"

Jessa reached out to the earth where Gregoor's potion lay, pooling and still warm in the snow. She touched it with her earth magic. There was the scent of green growing earth, strong and clean.

Cytherea turned back from the cowering demon. "What are you?"

Jessa said, "I am earth-witch."

The earth exploded upward, showering down dirt and rock. A figure stood full grown from the ground. It was ten feet tall, roughly man shaped, formed of rich black earth and the redness of clay. One eye was a diamond, the other an emerald. It took a heavy step forward and the ground moved.

The ice elemental grew like an ice fire and rushed over the earth elemental, shrieking like a banshee wind.

Cytherea screamed, "Then die, earth-witch!" She pointed her left hand and its ring at Jessa. A shriveling killing magic flashed outward. Jessa staggered from its touch, but it washed away and past her as if she were a rock in a stream.

Cytherea stared at her. "No!" Again she raised the ring. The ground began to smoke and pop to either side of Jessa.

Cytherea turned to Gregoor, "Die!" He stood unmoved and unharmed. "What is happening here?"

"We are both already cursed. You cannot curse someone twice." Jessa said.

The sorceress shrieked and tore her cloak away. She stood, hair streaming in the wind, the emerald necklace sparkling in the cold light. She put a hand over the emerald and began to chant.

Incased in ice, the earth elemental moved forward, its movements stiff. Ice froze the earth, until the earth-giant moved in agony. The ice wind shrieked its triumph.

Jessa felt the power growing. She felt the pull of the enchantment. It called to her magic; it beckoned, a poisoned seduction. Her magic answered it, flaring and shredding on the winter wind. It drew off the magic she had absorbed. Jessa drew her sword and started forward, but she could not move against the necklace. It was sucking her dry.

A throwing knife blossomed in Cytherea's side. She shrieked and staggered.

Jessa saw Gregoor coming forward, another knife in his hand. She fell slowly to her knees in the snow.

Gregoor screamed, "Jessa!"

Cytherea had regained her control. She gestured and sorcery flared in her hands. Blue flame enveloped Gregoor.

There was a crackling thunder and the earth elemental burst free of the ice. Then it was suddenly running, shaking the ground as it came. Cytherea was forced to turn her attentions to the earth-giant.

Gregoor fell facedown into the snow, unmoving.

Blue light and ice crawled over the earth elemental. Jessa felt its scream through the frozen ground. She began to crawl toward Cytherea, naked sword dragging over the snow.

Cytherea was bathed in blue flame, she crackled and seemed to glow. Jessa was almost close enough to touch her skirts. Stray bits of power crawled along Jessa's skin, burning with cold-fire. She staggered to her feet, sword held two-handed, for an upward thrust.

The ice elemental hissed, "Behind you, mistress."

It was too late. The steel bit into Cytherea's back, the blue fire shredded and vanished. Jessa shoved the blade upward, seeking her heart. Cytherea shrieked, but would not die. She put a hand on the emerald necklace and Jessa felt the power begin to grow.

Jessa screamed, "Die, damn you, die!"

The earth elemental leaned over them, one massive hand reaching. Cytherea yelled, "No the necklace is mine! You can't have it!" The earth elemental stood, the broken chain dangling from his massive fingers. Earth magic poured out of the broken enchantment, free at last. Magic that swelled and flowed and carried Jessa with it until she thought she would explode with the power. It rushed over and through her, a magically visible green fire.

Jessa drew her sword free. Bloody, but still alive, Cytherea turned and began another spell. Jessa's blade crawled with emerald fire. The silver-green blade sliced outward, cleanly. The sorceress' head spun off into the snow. The body toppled into the crimson-washed snow.

Jessa dropped to the ground, unsure how to cope with so much power. Gregoor was huddled against the earth, staring wide-eyed. Green grass showed in the snow. Summer warmth beat down. Earthmagic pulsed and spread from the earth elemental as it grasped the emerald necklace in one massive hand.

The ice elemental had fled. The demon bowed to Jessa. "Earth-witch, I am most impressed." As he faded from sight, he said, "Perhaps we will meet again some winter's night."

Gregoor crawled to her. "I can't stand up. The earth pulses like a great heart beat."

Jessa could not speak past the magic. She could feel it racing over the ravaged land, healing, awakening, reviving.

Finally, she said, "Begone, earthling, back to the depths from which you came. Thank you for your aid." The elemental melted into the earth, taking the necklace with it. Cytherea's body lay in a circle of black fresh-turned earth.

Jessa crawled to the dead sorceress and looked down at her. The face was blank as any dead man's. "Peace at last, Mother, peace at last."

Gregoor was scratching his face. "You did it."

"We did it, Gregoor."

He grinned, then grimaced as he tore at his coat to get to new itches.

Jessa smiled. "Perhaps the village of Bardou boasts a curse-maker."

He looked at her, a hopeful light in his eyes. "Oh, that would be a blessing indeed."

"Come, they should be grateful enough to remove a couple of curses." Jessa paused, staring at the pale hand, the ring of curses was still on the left hand. It was a slim band of black iron, empty now, but waiting. Jessa slipped the ring from Cytherea's finger.

"It's expensive to get something like that reenchanted," Gregoor said.

She slipped the ring into a belt pouch. "But well worth it, don't you think?"

"I can think of a few uses for it."

Jessa reached out and touched him, and green fire flowed from her across his skin. He gasped, then forced a grin.

"Extraordinary," he whispered.

They helped each other to stand and began to limp towards the village.

There was a strong scent of roses on the air, almost choking in its sweetness. Jessa turned.

There in the fresh earth was a rose bush, blossoms flared to the new sun. The roses were yellow, the color of Cytherea's hair.

Jessa called softly, "Mother." A breeze began to blow, gently, against them. The earth-fire began to melt into the ground. Jessa found herself crying. She walked alone to the roses, on unsteady legs. The flowers moved, stretching towards her hands without aid of wind. One small blossom rubbed against her hand.

Gregoor asked, "What is it?"

"I think I am being forgiven."

"Forgiven for what?"

Jessa did not answer; for some things there were no words. And some things were not meant to be shared.

STAYING BEHIND

by Jessie D. Eaker

Jessie Eaker, who is male in spite of the spelling of his name, appeared first in a story I bought for SWORD AND SORCERESS VI. He has also appeared in small press publications such as PANDORA and BEYOND. He also has a novel in progress; as I seem to have said before, "Doesn't everybody?" He has two daughters and a son, and currently owns no pets, saying that he and his wife Becki are finding the children keep them quite busy enough.

It's hard to call names; I still remember misjudging a "Terry" as female in an early anthology and mistakenly judging all contributors to a Darkover anthology as female. Maybe it's just as well names aren't gender-specific, because most people used to think my name "Marion" was male—or, when they know I'm not, demanded to misspell it "Marian"—but it's always been "Marion" in my family—or rather, my mother's family—Scottish—while my father and oldest brother were both named "Leslie" . . . and so was *his* oldest son. I recently found out that my mother's name, Evelyn, was a male name in England; so maybe no one can—or should—be able to tell gender from a name. Which reminds me of a memorable scene in a movie where a boy auditions for the High School of Performing Arts, finding out halfway through Juliet's speech that Juliet was the girl. What's in a name, indeed?

About this story I will only say that it's an interesting and slightly different story of a woman warrior "staying behind" when her friends have all gone to battle. Jessie dedicates it to his wife, "one of a very select class of mothers."

Freya stood silent, loosely at attention in the large meeting hall. Around her, talking excitedly in low voices, the other guardswomen of the garrison took their places. She didn't know why they had been awakened for the pre-dawn assembly, only that something was dreadfully wrong.

The torches lining the walls and illuminating the hall did nothing to take away the early morning chill. At her awakening, the sergeant had stressed the need for speed, so Freya—like the others—had donned only a tunic, and come with feet bare and hair undone. She shivered, longing to return to the warm furs she had just left.

The restrained whispers died and every woman drew to attention as their commander—fully dressed and prepared for travel—entered at the front of the room. She stepped up on a small raised platform.

"Guardswomen!" announced the commander, raising her arms and extending them towards the group. "A cry for help has reached us from the temple city Percillis. The Meninkinites have the city under seige and seek to steal the Goddess Mother's Amulet. We *must* go to our sisters' aid and prevent these animals from defiling our most sacred city. Therefore, prepare at once for a forced march. Travel light, taking only the barest essentials. We leave at dawn. Go now to make your preparations!"

Restraining their excitement, the disciplined body of guardswomen turned as one, and began an orderly exit from the building. But Freya stood motionless, eyes staring straight ahead, her mind in turmoil. She thought of her young daughter Neola, who slumbered safe and warm beneath the furs of their shared pallet.

She thought of her oath as guardswoman and the law she was oathbound to obey.

Ignoring the glares of contempt from some and the looks of pity from the others, she broke rank and made her way to the front of the hall. There she found the commander talking with her lieutenants. Freya dropped to her knees, bowed her head, and waited to be recognized.

After several moments, she felt the commander's light touch on her shoulder. Freya looked up, searching the elder's face. "Commander, I ask . . ."

Shaking her head, the older woman interrupted. "I know what you want Freya, and I cannot make an exception. I realize your daughter is four summers old, but the law is very clear about this."

Freya closed her eyes and dropped her head in shame.

"I am sorry, but until your child reaches her fifth summer, you are forbidden to go into battle except in defense of your child. You will have to remain behind."

Freya loaded another stone into her sling and took careful aim at the mark on the inside garrison wall. Concentrating on the throw and pouring all her frustration and anger into it, she twirled the sling over her head. She propelled it faster and faster until the sling's leather cords sang with their speed. Only then did she release the stone, which cracked against the wall and gouged a deep hole where the mark had been. She nodded once in satisfaction and dug in her pouch for another stone.

Two days had passed since the others had left, but her shame and anger still burned. Why the age of one's child determined who fought and who stayed behind infuriated her. Before the birth of her child, she had proven herself to be a fearsome fighter, earning herself a reputation for skill and bravery. And since coming to the garrison with her daughter in her arms, she had continued to prove herself an outstanding warrior. Only now the battlefield was denied to her. It was the ultimate cruelty, like stealing the air from a magnificent eagle.

She knew the intent of the law: to prevent hordes of children from being orphaned. Guardswomen had no fear of death and, for the Goddess Mother, would meet it head-on with sword in hand. But such dedication had its price. In the early days of the guard after a battle, the elders had frequently found themselves swamped with motherless babes. In the end, both the guard and the babes had suffered.

The commander sensed Freya's turmoil and had tried to ease the burden by leaving her in command of the garrison, but this only added to her frustration. Aside from one other exempt mother, she was responsible for thirteen children—from six seasons to fourteen—not to mention one old senile priestess. She wasn't a warrior, she was a nursemaid!

Once more, she loaded a stone and flung it at the wall. Having long since tired of hacking away with sword at the practice post, she had searched for another exercise. But the others had taken all but a few of the spears, bows, and arrows, leaving her with few tools to practice her trade. So she had returned to her childhood favorite—the sling. Her intent had been to teach the children after a few practice rounds, but she had enjoyed it so much, she had not stopped.

She loaded another stone and began her swing, when suddenly she was attacked from behind; the culprit attaching itself to her left leg and throwing her off balance. "I got you!" yelled her daughter Neola, hugging her mother's leg tightly.

Caught in mid-swing, Freya released both sling and stone to prevent hitting the child, and rolling, fell to the ground. The mother turned to glare at the daughter, and caught sight of the other children standing behind. Dessita, the eldest, who was supposed to be entertaining them, had her finger nervously clamped between her teeth as if to bite it off. She looked back to her daughter, who was smiling.

"You shouldn't sneak up on me when I am practicing," scolded Freya. "I could hurt you."

The child shrugged, indicating she did not consider that a possibility. "We were chasing each other. And I wanted to catch *you*!"

The child's smile was infectious. Freya smiled, too. She knew she should be more stern, but her daughter's smiling nature always melted her heart. She tousled her child's hair. "Be more careful next time, all right?"

"Yes, Mother." The child nodded and jumped up. She reached for Freya's hand. "Here, since I made you fall, I'll help you up."

Groaning in mock exertion, the child tugged on her mother's hand. Playing along, Freya couldn't help noticing how different they each were. The child had hair so blonde it was almost silver and eyes of the deepest blue, while Freya had dark hair and brown eyes. But Neola was strong and especially intelligent, outstripping most of the children her age. Freya took pride in her daughter.

That was when Freya noticed the makeshift necklace swinging loosely from around her daughter's neck: a piece of rough rock attached to a dirty and worn strip of cloth. "Where did you get the necklace, Neola?" asked the mother.

"From Amada. She said it was a piece of the sky that broke off and fell down." She held it out. "Isn't it pretty?"

Purposely, Freya stood and took her daughter's hand. "Come. Amada shouldn't give you gifts like that. That old priestess should know that sky-stones bring bad luck to warriors."

After retrieving her sling, Freya led her daughter toward the barracks—Neola having almost to run to stay with her mother. They climbed two flights of steep stairs outside the barracks to a small room sitting on top: Amada's building, placed there so she could watch and record the movements of the night sky. In Freya's opinion, another testament to the priestess' senility.

Out of respect, Freya knocked gently on the old woman's door. The elder was rumored to have been a great sorceress in her younger days, before her powers had waned and her senility had increased.

The door opened to reveal the older woman standing just inside, a towel thrown over her shoulders, but otherwise completely nude. Freya couldn't help noticing that despite her age, the elder appeared to be in reasonably good shape.

"What do you want!" demanded Amada. "I do not like being disturbed, *especially* when I am washing." The elder's eyes drifted down to Neola and brightened. They smiled at each other.

"I want to know why you gave Neola a sky-stone?" asked Freya. "It brings warriors bad luck."

Amada considered the woman briefly before answering. "True. But the child is obviously not a warrior, now, is she?"

Freya was taken back by the answer. "Of course, she's not *now*, but she will be. It is the same thing."

Ignoring the mother, Amada took the child's hand and led her inside. Freya followed. Belying her age, the elder easily lifted the child onto a rough wood table beside her wash basin and began to pull on a coarse, white tunic. "No," said the priestess gently shaking her head. "She is not a warrior, and I do not think she ever will be one. She *does* have the potential to be a great sorceress one day. Can't you feel the power coming from the child?"

Amada searched the mother's face and shook her head in disappointment. "No, I guess you can't feel it. But be warned. The child already has more power than you think."

"Show me," said Freya doubtfully.

Amada nodded and held out her hand. "Give me two stones from your pouch of the same size and shape."

The mother fumbled out two smooth ones, which Amada took and laid on the table two hand-spans apart. The priestess touched Neola's shoulder. "Remember what we did the other day with the stones? How like attracts like?"

Neola nodded vigorously.

"Then think hard and make these brother stones come together."

The little girl screwed up her face in what appeared to be intense concentration; Freya couldn't help but smile at her comic expression.

At first there was nothing and Freya opened her mouth to speak, but the priestess held up her hand. Glancing back at the stones, the warrior saw them begin to vibrate and then slowly slide toward one another. Suddenly, one of them shot to the other with a loud smack, cracking both of them.

"Excellent!" cried Amada, who hugged the smiling child.

Freya stared in shock at her child's feat. It could not be. The priestess must have done it.

Unexpectedly, Dessita opened the door and burst into the room. "Hurry! Hurry! You must go to the watch tower!" she said breathlessly. "Sonita says troops are approaching. And they are *not* guardswomen!"

A gentle breeze tugged at the loose strands of Freya's hair as she stared at the approaching troop. The garrison was strategically positioned on top of a steep hill to protect the shrine of the Goddess Mother beside it and to keep the road below open. From her vantage point, high within the watch tower, the warrior could see the whole road—and she didn't like what she saw.

Sonita, the other remaining guardswoman, stood beside her; her infant son, not yet weaned, strapped to her back and playing with a strand of her hair. "It looks like an outlaw troop," she said. "But I was unsure."

Freya shook her head and pointed. "No, you are correct. See that long line behind the main body. Notice how straight and perfect it is. No one can maintain a line like that unless they are chained. And where there are slaves, there are outlaws."

"But they approach so boldly, openly showing themselves, as if they have nothing to fear!"

The women exchanged glances. "Right now," said Freya, "they *have* nothing to fear."

* * *

Freya's back itched as she walked steadily toward the lone man. The outlaw troop had approached to the bottom of the hill and then started setting up camp. A lone man had climbed the path to the garrison and stopped half-way, holding his spear high over his head and then thrusting it point first into the ground: he wished a parley.

Freya had used the distraction to send Sonita out for help, using a rope to climb down the garrison walls. A single woman—out of sight of the outlaws and traveling quietly—stood a small chance of getting away, but it was doubtful she could return with aid in time. Behind her, on the garrison walls, patrolled the children. She had dressed them as guardswomen and given them what weapons they had. They were to pretend to be patrolling the walls; they thought it a great game.

Freya stopped ten paces from the man, dressed in light leather armor, but legs and arms bare with a gold band on each arm and jewels braided into his thick and slightly graying beard. He smelled foul. "Salutations, Guardswoman," said the man smiling. "My name is Jord, and as you have probably guessed by now, I deal in flesh. Not just any flesh, mind you, but *young* flesh. Flesh that doesn't die quickly in route and can easily be trained. Which is why I am here. The offspring of guardswomen are in especially high demand."

Freya resisted the impulse to cut him down where he stood. Instead, she laughed. "You cannot expect us to just hand over our children. You will have to *fight* for them, and judging by your meager numbers, your men will be slaughtered!"

Jord chuckled. "I am no fool, lady. It was *I* who sent your commander the call for help. I saw them leave and I know they have not returned. By now, they are two days distant and can be of no help to you." He pointed to the garrison. "And, I must say, a novel idea to make the garrison appear staffed. Had I not known better, I would have turned away. But you see, I *do* know better. We can easily overrun you." He took a deep breath, exhaled slowly, and smiled.

"Therefore, I make this offer in both our interests. At dawn tomorrow, I will attack. Anyone left inside will be mine. Since women are worth no more to me than a moment's pleasure, you and any other women inside may leave before then. *But all children must stay*."

Freya stood over her sleeping daughter, who was curled up beneath their furs. All night she had paced the walls of the garrison, keeping lookout and thinking, searching for some escape from their predicament. But she could see no way out. Which was why she stood looking down at her daughter: to exercise their last option. They must not be taken alive.

She had known it all along, but had not wanted to admit it. Now the sun had already begun to lighten the horizon and stirring sounds could be heard from the enemy camp. She was worried she had tarried too long.

Kneeling down beside their shared pallet, she kissed her daughter and brushed back her sleep-mussed hair. The dawn's dim light was already bright enough that she could make out the child's beautiful features. Although she had never admitted it to anyone, Neola was the most beautiful of all the other children.

Freya blinked back tears and drew her knife from her belt. Neola would be first, in case she did not finish with the others in time. The warrior kissed her child once more, said a silent prayer to the Goddess Mother, and held the blade to her daughter's throat. Tears filled her eyes, making it difficult to see. She wiped them with the back of her hand. "Bye, little one," she said and tensed to slash.

A firm hand pulled Freya away from the child. She rolled, expecting one of the attackers, but found only elderly Amada. "Hold, warrior!" said the older woman. "There is another way. We can defeat them!"

Freya shook her head. "Are you crazy, old woman? There are more than enough men out there to utterly destroy us—ten for every one I can kill."

Amada looked the warrior straight in the eye. "You may believe I am old and senile, but I know what I am about! There is hope . . . and your daughter is the key!"

Freya stared at her in silence, unsure.

Amada stood. "Unless you enjoy killing children, awaken them all and come to the garrison wall over the gate." Amada started out and called over her shoulder. "And bring your sling!"

The children stood frightened and cold on the garrison wall. Most stood numbly while a few whimpered softly. Only the older ones had an idea of the fate which awaited them.

Clearly visible at the bottom of the hill, their attackers were preparing their ropes and ladders to breach the walls. Their pace was leisurely. After all, what had they to fear?

Amada quickly positioned the children in an oblong circle, holding hands. Neola was positioned on the garrison's outer wall in front of the circle, facing their attackers. Freya couldn't help but think how insane this appeared.

"Neola, do you still have the sky-stone?" asked Amada.

The young girl nodded.

"May I have it?"

Neola took the necklace off and handed it to the priestess, who quickly snapped the strip of cloth and handed the stone to Freya. "Use your sling to place this stone at the center of their column."

"This is insane."

"*Do it*! There is not time to argue."

Freya measured the distance and shook her head. "I do not believe I can throw it that far. I will have to try a practice shot."

Reaching in her pouch, she pulled out a stone of roughly the same size, took aim, and let it fly. But it fell far short. Noting the outlaw party had begun marching up the hill, Freya selected another and tried again, angling it higher. This one went farther, but again fell short.

"There is no more time!" yelled Amada. "You must

do it now, before they get closer. But don't release it until I tell you to!"

Carefully slipping the sky-stone into the sling and starting it whirling over her head, Freya concentrated on the target: funneling all her energy and skill into that one shot.

Amada took her place in the circle of children and gave them their last instructions. "Everyone think of the sky-stone. Give Neola all the help you can." She looked to Neola. "Child, call to the sky, just like we did with the stones. Call to the sky-stones high above us. Make one come down to visit his brother! Now everyone, *concentrate*!"

Each of the children squeezed their eyes shut, doing as they were told. Neola's face became a solid mask of effort; all color drained from her face.

Over Freya's head, the stone whirled, faster and faster, whispering through the air with a speed she had never before reached. The very straps of leather seemed ready to tear.

A tension grew in the air as power gathered around them; the hair on each child's head stood up. Flickers of light danced between them, and the very wall of the garrison began to shake. The old priestess began to tremble and struggled to stand.

"Now!" screamed Amada.

Freya released the stone angled high; it arched toward the enemy, traveling farther than she would have dreamed possible, falling just inside their numbers. Then above, a streak of light appeared, glowing brighter and brighter: a star from the heavens streaking closer and closer. A piece of the sky.

With blinding speed, it shot toward the troop. The outlaws had time to look up and scream in terror as the falling star struck the earth, exploding in white light and a deafening roar. A burst of hot air knocked Freya to the wall floor, where she lay dazed against the low inside wall, pelted by falling stones and dirt.

Moments later, all grew still. Freya sat up and inventoried the children. All were covered with dirt and crying, but unharmed. Amada had pulled Neola down from the wall at the last minute and shielded her with her own body. The two sat holding each other.

Freya took the whimpering Neola from Amada and gathered the other children closer around her, spoke reassurances, and brushed back tears. In those few moments she came to realize that it was a good thing she had been there. If she hadn't, she would have come back to find Neola gone. When others went into battle, there was no shame in staying behind with the children.

Standing together, Amada and Freya looked over the wall to where the enemy had been. All that remained was a large and smoking hole. Freya turned and stared at Amada in horror, not believing the destruction.

The old woman smiled and swelled with pride. "I *told* you she had the power. *Now* do you believe me?"

HAWK'S HILL

by Gary Herring

In spite of the emphasis I put on plot in a story, I am not at all indifferent to other elements in a story; and this one contains a good deal of subtext; the important things in our lives are more than just "what happens." I firmly believe that a story should have a firm plot—but it should also have other things; real people, ethic patterns, searing moral choices—without ever preaching.

Why, then, am I always harping on plot, and "what happens" in a story? Because if nothing happens, people are not likely to read enough of it to find whatever message you are trying to put across.

Just for the fun of it, try reading this story—and all the other stories in this anthology—and figure out what point they're making, or why the writer bothered to tell this story about these particular people. Then go back and see if your point can be deduced from what you write. A story with no moral isn't worth writing; a story with no plot isn't worth reading. And if people get your point before they get your story, you ought to hire a soapbox instead.

Gary Herring is twenty-eight years old, and lives in Alabama.

Sharik stood at the foot of Hawk's Hill and swallowed nervously as she stared up its slope. With just the moon and two lanterns to see by, the hill was a huge, featureless shadow looming against the summer stars. At its top was the ruin of the Healer's shrine, where—according to Old Alfri—ghosts rose up some nights to do battle with one another. *Cursed ground,* the old storyteller would say. *There's a ghost for every tree.*

"There aren't any ghosts on Hawk's Hill," Sharik whispered to herself. That had been easy to say in the yard of her folks' inn, with the sun overhead. Now, standing dry-mouthed before the cobblestone path that led up to the old shrine, with owls calling to one another amongst the trees, the lanky twelve-year-old with the russet hair found the words a lot less convincing.

Not that she let that show to the little group of children that had been waiting for her here. Especially not to Gedr, Lord Kivan's only son, nor to Big Finn, who held one of the lanterns and, as always, stood right at Gedr's shoulder. Instead, Sharik did her best to look bored with the whole notion of haunts.

Gedr looked behind her and grinned. "Brung your bodyguard?" he asked.

Sharik looked over her shoulder at her ten-year-old brother, Solvi. He was staring anxiously up the path, as if he expected an army of ghosts and trolls to come howling down upon them at any moment. Nervous laughter rippled through the group of children and Sharik felt her face getting hot. "Runt's carrying my light for me," she snapped.

Gedr ignored her. "You gonna stay up here and protect your sister, Runt?" he taunted Solvi. "When the ghosts finish with her, they'll have you for dessert."

Solvi looked wide-eyed at Gedr, and Sharik gritted her teeth. The Runt always got like this when Gedr mocked him; stiff as a board and never so much as a squeak, even when taunts turned to pinches and blows. She was as surprised as anyone when Solvi suddenly chanted in a loud, clear voice:

Lord Osric is a mighty man,
With hair upon his chest.

'Gainst a ham in his dining hall,
He's at his fighting best.

Sharik grinned and the others snickered. One boy laughed aloud and was angrily shushed by Finn. That rhyme had dogged Gedr's kin since his grand-da, Lord Osric, had let the Healer's shrine be looted and burned. Old Alfri taught it to all the children of Rivermouth. Gedr turned red in the lantern light and took a step toward Solvi.

Sharik was between them in an instant. Gedr scowled, but he backed down, remembering the black eye she'd given him the last time he'd touched the Runt. He drew something from a pouch at his belt and held it up in the light. The ten-mark coin gleamed silver, and there were gasps from the other children.

"This says we'll find you hiding in your bed in the morning," Gedr said coldly. "I'll bet it against that knife of yours."

Sharik touched the hilt of the knife tucked in her belt. Her da had bought it from a peddler who'd visited the inn on her birthday. She'd spent the whole day pleading for the little blade after she'd seen it in his pack. If Da ever found out she'd lost it in a bet, he'd peel her.

But ten marks was as much money as they saw in the inn in nearly a week, and she'd sooner die than back down to Gedr now, in front of everybody. "All right," she said, angry at her voice for quivering.

"Let's go, then," Gedr said, taking the lead as usual. Finn and Solvi held their lanterns high and everyone trooped up the path to the top of the hill. It was tricky going with just two lights. Weeds had grown up through the paving, and some of the stones had been washed away. Halfway up, Solvi suddenly turned his lantern on the nearby trees. Sharik stumbled and went sprawling with a word she'd heard her father use on rowdy guests.

"Dammit, Runt," she hissed, fingering her scraped knee, "if you're gonna hold the light, shine it on the ground!"

"I heard something moving," her brother whispered. "M–maybe it's a Hawk's ghost."

Sharik rose to stand beside him and stared into the trees that covered the slope of Hawk's Hill, her hand on her knife. Solvi cast the lantern's beam back and forth, making the shadows dance crazily.

"Must've been a rabbit," she said. "We aren't at the top of the hill yet." Her palms were sweaty. She wiped them on her shirt and added loudly. "Besides, there aren't any ghosts on Hawk's Hill."

"Old Alfri says he saw a Hawk on the hilltop; all in armor, with a big sword. And I heard that a tramp spent the night up here when he got turned away from the chapel in town. The ghosts ate him."

"Where'd you hear *that*?"

"Finn told me so today."

Sharik snorted and resumed walking. Solvi had to hurry to keep up. "Old Alfri can't see his hand at the end of his arm," she told him, "and Finn was trying to scare you. You know he's just Gedr's echo. Nobody gets turned away from the chapel. Gedr says he slept up here last night, and if he can do it, then anybody can."

"He saw ghosts, too. Remember?"

Sharik remembered. Three times that day Gedr had told the story of how he'd slept in the shrine and seen the ghosts of the Hawks and the raiders fighting. The ghosts had gotten uglier—and Gedr bolder—with each telling. "He was just boasting, Runt. Like he always does."

Solvi was quiet for awhile, then he whispered, "You don't have to stay up here alone. When the others leave, I can come back. I'll hide when they come in the morning and you can just say you were alone."

Sharik snorted again. "Sure you will, Runt."

"I'm not scared."

Then why are you shaking? Sharik was about to ask it aloud when she recalled how Solvi had stood up to Gedr. He'd never done that before, not even with her around, and to do it with Big Finn to back Gedr up if there had been a fight . . .

"I know you aren't, Runt," she said, "but remember what Ma says? If you're caught cheating . . ."

"It's for life," Solvi finished morosely.

"I'll be all right." Sharik paused, then added, "There aren't any ghosts on Hawks' Hill."

The gateway in the shrine's courtyard wall stood empty. On the arch over the gateway was a carving of the Lady as the Healer, to whom this place had once been dedicated. Sharik regarded it with a little shudder. In the tapestries hanging in the chapel in town, the Healer always smiled gently. This worn stone face seemed to wear a hungry grin, like a ghost that hoped for a little girl to eat.

Just a trick of the light, she told herself as she took the lantern from her brother. "See you tomorrow," she said to Gedr as she strode past him and into the courtyard.

"We'll look under your bed first," Big Finn called after her, and Gedr's echo laughed as he and the others started back down the hill. Sharik watched Finn's lantern until it was out of sight, and then held her own up for a better look around.

Untended for forty years, the shrine's courtyard looked no different from the woods outside the wall, save that the trees were smaller. Sharik harked back to Old Alfri's tales of the fine gardens that the healing Sisters had tended here, and tried to imagine what the place had looked like when the storyteller had been her age, before the sea-raiders had come down from the North. She gave it up with a shake of her head. She couldn't picture this mess as having ever been pretty.

Everybody in Rivermouth knew the story about Hawk's Hill. The first priestess, Alwilde, had seen the town's founding, and she had left behind a staff of carved wood that could be used to cast healing spells. The sick and the faithful had come from all over the province and from up and down the coast, either to be healed or to watch the relic at work, and a squad of

Hawks had been quartered on the hill to protect the shrine and its precious staff.

The Hawks were a martial order of women sworn to the Warrior, taking a bird sacred to Her as their namesake. They guarded temples and fought bandits and the like. Sharik had seen some once, as they had ridden past town. Thirty or forty women bearing swords, with red, spread-winged birds painted on the shields slung on their backs. She'd been disappointed when they had ridden on by without slowing, but no Hawk ever visited Rivermouth anymore.

Carefully, Sharik picked her way through the waist-high grass toward the stone building that squatted in the center of the courtyard. The shrine's chapel was the only building still standing here. The others—hospital, barracks, storehouses—had been of wood. The first hints the folks in Rivermouth had had of something wrong on that long ago night had been the fires atop the hill and the alarm bell from down the shore.

Lord Osric had sent no aid to the shrine. Instead he'd prepared quickly for an attack on the town, passing out weapons and armor to the townspeople and sending messengers upriver to Adienne for reinforcements. The pirates had reached Rivermouth just before daybreak, and, failing to take the town by surprise, they had tried unsuccessfully to fight their way past the town wall. The soldiers from Adienne had arrived a day later, forcing the Northerners to break off and return to their ships. Only when they had disappeared over the horizon had Lord Osric taken his men to the shrine, along with a column of Hawks that had accompanied the town's relief.

Sharik found that the chapel doors were gone, just like the courtyard gates. Inside, the chapel was a larger version of the one in town—a single, circular room with several high, narrow windows and a hole cut into the center of the ceiling to let the moonlight shine on the altar for ceremonies. The altar was gone, though, and the floor was covered with leaves and twigs that the wind had blown in through the empty doorway.

The defenders had made their last stand here. Lord Osric and the Hawks from Adienne had found it a slaughterhouse. They had buried the dead with rites to lay any ghosts, and then searched the smoking ruins for Alwilde's staff. When no trace of the relic was found, hard words had passed between the Lord of Rivermouth and the Hawk captain.

The Hawks had ridden away the next day, and none had set foot within Rivermouth's walls since. Children, and sometimes even his own men at arms, had sung taunts behind Lord Osric's back. He'd built a fine new chapel on his own lands and dedicated it to the Healer, but no new priestesses had come until he'd been five years in his grave. With Alwilde's staff lost, Hawk's Hill was left to the dead.

Sharik examined the chapel thoroughly, just to make sure there were no rats or snakes about. Satisfied, she sat on the cold stone floor and leaned back against the chapel wall. Looking at the empty windowsills and the weeds growing through the flagstones, she debated whether or not to put out her lantern. She didn't relish sitting there in the shadows, but the oil would be used up before long and she might need light later. She blew out the flame, and the darkness closed about her like a fist.

Sharik wished she'd brought some bread to lay where the altar had been, and perhaps a little wine filched from the inn's stock. Would the Lady have been pleased, or would She ignore offerings made in a ruined shrine? Had She listened to the rites given for those slain here, or had She punished them for the destruction of Her shrine by abandoning their shades to walk?

"There aren't any ghosts on Hawks' Hill," Sharik reminded herself, but she expected a long and wakeful night just the same.

Sharik awoke with a start. She looked around at the gloomy old chapel and thought, *Lord and Lady, did I really fall asleep here*? Then she wondered, *What woke me*?

A sound came to her ears. A hammering sound, from somewhere outside. She listened carefully. There it was again. And again! Were those voices?

All of the stories she'd ever heard about ghosts and unwary travelers came rushing back to her. She took a deep breath and tried to swallow the sudden terror that made her stomach flutter. Her eyes were used to the shadows now, so she left her lantern where it was and crept to the doorway.

The noises had stopped, but there was a light moving around out there amongst the weeds. A lantern! Oh, Lady, had her parents missed her? Had Solvi been caught sneaking back home? She'd never sit down again, and if they dragged her back, she'd lose the bet, and her knife, to Gedr. But if it was her parents, why weren't they calling her?

Sharik grinned suddenly. Gedr! It had to be. Ten marks was a lot of money, even for Lord Kivan's son, so he'd come back with Finn and some others to scare her into running away.

Slipping out the doorway, she picked up a good-sized rock and moved quietly through the remains of the priestesses' garden, toward the light. *Let me get close enough for a good shot at you, Gedr*, she thought gleefully. *Then we'll see who runs home.*

But instead of some boys wrapped up in someone's bedlinen, she found a lantern resting on the ground by a spade and a mattock. The lantern shone on a pile of rocks and a hole in the ground. The rocks looked like old flagstones, and the hole was about three feet across with sides of mortared brick. Handholds had been cut down its side.

Sharik dropped her little rock and picked up the lantern. She held it down into the shaft as far as she could reach, but she couldn't see the bottom. One of the shrine's wooden buildings had stood here, she guessed, and the flagstones were from its floor, long since covered over with dirt and weeds. The pit must have been a well or a privy. But what were the handholds for, and why had it been sealed? And, Lord and Lady, who would come to Hawks' Hill in the dead of night to dig it up? Sharik didn't think she wanted to know. Better to get back to the chapel and hide until daybreak. She set down the lantern and turned . . .

. . . And found herself looking up at a giant, bearded figure whose eyes were empty sockets in its yellowy face, and whose teeth were bared in a skull's grin.

Sharik's mouth fell open, but her chest felt squeezed tight and no sound came. She took a step back and her foot came down on nothing. Flailing her arms, she began to topple back into the shaft. The ghost caught her by the shirtfront and hauled her back to solid ground. Then it dropped a bundle it had been carrying under its other arm, and its free hand came around to strike her hard across the face.

Sharik's last thought was that the ghost's hungry cries sounded just like the wailing of a baby.

"This is it! This sign leaves no doubt!"

The rumbling voice was the first thing Sharik heard. Her jaw ached and there was a taste of blood in her mouth from a split lip. She tried to put her hands to her head to stop its ringing, but they were tied behind her back. Her feet were bound, too. Carefully, she opened her eyes and found that her knife was gone.

Looking around, she saw a small, dry room lit by two lanterns hung on brackets set into the walls. The room was made of the same mortared brick as the sides of the wellshaft. Sharik saw a circular hole in one corner of the ceiling and guessed that the room was at the bottom of the shaft. Two big knapsacks and a little bundle wrapped in a horse blanket lay in the center of the floor. Two men stood before the wall farthest from the shaft, with their backs to her.

"They hid it well, the sly bitches," one of them said in the deep voice she'd heard before. He was a big man in a bearskin cloak—so tall that his head brushed the ceiling. When he turned, Sharik saw that his beard and braided hair were as white as snow, and that his face was seamed with age. It was the face of her ghost. His weird appearance before had been a trick of the lantern light.

"Bjan thought they must have hidden it with magic," he was saying, "but we didn't have a mage with us, so that did us no good. Can you open it, Jeral?"

The smaller man had dark hair and a smooth, pale face. If Sharik had seen him in the inn, she'd have taken him for a merchant. "I can open it, Ugi," he said in an accented voice. "They had no time for artistry with you and your comrades beating at the door, and the staff wasn't really meant for such things as this. The ward will be no trouble."

The man called Ugi grinned at this, but his smile faded and Sharik watched him come striding toward her. Had he seen her move? She held herself still and narrowed her eyes to slits, but he ignored her and nudged the blanket-wrapped bundle on the floor with the toe of his boot.

"Is this the only way?" he demanded.

"It is the only way that I know," the man called Jeral replied, coming up to stand beside him. "There are other ways, and perhaps I could learn them, but that would take much time, and the wrong people might hear." Sharik saw him nod in her direction.

Ugi followed his gaze. "Use her, then," he said. "She looks young enough, and that will make certain that no one will hear."

"We can't be sure of her, not at her age. These country brats give it away as soon as they can, and the requirements of the spell are very specific. Why should we take the risk when we already have what we need?" Jeral gave the big man a mocking look. "Does the age make such a difference to you? Who would have thought you so squeamish. Perhaps you do not want this prize so badly after all?" He laughed.

The old man's face didn't change, but his hand came to rest upon the hilt of a great dagger at his hip and Jeral's laughter stopped at once.

"I have sought the damned staff," Ugi said softly, "for almost all of my life." He nodded at Sharik. "I was scarcely older than her when I saw it last, on the day Bjan's band burned this place down around its keepers. I alone have never stopped seeking it." He shook himself and his voice became a rumble again. "Ready yourself. We'll do it as you say."

"And the girl?" Jeral asked.

"If you fail, she must not carry tales. If you succeed, it won't matter. We'll have nothing to fear, ever again."

Jeral nodded and began rummaging through one of the knapsacks, removing little bottles and pouches and carrying them to the back of the chamber. Sharik watched him light several fat candles and arrange them in a circle on the floor. With the additional light, she could see that there was something painted in red on the wall before him.

A great, spread-winged bird.

Muttering under his breath, Jeral opened a leather pouch and poured a line of white powder along the base of the wall. Then he set a small brazier at the center of the circle of candles and lit a fire in it. Chanting aloud now, in a tongue Sharik had never heard before, he knelt and poured dried leaves and the contents of a small bottle into the brazier.

A cloud of dark smoke welled up from the brazier, but instead of rising to the ceiling, it flowed along the floor toward the bird-painted wall and began to creep over its surface. Jeral clasped his hands together and his chant grew louder.

A noise like stone moving against stone echoed deafeningly through the room, as if the hill's bones were grating together. Sharik had to set her jaw tightly to keep from crying out, and Ugi cast nervous glances at the walls of the chamber. Then the noise stopped as suddenly as it had started, and there was an open doorway in the wall where the bird sigil had been!

The magician gave a shuddery sigh and stood. He peered into the shadows beyond the doorway and said, "Bring the child and a lantern."

Sharik's heart thudded against her ribs, but Ugi picked up the bundle on the floor and unwrapped it, letting the blanket fall. Sharik's eyes opened wide with shock and she drew a sharp breath.

For a moment she thought the baby Ugi held was dead, but then it moved in the man's huge hands. It was asleep, likely drugged. That had been the source of those cries she'd heard when Ugi had caught her. Lord and Lady, where had they gotten it?

Ugi took a lantern from the wall and joined the magician by the doorway. Setting the baby down, he raised the light and looked into the darkness.

"It's her, by Ult," he exclaimed. "The commander." Sharik craned her neck to see what the big man was pointing at, but she was too far away.

"See there," Ugi was saying. "Bjan always swore his mace had broken her arm." He took a step forward. "I don't see—"

Jeral grabbed his arm. "Careful, fool," he hissed.

There was a sudden sound from the darkness, like the wings of some enormous bird. Ugi stumbled back, pale-faced. The hand holding the lantern trembled. "Ult's thunder," he whispered, staring into the shadows. "What was—did you see?"

"I saw. She guards the staff yet." Jeral knelt and arranged his tools. "We will not walk past her, but we don't have to. I can bring the staff to us."

Sharik heard the thrashing of wings again, and this time she thought she saw something moving at the edge of the shadows. Ugi drew back another pace. "Are you sure she can't get at us?"

The magician laughed dryly. "Do not fear this Hawk; she is caged. She cannot cross over the salt, and she could do little even if she did. They used the staff to bind her to that spot. A few paces from her carcass and she has no more substance than a cloud of smoke."

Sharik recalled from some of Old Alfri's stories that salt was supposed to keep ghosts and such from crossing thresholds. She watched the two men carefully. Jeral had gone back to his work, and Ugi stared raptly into the shadows. Neither was paying any mind to her. Curling up tightly, she tried to slip her hands under her bottom. Her shoulders ached and her wrists felt as though the rope was cutting through them, but with a bit of work, she got her hands in front of her and wriggled toward the knapsacks.

Jeral set the baby next to the brazier and added

something to the flame that turned it a bloody red, then he stood and drew a slim dagger from his belt. In the light of the brazier, the blade glowed as if fresh from a forge. "I am ready," Sharik heard him say. "Once the chant is begun, do not interrupt."

The wingbeats came again, frantically, and Ugi's face cracked in a cold grin. "She knows," he said. "After all this time, after all she's done, she's failed, and she knows it." His voice rose in a bearish roar. "YOU HAVE FAILED, BITCH!"

"Silence," Jeral snapped. He waited, and when the echoes of the old man's outburst had faded, he began to chant again.

Sharik found her knife in one of the knapsacks and began sawing at the cord binding her wrists. It was awkward work, but the cord finally parted. She rubbed her bruised wrists and tried to work some feeling back into her hands, then she went to work on the bonds at her ankles. The sound of wings was almost constant now.

With her feet free, Sharik rose to a crouch. They had forgotten her. She could get away easily. Once up the shaft, she could run home and tell her parents everything. Lord Kivan would send his men to take care of it.

But they were going to kill that baby. No matter how fast she ran home, no one would get here in time to save the child.

A calm, blue glow hung in the shadows, overpowering the red light from the brazier like water damping a fire. It took the shape of a staff topped with a carved bird, and the wingbeats came from somewhere near it. The magician's chanting grew louder as he drew shapes in the air with the point of his dagger.

Sharik charged. She was past Ugi before the old man had time to react, slamming into the magician and driving her little blade into his back. He yelled—more in surprise than in pain—and wrenched away from her. Sharik's knife came loose in her hand and she fell, scattering the candles and knocking over the brazier. Jeral's dagger clattered to the floor near the baby's head, and the magician stumbled forward.

Through the doorway.

Limned by the glow of the bird-staff, Jeral stood perfectly still for a moment, then he turned and lunged for the doorway. Sharik heard wings, and the magician was yanked back off his feet and out of sight. There was a single scream and a wet, tearing sound, then nothing. Sharik got to her feet and stumbled back away from the doorway, trying not to be sick.

There was a noise behind her and she whirled, holding her little knife in front of her with both hands. In the fading blue light from the doorway, Ugi faced her with a blade as long as her forearm. The look on the old giant's face told her, more plainly than any words, that she was going to die right where she stood.

"Damn you," he growled, stepping toward her. "Damnyou, damnyou . . ."

Something flew through the doorway over a scuff the magician had made in the salt at the threshold, and Sharik had a fleeting sensation of wings folding gently around her. She looked at Ugi, who stared back slack-jawed, and something within her remembered him from a time when he'd been a beardless boy—a wild pup eager to kill and gain the respect of the older curs. That same something gauged the weight and balance of her knife, shifted her stance just so, and waited with a smile.

Ugi came barreling forward, dagger held low, his face showing as much fear as rage. Sharik threw her little knife, and the shrill cry of a hawk came bursting from her throat.

It was a little past dawn when Sharik heard her name being called. Rubbing her eyes wearily, she walked to the doorway of the old chapel and looked out. Solvi, Gedr, and a few of the other children were gathered at the empty gateway in the courtyard wall.

For just an instant, she saw the lovely garden that the overgrown and neglected courtyard had once been, but then the vision was gone and her brother was running toward her. Gedr stayed where he was, looking like a wife who'd found a rat in the butter churn. She gave him a grin and waved.

"You did it!" Solvi looked proud and relieved all at once. "Are you all right? Did you see any ghosts?" His eyes went wide when he noticed her split lip and the bruise on her jaw. "what happened to your face?"

Sharik laughed and hugged him. "I tripped in the dark. There aren't any ghosts on Hawks' Hill, Ru—Solvi. Gedr was just boasting, like always."

"Hurry up," Gedr called from the gateway. "We gotta get back." He turned to go.

"Hey, Gedr."

Gedr paused and looked back. "Don't forget," Sharik called, "you owe me ten marks."

Gedr scowled and marched back down the path.

"You go ahead, Solvi," she said. "I'll get my lantern and follow."

"Gedr's saying you cheated," Solvi confided. "When you weren't at home, he started saying you hid down at the bottom of the hill and came up here just before daybreak."

Sharik paused to consider this. She wasn't really surprised. Last night an accusation like that would have made her furious, but today she found that it really didn't matter to her what Lord Kivan's brat thought, and she wasn't really surprised by that, either. "Who cares what Gedr says," she told her brother with a smile. Solvi grinned and ran back down the path. Sharik watched him go, and then she went back into the chapel and picked up the baby.

Whatever the baby had been dosed with the night before seemed to be wearing off. She was making soft noises that would doubtless become hungry wails soon. *We'll get you fed at the inn, little sister*, Sharik promised silently, *and after I've explained how I got you, we'll see about finding your folks*.

Sharik grimaced at the thought of all the questions she'd have to answer, and of everything that had to be done. Lord Kivan would have to send someone to collect the bodies. The town priestess would likely have to send to Adienne for someone who could retrieve the staff and lay its guardian to rest, and a watch would have to be set over the chamber for however long that took. It wouldn't do at all for someone to wander into that chamber out of curiosity.

Thinking of the staff's guardian brought back the memories—places she had never been, the faces of friends she had never known, the feel of a sword in someone else's hand. They were fading. Soon they'd all be gone, but she didn't mind. She'd remember the happiness at having kept the treasure safe, and the warm gratitude that had filled her like a mug of hot cider on a winter's night. Those memories were enough.

Smiling, Sharik rested the baby on her hip and started on the path down the hill. From somewhere far overhead, a hawk's cry greeted the new day.

WATERWISE

by Mary Frey

Another theme that keeps coming up in the pile of stories on my desk—I almost said the never-ending pile—is a sorceress faced with a final exam in her craft. Like all the "old themes" I bought, this one strikes me as a little different.

Mary Frey has also appeared in one of my Darkover anthologies. Often, in writing, granting the basic skill of writing a literate English sentence—which can no longer be taken for granted even in college graduates—all it takes is determination. That and applying the seat of the pants to the seat of the chair—not to mention putting brain in gear before engaging typewriter.

Mary Frey teaches French for a living and is "still working on my novel, of course, while trying not to totally ignore the housework and not to forget to feed the cats somewhat regularly."

That's the way most writers work—trying to keep the house sufficiently picked up so the health department doesn't interfere—in the cracks and crevices of real life (which means what's happening in the book).

The elixir dripped with excruciating slowness from the tip of the crystal pipette into the ivory-footed chalice. Sitting cross-legged before the distilling apparatus, a woman whose silver hair belied her youth schooled herself to patience, forcing the muscles of neck, shoulders, and arms to remain loose beneath her blue silken robes.

There must be no error in decanting the mixture, no failure of any part over which she exercised control. She raised her hands that had been resting palms up on her knees, spread slender, ringed fingers toward the silver rim of the chalice, and recited the final lines of the spell. A last droplet quivered at the lip of the pipe and fell to join the others in the goblet.

Keilin exhaled, aware once more of her surroundings. A single ray of early sunlight through the chamber's crosspaned window set dust motes to dancing along its path. The chill of the stone floor seeped into her cramped legs. She breathed in the distinctive scent of the herbs and powders stored in pots on the workroom's many shelves.

Despite their age, the door's hinges made no sound, and the dark-robed newcomer slid into the room through the narrowest of openings. If Keilin had not been listening and watching for his arrival, she might have thought he used some magic simply to appear here. There had been a time when she first came to the Collegium, before she had learned the ways herself, when she could have been as easily fooled as the townsfolk.

"Good morn, Master Giraud," she nodded politely to the tall, thin man.

"The elixir is prepared," he commented, looking not at her, but at the distillery. There was no need to ask if she had performed the work correctly. Every student knew the price of inattention to task. Once you left the Collegium with whatever rank you had managed to achieve, there would be no one to check constantly that you had prepared your tools and yourself accurately. "Let us go to the water."

Of the four elements, water was to be Keilin's final trial, and if she fared no better than on the three previous occasions, her training would be ended. Not completed, merely ended. She would be entitled to call herself an adept and seek out any clientele she wished. Of course, they would be people who sought little more than a love potion or a fortunetelling. The prestigious, profitable commissions were for true sorcerers, those who had proven their mastery over one of the elements.

Wordlessly, Giraud led her out of the workroom and down a long, shadowed hallway. Keilin kept her eyes down, focusing alternately on the chalice between her hands and the flagstones beneath her feet. They passed other people, but no one spoke lest they disturb her concentration on what lay ahead. Master and student crossed a courtyard with its brief moment of morning sunlight and sweet scent of wakening blossoms.

It was not the thought of prestige or profit which had brought her to this day, Keilin reminded herself as they reached the stairs and she set her foot to the top step. Even an adept who had skills in only one or two elements in his repertoire could attract a good number of clients in a city the size of Iroania.

But there were more urgent wants than keeping one's stomach filled or the icy winter winds from one's back. Keilin wanted to know she had the skill necessary to master water. Regardless of what princeling's court or wealthy guildhouse might have use for a master sorceress, she wanted to know just for herself that she could be one of the waterwise.

The stairway wound downward, dark except for the torches spaced along the stone wall on their right which provided just enough greenish light to mark the steps. To their left was nothing but air, palpable with damp and the echo of unseen, unknown depths. It was not a place to misstep. Keilin followed Giraud down into the growing silence until he reached a perceptibly wider step and paused, indicating with one hand unfolded from his sleeves that she should precede him through an arched doorway in the wall.

Several steps along a darkened corridor brought them out into a high-vaulted cavern lit by a pervasive azure glow. The sounds of the sea reached her ears, setting every inch of her skin atingle. The stone flooring sloped downward, ending in an expanse of glittering sand lapped by dark seawater. Her heart thudded against her ribs.

Keilin walked slowly down to the water. She felt the sand tickle between her toes. At the first touch of the water on her skin, she paused. This was the last honorable chance to decline the test. Once she entered the water, chanted the words, and swallowed the elixir, there would be no halting the process.

Every student at the Collegium knew the four possible outcomes of an element testing. The worst, from the viewpoint of a would-be adept or sorcerer, was total rejection. This meant you had attempted the trial before you had acquired the necessary skills—an indication of arrogance that ended your training immediately. Having been accepted three times before, Keilin no longer feared this might happen.

There was always the chance the element would be too strong for your skills. You might be entrapped in the spell, doomed to live out the rest of your allotted days in some magic-wrought form. There were beasts and birds and other strange creatures within the walls of the Collegium who had once been students just like Keilin. They were cared for, but pitied. Keilin dreaded pity.

Every adept and sorcerer who had skill enough to use the four elements bore the signs of his or her testing. If you failed to master an element, it changed you in some way so that you remembered forever the limits of your skills. Three times before today, Keilin had emerged from a test changed.

She had struggled against the earth, feeling herself grow roots that drew nourishment from the soil, and returned to a body that would no longer be mistaken for a young boy's. She had drifted, insubstantial as any other cloud on the wind, and returned to gaze into a mirror that showed the brown eyes she had from her parents changed to the shifting hues of the sunset sky. She had burned as a white-hot flame, and returned with her once-dark hair silver white.

If you had the strength and skill to master an element, however, you were returned unchanged, bearing a talisman that became the focus of all your spell-weaving. Giraud, for example, carried with him a flawless jewel in which a flame of power burned. No mortal was master of more than a single element.

And the water was Keilin's last opportunity to attain her goal.

That thought strengthened her resolve. She shrugged off the blue silk robe and waded out until the seawater reached her waist, carefully holding the chalice raised before her. She turned to look at the master sorcerer who waited at the entrance to the cavern. There was nothing he could tell her, even if rules permitted it, about what would happen once she had swallowed the elixir. Everything up to that moment might be taught, but when you surrendered yourself to the Unknown, only the gods decreed your fate.

Still, Keilin thought, *some word of encouragement would be nice.*

As if she had actually spoken, Giraud turned his head to look at her for the first time since she had entered the water. She saw his mouth move before the words made any sense. "I will wait for you until sunset."

Keilin's hands trembled as she raised the chalice to her lips and her voice refused to rise above a whisper. She glanced down and saw the colorless potion she had prepared was changing, taking on all the colors of the rainbow as she spoke the formula.

She closed her eyes and gulped it down.

How will he know, deep inside this cavern, when the sun sets? she wondered fleetingly.

The stone walls around her began to spin, a roar like rushing water filled her ears, and she was suddenly too weak to stand. The chalice tumbled from her fingers and she felt the sea close over her face.

"Ahai! I've caught us a mermaid," a man's voice proclaimed as the net was pulled from the sea.

Keilin shut her eyes against the sudden brightness of unwatered sunlight and lay still so the fibers of the net would not grate any more painfully against her skin. The way it twined itself around her, trapping her arms behind her back so that she could not reach the help available in her rings, told it was spelled in some way. She cursed herself for seven kinds of a fool for having let her curiosity bring her so close to the the strange ship.

The net swung in the air as the water rushed off her and she cried out in pain as she was dashed against the ship's wooden hull.

"Leave her in the net, Ossig," a woman's voice said. "See the rings on her fingers? This is no sea creature, but some sorceress sent by Prince Rymon to spy on me."

"Shall I dispatch her now, milady?" Keilin's eyes snapped open just in time to see the glint of sunlight on a wickedly slender blade. The face behind it was pockmarked, half concealed beneath a curly black beard. A toothy smile appeared below the mustache. "Or get rid of that fish's tail and have myself a little fun?"

Keilin opened her mouth to protest that she was but a student, no sorcerer in the employ of Iroania's lord. She wished suddenly that she had been a tad less absorbed in her studies, so that she had paid heed to the common gossip about the prince and his enemies.

"Just slide your knife in behind her to keep those hands apart," the woman ordered. "That'll stop her singing." Keilin twisted her head around and saw tightly wound auburn braids, a beautiful face distorted by smugness, and the glittering silver and green of some court sorceress's robes. Once more she tried to explain, but at the touch of bare metal against her wrists, even the singing abandoned her. "Doesn't your fool of a lord know better than to send one of his beautiful harlot-witches against the likes of me? You'll do me no harm now. If you mind your manners, I *may* remove the knife after sunset."

Although the pain was intense, Keilin thrashed against the net. The young woman knew perfectly well that if she was still in this form when the last rays of the sun vanished into the sea, there would be no changing back. She would be the innocent victim of a quarrel she knew nothing of until moments ago. For the first time in her life, Keilin hated.

"Lady Ahai, a ship is approaching," another man's voice reported.

The sorceress leaned toward the net. "You'll keep safe here for the while," she promised in a way that sent shivers down Keilin's spine. "He'll not get you back, even if he does win."

The deck of the ship erupted in a flurry of footsteps and voices shouting directions for deployment of the sails. Keilin looked up and saw the great widths of red cloth fill with a wind that did not reach where she was imprisoned. The stench of sulfur filled her nostrils and her stomach heaved. The nausea increased as the ship rocked under an assault of contrary winds sent from the other, unseen ship. Overhead, a scarlet sail screamed as it was rent by the blast and tore lose from the spar. A flapping, grommet-studded end slapped onto Keilin's net, cutting into the delicate rows of scales. She cried out, but no one heard.

Sometime later she smelled woodsmoke as well as sulfur and guessed that some part of the ship was afire. At least if the ship were to sink with her still bound in the net and rendered helpless by the knife, she would not drown in her present form. She could lie quietly on the sea-bottom for hours until the spells in fiber and metal finally abated. It would probably be long after sunset, though, judging by the current angle of the sunlight—too late for her to resume human form. But she would not die.

It was little consolation to think that she would be entrapped in this form through no fault of her own, the victim of some fight not of her making and the malice of some sorceress to whom she had done absolutely nothing.

A new, fetid smell reached her now. With great effort, she turned her head in its direction and saw gigantic purplish, suckered tentacles grasping the side of the ship. Some waterwise sorcerer on the enemy ship—no, the prince's ship, she corrected herself quickly—must have raised the great creature from the depths. Would it know that she was not one of those who fought its master?

"Call it off!" Ahai's voice suddenly rasped in her ear, and she felt the blade slide away from her wrists. "I will cut you loose, Waterwise, if you will send the monster back where it belongs." In an instant, the net fell away and Keilin was flopping as helplessly as any just-hooked fish on the deck of the ship. "Do it!" Ahai knelt and pressed the blade into the hollow at the base of her neck. "Or you die right here, Waterwise."

Although her mind formed words, her mouth could utter only a strange song. She prayed that Ahai was spellweaver enough to understand she was saying that she was naught but a student in the midst of a testing, not waterwise at all. The deck tilted alarmingly beneath the two women, and Ahai let go of her as they slid down its length toward the gaping suckered mouth of the sea monster.

A sharp pain shot across Keilin's scalp at the same moment she realized the sorceress would reach that awful opening first. Her own silvery hair, loose and wet, was tangled in the remnants of the net in which she had been caught a few moments before. Immobilized, she watched as Ahai vanished into the mouth, screaming curses at Prince Rymon and all his kind.

Keilin looked away from the eagerly pulsing suckers, and tried to free herself from the last bit of the net. She told herself that this was not the moment to end the illusion—she had to get away from the creature and the whole nasty business, and she could swim much more quickly with the fish's tail than with two legs. The test would not be judged successful unless she returned to the cavern as she was and Master Giraud witnessed her return to her normal body. And she had not yet claimed a talisman from the seabed.

She plopped into the water, no longer awkward once she could use her tail as it was intended. Frantically, she dove beneath the monster's body and swam away. When no writhing tentacles were visible in any direction, she surfaced and looked around.

Behind her, the boneless mass of the creature's body

was undulating over what remained of the ship. She heard screams and surmised the rest of Ahai's crew was being consumed. She told herself it was no less than they deserved for having followed that evil woman in her battle with Prince Rymon, and she reminded herself that it was not *her* fight in any case. A half turn in the water showed her the sun, a fiery orange ball, just touching the horizon far out to sea. Talisman or no, she had to get back to the cavern.

Keilin used the last strength in her arms to pull herself partway up onto the strip of sand. She could not even raise her head to see if Giraud was still waiting at the entrance for her. A bit of red sun had been still visible above the horizon when she swam into the narrow channel in the rocks that led to the cavern. Now, she could only recite and pray it was not too late.

In the midst of the vertigo that seized her, she was aware dimly that hands were wrapping her in a warm length of soft fabric, holding up her head to force some fiery liquid into her mouth, pushing some kind of tasteless chewy food between her teeth. A voice ordered her to rest, to swallow, to chew, and to swallow once more. She obeyed.

At last her eyes were able to open. She felt she still lay on the sand, and that she had two legs once more. Gradually she became aware that Master Giraud was kneeling beside her, watching for some sign of returning consciousness. "You were very late returning," he said quietly, in a tone that was not quite concern, not quite reproof.

Keilin drew in a deep breath. "I have failed again," she admitted. So she would be a minor adept after all, with small-minded clients who sought no more than to know if a business venture would succeed or to find some magical way to make another person fall in love.

But was that narrow concern with personal affairs any less selfish than the efforts of princes and great houses who used sorcerers to advance their own interests, trapping and slaughtering the innocent as they struggled to overpower each other? No one died for the sake of a love potion, and if it failed, the only thing lost was a passing fancy.

She would take a small house in the city, hang out her shingle, and help the innocent. There would be no splendid, glittering court robes and no great financial rewards when she succeeded in pleasing her employer. But neither would she die as Ahai had, cursing all princes and their kind.

"But you have returned unchanged," Master Giraud protested. "I have looked carefully . . ." his face flushed as he said it, ". . . and there is no change in you this time."

Keilin sat up and drew the blue silk robe around her. "Yes, there is," she replied.

THE SECOND SONG

by I.F. Cole

Isabel Cole's first story, "The Brass Horsemen," appeared in MZB'S FANTASY MAGAZINE while she was—and for all I know still is—in Hunter College High School in New York City. She says she gets her ideas from "mythology, classical music, opera and ballet."

I seem to have spent an inordinate amount of time in these introductions talking about recurrent themes, and one of the themes that keeps coming up in fantasy is that of the magical harp; maybe one of the reasons it keeps coming up in fantasy is that it is a very powerful metaphor for the human psyche.

After all, what's a harp—except a means of making music? And what is fantasy if not the means of daydreams? Don't we all have magic harps one way or the other?

Franz and I were returning from our journey, sharing an ancient war-horse we had bought for a few coins after border guards had stolen our horses a few weeks ago.

We were still free enough to run off on quests with light hearts—the country Franz ruled was nothing more than one city and a few miles around it. As his seer, I had enough power to amuse myself and fulfill my largely ceremonial function. We felt lucky for what we had, and we did not have enough to weigh us down.

Faint singing rose from the bundle on the horse's shoulder. The horse's gait jostled the harp, that marvelous instrument fascinating enough to send us on quests when we had a city to govern. The Nixies had given it to us, and it was certain no human hands had first played it. Its golden figures twining to make its frame seemed almost to be alive, and three rows of strings were stretched between them. The inner row of strings were finer than hairs and were not to be touched, but sang at the slightest movement, and vibrated in sympathy when the other strings were played, creating strange harmonies.

Franz could play it much better than I could. I tried not to let this bother me, but it did anger me that he could draw more out of the magical thing than I, a sorceress. Indeed, during this journey, I had begun to realize how inadequate my powers were. It occurred to me for the first time that I might only be a mediocre magic-worker, no better than a village witch, the kind who needs to scrape her power together for the least spell. Never until now had I doubted that I would soon feel the rush of power, the great inward opening that would make me a high sorceress.

From the top of the hill we could see the Heldau River glittering beyond wide flat grasslands. Just ahead of us was a guard tower.

"They're going to wonder what a couple of poor merchants are doing with such a fine harp, just as the other guards thought our horses too good for us," said Franz. "Could you change it so that it looks ordinary, and they won't be suspicious?" I had to shake my head. "Maybe they won't notice," he said.

I felt the harp singing within its wrappings, and the sound brought up my new bitterness again. By now the harp felt like a part of me—but a part I could barely touch, however much I beheld it. I envied Franz for the time he spent playing the harp. It would never sing so sweetly for me. Now that I felt how small my magic was, it was painful seeing him so easily drawing song from something from which I could only draw halting notes.

At the guard tower a group of bored young soldiers looked us over perfunctorily. We told them we were brother and sister. We looked enough alike, although Franz's eyes were blue and mine green, for we both had fair hair and slightly similar faces. There was little use for the deception; had we told the guards we were Ruler and High Seer of Morvenna on the Heldau they would not have batted an eye—in those days Morvenna was not counted highly among world affairs—but it was much more fun to adventure with assumed identities.

The guards seemed about to let us pass, when one gave a closer look at the bundle with the harp, and exclaimed, "This is a strange shape; let's have a look at it." A stab of fear went through me; I could not think of a spell, although Franz was looking at me, waiting for me to do something.

A murmur of awe went through the soldiers as the wrappings fell away from the harp.

"Where did you get something like this?" asked the red-haired captain sharply. He brushed aside our attempts to answer. "I'd better take you in for questioning." Mercifully, Franz did not draw his sword, though I saw he was thinking of it; he was a good swordsman, but there were at least twenty soldiers. Our horse was led away into the stable, and we were taken into the tower and tied up. The harp was placed on a table in the middle of the room, and the captain sat at the table looking us over.

"Where did you get this?" he asked. "Don't bother lying. We can always check up on your answers."

"Not this one," said Franz. "The Nixies gave it to us."

The guards sputtered with laughter. I shrank back into myself. I could change my shape, but that would do little good, it would only warn them of my magic and it would not help Franz.

"Pretty sister you have there," said the captain to Franz.

I crimsoned. "Don't touch me." My mind froze, my tongue readied.

"What'll you do—scratch my eyes out?"

"Just keep away from me if you really value your pathetic life."

His face flushed with anger for a moment. Then he laughed. He caressed the strings of the harp, and jerked his hand back with a cry. "What's wrong with this thing?" Tiny raised white lines sprang up on his reddened fingers.

"It's not yours," said Franz. The captain stood looking at us for a minute.

"All right," he said. "So you won't tell me where you got it. Perhaps you'll feel more inclined later on. I've got plenty of time. I'll start with your sister." The guards dragged me to my feet and cut the ropes binding me. The silence in the crowded room beat against me and made my head spin.

I heard Franz's voice, and, coming through the warm, swarming silence, it steadied me a little. I did not catch his words, but a guard kicked him in the ribs for it.

". . . but first," the captain was saying, "a little music. Play us a tune, my dear. It won't bite you if it's really yours." The room echoed with laughter, and all the guards leaned forward, eager to see me caught in my own trap. For an instant I felt almost weak with relief. The captain watched me, flexing his burnt fingers.

A ripple of warmth went through me at the first sound of the harp, rising from the inner strings through my hands, passing through me like a wash of light. I saw endless spaces within me, places where I could retreat and never be found, but also an infinite source of strength. I was too angry now to hide, and the new strength rose from the strange and distant place within me into my mind and hands. My eyes must have changed visibly as they went clear, for Franz relaxed almost imperceptibly.

I drew a tune out of the humming strings, twisting threads of sound together as I had often seen Franz do. I could not play half as well as he could, but it would be good enough. The captain watched, surprised and angry. At last he laughed harshly.

"You play a sweet tune," he said. "If you can play that vicious thing, you can take anything." His men laughed nervously. I smiled and kept playing. Two magics waxed and waned within me as I explored the new strength, and one transfixed me for awhile, rising from deep within the roots of common anger. Anger had always heightened my power, but I had never known what a strong power it could bring now that the way was clear. I could rip the captain to pieces, watch him choke as I forbade the air to enter his lungs, make his very blood burst into flame, and bring the stones of the tower down upon the bodies of him and his men. Eagerly my fingers skipped across the strings.

I listened to the twin songs within and around me, a second one touched off by the first, fey and innocent and playful, full of delight with its own beauty. The second song held me, and I felt the bitter magic fall back. I forgot where I was, and I was flushed and trembling with happiness, as I realized I had at last found the opening, the beginning of power.

The joyful song broke free from the harp strings, reaching into the air around it, lifting a sweet smell with it, twining around every face, every ear, every limb, so that all the men were frozen and transfixed. An image came into my mind, and I was amazed to see it realized.

Branches sprang up from the captain's feet, and a veil of green leaves wrapped around him as quickly as a scarf thrown against him by the wind. Tiny thorns pricked against his skin as the roses pressed tighter about him, their fragile white faces waving. He fell to his knees on the floor that had become a tossing sea of leaves and tendrils, roses surfacing as pale as the faces and hands of the Nixies. The men against the walls did not move, choked with the sleep of the twining, prickling stems; roses covered them as if they were only the stones of an old wall.

I came down from the table, holding the harp, and waded through the roses. A perfume rose from them, sweet but damp and mossy, like the depths of the forest, where we had met the Nixies swimming in the dark silent streams. The roses had crowded up to Franz, but had not entangled him. I cut him free with my knife and helped him up.

"Take your harp," I said. He looked at it as if he did not recognize it. "Take it. I'm no musician. I can't even carry a tune."

"What was that you were just doing?"

"That was magic."

He laughed. "You'll make a musician yet."

We picked our way out of the tower, brushing aside curtains of roses and stepping over sleeping bodies, and the harp sang to itself.

THE THORNY PATH TO WIZARDRY

by Lawrence Schimel

I sometimes wonder how writers manage to master the short short story; I find I think in blocks of a hundred thousand words; but here we have a very completely realized short-short where there is character as well as plot. I wish I knew Lawrence Schimel's secret of getting so much character into so few words.

On second thought, I suppose it's the same thing all good writers use; to get very completely inside your characters. I say you should know your characters so well that if you were waked out of a sound sleep at 3 a.m., you would know how a character spoke to his mother-in-law.

I think this one meets this criteria; it's very short without being only a gimmick disguised as a story.

I stumbled on a stone in the path and more water sloshed out of the bucket. "Why did he have to build his stupid hut so far from the river?" I grumbled. "He should have been smarter when he built his hovel than the gruel-brained oaf he must have been to build it where he did. I don't know how he ever completed his apprenticeship."

I was so busy cursing I forgot about the roots which stuck out onto the path. I went flying into a bramble patch and even more water sloshed out as the bucket landed a few feet away.

The thorn pricks hurt, but it was worse when I moved. I closed my eyes and rested for a moment. Whyever had I wanted to become a wizard's apprentice? This isn't how it's supposed to be. Getting married off looked promising at times like these.

But then there were the times when Arden actually taught me magic. They were definitely worth it. If only he'd test me for my gray robes so that I could start learning some real rituals instead of just cantrips. Maybe one to create water so I wouldn't have to lug it from the river all the time.

"The water for supper!" I sat up and instantly regretted it. Pain lanced through my back as thorns were pulled out. They tore even deeper into my legs.

Slowly I disentangled myself from the brambles, snacking on any ripe blackberries I found. The water was getting pretty low. I stared into the bucket wondering if I should bother going back to the river to get more. The light made rainbows sparkle off its surface, but it looked like something else was swimming in the water as well.

A gasping water sprite lay at the bottom of the pail. I knew it was a sprite even though I'd never seen one before. "You must be drowning in the air." I rushed back to the river, trying hard not to let the bucket swing wildly. I scooped water into the bucket and pulled it onto the shore before the sprite could get away. Wait until Arden heard about this!

The door nearly tore from its hinges as I kicked the door in rage. "Arden," I screamed. "Where are you?" I burst into his bedroom as he got up from a nap. "Why didn't you tell me the water sprites provided an underground connection with the river for you? You made me lug water all those times."

"Yes," he said, "and how did you find out about it?"

"I met this water sprite down at the river and she told me."

"That's all I needed to hear. It's on the chair."

"What's on the chair?" I asked, even as I spun

around. There on the chair was a gray robe. "Is it for me?" I whispered, too hopeful to talk louder.

"Yes, You've passed your first test. An air sprite brought me the news so I could get the robe ready before you arrived."

"All I had to do was talk to a sprite?" I asked as I held the robe up against me.

"It's no small achievement."

"But you still never told me about the water channel. You made me make that trip so many times. And you lied to me! That's not a workshop, it's a bathroom!"

"Moyra, you're tired and excited. Why don't you go into my workshop and take a nice hot bath. Then you can try on your robes."

"You get hot water, too!"

"If you can talk the fire sprites into heating it for you."

I grabbed my robe and headed toward the bath. "They will. Have no fear about that. They will."

GRIM CALLING

by Patricia B. Cirone

I have bought two or three stories before this by Pat Cirone; this is a plot which is not new to fantasy or to science fiction, the yearly—or less frequent—call of the sorceress who tests the current crop of children and finds them acceptable or wanting; and as happens in fairy tales, the criteria by which they are examined turns out not to be quite what you think . . . another fairy-tale theme.

I am slowly coming to realize—though I had some dim inkling of it before—that the themes which recur in fantasy—and therefore in my slush piles—usually say something very profound about the human condition. But after all, what is fantasy? Simply very deeply buried inquiry about our dreams, desires, and hopes . . . and why else does anyone write? Or read, for that matter?

Nestled in the dip of a protective ring of hills, a small pond lay just beyond the reach of the woods. Crouched at its edge, a brown-haired girl delicately dipped one finger below its surface. She laughed softly as small gray-green fish gathered to stare. One more courageous than the rest darted up near to the finger, then dashed away again. They hovered closer. One swam up to nibble, then, with a quick flash, another. Startled by their audacity, the two dove back down amongst those who circled, eyeing the tempting finger. Fia smiled, waiting patiently.

The ripples on the water died, flowing together into an unnatural stillness. Fia's eyes widened as instead of the surface of the pond, she saw a dark street with tall, cold buildings. A woman walked alone down the narrow street, her way lit by the cold silver light of First-to-rise. Her long skirts swished against the strange surface of the street. Stone, Fia thought. Whoever heard of a street made of stone? Her eyes widened further as she noticed a figure. A figure that crouched, hidden by the turning of a building.

It inched forward. Evil seemed to emanate from the black folds of cloth that covered it from head to toe. Fia's breath was caught somewhere in her throat. She looked at the figure, at the woman approaching, at the figure inching closer, the gleam of moonlight on a long knife.

"No!" she cried, throwing out her hand. Instead of touching cold street, it splashed against the water, broke it into a thousand harmless ripples. Beneath the water, the startled fish darted away. The vision was gone; the pond was just a pond again.

"Ow!" Fia squawked as fingers grabbed and dragged her up by the ear.

"Are you bewitched, squatting and staring at a muddy pond? You're *supposed* to be watching the geese!"

"I *am* watching the geese," Fia replied, rubbing her ear.

"Huh!" Cenna snorted.

Fia glanced around guiltily. Only three of the flock were still by the pond. The rest were walking up the hills or wandering toward the woods.

"Oh, Fire!" she muttered, and took off at a run. She was out of breath by the time she had rounded up the geese and headed them back toward the woods-path that led to the village. It didn't help that Cenna just stood there, watching instead of helping. Not that she *had* to, geese weren't her chore this week, but still!

"I don't know, Fia," Cenna said, shaking her head as they walked down the path behind the geese. "You certainly act strange sometimes."

"I do not!"

"What do you call what you were doing at the pond, then?"

"I was just watching the fish," Fia replied.

"You were as slack-jawed as an idiot. What if I had been a wild dog after the geese? What if I had been . . . one of . . . *them*!"

"They never come anywhere near here. And besides, I would have heard!"

"Huh! You didn't even hear me calling your name two inches from your ear! You keep daydreaming like that, an' Grim will take you when she comes calling."

"No!" Fia protested, her face turning white. "That's mean to say!"

Cenna shrugged with all the superiority of being two years older. "it's not mean, it's real. It's the strange ones she takes."

"She didn't take *anyone* the last two times!"

"But she did the time before that. *I'm* old enough to remember. She took Donal, the boy who used to wander about talking in words that no one understood."

"I'm not strange like that!" Fia answered, near tears.

"It doesn't matter *how* you're strange. Just that you're strange."

"I'm not strange! I was just daydreaming!"

Cenna just shook her head. Both girls were silent as the geese, scenting home and anticipating their nightly ration of grain, led them down the twisting, turning path through the woods. Behind them, the trees rustled and half-closed the path. They were barely past the Sentinel trees when other village children came running up.

"Grim's here!" they whispered in voices that chilled her soul.

"She's come!"

"Grim's here!"

Grim had come calling. Grim, the woman who came every five, or six or seven years. Grim, the woman parents used to scare their children with when their patience was exhausted. Fia bit the inside of her cheek as a shudder ripped through her. The small ones who had never seen Grim before were wide-eyed with excitement. The older ones were wary, knowing they had passed once, twice, three times and hoping they'd pass again. Grim didn't take adults; it was only the children she winnowed.

Numbly Fia herded the geese into their pen. What Cenna had said echoed through her head. "Grim's going to take you." She was shaking so hard her fingers fumbled with the rope latch on the pen, and spilled the grain she tried to scoop into the wooden bucket.

"Fia, girl. Where are you?" her mother called. "Haven't you fed them yet?" she asked, spotting Fia motionless by the noisy, demanding geese.

Fia straightened, and flung the grain from the bucket over the side of the pen, scattering it into the jostling crowd of geese.

"Come along, now," her mother admonished. "You have to get dressed in your best."

Fia hated the thought of dressing as if it were a holiday, but it was always like this. The grown-ups dressed all their children and themselves in their best, and put on a feast when Grim came. They plied her for news, as if she were just another passing stranger, though Fire knew, there were few enough of those. But not even for strangers were the fattest geese killed, and the holiday clothes worn, as if it were a Fire feast. That only happened when Grim came calling.

Reluctantly, Fia donned her newest gown and wove bright kirtle leaves into her hair. She walked behind her parents to the gather place, nestled in the deepest shade of the trees. Her little sister Rune clung to her hand and chattered away, excited at the thought of a feast and not frightened she would be taken away. She was too young to understand. Thom, at her other side, was silent, but he was almost too old to worry. It was only *she* who had to worry, Fia thought. Cenna thought she was strange. Had the others noticed?

It wasn't the first time she had had one of the . . . dreams. They had started coming two years ago, soon after she had first used women's rags. She had never told anyone about them. They were too . . . strange. She shivered again at that hated word. But she never dreamed of cosy, tree-nestled villages, or people she knew, like all the other girls seemed to. Her dreams were of strange places, tall forbidding cities, cold lonely plains, or aching deserts. And always the danger. She would wake, heart pounding, eyelids twitching. Wake, when she hadn't even been asleep, for the worst ones didn't come at night. Usually her sleep was as free of dreams as were the other girls' days.

The gather hall with its low, carved branches and woven sides was already full. Fia took a deep breath to steady herself and smelled the lingering sweet smell of grain from last season's threshing. She followed her parents over to one of the hastily erected plank tables. Other times, children were bidden to the separate tables at the end of the hall. But when Grim came calling, families sat together as if it were the last time.

All too soon, the meal was over, and Grim began calling up the children to talk to her, one by one. Fia felt the fear rising in her as it never had before. The first time she had been about Rune's age, and like her, bemused by the fanciness and unexpectedness of it. Last time, she had known what could happen, but it didn't seem real, not real for *her*. She had worried more for her friends. But this year . . .

The youngest went first, tripping up like Rune, and talking happily to Grim as if she were the Gifter come to flesh. Next went the middling children, the ones old enough for chores but not yet old enough for rags or cracking voices.

And then it was her turn. Fia wanted to turn and run; instead she forced herself to walk up, stiff-legged as an angry cat. Grim smiled, reached for her hand, and looked right into her mind. The wrinkles on Grim's brow smoothed and her eyes half-closed in a look of peace. With dread, Fia knew that she knew.

"Ah. This one I will be taking."

Fia wrenched her hand loose, whirled, and ran straight back into the crowd. Shouts rose around her as she ducked and shoved her way through the startled people.

"Here, what are you doing?"

She shook loose of an arm and plunged into the night. Like a hare, she ran through the trees, doubled up, eyes wild. She went to earth deep in a tangle of gora bushes, far from the village.

Slowly her panting stopped, and she started to shiver. What was she to do? If she went back, they'd just hand her over to Grim, even her own parents would. The ones who were *gone* were spoken of in whispers, and no adult ever explained why they let them be taken. Tears welled up and trickled down Fia's face.

She had never heard of anyone living alone; besides the cervines and the wild dogs there were . . . *them.* Yet, what else could she do? It was go back to the village and be turned over to Grim . . . or live alone. She worried over the two choices like a dog over a bone, and between the impossibility of either choice and the fright of running, she drifted off to an uneasy sleep.

Third-to-rise lifted above the treetops and cast its dark red light down. Fia twitched, and rustled against the stiff branches of the gora bushes. Slowly her mind came to life.

She saw figures creeping down a hillside. Their gait was awkward, a hunched shuffle. Their beards were long . . . not . . . really . . . beards. With horror, Fia realized it was . . . *them* . . . the O-Mein, the yellow of their leathery skin made darker by the fitful shine of Lural, last-to-rise. Fia saw the hill they were creeping down and she knew it like she knew the goose pen near her home.

It was the hill by the pond where she had watered the geese just today.

They shuffled down, cast around, shuffling, sniffing. Fia strained against the edges of her dream, not wanting to watch, not wanting to see *them*, not wanting to see their shambling feet defile the ground on which she walked.

With a moan, Fia watched as they followed the goose droppings and entered the path into the woods, the woods that kept her and her people safe. *These* O-Mein did not seem frightened by it, and the trees let them pass. Fia watched in disbelief as the last of them disappeared into the woods, headed for her village.

She stumbled to her feet, shaking her head and blinking the last of the dream away from her eyes. She shuddered, expecting to hear screams, and then realized she was still bathed in the red light of third-to-rise and not the yellow of Lural.

There was time, then.

Fia pried herself loose from the branches of the gora bushes and ran swiftly to the heart of the village. It did not matter that her return meant she would be sealed to Grim; all that mattered was the safety of her people, of her family. She passed groups looking for her, but they did not see her. She was as silent and invisible as the Gifter. It was as if the trees were aiding her against her own people. She went straight to the gather place, seeking Grim.

That one, having plundered her mind, would believe her. Would know she was telling the truth, would know that her dream was real.

Grim was waiting for her.

"They are coming," Fia said breathlessly.

"Who?"

"Them."

Grim still looked confused. Fia had to say the dreaded word out loud. "The O-Mein!"

"Where?"

"Here!"

Grim looked at her in disbelief for a moment. Then her expression changed. "Call the people!" she ordered Sulir.

Fia felt the summons. It was not a call that was heard, or shouted but rather a warm feeling, coupled with a need to draw near. She found herself taking a step closer to Sulir without meaning to, as the yearning beckoned her.

Soon the search parties were returning to the village, gathering at the hall, pushing closer.

"Oh, Fia, you're found!" her mother said with a sob, moving forward to hug her daughter. But Grim put her arm between them, and her mother moved back as if burned, a look of longing on her face.

But Fia knew this was not the gesture of severance. That would come later. Now . . . there was the O-Mein.

"Tell them," Grim commanded, when all had returned.

"The O-Mein are coming," Fia said in a voice so small it was barely more than a whisper.

"What? To this area?" Kelor, the headman, demanded. "And how would *you* know? Is this another childish prank?"

"Fia is not a child," Grim said calmly. "And this is not a prank. She is a True-Dreamer."

Kelor took a moment to swallow this, and then asked, "Where are they coming?"

"To *Here*. Our village! By the goose-pond path."

Fia heard the murmurs of disbelief.

"But that's impossible! We're in the woods!" Kelor protested.

Fia shrugged, as mystified as he. "I *Saw* them," was all she could say.

"When are they coming?" Grim asked calmly.

"When Lural is high."

"We have time, then."

Quickly the men and women gathered their weapons, ran lightfooted through the roots and the leaves of the forest. They crouched, hidden, along the goose-path, by the entrance to their village, and even down the back-path . . . in case.

They waited patiently as fourth-to-rise sped its way across the sky and Lural began to rise.

When the yellow of Lural shone on the roots in the path, they heard the shuffling. Hands hardened around sharpened staves; arrows were notched into bows.

With a silent call, Sulir loosed the tide upon the fearful O-Mein. Two of them fell to the thud of arrows.

With a second, silent call Sulir led the charge out

from the protection of the tree branches. She was the first to pin an O-Mein to the ground with her stave. A second stave was thrust into its low, belly-riding heart. Despite their size and fearsome claws, all the O-Mein were dead within minutes.

Kelor got up from where he had fallen to his knees, wounded by one of the O-Mein. He turned one of the bodies over, searched it. Slowly he lifted up a thin chain. At the end of it dangled a splinter of true-wood. "This is how they did it. This is how they fooled the woods." His face looked grim.

"We're no longer safe, then," Fia's mother said. "Not even here, in our own woods." A shiver rippled through the villagers.

Fia crept up to see the bodies. It was the first time she had seen an O-Mein. With a shudder, she knew the outcome would have been quite different if she hadn't warned the villagers. Twice as tall as any of the people, with knives even longer than their claws, the twenty O-Mein would have been able to kill, or capture, the entire village.

"That is why we need you," Grim said.

"Then why take me away? I'm needed here. Especially now!" Fia asked.

"Your gift is less than half of what it could be. You need training. So you can use your gift freely, at will for *all* the people, not just one village. What of all those other dreams, all those other times when someone could have been warned?" Grim answered.

Fia bowed her head. She wanted to say, let someone else do it, let me stay here.

". . . all those you have taken. Are they *all* being trained? Not . . ." Fia trailed away, realizing she had never wondered what happened beyond the horror of being taken.

"Of course. They are trained to use their gifts more fully. And then they are sent where they are most needed."

"Why can't I ever come home again? See my family, my friends?"

"But you can! You might even be sent back here, if

this is where you're most needed. Sulir was trained and then came back home."

Sulir? Their caller? She had been taken by Grim, and come back? "Then . . . why don't the parents *say* so, instead of . . . it's so frightening."

Grim sighed. "It's because they are frightened. They are frightened if they say the word O-Mein, it will bring them down upon them. They are frightened if they talk of the war, and the gifted who are fighting it, it will swirl the war closer, catch them up in it. It is not like that everywhere. Only . . . only in the small places like this. You will see."

Fia thought of being in a place where the O-Mein were not just whispered of as "*them*," of a place where people were actually *doing* something about defeating the bearded evils. She was both attracted, and frightened.

"Will I have to live in a city of stone?" she asked.

Grim smiled. "Not at first. Besides, stone can be as warm as trees when you're with people."

Fia looked at her and no longer saw a woman wrinkled and terrifying, but one who cared very deeply. One who walked the paths alone, risking her life to find others gifted enough to sway the outcome of the war on the side of the people.

"It's not easy, being gifted," Grim said. "But it is not I who have chosen you, but your own body. It is a calling, if you would. In this time of war, it is rather a grim calling, but you are needed. You cannot let yourself drift in your own village, happy only for yourself."

Fia knew Grim was right. She thought of all the times when she had called out or thrust out a hand to stop the danger, the dying, and only been frustrated by the loss of the dream. She had calmed herself by saying it was only a dream. But now that she knew her dreams *were* real, she would not be able to do that, and she could not let people die because she was afraid of leaving everything she knew. She would have to master that fear and answer her calling.

Fia turned, and went to pack her way-bag.

WINTER'S DAUGHTER

by Diane Burrell

Diane Burrell describes herself as a "typical military brat" but says the most interesting part was the three years she lived in Libya. She has recently moved to Hollywood "to try my hand at script writing," and is fond of heavy metal and classical music. Strange; I'd think they'd be mutually exclusive, but perhaps that's a generation gap for me; it's surprising how often I seem to be reminded lately that I am a member of the older generation. After all, when I was growing up they told me in school not to waste my good mind on science fiction or fantasy, and they were very wrong; everything I ever learned which has contributed to real life came out of fantasy. Times have changed—and who knows, some day I may discover how heavy metal and classical music can be compatible—or even exist in the same head space.

Every year I indulge myself by buying one story for this anthology for no particular reason except that I like it and I am sure my readers—at least those who are wholly on my wave length—will, too. I simply couldn't resist this one.

I was born in the heart of winter, and my mother's cries were lost in the shriek and moan of the winter winds as they assaulted the high towers of my father's castle. I came into the world on those winterstorm winds, they used to tell me in the nursery, and though my father the king would frown and discourage me from paying any heed to the tales my nursemaids would spin, I still grew up with the details of that particular winter forever etched in my mind.

As was befitting the daughter of the king, I had many tutors and nannies, and I learned from them that the winters there on the shores of Lake Hyperberon once were mild and joyous, and that the snow used to settle like a soft blanket upon the stone cliffs from which Castle Beron was carved, rising high above the southern shore. But now, as I grew older and more aware, I saw how the season would descend with a fury, ravaging the land with bitter cold and choking snows, refusing to loose its grip until forcibly broken by the return of spring. Many a winter night I could remember huddling in my bed beneath a huge mound of furs, watching as my ladies in waiting would coax the fire in the grate into leaping brands of flame, chasing back the terrible chill that seemed to permeate every part of the castle.

Outside the winds would howl, raging as they crashed into the spires and turrets of gray stone, snow dancing wildly through the air. I always would wonder why the elements of winter seemed to spend so much time ravaging our kingdom . . . but then, as a child I thought I heard voices on those winds, and would assign them personalities, so it was only natural that I would wonder why they behaved as they did.

Winter meant a virtual imprisonment in the castle, and venturing free during the winter months was strictly forbidden. I didn't know why—I only knew that it was the king's decree—but it seemed so unfair to me to be unable to go forth into that glorious whiteness on the days the sun broke through the clouds and bathed the lake in shining light. I loved my father, after a fashion . . . but his denying my winter freedoms only hurt and puzzled me.

My mother, Leirinda, was a pale wraith in the background most of the time, and as I grew older, it seemed that my father, Valhar, did all he could to prevent us time alone, together. I knew her love for me was deep and encompassing, but he seemed to jealously guard her love from me. When she could, in the small moments we were mother and daughter—not queen and princess—she would shower me with maternal love, and I felt the deep sadness she carried, and tried to keep hidden.

I suspected that much of my father's behavior toward my mother and me was due in part to my gender. I learned at a very young age that it had been foretold to the king that his wife would bear him a son, and the birth of a girl child, instead, had disturbed him greatly. Nonetheless, my mother welcomed me and named me Kirin, and loved me, perhaps all the more so for my father's indifference.

What had transpired before my arrival I knew little about, except those tales that I gathered from the servants when they did not know I was in the room. I knew that although our kingdom was small, our neighbors did not dare oppose King Valhar, for it was said that in his youth he had conquered great magic, and had forced it to obey him. I knew nothing of this—and yet, there were times during the winter months, locked up in that dark and chill castle, that I thought I sensed a trace of . . . something . . . in the stonework. It always faded, however, and I made no mention of it to my parents. Peace prevailed upon the land, and whether magic played a part in that or not, I did not really care.

My thoughts were always upon my parents, for their relationship puzzled and saddened me. The queen would often call for me to attend her, and although my father was always near, would take great pains to show me her love. I knew her embrace much more often than my father's . . . and those times when my father was enraged, often at things I did not fully understand, her arms would shield me from the worst of his tirades. But also at those times, most often during high winter, I would be sent from my parents' chambers, hearing their voices raised in bitter anger in my wake. What they fought about I did not know—all I knew was that soon my mother's voice would break and fall into silence, sometimes punctuated by soft weeping. My father never wept.

Other things haunted me as I grew older, until by the winter of my seventeenth birthday, I had pieced together several things. My mother was a tall and graceful creature, fragile and disturbingly beautiful, with pale skin and hair, and large black eyes that shimmered in darkness, and my father did not just love her—he *possessed* her in some manner I could not fathom. He jealously guarded her, preventing her contact with almost every dignitary and visitor to our courts, and it was perhaps reflective of this possessiveness that I realized she did not love him. As this dawned on me, I began to see that my father saw in me the same traits as my mother—the tall paleness, the dark eyes, the fragility. It was for these things that I was kept so confined to the castle, a thing to be guarded, a child to be watched. My love for my father began to waver.

That winter, the elements ravaged the kingdom with such severity that the impossible finally happened—Lake Hyperberon froze over. We could hear the cracking and thundering of the ice floes as they thawed and refroze during those winter days and nights, and the sounds echoed through the stonework, disturbing all the inhabitants there for the season. I could hear the muffled booms as I wandered the huge corriders and rooms, and in the kitchen keep, the cooks and servants muttered and cast charms over their shoulders, suspicious of the weather elementals.

At night the storms beat so violently at the towers that all who dwelled in them were bade by the king to come down into the common rooms below, and sleep in the dormitories of the various servants and courtiers. It was feared that the weight of the ice forming on the masonry could cause a catastrophe, and there was much speculation in those rooms at night that some sort of vengeance was being paid upon King Valhar. These mutterings were quickly brought to an end when the women realized I was present. In the awkward silence that followed, my mind raced with half-formed thoughts and questions. *What is this muttering I have heard all my life? What secrets does my father keep? And my mother?*

Knowing I would hear nothing more within that room, I rose from my bench and left the warmth of the great hall, my furred slippers whispering softly on the smooth floors. My excuse was that I sought to retire to my rooms, but in truth, I searched for my mother. My father had left the castle that evening, and I knew she would be somewhere within the deepest parts of the great building, alone.

I found her in the great library, curled among the pillows on the floor, her long silver hair loose about her shoulders, a soft robe wrapped about her, and a book upon her lap. The fire was huge, filling the room with comforting heat, and her bare feet poked from the robe toward the flames. I hesitated within the door, unused to the sight of my mother, the queen, barefoot and alone in the library.

She heard me enter and looked up, a slow smile lighting her fire-bronzed face. "Come in, Kirin," she said, her voice soft. I crossed the room and lowered myself to the floor, spreading my heavy woolen skirts to cover her feet. She smiled again and lay her book down. Her eyes studied me a long while as I sat in silence, confused. Finally she took my hand. "What troubles you, kitling?"

"Mother—" I sat there, mouth open, suddenly realizing that I had not the slightest idea how to voice the questions within me. She sensed my confusion, as she always could, and smoothed the stray locks of hair that had escaped my braid and hung in my eyes.

"Kirin . . . ?"

I blurted it out before my trembling stomach got the best of me. I expected my father to burst in on us at any moment, as usually happened, and I wanted to say something before that time came. "Mother—why are there so many secrets in this house?"

She smiled serenely. "Every castle keep has secrets, kitling."

I shook my head. "Not like this."

Her dark eyes carefully searched mine. "What is it you ask, Kirin?"

"Mother—why don't you love the king?" Even I couldn't believe the audacity of my question, and I was relieved when Leirinda dropped my hand and looked away toward the fire. My face burned as I dropped my eyes to my lap, wondering if I had destroyed the delicate balance that existed between my mother and me.

I did not know when she looked back to me, but soon her hand reached over and again took mine. I looked up and saw the tears shining in her eyes. "Sometimes we must accept the things that happen to us in life, Kirin. We fight as long as we are able . . . but eventually comes the time when we give in and accept." I could not meet her gaze, for the tears threatened to spill down her alabaster cheeks, and I again dropped my eyes, listening as she continued. "I tried to love him . . . but it is not in me. It took all my strength to let go my . . . anger . . ." Her voice trailed off, but by this time I did not notice, for my eyes were drawn to my mother's slender wrists. I had never seen them before.

It was my mother's habit to wear long-sleeved gowns, even during highest summer, and although it was unusual to some, I had never commented on it. My mother was very pale and did not tan in the sun, and being like her, I, too, often covered myself completely to prevent a burn. But never had I seen her bare arms, even within the private apartments of the royal family.

They were, as I stated, slender and pale, very graceful to look upon, but in the firelight, I thought my mother's delicate wrists appeared . . . damaged. Only half-hearing the silence in the library, I drew a finger across the skin.

Immediately she started, and tried to withdraw her hand from mine, but I held her firmly and looked again. Leirinda's wrists were scarred, the skin drawn and white, even for her. She pulled against my grip again, but I just looked up at her, horrified. "Were you in chains, Mother?"

This time when she tugged, I let go, and she turned away, withdrawing behind her silences, as always. Something made her stop, however, and she stretched her arms out before the fireplace, staring a long moment at her wrists. Finally she nodded, dropping her hands into her lap. "A long time ago—before you were born. In another life." Her voice was very soft, and very sad.

My original questions forgotten, I stared at her. Who would have dared do such a thing to the Lady Leirinda, Queen of Castle Beron? "Mother—who? *Why?*"

For a long time she did not answer, and the logs on the fire crackled and snapped in the silence. Softly, almost inaudibly, my mother whispered, "Only one man could have done such a thing to me . . ." Her eyes met mine, and I felt certain that she would have told me the truth then—but abruptly the doors of the library flew open and my father stormed in. Although she did not move, I felt her draw away, from both myself and him. Her expressionless face lifted toward him as moved nearer to us.

He was clad in his winter gear, the furs frosted stiff about his face and boots, a trail of melting snow stretching behind him. His face, where it showed above the thick gray beard, was reddened from exposure, and his blue eyes sparked angrily when he saw us seated together on the floor. My mother demurely drew her wrists upward into the folds of her robe, but not before he saw the movement, and his eyes flicked down to her hands, then back to her face. Slowly he turned toward me. *My father was the one*, I knew with sudden clarity. *My father was the one who put her in chains.*

Valhar tensed, as if awaiting some sort of proclamation from me, and his expression grew blacker and blacker. Finally I had to look away, not knowing what it was he expected—or dreaded—for me to say. He cleared his throat and reached upward, pushing the fur-trimmed hood off his head. "Kirin—leave us." His voice was rough with suppressed emotion, and I wondered what he had expected to happen in those few tense moments.

I automatically rose to leave, but my mother amazed me by stopping me with a touch. "No—Kirin, stay." It was the first time I could remember hearing her counter one of my father's orders.

Valhar almost choked on his swift anger. "Leirinda—it is the storm."

Now we could hear it through the open library doors. The winds howled with such force that it carried down into the deepest part of the castle, and the air stirred faintly within the walls of the library. Again, as in childhood, I thought I heard voices in the wind, but they faded as I looked back to my mother. She rose from the floor, head tilted as she listened.

"Yes. I hear the winds." And then she smiled.

The king scowled. "The day watch spotted a crack running through the north tower that wasn't there yesterday. The storm—the ice—may cause a collapse."

Leirinda's smile faltered. "No. They would not."

They? I longed to understand what my parents spoke of.

Valhar smiled now, a slow, cruel expression. "You yourself had said it. They will." He looked at me, then back to the queen. "You must prevent it."

"No." Her features grew distraught. Afraid for her, I took her hand in mine. Her fingers trembled, ice-cold. My father saw this, and exploded.

"Kirin—leave, *now!*" I heard the tone and knew he was not to be disobeyed, but my mother trembled harder and I could not leave her there.

"Mother, what does he mean that you mu—" With two quick strides Valhar was beside me, gripping my arm in his vicelike grip. He propelled me toward the door and shoved me into the corridor. With a dangerous expression he glared at me and slammed the library doors shut, but I pressed my ear to the wood, listening to their muffled voices.

My father was livid with rage. His voice bellowed out. "What does she know?"

"Not enough . . ." Her voice was almost lost in the storm sounds straying at the edge of my hearing. ". . . I made a promise. Do you fear I would break it?"

"Yes! For the storms, for the winds—yes, I feared you would break it." There was only silence. He spoke again. "The winds grow stronger every year."

Bitterly, she replied, "What else did you expect?"

"That you would put an end to it!" Again, silence, and I shivered in that cold corridor, imagining my father's huge bulk towering over my mother's pale form. "Leirinda—you must do it. This year . . . I fear the castle will fall."

"Let it! I don't care anymore!"

There was the sound of a short scuffle, and my mother gasped. Valhar's voice was rough and cold. "Your daughter could lie in the wreckage!"

"No . . ." she moaned, and I curled my hands into fists, shaken that my father would use force on my mother. "Please don't ask me to do it, Valhar . . . I am not strong enough!"

"Your lack of strength is your own fault, my lady—you took it upon yourself to bear a daughter, instead of a son!" My mother made sounds of protest, and I could envision the king shaking her. "You thought to use her against me, did you not?"

"No, Valhar . . . please . . .!" There was the sound of a hand striking flesh, and I started at my mother's cry, followed by soft sobs. The anger welled up inside of me until I thought I would burst—and from somewhere else in the castle, the sound of shattering broke the wind-driven silence. I turned and looked down the corridor as a maelstrom of gale-force winds hurtled through the darkness, buffeting me violently about the hall. Snowflakes danced about as I cried out and crouched against the stone, the wind pushing and pulling at me.

The library doors flew open and my parents dashed out, the king stopping abruptly as I managed to climb to my feet within the whirling center of the wind. The cold was numbing, but the snow did not settle on the floor—it danced and sailed through the darkness. Frightened and bruised by the force of it, I cried out to my parents. "Mother—Father! *What's happening?*"

My father stared, his expression one of—terror!—as I stood in the corridor, my hair sailing about with the wind. I stretched my arms out to my mother, who rushed to me and took me within the warm circle of her embrace. The winds howled and moaned, but she held me tightly, her hair mingling with mine. With a shriek of near-defiance the wind abruptly died. The sudden silence was deafening.

I pulled away from my mother and saw the bruise on her cheek from my father's hand. Tears stood in both our eyes as she assured herself with soft touches that I was whole and unharmed, and then she turned to the king.

"You see what your secrets have done? *Do you see?*"

Valhar advanced, his expression no longer one of terror. "Kirin—go to your rooms, now." My mother stood straight before him, and I thought she would defy him once more . . . but she only wilted before his terrible gaze and released me.

"Do . . . do as your father says, Kirin." Her voice was very soft. Even softer was the whisper she spoke in my ear. "The southernmost dungeon." The tears spilled over and coursed down her cheek as she met my eyes. Her hand touched my face.

Voices up the corridor came to us, and dancing lanterns began to come toward us as the servants began to assess the damage the freak winds had done. Frightened, unsure, and shaking with anger, I turned and ran from my parents. My mother's voice reached my ears.

"Take me . . . to the winds, Valhar . . ."

I ran until I had to stop, gasping for breath. *The southernmost dungeon?* I thought, sitting on the stairs of the central tower. Why would my mother whisper such a thing to me? The winds, the terror on my father's face, and the bruise on hers . . . my heart pounded with its own terror. Secrets—my mother had flung the word at the king like an accusation.

Had my father kept my mother in chains? Why? What was happening to me, that I thought I heard voices in the winds, and that filled my father with such fear?

Before I knew that I had made up my mind, I was descending into the dungeons below the castle, a lantern in my hand, my heart pounding fiercely in my breast. The dungeons were unguarded as they were unused. Holdovers from a more savage past, they stretched the entire length of the eastern boundary of the castle, dank and dark rows of cells and chambers, metal-rimmed doors of wood rotting now in the silences. The king, though a hard and cold father, and perhaps an even harder husband, was a justice-minded ruler, and did not believe in imprisonment for those who did not always agree with him. For criminals, a more humane prison existed above ground, far to the west of the main township . . . and for now, the dungeons were mere architectural curiosities.

The air here was warmer than above, and it smelled of decay and abandon. I knew there was nothing to harm me but for my imagination, but I still shook with—with anger, with fear.

I walked the long length of the main corridor, the shadows retreating from the bright cheeriness of my lantern. Gaping holes of blackness opened behind the rotted doors I passed, and once or twice I had to pause, hands shaking, as I heard the creak of old hinges in that silent corridor.

Finally I reached the southern end of the corridor, and I lifted the lantern, seeking . . . what, I did not know. All that was there was the last cell—and the door stood open. A faint breath of wind played against my cheek, and I jerked back in fright, for there should be no wind beneath the castle!

Again that faint breath of cold wind blew against my cheek, and my skirt stirred, tugged by the air currents. It moved in the direction of the cell, then doubled back, lifting my hair in tendrils about my face. Almost too frightened to move, I stood there and let that strange wind move about me, its coldness not as unsettling as its very being there. Finally, with a faint sigh almost as audible as a human voice, that chill breeze blew past me and into the cell, the door stirring back, opening wider to admit me.

It followed me down here, I thought, half-mad with fear. *The wind followed me down.*

"*. . . yessss . . .*" whispered the wind. A rustle of straw from within the cell brought me back, on the verge of running in terror up the corridor. A few pieces of the mildewed rushes blew out on the breeze.

Rushes? These cells should have been cleaned out years ago. My mind grabbed onto that minor puzzle and I managed to push back the fear. With my heart beating loud in my ears, I lifted the lantern and entered the cell.

It was as all the others, small, cramped, stones slick with seepage—for the lake was very near to these castle foundations—and utterly empty, but for the rotting straw on the floor. *There should be no straw here. These cells have been unused since before my birth.* Puzzled, I lifted the lantern again. The wind blew against the little flame, and it flickered once. In the movement of the shadows, I caught a glimpse of something reflecting back the light. I bent and looked closer, and saw the manacles and chains bolted to the stone block wall.

I grew dizzy suddenly at the sight, and wanted nothing more than to turn and run from the cell, as I had run from my parents above. The wind circled me, caressing my face, and the coldness revived me, and gave me strength. "*. . . sssssseeeee. . . .*" the wind whispered. Almost against my will I reached out my free hand and touched the manacles . . . and saw the crusted blood, dried to a dark stain within the iron cuffs. There was blood on both manacles . . . and they had been drawn to fit an impossibly slender wrist.

"NO!" I cried, falling to my knees. The shadows danced crazily as the lantern tilted and then righted itself. My cry echoed through the corridors of the dungeon, and the wind caught at my fleeting echoes and brought them back to me. "*. . . no, no, no, no. . . .*" Abruptly the wind died.

I do not remember running from the cell, nor do I remember the long climb back up the stairs into the keep. When I came back to myself, I was standing in the great hall, the lantern still in my hand, the huge doors behind me bolted tight. Did I really descend? I looked down at the hem of my skirt and saw the dankness and bits of straw, and knew that I had. Tears stung at my eyes, and I knew that indeed, my father had chained my mother within the walls of that tiny cell. "Valhar!" I cried. "Valhar! How could you do such a thing!" No one answered my anguished cry, but that small wind that had led me to the cell suddenly sprang to life around me, lifting my hair, my skirts, dancing about the room, spinning tapestries from their places on the walls, tilting precious objects from their stands.

"Stop it!" I cried. The wind ceased its dance and whirled about me, its touch cool on my burning cheeks. My fear was replaced with anger, and I screamed out at the wind, "why?"

"*. . . theeee . . . Laaaadyyyy . . .*" An image of my mother, white as a wraith, trembling in the darkness, sprang into my mind. Her thin wrists bleeding from the bite of iron cuffs, she struggled against the chains, finally sinking down in exhaustion, her long silver hair obscuring the tears of pain . . . and fear . . . and . . . "*. . .beeeetraaaaaayaaaal . . .*" Again the wind died, and the image was gone.

I heard the heavy slam of a storm door, and suddenly realized that the winter gale was howling and tearing at the castle towers with a force I had never known before. The breeze touched my face and whistled down a hallway, toward the main courtyard. I followed its progress, knowing where it was by the way the tapestries flapped free from their moorings near the high ceilings, and soon heard the clamor and clatter of servants rushing about, securing heavy shutters on the high windows overlooking the lake. The winds had swept over the frozen water with such fury that the thick wooden beams from which the original shutters were constructed had splintered into thousands of ice-coated fragments. Snow piled high in the corridor, melting into slushy puddles of icy water that stained the luxurious carpets, but I paid no attention to the squish of my slippers as I followed my small wind to the great doors.

A hand touched my shoulder, other hands pulled at my arms, but I easily shrugged out of their grips and touched the great door. Servants yelled and called to one another, trying to stop my progress, but at the touch of my hand, the door exploded open, wind and snow battering it inward.

I stood there, unmindful of the white coldness, staggered by the power of the wind, and saw the main courtyard overlooking Lake Hyperberon. My small wind circled about me, countering the force of the snow hurtling toward me, and I was protected by its frantic dance. I thought I heard voices high on those gale winds, angry voices shrieking and moaning, and the small counterpoint of my protective wind.

My father stood near me, his back to me, facing the northern tip of the courtyard. His winter furs were white-rimmed with frost, and he struggled to remain upright in that violent storm.

My mother stood a little farther out in that white fury, and I saw her arms were raised toward the north. Her hair streamed out behind her, and with a shock I saw her feet were bare—and no snow touched her. It piled and blew into drifts about her, about the courtyard, even onto the king—but she was untouched by both the cold and the wet. "Mother!" I shrieked above the wind.

The king turned and saw me, and his eyes widened first with surprise, then with fury. "Kirin—go back! Now!" He advanced on me.

I backed away, hands raised. "No!" Suddenly he was pushed by the wind, and he toppled backward into a drift. As he struggled to rise, I heard my mother's voice over the shriek of the gale.

"Winds of winter, you must stop this! I command it! I command it!" The winds tugged at her gown, lifted her hair, and with a voice near to breaking, she cried out, "I cannot return with you! I cannot break my vows of marriage!" The winds howled and roared above her, striking at the high towers. "No! Stop this at once! You endanger us all with your fury!" Snow lifted in a whirlwind column and advanced on the castle, dancing and twisting on the frozen lake, and my father, finally regaining his feet, paled beneath his furs.

"Leirinda—the lake! The lake!" My mother turned and saw the snow whirlwind, and as she turned back, she saw me. Her eyes were dark smudges in that whiteness, and with a cry she called to the winds.

"You will kill me—and my daughter! I cannot allow you to do this!" Her hands raised again—and there was a great booming as the ice on the lake cracked and rose upward, the floes shedding water and snow as they blocked the path of the whirlwind. The twisting wind turned and bent, sucking up water from beneath the wall of ice, finally collapsing in a great wave of water and snow. With a moan, the winds swept back over the castle, circled once, and were gone.

Snow settled about as the air grew still. I shivered as the cold finally began to creep on me, my small wind retreating with the great ones, and my mother turned to me, her arms open. I ran to her warmth, and felt her slight form tremble as she hugged me to her breast. Hot tears cascaded down both of our faces. "Oh, Kirin, Kirin . . ." she whispered. "I wanted to spare you this."

I looked up at her. "Are you a sorceress, Mother?"

"No," my father interrupted. We looked up to see him standing in the snow, steam puffing from his nostrils, his face red with the exertion of clambering through the frozen piles. "She is not a sorceress." His voice was flat and dead, and I knew this was when my mother would tremble and give in to him.

This time, she did not. "I am not. I am Lady Winter."

"Leirinda!" His tone was sharp.

"She deserves to know!"

"*. . . yyyyyyeeeeesssss . . .*" The whisper was loud and mournful, and we felt the stirring of the winds again. My father glanced up and saw the clouds tossing high above us.

"Leirinda—Kirin. Into the castle, now!"

"*. . . nnnnnoooo . . .!*" With a shriek the wind hurtled down and slammed the great doors shut, leaving the three of us outside in the snow. My father clenched and unclenched his hands helplessly.

I stared at him, the memory of those iron manacles fresh in my mind. "I saw the iron cuffs." My voice was accusing, and he took a step backward, shocked at my words. "You put the queen in chains!"

"Kirin—you don't understand the circumstances!"

"I understand enough! How can you put in chains that which you claim to love?"

His mouth opened and closed. "She is held by no chains, now."

My mother drew me close. "No—for now the chains are around my heart."

The wind moved about me, and I heard again the sad voices. "*. . . beeetraaayed . . .*"

I looked up at Leirinda. "I hear the voices on the wind."

She nodded. "Yes. You have always heard them. That is what I gave you at your birth. The voices of winter are in you, as they are in me." She looked at the king, and her voice became strong. "We made promises—and you broke both of yours to me. Release me from mine."

Valhar stared at her, his face unreadable. Finally, with a slow nod, he turned away, to look out over the frozen lake. Leirinda spoke softly, her eyes never leaving my face.

"Years ago, when I dwelled in the north . . . your father came to me. His kingdom was being ravaged by his enemies, and needed far more than arms to defeat them. I was constantly being approached by suitors, unwanted and unworthy, and although my defenses were dangerous, he still managed to cross the mountains and brave the storms I sent to discourage him." Her voice trailed off, her eyes seeing a memory mine could not. With a trace of a smile she continued. "He was both courageous and determined. I was . . . impressed." Her eyes met mine again. "He promised that if I agreed to help him, he and his men would guard me from any other suitors that I wished to discourage. I agreed . . ."

Her voice faltered then, and I felt her tremble. "And when my winter winds had ravaged his enemies, he turned to me and proclaimed his love, and swore he would forever shelter me from others—if I would only agree to marry him. I refused. And he took me, by force."

I felt the courtyard tilt beneath my feet. *Am I a child of rape?*

Leirinda swallowed and continued. "He—took me—and brought me here, bound in chains. I refused to bow before his will . . . and he left me in that cell, alone . . . apart from the winds."

I felt the rage and sorrow within her as she trembled again. The winds blew about us, crying out in their whispery voices. "Mother—" My tears welled up again.

"I was helpless without touch of the winter winds. When I knew I was with child, I was forced . . . to give in . . . and he made me swear never to use my hold on the winds against him . . . and to raise his child ignorant of its heritage. He thought I carried a male child, an heir to his throne . . ."

Valhar turned, and I saw with a shock that his eyes were bright with tears. "All I asked was your love, and an heir."

"You asked too much!" Her tone was sharp, and her pale face flushed pink with anger. The wind began to pick up, small flurries of snow dancing across the lake below us.

My voice was very small as I asked, "What was the king's promise to you?"

"That he would never ask me to do that which I could not. He could not expect my love—nor could he expect me to command the winds which I had been forced to abandon."

The sharp sting of the winds grew colder. I heard the voices howl, high up among the towers, ". . . *aaabaaannnndonnnned* . . ."

I wiped away the tears which threatened to freeze on my face. "And the winter winds have sought revenge ever since . . . ?"

"Yes. Against the king. And my hold on them—and myself—has grown weak over time. It was only when they found you that I dared to hope. . . ." I remembered my sudden flaring anger as my father had struck my mother, and the crashing of the winds as they had torn through the castle to find me—*did I grant them the strength? And when my mother embraced me—was she protecting me from them . . . or demonstrating that I was her child—that I was to be obeyed as she was?*

My little wind danced about me, growing in force as the other, more powerful winds joined it. It had stayed when the others left, to guide me to the knowledge of who—and what—my mother really was.

My eyes found my father, standing apart from us. "Such treachery . . ." My voice broke. "How could you, Father?" The winds began to blow harder, colder, but the chill did not reach us.

"I did it—for love, Kirin!"

". . . *nnnnnnoooooo* . . ." sighed the winds. I felt their embrace as the world fell away, and the dancing snows lifted us into the sky, my mother and me, and carried us northward, carried us home.

THE BRIDGE OVER DARIKILL FEL

by Stephen L. Burns

As I said earlier, and probably more than once—true things don't get any less true for repeating—one of my major pleasures in editing is to welcome back to our readers people we've met before in this series. One—and not the least of these—is Stephen Burns, who lives on Wellesley Island, on the St. Lawrence River; he has "an ancient cat, a young whelp of a dog" and come August of this year—1989—he will be married to an herbalist named Sue-Ryn Hildenbrand. She has a booth at the Sterling, New York, Renaissance Festival, and helping her there has had, he says, "an odd effect upon my speech and wardrobe."

He has also appeared in small press magazines and to my great pride has achieved the status of a "semi-regular contributor" to the enormously prestigious ANALOG magazine. He would like to write a novel (or more) sometime in the future; he says that only last week a fortune cookie assured him there was immense wealth in his future. All I can say about that is that it probably isn't as a writer—writers don't usually get rich or famous—though if there were any justice in the world they all would—and especially those like Steve, who provide a whole society with their favorite dreams.

King Keronian had been back at his keep no longer than it took to change into dry clothes and boots when he summoned his chamberlain, Reege.

"Well?" he demanded when the old man presented himself. "Are they come?"

Reege looked like a man lately informed that he had been selected to join the ranks of the eunuchs. "Not so much *they*, lord," he replied evasively.

Having just spent six days mired hip-deep in mud while directing the failing efforts to dam the rain-swollen Wanderush River before it swallowed up and carried off most of the kingdom's best croplands, Keronian was in no mood for riddles. He scowled at his retainer. "Do you tell me that no one answered my call?"

"No," Reege answered, his face grown longer than his beard. "But weighed against our troubles, the difference between no one and what has come escapes me."

The king let out a tired sigh, wondering what god had decided to make sport of him and his kingdom. "Well," he said, "Unless I have missolved one part of your riddle, *someone* has answered my call. Time rushes faster than that damned river, and until it is dammed, I have nothing even remotely like an army to send against those blasted Irsikilliki savages when they invade."

He leaned forward, his voice going low and dangerous. "So stop mumbling these witless ambiguities and *send him in!*"

This display of kingly wrath sent Reege scurrying for the door. But he paused just before letting it close behind him, licking his lips and readying himself for a fast escape.

"It's not a *him,* lord," he cried through the crack.

"What?" Keronian demanded. But Reege was already gone.

Keronian laughed out loud. He could not help himself. Shaking his head in wonder, he addressed the lone respondant to his call for mercenary troops.

"Have I heard you truly? You demand a hundred gold talents—a price that would be high payment for a whole army—for you alone?" He leaned forward as if to better look at the one before him. "I am tempted to question that you are indeed a woman, for you show more balls than most men in this kingdom!"

Clea, known as "The Fox" by many, but as *that damned bitch Clea,* and other names less complimentary by those who had come in contest with her, smiled up at the king.

Slight of build and dressed in a long shift of black wool, she seemed not at all dismayed by the king's doubts. Her wide-set black eyes sparking with a good humor that might have been gilded with a filigree of madness, she answered, "I think you mistake common equipment for nerve, King Keronian. Coward and hero alike have the former, and the same will to use them. But as to the latter? When the call is for courage, they become mere ornaments, and I can purchase prettier trinkets at the meanest of marketplaces."

Keronian laughed again. "I swear, you tempted me to give you a hand of gold talents for simply providing me a reason to laugh at this dire time." His face grew sober. "There has been little enough to laugh at of late."

"I would never refuse gold," Clea answered, "Yet why pay me a pittance as jester to help you forget your troubles, when the price I have named will end them altogether?"

"You do not jest, do you?" Keronian looked her up and down. "You are no bigger than a slim boy. Your arms are not those of a sword-wielder. You are young, and bear not the stamp of some mantic who would carry out this task with magic. So unless you have some army at your beck . . ." He waved his hand and shrugged.

Clea dismissed his doubts with a wave of her own hand. "A knife-wielder needs not the thick arms of a sword-fighter. As for magics, I know a small trick or two. I make no boast when I say that not only am I sufficient to this task, but to much more than you could ever guess."

Her smile faded. "Hear me, Lord; I know your strait. You are but a year enthroned, replacing an uncle gone mad and strange. Your vaults are richest in dusty corners and empty shelves. An overlong rainy season has swollen the river beyond its normal bounds, and every available hand in your kingdom is turned toward keeping your best croplands from becoming a lair for the fishes."

She paused a moment, eyeing him intently. A prickle of unease ran up his spine. He was overtaken by the sudden, strange notion that she was weighing his soul. For just a moment the familiar stone walls of his keep faded around him. Visions flickered behind his widening eyes. Visions of a laughing old man crushed by falling rocks; of a black glass tower and some nightshade monster heroically fighting a hundred smaller monsters; other glimpses that came and were gone in the space of a single heartbeat.

The moment passed. Keronian let out his pent-up breath, wondering if she had enspelled him, or if what he had felt was simply exhaustion taking its toll.

"But," she continued as if nothing had happened, "I have no doubt that you would be equal to such setbacks. It is the Irsikilliki tribesmen on your northern border who have made necessary your call for help. Ever a nuisance—though rarely more than that—they have long been kept from invading in numbers by Darikill Fel, the great deep gorge between your lands and theirs.

"But now they have captured some learned man; a builder and architect from one of the great Southron cities. He builds them a means to cross the Fel."

"So they might strip this land like locusts," Keronian agreed, his equilibrium returned. "You know my situation well enough; that I will admit. But what can one woman alone do against a horde?"

"All that is needed. Besides, I will have aid."

Keronian's eyes lit with new hope. Perhaps this strange creature, so waiflike in appearance and yet so aglessly self-possessed was the mistress of an army after all! "Where are they camped?" he demanded, leaning forward in his eagerness. "Are their numbers sufficient?"

"There is only one, Lord, and she awaits without. Rest assured, this task will not overtax us." Clea turned toward the door. "Ask Maggrix in."

The guard looked to his king for permission, receiving a glum nod. Only one more than this weird weregirl, and another woman at that? Were this not some brawny swordmaiden, he might as well abdicate his throne and go into the boat-building trade.

Keronian's face fell when the newcomer shuffled in, leaning on a stick. He would have been willing to wager his crown that she was no less than a century old. Tiny and bent, her limbs were stick-thin and gnarled, and her face as wrinkled as a sun-dried grape. If she possessed any teeth, they had to be in a pocket of her ragged robe. She hobbled in to stand at Clea's side, staring up at the king with eyes as bright as ice chips.

"Too old," she said, baring her gums and cackling. "A pity. Has he a son, perhaps?"

Clea smiled at the smaller woman. "He has, though too young for your purposes. You will just have to wait."

"Then there best be savage bucks in plenty," the crone grumbled. "Young and hot-blooded." She cackled again, licking her seamed lips. "Ripe and tender, not like that old fellow up on the throne there. *Sweet.*"

"Enough!" Keronian roared, his patience frayed past the breaking point. "I am sorely tired, and can ill-afford to waste my time on whatever game you play. Begone with you, or I shall have you tossed in a cell for your impudence. I have plenty enough guards left in my keep for that!"

"Actually, you do not," Clea remarked mildly.

"I will remove them, sire," Reege volunteered, hoping to at least keep a place in the shadow of his master's good graces. He marched forward and started to grab the crone by the elbow. A surprised bleat escaped him when he found himself grabbed, snatched off his feet, and hoisted up over her white-haired head.

Maggrix eyed him critically, then shook her head. "Too old," she said regretfully, tossing him away like an overripe fruit. Reege flew across the chamber in a blur of windmilling limbs. Only his crashing into an arras hung over the open doorway into a side room saved his neck from being broken.

The guard at the door started forward, bringing his spear to the ready. King Keronian's eye was too slow to follow the speed with which Clea produced a long black knife from apparently nowhere, turned and flung it in one fluid motion.

The knife flashed across the room like black lightning. It struck the shaft of the guard's spear, splitting it lengthwise, half its length protruding through the splintered wood to point at a spot right between the guard's bulging eyes like an accusing finger.

"Stand to, guard," she said gently, another knife already in her hand. Beside her Maggrix primly rearranged her rags.

The guard swallowed hard, eyes on the knife, then stepped back. Reege groaned and heaved himself to his knees. Keronian watched all this but said nothing, for words seemed a bit beyond his reach at that moment.

Clea winked at the guard and gestured. The black knife wedged in his spear wrenched itself free and flew back to her hand like a trained bird. Once there it vanished.

She turned back toward Keronian, smiling as if nothing had happened. "No others have answered your call for a force to defeat the Irsikilliki. Do you not think that our energies would be better turned against *them,* Lord? I tell no lie when I say that they are already half-defeated, and I am loath to abandon a task already begun. We shall go now to finish our work, and you would be well advised to have the fee prepared against my return." She crossed her arms. "Have you any disagreement with this, Lord?"

He gave her a sour smile. "I have my doubts they would make any difference."

"Then our bargain is made." Clea and Maggrix

turned and departed; one shuffling along on her stick, the other's step light and confident. The guard let them out, taking care to stay well back from Clea.

When they were gone, Reege skulked to the king's side, limping slightly. "You will not meet their outrageous demands, will you, sire?"

Keronian started to answer, then frowned. "Who else offers to aid us? I have spent nothing, and since the gods seem in a capricious mood, they just may prevail. Whatever way it goes, there is naught else I can do for the moment but give myself some long-overdue sleep."

His face hardened. "All this has done little to help my much-shortened temper. I warn you, if my sleep is troubled I will take my next rest with your head as my pillow." He rose and stalked off toward his private chambers.

A pale, shaken Reege watched his departure. He was certain that his king was too kindly a man for such a barbarous act.

There were several matters that demanded his tending. But perhaps he had best tend them from a station outside the king's bedroom door just to be on the safe side. . . .

As Reege pondered these matters, Dessurne, a tall, fox-faced, fair-haired man dressed in silken finery gone to rags and tatters stood on a low knoll contemplating his own unhappy situation.

He watched the naked, paint-daubed Irsikilliki wildmen putting the final touches on the turnable reach-bridge which would allow them to cross the gorge called Darikill Fel.

He was tired of hearing them boast about how easily they would conquer the land across the Fel. A learned man and one for fine distinctions, he knew that conquering implied imposing some sort of new order on the victims of their assault.

If these savages had any sense of order, he had not seen any evidence of it in the three moons since his capture. Had the workforce been even halfway competent, the siege machine would have been completed over a moon ago. He was past counting the number of times he had been tempted to abandon the project.

But he had persevered for several reasons. One was that without the bridge he had no way of escaping to the kingdom they planned to invade; a land certain to be more civilized than this wretched place where the trench toilet was a new invention—one he had brought to them—and the closest they had to wine was a stuff called *urgsk*, brewed from fermented grass in muddy pits.

Another was that they had made it clear he would end up wearing his own entrails around his neck if he did not help them.

Below him an *urgsk*-sotted ass had begun lashing a brace on backward. Sighing, he started down to see that it was done right, the rude, heavy chains around his feet clanking in time with his steps.

He hoped with all his heart that the kingdom across the Fel had a big army waiting, and that he was not mistaken for another Irsikilliki wildman by some close-sighted soldier when they met it.

In two days the matter would be resolved one way or the other. The time had come to begin refining his plans.

Food. Shiny-pretties aplenty. Fine blades. *Women . . .*

Irsikubo could not help beaming with avaricious pride as he watched his battle-painted men swarm over the great making that was the gateway to those things and more.

No more skulking about and stealing this bit or that like mice. No more having half the men he sent out fail in their attempts to cross or recross the gorge; those returning able to carry little of anything valuable—and nothing of what was most ardently desired—because of the arduousness of the journey. At last able to . . .

His thoughts of high statesmanship flew from his mind like startled birds when his wife Omatoo grasped his ear and hauled him to his feet by it. Had he not been celebrating the nearness of the project's completion with much *urgsk*, he would have been warned by the stench of the rancid pig fat she and all the other Irsikilliki women customarily wore as a cosmetic.

She said not a word, only showed him her filed teeth in a leer that made what she wanted all too clear. As she outweighed him over two to one, there was little profit in resistance. All the women of their race were twice larger and thrice fiercer than the men. That went a long way toward explaining why the men did not forbid the filed teeth and pig-fat cosmetic the women so loved.

Too late he regained what the *urgsk* had driven from his head. He had planned to consult the Spirit-talker, seeking some reason to remain apart from his wife in these last days leading up to battle.

As headman, he was entitled to first pick of any women they captured. But unless he remained safe from Omatoo's endless hunger, he would be too drained to do anything with them.

Which would take most of the gloss off the invasion's bright promise.

King Keronian stared at the young man Reege had set to following the lunatic woman and her ancient accomplice who proposed to win his war for him. Reege did gain credit for thinking to put a spy on them, but why had he picked this lackwit?

No doubt the lad was a nephew, or worse.

"Let me see if I have it aright," he said with all the patience he could muster. "They bought a large horse-drawn cart and four casks of cheap dark wine."

The spy nodded timidly, his eyes downcast, but said not a word.

"Then they went to the Glass Master's Works and took delivery of one hundred glass-bladed, wooden-handled swords?"

Another slight nod.

"You went in after they departed and questioned Master Petchris on this matter. He told you that the young one hired him for their making a full three days ago, paying in advance."

A sigh this time instead of a nod.

Keronian sighed as well. This was where the story—and its teller—always fell apart. "You say that as you were leaving Petchris' Works you were taken captive."

A whimper.

He gripped the spy's shoulder. "Steady on, lad. Was it the young one, the one called Clea who took you?"

An anguished moan. The spy shook his head from side to side.

"Then it was the old one? Well, she is uncannily strong. I saw that myself, though I could scarce believe it. So the old one took you, and dragged you back into the alley behind the Works. Come, lad, I am your king. I mean you no harm. Can you not tell me what happened then?"

The spy's only answer was to burst into tears, hunching over with his hands trapped between his legs as if to protect himself from some terrible threat.

Keronian sighed, remembering the crone's interest in young men and suspecting he knew the fate that had left the lad so unhinged. He sat back to consider the matter.

The women appeared to be purchasing weapons and drink for the invaders. He could not think of any way to find this news reassuring.

As if that were that not enough to darken his thoughts, over the sound of the spy's sobs he now heard the rains hammering down once more.

Dessurne stood at Irsikubo's side, helping oversee the project's final stage, and praying that a combination of ill-suited materials and shoddy, incompetent workmanship did not cause the roughly built engine to fail.

Just below, a ragged line of warriors carried baskets of sand to the tightly woven, leaf-lined receiver at one end. The pile inside it grew larger, even though there was more drunken laughter and horseplay than order or industry in their labors.

He now knew the real reason for the upcoming invasion, and it was much the same as one of his reasons for wanting to escape.

The Irsikilliki women. The vast, insatiable, fat-smeared, sharp-toothed, sharp-tongued creatures who made most of the men's lives a living hell. The reason that the men tended to spend most waking moments drunk on *urgsk*.

It was no great task to find Irsikubo *urgsk*-addled; and last night he had sought the headman out and plied him with more of that vile libation. He had learned much.

When Irsikubo was but a boy and his father head-man, his tribe had captured an outlaw who had escaped the neighboring kingdom's Guard by crossing the Fel and fleeing into the Irsikilliki lands. He had taught the Irsikilliki a tongue more civilized than their own, and told them tales of that other land. It was from him that they had learned of shiny-pretties, of fine blades and other wonders. To be closer to this magical bounty the tribe had moved to the edge of the Fel.

The men had kept secret one thing they had learned from this outlander. He had told them of how different women were across the Fel. They had gifted him with a wife for this precious knowledge, and he had committed suicide some five moons later.

The women belived the invasion was being staged so the men could bring them gold, rare cloths, jewels, and other treasures.

The men's dearest secret was that *women* were at the top of their looting list. Diminutive, blunt-toothed, sweet-smelling ungreased non-Irsikilliki women.

The sand-bearers staggered on. Suddenly the massive device groaned. A shout went up, and more sand was dumped into the huge basket. It groaned louder. An awed hush spread as the great arm lifted like the head of a sleeping dragon to hang a man's-height above the stony ground. Dessurne let out a relieved sigh.

The men cheered and drank a round of *urgsk*. The women strove to look unimpressed.

Dessurne took a long swallow of the awful stuff himself, begging whatever gods there were that the thing held together. He had to get away.

Last night a drunken Irsikubo had given him one of the women as guest-wife. Though young, sweet, and comely by Irsikilliki standards, she had the face and disposition of a camel, and one seemingly endless night in her tender embrace had left his body a mass of sprains, bites, and bruises.

He still had no way of knowing if this was simply drunken generosity, or a cruel and crafty way of insuring that he did not sabotage the bridge at the last moment.

He wiped his lips on his sleeve, then nudged Irsikubo in the ribs. "Have them take up the ropes."

The headman nodded happily and let out a bellow. A hundred little painted men scurried to take up the ropes, then bent their backs to the task with a will.

The creaking of the ropes was drowned out as the massive reaching-bridge's weight began to shift. It pivoted ponderously on its timbered base, the long working end swinging out over the gorge. Once it was over the opposite ledge, the ropes were released and enough sand bailed out to let the bridgehead settle to the ground.

Dessurne had first planned to have them simply slit the counterweight basket's bottom. That would leave the Irsikilliki a line of retreat—and the neighboring land's army a way to follow after and wipe them out.

More than pride in his arts had made him change his mind. There was the matter of a subtle and perfect revenge for his capture and the uncountable indignities he had suffered.

He knew that the engine was too shoddily built to survive being lifted and turned away. It would collapse, surely as his name was Dessurne. That meant that the Irsikilliki had a safe line of retreat.

Right into the waiting arms of their women, never able to escape again.

"Our plans go good, hey?" Irsikubo cried, grinning and slapping Dessurne on the back.

He smiled back. "Our plans go very well indeed."

The paint-daubed army crossed their new bridge. Just under a hundred in number and armed only with stone-tipped spears, stone knives, clubs and slings, a score of mounted guards could probably have turned them back. But other than the handful of guards on duty at the keep, they were all at the far side of the kingdom, battling the Wanderush River instead.

Once across, they shambled forward in a loose knot. At the center of that knot was Dessurne, whose status had become somewhat unclear. The Irsikilliki warriors were treating him like a hero, taking turns thumping him on the back and offering him *urgsk*. Each one told him what a splendid fellow he was, and that they would name their children after him.

But then again, they would only laugh when asked to remove the chains from around their hero's feet.

The invaders had traveled less than a league when they came upon four large wooden casks in the center of the path. One cask had been set atop the others and tapped. Under the tap was a filled mug. Writ large on each cask was the word *WINE*.

They halted, frowning and muttering in confusion. They had before pilfered smaller casks—empty more often than full—but to see ones this size was not unlike seeing a mouse the size of a horse. The consensus was that they should give them wide berth.

Dessurne eyed the casks thoughtfully. They were obviously placed there to be found by the Irsikilliki. Could it be someone thought that if the savages became besotted enough, they might abandon their invasion? That seemed unlikely. The wine was more probably drugged.

Whatever the reasoning behind this offering, he was sure that his best interests lay in having his captors drink it.

"I do believe those casks contain wine," he told Irsikubo.

The headman looked suspicious. "Wine?"

"Did not the outlaw speak of it? It is like *urgsk*, only sweeter." He hesitated, seeking a way to make the offering more tempting. "Not only are the outland women fairer and more gentle, so is their *urgsk*. You really should try it."

Irsikubo squinted at him, a crafty look on his broad, paint-daubed face. "And maybe be poisoned, hah? If you so sure we should drink, maybe you should drink some first."

Dessurne had been half-expecting this. Irsikubo was not an entire fool. But he told himself that were there a truly subtle mind behind this offering, the first cup would be pure even if the casks were tainted.

"It would be my pleasure." He shuffled up to the casks, Irsikubo remaining right by his side. He picked up the filled mug, and after giving its contents a tenative sniff, tipped it back.

He had scented nothing amiss in the wine. But there was a fair chance that three moons spent among a folk not given to bathing had blunted his sense of smell. Wine spilled past both sides of his mouth, trickling down his chin and chest—more wine than reached the inside of his mouth. As this was the way the Irsikilliki drank, none thought him trying to pull some sort of trick.

It was a cheap, ordinary wine; one he might have once spurned as too coarse for a man of his refined tastes. But after three months of *urgsk*, it tasted like a flagon from the emperor's table. He could not resist allowing a swallow or two past his lips and onto his delighted tongue.

His canny captors waited all of ten heartbeats for any ill effects to show themselves before swarming over the casks like ants over a crumb of honey-cake.

When the Irsikilliki invaders staggered around a bend in the path not half a league distant from where they had conquered the casks, they found a stack of swords waiting for them.

Most of them had been drunk even before setting out on their sortie, and the wine had done little to sharpen their sense of caution. In a matter of moments they were reeling about, laughing like children and waving the swords about in delight.

Dessurne doubted that it would be noticed if he tried to acquire a sword of his own. But trying to stay out of the path of carelessly wielded blades was a much more pressing matter.

Bobbing and weaving through the melee, he sought the logic of arming the savages. The blades were glass instead of metal, but wickedly sharp and probably no more prone to shattering than their own blades of thinly-struck stone.

There had to be some subtle sense to it. He cursed that second—or was it third or fourth—helping of wine. It had turned his thoughts slippery as eels.

Irsikubo was the first to recover the reason they were in a position to find such treasures. He bawled out his orders, reiterating them with a certain amount of chivvying and cuffing.

Not long after they were on the march once more, loudly and boisterously congratulating themselves on how good they were at this invading and looting business.

Leaving their own weapons behind, lying scattered and forgotten on the path where they had dropped them.

Dessurne could not help wondering what would happen next.

He was even more curious about the mind behind the offerings of wine and swords. There was a plan at work here; a plan that showed a subtlety and depth of thought to perhaps equal his own.

What sort of man would the planner be? Wine-warmed and sure that freedom awaited around the next bend, Dessurne grew certain that the planner was a kindred spirit, another man of wit and learning. No doubt their meeting would be the beginning of a full and rich friendship.

The Irsikilliki invaders now moved at the pace of a ravening horde of snails. Still, it was not long before they crested a low, wooded hill and beheld a bonfire in the shallow depression just below.

A shout went up. Surely this was food, or women, or some other delight. Wine-brave and waving their fine new swords aloft, they staggered, rolled, tumbled and slid down to conquer.

Moving more slowly as befit his dignifed position, Irsikubo proceeded down to maintain control of his troops. Dessurne remained by his side because it was only his shoulder that kept the headman from falling on his face.

There were two people at the fire. One was a tiny, ancient woman all dressed in rags. The other was cloaked in black, hood pulled down to hide his face, hunched before the fire as if warming himself by it.

Pride swelled in Irsikubo's breast as several moons of training paid; his warriors more or less surrounded the pair.

He and Dessurne pushed through their ranks. The crone tottered toward them and flung herself at Dessurne's feet.

"Woe!" she wailed, clinging to his chain-decked ankles and gazing up at him in wide-eyed entreaty. "Oh, master, a doom is upon us! The daughter of my daughter! Witch! Monster!"

Dessurne stared down at her, blinking owlishly. This had to be another strand of the web of deception they had entered, yet surely the ancient at his feet could not be the weaver at its center. But what about the cloaked figure before the fire?

He spoke to the crone then, but pitched his voice so it was certain to reach the ears of the mysterious other. "I am but a prisoner, mother. A hostage. Do you understand me, a *captive.*"

He shucked Irsikubo off his shoulder. The headman swayed, but remained upright. "Here is the captain of this horde. The one who keeps me chained."

The old woman transferred her embrace to Irsikubo's ankles. "Kill her, master! The doom must be unmade! I beg you, kill her!"

"Kill who?" Irsikubo asked muzzily, scratching his head.

"The daughter of my daughter!" she wailed. "The poisoned fruit of the fruit of my loins! The witch, the witch, the *witch!*"

Irsikubo looked around in confusion. "What witch?"

"*This* witch!" answered the shrouded figure before the fire, standing and turning to face them. The hood was thrown back to reveal the cold, cruel face of a woman with close-cropped black hair and wide-set eyes the color of midnight. So forbidding was her mien that a nervous muttering went through the warriors encircling her, and the circle widened.

"Kill her!" the crone shieked again. "Kill the monster before you find out what she can do!"

"Silence, you stick," the monster in question hissed, "Or blood or no, I will warm my hands on you, too!"

Dessurne's mind was not so sodden that he missed the implications of this threat. He cleared his throat nervously. "Yon blaze was, ah, someone?"

The laugh that preceeded her answer froze his marrow. "Indeed it was. My dear gran thought to palm me off on some doddering old wizard in hopes that I would become biddable if controlled by a power greater than my own."

She laughed again, sweeping her hand toward the blaze. "So much for a greater power than mine! Ah, but he did put up a worthy fight, I will give him that! I had to take him apart in layers, like some tough old onion, and that gave him time to cast—"

"*A curse!*" the old one wailed. "A dark and dreadful curse! Oh, will no one save us from her infamy?" She scrabbled on her hands and knees to the Irsikilliki warrior nearest to her, a brawny young stalwart whose drink-bemused grin faded when she clawed at his legs crying, "You, young master! Will you not chance your life to save this land?"

The warrior glanced nervously at the fire, then shuffled back out of reach. The crone wept in dismay and threw herself at the next man in line, repeating her entreaty.

There was something like love in the witch's eyes as she purred, "It was a rare and beautiful curse. He cursed this land that spawned me who cut short his life. For so long as I live, any man who lies with a woman shall find himself unmanned and unable. This state of nonaffairs is supposed to lend urgency to the task of removing my head from my shoulders and seeing him revenged."

Dessurne heard Irsikubo grunt in dismay. A sidewise glance showed the headman's brow furrowed in wine-slowed thought.

The witch drew herself up, her gaze gone cold and haughty. "My head is mine to keep. I made the curse-caster into his own pyre, and as he burned I forged a curse of my own. Hear me and know that any man who raises arms against me will first find his weapon shattered, then his manhood will suffer a likewise fate!"

This warning had just been issued, but had not yet time to sink into Irsikubo's skull, when he at last untangled the incinerated wizard's curse. *"What?"* he roared, clutching his sword more tightly. "We go through all this trouble and now you say we can have no *women?*"

A nervous muttering passed through the Irsikilliki ranks, angry expressions appearing on the faces of the quickest witted. The ring around the witch tightened.

She responded by flinging her cloak behind her and moving her hands. They were instantly filled with a pair of long-bladed black knives. Her lips drew back from her teeth in a feral grin.

"I warn you one last time, you gutless snivelings: Come for me, and first your weapon shatters, then your manhood joins the broken pieces in the dust!"

"Kill her!" screeched the crone. "She lies! Her curse has no power! Kill her and all this land's women will be yours!"

"Kill her!" Irsikubo bellowed, brandishing his glass sword.

Dessurne's breath caught in his throat as he watched the young woman laugh and taunt those who encircled her. Although outnumbered a hundred to one, she showed no trace of fear. Those hundred looked to each other for the one who would attack first, but none stepped forward to accept that honor.

Irsikubo cursed, and enraged past all reason at the cowardice of his men and having that most precious booty denied him, made a lumbering charge at the witch.

The witch raised her knives and let loose a bloodcurdling war cry. The howl she emitted skirled higher and higher, reaching a note that raised the hackles on the back of Dessurne's neck.

Irsikubo held his sword down before him in a clumsy, two-handed grip. Suddenly the beautiful glass blade shattered as if struck with a hammer, leaving him holding only a blunt wooden handle. At that same moment all the other swords exploded into a thousand glittering shards.

The headman skidded to a halt, his bulging eyes fixed on the useless remains of his weapon. He paled as he realized what was supposed to happen next. In less than the space of a single heartbeat he got his feet turned around and sent them flying back toward Darikill Fell as fast as they would carry him.

Irsikubo's leadership was proved; his battle-painted army did not hesitate to follow their headman's lead. They dropped the sticks their weapons had become as if they had been turned to vipers and stampeded after him.

But an even dozen of them had sprinted no more than a dozen strides away before their feet were yanked out from under them by some unseen force. Those unfortunates hit the hard ground like sacks of wheat and lay there stunned.

Dessurne nearly screamed when he felt a hand on his shoulder. His head snapped around and he found himself face-to-face with the fearsome witch.

He fainted dead away.

When he recovered his senses, she was crouched over him, the expression on her face one of dismay. He sat up in sudden panic, startling her back. "The Irsikilliki—" he cried, looking about wildly. "You—"

"Gone," she said soothingly. "If I have frighted them aright, they'll not stop until they have recrossed the bridge you built them, swung it back, and broken it into a thousand pieces."

Dessurne stared at her in disbelief. "*You?* You were the author of all this?"

She blushed and ducked her head. "I am, my lord. My name is Clea."

Before Dessurne could recoup his wits sufficiently to remember courtly manners and introduce himself, he heard a scream. He jerked around to look, and the sight he beheld was so strange that it took him several moments to make sense of it.

The crone was scavenging the edge of the battlefield. The scream had come from a fallen warrior who had been stuffed in a huge sack. As he watched she tottered to the next one in line, and passed a knife through the air next to his feet. Then she picked him up like a straw dummy, her stick-thin arms hardly bulging, and wadded him in after the first. Cackling gleefully she dragged her sack—already laden with the weight of two—on to harvest the next.

"That is Maggrix," he heard the young witch say. "My accomplice in your rescue." Clea. Her name was Clea.

Dessurne shook his head, baffled. He had a thousand questions, but the old woman's actions first begged explanation. "What made those men fall? How can one so ancient be so strong?" He swallowed hard. "What is she going to do with them?"

"Maggrix is very learned," Clea replied reverently. "The men were brought down by this." She knelt before his feet. He had his eye on her hand, and could have sworn the knife that suddenly filled it just appeared there. She made a pass near his feet, then held up what looked like a strand of thread.

"This brought them down. Web-fine, it is nonetheless as strong as a heavy rope. The secret of its making, and the secret of her strength are known by only a chosen few, and most of those learned it from her. As for the men she has captured, well, she believes that if she beds enough young men she will herself become young again."

"That is ridiculous," he muttered.

Clea spread her hands. He frowned when he realized that the knife was gone again. "I myself have doubts that it will work," she said, "But she gets much pleasure from it, regardless of its efficacy, and who would gainsay her?"

He watched her hoist and bag a stout lad nearly thrice her size. He swallowed hard. "Not I."

"Nor I. Shall we depart and leave her to her pleasures?"

Dessurne had no argument with that; he was afraid that he, too, might end up in her sack.

"The sooner the better," he said, climbing to his feet. He pointed at his shackles. "But we would make better time were I free of these chains. They slow my pace."

"We need not walk back to the keep of King Keronian. I have a horse and wagon waiting nearby," Clea said. Then her face fell. "But as to those chains, it shames me to tell you that I neglected to bring the sort of tools needed to strike them off. I hope you can pardon my stupidity in coming to free you and yet letting something so important slip past me. . . ."

Dessurne patted her atop the head like she was an errant child. "Do not chastise yourself, fair one." Indeed, she was fair, and from more than the viewpoint of a man who not only had seen naught but Irsikilliki women for three moons, but also spent a harrowing night with one of their lasses.

He gave her a winning smile. "You have released me from my long imprisonment. Though these chains remain, they are now no more than an inconvenience."

A further thought occurred to him. "Must you report to this King Keronian upon your return?"

She ducked her head, looking unhappy. "I must."

"Then this is for the best. The king will be able to see proof that I was a prisoner of the Irsikilliki, not some paid conspirator."

She said, "You may be right, my lord . . ." But she still looked unconvinced. He was unsurprised that the brilliance of this argument surpassed her; this was not the woman's art of bending men's actions, but the man's art of political strategy.

He gave her his most winning grin; one that had lured many a woman to his bed. "Do not worry, my beautiful rescuatrix. You made no omission. This will all turn out for the best."

She looked up at him, gifting him with a shy smile that made him exult in how easily she could be manipulated. "If you think so," she said. "Although we could probably stop at some farm and have those chains off. . . ."

"We leave them on," he said. "I know best. You'll see. . . ."

"Sticks?" Irsikubo's wife Omatoo shrieked in red-faced outrage. "You come running back with your tail between your legs bearing nothing but sticks you say were once great weapons?"

Irsikubo made no answer. His wife bared her filed teeth and hissed in frustration, then grabbed him by her favorite ear—the one that had been pulled to near twice the size of the other. "We will discuss this, worm, to my full satisfaction!" She began towing him toward their mud hut.

He went meekly. He was tired, his head hurt, and he knew what she would want of him once the explanations were over. He could only thank the gods that he had escaped with the means to provide it all intact.

Irsikubo's dreams of conquest were broken, his captive builder was gone, and he was left with a question to plague his sleep for some time to come.

Would he have been better off had he remained behind, perhaps unmanned, but out of Omatoo's tender clutches once and for all?

One thing was certain. With that damned bridge over Darikill Fell broken into kindling, he was sure to have much time to ponder the matter.

King Keronian stared down at Clea, wondering if he dared hope. "So you are returned," he said tonelessly.

"I am, Lord," she replied meekly. "The Irsikilliki have been turned back. So I fear I must bring up, well, the matter of my fee. . . ." She hugged herself and stared at the floor in misery.

Keronian frowned, wondering at this sudden humility.

But Dessurne was unsurprised at Clea's diffidence. She was, after all, a woman. True, she had turned back the invaders and freed him, but all that had been wrought with deception and guile; women's traits all. But in a situation such as this—man to man—of course she was out of her depth.

He was resolved to intercede in her behalf. He was no stranger to discourse with kings and princes. Besides, did he not owe her that much for freeing him?

Beyond all that, such an act might earn him the sort of gratitude that is banked in bed. Although fairly certain that once he was bathed, shaved, and again made presentable the sight of him would draw her halfway there, he knew the wise man allowed for the unpredictable whims of women. This would be but one more brace buttressing an already solid structure.

"A fee well earned," he exclaimed, drawing himself up and meeting the king's eye.

"And who might you be?" Keronian inquired archly, fairly certain he already knew the answer.

He bowed. "Dessurne il-Apsangir, Chief Architect and Works-Master to Emperor Mansu of the great city of Sessaria." He glanced sideways at Clea to see what impression this recitation of his title and station made on her. The awed expression it had put on her face made him smile inwardly. Even King Keronian looked impressed.

"Behold these chains on my feet, Lord," he continued. "For three moons I have been a prisoner of the Irsikilliki savages."

"So," Keronian put in quietly, "you are the one who gave them means to invade my kingdom."

"Only on pain of death did I provide it," Dessurne protested. "Moreover, I found it hard to see how that drunken rabble could pose much of a threat to any halfway organized kingdom."

The king frowned. Too late Dessurne realized his last remark might be taken as a slur. "After all," he hastened to add, "A score of trained horsemen could have easily driven them back."

"You are right enough there," Keronian admitted

grudgingly. "At their worst they are no more than a nuisance. But I could not spare men to meet them. The rains, you see. The Wanderush River overflows its banks, sweeping away the levees we build faster than they are put up. Nearly every hand in the kingdom is turned toward that task." He sighed wearily. "And yet we fail."

Dessurne nodded in understanding. "Flood, you say? A pity you did not have me instead of the Irsikilliki. I will hazard that I have forgotten more of dams and dikes than the best man in this land. Did you know that there are simple engines that use the power of flowing water to remove what has been spilled? Or that what cannot be directly stopped can often be guided, like a stampeding horse." He tipped his hand to show how inconsequential such matters were. "The waterworks at Sessaria are fabled as the greatest in the world. I do not brag if I say that they are, and it is I who have made them so."

Keronian sat back and stroked his chin, his face unreadable. "Surely you must be bragging."

Dessurne laughed, looking smug. "I tell unalloyed truth. Why, were it I who managed your efforts, that river would be tamed like a dog, and you would have a means to irrigate your fields during the dry season afterward in the bargain!"

The king sighed, then shifted his gaze to Clea. She gave him a sweet smile in return.

He grimaced. "Well," he said, "I suppose I should thank you. But I will withold those thanks until I know how badly I am to be used."

Clea's smile grew brighter. "Not too badly. He is yours for one hundred talents over the one hundred I am already owed for defeating the Irsikilliki."

Dessurne turned to stare at her in slack-jawed surprise, struck dumb by this sudden turning.

"What if I do not pay?" Keronian asked sourly. "What mischief, then?"

Clea laughed. "Do you really want to know?"

He thought that over. "No," he sighed, "I suppose not." He turned to glare at his chamberlain as if this were all his fault. "Reege! Stop standing there with your mouth open to catch flies! Go fetch the gold she gouges from me!"

"But you cannot buy or sell me," Dessurne whispered. Or had he! His objections were paid no more heed than those of the kine on the auction block.

Keronian watched the graybeard scuttle off, then addressed Clea once more. "Do you care that you all but empty my coffers?"

"Have I not given you cofferdams in exchange? But as you feel cheated, I shall offer some free advice. As long as you have a builder, put up a permanent bridge to the Irsikilliki lands. Their invasion could have been forestalled with five talents' worth of gauds and a handful of prostitutes. Offer them service as a regiment. Promise them wine and women—and a chance to be away from their own women. You will have more volunteers than you can use. But be warned: If Maggrix finds the bucks she captured to her liking, the Irsikilliki may just have a new queen when you next meet them."

At that moment Reege returned, dragging two heavy saddlebags after him. Clea looked inside to verify their contents, then slung them over her shoulder. "Our business is concluded. By your leave, my king," she said, giving him an ironic bow.

Keronian managed a pained smile. "You have it. I fear that if you stay I will end up losing my crown to you as well."

Dessurne found his voice at last. "But what about *me?*" he cried, starting toward Clea, his chains clanking about his feet. He held them up and rattled them. "What about *these?*"

"It was you who convinced me they should stay on before," Clea answered sweetly, "And now they are in the king's hands. But if you find yourself needing an escort home once they are struck off, send word and I shall return."

"What?" Dessurne stared at her in disbelief.

She leaned close, giving him a lingering kiss and then whispering, "Surely the emperor would gift well the one who returned you to him. Without a proper escort, who can say that you will not again go astray?"

She kissed him once more, then left him there, listening to the fading sound of her laughter. He turned to face the king, shaking his chains disconsolately. "What of these?"

Keronian stood up. "They will come off once you have earned what I have paid for you." He beckoned. "Come, we must get you garbed for rain and mud before we set you to performing these wonders you promised."

Dessurne let his chains drop, defeated. He shuffled after the king, still a prisoner. *At least there will be wine instead of* urgsk, was his sole consoling thought.

"My lord?" he asked upon reaching the king's side. "The women in this land—do they smear themselves with rancid fat or file their teeth?"

Keronian looked at him as if he had gone slightly mad. "No, they do not."

Perhaps he had gone mad, for he found something like a resigned grin creeping out onto his face. "Thank the gods for small favors," he said, following the man who would be his master for a time.

And as for that day when he was set free—

Surely no mere woman could best a man of his education and experience twice in a row. . . .

WARRIOR'S OATH

by Lynne Armstrong-Jones

Lynne Armstrong-Jones embodies one of the first things I always tell everyone about writing: if they can't handle rejection, they'd better find another profession—because rejection is the first experience of all writers.

I once said flippantly—and yet I couldn't have been more serious, except perhaps in choosing my words—that I became a writer because I sent out manuscripts so often that the editors simply got tired of sending them back. Lynne Armstrong-Jones certainly embodies that advice; for a while, I found a story of hers in my slush pile every week, and even before I bought anything of hers I had begun to respect and applaud her persistence.

My first husband had the somewhat too common feeling that I should not send in stories to be rejected—he said the editors would get so used to my stories not making it that they would send them back unread. Fortunately I did not take his advice, but went—as I try always to advise my writers to do—to someone who knew what they were talking about, the late Sam Merwin; who said (which I knew already) that my husband was dead wrong . . . that all writers—here he named some of my own idols—had gotten, and still got—plenty of rejections. So I kept trying, though I didn't sell for about three more years. But the rest is history.

So I still say to young writers; keep trying. The editor doesn't know what he wants often till he gets it.

The tall rider eyed the turret which seemed to grow into the sky from the tops of the tall green trees. A fluffy cloud hid it from view for a moment, then split into two cottony strips as it passed by the high tower.

"There it is, then," murmured the rider, urging the gray gelding toward a nearby grove of trees. Here they could stop and prepare themselves for whatever lay ahead. The rider had some idea of what to expect, having been briefed by the nobleman as to the number of guards and what he and his spies knew of the castle layout.

Galaan hoped the information which she'd been given was correct. The thought of risking life and limb against sword and magic—for naught—held no appeal. She comforted herself, though, with the thought that, if he wanted his kidnapped niece returned safely, the nobleman would've been careful, indeed, to provide the rescuer with accurate information.

"Well, Jewel," said the tall woman quietly, reaching a finger to the bird upon her shoulder; "I shall need your assistance now. Fly yonder and scan the castle for signs of sorcery which might protect it from the outside. If you see none, return and sing your most pleasurable song. If magic you detect, offer me naught but silence when you've rejoined me. Off, now!"

With that, Galaan swept her hand forward and watched as the crimson bird took flight—no ordinary bird he! Galaan smiled as she recalled how she'd managed to free him from the enchantment which had, at one time, imprisoned him. His gift for detecting the presence of magic had proven a most valuable talent since then.

The sun on her face revealed Galaan's thirty years and more as lines gathering in the corners of blue eyes when she smiled. The nearly twenty years of mercenary work and a plethora of similar occupations had also left *their* marks here and there: the small scar on her chin and long one across her left forearm were permanent reminders of battles fought long ago.

Yet, to live without such challenges would have been unthinkable. She dismounted and and began to prepare her equipment.

She was sitting quite contentedly against the trunk of an oak when Jewel returned. She'd unbound her long, dark hair (which contained just a strand or two of gray here and there), and let it hang freely: it might be a long while before she'd have opportunity to do so again. Her jaws moved rhythmically as she chewed on her hard cheese.

Galaan watched, envying the bird's ability to soar so freely and gracefully above the ground. Her smile was broad, indeed, when the crested bird lit upon her outstretched finger and began to sing. So beautiful and rich were the tone and melody that the woman closed her eyes to shut out all distractions.

"Thank you, dear Jewel," whispered the woman, reaching into a small pouch. When she withdrew her hand, it contained a number of seeds—eagerly devoured by the bird.

Galaan watched as the sky became orange with the setting of the sun. She made sure that her hair was bound tightly in its braid. "Now," she whispered softly, and the bird flew to her, lighting upon her shoulder.

She mounted the gelding and headed toward the castle. It was not long before they came to an area only a few moments' walk from the building. Here Galaan tethered her horse.

Jewel flew upward as the woman dismounted. He came to light upon a trellis near a window.

Galaan was smiling once more as she considered how the redness of his feathers would serve as a beacon for her. Then she turned her attention to finding a good location for climbing.

She withdrew her hook from the small pack at her waist and began to swing the rope so it gathered momentum. Up it went, the hook hitting the wall and falling downward. Galaan was grateful for the breeze which rustled the leaves—and provided background noise to mask the sounds of the hook.

Finally, the device bit into the wall, a bit of pebble crumbling to the ground as it did. Galaan pulled firmly on the rope, and, satisfied, began to ascend. Her boots held the wall well, making her climb a relatively simple one.

Galaan eased herself noiselessly up to the top of the wall, gripping the edge with her fingers. Slowly, slowly, she pulled herself upward until her eyes could see over the rim.

Her ears told her footsteps were approaching, yet she could see no one. Suddenly, a bird chirped—and instantly Galaan had eased herself back down to the level of her hook. Now she heard the footsteps as the guard passed.

She waited. The bird chirped—twice this time. Galaan stretched her long arm to the top of the wall while her other hand pulled the hook free. She worked her way upward, easing herself over the edge, and tucking her hook back into her pack. Almost instantly, she was moving through the shadows, her dagger now in her hand.

She hurried along the walkway to a spot just below the window near the bird. She tried the trellis with her hand but didn't trust it to hold her weight.

The rope once more in Galaan's grasp, she hurled the hook and found a niche. Galaan climbed upward, as certain as a spider in her web.

Her fingers gripped the sill and she pulled herself up until she could gaze into the window. She nodded in the bird's direction. Jewel whistled softly in reply.

So, thought the intruder. *Jewel senses the presence of sorcery*. Not surprising, as there were no bars upon the open window nor any armed guards visible in the sleeping chamber.

All Galaan could see was the reclining figure on the bed, the light of the moon giving it a golden glow. She selected a small pebble and tossed it through the window—but the bird remained silent and there was no other hint of any magic which could prevent entry.

Mildly surprised, Galaan eased herself into the room as silently as a stalking cat. She felt a bit uneasy now, having anticipated a confrontation with some sort of spell before this. . . .

As she moved closer to the bed, though, a gentle whistle from Jewel told her where the magic began.

But it was too late—Galaan had already stepped through the boundary of the spell's power—

She fell backward, automatically shielding her face with her hand as the searing flames rose suddenly before her. Galaan began to pull back, away from the terrible heat—but as she did, she'd already blanked all thought from her mind save one.

I am looking at illusion—nothing more.

She had to move quickly, as the magician would've detected her presence—

She drew her sword and walked through the wall of fire, concentrating on a cool sensation as she did—

And she was through. It had been easier than she'd anticipated, as though the spell was not as strong as some she'd encountered before.

No time for speculation, though. The noblewoman was still sleeping. Galaan reached over and, gently, placed one hand across the woman's mouth to silence her. Eyes opened, wide with fear.

"You are safe, Lady Anna," whispered the rescuer, "I am Galaan, the warrior, come to take you home. . . ."

Poor Lady Anna looked quite distraught, and seemed beyond comprehension.

I must hurry, Galaan was thinking as she heard Jewel's warning of magic. Then, footsteps in the hall told her time was running out.

She sheathed her sword and grabbed the young woman around the waist. But the girl was struggling and cursing Galaan, crying that she would *not* go home.

Galaan had no choice. Carefully, not wishing to cause more injury than necessary, she struck the girl with her fist. She had just enough time to ease the unconscious form onto the window-seat and draw her weapon.

Three young men approached, their weapons ready. Galaan's blue eyes were moving slowly from face to face—but never allowing any of them out of her peripheral vision.

Which one first, she was wondering—but then she saw him. He looked to be the youngest of the three: the one prone to acting before considering.

He would also be the one with least experience.

So she left him. It was the most calculating of the trio that would be her greatest threat.

She could feel his eyes reading her movements, assessing her strength and body—and she saw his eyes relay their message to the third guard.

Instantly, her sword arm was up to block the blow while her foot kicked the older man's knee where she still saw him from the corner of her eye. His moan told her she could turn now and face the other two.

This could be difficult . . . the two charged her from different sides at the same moment. She dropped to the floor and rolled away, quickly regaining her feet as the two men collided.

Hastily she heaved the bulk of the girl over her shoulder. As she gripped the rope to descend, she caught a glimpse of a sorceress pointing her finger in Galaan's direction.

Fire—again—fire! Galaan inhaled sharply but forced the illusion out of her mind immediately in response to Jewel's twittered warning.

It was difficult to maneuver down the wall with the heavy burden. She looked upward to see the face of the sorceress peering downward—and hastened her descent.

The rope—the rope was beginning to break immediately above her—she was still too high above the ground to let go.

Then she shook her head, hearing Jewel's warning and angry that she'd allowed herself to be distracted. This, too, must be illusion! She forced it from her mind and continued as though she'd seen nothing unusual.

She was at the bottom of the lower wall and pulling out the hook when she saw the archers approaching. Time—she was running out of time—

She hoisted herself and her burden into the shelter of the leafy growth, whistling loudly, knowing that Jewel would fetch Grey. She staggered awkwardly through the trees' lower branches and heaved the girl across the horse's back, securing her with rope.

She bade Grey run quickly and leapt into the cover of the bushes as the arrows continued to fly, one catching her in the upper arm as she ran.

Galaan cursed, bursting through the bushy growth and rolling down the hill. When she'd finally come to a stop on the level ground—feeling quite bruised and battered—she found that the arrow'd been pushed completely through her arm. The bleeding rather heavy now, she lost no time in withdrawing from her pouch a cloth packed in healing herbs. Quickly she secured it.

That was all she could do for the moment. She rose, a bit dazed, and hastened into the wood as her ears picked up the sounds of voices somewhere behind her.

Galaan hadn't expected to see one of the guards appear before her so soon, but the sword was in her hand almost instantly as she faced the grinning young man. He was certain he had her.

It was then Galaan knew that the opposite was true.

She forced a look of surprise on her face, then fear. Her eyes were fixed on those of the guard.

In his gloating, he didn't notice that the woman's weapon was in her hand—neatly tucked behind her back. It happened in one smooth motion. He reached toward her, a sickening smile on his face, and she, still feigning fear, struck forward with her blade—and neatly sliced off his hand.

She ended it for him quickly and then hurried on her way.

Finally she'd arrived at the little grove. She looked over at the gelding munching the clover. The young woman had recovered her senses and was struggling against the ropes.

Anger surged through Galaan when she thought of how this "poor victim" had struggled against her attempts at rescue. Wincing at the pain in her arm, Galaan moved forward to release the young woman.

"So, Lady Anna," she said, almost spitting in her fury, "I have rescued you—and are you going to tell me yet again that I should not have risked life and limb on your behalf?"

The girl looked up, suddenly realizing Galaan for the formidable figure which she was, a tall, muscular woman with a glaring anger and hands on hips.

"I . . . I am sorry. I truly am—but I do *not* wish to return to my uncle's home!"

Galaan pulled her gaze from the gray eyes of the small woman with the pale yellow hair. She glanced toward the wood, wondering how long they might have. She eased the girl in the direction of Grey and helped her to mount, then climbed on behind her. There was something about this girl—something familiar, yet not. Galaan shook her head, trying to make the sensation leave, but it refused.

They rode in silence for a time until, at long last, Anna spoke again.

"Galaan? What is it like to be a great warrior?"

Galaan laughed at the question, never having considered herself anything "great." "Now, why might a young lady ask that?"

She continued, though, when Anna did not reply. "Well, Lady Anna," she sighed, "can you imagine never having fine silk gowns to wear? Can you imagine sleeping in a real bed so seldom that it begins to feel unnatural; or to be hungry for days at a time; or to see so much death it no longer disturbs you—"

They were interrupted by a brief melody from Jewel as he flew downward and lit upon Galaan's shoulder. "Ah, my little friend! So, all is well, is it? Good news! We shall sup here, then." With that, she directed Grey toward a sheltered area. Satisfied the rocky ridges could conceal them, she helped Anna dismount and then rubbed Grey's muzzle affectionately.

"But there is more to it than that," Anna was continuing.

"Nonsense! I do this because I am not suited to anything else," Galaan muttered as she removed supplies from the horse's back.

"You love the life. I can see it—I can hear it when you speak."

Galaan ceased her activities, a bit startled by the young woman's claim. She turned to look at Anna directly—and gasped.

That face—no wonder it had disturbed her so! She'd seen it before. A *very* long time ago. Galaan stood, unable to move. She was shocked by the familiarity of that face: the gray eyes, the round cheeks, the blonde hair. Even the shape of the lips spoke of Melanie.

Dear Melanie—my closest and dearest friend. My constant companion for nearly six years.

A memory flooded her mind: Melanie dying in Galaan's arms after the enemy's blade had pierced her chest.

"I said, are you all right, Galaan?"

"What? Oh, oh . . . yes, child. I am all right. I just thought of something. I—I am all right now."

"Galaan," Anna continued, "I wish to be a warrior, like you! Certainly, I like to wear silk gowns and sleep in comfortable beds—but there's much more to life than that. And you know it!" Anna was cleansing and binding the warrior's wound as she spoke.

"Like what, child?"

"Like the challenge of a battle when all you have are your strength, your wits, and your blade! Like knowing every area of the forest as your home! Like feeling the wind in your face as you guide your galloping steed! Like knowing that your action has saved the life of a weaker person—"

"Enough!" Had the words come from someone else, Galaan might not have hesitated to suggest that the speaker seek a warrior's training . . . but *Melanie's* daughter?

Galaan sighed, remembering her oath—a great oath. The Oath of the Warrior Sisterhood. For, when one's warrior companion died, the one still living was bound by her Promise to carry out the companion's wishes.

The image was all too clear, now: Melanie's lips gasping her last words—and Galaan's Promise. She'd been honored to carry out the Promise, even though it had taken her many months to find the old friends of Melanie who were willing to raise this toddler as their own.

The Promise, remembered Galaan. She could see Melanie's lips move as she spoke the words: *"Do not let little Annabel simply follow her mother's ways! Please, see that she learns a better life. . . ."*

So lost was Galaan in her musings she almost didn't see the hand reaching for her sword. Suddenly, she was looking into the eyes of Melanie's daughter, Annabel, her hand holding the girl's wrist.

"Whatever are you doing, child!"

"I wish to show you what my cousin has taught me since I've been staying at my uncle's home. Trust me, Galaan."

After a moment's hesitation, Galaan released the girl's wrist.

She watched the girl as she admired the blade in the sunlight, but Galaan wasn't prepared for what happened next.

Suddenly, Annabel turned toward her rescuer and lunged! Galaan had to move quickly to avoid the blow. Swiftly, she drew her dagger, grateful that it hadn't been her swordarm which was damaged.

"What are you doing, Annabel. Please, do nothing foolish—"

But Annabel only smiled, and lunged once more. Galaan again had to be quick to miss injury.

Anger began to fill her. She didn't dare risk wounding Melanie's daughter, but it was difficult indeed to protect herself without her sword.

Annabel had stopped her attack and stood, sword held tauntingly in Galaan's direction.

"My kidnappers were holding me for ransom, but

they were not cruel. And some of the warriors were women. Oh, Galaan, the stories they told me! You think me unworthy of the sword? Ha! Then take yours from me: I defy you!"

It was Galaan's turn to lunge forward, grasping at Annabel's arm. But the girl was quick—very, very quick. She feigned a blow but then moved away—

Galaan felt sick at the stomach. The girl was good. She had the natural speed and agility of her birth mother. Had they been strangers, Galaan would gladly have sought her companionship.

She sighed, her head hanging.

"You've convinced me, Annabe—Lady Anna. You have the quick reactions and wit of a fighter . . . but I made an oath. . . ."

Annabel walked back to Galaan and handed her the sword. She spat in disgust.

"Oath, Galaan? An oath to my uncle to return me to the boredom of being a 'lady' in his household and my parents'? Ah, yes! Embroidery and needlepoint. True excitement, these! Tell me, Galaan, would you wish to return to such?"

The warrior shook her head, not correcting the erroneous assumption that the oath was one made to Annabel's uncle. Galaan added, "An important part of being a warrior is that of honoring one's oath. A warrior's word is truth itself. As a warrior yourself, you must understand, then, that I must do as the words of my oath require me."

Annabel sighed and nodded.

Galaan placed a hand on the young shoulder. "All aspects of life at times require from us what we do not wish to give. Believe me, Anna. I speak truth when I say I sorely wish I could take you for a companion. I must return you to the nobility, however. I think, though, that should we meet, perhaps one year from now, and if you have then chosen the warrior's life, we might begin anew without my breaking the oath-words."

At this, Annabel looked up and began to smile.

* * *

A solitary figure sat by a small fire amidst a grove of trees. The nearby gray gelding was almost invisible in the shadowy darkness, but the flames made the bird's scarlet plumage seem to sparkle like a gem.

The woman sipped the steaming brew from her mug and sighed.

"Oh, Melanie—my Melanie. I wish you could have seen your daughter! What a fine woman she is! I truly wish I might have taken her as companion."

Another sigh, and then she continued: "I do not think I've broken my oath: I did, after all, return her to the life of the nobility. But, dear Melanie, surely it's not wrong to also speak the truth! She *does,* indeed, have the basic skills to fight! How it hurt to return her to a life she does not want! Surely, if she has already become a warrior—surely then I would not be breaking the oath if I took her as companion then. But—it is not for me to decide. Should she become a warrior or remain with the nobility, it has little to do with me, now."

Galaan passed her sleeve across her moist eyes. *Strange,* she thought; *I'd forgotten that even a warrior can become lonely. . . .*

A twitter broke her musings and, as she looked up, Jewel perched upon her arm. When he opened his tiny beak, the beauty of his song was like an herbal remedy for the fighter's aching heart.

LOST SOULS

by Alison Brooks

Once again we arrive at the end of a ramble through the stories chosen for this anthology; and for each story I've tried to tell you a little about the writer and why each story was chosen—letting you share with me my rambles through the slush pile, and telling you something about how and why I made the choices I did instead of sending you some others.

Alison Brooks is British and has a Ph.D. in fossil worms; as far as we know, that's a new one. She has sold one previous fantasy, a vampire story, which was published in a British fantasy role-playing magazine which "promptly went bust and didn't pay me." It's a classic experience; that happened to my first story, too. So you can have all the "fun" of trying to sell it again. She has also had a few stories—typical British understatement that—in various role-playing magazines. She says she's "working on a novel—but isn't everyone?"

Well, all my writers seem to be.

And so here, at the end of another anthology, is a piece which has the mythlike quality of a folk tale—while being written like a story. I found it strong and poignant—just right in mood to embody everything I've been saying about the writing—and the reading, too—of fantasy.

Fingers of wind moaned their way between the timbers of the cabin. Drafts circulated the air, preventing the fire from creating the usual glow of heat. Outside, the trees crashed their dance to the winter storm.

The older woman huddled in her blanket closer to the fire. "Stranger, can you hear them?" she whispered.

The younger woman, an outlander named Aldith, looked up from the knife she was sharpening. "Hear what?"

"The voices in the wind."

Aldith snorted. "Old woman, are you senile?"

The old woman looked round with a frightened face. "Old I may be, but at least I don't mock what I don't understand. You must hear the voices?" It was more a plea than a question.

"There are no voices out there." The young woman met the eyes of the older. "You yourself said it was a miracle that I managed to get here, and I arrived soon after the storm blew up. Anyone out there is dead meat."

The old woman nodded. "I know." Her voice took on an urgency, "But they are out there. I have heard them in every storm for the last thirty years. The lost souls, the dead children demanding revenge. 'Mother . . . mother . . .' Every storm."

Aldith had a strange look in her eyes, nearly gentle. "It is your superstitious imagination," she said quietly. "Why would the souls of dead children seek you out?"

The old woman laughed bitterly, only it sounded more like a sob. "You don't understand," she said. "You, a foreigner, a warrior, young. Things are different where you come from. Your parents—"

"I am an orphan," Aldith interrupted flatly.

"I am sorry. I meant no harm." The old woman turned her eyes back to the fire. She took a ragged breath. "Here, a child who is orphaned, or a child born out of wedlock, or even a child too many, is left in the forest. The women do this, for they are blamed for bearing a child it took two to create. The children's spirits haunt the forest, seeking revenge."

"On their mothers?"

"Of course. Who else should a child blame? Every storm for the last thirty years," she repeated bleakly.

"Since you left your own child in the forest?" Aldith guessed. The old woman nodded mutely.

The wind mounted higher. Aldith listened, but there were no voices for her. "Tell me about it," she requested. She moved over to the fire, and stood above the older woman.

She shrugged helplessly. "I, it's nothing special. A child out of wedlock, so they made me take it out into the forest. I didn't want to, but they would have killed me."

Aldith spoke with quiet fury. "You could have taken the child and left the forest. You did not have to do it."

The old woman's face spasmed with pain. "It was impossible. I was too weak from the birth. All these years since, I have cursed my weakness, thought of a thousand ways to save the child, but too late. Too late." She sobbed silently. Aldith waited quietly, until she was able to continue, brokenly. "I was married later. But no children came to me. Only the lost souls calling me. Everyone heard. My dead daughter." She looked up. "Can't you hear them calling?" she pleaded.

"No."

The old woman rose to her feet, wiped the tears from her seamed cheeks. "I have nothing left, stranger. My family are gone. No one wants me but my daughter. When they call to one person only, it means they will have her soon. No one can stop them. She will have me—let it be now." She threw off the blanket and strode to the door with decisive vigor.

Aldith reached her as she wrestled with the bar. "Stop that! Are you mad?" She tried to pull the old woman away from the door, but the old woman found manic strength, and shoved her away. She staggered back, collided with a rough wooden stool, fell over.

By the time she regained her feet, the old woman had opened the door and was stepping out.

"NO!" The wind battered Aldith, carried her yell away. She lurched to the door. Oudside was snow-dappled blackness, a faint trail erased by the wind as she looked. Without thinking, she launched herself out of the cabin into the darkness.

The open door provided a little light, and in a few paces she saw the old woman, a dark huddle in the snow. Above her, faintly luminous, several shapes were dancing. Shapes the size of small children.

Aldith cursed. "Leave her!" she screamed above the storm. She forced herself forward. Ignoring the ghosts about her, she scooped up the old woman and turned. She could see the light of the cabin. Little fingers reached for her, little nails scratched. She could hear the lost souls' cries on the wind. She shut her heart to them. She took a pace, another. *Think of the safety of the cabin ahead, there's nothing else. Take a step toward safety. Another. Another.*

Suddenly they were inside the cabin. Aldith carried the old woman over to the fire and laid her on the blanket, then went and put her back to the door. Fighting the wind's angry strength, she closed the door, and slid the bar into place. There was a sudden hush, but Aldith fancied she could hear frustrated wails in the wind outside.

Aldith went back to the old woman. She was icy but breathing feebly. Aldith brushed off the worst of the snow before it could melt, and put her arms around the old woman to warm her. There was nothing more she could do. The candles had been snuffed, but the fire still glowed fiercely from the wind.

The old woman stirred. "Where—?"

"In the cabin."

"But, didn't you see them dancing?" The old woman struggled into a sitting position, and looked at Aldith's face. "They scratched you."

Aldith put a hand to her face. The hand came away bloody.

"How did you do that?" the old woman quavered.

"How did you get me away from the lost souls? I thought no one could do that."

Aldith sighed. "Perhaps because I'm one of them," she admitted. "I was abandoned at birth, but I was lucky. A traveler came upon me, and adopted me. I—I always hated my own mother for abandoning me. Perhaps they knew that." Old tears pricked her eyes, and she bent her head.

The old woman touched Aldith's hair. "Are you—? No," she said sadly. "You're too young. Why did you save me? You should hate me, too."

"You've suffered for thirty years for your weakness," Aldith said. "My hate would not help either of us. When this storm is finished, we'll go away from here, away from the forest and the storms."

The old woman stared. "But how can I leave my daughter?"

"Everyone must move on at last. Your daughter has gone. If you wish, I will take her place for you."

The shock on the old woman's face was slowly replaced by disbelief and, finally, joy. Her tears, and Aldith's, mingled with the blood on Aldith's face as they embraced.

Outside, the cries faded away.